SHE WAS NICOLE, NADIA, AND NATASHA.
AND THREE MEN CLAIMED HER.

William Caldwell, the ambitious, blustering English
officer, swore he could force Nicole to love him. He
imperiled the entire British army trying.

Yuri Janov, the gentle serf with the soul of a poet and
the nobility of a saint, bought his Nadia from an auc-
tioneer and tried desperately to soothe her heartbreak
with his tenderness.

Dimitri Denisov, the irresistible nobleman who com-
mandingly took Natasha's body, awakened in her a
sweet fire that would never stop burning.

**Nicole wanted only to be Dimitri's Natasha, so des-
perately did she long for his love. But in the power-
mad court of Catherine the Great, only a fool would
put love before obedience to the Empress. Dimitri was
no fool. . . .**

YANKEE PRINCESS

The Best in Fiction From SIGNET

YANKEE PRINCESS

MAGGIE OSBORNE

A SIGNET BOOK

NEW AMERICAN LIBRARY

TIMES MIRROR

SIGNET TRADEMARK REG. U.S. PAT. OFF. AND FOREIGN COUNTRIES
REGISTERED TRADEMARK—MARCA REGISTRADA
HECHO EN CHICAGO, U.S.A.

SIGNET, SIGNET CLASSICS, MENTOR, PLUME, MERIDIAN AND NAL
BOOKS are published by The New American Library, Inc.,
1633 Broadway, New York, New York 10019

First Printing, October, 1982

1   2   3   4   5   6   7   8   9

PRINTED IN THE UNITED STATES OF AMERICA

To Aleon DeVore, with gratitude and affection

1

NICOLE DUCHARD WORRIED her full lower lip between her teeth and strained to overhear the angry murmurs emanating from the parlor below. For the past hour her parents had been closeted with the richly dressed strangers, speaking rapid-fire French which Nicole doubted she could have followed even if she had been able to hear clearly.

Absently she tucked a golden curl beneath the edge of her dust cap, then rose from her chair and wandered to the bedroom window, pressing her forehead to a frosty pane and peering into the cobbled street below. Soldiers rimmed the Duchard fence line; she hadn't imagined them. Others stamped through the snowy slush of last week's storm, protecting an elegant carriage more ornate than any Nicole had previously observed.

As she watched, a passing coach slowed and a man leaned from the window to gape at the soldiers' loose blouses and gleaming leather boots. Nicole heartily shared the passenger's curiosity. She knew the soldiers weren't British—she had reason to know the crisp arrogance of the redcoats—nor could anyone mistake them for the fledgling colonial militia. And despite the fluent French rising angrily from the parlor, Nicole doubted either the soldiers or the couple below were French. That both were personages of note, Nicole did not dispute; only those of wealth and position traveled with private guards. But who were they?

And why were they interested in her?

Her name had surfaced with worrisome frequency. Beneath her breath Nicole cursed herself for failing to be as proficient in French as she might have been, considering French was the native tongue of both her parents. On the other hand, Louis and Marie devoted themselves entirely to their adopted country; they seldom spoke French except between themselves. Language aside, a spark of rebellion lifted

Nicole's small firm chin. She chaffed at being excluded from a discussion so obviously concerning herself.

In the street below, a tall man appeared at the edge of her vision, striding toward the soldiers with the slight swagger of one accustomed to a uniform, although he did not wear one today. His pace slowed as he neared the unexpected presence of the soldiers; then he touched his hat brim in a near-salute and proceeded toward the Duchard gate, eyeing the guards inquisitively.

"William." Nicole's sapphire eyes reflected an ambiguous mixture of pleasure and doubt as she hastily puffed loops of flowered dimity over a quilted petticoat. If she hurried, she would have a moment to exchange her muslin cap for the frilled one before William reached the porch. She pushed from the window, then halted and abruptly leaned forward, her mouth dropping in astonishment.

A soldier stepped before the gate, solidly blocking passage. More men closed on either side of Major William Caldwell. Using the blunt hilts of their sabers, they nudged William away from the house. Aghast, Nicole blinked in disbelief as harsh guttural language exploded past the windowpanes. William indicated the Duchard porch and attempted to push past the soldiers. A blade glittered in the winter sunshine and one of the guards butted a massive chest against William's frock coat, forcing him backward. The threat was icily clear even if the language was not.

Nicole held her breath, for once wishing William had worn the hated English uniform; surely the soldiers would not have dared this affront had they known William's rank. As it was, William's heated protests served only to annoy the soldiers. Without ceremony, two seized him beneath the arms and roughly hauled him away from the Duchard property line. They hurled him into a soiled bank of snow.

Nicole gasped, and her hand leaped to her mouth. Instantly she recalled the substance of a dozen lengthy meetings held secretly in the Duchard kitchen; incidents provoking the British were to be avoided if at all possible. The scene below vividly called to mind her own private war of allegiance.

She leaned far to one side and watched William jump to his feet, slapping furiously at the mud and snow clinging to his coat and breeches. In a fury, he surveyed the guards and the Duchard house, then spun on his heels and strode rapidly up the street.

"Wait!" Nicole struggled with the latch. When finally it

2

gave way, she leaned from the window and called out, but William had vanished beyond the curve. As a man, the soldiers raised their faces and immediately saluted her with drawn swords.

Nicole stared at the spectacle. One of the men addressed her in the strange coarse language, then all dropped to one knee, oblivious of the slush and mud. They swept their fur caps from bowed heads.

Nicole's blue eyes widened; then she slammed the window and spun from view, her heart beating alarmingly. Who were these brutish people? Violent one moment, oddly subservient the next—she understood none of it. But she knew Louis Duchard would be outraged to learn a visitor had been forcibly barred from his gate.

"Nicole?"

Nicole whirled toward the soft voice floating from the stairwell. She wiped damp palms against her skirt. Minutes before, she had eagerly anticipated the summons; now she wasn't at all certain she wished to meet the people downstairs.

"Nicole?" Marie Duchard's insistent voice revealed an uncharacteristic strain, and Nicole quickened her step.

At the base of the staircase, Marie Duchard peered hard at her daughter, then suddenly swept her into an embrace. Puzzled, Nicole returned the fierce pressure. The oddities of this singular day mounted by the moment. She didn't recall Marie fully embracing her more than twice since childhood . . . and then only in the aftermath of catastrophe. She swallowed uncertainly.

"Mama . . . those soldiers refused William permission to—"

"Yes, yes," Marie murmured. "Remember your manners," she whispered. Her face had paled and was now almost as white as her hair and the starched dust cap above it. "And speak French, they don't understand English."

Before Nicole could protest, Marie gently propelled her through the parlor doors, and Nicole experienced a sudden wave of self-consciousness. A middle-aged woman lifted an ivory-handled lorgnette and examined Nicole with frank curiosity bordering on rudeness. The man stared but quickly recovered himself and crossed to bend over her hand, brushing warm lips across her fingers before she realized his intent.

"*Magnifique!*" he murmured, his voice a rich blend of resonant tones. When he straightened, he towered a full head above her. Smoke-gray eyes smiled an appreciation for her beauty, staring into Nicole's upturned face.

A rush of warmth colored her cheeks, and she drew a startled breath. Since the beginning of young womanhood Nicole had been accustomed to admiring glances from men. But none like this. The man's steady gaze pierced beyond her creamy translucent skin, into her thickly fringed blue eyes, and seemed to penetrate the small hidden core Nicole cherished as the private essence of herself. She shifted uneasily.

"Prince Dimitri Denisov, at your service."

The rich flow of flawless French was delivered in an intimate tone. His eyes continued to hold her as if they were alone.

Nicole pulled her fingers from his grasp with a deepening blush which both annoyed and embarrassed her. She stole another quick look at him and concluded uncomfortably that Prince Dimitri was easily the most handsome man she had encountered. For perhaps the hundredth time she wondered if accepting William's betrothal ring had been wise. Perhaps her parents were right: there were other leaves upon the tree. The unbidden thought rightly shamed her. Yet at the very instant she whispered an unspoken apology to William, she peeked through her lashes at the prince. In her defense she argued she'd never encountered a member of royalty, nor did she think it likely she would again. Still . . .

A tiny frown knit her smooth brow. She decided William Caldwell paled by comparison as she examined enigmatic gray eyes and thick blue-black hair tied with a satin ribbon at the neck. She hadn't suspected such elegance could exist without the sacrifice of masculinity, yet the prince's masculinity charged the room. A green velvet coat and buckled knee pants barely constrained the heavy muscles along broad shoulders and taut thighs. Her first impression was that of a lean tapered body, hard and physical in its impact. She could more easily imagine this man astride a flying stallion than indulging in polite repartee in a drawing room. He was a man born to command. Men would respect the easy authority in that chiseled face . . . and women would summon his image to delight private musings.

Nicole gave herself an annoyed shake and forced her attention to sharpen as her father's stiff voice introduced Countess Irina Ivanova. A gleam of voluminous rose-patterned brocade caught Nicole's eye along with an impression of powdered white curls beneath a plumed hat.

Countess Irina's voice was low and calculated. "You are very beautiful, *chérie*. As lovely as your mother."

Nicole curtsied, then sank gracefully to a ladder back chair near the door. Marie Duchard might have been attractive forty years ago, but Nicole secretly doubted her mother could have been considered a beauty. Marie's broad wrinkled face bespoke a rural background, and her large callused hands suggested a woman accustomed to work, not luxury. How Nicole had inherited her fine high cheekbones and patrician lines had become a family jest.

"Say what you came to say," Louis interrupted harshly. "The girl's bright, she knows this concerns her." He reached for his wife's hand; neither looked at Nicole.

Their odd behavior heightened a building apprehension. Nicole stared at the people crowding the small warm parlor, responding to a tension which seemed to electrify the atmosphere. Her small hands unconsciously curled into fists. And she blinked anxiously toward her parents, not comprehending why they avoided her glance. She was uneasily reminded of those still, charged moments before lightning forks the sky and a storm ravages the heavens.

Her gaze traveled slowly, leaping quickly beyond Dimitri Denisov's measuring gaze and settling upon Countess Irina. A predatory glint behind the woman's heavy lids did nothing to alleviate Nicole's expanding nervousness. The prince and the countess examined Nicole Duchard but recognized someone else. She swallowed and lifted an inquisitive brow.

"Will you begin, Prince?" Irina Ivanova inclined her head graciously, deferring to rank amid the rustlings of heavy brocade. But her small eyes did not leave Nicole. Nicole was unpleasantly reminded of glittering chips of granite.

A froth of white lace cascaded from Dimitri Denisov's wrist as he lifted a hand from the back of his chair. "You were present at the beginning, Countess, I cede to you." Though his tone was scrupulously polite, the gray eyes cooled, and Nicole intuitively sensed the prince and the countess cared little for one another's company.

Countess Irina nodded in satisfaction and returned to Nicole. Marie and Louis Duchard had become as invisible as servants; they did not exist for the woman. "Do you speak French, *chérie*?"

The endearment grated. "If you speak slowly . . ." From the corner of her eye Nicole watched Marie lift the hem of her apron to trembling lips. And an unnamed fear swept Nicole's small lush frame. A sudden incomprehensible urge to flee tightened her muscles. She decided she did not want to hear whatever Countess Irina was preparing to divulge. Mere words often possessed the awesome power of altering lives.

"Then we shall proceed." The countess edged forward in her chair, long jeweled fingers toying with the pleats of her gown. "Twenty years ago, a child was born in St. Petersburg. You've heard of the city? No?" An expression of astonished irritation flashed across her powdered face, suppressed before Nicole fully registered what she'd seen. "St. Petersburg is the capital of all the Russias. In any event, the young mother, Princess Varina Stepanova, considered the arrival of a child ... awkward ... as she was unmarried at the time. Do you understand what I am saying?"

Nicole nodded, her blue eyes bewildered and her mouth suddenly dry. She couldn't comprehend how this story concerned her, but her sinking heart warned that it did.

"The princess's condition was hardly a secret," the countess continued dryly, "but she treated the event as if it were. At the time of the birthing, and with the probable aid of Empress Elizabeth—"

"Elizabeth is now dead, Catherine is the czarina," Prince Dimitri interrupted.

The countess cast him a murderous glance. "—the child was spirited out of Russia and entrusted to the care of a childless French couple then residing in southern France." She paused as Louis Duchard leaned his elbows onto his knees and dropped his white head into his hands.

Nicole swallowed hard; her breath constricted. Her fingers balled her apron into damp clumps.

"Last autumn Princess Varina succumbed to a pox. It was her dying wish that the child be located and restored to her natural title and inheritance."

"Her?" Nicole's whisper strangled. Please, God, don't let this mean what it appears to! No.

"Surely you realize we are speaking of you, *chérie*."

Shock crushed the air from Nicole's body. The countess's voice echoed like traces of a nightmare. It wasn't true! This simply was not true! In a moment Nicole would awaken and the street would be cleared of soldiers, this man and this woman would have evaporated like steam from a kettle. Please, God, she prayed silently, let it happen now!

"Mama?" Nicole choked. Shaking fingers fluttered over her

6

cheeks and throat, and she tried again. "Mama?" Wide moist eyes pleaded with Marie to refute the Russian's claim.

Marie's lashes dampened. "We should have told you," she whispered. Her expression begged understanding. "We thought of you as our own, an answer to our prayers. We believed when we immigrated to the colonies that no one would find us again."

Irina Ivanova smiled and arched a coy eyebrow.

"Papa! Please . . . ?"

Louis Duchard spoke through his fingers, his weary voice muffled. "As the years passed, we told ourselves they'd forgotten." Heavy shoulders lifted in a Gallic shrug, his tone deepened into pain. "We should have known better."

Nicole blinked at nothing. Her safe, comfortable world slipped into an abyss, sweeping aside her sense of identity and everything she had believed herself to be.

A dark sickness churned through her stomach; layers of cotton swathed her thoughts. How was this possible? How could she be one person all of her life, then discover that person had never existed? Nicole watched her clasped hands flare red, then tighten to white against the flowered pattern of her skirt. Only a deep abiding pride stayed the tears building behind her lashes. In the space of minutes her life had spun upside down.

Irina Ivanova cleared her throat with a small discreet cough, then again leaned forward, displaying a generous expanse of powdered bosom. Nicole's numbed thoughts settled upon small details; she decided the countess was composed solely of powdered rice. Wildly she wondered if the countess would dissolve if a pot of water were dashed over her head. Perhaps nothing lay beneath the mask of powder but more powder.

"I realize this is abrupt, *chérie*"—small cool eyes swept the grieving Duchards with disapproval—"but we must proceed to practical matters. Arrangements must be discussed."

"For the love of God, Irina, can't you see the girl is stunned?" Dimitri Denisov's deep voice sharpened in irritation; he and the countess exchanged salvos in the harsh unknown tongue.

At the conclusion, the countess's eyes flashed resentment, but she lowered her head and lifted a hand heavy with emeralds and pearls. "As you please."

Gray eyes met Nicole's anguished stare. "Take as long as you like. If there are questions . . . ?" The dimming light cast

Denisov's face into shadow, highlighting sharp angles which at another time would have drawn and intrigued.

Nicole held herself stiffly rigid, her fingers gripping the arms of the chair. The candles should be lighted; someone should poke up the dying fire and see to dinner. The ticking of the mantel clock sounded unnaturally loud, striking down the old, ushering in the unthinkable.

"Is there . . . is there more?" she whispered.

"Yes, Princess."

Princess? Nicole started, staring into eyes which the shadows painted silver. Nicole Duchard—a Russian princess? The concept was fairy-tale ludicrous; had she not been so dazed, so disoriented, she might have laughed. Instead she shook her golden head so violently her dust cap slipped above one ear. Swimming eyes focused toward Marie and Louis Duchard. Not once had she suspected they were not her natural parents. Not once. A sense of loss gnawed her heart, interspersed with an unwanted feeling of betrayal. Nicole touched her forehead and closed her lashes.

"There must be a mistake." If she denied this vigorously enough, perhaps it would not be true. She would remain the person she knew, and her parents would remain her parents.

Though Dimitri Denisov's voice emerged in a gentle tone, his words fell like stones. "There is no doubt."

Countess Irina sniffed. "Many would gladly give ten years of their life to be a Russian princess!"

Fleetingly Nicole wondered if Irina Ivanova included herself in the number. She cast a despairing plea toward her parents, but neither would meet her eyes. Lowering her head, Nicole sensed what was to follow would be difficult to bear. And had been thoroughly discussed before she was summoned.

Denisov's tone commanded her attention. "Empress Catherine has generously declared you her ward. It is her wish that you present yourself in St. Petersburg to establish your claim to the Stepanova estates."

Nicole gasped. "I . . . Are you suggesting that I travel to . . . to Russia?" She clung to the chair arms as if they alone anchored reality, and her eyes swept the parlor as if seeing it for the first time. She had helped select the pale yellow above the wainscoting; her skill with a needle had fashioned the ruffles tying back the curtains. The yellow-and-blue needle-point cover on Marie's footstool had been Nicole's Christmas gift to her mother; the braided rug beneath her feet contained scraps and memories of a lifetime.

"The czarina wishes it."

Nicole stared into impassive faces, shaking her head in disbelief. "No," she blurted in a voice too loud for the hushed room. "Please . . . I . . . I accept what you claim as my parentage . . ." There appeared no alternative. "But I love my . . . my parents! I can't leave Boston! This is my home!" Helplessly she lifted her palms, indicating the familiar homey surroundings. The faint light of early evening harshened the rejection in their expressions. "Please thank Empress Catherine for her interest, but inform her that I relinquish any inheritance. I don't want to be a princess, I just want to remain who I am." Whoever that might be. Her eyes flicked toward the staircase, and she yearned for nothing more than to curl beneath her quilts and blot this infamous afternoon from memory.

Irina Ivanova's lips curved, but the smile failed to reach her heavy-lidded eyes. "Impossible."

"Princess . . ." Dimitri Denisov's voice strove toward patience.

And his tone stung through Nicole's confusion; she resented being addressed as if she were a stubborn child—and addle-witted at that.

". . . you don't appear to grasp the issue. Catherine—the Empress of all the Russias—orders you home." For the first time Prince Dimitri allowed a hint of an implacable authority. His gray eyes were soberly chill.

"It is not a request, *chérie*," Countess Irina added softly. Swirling undercurrents penetrated Nicole's desperation, swift-flowing rivers of suggested intrigue which she could not hope to navigate. Irina watched her without expression. "One does not defy the empress."

Nicole's bodice tightened around full breasts until each breath burned; her fingers shook. Rising on unsteady legs, she appealed to them, "Please . . . what you're asking simply is not possible. I . . . I'm to be married in two months!"

"Married? That is unthinkable," Irina announced flatly. "A princess wouldn't dare wed without Catherine's approval."

Nicole passed a trembling hand across her eyes. Nothing she said reached these people. An empress of whom she had known nothing an hour ago now dictated the course of her life. Her future, her very identity, lay rooted in the whims of a woman dwelling on the far side of the world. Despairing,

9

Nicole spun toward her parents, her skirts billowing about her house boots. "Papa! Tell them," she implored. "Tell them I don't have to go!"

Marie wept quietly into her apron; Louis shook his head in his hands. Chewing her lip and blinking rapidly, Nicole turned slowly toward the Russians, recoiling from Countess Irina's expression. Dimitri Denisov's face remained unreadable.

"We sail in one week," he said quietly.

"One . . ." Nicole raised a hand, warding off the darkness invading the parlor. ". . . week!" A curtain of black crept toward her. She had time to recall all she knew of distant Russia. A second was all she required. A schoolbook memory of a vast frozen expanse flashed before her vision.

"Who am I?" she whispered hoarsely. The bastard offspring of strangers from an unknown country. "God in heaven . . . I don't know who I am!"

She pitched forward, fainting into the strong enfolding arms of Dimitri Denisov.

2

Now CLAD IN his uniform, awesomely resplendent in red and black and gold braid, Major William Caldwell presented himself within minutes of the Russians' departure. The junior officers by his side gripped their sabers and growled a challenge to the soldiers Prince Dimitri had posted beside the Duchard gate. An ugly altercation would certainly have ensued had not Louis Duchard hastened to intervene. With unusual cordiality in view of his political convictions, Louis invited William inside. He surprised everyone by granting the couple an unprecedented moment of privacy.

The meeting went badly from the beginning.

Continuing to smart from his unceremonious deposit in the snowbank, William fumed and stormed about the parlor until Nicole found it necessary to press her lips tightly against an outburst of frustration. The image of the Russians lingered behind her lids. A heavy, powdery scent clung to the chair upon which she sat, and compelling silvery eyes teased her memory.

"William, please! We have so much to discuss!"

"Of course." But his thoughts obviously remained upon the insult to his honor. He poured two glasses of sherry from the decanter on the table between Louis and Marie's chairs and presented one to Nicole with a distracted frown.

Drawing a breath, Nicole related the afternoon's events, concluding the tale by explaining the necessity of postponing their wedding. William's thin lips opened and closed.

The only sounds in the small parlor were the ticking of the mantel clock and the angry click of William's heels as he paced the length of the room. Watching his candlelit shadow marching along the wall, Nicole discovered herself comparing William to Dimitri Denisov. For the first time she began to glimpse the man behind the uniform, began to note the abrasive qualities Louis and Marie continually hinted at. Annoyed with herself, Nicole guiltily reminded herself that it was no crime to swagger; soldiers were expected to comport themselves with a certain arrogance. And William's ironclad control was to be expected; emotional outbursts would be unseemly in an officer. Nor could he be blamed for an unprepossessing set of ordinary features instead of an aristocratic profile.

But William's greatest drawback, Nicole admitted with an inner sigh, was his predictability. There were few surprises; William was precisely what he appeared to be, a grimly ambitious English officer of rather humorless cast who would prove a devoted husband, father, and provider. Even her parents agreed on these points.

Nicole released a breath and studied her hands. She was fond of William, really she was, but occasionally she wished he would step out of character and do something unexpected and utterly frivolous, something a trifle foolish and romantic. She wished he weren't so conscious of his image and position. Surely it would do no harm to unbend just a little. She turned his pledge ring upon her finger, contemplating the narrow circlet of silver. She was being silly. She had spurned a dozen offers, choosing William from a crowded field of suitors and over her parents' protests. William's primary attraction was not the dashing uniform, as Marie had suggested . . . was it? Or the romantic notion of defying parents and politics for love? Love? Buffeted by sudden doubt, Nicole bit her lips and frowned. Did she really love him?

Gradually becoming aware of William's polished boots near her hem, Nicole started and glanced upward, spilling drops of wine across her fingers.

William dropped to his knees and gazed into her smooth, untried face, his pale eyes angry, as if Nicole were to blame for the situation. "Outrageous!" he muttered. Short jerky fingers combed through a shock of sand-colored hair. "You won't go, of course."

"William, I must. There is no choice." A fleeting wisp of bitterness cooled her eyes as she struggled to accept the stunning revelations of this remarkable day. She answered his next question before he asked it. "We'll have to postpone the wedding until . . ." Mentally Nicole calculated the time required for two ocean voyages and a brief sojourn in Russia. ". . . until this time next year." As she examined the controlled lack of expression on William's features, a lump of disappointment lodged in her throat. She watched the thought processes flickering in the depths of his gaze, observed his outrage melt to anger and then eventually to resignation. Her shoulders drooped and she wondered briefly if Dimitri Denisov would have surrendered without a daring countersuggestion. She thought not. Circles of color dotted her cheeks, and she hastily lowered her gaze from William's eyes.

He shoved at a lock of unruly hair falling across his forehead, and his narrow lips tightened. "When do you . . . ? A week?" He stared. Awkwardly he gathered her hands and pressed them between his palms. Intense pale eyes dropped hungrily to her full surprised mouth, and he licked his lips nervously.

But he didn't attempt to kiss her. William Caldwell could always be counted upon to do the right thing; an English officer did not press an advantage. Nicole expelled a tiny breath, fighting waves of depression. She knew she should admire his restraint, but her shocked system craved the comfort of a man's arms, and this was, after all, the first time Louis had granted them any privacy.

After squeezing her hands until they ached, William took his leave amid promises to call each night. The promises provided little comfort; she would have preferred action.

Nicole's moodiness intensified as she moved haltingly through the most hectic week of her life. She attempted valiantly to entertain nothing but positive thoughts, and failed, as she might have predicted. Despite the best intentions, she worried about her unknown future incessantly and wept when she considered leaving the home she loved.

Throughout the greater part of the week, thick leaden clouds scudded low over Boston's chimney tops, reminding her of an upturned bowl of gruel and matching her mood exactly—gray and lumpy and near to bursting. Her parents glided silently through the house, their misery evident in averted eyes and hesitant steps. The nightly chats with William were strained and unsatisfying.

During the activity and routine of daylight hours, Nicole thrust him entirely from her mind. At first she questioned how this was possible, then gave herself up to the wild swings of mood. One moment she wandered aimlessly through the Duchard house, responding to tides of nostalgia; the next moment her thoughts flew forward, riding a crest of speculation.

As she resigned herself to the voyage, Nicole experienced the surprise of anticipation. There were moments when the allure of far-off lands was intriguing, moments when she secretly tasted "princess" on her tongue and unconsciously stood a little straighter, striving for a dignity of carriage and a serious demeanor in sparkling blue eyes better suited for laughing.

The days elapsed in a bewildering swing from apprehension to building excitement.

Then at last her trunk was packed and the last-minute errands were completed. All that remained was her farewell party, and Marie had the preparations well in hand. The week had passed in the blink of an eye.

"Sit down and draw a breath—you've been on the run for days." Marie glanced upward from a circle of pie dough and wiped a hand across her cheek, leaving a trail of flour. "Molly and I can manage the party doings." The servant girl nodded from the hearth, regarding Nicole through timid awed eyes; she'd overheard the talk of royalty and sea voyages.

"Oh, Mama!" So much needed to be said, and no opening existed in which to say it. Although Marie Duchard's pillowy plump body appeared created for easy embraces, and her honest open face invited confidence, she had never been comfortable expressing those emotions lying nearest the heart.

Marie's sturdy face struggled to combat a lifetime of reticence; then she bit her tongue and lowered her eyes to the pie dough, attacking it vigorously. "You should brush out your gown for tonight, and you mentioned washing your hair. Mind you don't dry it near the window. It wouldn't do to catch cold . . . not now." Beneath Marie's assault, the pie dough widened into a thin wheel.

"Mama . . . ?" Marie would always be her mother; the Russians could not alter Marie's position in Nicole's heart—this she would never allow! Her eyes misted and she hurried from the kitchen lest she embarrass her mother with an impulsive hug. A thousand words died on her lips, and her only comfort existed in knowing her pain was matched by the ache in her mother's eyes. In the final analysis, perhaps words had no need.

Throughout her final day at home—Nicole rushed past this desolate thought—memory unreeled in flashing frames. She recalled a younger Marie bending over scraped knees, kissing the hurts away. She remembered Marie's glowing pride as Nicole's skill with a needle surpassed her own; and the day Marie shyly presented Nicole with her first grown-up stomacher, one featuring a trim of fine Irish lace and genuine whalebone molding. Marie appeared in the hundred guises of motherhood, in the kitchen unveiling the mysteries of treasured family receipes, in the bedroom with a cool cloth for a hot brow, in the parlor nodding approval as Nicole demonstrated the grace of a thoughtful hostess.

And Louis Duchard. Nicole peered into the mists of memory and saw her father before white leached the vigor from his dark hair. When Louis Duchard first arrived in the colonies, he had been a man of the soil; he understood farming, but not a word of English. Willpower and determination had fueled the ambition to succeed, to develop a new trade and a new language. He'd parlayed an appreciation of fine leather into one cobbler's shop and then three, prospering to the extent of now employing five apprentices in each.

Nicole's distraction settled upon a snow-frosted elm to the left of the front porch; two arms could not circle the girth. And her eyes stung as she recalled her seventh birthday, when Louis had helped her spade a hole for the little sprig which would grow into that elm. So long ago—had it really happened?

Nicole bowed her head on Sunday, and when she raised it, the calender had leaped forward.

The *Kiev* would sail in the morning, voyaging into the unknown, leaving behind everything dear and familiar.

"Nicole? Are you dressed?" Marie rapped lightly, then entered Nicole's small bedroom wearing her Sunday gown, a pale blue taffeta with black ribbon edging. "Shouldn't you come downstairs? Your guests are asking for you." Gently she touched Nicole's shoulder, meeting her daughter's eyes in the chipped bureau mirror above the washbasin.

Nicole clasped Marie's fingers, holding tightly until Marie returned the pressure and lowered her lashes.

"Is William . . . ?" A chatter of voices and the tinkle of glass drifted up the stairwell. The house had filled to capacity as Nicole dressed and wandered in melancholy musings.

"Not yet." Marie was unaware her lips pursed in the disapproval William's name aroused. "But nearly everyone else is here." Habit directed Marie's fingers, fluffing Nicole's green silk over a hooped frame, tucking an errant curl of honey-gold into an intricate arrangement.

Nicole bit her lips, reluctant to join the gaiety, without understanding exactly why. Delaying, she examined her reflection. She had seldom looked lovelier. Green silk tucks molded her firm young breasts, then dipped to define a waist so slender a man's hands could circle her sash with ease. White lace and pink ribbon hid a curve of hips and long shapely legs. Small satin slippers peeped from beneath a ruffled hem. She leaned to study the loops of golden curls framing an oval face and then adjusted a long shining coil over one bare shoulder.

"Prince Dimitri and the countess . . . have they arrived?" She decided her eyes were a touch too bright, her cheeks too pink with nervous color. Hiding her expression, Nicole dotted a few drops of rosewater on her handkerchief and pushed the lace between her breasts. She located her favorite fan, the one with lacquered scenes in pink and green, and tied it around her wrist.

Marie sighed softly, leading toward the stairs. "From the instant the prince arrived, Mr. Revere has inundated him with political talk. And the countess . . ." Marie sniffed and her mouth pinched. "The countess is wearing a French gown which . . . well, you'll see. The neckline is positively shocking! And the waist hoop is so wide she's forced to enter and depart a room sideways. Like a crab."

Nicole smiled at the image, and held the smile as a crowd converged on her as she descended the staircase. Younger friends struggled to suppress expressions of envy, and everyone good-naturedly addressed her as "princess" and dropped into teasing bows. It seemed as if everyone laughed and shouted at once. Someone thrust a mug of Marie's famed mulled cider into Nicole's hands; someone else insisted she sample Mrs. Revere's lemon cake. Smiling over the shifting crowd of noisy friends and neighbors, Nicole concluded that Molly had polished the house in vain. Furniture vanished behind flaring frock coats and voluminous silk skirts.

None were as voluminous as those worn by Irina Ivanova. Eventually Nicole located the countess in the kitchen, surrounded by curious women and a few smiling men. Irina's mountainous powdered bosom threatened to spill from a deeply cut gold brocade, the bodice of which appeared two sizes too small. It was necessary to pause between sentences in order to force fresh breath past Irina's tight lacings. The gown was as enormous as Marie had promised. Brocade and lace ruffled lavishly over an oblong pannier under which a small child could have stood comfortably. Coupled with the massive white wig sailing back from Irina's forehead, the skirt was indeed an awesome concoction, creating an overall impression of stately foolishness. The countess was unapproachable from the side. And Nicole doubted the Duchards possessed a single chair upon which Irina could sit; none would accommodate the pannier.

"Ah, there you are, *chérie!*" Those in the countess's audience who spoke French turned to face the kitchen doorway.

Unfortunately, little Mrs. Trimbridge was not among the linguistically gifted, and the poor woman was nearly knocked into the hearth by the swinging pannier. Irina murmured apologies the confused little woman did not begin to understand; then the countess arranged rouged lips into a strained smile and stepped forward to clasp Nicole's hands.

"How coy of you to stage a late entrance! And what a stroke of genius to dress simply and wear your hair unpowdered!" An artificial laugh trilled. Irina rolled her eyes above the edges of an ivory fan. "The unadorned freshness of youth diminishes the artifice of those who approach thirty." A few heads smiled and nodded.

Quickly Nicole raised her fan to cover the beginnings of a smile. Standing as close as the swaying pannier permitted, she could observe lines of powder settling into valleys beside Irina's mouth. The heat in the kitchen had glazed additional powder into horizontal strings along her brow. If Irina Ivanova was anywhere near thirty, then soup caldrons could fly.

"You look lovely," Nicole murmured. She hoped heaven

16

forgave the white lies demanded by society, and she tried not to stare at a glittering speck of gold pasted to Irina's cheekbone.

Recognizing the object of Nicole's fascination and measuring the amusement dancing in the girl's eyes, Irina abruptly dropped Nicole's hand. "Run along and see to your guests, *chérie*. You and I will have weeks to develop our acquaintance. For these . . . charming . . . people, you have only tonight."

Nicole's eyes flared, then narrowed. Perhaps she had imagined the scorn underlying the countess's tone. But she didn't think so. Watching Irina return to the small informal court she had assembled, Nicole attempted to decipher the countess's hints of hostility.

And failed. Disturbed, she withdrew to the crowded parlor, discovered it to be hot and noisy, then repaired to a niche in the hallway where she could catch her breath and enjoy a moment of unobserved quiet. She watched Louis and Marie moving among the guests, seeing to their comfort, and she wondered what had detained William.

"Are you enjoying your party, Princess?"

Nicole met the smoky gray eyes smiling down at her. Prince Dimitri bowed and offered her a glass of wine. Tonight he wore black satin breeches and matching coat. The satin was as black as his hair and captured the mellow glow of blazing candlelight and returned soft reflections with each graceful movement. Dazzling white lace frothed at throat and cuffs. A quick glance confirmed his shoe buckles were indeed a cluster of diamonds. As were the buttons sparkling at wrist and breast. No guest was as elegant; in fact, Nicole privately admitted she had never observed such rich clothing.

At her sidelong examination, Dimitri's eyes twinkled, an amusement which offended Nicole's sense of loyalty. Suddenly she perceived her friends and neighbors as the Russians must, shabby and ill-clad by comparison.

Her golden curls tossed and her eyes flashed. "How can I enjoy anything? Tomorrow I'm being dragged from my home; my every step is tagged by your soldiers; and the most important event in my life, my engagement is completely disrupted!" The sheer physical power of the man unnerved her. She edged backward until her spine gently bumped the wall. His broad shoulders blocked the party from view.

Sensual lips smiled, and Nicole drew a quick breath at sight of a tantalizing hint of cruelty she'd previously overlooked. It would be foolhardy to cross this man. He sipped his wine before answering. "First, you are not being 'dragged' away, you are returning to your homeland, an occasion for joy. Second, the soldiers are not mine, they are yours, an elite corps permanently attached to your service and charged with your protection. Third . . ." His eyes traced the curve of her moist lips, dropped without apology to a swell of creamy breasts. "Having met your fiancé, frankly I'd think you'd view the 'disruption' more in light of a rescue." Grinning, he lifted his wine and drained it with a nonchalance which indicated he was either unaware of his appalling rudeness or didn't care.

Nicole glared, snapping her fan open across her breasts. Heat circled her cheeks as she hid the hollow of cleavage from his appraisal. "I think," she responded through clenched teeth, "that we had best abandon the subject of my fiancé. William is none of your concern." If the prince had not blocked her passage, Nicole would have brushed past him and flounced into the parlor.

An eyebrow lifted, and his grin broadened. "As you wish, Princess."

The ensuing moment of quiet scraped Nicole's nerves, as did his steady appreciative gaze. His eyes held her, releasing butterflys in her stomach.

"What are those medals?" Prince Dimitri wore a silk sash looped over one wide shoulder; the white silk was nearly obscured by a multitude of medals and ribbons. Though she was curious, Nicole inquired more to end an uncomfortable silence than from any great desire to learn each medal's merit.

"Mostly nonsense," he replied with a shrug. Examining the precious stones circling many of the pieces, Nicole doubted his modest disclaimer. "In the main, this is to remind your friends, such as the astute Mr. Revere, that Russia and England are on amiable terms. At least for the moment. The unrest in the colonies is well known, as is a reputation for outspoken opinions. I'd not like some hot-head to forget himself. What politics are voiced will reach the ear of the empress and possibly King George."

"You're . . . you're a spy?" Flustered, she thought of the crush of people straining the limits of the parlor. Some of her guests had participated in the Boston Massacre; many were actively engaged in harassing the redcoats whenever and wherever opportunity presented, including Louis Duchard. The colonies were a tinderbox awaiting a match.

Not for the first time she felt her heart divide into a tug-of-war of loyalties. In spirit she sided politically with Louis and the colonial rebels; more than once Paul Revere had paced the Duchard kitchen and stirred souls with his impassioned rhetoric. At the opposite end of the mental rope stood William with his stoic condemnation of rebel demands, arguments stated reasonably and cogently, which raised storms of confusion in one small listener. It bewildered her that William stubbornly refused to admit any validity to the colonies' wish for independence, and it shocked her to suspect he would prefer war to conceding a single point. It was painful to observe friends suspiciously curtail their conversation in William's presence. Had William arrived on time tonight, the pockets of lively chatter would now be concerning themselves with more mundane topics.

Her guests didn't realize an additional spy was concealed in their midst. "Additional . . ." Nicole winced at the thought. William was not a spy.

"You think I'm spying?" To her astonishment, Dimitri Denisov threw back his head and laughed, a deep rich sound which reverberated along her nerves. "A spy?" He placed his wineglass beside a darting candle and wiped his eyes with a square of spotless linen. "Your innocence is refreshing. We don't refer to it as spying; mine is a diplomatic reconnaissance." He smiled, reading her mind. "There's no need to warn anyone. I'm in private agreement with your friends' principles and aims, I assure you; my only regret is that I can't join the fight. My public position, however, is a different matter. And Mr. Revere and the others are well aware of the differences." The smile became annoyingly patronizing, and Nicole blushed. "My position as diplomat can be used to advance the rebel cause . . . your friends have a possible opportunity to approach the English king through a new channel." He shrugged. "If used wisely, the conduit may be beneficial to all." He continued watching her, then added, "Would it ease your mind to know that I believe so strongly in the colonies' future that I've purchased a large tract of land near Salem?"

She had no way of judging whether the sympathies he expressed were genuine or an effort to mollify her concern. The duality of duty versus personal conviction was a concept Nicole could not comfortably align. "But . . . spying?" She stared. No matter how he glossed the label, he was gathering information—spying—and spying was the most despicable duplicity she could envision. What had life sunk to when Louis Duchard's modest home was invaded by foreign spies? "What exactly is your position?"

She pressed farther into the corner, grateful her own skirt wasn't as obstructive as Irina's. Dimitri stood too near, closer than refinement allowed. She felt a heat which made her alternately weak, then giddy. Nicole frowned into her wine. She hadn't noticed this peculiar tingling sensation when standing near other men. Her gaze dropped to his strong tapered hands, experienced and capable, now deceptively relaxed. A flush of pink climbed her throat.

"I serve the Russian throne as my father did before me, as an ambassador-at-large in the service of the czarina." He smiled. "I'm not always a spy."

She ignored the jibe. "What does that mean?"

"It means I go where the empress sends me, wherever she finds need of my talents. To conclude a delicate negotiation, to solve problems affecting the empire . . . When I'm not needed, I retire to my estates in whatever country I happen to be." Leaning a hand against the wall, he bent near her ear to be heard. Nicole's breast lifted unsteadily, and she quickly unfurled her fan above the plunge of green silk. His breath smelled wine-warm, his gray eyes appeared bottomless. An explosion of nervous heat stole across her lower stomach.

What on earth was happening to her? Was she catching cold? Developing a fever? "Why doesn't Irina like me?" she blurted. Maybe he wasn't a spy, or maybe spying was complex and had more positive attributes than she knew. The entire issue was confusing.

Surprise darkened the slate eyes, and he drew back, regarding her with sharpened interest. Nicole expelled a tiny sigh of relief at the restored distance.

"Has Irina said or done anything to offend?"

"No . . . I just sense that she resents me. Perhaps that's too strong a word." Nicole caught her lower lip between her teeth, swirling her wine in the glass. "I feel as if I'm missing a piece of a puzzle, as if I'm being shown the twig but not the tree."

Without speaking, Dimitri exchanged Nicole's full glass for his emptied one, lifting the wine to his lips. Above the rim he studied her soberly, as if seeing her for the first time. "There's more beneath those honey curls than beauty," he murmured. "You must forgive Irina's lack of warmth. She is passionately devoted to Catherine. Irina views you as a possible threat to the Empress."

Nicole wasn't certain she'd heard his quiet words correctly. Her lips parted and she started to ask for an explanation, although his face suddenly closed as if he'd revealed more than he intended. Had Nicole proceeded with her inquiries, and had Denisov chosen to answer, no force on earth would have induced her to sail from Boston's safe harbor. Later, when so many destinies had been irretrievably altered, when many had suffered and died, Nicole would look back to this moment and torment herself that she had allowed the opportunity for answers to slip away.

But at that moment William strode past the soldiers posted inside the doorway, and problems of a more immediate nature invaded her thoughts. It was imperative that she speak to William. And escape the disturbing nearness of Prince Dimitri.

"Major."

"Prince."

The men shook hands with a wariness born of instant dislike, cold eyes measuring and cautious. Intuitively each viewed the other as a dangerous adversary, although neither could have precisely stated the reason.

The icy politeness puzzled Nicole, and she turned to face William, a question in her wide eyes.

A question he deliberately misread. "I apologize for being late—the regiment was detained on maneuvers." While his narrow face retained its usual implacable control, his eyes signaled an urgency which Nicole immediately recognized as matching her own need for a moment's privacy.

Head held high, Nicole tucked her arm around William's sleeve, acutely aware the hum of conversation had taken a different turn the instant a British officer entered the house. She wished he had thought to don civilian clothing before arriving. "Please excuse us," she murmured to Dimitri, who executed a graceful bow at the end of which she couldn't be certain who was dismissing whom. William instantly stiffened, his hand dropping to his saber and his eyes narrowing. Hastily Nicole tugged his arm, leading toward the kitchen.

"I need to talk to you alone," William insisted beneath his breath.

"I know." She shook her head in annoyance, attempting to banish the chill amusement she'd read in smoky eyes she con-

21

tinued to feel at her back until she and William entered the crowded kitchen.

Irina and her admiring circle had been dislodged, replaced by a noisy gathering of men who had been heatedly discussing tax reform and British oppression until William's arrival. Now they passed a hot flip iron from hand to hand, thrusting it into sizzling mugs, then back to the fire to reheat, and the conversation centered upon business and weather and inconsequential matters. Louis had produced a barrel of rum and the libation flowed freely, but not so freely as to render tongues careless. They pretended not to notice as Nicole guided William past the edges of the gathering and into the small buttery at the back of the house.

She closed the door quietly and fumbled in the darkness to light a candle, placing it on a shelf near rows of covered crocks. The flame wavered uncertainly in a flow of cold air leaking from the outside door and stirring the scents in the pantry. The tiny room smelled of freshly churned butter, smoked hams, and baskets of apples beginning to turn vinegary.

"Nicole," William whispered. An unaccustomed agitation broke past his control, and he placed his hands on her shoulders, peering into her face. A torrent of astonishing emotion flowed from his thin lips. "What are you trying to do? All week you've been a hundred miles away! You're tormenting me, do you know that? I can't work, I can't think!"

Nicole blinked in surprise and examined the unexpected depths within this man whom she had believed she knew. The intensity matched her perception of him, but the lapse of control did not, nor had she anticipated the words tumbling from his mouth. The raw emotion twisting his features alarmed her. There was an obsessive quality behind his pale stare and in the bruising force digging into her shoulders.

"William . . ." Flickering candlelight shone directly upon his impassioned features, imparting a feverish glow to his eyes. Grateful that her own countenance remained in shadow, Nicole began slowly, uncertain what she would say. "A year is a very long time. It's unfair to ask you to wait. I . . . I think it best to release you from your pledge." Immediately she recognized the wisdom in her statement. Far from reassuring her, his outburst of emotion repelled her, impressed her as excessive and out of character. Quite suddenly she perceived that William was not what he seemed; he was not predictable at all—there were hidden layers she hadn't suspected. That he was prepared to marry without divulging his entire character both fascinated and frightened her.

His hands tightened, crumpling the green silk and biting into her flesh. "Never!" Pale eyes blazed and his voice sank into hoarseness. "Our pledge binds us forever! If I must wait a year, I'll wait, but I'll never let you go! Not now, not ever!"

"William . . . you're hurting me!" She swallowed her surprise, and her wide eyes flicked toward the door. Not once during the last year had they discussed love. In fairness, they hadn't been granted the privacy for intimate declarations, but surely she couldn't have overlooked what her heart so yearned to see. Yet somehow she had. She stared at him with an expression akin to awe; his control had been miraculous. And the realization triggered a warning alarm within her breast.

"I'm sorry, forgive me." He released her abruptly and ran a hand past the sandy lock on his forehead. "I despise this!" Pale eyes hardened to marble. "I can't tolerate the thought of you spending weeks with Denisov!"

The emotional outburst astounded Nicole. She licked her lips and lowered her hands, forcibly pushing them down by her sides. "William, our betrothal—"

His eyes glittered. "Enough of that nonsense! No one jilts William Caldwell!" The look in his eyes sent a shiver up her spine. "Don't you understand? I love you, dammit, I love you!"

What Nicole understood was that her impending departure had unleashed a strange new William, one she had never suspected. She answered carefully. "And I'm . . . fond . . . of you, William, truly I am, but I think . . ." His stare halted the stumbling words. And it felt as if they had been standing in the pantry for hours. The small room closed around them, hot and suffocating.

"I want to kiss you."

"What?" The blunt vulgarity of his flat statement jolted with its impropriety. Was this really William? Always correct, always obedient to authority and convention . . . William?

"In all this time, we've never kissed."

"My father—"

"—is not here now. Nicole! For God's sake, grant me *something!* Can't you see that I'm suffering?"

Yes, she could see it. And the knowledge stunned her. She was watching a placid stream rage over its banks, flooding out of control.

He banged his fist against a shelf, his head hanging and his voice muffled. "I've dreamed of holding you and kissing you! I've imagined it a million times! You don't know how often I've wanted to strangle your father, anything to get him out of the room and you into my arms!"

This, then, was the romantic gesture Nicole had long awaited. She shifted from one slipper to the other, sifting through veils of confusion and wondering why his declaration alarmed instead of pleased her. Perhaps it was an uneasy suspicion that if she refused the kiss, he would not allow her to leave; there was something wild and fixated about his eyes.

She licked her lips nervously and ran damp palms over the cool green silk. "I . . . If you wish . . ." And she prayed she would find a way to escape without a scene.

His head snapped upward and his pale eyes blazed. He crossed the pantry in a bound, clasping her tightly against the gold braid running down his red jacket. A groan issued from deep within his throat, and then hard dry lips met hers in a closed kiss, alternating between a force of passion and the tenderness of emotion.

Nicole winced, and she watched his sandy lashes close against narrow cheeks, and her hands lifted to his shoulders, increasing the pressure in a growing compulsion to break free. And deep inside she acknowledged that Dimitri Denisov had been correct: she had been rescued. William's kiss was hot and clutching and repugnant.

Without warning, the outside door splintered inward with a deafening crash. At the same instant, the kitchen door slammed open. In the sudden spill of light, jars and crockery smashed to the floor, food and glass exploded across Nicole's satin slippers.

In less time than she could draw a breath to scream, soldiers jammed the pantry. They ripped William from her halfhearted embrace and hurled him brutally against the shelves. Two soldiers wrenched his arms behind his back, and a flashing dagger appeared at William's throat; another man positioned himself protectively before Nicole, his saber drawn and ready.

Eyes wide with fear, Nicole gasped as a ruby bead welled from William's throat and stained the tip of the dagger. She couldn't grasp what her eyes registered. At a sound, she whirled to face a tall dark form filling the kitchen doorway, blocking a ring of horrified faces beyond. They too were confronted with soldiers; Nicole had time to see the glitter of swords before Dimitri Denisov's broad shoulders blocked her line of sight.

"This man's life is in your hands, Highness. If he offended you in any way, you have only to speak and he dies." The words emerged flat, as hard and final as death.

"What are you doing?" Nicole wrung her hands, blinking desperately past terrified tears. The soldier pressing the dagger to William's taut throat stared at her over his shoulder, waiting. William's eyes rolled in disbelief; the beginnings of fear sounded in the terrible gagging noise he made.

"Does he live or die? *Da* or *nyet?*" Dimitri's slate eyes bored into hers.

"Let him go! For the love of God, release him! I beg you!" The silence beyond the kitchen door was as thick as paste.

An eternity elapsed before Denisov nodded curtly and turned sharply toward the soldiers. Harsh commands reverberated within the pantry; then he stood aside as the soldiers dragged William toward the door.

"You son of a bitch!" William screamed, struggling against the soldiers. "I know what you're doing! If you touch her, I swear I'll find you and kill you!" The pale eyes boiled hatred. "She's mine!"

Denisov's lips curved in a cold smile which matched the icy granite in his eyes. "It seems you are in no position to make threats, my friend." His pointed glance indicated the soldiers' rough hold. "And if you're considering any foolish melodramatics at the dockyard tomorrow, I suggest you discuss the situation with your superiors. I believe they will remind you that the current political climate is delicate . . . I suspect your career would suffer for any refractory incident."

Their eyes locked in mutual loathing. Then William hissed, "Just remember! She's pledged to me!"

Dimitri shot his cuffs and smiled. He nodded to the soldiers, and they dragged William from the buttery. A swelling buzz hummed through the kitchen as more people pressed forward, straining to see.

Shame flamed across Nicole's cheekbones, and she fell limply against the shelves, covering her face with shaking hands. The disgace of it! The sudden heart-stopping fear when the soldiers . . . Her head jerked up, and she raged at Denisov. "How dare you humiliate us like this? How do you dare such an outrage! and William . . ." It was unforgivable. The soldiers had drawn blood! He'd behaved as if he actually meant to kill William!

Dimitri Denisov's eyes hardened to flint. "This is not a game, Nicole, those are not toy soldiers! Listen to me, and this time hear what I tell you. Those soldiers are pledged to protect you; if any harm comes to you, their punishment is death."

Her face paled to chalk. "That is barbaric!"

"Perhaps. But that is also the truth."

"But if they . . . How can I hope for any privacy?" Behind him, Marie and Louis pleaded with their guests to remain, but an exodus streamed hastily toward the front porch, scrambling for cloaks and hats. It was just as well; Nicole's shame precluded facing anyone.

"You may secure whatever privacy you wish simply by informing the captain of the guards that you desire solitude and telling him where you will be."

"That's impossible—I don't speak their language."

He grinned, relaxing against the door. "Then you had better learn quickly, hadn't you? In the meantime . . ." The infuriating grin widened. "The next time you arrange a tryst with a lover, I suggest you inform me, and I'll alert the guards on your behalf."

Nicole's eyes flashed. "William is not my lover!"

He laughed and settled against the doorjamb, folding his arms across his chest. "Obviously. If what I observed is the standard, your William is about as skilled in lovemaking as he is at defending himself."

Furious, Nicole stiffened her spine. The green silk crackled. "Well, perhaps you're mistaken! Perhaps what you observed was the last kiss following . . ."—she waved a hand—"following a dozen passionate embraces!" The words astonished her; she hadn't the vaguest idea why she claimed such foolishness. She sensed uneasily that she was edging herself into a corner, but she couldn't stop until she'd erased the arrogant amusement from those knowing eyes. "William is the most romantic man I've ever met!"

"Oh?" The amusement vanished, replaced by a hard sweeping stare which snatched at Nicole's breath. He crossed the buttery in two strides. "Did he take you in his arms like this?" Dimitri's hands circled her waist, and he pulled her roughly against his black satin breeches. Nicole gasped as a rod of heat thrust against her body and his eyes smoldered into hers. "Did he demonstrate the effect of a desirable woman upon a man?" Strong hands rocked her hips against the unmistakable strength flaming between them. "Did he sample the honey moistening a woman's tongue?" His hands swept upward to cup her golden head. For a moment smoky eyes burned into hers; then his mouth crushed her lips in a kiss that scorched, that explored, that pulled the breath from her body and left her weak-kneed and deeply shaken.

He released her suddenly, and Nicole fell against the shelving, her legs rubbery and her pulse thundering in her ears. A hand rose to trembling lips, and she stared at him from eyes the size of saucers. He laughed softly and paused in the doorway. "No, I thought not." Then he was gone.

Nicole waited for her breath to return, for the hurricane in her breast to subside. She stared into the empty kitchen.

One cycle of life had ended abruptly, and another, more disturbing, had begun.

Lifting her finger, she twisted off the band of silver. She placed William's pledge ring on a shelf where Marie would find it in the morning. The discovery would gladden her parents' hearts.

Her bridges were burned; Russia awaited. There would be no turning back.

She stared at the vacant doorway. Then she slowly bent and gathered shards of crockery into her skirt.

3

THE FRIGATE *Kiev* waited in Boston's harbor, her great oaken hull dwarfing the bobbing barkentines, merchant ships, and fishing vessels. Her wooden masts accused the leaden sky like spiny fingers. A crowned double eagle challenged the sea from the bow; a bank of misted windows wrapped about the stern. The sheer size of the ship swept Nicole's breath away and helped divert her thoughts from the distressing farewell scene on the docks. Her parents' grief and her own lingered darkly in her heart.

Dimitri assisted her from the longboat and up a rope ladder onto the decks, smiling as she flung out her arms for balance.

"Until dinner," he said, his warm hands releasing her shoulders.

Through eyes dark with mistrust and resentment, Nicole watched him run lightly toward the forecastle, taking the steps two at once. Today he wore woolen breeches and a blue cotton shirt, its flowing sleeves restrained beneath an unadorned coarse jacket. His black hair was tied at the neck with a strip of cord. She noted how his rugged body responded joyously to the open salt air; then she dropped her eyes in a confusion of embarrassment. She had promised herself to ignore him, a promise she meant to keep.

Uncertain what was expected of her, Nicole backed against the railing. Riotous color jumped forward wherever she looked—reds and blacks and bright yellows. Then she blinked hard and leaned forward. Near the waist of the ship, distant enough to be observed without undue fear, an enormous cage was lashed to the main mast. Inside paced a mammoth black bear. The animal responded angrily to the tensions of a ship preparing to get under way. Its protesting bellows added to the noise of blasting whistles, clanging bells, and shouting men.

Racing feet pounded past Nicole's hem, and she shrank into the railing; men swarmed up the ratlines, their agile bodies swinging like monkeys through a jungle of rigging. Caged pigs, sheep, and chickens squealed, bleated, and cackled as men hastened to secure the hatches of the holds.

Sharp retorts sounded from above, and Nicole shaded wide eyes to stare upward as clouds of sail spilled from the yards. Chill wind battered the canvas, then cupped it full with a crack like cannon shot. The *Kiev* shuddered along her planking, straining at the anchor like a sleek animal eager to run free.

Voices rang from above and below; the leadsman sounded the depths in a singsong chant. A clank of heavy metal screeched as the anchor chain wound up and up. Dripping iron broke above the waves with a heavy sucking noise.

And a cheer roared from cold-hoarsened throats as the *Kiev* dipped forward, then sprang toward the open sea. Alone at the railing, Nicole whirled to peer longingly toward the receding shoreline, attempting to engrave upon her memory the snow-frosted town, the graceful church spires against a gray sky. She swore she could identify Louis and Marie, though her heart knew it was impossible to isolate the dots moving about the wharf. She touched her temples, blinking hard. Her

28

parents had aged a decade in the last days; she had seen it in their eyes. A sudden spate of tears fogged her vision, and she battled to cork an outpouring of grief. She didn't belong on this noisy ship; she wanted to go home. Only a deep reservoir of pride stayed the tears stinging her lids.

Cold fingers of wind caught her bonnet and tore it from her head, fanning golden strands about her pale face like a halo. A small distracted sound broke from her lips as she watched her hat sail above the water before tossing waves snatched it away. The circle of brown velvet vanished as completely as her own identity had vanished, in a swirl of turbulence.

Deer Island passed on her left; then nothing lay ahead but vast endless sea flowing invisibly into the leaden horizon. Nicole brushed helplessly at her wind-tossed hair and wondered where Irina had disappeared to. Even Irina would be a comfort now.

"Some hot tea and a splash of vodka will restore the sparkle to those lovely eyes, I'll wager."

For an instant the flawless French and deep voice brought Dimitri to mind, but when Nicole peeked through her fingers, she was looking into the bearded face of a much older man. Snow-white hair fluttered beneath a beaver cap, contrasting violently with prominent jet-black eyebrows an inch wide and as heavy and dark as the mustache and beard. Steady black eyes appraised her with the open admiration of a man who appreciates beautiful women. The giant bowed over her glove. "Vadim Ivanovich Nevsky at your service, Princess."

Nicole's tongue stumbled over the name, and the man laughed, the twinkle in his eyes softening the frightening boom of humor. He was the largest human being Nicole had ever seen.

"Russian names are impossible until you understand the system. Then it's simple. The middle name is the father's first name; 'Ivanovich' means 'son of Ivan.' You won't be far wrong if you assume every third male's mid-name is Ivanovich." He smiled broadly, the black beard framing strong white teeth. "I am called Vadim. No title . . . I'm a freeman and proud to be one. I wouldn't give a kopeck for a title."

"Who . . .?"

"Am I?" A hamlike hand turned her from the shore. "An old *diad'ka* who should have been turned out to pasture years ago." He winked. "I refuse to go." Tucking her gloved hand firmly around his sleeve, he guided her toward the stern, stepping over thick strands of rope, glowering menacingly at sailors dashing across their path. His arm felt like a log beneath her fingers.

"A *diad'ka?*" Nicole asked timidly. She hadn't imagined any living person could be so huge.

The man was simply enormous; taller than Dimitri by a foot, barrel-chested and thick-limbed, he was a bear of a man, a giant. Even with the sparkling black eyes and carefully modulated voice, Vadim Nevsky was a terrifyingly awesome specimen. Sliding an alarmed glance toward his bearded profile, Nicole suspected few would dare oppose him, even though he'd attained an age when most men preferred to rest before a fire and dandle grandchildren on their knees. She was dwarfed, a slender reed in the shadow of an oak. Uneasily Nicole wondered where he led. Her glance swept the decks, searching out a familiar face.

"How best to explain a *diad'ka* . . . a *diad'ka* is the person responsible for the care of a young nobleman in those years when he is too old for a nursemaid but too young for a tutor. Sometimes when the *barchuk,* the little master, is particularly thick-headed and backward, his *diad'ka* must remain with him well into adulthood." Vadim halted, his black eyes dancing. His voice coarsened to a semiroar, raising bumps along Nicole's skin. "My *barchuk* is especially slow and idiotic. Almost thirty, and the dolt still has need of a keeper!"

"Don't believe everything this old reprobate tells you! Age and vodka have scrambled whatever brains he might have had." Dimitri Denisov strode down a flight of stairs leading from the poop. An affectionate grin widened his lips. He had discarded his jacket, and the wind plucked at his wide sleeves.

"See? Didn't I tell you my *barchuk* was stupid? As ranking official, he should be counseling the captain on the forecastle. But where do we find him? Sniffing about the entrance to the women's quarters like a mongrel dog!" Dimitri laughed as Vadim lowered thick black brows and glared. "Why didn't you tell me she was so beautiful? Are you afraid of exposing our little princess to a real man?"

Smiling, Dimitri responded in Russian, and both men laughed. He settled a fur cap over wind-tumbled hair. "When you have the princess settled, come back up here and let's see if those muscles are capable of elevating something heavier than a woman's hand." Before he departed, Dimitri directed his smile toward Nicole. His silvery eyes lingered provocatively on her lush full breasts, molded by the wind's force. Blushing furiously, she jerked her cape over her bodice and ground her teeth.

Not for one moment did she understand her conflicting reactions to him. His masculine confidence attracted at the same instant his appalling insolence repelled. Ignoring the sudden rush of heat tingling through her body, Nicole tossed her hair and lifted her skirts, stepping into a wood-paneled hallway without waiting for the giant Ukrainian.

A roar sounded at her back. "Hold on, there, Princess, you're more brave than wise to wander about a ship housing a hundred lusty men!" Vadim caught her in two strides and firmly clamped her hand around his massive arm.

There was no resisting. "Your *barchuk* should be taught some manners!"

Vadim laughed and slid a knowing smile toward the golden crown held stiffly below his shoulder. He patted her fingers and answered in a surprisingly gentle tone. "Dimitri Mikhailovich Denisov is the finest man I have the honor to know. I would lay down my life in his service."

Nicole tilted her head upward, startled by the unexpected depth of emotion.

Sandwiched between the harsh black of cap and beard, Vadim's serious eyes flickered dark warmth. "Place your trust in the *barchuk*. When we dock in St. Petersburg, you'll be glad of such a man as your champion. You won't find a better friend."

Nicole's jaw set and the pink deepened in her cheeks as she recalled the scene in the buttery. "That sort of friend I neither want nor need!"

Vadim smiled. "We'll see. In the meantime, I'm to deliver you into Countess Irina Ivanova's care." He peered into Nicole's face. " 'Ivanova'—'daughter of Ivan.' See how it works? The countess will see to you." Black eyes rolled and his mouth puckered into a droll circle. "A formidable woman, our countess. Outlived three husbands—they died in self-defense. If she and I were younger, I'd sweeten that vile temper!" Sighing, he shook the white hair, then knocked aside a guard in a red tunic as if the man were no weightier than a fly. The wooden door buckled inward beneath the energetic impact of his fist.

A young girl in dust cap and apron opened the door a crack, then swung it wide enough to allow Nicole entrance. As Vadim bid her good-bye, Irina's voice bawled from the interior, "For God's sake, shut that door! You're letting the heat escape!"

"A harpy," Vadim confided. "What she needs is a good——" the closing door cut off his theory, and Nicole decided it was fortunate that it had.

A blast of hot air rising from glowing coals within hooded braziers struck Nicole with oppressive force after the fresh chill above deck. She peeled off her gloves and untied her cape strings, gazing about in openmouthed wonder.

Irina's quarters were more lavish than Nicole could have imagined. Only the roll and pitch beneath her boots reminded her that she had not stepped into a fairy tale of Oriental splendor.

Tapestries interwoven with silver thread concealed the walls; animal skins covered the planking. Brass lanterns swung from the ceiling, illuminating first one part of the cabin and then another. A pencil-post bed draped in emerald velvet was bolted to the far wall; servants' pallets formed a ring around it. Various gilded chairs and low tables and thickly upholstered ottomans slid with the motion of the ship. The tang of incense spiced each breath.

"It's good to be going home," Irina sighed. She'd exchanged her traveling gown for a flowing robe of violent yellow. Waving Nicole inside, she leaned to the mirror above her dressing table and raised the lid of a jeweled snuffbox. Studying her image, she inserted a pinch of snuff first into one flaring nostril, then into the other. She sneezed, then leaned backward with a contented sigh, motioning to one of the women digging into the trunks Irina had required throughout her Boston visit.

The young girl who had answered Vadim's thunderous rapping hastened forward to assist in removing Irina's wig. She placed the ponderous mass on a wooden form clamped to a small table. A cloud of powder rose like fine mist, sifting slowly over the polished surface.

Irina gestured toward Nicole impatiently, then called another of the servants. A young woman a year or two older than Nicole hurried to draw boiling water from a silver samovar steaming beneath the porthole. "Do you take vodka in your tea, *chérie?*"

"I . . . No."

Freed from the wig, Irina's hair emerged yellowish gray and streaked with traces of auburn. Long thin strands matted close to her head, darkening at the temples as perspiration glued loose wisps to her skin.

Lifting both hands, Irina scratched vigoriously at the pink scalp showing beneath gray and auburn. "I thought we'd have tea, then Pavla will see you to your room. Pavla is one of yours."

Nicole accepted a glass mug from the sturdy servant girl and murmured a word of thanks. "Are you Pavla?" The girl frowned and bit the end of a long dark braid falling over one shoulder. Clearly she didn't understand French.

Immediately Irina sprang from her chair and turned on the girl in fury. Her hand lashed out and stung across the girl's cheek. A fusillade of harsh words erupted like bullets. Cheek flaming, the girl dropped into a deep curtsy, her stony eyes riveted to the floor.

Nicole's mouth dropped, and she stared, forgetting the glass of tea until her fingers burned. Shakily she placed the mug on Irina's dressing table. "What was all that?"

Irina seated herself and leaned toward the mirror, peeling a heart-shaped patch from her cheek. "If you allow it, they take the most outrageous liberties! Then look you square in the eye and plead innocence!" She met Nicole's wide gaze with a sidelong squint of reproach. "It's fortunate none of them speak French, or they'd be laughing their fool heads off! A princess does not deign to thank a servant!" She dropped the heart shape into a small pearl-studded box containing a collection of patches. "Did you see her? She knows a princess ranks more than a cursory bobbing; she knows how to bow!"

Nicole stared at the girl's bent head and swallowed uncomfortably. "Why doesn't she rise?"

"She doesn't dare, until you permit it, of course, which I wouldn't advise immediately. Teach her humility; that one's too proud by far! And a thief and a liar, if you ask me—they all are."

Nicole shifted uneasily. She'd stepped into a strange harsh dream where nothing was as it should be. The tapestries lifted and sank with the plowing thrust of the ship; the sweetish drift of incense tickled her nostrils. Suffocating heat, combined with the bilious yellow of Irina's dressing gown, elicited a nauseous roll in the pit of her stomach. Hesitantly she stretched a hand and touched Pavla's shoulder. The girl straightened. She held her face carefully blank, but her expressive dark eyes flickered resentment.

Watching in the mirror, Irina shrugged. "She belongs to you—you can do with her as you like. But it's a mistake to coddle serfs. They'll repay you with treachery, mark my words."

"I believe most people act as we expect them to," Nicole answered softly. "Expect the worst, and you receive the worst. Expect the best, and . . ."

Irina smirked indulgently. "A charmingly naive concept."

Nicole lifted her tea, watching the servant girl bow deeply, then withdraw. "When you spoke to her, you indicated me . . . but I didn't hear my name . . . ?"

"Oh . . . well, that's because your name's been changed, *chérie*, you didn't recognize it."

"What?" Boiling tea scalded across Nicole's fingers. She couldn't decide which was the greater shock, Irina's offhand manner or the outrageous liberty they'd taken in changing her name. "But what's wrong with . . . ?" The Russians were simply incredible! First they deprived her of her background and her parents; now they stripped away her name. When they finished with her, would she retain any shreds of her original identity? Nicole Duchard appeared to be melting away.

Irina's shoulders lifted and dropped. She splashed a generous dollop of vodka into her tea. " 'Nicole' is too . . . French." As Nicole continued to stare in disbelief, Irina explained. "While the Russian court emulates French culture—fashion, art, literature, manners—we don't admire the French themselves. Do you understand?"

Nicole did not. But it didn't matter; what mattered was her name. Blinking, she gazed into her glass. There was no point in resisting; her wishes were of no consequence. "So . . . who am I now?" she whispered. It was a question she'd asked herself frequently throughout the last week.

"Princess Natasha Stepanova. Catherine selected it herself, in the event you'd been christened with an unacceptable name."

Nicole sank slowly to the ottoman pressing against the back of her knees. The Russians had stolen everything; they had taken the clay of one personality and sculptured a new form more to their liking. A disturbed laugh brushed across her lips. "What else? Is there anything left of me that you plan to alter or erase or mold into something else?"

Irina frowned. "All in good time. I think perhaps you're overwrought. Perhaps a rest before dinner . . ." She snapped her fingers, and Pavla hastened forward, leading several older women also wearing caps and aprons. Irina instructed them, then waited impatiently as they assembled by the door. "They'll attend to your needs throughout the journey."

Nicole gazed desperately into one stoic face and then another. "But how? I can't communicate with them!" She lifted her palms and looked to Irina.

Losing interest, Irina returned to the mirror and raised a silver brush. "We'll begin language lessons in the morning." Removing her hairpins, she drew the brush through thin strands of gray and auburn. "I expect you'll prove an earnest pupil." The heavy-lidded eyes smiled into the mirror: a hint of malicious satisfaction edged her voice. "You're motivated."

Rising to her feet, Nicole firmed her chin. She would not allow Countess Irina the pleasure of observing her dismay. She spun on her heel and stormed toward the door.

Outside the smothering heat of Irina's cabin, Nicole drew a calming breath of frosty sea air. One of the red tunics bowed, and the guard guided them down a paneled hallway past a galley and several latched doors. The party halted before two soldiers. Both saluted crisply, fists thumping against chests; then one leaned forward and pushed open the door.

Once inside, Nicole gasped and halted abruptly. The women behind nearly trampled her hem. She had expected a duplicate of Irina's cabin; instead she faced a magnificent bank of windows overlooking the foaming bubbles churning in the ship's wake. A sinking sun flooded the cabin with tones of gold, as softly mellow as the gleaming gold fittings wherever her eye touched. Minutes ago, she hadn't believed anything could surpass the sumptuousness of Irina's quarters; now she stood in the midst of undreamed luxury.

Polished mahogany shone about the edges of vibrantly colored wall tapestries, and the canopied four-poster was covered by a spread of rich dark mink pelts. Thick warm rugs scattered over shining planks, and the draperies beside the windows were of the finest rose-colored brocade and velvet. She'd been provided an inlaid writing desk, a dining table, two satin sofas, and several side chairs, one of which appeared to be solid silver.

Nicole walked slowly toward the cabin's brazier, staring in astonishment. She held her palms above the hood, whispering a word of gratitude for the slight chill—otherwise everything would have seemed to be an hallucination.

The surfeit of new sensations dulled her mind. She wanted

nothing more than to sit quietly over a cup of strong hot coffee and ponder the day's impressions. Even Cinderella must have required a period of adjustment, she thought wearily.

Drawing a breath, Nicole turned from the brazier and surveyed the large open room. The older women had flipped open her trunk. They shook out Nicole's gowns with tiny murmurs of disappointment; evidently they had expected grander attire. Pavla unpacked Nicole's books, arranging them by color groups within the shelves along one wall.

Nicole bit her lip uncertainly. "Pavla?"

"Princess Natasha." The girl curtsied deeply.

They had spoken the only words either could hope the other would understand.

Nicole had to begin somewhere. "I'd like a cup of coffee, please, black."

"Ya ne panemah 'yo."

Nicole sucked in her cheeks and released a long breath. She nodded to herself. "You knew it wouldn't be easy." She could forgo the coffee, or persist until she somehow made herself understood. Near the bed, the older women slowed their movements, exchanging glances and watching without appearing to. "Nicole Duchard is not a quitter!" Their expressions didn't alter. Sighing, Nicole embarrassed herself by raising her voice. Loud did not equal comprehension. "Coffee?" she repeated, shouting and feeling foolish.

Pavla shrugged helplessly. Her broad square face was plain as vanilla pudding, she was nondescript in those areas a woman most dreads being nondescript, but she possessed fine dark eyes. Those eyes showed themselves anxious to please—and as frustrated as the woman she faced.

Releasing another sigh, Nicole rebelled at her predicament. The silver chair upon which she leaned was easily equal in value to three coffee plantations. And all she desired was a single cup. She had smelled fresh coffee in the galley, and she was surrounded by servants willing to provide; the entire situation was idiotic.

Signaling Pavla's attention, Nicole formed her fingers around an imaginary cup and lifted it to her lips; she raised an eyebrow. Immediately Pavla's expression brightened in relief, and she hurried to an ornate silver samovar twice the size of Irina's.

"No," Nicole cried in frustration. "Not tea!" What was the word? "Nyet!"

Puzzled, Pavla frowned, replacing a glass mug upon the table. Cocking her head, she pointed inquisitively toward a vodka bottle. Nicole shook her golden curls into disarray.

Not knowing what else to try, she again mimed drinking coffee. This time, Pavla duplicated the motions, seeking a clue in action.

Aware of the other servants watching two adults enact a childhood tea party, Nicole smiled with tired amusement. She read a corresponding sparkle in Pavla's expressive eyes. Impulsively Nicole lowered her pretend cup from her mouth and extended it in a toast. "To your health!"

"*Na zdorovie!*" Pavla touched her imaginary cup to Nicole's; then both sipped with exaggerated sounds of noisy pleasure.

The women by the bed froze and their mouths dropped.

Suddenly, wonderfully, both Nicole and Pavla burst into gales of delighted laughter. One had only to lift a curved hand to her mouth to send the other into a paroxysm of helpless hilarity. At the finish, both gasped for breath and wiped damp eyes, and Nicole understood they had become friends. They had shared frustration and laughter, and in the process given something of themselves. It was a beginning.

Still smiling, Nicole did what she should have thought of to begin with: she rummaged through the desk until she located paper and ink. With Pavla bending over her shoulder, she sketched a bean, then a rather poor representation of a coffee grinder. Before she completed inking a steaming cup, Pavla had happily disappeared through the door.

Ten minutes later Nicole had her coffee and was settled comfortably before the windows, watching a glowing orange orb suspended above the waves. The sun had emerged in time to set; somehow it struck Nicole as fitting. Her smile faded.

Marie would be in the kitchen now, preparing dinner, perhaps a fragrant wine-based stew or a plump chicken roasting on the spit. Louis would be inspecting his tanning shed, adjusting the heat, checking the progress of various hides, his skilled eye gauging the number of boot tops he could scissor from each skin. When they sat down to supper, would they gaze at her empty chair and think of her?

When Nicole began to remember William with fondness, she shook herself from her reverie. Removing a square of linen from her pocket, she blotted swimming eyes, hoping the servants didn't notice.

Pavla touched her shoulder gently and pointed toward an

exquisite ormolu clock. She acted out the motions of eating, her dark eyes sparkling above an imaginary spoon.

But the game no longer amused. Nicole pressed the girl's hand but shook her head. *"Nyet."* Rising slowly, she penned a brief note to Irina, excusing herself from dinner.

Tonight she wished to devote exclusively to Nicole Duchard. Nicole Duchard had died, to rise like a phoenix in the form of Natasha Stepanova. It seemed unthinkable that Nicole Duchard should slip away unmourned. Tomorrow the person who had been Nicole would be relegated to the dustbin, and Natasha Stepanova would step forth in her place.

A wan smile teased the corners of Nicole's lips. Considering the difficulties of communicating, she certainly hoped Natasha was quick to learn. And she prayed Natasha could cope with silvery eyes and a man's smoldering hunger.

4

THE WEEKS AT sea settled into a monotony of unvarying routine. Each morning at seven, Irina knocked at Nicole's door, yawning and grumbling until coffee and vodka restored some semblance of good humor. Surprisingly, the countess emerged as a competent if impatient tutor. Subject to Irina's exacting standards, Nicole progressed rapidly.

Following a hesitant beginning, that is. Her initial glimpse of the Greek-derived Russian alphabet defeated her. It was with relief and gratitude that Nicole learned she was expected to speak Russian, but not to read or write it, a task she considered nearly impossible. Once she conquered her fear of the strange alphabet, the basic words came easily. Not as simple were the verbs, which splintered into more transmutations than she would have believed possible.

Despite occasional discouragements, Nicole took pride in the pace of her accomplishments. And gradually she began to appreciate a language richer in concrete words than French, more energetic and expressive than English.

"Vinovata?" Irina sipped vodka-laced coffee with moist sighs of pleasure.

"I beg your pardon?" Nicole answered promptly.

"Vinovaty?"

"We beg your pardon."

"Good. Your accent is nearly perfect. Excellent." Nodding, Irina closed her folder. After glancing toward the clock, she pressed both hands against the small of her back and stretched. "It's twelve o'clock, time for your walk." Vadim's forceful knock confirmed the observation. "After lunch, we'll schedule another gown fitting and review court etiquette." She frowned at the servant women sewing near the windows, deploring their slow stitches. "Only one gown complete—and you'll require at least five for court appearances!" Muttering, she fisted her hands on her hips, and her frown intensified into a glare.

As spacious as Nicole's cabin was, Vadim's presence made it appear crowded; the large Ukrainian required open spaces. Sweeping off his cap, he inclined his shaggy head to Irina and grinned at Nicole. She'd insisted he dispense with bowing; his giant's physique was not intended to bend.

"You're pale as a fish belly, Countess." Twinkling black eyes winked at Nicole. "A little fresh air would restore some pink to those cheeks. Will you join us?"

Each morning he extended an identical invitation, and each morning Irina's disdain increased. She sniffed and presented her back. Not once had Nicole overheard the countess address Vadim directly. He was beneath Irina's notice.

Massive shoulders lifted Vadim's short seaman's coat in a shrug. He replaced his fur cap, then extended both arms to Nicole and Pavla. "Ladies?" He ignored Irina's over-the-shoulder glare. "Tie your bonnets and cloaks, a storm chill rides the wind."

"It is disgusting how some men treat servants like royalty, and equally abominable that royalty would permit it!" Irina shoved irritably at the white curls glued to her forehead. A rain of powder drifted past her nose.

"Ah, Countess." Vadim winked. "You're in good humor today. What a pleasant surprise!" He pushed Nicole and Pavla into the corridor, slamming Irina's shout in the door. Grinning hugely, he escorted them to the decks.

Nicole stepped across the planking and drew a blissful breath. Undoubtedly this was her favorite hour of the day.

Beneath a crisp sky, foam-tipped waves glittered as if strewn with diamonds. Clouds of dazzling white sail puffed against the cold blue overhead. Lifting her skirts, Nicole nimbly traversed a patchwork of ropes and netting to lean her elbows against the railing. She inhaled deeply, closing her lashes; the tangy scent of salt and water and brisk frosty air cleared her head of cloying powder, coffee, and oppressive heat.

Vadim nudged between Nicole and Pavla, placing his broad spine to the water and glowering to discourage any of the watching sailors from approaching too near.

"A beautiful day," Pavla observed shyly. "It reminds me of the village where I grew up . . . nothing to break the horizon as far as the eye can see." She enunciated slowly so Nicole could understand.

"Not quite," Vadim corrected. "Lean this way and look to the east. See that wedge of cloud? There's a storm brewing, you can taste it." He folded his arms across his chest. "Time for lessons. What will it be today? History or law?"

"Couldn't we skip today? Can't a *diad'ka* have just one holiday?" Nicole pleaded charmingly through a fringe of dark lashes. Her head was stuffed with tales of Peter the Great, the Ivans, and the Annas. She favored Vadim with a smile few men could resist. "Couldn't we just stroll the decks and enjoy the day? Just this once?" The spell of creaking rigging, the smell of pine pitch, and the snap of fluttering canvas were exhilarating . . . and erased any impetus toward lessons.

Black eyes sparkled as the wind teased Nicole's honey-colored curls from the ruffle framing her face. "What? And drive the crew mad with passion?" A mock glare slid the unruly black brows over his eyes. "I'd have to fight half the ship!" Nicole suspected he'd enjoy nothing more. After winking into Pavla's smile, Vadim pretended a great sigh. "Ah, Natushka, as a babe in the cradle you learned the weakness of old men—we can't resist rosy cheeks and flirting eyes. Come along, then."

They paraded leisurely about the decks as Vadim explained intricate knots, then halted to observe a group of sailors busily polishing brass cannon. If any man dared display too great an interest in the women, Vadim gripped the hilt of his dagger threateningly. And Nicole couldn't resist teasing him when he showed an obvious disappointment that no man accepted his challenge.

Vadim grinned. "A man needs a good fight on occasion to

blow the cobwebs from mind and muscle." He placed his boot on the first step leading to the forecastle.

Looking upward, Nicole hung back. On the higher deck, Dimitri bent above a breeze-fluttered chart, deep in conversation with the *Kiev*'s captain. She bit her lip. For perhaps the hundredth time Nicole asked herself what she felt toward Dimitri Denisov. To her extreme annoyance, her fingers shook in anticipation each night as she dressed for dinner. Yet, at the same moment, she feared his smoky probing stare and his imperturbable assurance. She sensed he bided his time, waiting for . . . For what? She wasn't certain, but when she pondered those eyes and that lean responsive body, a strange moist heat shot into forbidden areas.

She squirmed uncomfortably, then looked up at Vadim, speaking slow, careful Russian. "Could we visit Zinka instead of going above?"

"Da!" Pavla agreed enthusiastically. "I brought some scraps for her."

Vadim glanced at Dimitri, then toward Nicole. He grinned. "It's your holiday."

Retracing their steps, they approached the cage lashed to the main mast and then perched on barrels Vadim rolled forward. Perhaps due to the gathering storm, Zinka appeared nervous and restless today.

The bear paced forward three steps, lowered her great shaggy head, and shook it violently from side to side; then she rose to an awesome height, dropped back onto her paws, and paced to the opposite end of the cage to repeat the pantomime. Someone had tied a bright red cone to her head, and each time she halted, Zinka's huge clawless paw swiped at the strap securing the cone. She roared and slapped a blue ball against the iron bars, then resumed the monotonous pacing.

"It's cruel to pen an animal like that." The caged bear disturbed Nicole. She never tired of visiting Zinka, but afterward she experienced an inexplicable depression.

Vadim agreed. Leaning against a sturdy pile of folded canvas, he rummaged in his coat pocket until he located a stained clay pipe. He lit it, speaking around strong teeth clamped to the pipe bit. "But it would be cruel to the men to forbid it." They watched Pavla pushing food scraps between the bars. "Nearly all the Russian fleet disobeys the rules; most ships have a bear. A mascot, you might say, and as important to the men as the ratters."

"But the ratters serve a purpose. Without the dogs, the holds would be overrun with rats. You said so yourself."

He nodded, exhaling a stream of fragrant drifting blue. "The bear also serves a purpose. Zinka represents a piece of home to the men. It's a poor village indeed which doesn't keep a bear." After a moment he removed the pipe and looked at her, adding softly, "What upsets you is not the bear but the cage." He lifted Pavla onto a barrel top. "The iron bars remind us of the cages we build around ourselves. No matter how grand or how lowly our station in life . . . we all dwell in cages of our own making."

Both women fell silent. Pavla stared at the swelling waves with an unreadable expression; Nicole uneasily considered the new cage of identity Irina insisted upon, bar by constricting bar.

Vadim knocked his pipe into a bucket of wet sand. "I smell borshch and pelmeni—it's time for lunch," he announced briskly. "And not a minute too soon. I've seen happier faces at a funeral!"

Dusting her skirts, Nicole rose to her feet. She didn't care for beet soup, but she relished the small boiled dumplings stuffed with spiced beef. Anticipating lunch was preferable to pondering self-imposed cages.

Later, she and Pavla joined Irina in the countess's quarters, resigned to several hours of tedious fittings. This portion of the day Nicole preferred least, standing motionless while Pavla and the women pinned and tucked and hemmed, and Irina tested the morning lessons, then read long dry passages from Orthodox texts. Secretly Nicole suspected the church lessons bored Irina as greatly as they did her.

"If you fidget today, I'm going to stick the pins in you," Pavla murmured, slipping a half-sewn brocade bodice over Nicole's golden head.

"If you do, I'll report you to Ivanova the terrible," Nicole whispered. She glanced at her full satiny breasts mounding above a band of stiff ribbon. "Isn't there something to go above this?" A blush tinted her creamy skin as she imagined smoky eyes lingering. A light shiver rippled along her half-naked body.

Pavla smiled around a mouthful of pins. She leaned near Nicole's curls. "He'll find you enchanting!"

The blush deepened to crimson. "That isn't what I was thinking!"

Pavla rolled disbelieving eyes and sank to her knees, joining the circle of women and taking up a length of hem.

Observing the whispered exchange with heavy-lidded disapproval, Irina commented in French, "It's all well and good to practice your Russian, but you'd be wise to remember your position . . . and hers."

Nicole's chin firmed stubbornly. "Pavla and I are friends."

"Friends! With a serf?" Irina's hiss was sharp. "She is a commodity! You can buy a dozen better than she for less than the cost of a pedigreed dog! I've examined the titles of your books; anyone who enjoys Voltaire and Shakespeare can hardly find anything in common with a creature who can't write her own name!" She nodded curtly to the woman attending the samovar. *"Chai?"* Coffee braced the mornings, tea propped the afternoons.

"Da, with lemon." Nicole's gaze cooled. She had no intention of allowing Irina to sabotage her relationship with Pavla. The girl might be illiterate, but she possessed a wealth of common sense and loyalty. Everyone needed a friend. "We've discussed this before, Irina. I don't understand serfdom, and I disagree with the concept. You view serfs as beasts of burden, I see them as people like you and me. As we can't be reconciled, I think it advisable to avoid further discussion of the topic." Nicole didn't often defy Irina, but she refused to be intimidated on this point.

"Like you and *me?*" Irina's backbone stiffened in a shudder, and she added too much vodka to her tea. "Serfdom is the basic foundation of life! Without it, I ask where you would raise the taxes to support the government? And where would you recruit soldiers to supply the army? Not to mention who would see to the needs of the nobility. Serfs are vital to the economy, but they are not—and I repeat, *not—* like you and especially not like me!"

"Irina, I would really prefer—"

"And Vadim Nevsky! You treat him as an equal! An equal! Prince Dimitri's father freed Nevsky, yes, and even educated him in Europe, but he was born a serf. Once a serf, always a serf; it's in the mentality. You dishonor yourself with this shameful conduct. I assure you the court will not tolerate these appalling liberal attitudes!"

"We will *not* discuss this further!" An angry flush accentuated the flash in Nicole's eyes. Everything about serfdom offended her sensibilities.

"As you wish . . . Princess Natasha." Equally angry, Irina

stressed Nicole's title, making it abundantly clear that she de-ferred to rank and not to preference. Following a period of awkward silence, she removed an item from the drawer of her dressing table and concealed it behind the yellow robe. "I was saving this until we approached St. Petersburg, but I think now is as good a time as any."

"What is it?" The clashes of temperament distressed Nicole. She'd learned the extent of rank at the expense of Irina's possible support. The countess maintained a deliberate distance, and the small skirmishes had the unfortunate effect of increasing the woman's hostility. Nicole did not understand Irina's dichotomy of approach. The countess appeared genuinely eager to assist with Nicole's lessons and seemed pleased by her progress; yet Irina's resentment was as obvious as the powder lining her face.

"Haven't you experienced any curiosity regarding your mother?" Irina's lazy smile emerged nasty and calculating.

"Of course," Nicole lied. In truth she hadn't expended two thoughts for Princess Varina. Louis and Marie Duchard were her parents; they would always be.

"Well. As an example of Empress Catherine's generosity—she located a portrait for you."

Nicole's head snapped upward, and Pavla released a tiny groan as the hem jumped through the servants' fingers. The task was proving difficult enough with the ship's increasing roll.

"A portrait?" Nicole's heartbeat quickened, and heat suffused her cheeks. "May I . . . may I see it, please?"

Into her suddenly shaking fingers Irina pushed an oval frame sparkling with small precious stones. Nicole drew an unsteady breath. So long as Princess Varina had been no more than a title, she had remained a shadowy make-believe figure. But would she continue so when an image attached to her name? No. Nicole thought of Louis and Marie and her heart ached.

Nicole slowly lowered her gaze to the small portrait shaking in her palm. The painting was of two remarkably beautiful women. Nicole stared, forgetting the servants at her feet and Irina's hooded scrutiny.

Both women were light-haired, their shining curls drawn up into old-fashioned coiffures. Both were blue-eyed above delicate porcelain complexions. Each possessed patrician features and full lovely bosoms rimmed by silk roses. They might easily have passed for sisters, so alike were they in physical charms.

Puzzled, Nicole raised her eyes. "Which is my mother?"

Secrecy veiled Irina's sly gaze. "Guess," she suggested coyly, her tone hinting rehearsal.

Frowning, Nicole tilted the oval frame toward the light. The nearest lantern swung in wide arcs, casting alternate bands of illumination and shadow across the painting. Nicole shifted, balancing automatically against the growing pitch of the ship. She thought perhaps Vadim would have his storm. Then she returned her full attention to the portrait.

The woman on the right avoided the viewer with serious downcast eyes; Nicole's immediate impression was one of deep sadness, although the woman's lips had been portrayed in the beginnings of a smile. The second woman faced the viewer directly, a challenging sensuality in her bold glance, an unmistakable vibrancy and energy in her confident smile. Nicole selected the woman whose attitude she unconsciously identified with. "This one?" she inquired, indicating the woman who posed full-face.

A blaze of mottled color infused Irina's powdered cheeks, her expression twisted into a startling blend of triumph and horror. "No!" She snatched the frame and stabbed a finger toward the sad-eyed woman. "*That* is Varina!"

A sting of disappointment furrowed Nicole's brow. "Then who . . .?"

"You chose Empress Elizabeth!" Irina's shrill voice accused, as if Nicole had committed an unspeakable blunder. Something resembling fear and hatred flickered behind Irina's cold eyes. She thrust the portrait into Nicole's hands, then sank abruptly into her chair and reached for the vodka bottle. "We've finished for today." Rapid-fire Russian dismissed the servants. Obediently they dropped Nicole's hem and packed away pins and needles and scissors.

Ignoring Pavla's questioning brow, Nicole squirmed into her own gown and stepped from the ring of servants. The women in the portrait haunted her thoughts. They had been so lovely; and now both were dead. She hoped they had been as beautiful at the end of their lives as they had been during the first bloom of beauty.

"I don't understand why you seem so upset." Irina's strange expression baffled her. "You refused to identify Princess Varina; you insisted I choose. I can't see any harm.

Didn't you teach me that Empress Elizabeth was well-loved by the Russian people?"

Raising the portrait to the swinging lanterns, Nicole studied Elizabeth's familiar eyes and brow, wondering where she might have seen them before. With a start, Nicole suddenly realized she looked into those eyes whenever she approached a mirror. Confused, she transfered her examination to Varina. Before slipping the portrait into her pocket, she identified her nose and sensitive mouth. She fidgeted uneasily. If she were honest, she would have to confess she resembled Elizabeth more than Varina. She wondered if Irina could possibly have mistaken the two women.

"Yes. Elizabeth was loved by the people," Irina snapped. Her head jerked upward, eyes furious. "But so is Catherine, and don't you forget it! Catherine is twice the empress that Elizabeth ever thought of being! Elizabeth was lazy and immoral—everyone knew about Alexei Razumovsky, her lover! All her piety . . . nothing but sham to impress the populace, you can't tell me differently! And she was a wastrel—she owned four thousand gowns! That's all she cared about, her lover and her gowns! Now, Catherine . . ."

Wide-eyed, Nicole backed toward the door, motioning to Pavla. Both girls watched as Irina hurled her hairbrushes about the dressing table. A shower of spittle sprayed from her lips. Nicole pressed the latch and hastened into the corridor, drawing a deep breath of cold air.

"Did you and the countess have a spat?" Pavla asked dryly.

Nicole explained as a red-tunic escorted them to her cabin. "It makes no sense, but Irina interpreted my selection of Empress Elizabeth as a disloyalty to Catherine." They gripped the ropes fastened along the paneling as the *Kiev* mounted swelling crests, then swooped down the walls of deepening troughs.

Inside her own quarters, Nicole's eyes flicked to the bank of misty windows. Outside, the sky had blackened to ebony, and angry waves hurled tons of water toward an inky low ceiling. The building storm charged the atmosphere with tension. Nicole hastily asked Pavla to draw the draperies.

As Pavla raised her arms to tug the heavy brocade, the ship rolled and a small glittering object tumbled from her pocket. Instantly she froze, a stricken expression contorting her broad features. The other servants halted as if transmuted to stone.

"That . . . that's Irina's snuffbox!" Bending, Nicole retrieved the jeweled box before it skittered across the planking. She stared at Pavla. "You didn't . . . Did you *steal* this?"

Pavla lowered her head, her one long braid swinging over her shoulder. She wrung her hands.

"You did!" Nicole whispered. She sank slowly to a bolted chair before the desk. Placing the snuffbox beside a pile of stationery, she shook her head in stunned disbelief. "But why? You have no use for this . . . I've never seen you take snuff."

"I . . . Will you order my hands cut off?" Pavla's voice choked, her face blanched to paste.

The beginnings of a headache throbbed behind Nicole's brow. She shoved back her hair and rubbed her temples. When Irina missed the box, she would erupt like an exploding volcano.

"The knout? Flogging?" Pavla's voice cracked.

Face cupped in her hands, Nicole stared. "I . . . Have you taken anything else?" She didn't know what to say.

Pavla hesitated, then woodenly approached her pallet and withdrew a kerchief from beneath the pillow. She untied it on the desk before Nicole. The kerchief opened to reveal a multitude of small items: a comb with two broken teeth, a scrap of velvet ribbon, one pearl earring, four keys, and two ivory buttons. There wasn't a single item worth stealing.

"Oh, Pavla!" Uncertain how best to proceed, Nicole fingered one of the keys. Her voice sank in dejection. "To whom do . . . did . . . these belong?"

Pavla shrugged, her hands twisting in her apron. "I forget. I think one belonged to the guard captain, and . . . and one came from Prince Dimitri." Her ashen face screwed in concentration, straining to remember.

Dimitri! Nicole's eyes darted toward the clock. She and Irina and Dimitri rotated quarters each night for dinner. Tonight it was her turn—Dimitri and Irina would arrive in thirty minutes. She stared dully at Pavla; decisions must be made, plans laid.

Dropping the keys onto the kerchief, Nicole examined Pavla's plain sober face. "This is very serious. Do you understand what you have done?" The jeweled snuffbox was worth a small fortune. And although Pavla enacted the motions of contrition, Nicole suspected the girl rued being discovered more than she regretted the crime.

47

Pavla wet dry lips. "Please, Princess Natasha! Don't let them cut off my hands! I'll never steal again, I swear it!"

Nicole blinked. Pavla's fear sliced through her distraction. "Cut off your hands? My God!" She swallowed hard. Just as she began to grant admirable qualities to the Russians, a fresh barbarism surfaced.

Pavla nodded hysterically. *"Da!* The countess will demand my hands when she learns I borrowed her box!" Chapped red palms covered her face. "I didn't mean any harm! It sparkles . . . and I . . . I just wanted to touch it, to hold it and look at it—I would have put it back!"

There was cause to doubt the last statement, but not the first. Nicole concluded Irina would indeed insist upon the ultimate punishment. Thinking hard, she tapped a fingernail against the jeweled lid of the snuffbox. Conscience would not allow Pavla to be maimed, no matter what the offense.

"Quit weeping and listen!" She spun on the chair and patted Pavla's arm. "We have to return it, that's all. If we're lucky, we can replace the box before Irina discovers it's missing!"

Pavla's face flamed cherry red and then white, and she dropped heavily to her knees. Snatching up Nicole's fingers, she covered them with kisses. The dark expressive eyes dissolved to liquid. "Thank you! With all my heart and soul I thank you! I will serve you until the day I die! I'll never forget your kindness! Never!" She would have battled the giant waves beyond the panes if Nicole had suggested it. Instead, Pavla glanced at the clock and hastened toward the wardrobe. She shook out a blue off-the-shoulder gown which she knew deepened Nicole's eyes to a shade of brilliant sapphire.

Nicole nodded firmly. "Here's what I'll do . . ." She lifted her arms as cascades of soft blue velvet outlined her figure and swirled about her slippers. "After dinner I'll complain that it's stuffy in here, and I'll suggest we retire to Irina's cabin for our coffee." It was laughable to suppose anyone would prefer Irina's overheated, incense-permeated quarters, but Nicole would insist. "While Irina's occupied, I'll replace the box on her dressing table. Somehow."

"Thank you! As God is my witness, I thank you! If there is anything I can—"

"Just promise me that you won't steal again!"

"Never! I swear it on my sister's grave!"

"Good. We'll talk about this again later." Each looked

toward the knock at the door. Quickly Nicole swept the kerchief into a drawer and thrust the snuffbox into her pocket. She pinched color into her cheeks and hastily smoothed her skirts as Dimitri Denisov strode forward. He had exchanged his usual coarse sailor's attire for maroon satin evening dress. Lace frothed from throat and cuffs; a black ribbon secured his thick hair at the neck. He smelled of strong soap and salt spray. Nicole swallowed, irritated by the sudden weakness in her knees.

"Will the countess be delayed?" Rising on tiptoe, she attempted to see past his shoulder.

"The countess sends regrets, she isn't hungry." Dimitri smiled engagingly. "Our countess is in foul temper this evening." After bowing, he gazed down at Nicole, regarding her through smoky teasing eyes. "We'll dine alone. Just you and I and ten servants."

"Alone?" Nicole wet her lips. The snuffbox weighed like granite. The plan died, and she didn't see how the snuffbox's disappearance could continue undetected. Stammering, she instructed the servants to remove Irina's place setting. Pavla's eyes flared alarm, and Nicole answered with a tiny helpless shrug.

Dimitri poured wine into two glasses. "Come, now, is my company so distasteful?" A half-smile deepened an intriguing line near his mouth. "And here I thought I was an acceptable dinner companion. I don't chew with my mouth open, I don't spit on the floor . . ." Gray eyes teased above his glass. He balanced the ship's roll with widespread legs. "My stockings match, I buckle my shoes on the right feet."

Nicole lowered her eyes from the muscles tensing along his thighs. "I . . ." A blush flamed from her bare throat and climbed to the roots of her hair. The ship heaved, and she caught the rungs of a chair for support. "I was thinking of something else."

He waited, a dark brow lifting above his grin.

"The storm—I'm worried about the storm!" Impulsively Nicole threw back the draperies, staring through the droplets pebbling the glass. Immediately she wished she hadn't looked outside. The portrait of her mother, the scene with Pavla—both had distracted her attention from the increasingly heavy pitching of the ship and the roar of fury beyond the panes. A jagged fork of lightning carved the blackness, pulsed, then died as furious waves flung the *Kiev* to a dizzying height before hurling it down a sickening slide. Nicole cried out and struggled to remain upright. Books spilled from the case before one of the servants managed to snap a restraining rod into place.

"We can't eat during this!" Nicole gasped. Her stomach rolled in a sour loop as she stared at Dimitri, who calmly balanced near the desk, a glass in one hand, the decanter in the other.

He smiled. "That depends upon how hungry you are."

Silverware and napkins and hand-painted china flowed across the table and smashed to the planking. Moving cautiously from one bolted chair to another, the servant women approached the table and collected the pieces in a tray. Their wide frightened eyes continually strayed toward the windows.

"This is dangerous, isn't it?" Nicole inquired nervously. A large heavy object crashed above their heads; the impact shivered through the ship. "Shouldn't you be up there? On deck?" Nicole gained the table and sat, hooking her toes around the chair legs. She rescued her wine as it plunged toward the table edge.

Dimitri straddled the chair across from her. "If the captain needs me, he'll send someone."

Tilting her head toward the thumps and crashes overhead, Nicole doubted the captain could spare anyone for errands. A wild din assaulted her ears. Giant waves battered the ship; her timbers groaned and creaked and popped and emitted splintering cracks which froze the blood. Nicole's wide eyes fastened to Dimitri's steady gaze, and she suddenly prayed no one came to fetch him. The thought of riding out the storm alone terrified her.

Reaching across the table, he refilled her wineglass. "I don't know how much assistance I could render in any event. My naval experience is more academic than practical. I suppose I could pilot the *Kiev* in an emergency; otherwise it seems wise to leave operations in the captain's very capable hands." He smiled. "I'm reminded of the old saying concerning too many cooks spoiling the broth."

A wall of water crashed over the windows, and one of the servant women shrieked and held a bucket to her mouth. The others stowed loose objects into the trunks and wardrobe. As she worked, Pavla continued to stare at the door as if expecting the devil himself to burst in; the fury of the storm paled next to the avenging rage of the countess.

"Frightened?" Dimitri crossed his arms on the chair back,

his wineglass dangling from his fingertips, his gray eyes calmly curious.

"No!" Nicole lied. Her greatest wish was to scream and pray and fling herself headlong into his arms and hide her face in his neck. But Dimitri Denisov and his damnable mocking stare tested her mettle; from some unknown depth she dredged forth a quavering bravery.

Fixing her gaze steadfastly on his rugged features, she refused the temptation to stare at the windows. Desperately she sought a topic, something—anything—to submerge her fear. Raising her voice above the howl of wind and water and the terrifying thuds overhead, she asked, "Didn't you mention you'd grown up near water?"

He nodded. His knowing smile infuriated; Nicole could almost believe he enjoyed her discomfort.

"My father's estate, and now mine, is located in Temnikov on the Moksha River. But a river is not an ocean, and a sailing skiff is not a frigate."

The servant women wailed and wept and repeatedly crossed themselves. They prayed noisily to an icon one had produced from her pallet. Nicole licked her lips. "Both your parents are dead?"

"Yes."

This was sheer insanity. The floor beneath Nicole's chair vaulted upward, then dropped with a spine-jarring jolt. Her neck ached. Her toes cramped from clinging to the chair legs. And she and Dimitri chatted pleasantly of past ages, past locations. It was madness. She had never behaved so foolishly in her life.

"Did you mention that your mother was French?" A deafening crash impacted throughout the ship, lightning savaged the sky. Both hands jumped to Nicole's lips, smothering a scream, and her wine sailed across the table. She forced a smile. "Your mother?"

Dimitri retrieved the glass, extending it toward her. His steady eyes met hers as their fingers brushed. "My father served as Elizabeth's ambassador; he met and married my mother in Paris. Although they resided in France for the greatest part of each year, my father insisted I be raised in Russia. Vadim was more a parent than the prince." He grinned. "If you're interested, and I can't think why you would be, I enjoyed a typical young noble's upbringing, spoiled, pampered, every whim catered to . . . that is, when

Vadis was otherwise occupied." He studied her. "Natasha—"

"Nicole . . . please, I prefer Nicole."

"Nicole, then. It isn't necessary to pretend. There isn't a soul on board who isn't quivering in his socks, praying to God that the *Kiev* will ride out the storm. If you clench that glass any tighter, you'll snap the stem."

Nicole's jaw set and she ground her teeth. Forcibly she commanded her fingers to loosen. "You aren't quivering in your socks," she snapped.

He shrugged, and the maroon satin straining across wide muscled shoulders caught the light from lanterns swinging wild. "We either sink or we don't. It's God's will. There is nothing we can do to alter the outcome." The smoky eyes flickered and settled boldly on the creamy swell above a weave of blue ribbon. "You're particularly beautiful this evening, Princess."

She didn't feel beautiful. Wisps of loose gold flew about her cheeks; her eyes were large as teacups. If she could have spared a hand, she would have covered her breast from his bold silvery stare. But she gripped the table edge as the *Kiev* trembled and sighed and began the long climb out of a heaving trench of ebony water. The ship attained the crest, clung for a precarious moment, then hurtled downward. Nicole swayed, her fingers turning chalky against the table, her skirts swinging wide to one side. The snuffbox bumped from her pocket as the ship slammed into a valley of water. The box shattered against the planks, and the pieces slid to lodge against Dimitri's heel.

He bent, then straightened, examining a wide fragment between his fingers. Behind him Pavla cried out and buried her face in her arms. "This is Irina's, isn't it?" Pavla wept and tore her hair.

"I . . . no! It's mine!" If she could convince him the snuffbox belonged to her, perhaps all was not yet lost. Nicole had no idea how to repair the box, but she and Pavla would conceive of something. When the ship leveled at the bottom of the next trough, Nicole seized the brief respite to jump from her chair and rush around the table. "Give it back . . . please!"

Dimitri indicated no desire to surrender the fragments. "I'm certain I noticed this on Irina's dressing table." He arched a black eyebrow and held the piece beyond Nicole's grasp.

She judged she had ten seconds either to attempt a rescue

or to dash back to her chair before the *Kiev* ascended the next swelling crest.

With Pavla's cries ringing in her ears, Nicole bit her lip and lunged forward, stretching out her fingers.

Lightning cracked the heavens; a heavy piece of mast struck the deck with a thunderous splintering shudder. The ship rolled dangerously, and Nicole would have catapulted across the room had not Dimitri caught her wrist and pulled her onto his lap, smothering her terrified screams against his shoulder.

Nicole's fingers dug into the satin; her heartbeat thudded wildly against his chest. They were sinking, she knew it! This fragile manmade cradle could not withstand nature's fury. Dear God! There was so much she hadn't experienced, so much she hadn't accomplished! She didn't even know for certain who she was. Whimpering softly, she clung to Dimitri's neck as the *Kiev* slowly righted. A terrifying black wall roared up to the window, then crashed in upon itself, splattering icy bullets against the panes. Nicole pressed her face tighter against his collar, inhaling the salty sea tang she believed would soon envelop them forever.

Dimitri's quiet chuckle pierced her fear, and she gradually realized his large warm hands explored her waist. Firm fingers steadied her just beneath the curve of her breasts. Outraged, Nicole shoved from his neck and struggled to rise, but a man's strength coupled with the raging elements defeated her purpose. The ship pitched, flinging her against his broad chest. One breast filled the palm pinned between her body and his white shirt front. To her horror, she experienced an immediate humiliating response; beyond her conscious control, her nipples grew as hard and taut as the tensed thighs beneath her. Quickening breath bathed her cheeks; smoke-gray eyes traced the curve of moist lips, then moved upward and locked to hers, smoldering past her lashes. A gray whirlpool drew her into flickering heated depths. His stare was hard, searching, without a trace of amusement. And she recognized the man's need growing powerful between his outspread legs.

"Sooner or later I will have you," he murmured hoarsely. Burning eyes confirmed the promise. His fingers edged upward until they caressed the soft smooth skin above her bodice.

"No," Nicole whispered, her choked voice disappearing in the din. She fought to wrench her eyes from silvery-gray flame. "No!" The storm in his eyes was as impassioned as the raw savagery ripping at the ship. Wind and water pounded the windowpanes, the ship groaned and creaked, and the servant women cried and wailed into a mind-numbing pandemonium of noise.

His eyes locked to hers for an eternity; his iron fingers clamped her on his lap. Then his dark head descended and his lips crushed hers in a bruising kiss of fire. And the madness of the heaving ship, the threat of a watery death, the shrieks and howls of wind and splintering wood, whirled together in a hellish symphony.

Nicole's lips opened beneath his savage kiss and her head fell backward as skilled hands covered her breasts, meshed her thrashing body to the hard heat between his legs. And she clung to his shoulders as his lips found her throat and the careening ship pressed her fast against his searching mouth. Her lips swelled from the bruising force of his kisses; fingers of scorching flame trailed his touch. A great weakness swept her flesh as tingles of shock quivered beneath his stroking hands. And she yearned for his demanding kisses, craved the comfort of his hard tensing body, and believed herself to be going mad with storm fever and the abandoned passion of insistent lips and exploring fingers and the gathering urgency growing in his body and in hers.

They would all die. As surely as God had opened the murky void, the *Kiev* would spiral downward to a watery grave.

She lost herself in the hard chiseled planes of his face; she buried her hands in thick black hair and raised his face until she could stare into deep eyes the color of melted granite. And she no longer remembered that the servant women watched. She met his lips with frightening, sweeping abandon, clinging as he drank a hundred honeyed kisses from her open mouth. And a sound midway between a sob and a moan caught in her throat as she pressed his head to her warm thrusting breasts.

His arms tightened convulsively as a deafening crash imploded near the bow. Splintering shock ripples tore through straining planks, and for a heart-freezing moment the *Kiev* halted its labored tread. The ship wallowed in a trench of liquid blackness, listing perilously.

No one dared breathe. All eyes swung upward, following the thud of pounding feet. In a moment the door slammed inward and Vadim filled the frame. Ice glittered in his beard, and seawater streamed from his coat and cap.

"We've been rammed by the frigate *Kreml*! We're taking on water!" He flung his arms outward for balance. "For God's sake, move! We're going down!"

5

LIGHTNING, SLEET, AND roaring funnels of seawater birthed a living nightmare; chaos screamed across the decks. Broken lanterns swung in tormented arcs, casting ghastly shadows over a scene of utter devastation.

The mizzenmast had crashed through the center of Zinka's cage, forever ending that great animal's tireless pacing. Tattered rigging flapped in shreds; the decks were an obstacle course of debris and wreckage. Two cannon, ripped loose from rusted moorings, wheeled aimlessly with the roll and wash of the ship, crushing all objects in their path. Bells clanged into the tempest, whistles shrieked distress, and driving sleet glazed the planks into sheets of glass.

The *Kiev* nosed slowly downward, at the mercy of mountainous waves. She wallowed drunkenly, like a tree trunk whose limbs have been amputated.

Golden strands of hair stung Nicole's cheeks like barbed nettles, and she bent out of the wind to thrust the wisps inside her hood. Already her cloak and gown were soaked, and she was chilled to the bone. She'd forgotten gloves, and her slippers had not been designed for outside wear.

"Let me rub your hands," Pavla shouted. Above their heads the torn rigging snapped and groaned like a demented animal fighting to rip free.

Nicole shook her head. The women huddled at the railing, struggling to maintain balance. She edged nearer Dimitri and Vadim. Both men stared across a raging valley of black waves, squinting into a slanting curtain of sleet and water. They studied the pitching hull of the *Kreml* with intense concentration.

Nicole followed their eyes as a dozen grappling hooks flew over the roaring abyss. In seconds, thick cords of hemp knitted the ships like icy threads stitching a seam. Immediately men from the *Kiev* crawled out on the ropes and began to cross to the other ship. Pockets and shirtfronts bulging with brandy pilfered from the holds, they flung themselves into wet black space, inching along the ropes hand over hand. A tunnel of water boomed through the channel between the ships, and Nicole smothered a scream as a man sagged dangerously near the clawing waves. Far below, he struggled frantically, feet kicking; then he recovered and began the long upward pull. A dozen hands dragged him aboard the *Kreml* and reached for the next man.

She couldn't bear to watch. Before she spun away, a man dropped shrieking into the watery chop below. He vanished instantly.

"I can't do it!" Irina wailed, wringing her hands. "I can't swing along that rope like a monkey! I'm going to die! Oh, God, I don't want to die!" Wind and sleet ripped away her wig. Pounding water plastered her thin hair to her scalp.

Nicole conquered the image of a shelled peanut. "Yes, you can!" she shouted into Irina's ear. "You can do it!" She didn't believe this for a minute; none of the women would survive the ropes. Their skirts hung like sodden lead weights against their hoops; none possessed the strength or endurance of work-toughened sailors. A scream pierced the din of clanging bells, snapping timber, and yapping dogs as another man dropped.

Nicole bit her lip hard. For an instant a unique snuffling roar lifted above the chaos. She squeezed her eyes, attempting to isolate the bellow. When she identified it, she almost smiled. The *Kreml*, like the *Kiev*, had its bear—angry and frightened, from the sound of it. But comfortingly familiar, an assurance that friends waited at the end of the ropes, laboring frantically to rescue fellow Russians. She wondered fleetingly if anyone else had placed the sound.

Evidently Dimitri and Vadim had not. Nicole didn't understand their tense silence. Surely they should be manning ropes instead of staring intently into the sleet. As she watched, the captain of the doomed *Kiev* hastened forward, joining the captain of Nicole's guards. Both shouted into Dimitri's ear, and he nodded. Nicole would have given much to overhear the conversation, but Irina dashed her hopes by plucking insistently at her cloak.

56

"My debts aren't paid . . . my soul will go to hell!" Her fingers clawed Nicole's arm. "You're younger, you might survive. If you do, I beg you to convince Catherine to retire my debts and free my soul! In the name of God, beseech her to grant me this last favor!"

Nicole couldn't conceive of a God who bartered souls for coins, but she responded to the intensity of Irina's plea. "I promise!" They screamed inches from one another's ears, continually wiping at the rain and icy sleet. Nicole's eyes swung toward Dimitri and Vadim. The captains had departed, and Dimitri cupped his hands to his mouth, shouting her name, although she clung to the rail but a few feet distant. Slipping and sliding on the treacherous deck, Nicole picked a path along the railing and gratefully accepted the shelter of Vadim's arm.

Dimitri's slate eyes searched her face, and Nicole's heart sank. She saw nothing to remind her of the heat of mere moments ago—a lifetime ago. Those hard eyes demanded courage. "Both captains are going across to requisition a pulley basket for the women."

Nicole parted her lips to inquire why both captains should be dispatched on an identical errand; then a shout drew her horrified gaze toward the heaving chasm below. The *Kiev*'s captain dangled from the slippery ice-caked rope by one hand. Fingers of water boomed upward, and the captain vanished. Screaming, Nicole pressed her face against Vadim's wet coat. "Oh, God!"

"Listen! There's no time to waste!" Roughly Dimitri spun her to face him. The sharp authority in his voice penetrated her numbed thoughts. "We don't know what will happen on board the *Kreml*. Offer each woman a choice to cross or to remain here."

To remain was certain death. "I . . . I don't understand." Once the women realized they would be transported in a basket, they would fight for the opportunity to depart first. The *Kiev* listed dangerously, and minutes assumed precious significance.

Dimitri twisted her toward the *Kreml*. "Look hard. You won't see a Russian uniform which isn't ours." Nicole peered into the hammering sleet and spray, wiping her eyes.

"We're guessing Spanish," Vadim confirmed near her ear.

"Pirates?" The word strangled. And a new fear superseded all else.

Dimitri nodded tersely, water streaming from his face and

57

hair. "They're permitting the men to cross in order to retrieve the brandy." His flinty stare explained the reason the women would be welcomed on board. Nicole swayed. "The choice is certain death on the *Kiev* or probable death on the *Kreml*." Dimitri's eyes glittered, as icy as the droplets clinging in his dark hair and lashes. He glanced toward Vadim. "Unless we can arrange a few surprises."

"I . . . We'll cross," Nicole blurted. The will to live flourished powerfully, even if the hours would be measured. The unknowns aboard the *Kreml* were preferable to immediate death here. Later she would question her reasoning; for the moment, she focused on informing the women, then helping to tie them into the basket.

"You go before me," Pavla implored. Frightened eyes measured the cant of the planking, then peered down into the ebony gorge roaring far below.

Nicole secured the strap across Pavla's sodden skirt. She dashed stinging salt spray from her lashes and attempted a weak smile. "Off you go. The quicker the basket returns, the sooner we'll all be safe." She tugged the signal line, and Pavla emitted a choked squeak. The basket lurched, dropped, and disappeared into a veil of black rain and sleet.

"You've been foolish to linger. You go next," Dimitri ordered, his large hand a spot of warmth on her shoulder.

They waited in howling darkness, braced against a wildly tilting deck. One of the loose cannon rumbled past and smashed through the forecastle bulkhead. Another yardarm crashed to the planks, trailing rigging and shreds of canvas. The ratters barked furiously, their eyes rolling. They raced back and forth between the few people remaining on board.

"We still have two more."

"You go next." His fingers tightened. "I'll send the last two together."

"And you?" When the sea snatched the *Kiev*'s captain, Denisov had assumed command as ranking officer. Nicole prayed he harbored no nonsensical ideas of going down with the vessel.

He grinned, as if reading her thoughts. "I'll cross on the ropes the minute the last basket departs. And I'll wager I beat it across."

She stared up at him, blinking at the ice frosting her lashes. So many had vanished into the jaws of the sea. Despite the driving sleet, her mouth dried to sand.

The basket thumped against the railing, and before Nicole

could protest, he'd lifted her up and tied her inside. "Dimitri!" But the wind swallowed her cry. And suddenly she was dropping, down and down into a clawing snarling void, her hands clamped white on the basket's edges. Fear stopped her breath; then the basket struck the lowest point, bounced above the hissing water, and crawled upward. Vadim swung her on deck, and Nicole lurched against the railing, her knees rubbery and shaking. If she lived to be a thousand, she never again wanted to swing through howling blackness in a flimsy basket!

When she caught her breath and glanced upward, she might have been staring at the decks of the *Kiev*. The storm had damaged the *Kreml* almost as badly. Barking ratters leaped over fallen chunks of mast. Tumbled piles of canvas, smashed glass, and a litter of splintered wreckage obscured the decks. Overhead, fractured yards dangled in the wind, ropes twisted like broken cobwebs flying from tenuous moorings. A shattered length of railing gave evidence of the final rumbling plunge of a wandering cannon. Nowhere did Nicole see Pavla or any of the *Kiev*'s people.

She whirled to peer into the crashing canyon between the vessels, searching for Dimitri as the basket bumped the rail and Vadim pulled two terrified women onto the deck. Through the sleet-shadowed blackness Nicole watched the *Kiev*'s stern rising high above the *Kreml*'s decks as the bow sank beneath greedy waves.

A commanding voice, harsh with urgency, drove the *Kreml*'s crew to the ropes, slicing them free lest the wounded *Kiev* drag the *Kreml* along to her grave.

Nicole's icy fingers clawed Vadim's arm. "Dimitri!" She pointed frantically toward the nearest line. "He's on the rope!"

Vadim responded instantly, knocking aside a swarthy figure bending to cut the line. Immediately another man appeared before them, materializing out of sleet and rain like a menacing specter. Only Vadim's awesome size stayed the hand reaching for a cutlass.

Vadim and Nicole shouted simultaneously, one in Russian, the other in English. The man stared through cold dead eyes, understanding neither. Vadim tried French, and this the man understood.

"Stand aside," he commanded flatly. "Better one dies than all."

"Not this one!" Dimitri's head appeared above the railing

and Vadim pulled him over as Nicole mumbled a silent prayer of relief. Ice coated Dimitri's hair and lashes; the maroon satin had blackened with salt water. His hands bled where the rope had scraped. "Cut the line," he ordered.

The last rope dropped into the abyss and the *Kreml* sprang free. Within seconds the *Kiev* vanished behind a gigantic wall of water and sleet.

The Spaniard addressed himself to Dimitri. "I am Captain Domingo Santine. You are my . . . guests."

Santine's flat stare originated at an arctic distance. His were dead eyes which had looked upon atrocity and remained untouched, graveyard eyes no misery or suffering could awaken. Vaguely Nicole noticed a puckered scar twisting a thin mouth, but it was the empty sepulchral eyes she would remember all her life.

Dimitri Denisov and Domingo Santine scrutinized each other cautiously. They stood at the same height; they were an approximate age. There the resemblance ended. One possessed the innate elegance of humanity; the other had long since abandoned human emotion.

Dimitri's measuring gaze broke to sweep the deck. He watched the Spaniards kick the last of the Russian soldiers into the hold.

At Denisov's side, Vadim grinned a challenge to the circle of men closing around them. Speaking rapid Russian, he observed, "There are only nine of them and two of us—I'd judge the odds in our favor. Do we take them, *barchuk*?"

"Nyet. Not yet. Behind these nine are fifty more." Dimitri swung from Vadim's resigned sigh and regarded Santine through narrowed eyes. Neither man appeared aware of the rain and spray streaming from hardened features. "Your intentions?" Dimitri snapped in French.

Santine's malignant grin did not reach the dead gaze. "I believe you know. If I could spare my men from storm duty, you'd already be dead. Once the gale blows over . . ."

"The women?"

A one-eyed Spaniard spit. "Russian whores are only fit for dogs!"

"That one . . ." The cold eyes shot a freezing quiver through Nicole's flesh. "That one is not Russian."

Nicole lifted her chin defiantly, not realizing the wind and rain enhanced her startling beauty. Cold tinted her dewy cheeks with rose, and her golden hair clung in shining damp tendrils to a flawless face. And the wet blue velvet molded her jutting breasts like a second skin.

Dimitri's voice was harsh. "This is a blooded princess of the Russian nobility!"

Santine laughed. "Then I'll honor her by taking her myself."

Nicole's heart stopped. Three men jumped to restrain Dimitri, and six more prevented Vadim from rushing Santine.

Domingo Santine watched with bored amusement. "Throw them in the hold." The deadened eyes fixed upon Nicole, and something dark stirred the arctic depths. "Put her with the others." Any hint of emotion died from the empty eyes. He strode into the rain toward the mainmast. With his spine to the roaring bear, Santine brandished his cutlass above windwhipped hair. "Back to work, you bastards! Time enough to swill brandy when the storm's behind us!"

Before rough hands shoved Nicole into a dark corridor, she glimpsed the Spaniards hurl Dimitri and Vadim into a black hole and then padlock the cover. Blood appeared beneath her teeth, and she pressed the back of her hand to her mouth. "God! Dear God!" The formless litany whispered past trembling lips.

When Nicole stumbled into the captain's cabin, the servant women stared upward, their eyes flaring fright until the door locked behind her. Pavla ran forward with a cry and clasped Nicole's hands until they ached.

"Thank God! I thought you . . . I thought . . ." She scrubbed a hand across her eyes, then shut them, erasing the storm beyond the windows. "It would have been better if the basket had fallen." Dark lashes quivered against a pale face, and her voice sank. "It isn't hard to guess what they'll do to us!"

There was no assurance which Pavla would not recognize as a lie. Nicole lowered her hood from wet hair and gazed about the room. It was warm, thank heaven; otherwise there was nothing to recommend it. The filth and disorder were appalling. The planks underfoot were slippery with grime, scarred by streaks of tar and pitch. The original color of the walls lay buried beneath a coating of grease and smoke and dirt. And the bed . . . Nicole's eyes dropped from the captain's unmade bed; it turned the stomach. The sheets were an unwholesome gray crawling with vermin. "I . . . Is there a clean place to sit?"

"I guess the floor . . ." Pavla indicated a space against the

61

wall, near a brazier but away from the wailing servant women. Both braced themselves against the greasy bulkhead, extending cold feet toward the heat.

Nicole stared at Irina.

Irina occupied a chair before the captain's table, her slippers hooked about the bolted legs. She appeared as oblivious of the raging elements as she did of the rotting food stuck on the table surface. The countess smiled and dipped her head and conversed with an invisible companion. At one point she laughed gaily, and her bluish lips formed a coquettish pout.

"She's been like this since they threw us in here," Pavla explained softly. Her large eyes saddened. "She believes she's dining with the empress."

Nicole's heart ached. Without the wig and the powder and paint, Irina had faded into a plain, time-ruined old woman. When the lantern swung over her wet thin hair, harsh light gouged pits and crevices into her face, carved dark hollows around eyes grown feverish. Nicole blinked rapidly, unable to bear Irina's disintegration.

She wrapped her arms around the bare shoulders above her gown. She would have liked to pull a sheet or a blanket from the bed and dry her hair and limbs. But, as the others, she resisted the urge. Imagining the multitude of bugs in the linen, she released a mirthless laugh. Pavla lifted an eyebrow.

"We all crave a dry blanket . . . yet we desist from fear of lice and fleas and God knows what else. We're disgusted by a few bugs, when in the morning we . . ." She didn't continue; the pain in her eyes finished the sentence.

They lapsed into silence, enduring the storm's howl and Irina's babble and the wailing sobs of the women. And they drew comfort from one another. Neither wished to cause distress by giving voice to the nameless fears within. After a time, Nicole shifted and glanced out the windows. The waves didn't appear as violent or as mountainous. Needles of tension pierced her heart; when the storm ended . . . She pounded her knee helplessly.

"The worst is the waiting! Just waiting! I wish we could do something!"

Pavla nodded, chewing the tail of her braid. "But what? We're locked in, the men are locked in . . ."

Nicole dropped her head against the wall, watching as the far end of the room swept upward, then fell. The upward thrust appeared less than it had an hour ago. She worried her

lower lip. Then bolted upright and stared at Pavla. "You said
. . . you said the men are locked in the hold!"

"*Da.*" Pavla's dark eyes frowned in puzzlement.
"What . . . ?"

"Keys! Pavla, if you could steal the keys, do you think you
could somehow reach the hold? The hatch cover is an open
grid! All you have to do is drop the keys through!"

Pavla stared. Behind her broad brow, her mind worked visibly. "Anything is possible," she answered slowly. "If I could
get near enough for an accurate toss . . ."

Nicole gripped Pavla's hands until the girl winced. "Could
you try?" Her eyes widened and she groaned as an unfore-
seen objection sprang to the surface of her mind. "Oh, dear
Lord! You pledged a sacred vow on your sister's grave never
to steal again!" The Russians regarded a vow as binding as
death.

Pavla cleared her throat. "I never had a sister," she
confessed sheepishly. "The vow doesn't count."

"You never . . . ? But you said . . ." Nicole touched her
forehead and began again. She'd consider vows and sisters
and lies and snuffboxes another time. If another time was
granted. "Then you'll try?"

Pavla nodded hesitantly. "How do I get the key?"

"The man who locked us in here has a key ring." Nicole
drew a reluctant breath. "He must be lonely guarding the
corridor by himself . . ."

Comprehension dawned in Pavla's stare. She licked her
lips, and both hands fluttered to her throat.

Nicole swallowed hard. "I know . . . but I can't think of a
better method . . ." Her voice trailed miserably, and she
dropped her gaze from Pavla's expression.

Pavla released a ragged breath, then shrugged. Reaching,
she ripped her gown to the waist, exposing a rounded cleft of
soft white flesh. "It's now or later; what difference does it
make?" Another shrug widened the gap of torn cloth above
her breasts. "And it won't be the first time . . . Once the loaf
is sliced, another slice can't make all that much difference,
can it?" She attempted a smile as she pushed to her feet.

Nicole stammered soundless words. "*S'Bogem*—Go with
God."

" . . . with God," Pavla repeated. She stiffened her shoulders, looked at Nicole, then strode past Irina and the women.
She didn't hesitate; she lifted a fist and pounded the door. A
volley of Spanish responded from the opposite side. Pavla

continued knocking and kicking until the door clicked open a crack and an angry voice shouted.

Leaning against the dirty wall, Pavla arched her spine, thrusting out her exposed breasts. "See anything you like, you ugly son of a whore?" The whispery Russian extended a clear invitation.

A filthy hand dragged Pavla into the corridor. The door slammed.

Squeezing her eyes shut, Nicole ground her forehead against her knees. Despairing sobs convulsed her shoulders.

6

WHEN NICOLE'S EYES fluttered open, dim morning sunlight filtered through a layer of high thin clouds. The sea was running high, but the gigantic swells of the night had diminished in size and fury. As she had dozed, the storm had ended.

And the horror began. Dirty reeking men burst into the cabin. They slapped the cringing women to their feet. Exploring hands fumbled at breasts and reached beneath salt-stiffened skirts. Screams and laughter assaulted the mind, shredded the nerves.

Striking with the flat of their swords, the pirates herded the women toward the corridor door. With the exception of Nicole. They pointedly left her behind. And she tried desperately to judge if she should thank God or if she'd been spared for a worse fate than the others. She pressed against the wall, watching from wide eyes.

Irina shuffled forward in the center of the group. She paused and calmly removed a pill from the locket circling her neck.

Immediately one of the Spaniards shouted and prodded her with the tip of his cutlass.

Irina bared her teeth. *"Malchi razboinik!* Shut your mouth, you brigand! The empress will learn of any disrespect! Catherine and I are dear friends; anyone will confirm it! Wasn't it I whom she entrusted with this delicate mission?"

Irina nodded wisely, peering over her shoulder toward Nicole. She appeared unaware of a pinkish trickle leaking from her mouth. "Don't worry about a thing, *chérie*, Catherine will retire my debts. I spoke of the matter less than an hour ago, and she issued a ukase to that effect."

"I . . . I'm happy for you," Nicole whispered.

One of the pirates flung Irina into the corridor.

The bolt slid into place with a terrible click of finality, abandoning Nicole to her imagination and the sounds of fear and outrage. Both sickened her.

She tilted her head and strained to hear. The frightened screams were dimmer, the raucous laughter further removed, but each clawed the heart's sensibilities. Nicole groaned and covered her ears, pacing aimlessly before the bank of windows. What were they doing? Was it worse to know or not to know? Had Pavla succeeded, and where was she?

Nicole flattened her hands against the gritty panes and stared unseeing at the tossing water. What did the screams signify?

A violent chill swept up from her toes, and she rubbed her arms and stamped her ruined slippers. Her eyes probed the ceiling, following the din of barking dogs, a roaring bear, and the screams . . . the terrible rending screams!

She tightened into a ball near the brazier and waited for the Spaniards to come.

They did.

Two men half-carried, half-dragged Nicole up a short flight of stairs, then across littered planks toward a shouting, laughing audience crowding the mainmast. And they supported her weight as Nicole's knees buckled and spasms of shock wrenched her stomach. Her wild eyes gazed upon a public outrage, an abomination of humanity.

All the women were naked, regardless of age. Two of the oldest sprawled in congealing red pools, their arms outstretched. Sightless eyes stared into eternity.

Nicole doubled over and vomited until her throat burned acid and nothing more came up; then she searched frantically for Pavla amid the nightmare within the ring of pointing, laughing men.

Pavla knelt on hands and bleeding knees, a slavering Spaniard mounted behind her. Her braid had loosened and a merciful curtain of dark hair obscured her face. She was a thing. A naked inhuman thing to be used brutally and without the blessing of privacy. A thing, as the other women were things, coupled in postures of unthinkable sadism.

Nicole swayed, staring at black circles speckling her vision. Raw bile scoured her mouth; cramps twisted her stomach.

Then she spied Irina.

They had given Irina to the bear when they finished with her. At first Nicole's numb mind believed the Spaniards had dressed Irina in a red-and-pink-striped shift. Then her vision cleared, and if the men hadn't tightened their grip, she would have collapsed.

This bear had not been declawed.

"Oh, God!" Nicole whimpered, covering her face. "Oh, God . . . oh, God!" The evil of what she witnessed shrieked through the canyons of her mind, trailing echoes of blackness and blood.

Domingo Santine directed the Spaniards' amusements from a reclining position atop a pile of stacked canvas. A bottle of the *Kiev*'s brandy swung from one hand. He drained it and hurled the empty container over his shoulder. The dead eyes flickered with cold malignancy.

"The princess joins us." His voice lilted drunkenly, but the empty eyes were icily sober. No hint of compassion rippled his flat stare. "We saved our best in your honor." The men laughed.

Nicole's head swiveled and her blood curdled. Two grinning pirates led forward an immense black dog on a chain. They had excited the animal to a frenzy, and he strained at the heavy chain, plunging and panting toward the scent of the women and the sweating Spaniards.

Santine yawned. Then he nodded, and the men restraining Nicole cut away her velvet skirt and ripped down her pantaloons, exposing her golden vulnerability to the feeble sunlight and the men's lust-filled eyes.

Santine smiled at Nicole's wild, sick expression. "You are the main entertainment, my dear," he drawled. The Spaniards roared a drunken delight and raised their brandy bottles in hoarse cheers. One man staggered forward and kicked another from behind a woman. He fell on her with savage snarls. And all the while his narrowed eyes were fixed upon Nicole.

"Please . . ." She couldn't think past the horror. "Please . . . please . . ." She stared at the dog, unable to comprehend what Santine meant to do.

An emotionless smile twitched Santine's lips. "Release the dog."

The dog bounded forward and buried his snout in the triangle of gold. Nicole jerked backward and shrieked, a long quivering scream of terror and anguish and shock. Blackness rushed forward—the black dog, the Spaniards' leering eyes, the ebony horror blanking her mind. She crumpled to the deck in a merciful faint.

Pain was her first impression upon regaining consciousness, but not the pain she had feared. Rope cut into her wrists and ankles; needles of cold wind lashed her skin. They had torn away her gown and bound her naked body to the mast. The nightmare continued. Below her, the Spaniards savaged the women; their screams had diminished to whimpers of mindless endurance.

Domingo Santine swayed on the deck before her, hands splayed on his hips, a sneer stretching the scar over his lips and chin. "You're a virgin," he accused.

Nicole tilted her head toward the crisp blue sky. The clouds had parted, and bright sunlight burst forth, shining from another dimension where the world was young and innocent. Sunshine had no place here.

She looked into hellish eyes and her spirit shrank. A well of hatred exploded within, and she did the only thing possible to her: she hawked her head forward and spat.

Santine's expression did not alter. The glob of spittle glistened upon his cheek. "There are amusing methods of deflowering a virgin," he commented. The voice was frozen. "You've earned a demonstration."

At Santine's nod, the one-eyed man rose from the waiting circle, strutting forward in pride. With great care and much advice from onlookers he selected a short thick belaying pin and flipped it in his hand. He cast a questioning glance toward Santine, then grinned and rubbed his hand across the bulge growing against his dirty breeches. Gripping the wooden pin firmly, he strode toward the mast.

Nicole's eyes widened and blurred. Her lips twisted in dry appeal, but only a croak emerged. Finally a scream exploded at the back of her throat and she thrashed and wrenched at the ropes until flesh bled and her arms threatened to pop from their sockets. Insanity approached in the form of a grinning man and a thick wooden pin.

For one teetering instant she believed her mind had slipped into the netherworld of madness. Her scream was joined and drowned by voices inside and outside her head. Dazed, she blinked as the Spaniard halted, then spun and swung the belaying pin as a weapon. A man in a torn red tunic drove a sharpened point of a barrel stave deep into the Spaniard's groin; then he snatched a dagger from the man's belt and ran on. The Spaniard clasped both hands around the barrel stave, staring in disbelief. He sank to his knees and fell forward.

Men poured from the hold, brandishing discarded lengths of planking, barrel staves, primitive clubs fashioned from scraps. The Spaniards possessed superior weapons, but the Russians had surprise and the pirates' drunkenness in their favor.

"Yes," Nicole screamed, straining at the ropes. "Yes, yes! Kill them!" Her teeth bared, and madness colored her mind. She heard someone screaming but did not recognize the voice as her own. She had only to glance toward the bear's bloody cage or look at the women sprawled like discarded playthings to experience a black surge of blood lust and hatred. "Kill them!"

Men shouted and flashing metal rang and clashed as the battle raged across the decks. Dimitri and Vadim fought side by side. Dimitri had captured a cutlass, and he employed it like a man possessed, slashing and thrusting and widening a bloody path.

Unlike the others, Vadim felt no need of artificial weapons. Grinning hugely, the giant Ukrainian advanced, his massive arm sweeping aside the Spaniards' paltry swords, and he gathered them into a fatal embrace. His arms tightened until black eyes bulged and spines and bones snapped and cracked. Vadim flung aside one lifeless body and roared as he wrapped his arms about another man and lifted him off his feet.

As suddenly as it had begun, the assault ended. Dead and wounded lay scattered across the decks.

And Dimitri appeared in Nicole's line of vision. Stormy eyes as cold and hard as stone held hers for a moment; then he sliced the ropes circling the mast. He tore off his shirt and draped it over her trembling nakedness. His bare chest gleamed with sweat and exertion. "Can you walk?"

"Yes, I . . . Another minute and I . . ."

"Rouse the women," he commanded tersely. Vadim directed the soldiers, rounding the Spaniards into a sullen group.

Limping, Nicole approached Pavla and knelt to touch the

girl's cold cheeks. She lifted her face to Denisov. "Something warm . . . Is there . . . ?"

A dozen red shirts flew toward her, and Nicole gently lifted Pavla and wrapped her in a soldier's tunic. Pavla's wounded eyes fastened to Nicole's face. "Is it over?" Nicole bent to hear. "Did they find the key?"

"Da, da!" Nicole dashed the tears burning her eyes. "Can you stand?"

Slowly Pavla crawled to her feet, tiny quivers of pain leaking past her clenched teeth. "It hurts . . . it hurts!" Gasping, she leaned against a barrel, a hand pressed to her stomach. "The others . . . ?"

Miraculously, only Irina and the two older women were dead. The others accepted the tunics and moaned to their feet, eyes vacant and glassy with shock and pain. Slipping her arm around Pavla's shoulders, Nicole stared up at Dimitri.

"Hear this," he shouted, and no person hearing that voice would ever forget it. "No man who touched our women or who witnessed the atrocities done to them will live out this day!"

The Spaniards did not understand the language, but they recognized the murderous intent of the man before them. All but one dropped to his knees amid a babble of drunken supplication. One stood unbending in the center of the rabble.

Domingo Santine bowed to no man. His gaze locked to Denisov's, and the dead eyes flickered to life. They glowed with intense emotion, fixed upon Denisov as the deliverer awaited for endless aeons of black time.

Denisov returned the stare. "You guided your men to the gates of hell—you'll lead them inside!" A whipcord command ordered the guards to drag Santine before him. Neither man looked from the other.

"I knew you would come one day," Santine murmured. "I knew the man you would be, but I didn't know you . . . Do you understand?"

"Strip him," Dimitri snapped, and in that instant his cold silvery eyes were as frozen as Santine's had been.

Every eye watched. Slowly Denisov withdrew the dagger from his belt. Without speaking, he presented it hilt-first to Santine.

"There is no salvation," Santine whispered, his jaw knotting in cords. He looked at Denisov, then plunged the dagger deep into his stomach and squeezed his eyes shut as he sank to his knees. He grasped the hilt with both reddened hands and sawed upward. Blood trickled from smiling lips. With one last immense effort he jerked the dagger free and dropped it before Denisov's boots. No peace softened the vacant opaque stare as he rolled on his side.

Denisov wiped the dagger against his breeches. His eyes swung to the women's dull faces, gauging their silence. "Korsakov!" he barked. His harsh shout was the only human sound amid the creaking of torn rigging, the groan of battered timbers. "Take the women below. Divide them into two groups. Put one to work cleaning the captain's cabin; the other is to prepare decent quarters for the women and the crew."

Nicole gasped. Sick eyes widened in shock. Denisov was as inhuman as Santine. Her wrists and ankles bled from the ropes; she ached between the legs from whatever the pirates had done while she was unconscious. The other women had suffered far worse. What good was Santine's death if additional outrage followed? Eyes blazing, Nicole struggled to her feet. "Are you mad? These women need rest and care!"

Denisov continued as if she hadn't spoken. "Provide them buckets and water and rags and whatever else they require."

"Monster!" Nicole choked on raw liquid. "How can they work when they can scarcely walk? How can—?"

"If any woman refuses or displays signs of malingering . . . beat her." Flinty eyes singled out Nicole. "Including Princess Natasha."

Nicole recoiled as if he'd struck her. Hatred exploded in her heart. Denisov and Santine were poured from the same mold. Their code was brutality and violence. Their souls were insulated against human compassion.

Captain Korsakov slid an unhappy glance toward Nicole. "*Da*, my prince. It will be done." He selected additional soldiers and they formed the women into a shuffling file, prodding them downstairs, out of the healing sunshine and into the filth below.

While the soldiers located supplies, the women huddled like dumb animals. They stared at brushes and buckets as if they didn't recognize such objects. No one spoke.

Captain Korsakov examined them impassively. He drew back his fist and smashed his hand across Pavla's streaming face. Nicole screamed, and tears stung her lashes. Barbarians! Cruel, sadistic pagans!

Fear of pain curled her fingers about a bucket handle, and she dragged the heavy pail to the windows, wringing out a rag as if she strangled all men. With tears burning her lids, Nicole lifted aching arms and attacked the smoke and grit on the panes, rubbing with all her strength, her teeth grinding. One polished square emerged from the checkerboard of dirt.

She demanded and received a pail of clean water and assaulted the next pane, listening to the dull scrape of brushes behind her. The women labored silently, listlessly. One swayed beside the bed, staring at louse-ridden sheets, lost in a scene of private horror. Only when Korsakov threatened did she slowly stoop and strip the crawling linen.

The first of a shower of bodies dropped past the windows.

Every woman paused and looked up from hands and knees as another Spaniard splashed into the ship's foaming wake. And then another. The women stared, and grim life returned to ashen expressions. One by one they turned from the vengeance enacted above deck and fell to their work with a vengeance of their own. Strength flowed into battered muscles, and the wire brushes plowed the wooden planks with furious violence. Angry voices shouted, demanding additional water, more lye, and clean rags. The pent fury of the women exploded against planks and walls and furniture and ceilings. They scrubbed until their fingertips bled, until their arms trembled with fatigue, and no force on earth could have halted the onslaught. Korsakov and his men slipped away unnoticed.

When the rain of dead Spaniards ended, Nicole had cleared two-thirds of the windowpanes. And, ashamed of her outburst, she understood Denisov's motives. He'd restored the women's humanity; he'd provided them an outlet for unspeakable rage. As he obliterated the pirates above, the women erased all reminders below. When they sank into freshly made pallets tonight, the women would not toss and scream into nightmare memory; sleep would blank their thoughts before tired heads settled into the straw pillows.

Nicole bent and squeezed out her rag, the motion no longer a vicarious violence. Through the open door airing the cabin, she sensed a heavy silence overhead and paused as men's voices blended in a mournful Russian lament. The women crossed themselves and lowered their heads.

A canvas-shrouded oblong dropped past the window and splashed into the waves below.

Nicole met Pavla's steady eyes as the girl's callused hand reached for hers. Neither spoke. They clasped hands and watched until Irina bobbed from sight. Pavla pressed Nicole's fingers, then returned to rub sweet soda into the scoured wood on the captain's table.

By dinnertime the women were too exhausted to finish the bread and cheese and sausage they were served. Slowly they filed past Dimitri, stopping in the corridor entrance to kiss his fingers or express with moist eyes what words could not.

Nicole and Pavla were last to depart for the women's quarters. Dimitri stopped them at the door. "Pavla, the empress will hear of your valor." He held her lightly by the shoulders. "Every person on this ship owes you his life. We heard you drop the key, but we didn't find it until the sun struck the hatch cover." Before releasing her, he formally kissed both her cheeks.

Pavla touched her face, her eyes shining. "The empress will hear about me? About *me*?" The wonder of it glowed, chasing the fatigue from her features. Dazed, she stepped into the corridor.

Weary and longing for sleep, Nicole followed Pavla's swinging braid, but Dimitri's arm blocked her passage.

"It's been a long and strenuous day," he commented dryly, stretching his neck against his hand. "Will you join me in a glass of wine?"

Before Nicole could reply, the door closed and she discovered herself maneuvered into the center of the room. Her eyes flicked to the bolt, uneasily aware they were alone. Totally alone.

Denisov removed a bottle from a polished silver tray atop the desk near the wall and examined the label. "We're in luck ... it's French wine." He poured into two sparkling glasses.

"Stop! Don't come any nearer!" Eyes flaring, Nicole backed toward the windows. Denisov's strong masculine scent catapulted her mind backward. That smell signified sex and violence. A trembling hand rose to the collar of his borrowed shirt. She'd learned sex and violence were opposing sides of the same coin, each an expression of the other. And she associated both with his powerful male scent.

Denisov paused, staring at her through smoky speculative eyes.

"Put the wine on the table!"

He did so, placing both glasses on the powdery white surface.

Nicole blinked at the glasses. Beads of ice broke along her brow. Shivering, she wrapped both arms around her shoulders, pressing Dimitri's shirt close to her body. The cuffs dangled below her fingertips, hiding the rope burns; the tail brushed the back of her knees. The shirt provided little protection; she felt naked and cold and exposed.

"Natasha . . . Nicole . . ."

"No! Don't come any nearer!" She stared into flat dead eyes, imagined scarred lips. Spinning, she snatched up a forgotten mop and swung it into position at her shoulder. "If you take one more step, I'll smash the glass and throw myself out. I swear it!"

Slanting rays of a dying sun burnished his features in gold as rich as the tendrils flying about Nicole's fevered face. The lines beside his mouth deepened, and he appeared older than his years.

A hand lifted to tired eyes, and he murmured more to himself than to her, "I feared this . . ."

Nicole didn't hear. Blue eyes darted from side to side; her voice spiraled hysterically. "Don't move!" Denisov was everyman. And she'd seen the rapacious cravings of everyman, seen the abominations with her own eyes, listened to the agonized screams. And as long as breath coursed through her body, no man would touch her!

Denisov studied her tensing limbs, and the silvery eyes saddened. Without warning, he rapidly crossed to the windows and raised his arm, brunting the force of the swinging mop.

Nicole screamed as he threw aside her flimsy weapon and swept her into his arms. She fought like a wild animal, hissing and scratching and kicking, sobs choking her cries.

No trace of pleasure softened his hard face as he dropped her onto the bed and ripped the shirt from her breasts. Thrashing and gasping in terror, Nicole crawled to the edge of the mattress, but bruising fingers clamped her shoulder and hurled her roughly into the pillows.

The maroon breeches dropped, and he fell heavily onto the bed, pinning her ruthlessly beneath his weight. Nicole bit the hand covering her mouth until she tasted blood, but nothing would stop him. His knee brutally forced her legs apart; fingers of steel captured her wrists and slammed them into the mattress.

"No! Nonononono . . ." She bucked and twisted, and the cold sweat of fear slicked her brow. And then a brutal fiery pain cleaved her body, and she screamed until her throat swelled and closed.

Denisov raped her deliberately and without passion. When he finished, he rolled away and stepped from the bed.

She sprawled as he'd abandoned her, naked and used. A thing. Unaware of hot silent tears leaking down her cheeks, Nicole hid her face in the bend of her arm. Her mind retreated to an icy region nothing could penetrate but the throbbing pain between her outflung legs. She yearned to die, and cursed God for each unwanted breath.

Her flesh shrank as his weight depressed the side of the bed, and she buried her face deeper in the crook of her arm.

"Look at me." A surprisingly gentle quality softened his deep voice. Firm fingers guided her arm from her face.

Having learned the futility of resistance, Nicole dropped her arm listlessly, edging from his touch. Hatred gleamed from dull eyes.

He wrung a cloth in a basin of water and cleaned the rusty smears along the inside of her thighs.

Fresh tears welled in Nicole's eyes at this simple unexpected act of kindness. She pressed her face into fresh linen smelling incongruously of sunshine and soap.

He lowered the basin to the planks, and she felt his smoky eyes trace her body. "You have now experienced the worst violation man can perpetrate against woman. You need fear it never again. Because the pain and the outrage are survivable." Insistent fingers cupped her chin and forced her face toward eyes nearly black with intensity. "Those few minutes are what you were willing to kill yourself to prevent. Would your life have been a fair exchange?"

She refused to answer. She stared into the pillow and chewed bloodless lips.

His tone dropped to a hoarse whisper. "I've given you the worst . . . and now, my beautiful little Natushka, I intend to give you the best."

Her golden head snapped toward him and swimming eyes widened in horror as she understood what he intended to do.

"Shhh," he soothed, long fingers stroking the tangled hair from her forehead. "You can't conceive of it now, little Tasha, but there are delights between men and women which you haven't dreamed. Delights a woman will beg for . . . and you will." He met her eyes. "You will."

"Never!" she whispered, squirming from his lean naked body. "Please, no!"

"Shhh." Gentle lips brushed her dry mouth. His palm caressed her breast with the lightness of warm velvet. "You're so beautiful!" He gazed at her shivering body and sucked in his breath.

Rigid with fright, knowing the hopelessness of struggle, Nicole submitted helplessly, her teeth clenched in fear and revulsion.

He kissed a trail across her stomach. And skilled hands and teasing lips stroked and embraced and tantalized, approaching, then withdrawing, until all resistance melted from her heated thoughts, until nothing remained but the exquisite torture of physical sensation.

Driven by a force beyond her control, her hands slid up the muscles tensing his chest and circled his neck, urgently guiding his lips to her breathless mouth. And she cried his name in astonishment, and her body arched, seeking his with a will of its own. All thought faded from her mind until nothing existed but this man, this moment, and an ache, a sweet ache yearning for release.

"Now?" he murmured knowingly against her swollen lips.

"Yes! Oh, yes, now!"

"Say it!"

"I beg you . . . please, Dimitri . . . now!"

And he gathered her into his arms and cupped her cheeks between warm hands, staring into her eyes as he thrust into an inner sweetness and felt her eager response. And he led her slowly, then faster . . . lighter, then deeper . . . harder, and suddenly more urgent, until flesh and spirit soared. Her lashes swept open as amazement gave way to ecstasy and then all thought vanished in a shuddering explosion of unimagined bliss.

7

NICOLE AWOKE ALONE, thank heaven. She buried her tousled head in the rumpled sheets. Dear God! Darkness had played a cruel trick, causing intolerable events to appear reasonable, even desirable. But when these same events lay exposed to sunlight and conscience, they appalled; they accused. She couldn't have faced Dimitri Denisov if life depended upon it. Not until she discovered how to confront her shame, not until she'd had time to invent some justification for his actions. And for her own.

Once again the inner cogs of self-knowledge slipped into unfamiliar patterns. Nicole chewed her thumbnail and stared darkly toward sun-dappled waves. Remembering flooded scarlet across her cheeks. A dormant sensuality had exploded into life, and she could not accept this new shameless image of herself. Surely it had not been Nicole Duchard whimpering and moaning against his chest! Surely she had not clung to his neck and fought to satisfy his demands . . . and the demands of her own awakened body. Had that wanton creature borne any resemblance to Nicole Duchard? No, a thousand times, no! It couldn't have been her! Then who?

"I don't know!" Nicole covered her face, a golden tangle cascading past her fingers and across her naked breasts. "What have I become?" She punched violently at the pillows. Nothing made sense in this world; nothing was safe and familiar. She yearned to spin the calendar backward to a time when she had understood herself, when she had cherished a confidence in the world and her place in it.

Her heart leaped as the door opened; then she released a low breath of relief as Pavla entered instead of Dimitri. Praise be to God. A furrow creased her brow as she struggled to sit. To outward appearances, Pavla remained as natural and placid as she had been before the . . . Just *before*. Either that or she chose not to display her scars. Nicole closed her eyes, grateful the abominations would not be discussed . . . and all the while wondering how Pavla could think of anything else.

"I've brought you something to wear." Smiling, Pavla tumbled an armload of clothing upon the foot of the bed. If she was surprised to discover Nicole installed in the captain's bed, no hint of censure marred her sturdy features. Nor did she remark Nicole's miserably flaming cheeks. "We opened the legs of some sailors' pants and sewed new seams." A crude skirt appeared from the pile, fashioned of rough canvas material. "The length should be about right . . . we'll have to make do with the tunics for blouses, but belted they aren't half-bad." Pavla flipped her braid over one shoulder and struck a whimsical pose. "Stylish, no?" She laughed.

Nicole stared in wonderment. The Russian women were truly incredible. While Nicole languished in bed vainly attempting to unravel skeins of darkness, the servant women turned minds and hands to practical matters. Hardship was an old comrade. Life went on.

"Pavla?"

Pavla shrugged off Nicole's questions. "It was God's will." She relied upon the standard peasant reply to any calamity, no matter how catastrophic or how insignificant. It was unarguable.

Sighing, Nicole swung long shapely legs over the edge of the mattress and eyed the clothing doubtfully. Despite the women's efforts, the skirts resembled hasty makeshift contrivances. As they were. Smothering another sigh, she gazed down at her breasts, and then toward her long bare legs. Neither would do at all in their present state. Indeed, it was time to forget the past and consider practicality.

Pavla produced a large basin of soapy water and tidied the bed while Nicole washed gingerly, then slipped into the coarse skirt and red tunic.

"It's a wonderful day," Pavla commented. She ignored Nicole's disbelieving stare. "Crisp, but not too cold. Most of the storm wreckage has been cleared." Pushing aside a rack of men's shirts and breeches, she hung Nicole's second set of clothing in the wardrobe. "We've almost finished cleaning the galley, and—"

"Don't put my things in there!" Nicole concealed her crimson face, concentrating on knotting a cord about her slim waist. "I won't be returning here."

Pavla blinked. "Why not? I thought you liked Prince Dimitri!" A rural innocence rendered the words without sting. Morality was not at issue for Pavla; no one debated the morality of breathing or sleeping or eating. And in her opinion, the union of men and women was as much a necessity of life as the previous functions.

"I . . . It isn't right!" Pavla's honest bafflement upset Nicole. Why were right and wrong so clear-cut in Boston and so murky among the Russians? Moral premises were concrete; they weren't subject to geography or nationality. Were they?

"Why isn't it right?"

Nicole's slender shoulders drooped. How did one explain morality to a thief and a liar? Instantly she regretted the ungenerous thought. Pavla was her friend, and Pavla had rescued the ship. The circumstances of the rescue were an event Nicole didn't feel adequate to examine too closely. Expecially after last night. And if Pavla were to inquire why

77

stealing was condemned in one instance and condoned in another . . . Nicole shook her head.

"It just isn't!" Her answer emerged more crossly than she had intended. The cord at her waist tightened with an irritated tug. "I'd like some coffee if we have any," she added abruptly.

Pavla shrugged and removed Nicole's clothing from the wardrobe. "We do. I'll bring you a cup and then tell Vadim you're up and around. He promised he'd take you above if you want to go."

"Later, when the work is finished."

"Oh, no, you can't work . . . that was yesterday!"

Nicole's eyebrow soared and her fists balled on her hips. She felt as exasperated as she had when she and Pavla couldn't communicate. "I don't understand."

"You can't do serf's work!" Pavla's expressive eyes flashed indignation. "It wouldn't be right!"

Nicole grimaced. Right and wrong again, only now it was she occupying the side of incomprehension. Sighing heavily, she attacked her hair with the brush Pavla extended. "All right. Why wouldn't it be acceptable?" Unwilling to be easily persuaded, she pinned her hair into a utilitarian bun at the base of her neck. Work was a balm for troubled minds. If she had learned nothing else from yesterday, she had learned that. And she certainly admitted to a troubled mind.

"You are a princess!" This fact explained everything. "A princess does not stoop to physical labor."

For a moment Irina's voice echoed in her ear. "Well, no one minded when this princess stooped yesterday!" Irina would haunt for a long time to come.

Vadim's voice boomed from the doorway. "That was yesterday." Instead of the amusement Nicole had hoped for, his black eyes accorded agreement. "The quicker we restore normalcy, the quicker yesterday will be forgotten." He touched Nicole's shoulder gently. "If you take up a broom today, you'll shock your servants and forfeit their respect." Standing in the shadow of his towering bulk, Pavla nodded emphatically.

Knowing herself outnumbered, Nicole glared at each and opened her lips to argue. But she recognized her defeat before a word was spoken. Her earlier observation required amendment: work was a balm for troubled *peasant* minds. The aristocracy was forced to stumble along by other means.

She fervently wished she knew what those other means might be.

"I don't see the harm," she responded sullenly. And hated herself for defending a lost cause and for sounding petulant. The morning had not begun well.

Vadim studied her thoughtfully; then his gaze shifted to the bed, and his frown slowly dissolved. A knowing stare scrutinized her flushed cheeks. When he spoke, his thunderous voice had softened. "Bring your coffee and come topside. You'll feel better in the fresh air."

"I feel fine," Nicole snapped. She firmed her chin and ignored the offer of his arm, sweeping toward the door unassisted. Immediately she felt like a churlish adolescent. None of her problems could be laid at Vadim's door. Heaving yet another frustrated sigh, she paused in the hallway and murmured a low apology.

"Accepted." Vadim's dark beard split into a smile, and he tucked her arm comfortably around his sleeve. "In my village there lived a man named Ivan Ivanovich . . ."

"All your stories concern Ivan Ivanovich. Doesn't anyone else live in your village?" It irritated her to realize she continued to sound waspish.

"Ivan marched from field to *izba* in a continual state of anger." He glanced down at her. "An *izba* is a peasant hut."

"I remember what an *izba* is!" Stepping onto the deck, Nicole drew a breath of clear cool air deeply into her lungs. The spicy smell of freshly sawed wood delighted the senses, rising stronger than the tarry heaviness of pitch or the lighter tang of salt and water. Overhead, men shouted and cursed as they fought to untangle and repair the shreds of rigging. Others labored to clear the remaining storm debris. She winced and quickly spun toward the rail at the sound of Dimitri's commanding shout ordering men over the side as he directed an inspection of the *Kreml*'s hull.

But she decided Vadim was correct. There existed an uplifting quality to the smells and sounds of a trim ship cutting briskly through cold sparkling waves. She leaned her elbows upon the railing, cradling her coffee between her palms, and she gazed far below at a school of porpoises flirting with the stern.

Vadim poked through pockets the size of pie tins until he located his pipe; then he joined her, exhaling a jet of cherry-scented smoke. "Ivan was furious at the world." He slid a glance toward her bowed head, watching the sunlight transform honey to gold. "But the village forgave Ivan his foul temper. They understood his anger had little to do with them and everything to do with himself."

Nicole chewed her lip. Most often she enjoyed Vadim's stories; at other moments they irritated beyond measure in the transparency of the moral lesson. "Maybe so," she muttered, "but haven't you ever done . . . something . . . which you deeply regretted?" Bright pink flared upon her cheeks. In fairness, she had to admit Vadim's corollary: she did resemble his Ivan this morning, mad at the world and firing her anger like bullets.

Vadim shifted the pipe stem to a corner of his mouth. "I've lived many years, done many things I shouldn't have." He paused. "But what I most regret is not what I did, but that which I did not do." Black eyes hardened upon the horizon. "Mankind's greatest regrets are reserved for opportunities missed."

Nicole studied his profile. Her own experience didn't bear out his observation. She couldn't remember a single restraint she had ever rued. But if she wished to experience poisonous remorse, she had only to recall her actions of last night. "I don't agree."

He didn't appear to hear. Vadim stared out to sea, but his intense dark eyes examined a private space. When finally he spoke, his deep voice had gentled into memory. "In my village there lived a girl with sunshine in her soul. It shimmered about her like the brightest aura. When hardships befell them, her husband thought the burdens lighter because of her quiet radiance and her gentle smile." He removed the pipe, and his large fist tightened around the bowl.

"One day the village landowner noticed her laboring in the fields, and he lusted for her. The girl and her husband worried and whispered throughout the remainder of that long day. They talked of escape but feared the penalties for runaways. They spoke of buying their freedom, but their debt to the landowner already exceeded the ability of a lifetime to pay. Finally they considered resistance, but neither wished the other to suffer punishment."

His voice trailed, and Nicole shifted uneasily. She wished he had begun the story with his usual mention of Ivan Ivanovich.

"Each night the girl rode a cart to the manor house, and each dawn she returned, bleeding and battered. The husband did what he could to ease her pain, and then, when he understood nothing would heal the wounds in her mind, he beat his head against the walls of his *izba*."

High in the yards above them, men yelled and cursed and then cheered as mended canvas showered downward and blossomed. The air vibrated with carpenters' hammers and shouts and the whir of machinery. Nicole heard nothing but the pain cracking Vadim's low voice. She stared at his big hand clenching the pipe.

"When she conceived, the husband thought he would lose his own mind. And when she died in childbirth, he believed that he had. The sunshine vanished from his life, as it had died from hers months before." The pipe shattered. Vadim opened his fingers and watched the broken chunks tumble toward the waves.

"And the baby?" Nicole whispered.

"The child was christened Gregor Gregorovich Repinsky for his father. The husband delivered the master's son to the manor. Three days later a small mound disturbed the orchard." A shadow darkened Vadim's features, and now Nicole saw the white hair and the man's age. "The husband sat before his stove like a dead man, his fields forgotten, his animals roaming the village. And the need for revenge ignited a fire in his belly, growing hotter with every breath. But when his senses returned he rushed to the manor house, it was too late. Repinsky had moved his immediate household to Moscow for the winter. Leaving orders that the husband was to be sold before spring."

When he didn't continue, Nicole cleared her throat, then asked faintly, "And you were sold to the Denisov estates?"

Vadim's shaggy head moved and he looked blankly at his balled fists curling about the rail. "What?" He patted his pockets absently, as if searching for his pipe, puzzled not to find it.

Nicole peered into the craggy lines creasing his face. "Did you ever have your revenge?" She longed to learn he had avenged the gentle girl with sunshine in her soul. But considering his viewpoint on regret . . .

The blindness cleared abruptly from Vadim's black eyes and color flooded his cheeks. Once again he resembled the Vadim she knew, ageless and invulnerable. "Ah, Natushka, whatever gave you the notion I was speaking of myself?" He leaned his spine against the railing and shaded his eyes, studying the progress above. "Did I neglect to mention the husband's name was Ivan Ivanovich?"

Nicole's eyes welled with pity. No, revenge had eluded him; opportunity had flared briefly, then fled to Moscow. Leaving regret to fester like a thorn in the spirit.

He spoke softly, not looking at her. "Revenge is futile at best. In the heat of passion, revenge is never enough, and later . . . later one learns that revenge wreaks more damage upon the perpetrator than upon the subject." He shrugged. "Education and distance in time render vengeance impotent."

She didn't believe him. She had gazed into flat eyes and mourned the fire still charring his heart.

"But regret . . . ah, yes, Natushka, every person succumbs to the disease of regret . . . for those actions left undone, for those opportunities forever vanished."

"The opportunity for work isn't going to vanish. What are you two malingerers doing here while tasks cry out to be completed?"

Both Nicole and Vadim turned to watch Dimitri striding toward them, a freshening breeze ruffling his black hair. Hot color instantly rushed into Nicole's face, deepening as her eyes touched crisp dark hair curling from the open neck of his shirt. Her mouth dried and her heart raced, and only with difficulty did she conquer an urge to lift the canvas skirt and run. She desperately wished Dimitri Denisov's nose was flat or crooked, that his silvery eyes were close set or too widely spaced, or that he lisped or limped, or that he was too fat or too thin. She wished he was anything but so startlingly handsome that her knees weakened and her breath hitched and stammered in her throat.

Vadim lolled against the railing and deliberately crossed his boots at the ankle. Grinning hugely, he pretended a yawn. "I was considering the possibility of a nap."

Dimitri laughed, and his warm eyes smiled down at Nicole, intimate with memory and promise. "And what is your excuse, my lady?"

"I was informed a princess isn't allowed to engage in physical labor," Nicole snapped. The words emerged clipped and haughty. She clamped the inside of her cheek between her teeth, feeling a deep anger tighten her throat. She'd never felt as confused in her life. Seeing him, standing near, she responded against her will to the prowling animal force of the man. And she despised her involuntary reaction, and him for drawing it forth.

His eyebrow arched, and he looked a question toward

Vadim, but Vadim shrugged and smiled and offered no explanation. "In a bad temper, are we?"

"*We* didn't sleep last night! *We* are tired!" Immediately Nicole grasped the implication of her intended sarcasm, and embarrassment scalded her cheeks. Shaking fingers plucked at the red tunic, and she angrily averted her face.

Placing his hands on his hips, Dimitri studied her thoughtfully. "I think work might help you forget how . . . tired . . . you are. Naturally we don't want a Russian princess soiling her dainty little hands, but there is no rule preventing you from directing the cleanup operations." A clash of argument shouted from below deck, and Dimitri smiled. "I think your women might welcome a bit of leadership."

Nicole whirled on him, her eyes flashing. "You have all the answers, don't you? You believe you know what's best for everyone in any situation whatsoever!" She had to be losing her mind—it was the only reasonable explanation. An hour ago she'd been furious because she was denied the release of labor; now she raged at him for suggesting what she had demanded in the first place. She touched her forehead, surprised to discover it cool instead of feverish.

His smile faded and he considered her for a long moment before replying. "That's right. The instant I was placed in command, a great light descended from heaven, and suddenly I knew everything. It goes with being a captain. Ask me anything, and I shall answer." The tone was light and bantering, but his eyes were not.

"Don't patronize me!"

"Don't prattle foolishness!"

"I think . . ." But she didn't know what she thought. She glared from Dimitri's silvery speculation to Vadim's sparkling eyes; then she clenched her jaw and lifted the heavy make-do skirt and stamped toward the stairs, summoning what dignity she could muster. It made her furious to know she acted the fool and was powerless to prevent it. Damn! Damn guilt and damn regret and damn those silvery eyes and that hard-muscled stance! She said it aloud. Forcefully. "Damn!" And felt better, although she glanced around quickly to see if she'd been overheard. Marie would have been appalled.

The instant she stepped into the galley, three flushed faces converged upon her, spouting recrimination and gesturing angrily. "Slowly! Speak slowly or I can't understand!" Nicole settled the dispute, to no one's satisfaction; then she earned dark glares in the women's quarters, and raised annoyed mutters in the captain's cabin, before hastening to the storeroom to extinguish a near-rebellion. She arbitrated the skirmishes as best she could, eventually realizing she couldn't please everyone. Least of all herself, she thought glumly.

By the end of the day, surfaces gleamed, floors shone, and no one had come to blows. Nicole had discovered a skill for organization she hadn't previously suspected. The knowledge eased her bruised pride, and she took pleasure in the grudging respect in the women's eyes as they stored mops and brushes and then washed for dinner.

Nicole accepted her turn at the basin and smoothed her hair, wishing she could share the servants' table instead of dining with Dimitri.

"I know what you're thinking," Pavla murmured behind her hand, "and it wouldn't be right. Rank has its privileges . . . and its obligations." She tied a fresh kerchief above her braid, her level eyes reminding Nicole of a princess's limits and duties.

"You're advising me to remain in my cage, aren't you?" Nicole asked, smiling without humor. She hadn't forgotten Vadim's observation, nor was she comfortable with her own set of bars.

Pavla grinned and patted Nicole's fingers. "A doe doesn't squeeze into a rabbit's cage with any degree of comfort for either."

Nodding reluctantly, Nicole sighed, waved, and directed slow steps toward the captain's cabin, wondering what on earth she would say to Dimitri Denisov and dreading the necessity of speaking at all. She rapped lightly on the door, hoping miserably that he wouldn't respond.

"Ah, just in time." Dimitri gestured her inside and poured a second goblet of wine. He indicated the windows with the neck of a leather decanter. "A glorious sunset, I arranged it especially for you." Moving with fluid grace, he crossed the room and extended the wine, smiling as Nicole accepted the goblet without meeting his eyes.

An annoying blush had risen to embarrass her the moment she entered the cabin. She continued to chafe at the heat in her cheeks. It was impossible to conceive how wives faced husbands in the mornings. Licking her lips nervously, Nicole edged nearer the windows, acutely conscious that she and Dimitri positioned themselves much as they had last night. She tucked a golden wisp into the bun at her neck and attempted to swallow a lump of intense discomfort. She determined to follow his conversation, if the effort proved the death of her. Pride would not allow her to be bested in this game.

" . . . carpenters making rapid progress. We won't know we suffered a storm, within two weeks. . . ."

The words faded in and out, rich melodic sounds she didn't care a jot for. She couldn't look at him. Her eyes strayed continually toward the door, and she wondered what could be delaying their dinner. It couldn't arrive with enough haste. The sooner they ate, the sooner she could escape.

" . . . minor damage to the hull, nothing a shot plug can't temporarily repair. . . ."

Nicole stared into her glass, watching as the ruby liquid captured the final rays of a dying sun. It astonished her to hear him conversing so effortlessly, with no hint of strain or discomfort. Without appearing to do so, she studied him warily through a fringe of dark lashes. Nothing in his manner suggested that anything out of the ordinary had occurred between them. A sudden thought heightened the rose in her cheeks to scarlet.

Perhaps he was long accustomed to bedding women; perhaps nothing out of the ordinary *had* occurred—for him. A sharp intake of breath shifted her red tunic. The idea shouldn't have startled; from the first, she had admitted his powerful appeal. He was handsome, elegant, possessed of easy charm, and when his gray eyes darkened into that bottomless smolder . . . Oh, yes, there would be women in his past, many women. An odd twist knifed through her heart. Not jealousy, she vowed hastily, just . . . an odd twist.

"What?" she stammered.

"I said, I thought that would please you." Opening the door, he admitted a sailor carrying a heavily laden tray on his shoulder. The man cast a sidelong glance toward Nicole, then covered the table with an array of dishes. Whoever had stocked the *Kreml*, pirate or Russian, had provided amply. Roast lamb steamed beside crisp golden capons, mounds of pearly rice competed with noodles swimming in a sour-cream sauce, and Nicole counted at least three vegetables.

"Would *what* please me? I'm sorry, I . . . I wasn't listening." Seating herself, she flicked a linen across her skirt and watched the sailor's practiced movements, praying he would remain.

He did not. After lighting the candles in the center of the

table and trimming the wick on the lamp near the bed, the sailor departed.

Intelligent gray eyes took her measure, and Nicole bristled at the sympathy in their depths. Far from pleasing, his efforts to ease her discomfort raised an image of a child requiring nursing through an unsettling incident. Choking on the sudden return of an unfocused anger, she dropped her head and toyed with her silverware. The focus narrowed with each breath, and his obvious bid for patience did nothing to appease her.

"We discovered two bolts of silk in the hold, pink and brown. If your women begin immediately, you'll have a gown or two before we dock in St. Petersburg. I supposed you would be pleased to know you needn't arrive at court wearing . . ." His gaze swept her ill-fitting ensemble, and he grinned as she quickly raised a hand to the open collar of her red tunic. " . . . that."

Thick slices of roast lamb appeared on her plate, and she couldn't recall if she'd selected them or if he had when he finished carving. "I'm happy to have the material." No one would have suspected it from the tone of her voice. Lapsing into irritated silence, Nicole spooned beans and rice onto her plate, realizing as she did so that her appetite had vanished the moment she saw him. She decided to wait five minutes, then plead a headache and escape.

"All right," Dimitri said softly. "You haven't spoken two words since you arrived." He leaned backward in his chair, studying her above the rim of his wineglass. "What's wrong?"

"What's wrong?" Her jaw dropped and she stared. "What's wrong?" To her dismay, she couldn't control the shrill tone spiraling her voice. She simply could not believe what her ears registered. Throwing down her knife, Nicole leaned forward, fists forming beside her plate. "*You* are what's wrong, as if you didn't know!" she hissed. "I resent sitting here with a rapist! I'd rather eat salt fish and black biscuit by myself than share a feast with you!" Anger evoked a stammer, and golden tendrils flew about her flushed face. Once begun, she couldn't halt the tirade; she berated him for kidnapping her, for ruining her future and her image of herself, for treating her as a child. She raged and nearly wept, and spoke of everything but the incident which burned at the front of her mind, everything but her true feelings. When her voice finally trailed into silence, she glared at him, feeling drained but not yet free of the anger simmering in her chest. "People like you trample through life seizing what you want without a thought for those you hurt!" Her palms flew outward, then dropped. "Don't you ever regret the destruction you leave in your wake?"

Throughout her wild speech, he'd remained silent, watching as she paced before the table. Now he pushed aside his cold plate and refilled his glass. "Of course I have regrets," he answered quietly. "No one lives a life free of regret. I've done things I would undo in an instant if a magician offered to make it possible."

This was not the answer Nicole had expected; she had expected he would defend, justify. Deflated, she sank into her chair, averting her eyes from the cold lamb congealing on her plate. His admission surprised, but still . . . she believed it cost him nothing. She saw no dent in his confidence, no ripple of humility softening that elegantly aristocratic face. She scowled at him, resentful of his authority, his powerful male assurance. A stranger would have guessed him the commander, and this knowledge irritated her, although she couldn't have explained why.

A shaking hand rose to her forehead. She didn't understand her emotional vacillation. Once she had smugly viewed herself as even-tempered, not subject to swings of mood, not easily rattled. Now her feelings ran full-tilt in first one direction and then in another. One moment she experienced intense anger, the next she astounded herself by stealing glances at the candlelight shadowing chiseled planes. Intriguing patterns of light and shadow bathed his features in mystery. One moment she yearned to flee; the very next instant she felt hot and strange, as if her nerve endings lay exposed on the surface.

"I regret last night," he offered. "Is that what you want to hear?"

Her spine stiffened and she stared into his sober slate-colored eyes.

"I had no right to act as I did. I have nothing to offer in my defense. The gift of a woman's body should be freely given, not seized."

Night sounds disturbed a web of quiet as Nicole searched his steady gaze for hints of mockery. There were none. From above deck floated the sound of men's quiet greetings as the night watch changed; dark waves whispered around creaking timbers. Nicole swallowed and clasped her hands tightly in her lap. He had admitted what she wished to hear, but instead of feeling vindicated, she experienced a disturbing urge to defend, to forgive, to assure him that he'd done as he believed right. Confusion spun her thoughts upside down; she absolutely could not comprehend her sharp swings in viewpoint.

"Thank you," she whispered. Beyond the windows, full darkness had descended and a carpet of stars spangled the sky. Pinpoints of candlelight reflected from eyes as enigmatic and changeable as quicksilver. A shiver tensed along her thighs, then coiled in her lower stomach.

Abruptly she pushed to her feet. Had her chair not been bolted, it would have toppled. She met his gaze with an embarrassed blush and watched the heat of desire flicker and build behind his eyes. Her heart sank. "I . . . I think I . . ."

"Nicole . . ." His voice dropped to a husky register.

". . . had better leave."

"Come to me," he said quietly, not moving.

She couldn't step forward; her feet refused to carry her toward the door. "No," she moaned, swaying. "No."

"Tonight the gift is yours to give. Come to me."

"No."

Then suddenly, inexplicably, she was in his arms without remembering who had moved first, and the candlelight glowed silky across her bare throat as he swept her against his chest and her arms reached to circle his neck. "No," she whispered.

Wide blue eyes pleaded as he lowered her gently onto the bed; then he tore open her red tunic with a soft intake of breath.

And she knew she would not be returning to the women's quarters. As she surrendered, as her lips opened beneath his, she wondered wildly, helplessly, if she was falling in love with him.

8

"Dimitri, do you ever wonder who you are?" The sailor had cleared the dinner dishes and lit the lamps and departed, leaving them to Nicole's favorite hour of the day. Carefully she eased a length of silk along a double thread, gathering the material into a pink ruffle that would adorn the throat of her new gown, one of three taking shape from the bolts of silk. She extended the ruffle toward the windows, examining her work in the last hints of twilight, absently noting the days had lengthened.

Dimitri's dark head lifted from a clutter of charts and papers, and he smiled. "Ah, Tasha, how on earth do you come up with such ideas?" Several weeks past, he'd begun calling her Tasha; Nicole had decided she liked the way his deep resonant voice framed the name. "Of course I know who I am, don't you?"

"And who are you?" she asked lightly, directing the question away from herself. In the face of his self-assurance, she felt foolish exploring the mysteries of her own identity. Nicole, Natasha, and now Tasha—they were separate entities sharing an uneasy alliance. But she told herself that she had made progress; she didn't worry the void as frequently as in the near past. She resisted any thoughts which might cast a pall over her radiant happiness. She contented herself with being the person of the moment. And that was the person who treasured each day—with him.

Dimitri pushed his charts into a pile, then leaned back from the desk and ran a hand through his hair. "You're determined I'm not going to work tonight, aren't you?" His indulgent smile warmed the cabin, and for an instant Nicole considered laying aside the pink ruffle and running to sit on his lap . . . but there would be time later. A lifetime opened before them.

She tilted her head and formed her lips into a charming pout; her blue eyes sparkled flirtatiously. "Are you suggesting that you prefer your charts to me?"

His voice teased. "They don't talk back, they stay where they're put, and they don't scratch." Grinning at her blush, he touched his shoulders and pretended a wince.

Smiling, she lowered her head, tied a thread, and bit off the ends. "I'm anxiously waiting to learn who you are." She scissored a length of pink silk smaller than the first and began the ruffle to circle her upper arm.

"I'm the person who adores you, the same person who kisses you awake each morning when you'd rather sleep." Smiling, he drained his glass and reached for the wine decanter. "Do you know how domestic you look? Not at all like a princess." The deep voice roughened. "And do you know the lamplight spins gold from your hair and gleams like satin on your throat?"

"Seriously."

"Seriously?"

"Please. I love the compliments"—she blew him a kiss and a smile—"but I'd like to know what's important to you, what you aim for in life, your dreams and ambitions." She wanted to learn every small detail, even though he swore he'd told her everything. They had explored each other's history until he claimed she knew his past better than he did. If she closed her eyes; she could picture the woody estates surrounding Temnikov, could see the manor house and the peasant villages circling it. In her imagination she watched a younger Vadim pulling a small child from tree limbs and rafts, then teaching an older boy to ride and shoot, and finally directing the young man through the first levels of government service. She understood Dimitri's past, at least she believed she did, but not his reluctance to address the future.

He rolled his eyes. "My goals reveal who I am? Don't you require tea leaves or cards or something?"

"In part." She answered his first question and ignored his teasing.

A pointed glance traveled toward the charts. "You won't accept a postponement?"

Smiling, she shook her head.

"Ah, well. I was nearly finished anyway." Leaning back, he lifted his boots and crossed them upon the desk. "What do I want from life? . . ." He balanced the wineglass on his chest and gazed at the ceiling. "Like most men, I strive for recognition, honor, advancement. Catherine's approval. I aspire to increase my holdings both inside and outside Russia, and one day to produce a son to build on my accomplishments. I suppose every man dreams of founding a dynasty."

Circles of crimson dotted Nicole's cheeks, and she hastily lowered her face above the ruffle, her heartbeat quickening. If they produced a son, would his hair be gold or blue-black? Would Dimitri be disappointed if his dynasty began with a daughter instead of a son? She smiled softly, looking inward. Someday . . . someday. Forcing a normal tone, she inquired, "Just how far can you advance? Surely you've attained the top?"

"Hardly," he answered dryly. "No position is secure in Russia. No one knows what he'll discover following an absence. A man can depart enjoying the highest favor and return to discover himself banished into exile. For each friend at court, five foes are plotting destruction. A man can progress two ranks and fall three through no fault of his own. Service is all. By law, each noble gives twenty-five years to the state; *chin*, or rank, is awarded based solely on service. Being of noble birth is not alone sufficient to advance." He stared unblinking at the ceiling, the wineglass turning slowly between his fingers. "Unfortunately, the value of any service can be shaded with implications to suit the interpreter, and service performed at a distance is particularly vulnerable to denigration. There's no security in attaining the top, as you called it, not when the top rests upon quicksand."

"Why doesn't someone inform the empress of this appalling backbiting and intrigue?" She threaded the needle and bent above the emerging ruffle.

Dimitri's head lifted until his chin rested upon his chest, and he looked at her. "I forget your innocence. My dear Tasha, there is none so skilled in intrigue as our Catherine—she would be the last to condemn the practice. Consider for a moment. The lady hasn't a drop of Russian blood, yet she's risen to become absolute ruler of the largest nation on earth. She was born to an obscure German prince, yet managed to marry the Grand Duke of Russia. She arrived in Moscow with scarcely more than the shawl on her back and a year later was the central attraction in the most lavish wedding the world has seen. For seven years Grand Duke Peter avoided her bed, yet she suffered several miscarriages and eventually produced a son whom she convinced Peter to acknowledge as his own. Intrigue? Catherine thrives on it!"

Interested, Nicole dropped the ruffle into her lap. Irina had mentioned none of this. A shadow crossed her brow at the thought of Irina, and she hastened to ask, "No one speaks of Catherine's husband. Was she married when Elizabeth died?"

"Certainly."

"I don't understand. Why didn't Peter become emperor?"

"He did." His boots struck the planks, and Dimitri reached for the decanter. "Wine?"

"Please."

He filled her glass, lightly kissed the top of her curls, then wandered toward the windows. "Peter was murdered."

Nicole's mouth dropped. "I beg your pardon?" Wine spilled across her fingers. "But that's . . . Irina didn't hint a word . . ."

"Irina was fanatically devoted to Catherine. Catherine has faults, but among her talents lies an ability to inspire passionate loyalties. She possesses great charm when she chooses to exercise it."

Nicole blinked, fascinated by this new view of the empress. "Tell me about poor Peter."

"Poor Peter . . ." A grimace twisted Dimitri's lips. "For years Elizabeth made it obvious she considered her nephew unsuitable to inherit the crown, which God knows Peter was, but . . ." Dimitri paused beside the windows, staring beyond the panes toward moon-tipped waves, his face in shadow. "No document was found to prove Elizabeth had altered the line of succession. Gossip insists that such a document existed but was destroyed." Turning, he leaned against the window frame, regarding Nicole with an unreadable expression.

"Peter . . ." Nicole prompted impatiently. "He became czar, then, when Elizabeth died?"

"For a few disastrous months. He was addle-witted, immature, and committed to Germany at a time Germany had engaged Russia in war. In a most unpopular move, Peter ended the German war and pledged his loyalty to the German king. What few supporters remained after this outrage he managed to alienate by openly vowing to marry his mistress, a coarse woman as offensive as himself. To accomplish this, there is reason to believe he planned to have Catherine assassinated or, at the very least, confined to a nunnery. He viewed his wife as a threat. And with probable reason. Despite her German birth, Catherine genuinely loves Russia, a fact which has endeared her to the army and to the people; she's always enjoyed a popularity Peter lacked. Additionally, she is the mother of Grand Duke Paul, the son Peter acknowledged. She and Peter despised one another. Even a dull-wit could sense an eventual confrontation; it had to be one or the other."

The story contained a fairy-tale unreality. Nicole reminded herself that these were real people, one of whom she would soon encounter. Slowly she asked, "Are you hinting that Catherine murdered her own husband?" The thought chilled. Her eyes fixed on Dimitri and she wondered what she sailed toward. Irina had sculptured Catherine as a saint . . . now it appeared the saint possessed feet of clay.

Dimitri waved his wineglass, the gesture unconsciously elegant. Caught up in the story, he paced the room like an uneasy animal, as if the tale held personal significance. "That question has been endlessly debated for the last ten years. It is certain the Orlov brothers were involved in the murder. And Gregory Orlov has been Catherine's lover for years, the father of one of her children. The threads appear to lead back to her. On the other hand, the circumstances are too blatant; Catherine is too brilliant to so obviously implicate herself."

"Her lover? One of her children?" Nicole echoed weakly. She found it extremely difficult to reconcile Dimitri's Catherine with Irina's Catherine.

"When Catherine effected her coup, the most pressing problem was the deposed emperor, her husband. As long as Peter was alive, the danger existed that he would mount an offensive to reclaim his crown. His death was . . . convenient. Although the Orlovs' complicity is common knowledge, they've never been punished; in fact, they have all prospered under Catherine's largess. Whether or not she was directly involved, she was grateful to have the threat removed." Once again he glanced thoughtfully at Nicole. His lips opened, then closed decisively, and he drained his wine in one long swallow.

"Do you believe the Orlovs acted on Catherine's orders?" Palace revolts, lovers, illegitimate children, murders . . . Nicole twined a loose curl around her finger and worried her lower lip. Murky undercurrents swirled about the Russian court. The image of Catherine as gracious benefactor wobbled; there was a darker side as well.

Shrugging, Dimitri capped the decanter and placed it atop his desk. "Only Catherine knows the truth."

Nicole considered the elements of the story. "Paul . . . Catherine's son . . . wouldn't he have a stronger claim to the throne even than Catherine? Why didn't he become emperor, with Catherine as regent?"

"He was a child at the time of Catherine's coup. But our little Paul has grown up. . . . I'll wager he asks himself that very question every day of his life." Dimitri stretched and smiled. "Enough history. Are you finished sewing?" His eyes, those wonderful hungry eyes, melted from slate to silver.

Quickly Nicole folded away her sewing; then she cocked her head to one side and eyed him quizzically. "We seem to have strayed from Dimitri Denisov, haven't we? Am I ever to learn who he is?"

"Come here and I'll show you."

Nicole laughed and ran into his arms.

Thus the days blended into weeks, happy days spent laughing with Pavla, being fitted for new gowns, strolling the decks with Vadim, practicing her Russian—and eagerly anticipating the blissful nights of exploration and delight.

Occasionally as she smiled toward Dimitri's dark head bending above his charts or listened as his strong voice rang from the forecastle, Nicole was brought up short by the depth of her happiness. Regret? Vadim was correct; had she missed knowing Dimitri, had she missed knowing the rapture of men and women, she would have regretted the lost opportunity all the days of her life.

"Pavla, have you ever been in love?" The question slipped from her lips unaware; she hadn't intended to ask any such thing. Flushing, she realized the topic had occupied her thoughts for weeks.

"Me?" Tossing her braid over her shoulder, Pavla glanced up from a brown silk hem, her lips clamped around a dozen pins. "Turn to the right, no, not that far!" Nimble fingers flew as she talked. Near the windows a row of women bent over pieces of dark silk. On occasion one or another crossed to mold the material against Nicole's bosom or slim waist or around her upper arms.

"*Da*, you, who else?" She laughed as Pavla threatened to pin the hem to her toes.

"Well, maybe once."

"Who was he? What happened?"

Rocking back on her heels, Pavla removed the pins from her mouth, and her fine dark eyes assumed a dreamy cast. "He was the son of a wealthy landowner, visiting our village from Moscow. This was before I was attached to the palace in St. Petersburg. Anyway, his hair was as bright as yours, and his shoulders wider than I ever saw. He was even more handsome than Prince Dimitri."

Nicole couldn't imagine anyone more handsome than Dimitri. It wasn't possible. Interested, she fixed her gaze on Pavla's faraway expression.

"He saw me and my sisters bringing the cows back to the village, but he didn't pay the others any attention, only me. He rode right into—"

"Pavla! You don't have any sisters!" Nicole released a deep sigh and looked toward the ceiling. If Pavla had sworn the sky was blue, Nicole would have felt compelled to verify it. It wasn't that Pavla was malicious—Nicole knew this; Pavla simply couldn't help lying. She lied to protect herself, to amuse herself; she lied for a hundred reasons a person valuing truth could not hope to comprehend.

"That's right," Pavla agreed blandly. "Did I say sisters?" Unless she suspected punishment, Pavla readily confessed if caught out. And to Nicole's dismay, she did so without the appearance of remorse.

"You know you did." Irritated, Nicole clamped her lips into a disapproving line. She'd long since abandoned lectures or moralizing. Neither produced results. But she had learned Pavla's truth generally surfaced if she demonstrated anger or disappointment.

"Boris Horev," Pavla offered when Nicole's silence became uncomfortable. She bent above the ragged hem, folding, pinning, taking up another length. "His name was Boris Horev. He died." The dreamy expression had vanished; her voice emerged flat and dull.

"Oh, Pavla!" Now Nicole wished she hadn't forced the issue, wished she hadn't raised the subject. "I'm sorry!" She'd acted thoughtlessly, swept up in her own happiness and forgetful that not all stories ended happily ever after.

"He couldn't pay his taxes, so he became a coiner . . . he melted down a silver icon and made his own money so he could pay. The coins weren't a good likeness." The hem crumpled in her fist. "They knouted him, then they poured molten silver down his throat."

"Good God!" Nicole gagged, and her body stiffened in horror. "That's . . . that's barbaric! Didn't anyone try to stop it?"

"Who? God is too high to hear pleas for help, and the czarina is too far away. Who is there to help?"

Neither spoke. Nicole turned when Pavla prodded her toes.

She listened to the servant women's quiet murmurs and occasional humming, and she swayed instinctively with the rhythm of the ship's motion. But her mind raced, sorting through what she had learned of serfdom. Her knowledge was limited, and none favored a condition she equated with slavery. Vadim's story, and now Pavla's, offended the senses, shocked a spirit raised under the shelter of democratic principles. It disturbed her to realize Dimitri owned villages of peasants—and so would she when her inheritance was settled. Yet, to her astonishment, both Vadim and Pavla objected to any impulsive statement suggesting she would free the serfs she inherited.

"Where would they go? Remember, the land belongs to the master; how would the peasant survive without land?" Vadim had asked, his black brows lifting. "In times of trouble, the landlord provides seed and animals. He watches over his peasants like children—that's why they address him as *otets*, father. The title is not always deserved, but it is not altogether without reason."

"You would defend a system which killed your . . . Ivan Ivanovich's wife?" Nicole's confusion had shown in troubled eyes and in the slump of her shoulders.

"Defend? A thousand times no! But before the system can be overhauled, the people must be educated. They need schools and land of their own, they need to see themselves as men and not as dependent children! The time won't be ripe until these conditions are met; would you abandon small children without preparation?"

Pavla expressed similar opinions. "Don't judge the whole barrel by one piece of fruit! Some landowners are well-loved and respected. It's the abuses you hear discussed. Not all masters are evil."

Nicole rubbed her temples, recalling the conversations. At times she despaired of ever understanding the Russian mind. Pavla and Vadim, who were or had been serfs, appeared to defend, whereas Dimitri, who owned serfs, violently opposed the system.

Often he had stated that his holdings in other countries far outproduced his Russian estates in goods and profit. He attributed the disparity to free enterprise versus a system binding people to land and landowners. "A man works best when the lion's share of his labor benefits himself. No man should live solely by the labor of others." If Catherine had sanctioned it, Dimitri would have immediately freed every serf he owned.

However, when Nicole pressed, repeating Irina's views, Dimitri admitted wide-scale freedom would indeed result in economic disaster. But he also stoutly maintained that freedom would come. In time, and in blood, if his predictions proved accurate.

A light shudder raised Nicole's skin. Sometimes the Russian civilization impressed her as an artificial veneer rubbed raw in some spots, exposing a decaying interior.

She stared down at Pavla's glossy swinging braid. "What is a knout? I've heard you mention it before."

Without glancing from the hem, Pavla answered, "It's a whip. A parchment whip cooked in milk until it's so hard it's like a sword. Three well-placed strokes can kill a man."

Nicole's spine prickled and shrank, and she hastily changed the subject. But she didn't forget. The information gathered like a burr and lodged beneath her skin.

As the weather warmed, spirits lifted and soared. Soon the *Kreml* would enter the English Channel, and home was but two or three weeks distant. In the mild spring evenings, the men gathered around the masts, smoking and singing Russian folk songs as they shared out tin mugs of vodka. The women often joined them, sitting on barrels near the lanterns as they worked to finish Nicole's gowns.

"The pink is my favorite," Nicole commented idly. She and Dimitri leaned against the railing beneath a star-studded sky, watching as Vadim and Korsakov linked arms and danced within a clapping, cheering circle of song. With strained good humor Korsakov flopped alongside Vadim, having little option but to leap upward when the giant Ukrainian did and to sink when he did. The men clapped in rhythm, urging the dancers to greater feats until another man spun into the ring, crossing his arms over his chest, whirling, sinking, boots kicking. Vadim relinquished the stage reluctantly, Korsakov with a weak smile of relief. "They're wonderful," Nicole observed, her eyes glowing. "I could watch them dance all night."

"I'd rather watch you." Dimitri captured a loose golden curl and pressed it to his cheek, stroking the silky texture with a groan of pleasure. "Why do you prefer the pink?" Moon-deep eyes slid to Nicole's breasts, and she drew a soft breath. "Will I like it better than the others?"

"You'll have to wait and see," she teased, lightly touching

the triangle of skin at his open collar. Smiling, he stepped behind her, his arms circling her slender waist, his chin resting on top of her head. She leaned comfortably against his broad chest and smiled at the dancers. "The pink reminds me of the gown my mother wore in the portrait. I think that's why I..."

Abruptly Dimitri's arms stiffened and his head lifted from her hair. "You saw the portrait? Why didn't you tell me?"

Surprised, Nicole attempted to turn in his arms, but he held her fast. "Is it important? I thought I'd mentioned it ... the night of the storm."

"No."

His clipped tone alarmed her. A knot of frustration unwound in her stomach; it was difficult being the outsider. She thought hard, casting her mind backward in time, but she discovered nothing to explain why the portrait would disturb Irina, and now, Dimitri.

"Do you have the painting?" He released her and spun her to face sober eyes. Behind him, a long graceful form splashed through a ribbon of moonlight, a silvery flash, then gone.

"No, it sank with the *Kiev*."

"I see." The lines beside his mouth deepened. "Tell me what you remember about Varina." In the starry light, the eyes probing her expression were nearly black and the pressure upon her shoulders almost painful.

"Did you know Princess Varina?" she asked. She winced pointedly, and his fingers loosened but did not relax.

"I never met the lady. Describe her for me," his voice commanded, employing an authority Nicole overheard every day above decks but had seldom heard directed toward herself.

Uncomfortably she began, "Well, Varina and I resemble each other closely, as I remember ... blue eyes, blond hair, the mouth..."

"Go on."

"She impressed me as possessing great vitality—I believe that's what I most recall. The manner in which she faced the artist, frankly, openly, as if she welcomed life and everything in it. Also, she radiated an unmistakable ... sensuality." Blushing, Nicole dropped her eyes. When first she had viewed the portrait she hadn't recognized this parallel between her mother and herself. Now ...

Dimitri released her and passed a hand over his eyes.

When he spoke, he sounded suddenly weary. "You're describing Elizabeth."

"I am?" Nicole's brows arched, and she attempted to isolate her memories. The task proved difficult if not impossible. Time had blurred the painted women's differences for someone who had known neither. She touched his arm and peered upward, uneasy at his disturbance. "What's wrong? What is it about this picture that I'm not seeing?" She was impatient and frustrated by the mystery, by being excluded from information clearly concerning herself.

A long moment elapsed before he answered. "Tasha. My little Tasha," he said finally. "There is an old saying: Too much knowledge can be as dangerous as too little. In this instance, I agree."

"There is another old saying," she replied tartly. "Ignorance is bliss. And in this instance, I do *not* agree."

He smiled and refused to be baited, lifting a palm to smother her protests. Strong arms wrapped about her waist, pulled her close to his heartbeat. And they watched the dancers in silence, but the pleasure had diminished for Nicole.

When she fidgeted in his arms, he murmured against her hair, "Choose your St. Petersburg friends with care, Tasha. Resist the intrigues."

She tossed her curls. "Haven't we progressed beyond mysterious advice? If I should know something, I'm entitled to hear it without having to decipher some code. Must you treat me as a child?" The child analogy was apt. She felt as she had when she was young and a friend taunted her with a secret. Irritation clouded her eyes.

"I can't tell you how many times I've asked myself if . . . more history . . . would aid or imperil you. For the moment, at least, I ask you to trust my judgment." He paused, then added quietly, "I promise you this: if I discover I've erred, I'll find you and reveal everything you wish to know."

Nicole's heart lurched. All the questions died on the tip of her tongue. "Find me?" She twisted in his arms until she could examine his face. "Won't you be with me in St. Petersburg?" The possibility that he would not hadn't entered her mind. She rejected the thought.

"I hope so." Pulling her close, he pressed his lips to her forehead. "Remember, I'm at Catherine's disposal. In any case, I'll be staying at my city house, for a time at least, and you'll be residing in the palace. I won't be far away." He kissed her alarm-filled eyes. "I anticipate a trip to Temnikov at some point, but I'll call on you as often as possible."

The ground fell from beneath her feet.

Throughout the following week, Nicole worried the unsettling information during each waking hour. She had expected commitments, not good-byes.

The *Kreml* cleared the channel and entered the North Sea, and then the Baltic. The sailors invented tasks near the rail, their eyes avidly scanning distant shores for familiar landmarks. Gulls wheeled in the brilliant spring sky, circling the masts of a ship scoured and polished for her voyage up the Neva River and home. The long weeks at sea were coming to a close.

And Nicole's anxiety increased. She didn't know what to expect from the Russian court, or, more important, from Catherine. Most important of all, she couldn't bear leaving Dimitri's strong arms and his warm bed. She admitted it. The realization did not mesh with her ideas of herself, but it was a fact. She didn't want their time together to end, couldn't tolerate the thought of bidding him good-bye, of dividing their lives into two residences. Surely a more permanent, a more secure solution could be resolved?

"Dimitri? Are you awake?" His lean naked warmth curled about her, one large hand gently cupping her breast. And Nicole marveled at the curious comfort of habit; would she ever again choose the left side of a bed? Or fall easily asleep without the shelter of his arms about her, without his hand warm on her breast?

"Hmmm. It's too hot to sleep." He kicked the sheet away from their bodies, then kissed her hip with a smile and lay back against the pillows, folding his arms behind his head.

"Only a Russian would think this hot!" She laughed, retrieving part of the sheet for herself. She turned and nestled into his shoulder, pressing her hand flat against the crisp mat covering his chest. She liked the touch of the springy hair beneath her palm, the contours of sharply defined muscles. "Dimitri?"

"Hmmm."

"Do you think Catherine will dispatch you on another mission?"

"Not immediately. It's customary to allow several months between assignments. Time to attend to one's estates, reestablish oneself at court . . ."

The rocking motion of the ship cradled them in pleasantly

creaking darkness. She wished the voyage would never end. "And you must go? You have to go whenever she says for the next twenty-five years?" It seemed so unfair. She wondered why anyone agreed to this, forgetting for a moment the lack of choice.

He smiled down at her, stroking tumbled gold strands as their legs tangled lazily. "I've already given ten years. But, yes, every noble owes the state twenty-five years."

"It appears to me the noblemen are bound as tightly as the serfs."

He laughed. "The observation has been made."

"Can't you refuse?" Her head fitted perfectly into the hollow of his shoulder. She couldn't imagine that she had ever preferred a pillow.

"No one refuses an autocrat. The empress commands, and we obey."

"Haven't you ever wished to refuse some act of service?"

The warm intimacy chilled. His body tensed and his hand slowed its stroking motion.

Raising her head, Nicole frowned at his profile, angular and shadowed by the pale spring moonlight. "Dimitri?"

"Yes," he answered quietly. "Yes, I've performed a service for the state which I would have preferred to refuse."

His expression alarmed, and she hastily returned her head to his shoulder, seeking to reestablish the previous easy mood. Drawing a breath, she attempted to inject a playful note into her tone, although she suspected he would guess she spoke seriously. She drew slow circles across his chest. "Maybe I won't live in the palace, maybe I'll follow you home like a puppy . . . and live with you." Her voice rose on a question mark, her pride suffered at raising a suggestion better initiated by him. She cursed herself for impatience; if she had waited, surely he would have asked for himself.

To her surprise, he didn't respond. But his arm dropped from behind his head and circled her shoulders, holding her tightly.

Hating herself, but unable to stop, Nicole closed her eyes and pressed her face against warm skin which smelled of salt and soap and musky memory. "Could I do that?" she whispered.

When he didn't respond, she sensed something was terribly out of balance, and a tiny chill encased her heart. An odd sense of foreboding tensed her throat. "Could I follow you home?" she repeated.

"No." Pain hoarsened his voice, rippled through the muscles beneath her cheek.

And she knew. Knew something terrible rushed toward her, one of the missing pieces. She caught her breath and fought to restrain a tremble as her hand unconsciously closed into a fist. Everything sensible warned her to drop the subject; but she could not. "Why not?" she asked in a small voice.

"I'm married, Nicole."

His quiet reply exploded through her mind with the force of a volcano. She sagged against him, her body suddenly deadweight, her breath crushed from her lungs. It had never occurred to her. Not once. Suddenly she remembered him stating his ambition to sire a son.

And then the pain came. Silent white blades of pain slashing through mind and heart. Crippling, mutilating pain.

"Catherine desired to cement an uneasy alliance with Austria; Darya is Maria Theresa's niece. When Catherine requested that I marry Darya, I agreed. The match is beneficial for Russia."

Beneficial for Russia. Always the state. Didn't people matter? Or was it just a convenient excuse? Nicole clung to his warmth, her own flesh cold and rigid. And she listened but did not hear. Torturous images flickered behind her lids: Dimitri and another woman. Dimitri and . . . Darya. Princess Darya Denisovna. Dimitri kissing another woman, bending over her, stroking her. . . . Nicole's stomach convulsed in a bath of acid. Beyond the shell of numb isolation, her mind shrieked and protested and screamed a jealous agony. Moving like an automaton, she untangled her legs and slowly pulled away. She sat forward, covering her nakedness with her arms, staring dully at a patch of moonlight as her world and her pride curled into ash.

"Is she . . . is she beautiful?" Against her will, against her better instincts, her pain demanded more pain.

"Yes."

"Oh, God," she whispered. Then she buried her face in her hands, and now the tears came, wrenching scalding sobs that ravaged her throat and eyes, stung her heart like poison. "Oh, God, I've been such a fool! A blind, shameless fool!"

Gentle fingers closed on her shoulders as he attempted to gather her into his arms, but she tore from his grasp and threw herself flat to the wall, kicking him away. The storm of anguished weeping humiliated her, mortified her, and she would gladly have traded ten years of life to conceal her pain from him.

"Tasha . . . Nicole, listen to me! This isn't what you think. Darya is—"

"Stop!" she screamed, whirling on him in a fury, lashing out at his reaching hands. "Not another word! I don't want to hear your justifications, I don't want to hear about *her*!"

"Nicole, just listen! Darya—"

"*No!*" She covered her ears and buried her face in the pillow, rocking back and forth like a wounded animal. "You deceived me! I thought you . . . I wanted . . . Oh, God! I was such a stupid fool! I gave myself to you, and I thought . . ." The sobs gasped between her words like liquid punctuation. She wept until she was exhausted, hating every degrading moment. She sobbed until her eyes puffed and her throat felt raw. And always she was agonizingly aware of his silent form stretched beside her.

Toward dawn the rage and grief subsided into emptiness and she was powerless to resist when he quietly guided her into his arms, holding her without speaking until the bells sounded the early watch, and the *Kreml* stirred to morning life.

"Nicole, please. Now that you're calmer, can we discuss this?"

Her voice was dead. "There's nothing to discuss. Nothing. Don't insult either of us further."

He released her.

And she turned a stony face to the wall as he silently dressed. She stared into a vast wasteland of shame and abandonment. She had believed. She had trusted. And he had betrayed her. He had betrayed them both—her and . . . and Darya.

When the door softly closed, she cried out and fell across his pillow, clinging to the familiar warm scent, bathing his pillow in her tears. Then she dragged herself from his bed, gathered her things, and directed wooden steps toward the women's quarters.

And wished with all her aching heart that the planks would open and drop her into the endless tranquillity of the sea.

9

THE *Kreml* PUT into Riga for a day and a half, long enough to board fresh fruit and vegetables and to dispatch an overland rider to St. Petersburg carrying Dimitri's account of the *Kiev*'s fate and the *Kreml*'s imminent arrival.

Though Pavla coaxed and wheedled, Nicole resisted all exhortations to ascend above deck for a glimpse of the Russian coastline; she dreaded a glimpse of Dimitri as well. She had steadfastly refused to see him or read his letters. She sequestered herself in the women's quarters, wrapped in a blind bitterness of pain. The poison of betrayal seeped through her system, destroying appetite and transforming the nights into spans of torment, aching vigils of loneliness and recrimination.

When Nicole overheard the whir and clank of the anchor chain signaling the *Kreml* was leaving Riga, she willed her tensed muscles to relax and pressed her lips in grim relief. The sooner the voyage ended, the better! She longed to slam the door on this chamber of her life, to forget Dimitri Denisov and the brief existence of Tasha—whoever that vulnerable little fool had been.

"You must eat something!" Pavla scowled at Nicole's untouched trencher; then her dark eyes worried the violet smudges brushed beneath Nicole's lashes like delicate bruising.

"I'm not hungry."

Frowning Pavla chewed the end of her braid thoughtfully. Perhaps an appeal to pride would succeed where reason had failed. A sly expression stole across her wide plain features. "Do you want him to see how you suffer?" she inquired softly.

"What?" Nicole's head snapped upward, and her eyes sharpened to hard points of sapphire.

Pavla's red tunic lifted above an elaborate shrug. "Your cheeks are thin and drawn, your eyes don't sparkle, your hair is lackluster . . ." She watched the instantaneous effect of her observations. And hid a smile beneath her thick braid.

Nicole's shoulders squared and her eyes flashed blue fire. She thought hard, then jerked the trencher forward, and, gagging, forced herself to swallow. "I won't give him the satisfaction!" She hissed. Furiously she spooned cold food into her mouth, wondering why she herself hadn't anticipated this affront to her pride. Dimitri Denisov would not observe another humiliation; her heart might lie in pieces, but, by heaven, her pride was intact!

"You're right," she muttered between bites. "I've grieved enough. No man is worth this!" She didn't wholly believe this stubborn avowal, but perhaps, if she stated it often enough . . .

Pavla scrubbed the table, nodding agreement. "He isn't worth it." Loyalty prompted the echo; not conviction.

Nicole mopped her trencher with a crust of bread and wished for more, not to appease an eager appetite, but because she recognized the importance of building her strength. She rejected the debilitating grief; the period of mourning had concluded. And in its place burned a knot of prideful anger. It was time to inject iron into her spine and to lift her golden head high. She'd been behaving like an idiot. It was humiliating enough to have been played for a fool. Would she allow him to ruin her health as well? Never! Dimitri Denisov would observe only the cool, unruffled exterior she intended for Natasha Stepanova. She had finished wearing her emotions on her sleeve for all to mock; Dimitri would never suspect her anguish had endured for longer than a fleeting moment. This she promised herself.

Fresh purpose infused her stance as she pushed from the table and addressed the women. "Fetch me a tub of hot bathwater," she commanded briskly, "and soap enough to wash my hair." She flung open the wardrobe and critically examined her three gowns, eyes narrowed, hands on hips. "The brown needs to be pressed, and I want the neckline lowered on the pink. Were there any brown scraps?"

Pavla nodded happily, a relieved smile curving her lips.

"We'll make ribbons." Nicole's hand waved above her head. "I want a wide band for my throat, and smaller ribbons for my hair." The servants scattered in a burst of activity. "I'll have a glass of tea while I'm in the bath. And my shoes . . . what's being done to salvage my slippers?" The determined smile she directed toward Pavla failed to reach her stormy eyes, but it was a beginning, her first smile in days.

She tossed her head, discarding the kerchief covering her hair. "When I step off this cursed ship, I intend to be remembered!" She didn't explain whether she referred to the people who would meet the *Kreml* or if she wished to be remembered by someone else.

When the *Kreml* entered the Neva River, Nicole's mirror confirmed a beauty no man would forget.

Accompanied by blaring horns and blasting whistles, the *Kreml* trimmed to short sail and moved majestically past the low, flat outskirts of St. Petersburg. Escort vessels sailed fore and aft, adding their whistles to the din, their bows plowing aside the small melting ice floes dotting the Neva's silvery waters.

Standing beside Pavla at the rail, Nicole watched the chunks of ice bobbing toward the Gulf of Finland and struggled vainly to convince herself this was indeed May. The ice and the cool breeze lifting her hood mocked the balmy New England Mays she remembered.

But Pavla excitedly assured her that spring had arrived in Russia. Pavla pointed toward carpets of green flowing upward from the riverbanks to surround sprawling stone palaces interspersed with older wooden edifices painted startling shades of vivid red and blue and green. Between the buildings Nicole glimpsed early gardens and leafy trees overhanging the canals and bridges of the city.

St. Petersburg glittered in the crisp spring air like a newly cut jewel, a testament to man's ingenuity. Against overwhelming odds, the city had risen where once a great marsh had stretched. Magnificent buildings rested on wooden pilings driven deep into swampy ground. If St. Petersburg wasn't the "Paris of the East" that her residents claimed, the city was certainly a breathtaking triumph of planning, an enchanting collection of gondolas and canals, broad avenues and grandiose palaces, a conglomerate of the finest Russia could offer, from the gold leaf ornamenting the onion domes of soaring cathedrals to the neat cobbled squares reminiscent of English influence; from the meticulously landscaped parks to an unsurpassed market offering goods from every corner of the globe.

"There's the Peter and Paul fortress," Pavla explained, indicating a forbidding stone edifice. "And on the opposite bank, the Winter Palace!" Home softened her eyes, animated her voice.

Before responding to Pavla's impatient tug, Nicole inspected the Peter and Paul fortress. From within its thick rock walls, a gold-sheathed spire pierced the cobalt sky like a needle. Suspended beneath a cross at the top, an angel on a chain swung in the breeze. Nicole's gaze fixed on the twirling angel, and for a moment she sensed an affinity for the small form dancing to the winds of fate. She squeezed her lashes tightly and isolated the stream of commands issuing from the forecastle. And thought Dimitri's authoritative voice harsher, more demanding than she had previously noticed.

Men raced along the decks in response to his shouts, and the *Kreml* maneuvered slowly toward a stone quay jutting from the riverbank directly below the imposing Winter Palace. A cluster of people waited there, but Nicole ignored them for the moment and concentrated her attention upon her new home. She drew a soft breath. She hadn't imagined the existence of such an immense building.

Three stories of baroque splendor towered above the Neva's waters, sunlight gleaming against protruding facades of white and apple green that appeared to stretch the entire length of the river. As Nicole scanned the profusion of high reliefs and a roofline ornamented by vases and pale statuary, she felt diminished and very small. In this land of extremes, everything appeared enormous, in sharper focus, and more vivid than anything in her previous experience.

She started, and looked into Vadim's smile as his familiar voice rumbled above her ear. To honor their arrival, he'd trimmed the black beard, and his white hair was neatly tied at the neck with a braided leather cord. "Nervous?" he asked, leaning his elbows on the railing beside her.

"A little," she admitted, stubbornly understating the truth. Her fingers gripped the rail, and it was necessary to continually remind herself not to bite her lips. And not to seek the source of a certain shouting voice. "Pride," she bolstered herself silently. "Remember your pride." Her chin firmed, and she resolutely trained her eyes upon the quay and away from the frantic activity behind her.

"I've missed you the last days," Vadim commented, watching as Nicole dropped her hood to expose an elaborate coiffure streaming brown silk ribbons. His black eyes registered approval. "We're bringing the empress a treasure!" The pride in his booming voice could not have been greater if he'd created Nicole himself.

"I've missed you too," she responded affectionately, curling her fingers about his massive arm. Sudden consternation clouded her eyes. "Vadim! Will I see you again, or . . . ?"

He patted her hand, the gesture awkwardly sentimental. "Certainly! The *barchuk* and I didn't bring you this far to abandon you."

A flash of pain dimmed Nicole's vision. "I want to see you, but I don't want to see him again." Blank eyes stared unseeing at the elegantly gowned ladies on the dock. "I . . . That's a closed chapter."

The *Kreml* swung in a controlled drift toward the quay, and the anchor splashed into crystal waters. Signaling endings. No, Nicole determined, her eyes fixed upon the palace, signaling fresh beginnings. Coils of rope hissed toward the dock like unfurling serpentine; men gathered at the waist of the ship and hoisted planking into place. The leading edge of a gangplank bumped against the quay, where quick hands hastened to secure it. And an eager cheer rang from the decks, echoing in the rigging high overhead. Carefully Nicole arranged her countenance into a smile corresponding to the jubilation which met her eye wherever she chanced to look.

"About you and the *barchuk*," Vadim began carefully. "In my village there lived a man named—"

"Ivan Ivanovich," Nicole finished. "Oh, Vadim!" Her artificial smile became genuine and she pressed her palm to his cheek, mildly surprised by the softness of his heavy beard. "I really will miss you. Terribly!" The vastness of the palace and the surrounding countryside and the empty stretch of sky intimidated her. She experienced an acute awareness of being alone, a stranger in a strange country. When Vadim clasped her small hand between his meaty palms, she clung to him, reluctant to part with this great bear of a man.

"Don't worry," Vadim offered softly. "You'll have the court at your feet within a week, like a new scythe cutting spring wheat. And if any dandy presses an unwanted suit, you mention Vadim Nevsky by name." He grinned, failing utterly at modesty. "I enjoy a certain reputation."

Nicole smiled, blinking back an unexpected sting of tears as he guided her gently toward the gangplank.

Someone had attached banners to the ropes along the planks, and they snapped and fluttered in gay profusion as brightly colored as the waiting women's gowns. Nicole hesitated. This truly was the end. A dozen curious faces peered upward, faces which soon would attach themselves to names and personalities, perhaps to friendships. Yet she encountered an inexplicable reluctance to depart the *Kreml*'s familiar creaking timbers. And could conceive of no excuse for delay.

Still, she could not believe Dimitri would allow her to disembark without a word. What they had shared simply had to possess more meaning than that! Impulsively she whirled from the gangplank, his name forming on her lips. And she nearly fell into his arms.

Strong hands restored her balance. His hard stormy eyes swept the ribbons adorning her hair, dipped to the swell of milky flesh above the brown silk, then locked to her wide confused gaze.

A band of iron constricted Nicole's chest; she felt the heat of his hands burning upon her shoulders as if her cloak had melted beneath his touch. The indifference she had planned, the scathing remarks she had mentally rehearsed—they blew from her mind like dry leaves before a hurricane. The pain and the love she'd struggled to deny leaped unbidden into her eyes, and her pride's only salvation hung on the fact that he did not see.

He dropped into a graceful bow before a man and a woman who had mounted the gangplank behind them. "Princess Natasha Stepanova, I have the honor to present Vice Admiral Basil Vrubel and the first lady of the bedchamber, Princess Lilia Ulanova."

Nicole inclined her head and sank into a deep bow as Irina had taught, her racing thoughts attempting to judge the future importance of the man and woman examining her. Vice Admiral Vrubel she discounted immediately; his interest clearly centered on the vessel, not upon the ship's passenger. Princess Lilia Ulanova, in contrast, regarded Nicole with a cool blend of appraisal and speculation. Intuition warned Nicole it was vital to favorably impress this woman with the sharp eyes and superior air. Catherine had chosen Lilia Ulanova for a purpose; this Nicole did not doubt. A woman of Catherine's character abandoned nothing to chance; all her choices would be reasoned.

Nicole straightened from the bow with her most winning smile. She addressed Princess Lilia in careful Russian, enunciating slowly and clearly. "I am pleased to visit the land of my birth."

Lilia Ulanova's smooth brow shot toward a lightly powdered hairline. A smile of genuine pleasure curved her full lips as she offered a slight correction to Nicole's pronunciation.

"*Vinovata*," Nicole murmured. "I beg your pardon."

The princess pressed Nicole's hand with warmth, switching into French, the court language. "Her Majesty will be delighted by your diligence and progress." Sultry dark eyes traveled toward Dimitri. "Is this surprise a result of your efforts, Prince?"

"*Nyet*." Dimitri's stare dried Nicole's mouth, and she hastily averted her eyes. "Countess Irina must be awarded any credit."

The princess arranged heavily rouged cheeks into an expression of sympathy. "Ah, yes, poor Irina. A tragedy." Shrewd eyes flicked between Dimitri and Nicole, her curiosity as obvious as if she'd given voice to it.

Vice Admiral Vrubel interrupted the measuring scrutiny. His ruddy features drew into a frown and he balanced first upon one gleaming boot, then shifted to the other. "I'm most anxious to inspect the log," he announced briskly.

Lilia Ulanova's glance was withering. "Propriety," she sniffed haughtily, "must be observed." However, a businesslike crispness stiffened her demeanor. "When you've concluded the exchange of command," she addressed Dimitri, "Her Majesty will be pleased to receive you." The dark eyes hinted that Lilia Ulanova would also be pleased to receive Prince Dimitri. With flirtatious reluctance she returned her attention to Nicole. "Would it be correct to assume your wardrobe vanished in the tragedy? Ah, yes, we feared as much. When suitable gowns are readied, you'll be formally presented at court. The empress, however, will receive you privately tomorrow morning after you have rested and refreshed yourself."

Nicole's smile wavered before settling into a contrived calm. She inclined her head. "Please inform Her Majesty that I anticipate the honor with eagerness." Her eyes slid toward the women on the quay, and she wondered which was Darya Denisovna. Her heart contracted sharply. All the ladies watched Dimitri, and more than one interested blush heightened the heavy rouge which appeared to be Russian fashion. But none wore that special glow Nicole would expect from his . . . his wife.

She bit the inside of her cheek, and her blue eyes hardened as her jawline firmed. She drew a deep breath and turned to face him, her eyes sparkling with a chill brightness, her head tilted at a charming angle to best display Pavla's artistry with curls and ribbons. Knowing Lilia Ulanova observed closely, she extended her glove to Dimitri and curtsied, allowing her cloak to fall open above her breasts. "Prince Dimitri," she gushed, "how can I ever thank you for all your kindnesses throughout the voyage?" A sweep of thick lashes raised, then lowered. And she experienced the bitter satisfaction of knowing her blatant artificiality underscored the distance between them more cruelly than hostility would have.

"I've received what thanks I deserve," he murmured above her fingers. His tone revealed nothing, but his gray eyes were stony.

Nicole winced at the double meaning. But Lilia's knowing smile validated Nicole's coquettish mask; Lilia would obviously have thought it curious had Nicole not responded to Dimitri's powerful masculinity. How better to disguise her feelings than through exaggeration? She moistened her lips and tossed him a teasing smile over her shoulder as Lilia escorted her down the gangplank. And she felt his eyes boring into her spine until Vice Admiral Vrubel demanded his attention.

Before introducing her to the multitude of smiling women, Lilia leaned near the ribbons fluttering in Nicole's bright hair. "I envy you the trip, my dear." Lilia rolled dark eyes and chuckled softly.

Names and faces blended into a confused blur. Nicole recalled three Annas, a Galina, two Elizabettas, and a Sophia; the rest eluded her. Laughing, she threw up her palms in an engaging gesture of helplessness, begging forgiveness for addressing one of the Annas as Helene.

A timid glove patted her shoulder. "Everyone will sort themselves out eventually." Someone else presented her a ceremonial basket of bread and salt, Russia's traditional welcoming gift. A sound resembling the chirruping of a dozen birds surrounded her with questions.

"Patience, ladies," Lilia insisted, her voice rising authoritatively above the others. "I beg you to allow the princess to be shown to her rooms. There will be time later to develop acquaintances. For the present, however, I'm certain the princess would prefer to rest."

Nicole protested demurely, but in truth the promise of solitude was appealing. The exchange with Dimitri had dampened her spirits. And she felt her heart sink as she realized she would view every beautiful woman as a threat until she attached a face and a form to the name Darya Denisovna.

Thankfully she'd been spared an immediate confrontation; none of the women on the quay had borne that name.

Inside the palace, Nicole halted and her soft mouth rounded. Lilia smiled and waited patiently as Nicole looked about with undisguised wonder. A magnificent white marble staircase soared toward the upper stories; pillars of pure malachite created intimate alcoves adorned with priceless treasures. The main hall glittered with gold and bronze fittings, and polished marble gleamed beneath her slippers. Once again Nicole was awed by the vastness, by the excesses. As Lilia guided her through a bewildering maze of corridors and galleries and narrow passages, she couldn't help speculating that less might have proved more appealing. Three paintings jammed into space for one, four statues crowded corners large enough to comfortably accommodate two. Instead of one vase gracing a hallway table, a collection gathered. Rugs overlapped, sconces relinquished individual beauty to busily patterned walls.

Not all the rooms were as lavishly garish, however; they passed through areas which were surprising in their tasteful and restrained appointment, and then into hollow empty rooms bereft of furniture.

Noting Nicole's puzzlement, Lilia smiled. "We're in a perpetual state of renovation. In Elizabeth's time . . ." Nicole marked a barely perceptible pause. ". . . the palace was allowed to deteriorate. Her Majesty has undertaken a massive restoration program, but the necessary funds . . . well, the work progresses slowly, as you can see."

Nicole nodded, panting slightly from the exertion of climbing stairs. "I'd think it an endless task."

Smiling, Lilia adjusted a fur-trimmed satin cloak about her shoulders. The interior passageways were chill. "We've taken the liberty of providing you with a map. In the meantime, you might be interested to learn the palace has one thousand and fifty rooms, one hundred and seventeen staircases, and nearly two thousand windows. . . .

By the time Nicole arrived outside a heavy door guarded by two men wearing the familiar red tunics, the large numbers had blurred in her brain; she despaired of ever moving freely within the palace as Lilia appeared to. At the far end of the corridor she spied Pavla emerging from the gloom, and she restrained a cry of joy at sight of that friendly face.

Lilia deigned to notice a serf's arrival, she nodded to the

guard, who opened the door, and they stepped inside. "Do you like it?"

"*Da*. Please thank the empress." Nicole fervently hoped her voice didn't betray her disappointment, although from the manner in which Lilia held her skirts close to her body it was apparent that she too considered the accommodations less than adequate.

The two rooms assigned to Nicole were a surprising mixture of luxury and squalor. In contrast to the opulence of the public rooms, Nicole's living quarters appeared Spartan. A quick glance confirmed that the door between her salon and her bedroom was too warped to close. A strong draft ruffled draperies and wall hangings, and Nicole correctly concluded that the rooms would be icy in winter. Cracks diagramed the walls, some large enough to thrust a hand into, others oozing damp. She tried not to stare at trickles of condensing moisture leaking down the walls and soaking into ancient tapestries.

What furniture there was, however, Nicole thought exquisite, beautifully upholstered in complementing shades of blue satin and mauve velvet. Stepping into the bedroom, Nicole drew a delighted breath at sight of an elegantly carved four-poster canopied in lengths of gauzy pale blue. An open armoire displayed quilts of mink and fox fur; her dressing table had been painstakingly outfitted with heavy silver brushes and crystal decanters housing French perfumes. Suddenly feeling as though she had stumbled into an occupied room, Nicole hesitantly opened a drawer and touched frothy piles of fine lawn undergarments edged in gold lace. "Are these for me?"

"We provided what we could to replace the wardrobe you lost." Lilia crossed the small salon and paused, looking back at Nicole standing in the bedroom doorway. "If you feel equal to the exertion, the seamstresses will arrive this afternoon . . . there's a ball Saturday which Her Majesty invites you to attend."

"Saturday? Can the seamstresses possibly . . . ?"

For a moment Lilia appeared perplexed; then her brow cleared and she smiled indulgently. "My dear, if the empress wishes you to have ball gowns by Saturday, you shall have ball gowns by Saturday." Her hand cupped the latch. "Is there anything else . . . ?"

"I . . . It's very warm." Despite the stubborn cool draft, a blazing stove in the corner of the salon threw off a prodigious heat. The contrast wilted Nicole's ribbons, and her skin felt alternately sticky, then clammy. She mustered a light smile. "Is there a trick to opening the windows?"

A jeweled hand flew to Lilia's throat, and her mouth pursed beneath keen eyes. "The empress has not yet ordered her own windows raised."

The statement didn't register initially; then Nicole understood, and she responded weakly. "Thank heaven I thought to inquire. I wouldn't wish to give offense." Her New England upbringing laid a groundwork for easy blunders. Recognizing this fact, Nicole filed a mental note reminding herself to assume nothing; even the smallest events were legislated by autocratic whim.

"Her Majesty will be pleased to learn of your compliance. Attitude is so very important, don't you agree?" Lilia inclined her dark head, then stepped through the door.

Nicole stared at the empty space with a thoughtful expression. She suspected her every gesture and word would be faithfully reported. At least she hoped she could rely on accuracy. Sighing, she turned toward Pavla's explosion.

"Look at this! They've stuck us in the west wing, the oldest section!" Pavla lifted a tapestry from the wall with thumb and forefinger, wrinkling her nose in distaste as a musty cloud of dust and mildew wafted outward. "No one has used this room in a decade. I'd wager my last kopeck on it!" She shoved one of the blue satin chairs nearer the wall to conceal a gaping crack, her movements sharp and angry.

"The furniture is lovely," Nicole offered faintly. She felt as unsettled as Pavla; these were not the surroundings Irina had led her to expect.

"What there is of it!"

Nicole wandered toward the window and pressed her forehead against cool glass, feeling the oppressive heat of the stove at her back. Dimitri had often referred to Russia as a land of contrasts. She began to understand. For every plus, a minus appeared; and for every familiar, two unknowns surfaced.

Sighing, she directed her attention downward, watching chunks of ice bouncing like corks in the currents of the Neva; threads of perspiration unwound between her breasts and at the hollow of her throat. She thought of two thousand windows—and all of them sealed until such time as Catherine desired a breath of fresh cool air. Absently Nicole wondered how many people resided in the palace and how many of them gasped and panted and stared toward the windows with agonized longing. It was a pointless line of thought. She lifted her gaze from the deep rapid currents and inspected the bastions of the Peter and Paul fortress, which lay directly in her line of vision.

Across the wide river, the dancing angel was lost to view, but Nicole could hear the fortress's clock tower strike the quarter-hour. The gray stones and thick walls depressed her; even washed in sunlight, they appeared stark and forbidding. "Is the fortress for defense or is it a prison?"

Hands on hips, Pavla stepped backward to survey a new arrangement of their meager furnishings. The major cracks were hidden, but the seating was awkward at best. She sighed and tugged at a chair. "Both."

"I see." Nicole did not see. At some point during the long trek to her quarters, Lilia had paused to proudly display the square before the palace. They had strolled across a lovely balcony overlooking the square, and Nicole had clapped her hands in delight at the glorious vista spreading before them. It occurred to her now that a view of charming bridges and gold-leafed domes and leafy gardens was an infinitely more appealing view to present a stranger than the grim fortress glimpsed from all her windows.

What most disturbed her was recalling Dimitri's insistence that Catherine never acted without reason. This room, and this particular view, had been selected for a purpose. But what?

Smothering another long sigh, Nicole turned from the windows and considered the tedious hours of gown fittings yet to come. She would far rather have curled into the inviting four-poster and slept, blotting her questions and disappointments from mind.

Counting the days since she had enjoyed a full night's sleep reminded her of Dimitri. But then, everything reminded her of Dimitri. He would deliver his accounting to Catherine, and then . . . ? She couldn't tolerate contemplating where he would go then—to his town house and Darya.

"I'm going to lie down," she announced shortly, jerking the ribbons from her hair and flinging them toward a chair. "Wake me when the seamstresses arrive."

Pavla nodded absently, absorbed with the problems of interior decorating.

Nicole could see the fortress from her bedroom windows as well. She tossed onto her side and squeezed her lashes against her cheeks. A pain of remembrance sapped the energy from her limbs; it annoyed her that she automatically selected the right side of the bed, leaving the left for him. Frowning, she wiggled into the center of the quilts. But deciding not to think of Dimitri and achieving that aim were not the same thing. Her eyes blinked open in irritation, and she stared at the upper battlements of the fortress.

There was so much she failed to understand. She loosened her laces and composed herself for sleep, although she doubted her active mind would allow it. Perhaps tomorrow, when she finally met the woman of whom she had learned so many conflicting opinions—perhaps then the mysteries would begin to unravel.

Nicole drifted to sleep on the wings of a sigh, little suspecting the answers to her questions might be disturbing, might set in motion a chain of turbulence.

10

THE LONG NARROW room into which Nicole was shown revealed itself to be smaller and more intimate than most of the official chambers, but still more grandiose and opulent than she would comfortably have preferred. Recalling the vast intimidating throne room Lilia had displayed yesterday, Nicole released a tiny breath; it could have been worse. Looking about her, she judged the room to be a gallery housing Russia's ancestors, none of whom appeared welcoming. Her guard bowed and the heavy carved doors swung shut, abandoning her to a collection of enormous gilt-framed portraits, the eyes of which appeared to follow her as she hesitantly stepped deeper into the room. Nervous apprehension directed her feet away from an inlaid desk of curving cherrywood occupying the center of the gallery . . . and a lone chair positioned before it.

Nicole smoothed damp palms across the pink silk she had chosen for this occasion. And she wondered wildly what an insignificant girl from the English colonies was doing here, awaiting an audience with an absolute ruler who controlled millions of lives. The improbability of the event staggered her senses.

An odd sensation of foreboding affected her normally flawless grace as she slowly circled the gallery, staring at men and women painted in clothing of an outdated Oriental flavor. They smiled their frozen smiles and peered at Nicole as she unconsciously twisted a wisp of pink lace between her fingers.

A thousand questions nibbled her mind. And now, with the answers so tantalizingly near, she prayed she would be granted the opportunity to present her inquiries. She reflected upon the sealed windows and expelled a soft breath, her eyes fixed upon the portrait before her.

She tilted her head backward until a shower of golden ringlets cascaded past her pink-silk shoulders. The brass plate below the frame identified an extraordinarily handsome figure as the man history had labeled Peter the Great—Elizabeth's father.

And Nicole asked herself for perhaps the tenth time why Elizabeth's name surfaced with such tiresome regularity. Why was Elizabeth, dead for more than a decade, not forgotten?

And why had Catherine undertaken the expense of summoning Nicole Duchard, the daughter of a woman Catherine had apparently scarcely known?

What was the significance of Irina's enigmatic remarks? Or Dimitri's?

Questions . . . so many questions! Nicole rubbed her throbbing temples, her thoughts spinning in circles.

"Are you unwell?"

Absorbed by her own distractions, Nicole hadn't noticed the empress's quiet entrance until a soft German-accented Russian was spoken from directly behind her.

Pink silk billowed around her hoop as Nicole spun to face a woman of medium height, although an erect and regal carriage imparted an impression that the empress was much taller. Nicole sank into a deep bow, centering her eyes upon the hem of a black brocade gown, discreetly embroidered with silver bees, Catherine's personal emblem. Heart pounding, Nicole accepted the small plump hand extended toward her and pressed her forehead to the back of the fingers as Irina had instructed. "Your Majesty," she murmured, framing the address in careful Russian. To Nicole's surprise, Catherine retained her fingers, gently tugging upward until the two women faced one another.

With a slight start Nicole saw at once that Catherine had elected to minimize her official capacity, choosing instead to greet Nicole as simply another woman. She wore no tiara of rank in the masses of upswept chestnut hair beginning to gray at the temples, and her gown was impressively simple. Free of gaudy adornment, the gown's elegant cut aided in slimming a body inclined to corpulence. It was the understated choice of a woman who understood she wore clothing well, who rejected an overabundance of frippery and refused to allow her ensemble to diminish the woman inside.

Like the other Russian women Nicole had observed, Catherine affected a dusting of rouge across cheeks bearing faint evidence of childhood pox, but the empress did not apply the cosmetic with a heavy hand as did the others. The blush of pink softened the natural pallor of fine healthy skin and brightened dark blue eyes above a firm intelligent mouth. Her long nose and a chin hinting at the prominence it would assume in later life imparted a look of breeding if not beauty, for Catherine possessed that combination of features and form best described as "handsome." At age forty-three, hers was not a countenance to inspire violent passions, nor had it ever been, but neither would she lack for male admirers.

Warmly she clasped both Nicole's hands between her own, and the smile which Nicole would learn seldom left her lips deepened. Catherine prided herself on a charm as famous as her fine quick mind; the practiced smile illuminated her features with warmth. "I'm so pleased you agreed to visit us," she murmured. Her low, well-modulated voice transmitted sincerity interlaced with shadings of speculation.

Nicole blinked, then sought the presence of mind not to reveal a rising tide of bewilderment. Catherine's clear gaze and the welcoming pressure of her fingers suggested that Nicole's long voyage to Russia had been entirely voluntary. Flustered, Nicole dipped her golden curls and stammered a reply. "I'm honored to have been extended the opportunity."

"My dear, your Russian is exemplary! Lilia was correct. I applaud the effort and diligence which accomplished this feat. Your achievement in so short a period is laudable."

The compliment fired a flush of pleasure across Nicole's cheeks, and her face reflected the rosy hue of her gown. "Thank you, your Majesty."

Catherine tucked her arm about Nicole's sleeve as if the

companionable gesture were the most natural in the world, and she indicated the desk with a graceful wave. At her first step, an English whippet darted from beneath her hem and raced joyously about the room, his paws clicking upon the polished floor. Catherine laughed at Nicole's expression.

"This ill-mannered creature is Sir Tom. I've spoiled him outrageously, I'm afraid. He misbehaves unless he's allowed to accompany me wherever I go." The trick of speaking as if she imparted a confidence was one Catherine had learned early during her difficult years in Elizabeth's court; a confession of human weakness was more endearing than delusions of grandeur.

Releasing an exaggerated sigh over Sir Tom's antics, she seated herself behind the desk and invited Nicole to accept the facing chair as she called the dog to her side, stroking him affectionately until he settled into a ball on her hem. "Would you enjoy a glass of coffee? Or tea? I confess I'm practically useless without my daily ration of coffee." Again she hinted that she divulged information not generally known, the confidence delivered with an easy natural smile.

Nicole nodded, too off balance to speak. She had expected a queen and was confronted by a woman instead. Catherine's simple gown, her open manner, the homey presence of the whippet, and now the coffee which appeared at an invisible summons—nothing fit the picture of Catherine as autocrat, Catherine as commander against the Turks, Catherine as a skillful navigator through labrinths of intrigue, Catherine as the usurper of her husband's throne.

Nicole shook her head slightly, attempting to clear the cobwebs from her thoughts. She covertly examined the empress from beneath a sweep of lashes and found it nearly impossible to reconcile her previous conceptions of the woman. How could one assign harsh qualities to the smiling countenance seated across from her? And yet . . .

And yet a hard sensual line lay beneath the ever-present curve of lips, and while the eyes were bright and alert, a hint of cool calculation flickered in the depths. And the fabled charm, while undeniably potent, possessed a certain practiced quality which suggested a role—one acted to perfection—but a role nonetheless.

And yet . . . Nicole abruptly realized the desk had been positioned beneath a full-length portrait of Elizabeth, an Elizabeth whose radiant blond beauty dominated the quiet elegance of the woman below, an Elizabeth opulent in a bold pink gown which despite the multitude of drapes and folds and laces and jewels could not diminish the startling impact of the woman. Of all the portraits in the crowded gallery, Catherine had chosen to position Nicole's chair facing Elizabeth.

Coincidence? Accident? It wasn't likely. Nicole sat beneath Elizabeth's vibrant smile for a reason. The sense of foreboding returned in force. Shifting in her chair, Nicole balanced her coffee glass in the silver filigreed holder against her lap. And the questions burned like acid on the back of her tongue.

"I understand we are fortunate to have you with us at all . . ." With tact and sensitivity Catherine led into a discussion of the voyage, although Nicole understood the conversation was superfluous, designed to place Nicole at ease rather than to increase the empress's fund of knowledge.

Politely Nicole recounted her version of the trip. Before concluding, she swallowed and hesitantly repeated Irina's plea as she had promised, wondering if she blundered by requesting money for Irina's soul. Lilia had stressed the drain on state coffers occasioned by the Turkish war and the current problems surrounding collection of the poll tax.

Catherine laid her fears to rest. "But of course. How thoughtful of you to remind me. Irina was a loyal friend both to the state and to myself. I'll see that her soul does not languish in the nether regions." Catherine maintained an impassive expression, but her tone suggested that she too considered the idea ridiculous. As if realizing she had revealed more than she intended, she leaned to stroke Sir Tom's head, her face momentarily concealed. "Did I understand correctly that Irina presented you with the portrait?"

"Yes." Nicole released an inner sigh and steadied her hands about the coffee glass. Finally. Please grant me the answers! A subtle shift in Catherine's tone alerted Nicole's defense system. And she experienced a consternation whether to feel pleased or whether the sudden tightening in her stomach signaled a warning.

Catherine's clear, dark blue eyes met Nicole's gaze. "There is much you wish to know," she observed softly.

"I . . . yes, your Highness." The intimacy of the audience invited frankness, and Nicole leaned forward eagerly. "I've been so confused. I feel as if I'm surrounded by mystery, and I don't understand the reasons for it." Her liquid eyes beseeched. "I've dared to hope you will decipher the riddles."

Each motion deliberate, Catherine set aside her empty glass and folded her hands atop the desk. She gazed openly at Nicole, studying her thoughtfully. It was obvious she carefully weighed her next words. "Prince Dimitri praises your intelligence. Now that I've met you, I must agree with his judgment. Therefore . . . I've decided to be candid, a tactic I had initially rejected."

Nicole rushed past the mention of Dimitri. But her senses sharpened and the edge of apprehension deepened. Quite abruptly it occurred to her that a private audience might be somewhat unusual, that Catherine might wish this conversation to remain unrecorded by others. She moistened her lips and fastened expectant eyes upon the empress's face.

"Yes," Catherine murmured, "you resemble them both." She sighed heavily and nodded to herself. "The answers will not be easy."

Nicole caught a startled breath. It hadn't entered her thoughts to suppose Catherine might have questions as well. Taken aback, she could only stare, and fight the heaviness of unease which quickened at Catherine's sober tone. The empress's smile had faded, revealing a long narrow face, slightly pinched.

Catherine pressed her lips and began. "Twenty years ago a female child was born in this city." Her direct gaze measured Nicole's frown. "But you've been informed of that fact. What you do not realize is the importance of correctly identifying the parents."

Nicole didn't realize she interrupted as she leaned to ask, "But surely you refer to the identity of the father?" She had devoted little thought to her father, assuming him unknown.

"No," Catherine corrected, her face expressionless. "Your father was almost certainly Alexei Razumovsky."

Nicole's lower lip dropped, and she stroked her temples. One piece of the puzzle fitted into place, but it served only to open new empty spaces. She passed her hand across her brow, feeling as if she heard a totally different story. Alexei Razumovsky. The name carried a faint ring of familiarity, but she couldn't think why.

"Alexei was one of the most handsome men I have ever seen," Catherine mused. "A sweet man, one devoted to simple pleasures. He affected no interest in politics—he preferred his dogs and his music." A fleeting perplexity shadowed her face; the empress possessed no ear for music and lacked understanding of those who did.

Totally confused, Nicole raised a palm. "Your Highness, I . . . Could we start from the beginning? I don't think I . . ."

"Ah, yes, of course." Catherine eased backward, her eyes traveling toward a high scrolled ceiling, her voice assuming an oddly flat tone. "Varina Stepanova remained a lady-in-waiting and a loyal friend to Elizabeth until the day she died." Dark blue eyes stared into memory throughout a lengthy pause. "When Elizabeth died, Varina retired to her estates near Moscow, where she remained in seclusion until her own death last spring." Catherine drew a breath, and her smooth brow knit. "Certain information surfaced before the princess died." Thoughtful eyes considered Nicole. "And now events long buried must be dealt with."

The sad-eyed woman of the portrait appeared behind Nicole's lids with startling clarity. For the first time she experienced a bittersweet longing to know the woman who had given her birth. "What was she like—my mother?"

Catherine's charm retreated an alarming distance, distilling into a wary appraisal. "First," she answered quietly, "we must determine exactly who your mother was."

Bewilderment pinched Nicole's lovely face. And once again her sense of self swung into suspension. Just as she anchored to one rock, the rock dissolved, setting her adrift once more. "But I don't understand," she blurted, lifting her hands. "I thought . . ."

"Yes. And Varina may very well be your mother." Catherine's narrow features tightened, and suddenly Nicole glimpsed how torturously difficult the conversation had become for the empress. Catherine's gaze leveled as she added softly, "There is an equal possibility that you are Elizabeth's daughter."

Nicole's mouth dried to pebbles of sand. The back of the chair struck her spine with sudden force, jolting her coffee glass from nerveless fingers. It splintered across the floor. Neither woman gave notice.

Instinctively Nicole's stunned gaze swung to the portrait above. And she experienced a shock of recognition as she stared into her own vivid blue eyes, acknowledged her own inviting mouth. Elizabeth's smooth blond hair had been depicted in a startling replica of the coiffure Nicole now wore. Staring until her eyes ached, Nicole mentally subtracted twenty years from the beautiful face above her and she stripped the ornamentation from Elizabeth's rose-colored gown which so closely resembled her own. A chill raced over tensed muscles, and Nicole shivered.

She struggled to reassemble the shreds of her composure, forcing herself to look into Catherine's flat stare. "But . . . but that would mean . . ." She licked dry lips.

"Yes." A tinny edge sharpened Catherine's controlled tone. "As Elizabeth's daughter, you would have a direct claim to the Russian throne." It wasn't necessary to add that Elizabeth's daughter would have a claim superior to Catherine's or to Catherine's son's. The empress examined her clasped hands and continued quietly. "There is gossip that Elizabeth secretly married Alexei Razumovsky. It is certain that he was Elizabeth's lover for nearly all of their adult lives, though each experienced lapses toward the end. One such lapse may have been Varina." She studied her fingers absently, as if translating the precedent into personal terms. "It is rumored that Elizabeth bore Alexei as many as eight children. Gossips would have it that most of the children were stillborn or died in infancy . . . but not all."

Nicole was unable to speak. Her fingers fluttered like pale disturbed birds, flying to touch bloodless lips, then falling again to her lap. Disconnected phrases tumbled through the whirlwind of her thoughts like whispering leaves: the Empress Elizabeth's daughter . . . granddaughter of Peter the Great . . . Catherine's strained expression . . . revolt. The power of life or death resided in a single stroke of Catherine's pen. Would she acquiesce to replacement without struggle? A sick feeling boiled in Nicole's stomach. She utterly rejected what she was hearing.

As if musing aloud, Catherine continued. "There are two possibilities. First: the affair between Alexei and Varina existed as rumored, and Varina dispatched the resulting offspring to France rather than offend her dear friend Elizabeth. In argument: Elizabeth knew of Varina's pregnancy. Their friendship suggests the empress would have been informed as to the father. Yet she displayed Varina no ill will. In fact, if I remember the incident correctly, Elizabeth showed Varina particular affection during her pregnancy."

Nicole's jaw tightened, her lungs burned. Nervous fingers shredded the wisp of pink lace twisting about her hands.

"The second possibility is that Varina faked a pregnancy to account for Elizabeth's infant. An unnecessary precaution if, as it would appear, Elizabeth then decided to send the child out of Russia rather than encumber herself and the state with a bastard. Against this hypothesis stands Elizabeth's well-known yearning for children." Catherine dropped her head and contemplated her laced fingers.

And Nicole recalled Irina's outraged tale relating how Elizabeth had removed Catherine's son from the birthing bed and taken him as her own, allowing the young grand duchess visitation rights only when the child had passed his first birthday. Would this event exert an impact on Catherine's thoughts?

"If Elizabeth had surviving children of her own," Catherine added, "it seems likely she would have secured their succession. But she did not alter her decision in favor of her nephew, my husband, despite the fact that she made it known she detested him and questioned his ability to rule." Catherine's eyes revealed no flicker of emotion at the mention of her murdered husband. If she experienced any guilt, the guilt had long since been buried in a vault of carefully constructed justifications.

Peter III's fate no longer concerned Nicole. Her own problems soared into precedence. A taut silence stifled the dim gallery, broken only by Sir Tom's whimpering dreams. Deeply shaken, Nicole dropped her eyes from Catherine's steady speculation, feeling the eyes of the painted figures focusing upon her as accusers. She touched the ball of lace to her moist forehead as her mind raced ahead. She required no oracle to announce the danger she faced. When she could trust herself to respond, her voice, though scarcely above a whisper, seemed too loud in the hush. "Please believe I have no desire to wear a crown!" She prayed the empress would recognize the truth in her voice. Beseeching eyes lifted to Catherine's pale face. "I'm no threat to anyone! I wish only to pay my respects to you and, to your son, the grand duke, and then to return to the colonies. My home." She stressed the last word, underscoring the site of her loyalties and ambitions.

"That is no longer possible," Catherine stated softly. "Too many people are aware of Varina's dying wish: 'Restore the child to her rightful inheritance.' Until the question of your parentage is resolved, plots are inevitable. Varina's statement will be interpreted as individual ambitions dictate."

"But if I return to Boston—"

"I found you, others could as well." Catherine's brow knit, her hands tightened, and hints of an implacable will tensed her jaw. "Not everyone agrees with my policies. Many object to the war with the Turks, some believe Russia should remain unattached to Poland, tax collection is in arrears . . . The simplest method of changing policies is to change sovereigns. There are those who would seize on any opportunity to do so."

"Sweet heaven!" No sound braced the formless words. Nicole's lungs felt hollow; each breath scorched her throat. "Please . . ." She swallowed a heavy stone. "Please be assured that I'm a most unlikely candidate for . . . for political intrigue." Her hands fluttered in appeal. "I know nothing of government, even less of wars and finances and . . ." A drifting sense of unreality spun lazily through her mind. Not one word seemed real. The problem of identity had escalated into a political situation, and she couldn't grasp how this was possible. Her goals were simple and uncomplicated: she wished only a quiet, happy life surrounded by a loving husband and a healthy family.

"Which creates an ideal candidate in the minds of those who would install a pawn upon the throne—a puppet through whom to exercise power."

Nicole's lips pressed into a white line and she struggled to suppress a tremor of fear and disbelief. She hadn't imagined this denouement in her wildest dreams; Catherine's revelations both appalled and frightened her. Throwing out her palms, she inquired with more spirit than she felt, "If you perceive me as a threat, then why did you summon me?"

A dark smile toyed with the corner of Catherine's lips. "I considered it wiser to reach you before . . . others did." She transferred a distant gaze to a point in space. "Consider. If you knew a poisonous viper nested in your chamber, would you prefer the creature roaming loose, free to strike without warning? Or would you cage it, in order to observe its smallest action, in order to have it within reach should you judge it necessary to strike first?" Catherine's small elegant head moved, her gaze locked to Nicole's wide troubled eyes. "Do we understand one another?" she asked softly.

Staring, Nicole suddenly understood a phrase she had not previously comprehended: the iron fist in a velvet glove. Catherine's silky-smooth voice masked a will of iron. Without a single unpleasantry, the empress had served notice that she would not be deposed. Power rode her features like a visible mantle. And Nicole understood her own continued existence was perilous at best.

"I . . ." She relaxed her jaw and began again, urging her tone above a whisper. "I would be willing to publicly swear that Princess Varina was my mother." There was nothing whatsoever upon which to base this assertion except a desperate and abiding will to survive.

Catherine, too, recognized the confusion of conviction. She sighed and touched a lock of chestnut hair before arranging a smile upon her lips. "I fear such an avowal would be of little merit."

"Then how is the issue to be resolved?" Desperation exploded in a small burst of dry breath, flawing the smooth French which had emerged so effortlessly until this interview.

Catherine's eyes cooled in a measuring stare. "As there is no possibility of absolute proof . . . I alone shall make the determination." A tiny shrug lifted the black brocade. "I shall observe and consider."

Whim! Nicole's future depended upon Catherine's goodwill and sense of fairness. A drop of blood appeared beneath her teeth. In a moment of whimsy or pique, Catherine could sign away Nicole's life as easily as she signed a new bridge into existence or demolished an old one. Nicole's heart plummeted, and shaking fingers sought the shelter of pink silk folds. Good God!

With graceful rustling movements, Catherine rose to her feet, signaling the conclusion of the audience. Nicole hastened to follow suit; Sir Tom yawned and wagged his tail.

After drawing a level breath, the empress studied Nicole, and her words emerged reluctantly. "I am revered throughout Europe for a cautious and generous turn of mind, if I may say so. I would not endanger that hard-won approbation by a hasty course of action. I do not rush weighty decisions. We are each aware of the supreme importance of the outcome. We shall trust to time, fate, and God for the answers we seek."

Her assurances provided little comfort. An ax had been positioned above Nicole's small bright head, with no indication as to when it might drop. Twisting her handkerchief between frozen hands, she stared helplessly as a dozen new questions tumbled her thoughts. What criteria would be employed to determine her parentage? Could others exert influence? Could she herself?

"In the interim, Princess, we shall proceed as if Varina Stepanova were indeed your mother. Your rank and income will be awarded on that basis . . . but we'll not settle the estate just yet."

"I understand, your Majesty," Nicole murmured. She understood Catherine's viper was securely within the cage, while her own roamed at will, free to strike as fancy dictated. She'd been very wrong to assume she faced Catherine the woman; it was Catherine the autocrat who extended her fingers to be kissed, Catherine the supreme czarina who balanced Nicole's life in her smooth plump hand. Nicole bowed and withdrew, thinking Catherine surely smiled at the pounding thudding within her breast. Wooden steps had nearly carried her to the door when Catherine's soft, low voice called. Nicole turned to find the empress standing pointedly to the side of Elizabeth's portrait.

"I think it advisable to eliminate pink from your wardrobe," she suggested pleasantly. She did not raise her voice, but it carried across the polished gallery like a flint-tipped arrow.

Immediately Nicole's eyes flashed toward Elizabeth's painted smile, rosy with reflected color. She dropped into an unsteady bow, the air rushing from her lungs. "Thank you for the suggestion, your Highness." But it was not a suggestion; it was a command couched in iron encased within the velvet glove.

When the heavy doors clicked shut behind her, Nicole fell weakly against a brightly stenciled wall. Both shaking hands flew upward to press the drumbeat of her heart. Hot wind scraped her throat, and a brackish nausea roiled her stomach. Alarmed, the guard hastily took her arm and piloted her through the dim palace passages. And Nicole prayed she reached her chambers before the sickness erupted.

Once inside her own quarters, she rushed to a silver basin atop her dressing table and pitched forward, giving vent to the poison, her stomach convulsing until she thought she would die of it. At the finish, her eyes stung and her legs felt weak and rubbery. Weaving unsteadily, she emptied the basin into the chamber pot, then rinsed her mouth and blotted beads of perspiration from her brow. With all her heart she yearned to smash a window and inhale one deep breath of cool fresh air. Instead, she surrendered to the tremble in her limbs and climbed onto the four-poster, curling into a ball and burying her hot face in the pillows until she heard Pavla enter humming bits of a Russian folk tune. The snatch of melody seemed a profane intrusion into the heavily silent rooms.

"There you are." Pavla's sturdy body followed her peeking eyes into the bedroom. "You can't imagine all that's happened since I left!" Absorbed by gossip, she bounced about the room, straightening, dusting her apron over the furniture, unaware of Nicole's silence. "Gregory Orlov is on his way out of favor—can you imagine it after all these years? The empress sent him on a fool's errand to Fokshany to negotiate with the Turks. Practically the moment his horse cleared the gates, she ordered all his belongings removed from the apartments adjoining hers, and she ordered all the locks changed on the private chambers."

Pausing before Nicole's dressing table, Pavla tossed her long braid over her shoulder and opened a crystal decanter of perfume. She dabbed the stopper over her wrist and sniffed the result. Nodding happily and without conscious thought, she lifted an ivory comb, examined it, and dropped it into her apron pocket. Nicole watched the small theft through blunted eyes, not registering the flow of court gossip. But Pavla's next revelation pierced her ennui, and she bolted upright, her pale eyes wide and staring.

". . . in the Peter and Paul fortress. He won't be dealt with gently, you can wager your eyes on that! Pretenders to the throne never are. His foolish claims will earn him the knout, and he'll be branded and have his nostrils slit before he's banished." Pavla shuddered deliciously. "He'll wish to God that he'd never claimed to be Peter III before they finish with him!"

"Peter's dead." Fresh darkness engorged Nicole's raw throat. "Oh, Pavla! Oh, my God!" Shaking hands covered her ashen face in a fluttering motion of despair.

One long look brought Pavla rushing to the bed. Sharp eyes swept the rumpled pink silk, the honey-colored hair flying in disarray. Gently she tugged Nicole's hands away and stared into eyes streaming frightened tears. "What on earth has happened?"

Nicole's report tumbled from bloodless lips in disconnected starts and stops, jumps and bounces. At the conclusion, she shoved distractedly at a loose coil of gold and stared helplessly at Pavla. "What will I do? How can I possibly convince the empress that I'm no threat to her?"

As the story had unfolded, Pavla's expressive eyes had widened alarmingly; her hands pressed white lips against her strong teeth. "There's only one thing we can do," she whispered, her voice strangling on a shrill note. Scrambling from the bed, she crossed herself rapidly, then threw herself to the floor, prostrating her body before an icon hanging near the wardrobe. She pounded her forehead against the floorboards in ancient ritual, a frantic torrent of prayer issuing from her lips in an uninterrupted stream.

Nicole fell backward on the bed, listening without hope as Pavla wrestled with God, cajoling and pleading and promising. Slowly Nicole's blank eyes traveled to the windows, fastening on the far bastions of the Peter and Paul fortress. She thought of the small brass angel dancing on the spring wind.

And understood why her chambers faced the fortress instead of the city.

11

TRUE TO HER promise, Catherine evinced no evidence of haste in deciding Nicole's parentage; she would bide her time and move cautiously, as was her custom. In the following weeks, Catherine regarded Nicole with a special favor remarked by the entire court. She skillfully disarmed speculative rumors by welcoming Nicole into her circle of intimates as though Nicole were a cherished friend . . . instead of a viper to be kept within sight and striking range.

Upon discovering herself frequently sharing the empress's table or theater box, or invited to the empress's private apartments for a lively evening of whist, Nicole swung between anxiety and the honor of Catherine's solicitation. When Catherine's natural gaiety and charm were especially engaging, Nicole felt tempted to overlook her perilous situation and to surrender to the many pleasures of a luxury-loving court.

But eventually a conjecturing glance from a member of the shifting political factions would abruptly catapult her problems to the front of her mind, and again she would experience the gnawing consternation of the unsteady fence she straddled.

Within a few days of her arrival, Nicole had observed that while Catherine's court was conducted with impressive dignity and exterior decorum, all was but a sham, a gossamer curtain drawn across a scandalous interior. The decorum of stately dignitaries in powdered wigs and the graceful ladies in swaying silk was but a mask thinly disguising blatant affairs of which everyone was aware but blithely ignored. A tangled web of jealous lovers, both past and present, made the gathering of congenial groups a hostess's nightmare. Great skill and tact were required in arranging invitations and seating so as not to irritate current lovers, previous lovers, or spouses. Rank and the claims of birth added additional headaches for a concerned host. As did the ever-present complications of political machinations.

Nicole rapidly concluded the political climate of Russia might best be described as appalling. Unless a person hovered near death, he was likely involved in a series of plots, many of which overlapped and spilled into cascading springs of intrigue too convoluted and intricate for anyone to follow.

Amid bursts of delighted laughter, Pavla reported Count Panin had recently discovered himself embroiled in the awkward position of plotting against himself through the conspiracies of splinter groups he supported outside his primary faction. The situation was by no means unique.

Some groups favored Catherine's son, Grand Duke Paul, pressing his case and suggesting Catherine be relegated to regent. Other factions connived to install Catherine in a distant nunnery and enthrone Paul with full power. Still others whispered that the German skirt and her bastard offspring should be ejected entirely and a person of authentic royal blood be installed upon the Russian throne; if one could be found. Then there were those who supported Catherine with passionate devotion, but objected violently to her policies. Factions eroded into splinters which broke into smaller groups, and so on it went.

Nicole's introduction to court, and the titillating gossip attending her lineage, added a fresh element into the various equations. It was quickly noted that no one could afford to regard Princess Natasha with indifference. She loomed as a distinct threat to the ambitions of some, as an intriguing new possibility for others. Her vivid rare beauty and considerable charm were applauded in some quarters, reviled and feared in others. As invitations poured into her rooms, a few accompanied by extravagant gifts, Nicole wryly decided Catherine was not alone in judging the best possible location for a viper was beneath watchful eyes. Would-be friends and thinly disguised enemies avidly sought her company.

She accepted the invitations of all, carefully displaying favoritism to none, as she wound a cautious path past the snares of intrigue. She exercised great care not to align herself with any one person or faction; she trusted no one. The charming courtier at the midnight picnic or the dimpled partner at whist—either or both might be Catherine's spies or might be tools of those who would use Nicole to further their own ends. Or, or, or. Attempting to decipher the intent of those who clustered about her resulted in splitting headaches. As Nicole viewed the situation, her only sensible recourse was to maintain her own counsel. She labored to treat all in precisely the same manner, with charm, courtesy, and deference, while at the same moment establishing an invisible barrier of distance. And praying Catherine did not imagine alliances where none existed.

"You're doing wonderfully well," Pavla insisted. "The empress has no reason to fear you." She repeated the daily litany of encouragement and hope which they each needed to hear. Concentrating, Pavla pinned Nicole's hair into a luxuriant silky coronet at the crown, artfully accenting a smooth brow and the river of honey-colored curls spilling over Nicole's bare shoulders. Stepping backward, she squinted critically at her creation, then clasped a string of Lithuanian amber about Nicole's slender white throat, a gift from a young count who professed himself desperately in love. "I believe Baron Rupp or Prince Kulov sent you a matching bracelet. . . ."

Nicole absently rummaged through an ivory box which had been empty on her arrival but now overflowed with expensive jewelry. "I can't find it," she murmured.

Pavla appeared surprised, then sheepish. Wordlessly she bent to fumble beneath her pallet, eventually producing the missing bracelet plus two rings, a comb, and a half-empty bottle of smelling salts. "I wasn't going to keep any of this, you understand, I just wanted to look at the jewels, then I would have returned them."

Nicole sighed. It didn't merit the expenditure of breath to discuss the stolen items. They had enacted this scene once a week without any alteration in Pavla's behavior. Nicole supposed it didn't matter, as the items were always returned. At least those belonging to her were returned. Always there were one or two objects she could not identify, and these she and Pavla ignored by silent agreement.

As Pavla fastened the sparkling chain of amber about her wrist, Nicole released another quiet sigh and wondered idly who the smelling salts had belonged to. It was hopeless to speculate. Instead, Nicole admired the bracelet against the clear gleaming blue of her satin gown, then leaned to the mirror and looped amber eardrops about her ears. She frowned.

"Grand Duke Paul will be at the ball tonight." Her eyes flicked toward Pavla, raising a subject they had discussed more than once. "I think he believes I'm involved in a dozen plots to unseat his mother and dispose of him."

The comb in Pavla's hand paused in midair and her dark eyes drifted toward dreams. "You know . . . have you ever wondered what it would be like if you . . . ?"

"Never!" Aghast, Nicole felt a shudder begin at her ankles and ripple upward. She could not pin down who she was, but she knew emphatically who and what she was not. She understood her limitations and her personal convictions; she cherished no dreams of wearing a crown. Those who ruled required an obdurate ruthlessness which Nicole understood she lacked—thank God! Ruthlessness and a love of power and the arrogant conviction that one person alone possessed the wisdom and the right to dictate the destiny of a country. For a moment Nicole recapped her thoughts and applied her judgments to Catherine's rule. She discovered nothing she would amend.

Although Catherine labored unceasingly to project a pliant femininity, one could not remain long in the Russian court without sensing the fierce adulation of power which simmered beneath the czarina's soft exterior. A masculine force existed side by side with the feminine temperance. No one would seize the scepter from Catherine's grip without a brutal battle, not an alleged daughter of Elizabeth, not even her own son, whose actual claim to rule was stronger than Catherine's own.

Nicole worried her lower lip between her teeth and stared at her pale oval face in the mirror. "Paul watches me." A delicate shiver of distaste rustled the velvet-banded satin dipping low above her breasts. "He . . . watches me. Not like the others, it isn't a flirtation. He just . . . Every time I turn around, he's . . . watching!" She met Pavla's troubled eyes in the glass. "I try to be charming, but . . ." Sighing, she touched the perfume stopper behind her ears, then to her wrists and between her breasts. "I wish he wasn't so . . . I don't know . . . he makes my flesh crawl!"

Paul concerned her greatly; disarming his obvious hostility was proving an uphill task, though Nicole fancied she understood the reasons. For years a crackling animosity had existed between Catherine and her sullen son, each viewing the other as an obstacle to safety on the throne. For her part, Catherine kept her son well isolated from the seats of government and power; she ensured his ignorance, then deplored it by granting him an audience as seldom as possible. Paul retaliated by openly stating that his mother had usurped his rights; he repudiated Catherine and emulated Peter, Catherine's late and hated husband, refusing to acknowledge the rumors whispering Peter had not been his true father. Knowing it would enrage Catherine, Paul patterned himself after a man most of Russia had reviled.

Nicole released a heavy breath. Her arrival had provided mother and son an issue they could finally agree upon. Nicole must not be allowed to endanger the rights of either.

A sudden bone weariness invaded Nicole's small frame, an exhaustion initiated by mental fatigue and accelerated by the constant assault of balls, card parties, theater engagements, carriage outings. She leaned her chin into her palm and averted her eyes from the shimmering image of blue and silver and amber in her mirror. She did not belong here amid the extravagance and the luxury, the servants and the resulting idleness. Her nerves quivered on edge; she experienced guilt in coping with idle hours while an enserfed humanity performed the simplest tasks. Nicole's open nature rebelled at the intrigue and the murky currents gathering about her.

"I want to go home," she whispered, staring at herself. The elegant coiffure, the wide-hooped French gown, the jewels glittering at her throat—this was not the Nicole Duchard she chose to be. She attempted to clothe her image in a plain woolen gown beneath an apron, attempted to recreate a simple arrangement of curls beneath a dust cap. Was that Nicole Duchard? She didn't know. She simply didn't know anymore. The private core of self which she had treasured had disappeared in changing circumstances, in the whirlpool of mystery surrounding her birth. Her true self lay imprisoned somewhere in veils of confusion and strange new impressions. Nothing was as it should be, as she wanted it to be. Her body dwelt in one space, her heart resided in another; her mind had splintered into protective small compartments. "I just want to go home!" A desperation of longing cracked her voice.

Gently Pavla touched her shoulder. "But you are home," she said in a low tone.

Nicole gazed about her room through saddened eyes, noting the painted icon, the samovar bubbling near the window, the Oriental tapestries veiling the cracks in the wall. Beyond the panes she saw the Peter and Paul fortress; in the hallway outside her door sounded the arrival of the guards who would escort her to the palace ball.

She shook her head in disagreement. "No. No, this is not home." Home lay in another universe, spoke another language, lived by a different morality. Home was friends and genuine laughter and never feeling the ache of loneliness. Home was a concept best forgotten.

Ignoring the tremor along her chin, Nicole gathered the folds of blue satin, then clasped Pavla in a fierce embrace before she surrendered herself to the evening's festivities. "Don't worry, I'm all right." She set forth armed with a supply of artificially bright smiles and polite murmurs, knots tying her stomach as she valiantly prepared to gauge intentions and alliances.

The grand ballroom sparkled with gilt-and-crystal chandeliers and ladies' jewels as brilliant as anything adorning the heavens. Nicole returned enthusiastic greetings and slipped into place among Catherine's ladies at the edge of the dance floor.

Catherine opened the ball with a light gay step, choosing as her partner a strapping young guardsman named Alexander Vasilchikov, whom the gossipmongers predicted would be the next "emperor of the night" despite a fourteen-year age gap between the young man and the empress. Privately Nicole wondered at Catherine's choice, agreeing with those who hinted Vasilchikov's mind was too limited to be of interest. As for his appearance, Nicole thought him too vacuously pretty to be appealing. She preferred a more rugged type, a man who looked like . . . She bit off the thought.

Paying the opening dance but desultory attention, her eyes sweeping the vast ballroom against her will, she sought a smoky gray stare which robbed the limbs of strength, searched for a certain head of blue-black hair. Though Dimitri Denisov was seldom far from her thoughts, to her continuing annoyance, she hadn't encountered him since departing the *Kreml*.

Discreet inquiry had elicited the information that Prince Dimitri had immediately departed for Temnikov. The news had been accompanied by a dart of pain . . . and a quiet sigh of relief. That chapter of her life was firmly closed—so she repeatedly promised herself—and yet at every gathering she looked for him. And felt relieved to be spared an encounter, yet deflated and empty because he was not present.

Quickly Nicole scanned the ballroom, sighed quietly, and returned her attention to the empress and Vasilchikov.

And then a shock of recognition shot through nerves suddenly raw and exposed. Her fan slipped from shaking fingers and she blindly grasped Anna Kamorova's hand, steadying herself by gripping the countess's glove so tightly the ancient woman leaned to whisper, "Princess Natasha, are you ill?"

Nicole could not answer. Her mouth dried to dust, her lower lip quivered. Her ears rang, not with the lilting music, but with a swelling rush of emotion.

Dimitri Denisov stood wide-legged at the far edge of the dance floor, directly across from her, his arms crossed on his chest. Unreadable eyes spanned the distance, staring into her soul. And Catherine and Vasilchikov vanished into a mist, as did the circle of onlookers ringing the floor. Nicole saw nothing but a hard angular face and intense smoky eyes.

She swayed and pressed her glove to pale lips, strangling a cry of joy and anguish. Her resolve and her intentions died in his steady gaze, and she returned his stare helplessly. And recognized how foolish she had been to believe she recalled every small detail. She hadn't allowed herself the memory of the powerful sexual presence now confronting her. The lean, darkly elegant man facing her across the floor transmitted an animal magnetism. The broad, muscled shoulders strained his satin coat. The lace at his throat frothed dazzlingly white against deeply tanned skin. And his eyes. Hungry, stormy eyes that made love to her across the misty space, eyes so deep with passion they appeared as black as his hair or the satin ribbon at his neck.

Other couples brushed past Nicole's frozen figure, stepping onto the floor at Catherine's signal. But Nicole could not move, could scarcely breathe. The only rhythm she comprehended was that of her wildly pounding heart. Stately powdered couples obscured her line of vision momentarily, and when they swept forward, she watched Dimitri step onto the polished floor, his silvery eyes locked to hers above the heads of the dancers.

The ground tilted beneath her satin slippers; his burning gaze transformed her knees to water. The multitude of bright false comments she had rehearsed evaporated from her mind. Time, Nicole thought frantically. She desperately needed time to compose herself, to think this through, time to deny what her heart cried was true.

Blue satin ruffles billowed from her hoop as she spun, rushing blindly forward, only to stumble into the thin arms of Grand Duke Paul. "I . . . Forgive me, your Highness, I wasn't watching where I . . ." The grand duke's youthful sullenness repelled her. Nicole hastily lowered her eyes, sinking into a deep curtsy as her mind dashed forward in its flight.

Paul inclined a narrow head. Wizened and stunted by childhood illness, he moved without grace. "Princess Natasha. You're lovely tonight, as always," he intoned politely. His voice was bored and flat and artificial.

Biting the inside of her cheek, Nicole prayed the grand duke would not engage her in conversation. From under damp lashes she watched Dimitri winding steadily through the dancers, his expression hardening as he recognized her intent to escape.

"You're too kind, Highness," she murmured. Inside her long white gloves, her palms moistened, and her eyes flicked toward the door. How quickly could she extricate herself? Even without Dimitri closing the distance, she would have desired a rapid withdrawal. Paul's morose character exuded resentment. Believing himself unloved, he made a point of being unlovable. And a receding brow and chin, a protruding underlip, and a fondness to offend added to his deficiencies of personality. The years had transformed a rather handsome child into a distasteful caricature of a man, one whom Nicole was not alone in finding singularly unattractive. "If your Highness will excuse me . . . ?"

"I will not." Lazily Paul extended his arm, speaking above the fleshy lower lip. "I think it time we had a little chat, don't you? I request the honor of this dance."

Nicole could not recall to whom she had promised the first dance; her card seemed to have vanished. "I . . ." Her heart plummeted toward her knees. Paul disliked the gentry who spurned his claims in favor of his mother; he in turn spurned that which pleased the gentry. He was an abysmal dancer. Casting a final longing glance toward the door, Nicole sank into a bow, soft golden curls falling across her bare shoulders and concealing her expression. "I would be honored." She wondered how on earth Catherine would secure this boy a suitable wife.

She accepted his arm with reluctance and stepped forward on wooden legs, realizing immediately they would pass Dimitri. She lowered her burning cheeks toward the floor, hoping they would pass without greeting, but the grand duke halted, regarding Dimitri through cold eyes.

"We didn't expect your return to court for another month, Prince Dimitri. Did you discover Temnikov too dull for your taste?"

Dimitri elegantly returned the grand duke's curt bow; then he directed his attention to Nicole. "Princess Natasha," His hard eyes glowed like smoky embers. But he did not reach for her glove, nor did Nicole offer it. "Temnikov was refreshing as always, but my duty . . . and my interest . . . drew me to St. Petersburg." His deep vibrant voice addressed Paul but his eyes didn't move from Nicole. He traced the sweet tremble at the corners of her lips, stroked the curving swell of each shallow breath.

Paul's lip curled. "Ah, yes. Your sacred duty and your so very important interests." His eyes paled with the loathing he reserved for rank and breeding, the requisites of his mother's court. "But duty to whom?" he hissed. "Interest in whose service?"

Denisov's features hardened to chiseled stone; his eyes swung sharply toward the grand duke, and now they were slate-colored and icy. "Do you question my loyalty?" he inquired in a dangerously quiet voice. A gray suede glove dropped lightly to the hilt of his saber, an easy natural stroke, but a motion clearly stating that not even a grand duke could denigrate the loyalties of a Denisov.

An impotent fury narrowed Paul's eyes to slits, and he waved a hand in angry chopping gestures, carefully avoiding any suggestion that he might reach toward his own ceremonial saber. "There will come a time when none of you can hide behind my mother's skirts any longer!" A fog of spittle showered from the fleshy lips. "When I assume my rightful throne, all who dared laugh down their noses will wish they had never been born!" Raw hatred spread across his features like a dark malignancy.

Dimitri Denisov smiled and examined his gloves. The arrogant set of his shoulders and his confident stance presented a keen contrast to the grand duke's stunted growth.

Paul's eyes blazed. "You'll see!" he spat. You think me a powerless child. But you'll all discover that I can act on my own. I'm not the insignificant object you think. I, at least, don't place my sword and my service at the beck and call of a murdering bitch!" Eschewing the courtesy of a bow, he spun on his heel and strode furiously toward the dance floor, dragging Nicole by the hand.

Once on the floor, Paul jerked into an obligatory bow, then raised Nicole's damp glove to eye level, stepping heavily against the music, with no concession to form or rhythm. He ignored the stately minuet performed by musicians secreted high above within the immense glittering crystal chandeliers. A rainbow collage of dancers dipped and swayed about them, but Nicole was aware only of the painful grip squeezing her fingers and the mottled anger swooping toward her and then mercifully away.

"I know what the two of you are plotting!" His hiss spewed droplets of spittle around Nicole's bare shoulders. She pitted her willpower against a shudder. "Denisov rallies the provinces while you gather support right here beneath my stupid mother's nose!"

Nicole's jaw dropped. The blood rushed from her face, and she stumbled. "Your Highness! I beg you not to speak of such things! You can't believe—"

"I've pleaded with her to denounce you, I've shown her the wisdom of chaining you in the fortress where scum like you belongs! But, no! She'll wait until your troops storm her apartments before she'll admit who you are and what you're after!"

Nicole stared in dry horror. He was less than twenty, and already the madness of paranoia flamed in his eyes. A sick desire for power and respect had eroded his reason. Stammering, she struggled to find calming words. "Your Highness! I hold nothing but love for you and your esteemed mother. I wouldn't dream of—"

A bitter laugh clawed along her spine like fingers of ice. "Oh, yes, throw the boy a few pretty words and he's stupid enough to vanish happily!" The strains of music faded before he halted, his grip crushing Nicole's fingers as he stared hatred into her wide eyes. "Well, I am not going to happily vanish! And I am not going to tolerate a scheming chit like you, plotting to cheat me of my birthright! If the usurper won't act . . . then I will! You remember that!"

She stumbled and nearly fell as he abruptly released her fingers. Paul stormed from the floor, abandoning Nicole in what would have been an embarrassingly awkward position had not Dimitri materialized by her side. Smoothly, he tucked her icy hand around his sleeve and escorted her from the floor toward a distant table laden with silver and crystal.

"Smile," he commanded beneath his breath, bowing as they passed chatting couples forming for the next dance.

Nicole raised wide frightened eyes. "Good God in heaven! He believes that you and I are planning a coup!"

"Smile!" Dark silvery eyes swept her white face, and his strong hand tightened around her fingers, the warmth traveling through her chilled flesh in dizzying waves. They moved toward the long table slowly, pausing to exchange pleasantries with one laughing couple and then another.

Nicole smiled until her cheeks ached, and not a single word penetrated the cold encasing her heart. At once she perceived the sheltered existence she had enjoyed throughout her life. Until now she had escaped the molten heat of hatred, pure hatred. A shiver raised bumps along her skin at the memory of Paul's intensity.

When at last they gained the table, she waited upon unsteady legs as Dimitri directed the servants to fill china platters with caviar, blini, smoked salmon, and pirozhki, the delicious little meat-stuffed pastries Nicole usually relished.

"There's liver paté and sturgeon in aspic . . . ?" Gray eyes cautioned that a group approached from behind.

"It sounds delicious." Nicole prayed the gaiety trilling her response sounded more genuine to others than to her own ear. An eternity elapsed before Dimitri selected a secluded small table far from the ballroom floor and away from laughing groups and murmuring couples. Excercising great control, Nicole sank gracefully into a chair and clasped her hands in her lap.

A servant placed the laden china before them, then bowed and withdrew, indulging a knowing smile as Dimitri edged his chair nearer Nicole's. The appearance of a tryst would ensure their privacy.

He looked at her for a long moment, absorbed by the golden glow of candlelight brushing her shoulders and breasts with warm tints of ivory and rose. "Not one hour has elapsed that I haven't thought of you," he said softly. His smoky eyes devoured her as if seeking to quench an inexhaustible hunger. "Not one day . . . and not one night."

"Please, Dimitri . . ." And in her anguished whisper dangled the remnants of shattered dreams. She closed her eyes against a violent tide of longing; she yearned to hurl herself into those powerful arms and find solace from the fear and loneliness.

"I love you."

His simplicity struck with a powerful force, and Nicole covered a sudden sharp pain with her hand, watching it tremble above her breast. His intensity plucked at raw nerves, reverberated through the harp strings of her being. And where his taut thigh pressed against her leg, her satin gown melted to ash. "Dimitri . . . don't. I beg you, don't speak like this." Her painful whisper reflected in eyes suddenly scrubbed of color. And she winced as another thought flashed through her overburdened senses. "Darya . . . is Darya here tonight?" The name choked. As did the idea that Darya might be watching them. A weight of despair descended upon slim shoulders already heavy with anxiety.

"No. The journey was tiring, she remained at home."

Nicole tilted her head toward the ceiling, biting her lips. Home. Silently she tested the word, considering its meaning for Darya Denisovna. And what it meant to Nicole Duchard.

Lowering her curls, she touched her fingertips to her forehead, conscious of Dimitri's nearness as she was conscious of her own labored breathing, her own racing heartbeat. "Nothing has changed, has it?" she whispered. And understood she had cherished an illogical hope that when again she found him everything would be different. The obstacles would have evaporated. He would gather her into his arms and press her to his heart, and her world would right itself.

It could not happen.

Instead, Dimitri would leave the palace and return to his wife—the woman waiting eagerly in his bed. Mental images unfolded behind Nicole's moist lids and created a stab of agony that pierced her spirit. She shrank from the soft wine-scented breath on her cheek, knowing if she did not immediately alter the torture of her thoughts, she would certainly go mad.

His warm fingers reached for her hand and his grip tightened as she struggled to pull away. Bottomless gray eyes swirled like smoke, commanding her attention even though she desperately wished it otherwise.

"If you mean do I love you . . . yes. That hasn't changed, it will never change. Do I want you? Yes. Yes, with every breath I want you!" His silvery eyes darted hungrily over her lips, her breasts, and she knew he would have taken her in his arms had they been anywhere but here. "I remember it all . . . your hair fanned across the pillow like a flow of honey, your eyes soft and drowsy. Skin like dewy satin, lips of—"

"Dimitri! I implore you! Don't do this!" Jerking her hand

free, she clutched her skirts and struggled to rise, tears glittering like jewels in her lashes. Words which had once warmed her heart now sliced it to ribbons.

"Tasha . . . Nicole!" An iron band circled her wrist, and he stared at her, his hard face lined with the same pain trembling along Nicole's ashen countenance. "Forgive me. I won't speak of it again." His eyes commanded. "We'll talk of other matters."

There was never a choice. The only place on earth Nicole wished to be was here—with him. She met his gaze, then returned to her chair and silently lifted her fork for appearances' sake. The food was tasteless, and she swallowed with difficulty. He loved her. And the tragedy of it raised a leaden stone in her throat. She pushed aimlessly at a pink slice of salmon. Was the joy of being with him worth the torment of saying good-bye? Of knowing he rode home to another woman? Nicole placed her fork across the platter. The ache in her throat made a mockery of eating.

Dimitri leaned to extinguish the candle as a laughing couple called their names. The couple smiled, arched teasing brows, then turned aside, choosing another table.

"Tomorrow," he said, looking at her, "the entire court will whisper of our affair."

"Or our conspiracy." Her skin rose in icy bumps of memory. "Paul believes you and I are plotting to overthrow his mother and himself." Wrinkling her small nose in resignation, Nicole pushed aside the platter of food and accepted the glass of wine Dimitri poured. Their fingers brushed in a flash of heat lightning, and Nicole drew a sharp breath, feeling the rush of longing churn her stomach. She refused to think of such things—she would not! She squared her shoulders and gazed into the face she yearned to touch. "Some time ago I was granted a private audience with Catherine, not long after I arrived . . ."

"I can guess what she revealed, but tell me anyway." His low voice, rich with emotion, murmured above the music lilting from the dance floor. Shadows accentuated the angular hollows and crevices of his elegantly handsome features. And his long fingers tapped the table so near that Nicole could feel the warmth and vitality.

She had progressed well into the story before her mind caught pace with her words. At the conclusion, she attempted a shrug of bravery. "So. My fate hangs on Catherine's decision." She wasn't certain if she voiced bravery or bravado; she hadn't yet been tested.

Dimitri drained his glass and reached for the decanter. He'd remained silent throughout Nicole's recitation, and when he spoke, his voice was thoughtful. "Catherine is struggling with a difficult problem."

Nicole blinked surprise. "Catherine? It would seem that I'm the person with the problem!" She leaned forward, her golden ringlets spilling over ivory shoulders. "If the decision goes against me, prison will be the least of my troubles!" she said tartly.

"Not immediately." Responding to the anxiety widening her eyes, he continued quietly. "I've been in St. Petersburg but two days, yet have several times been informed of the speculation regarding your future. My point is: too many people know the story. Catherine is certainly aware of this."

"I don't understand," Nicole responded slowly.

"If Catherine moves against you, the city will know it is because she is convinced you are Elizabeth's daughter." He covered her cold fingers with his warmth. A fragrant blend of spiced cologne, wine, and sea spray filled Nicole's nostrils, and she wondered how he smelled of the sea, wondered how she could be distracted when they discussed her fate. "Consider what that could mean."

Forcing her mind to the issue, Nicole felt her mouth sour, and her liquid eyes closed in denial.

"The instant Catherine confirms the rumors, a hundred plots will hatch to place you upon the throne. As Catherine well knows, she has enemies who would welcome a legitimate reason to mount an overthrow."

"I don't wish to be the cause of bloodshed or revolt! Catherine has been generous and kind, I wish her no harm!" Nicole's whisper gained strength. "I have no ambition whatsoever to be an empress!" Few but Dimitri would have believed her protest, but she knew it as the truth. She had grown to young womanhood in a colony chafing beneath the reins of royalty. Everything she had been taught, all she had overheard in the secret meetings in her father's kitchen, had convinced her that rule by decree was an injustice. Her heart and principles rebelled against the tyranny of royalty. "I want a normal life like other women, with a loving . . ." But she could not allow herself a topic she had forbidden Dimitri. A blush stained her cheeks, and she averted her eyes.

"What you want will not be a consideration, my darling

Tasha. If this comes to fruition, men will act in your name, and you will simply be swept along without choice."

Nicole covered her eyes, recognizing the truth in what he said. "That can't happen! How can I live with this threat?"

Fine white lace whispered about his wrist as his hand rose to cup her chin. "Your threat is also your protection. Catherine will not act hastily."

"Yes," Nicole whispered. Briefly she rested her cheek against his palm, feeling the calluses, wanting to kiss each one. "The empress won't dare denounce me." Comprehending that curious eyes judged, she straightened in her chair, lowering eyes moist with the ache of desire.

"Not for that reason." When Nicole's head snapped upward, Dimitri explained softly, "The empress wishes to dispose of her problem—you—sooner rather than later. But her hands are tied on a direct approach. Catherine is shrewd. When she denounces you, it will be for a reason unrelated to parentage; she won't give her enemies any justification—she'll give them a reason they can't dispute."

Nicole swallowed. She understood her life must be blameless if she were to continue living it. Her future loomed as a series of tightropes. "And Paul?" Her chest constricted; her laces suddenly pinched off her breath.

"Paul is a child," Dimitri answered flatly. "He won't dare act against his mother's wishes unless pushed to extremes. And you may be assured that Catherine has made her wishes clear."

Nicole nodded, but an edge to Dimitri's voice suggested he wasn't as confident of the grand duke's stability as he would have her believe. She repeated a silent vow to avoid Paul at all costs.

"Enough," Dimitri said, rising and extending his glove. "May I have the honor of this dance?" Teasing eyes sparkled above a stage whisper. "If I don't hold you in my arms within the next two minutes, I'll be forced to a rash and desperate act." White teeth flashed in a grin against his darkly tanned skin, lightening the mood between them. "Like ravishing old Countess Kamarova, who is staring at us."

Nicole followed his bow and smiled politely, inclining her curls. Countess Kamarova returned the greeting solemnly, displaying a dark smile, her teeth cosmetically blacked in the old fashion.

"If ever you black your teeth like the older women, I

swear I'll wash your mouth with lye, then spank your delicious bottom!"

Nicole laughed and stood. But when she turned her face upward to meet his eyes, her smile faded. She drew a shaking breath at the hard passion smoldering in his silvery eyes. And she whispered the most difficult words of her life.

"We can't meet again." Her gaze dropped from his hard stare and settled fleetingly upon the firm sensual line of lips she had tasted and loved. "It would be too dangerous. And . . . and there is Darya." The words ripped bits of flesh from her heart.

"For tonight the damage is already done," he responded in a voice deep with desire. "Come into my arms, Nicole. Dance with me and allow me to pretend that when the music ends I'll carry you away and undress you slowly and make love to you until you're drunk with kisses and love and can speak nothing but my name."

Nicole swayed and choked on the moan swelling her breasts. Then she touched her trembling fingers to his arm and accompanied him to the floor. They danced in a private capsule of music and longing and locked eyes and flesh that tingled and burned when their bodies brushed.

When the strains of the last dance faded, she watched through a film of tears as he bowed and pressed her fingers to his lips. And left her. And she knew the best part of herself went with him.

12

IN MID-JUNE the court removed to Oranienbaum for the summer, as had been Catherine's habit since ascending the throne. The brief journey sparkled with gaiety and high expectation; laughing voices called back and forth from beribboned carriages. Though the expedition set forth at midday, horses and vehicles cast long slanting shadows and the smiling faces were bathed in a strange dusky twilight. It was the season of the famous June "white nights." An arctic sun suspended above the horizon like a dull orange globe, unmoving and static, bestowing a pale eerie illumination upon the ladies and gentlemen of the court and the following carts containing courtiers, pages, cooks, stablemen, pastry chefs, seamstresses, cobblers, goldsmiths—all the various and sundry servants required to ensure that country life proceeded with a minimum of inconvenience.

"Now, this is more suitable," Pavla enthused after inspecting the airy whitewashed rooms Nicole had been assigned.

A cool breeze blew from the waters of the Finland Gulf and ruffled light lace curtains at the windows. Pavla approved the silk-upholstered furniture as comfortable and easy to rearrange should the need arise. Satisfied, she briskly set about unpacking their trunks, shaking out Nicole's new riding habits and voluminous formal court gowns, and then the more simple attire for everyday wear. She carefully spaced them in a carved cedar armoire painted a vivid cherry red.

"The view is breathtaking!" From the windows Nicole could glimpse the gulf waters sparkling through tall forests of larch and birch. Nearer, the strange shimmer of half-light endowed the velvety parks and statues and pavilions with a quality of dreamlike unreality. An air of silver expectancy overhung the atmosphere. Or perhaps the faint edge of excitement was merely an effect of the unchanging dusk or the holiday anticipation. She leaned to inspect more closely the thick draperies tied inside the windows in readiness for the night. The heavy velvet would be employed to block the sun's midnight rays. "How long do the white nights last?"

"Through the first week in July." Bending, Pavla aligned rows of slippers along the wall, pleased by the array of color. A mischievous glint sparkled in her dark eyes as she tossed aside her braid and arranged brushes and rouge pots and silver boxes and stacks of gloves. "You'll begin to appreciate the long nights when you discover all the uses for them."

Deliberately misunderstanding, Nicole smiled. "I can't imagine summer will make much difference to the empress. I'll wager she's up and dressed by five-thirty, exactly on schedule, and the palace will be still as death before eleven each night." The czarina's habits were unvarying, all of which revolved around affairs of state. Catherine thrived on work; work was more intoxicating than strong drink or love.

"Not this summer," Pavla predicted. An armload of whalebone corsets and lacy camisoles disappeared into the deep reaches of a blue-and-red bureau. "I notice Vasilchikov was included on the list. There'll be more parties this season than ever before." Catherine's budding romance whispered across all tongues, from the highest placed to the lowest.

The dubious charms of Vasilchikov versus Orlov did not interest Nicole. From what she had learned of Orlov's temper, the vapid Vasilchikov was no doubt an improvement. There was no accounting for imperial tastes.

Turning from the window, she smoothed her palms over a gown as dusty golden as the uncertain light beyond the panes. The list. Not an hour passed that she didn't wonder if Dimitri had been included. "Did you actually see the list?" Pavla's cunning in such matters bordered upon the miraculous. Nicole conceded it would not have surprised her if Pavla had managed to appropriate a copy of Catherine's summer guest list. For once she wished this might be so.

"I can't read. But I have eyes to see." Noticing Nicole's sinking spirits, Pavla filled a goblet of wine from a pitcher on a small lacquered table. She arched a question toward Nicole's nod, then poured another for herself before sinking to the edge of the bed and fanning her apron above a striped wool skirt. The wool was none too warm for the cool freshness crisping the air. "If you wish to confirm an invitation, just look about you."

But it was not all that simple. Catherine's immediate entourage was quartered in the large-domed Summer Palace or, like Nicole, within one of the wings connecting to the palace by covered walkways. Others of the court occupied private estates nearby. Nicole hoped Dimitri formed part of this second contingent, as she knew he was not within the palace grounds. Her buoyancy slipped another notch.

Pavla gulped her wine, then rose and dusted her hands. "The summer begins. No long faces, please. Now. What will you wear for the opening banquet?"

"My pinkest pink, of course." Nicole responded in a tease, as she guessed Pavla wished. The responsibility for another person occasionally weighed heavily. Her moods and her problems reflected upon Pavla's plain, generous face. Nicole bit off a sigh, recalling an earlier life when privacy had been a reality. On the other hand, she reminded herself, it was comforting to know someone cared in this hostile land. Someone was always nearby to disrupt periods of loneliness, to share the fears and triumphs. A friend. "Pavla," she blurted, voicing a desire she'd long held, "I wish we could attend the balls together! I wish the seamstresses were designing gowns for you too. Don't you ever think about such things?"

An invisible hood dropped over Pavla's expression. Her broad peasant shoulders lifted, then fell. "I know my place. If there is no one to wear wooden shoes, there will be no one to wear velvet. It's an old saying in my village."

Nicole sighed and nodded. "Well, I wish you were included," she repeated wistfully. "The instant my inheritance is settled, I promise you'll have your freedom!"

Pavla's shrug deepened. "It doesn't matter. Whatever happens is God's will." The veil dissolved in the heat of affection. "I'm grateful being where I am. You're the kindest owner I've ever had!"

Nicole winced. She could never be comfortable owning people. The concept grated on her sensibilities. An image of St. Petersburg's serf auctions rose to offend her spirit.

"Besides," Pavla offered brightly, "look at me. Can you imagine me—me?—all trussed out in hoops and diamonds?" She pirouetted before the mirror, her wooden clogs clumsy, her kerchief and apron emphasizing a round face and a sturdy shapeless body. She grinned, smothering Nicole's protests. "A princess should look like you, not like a bag of beans." She maintained a barrage of teasing remarks until she coaxed a small distressed smile from her mistress's lips.

Later in the evening, the subject arose at Catherine's table. The empress and her guests dined beneath a silk awning covering a multitude of tables arranged upon the shadowed lawns. Nicole discovered that she and Dimitri were not unique in their attitudes. Count Boris Zeprin persisted in a heated denunciation of serfdom even as the others at the table lapsed into uneasy silence as they observed the empress's smile thin to a pale line.

"As you know, my dear count"—Catherine leaned her rounded elbows on the table and rested her chin on the backs of folded hands.—"I am the first to admit serfdom is a generalized evil. Have I not said so in my correspondence with Voltaire? All of Europe knows of my enlightened attitudes. But what is one to do? What we must realize is that nature is at fault, not human law. Just as cream rises to the top of the pail, men of superiority will rise to rule over lesser beings." She added softly, "And one can scarcely dare speak of a serf as a man."

"But they are men, your Majesty! Ignorant men, yes, and childlike. But not by nature. By oppression! We ensure ignorance by denying education to the peasants; we enforce their image as children by debt and dependence. What recourse do they have? The law forbids a peasant to lodge a complaint against his landlord." The count spread his palms and uncomfortably sought support from the faces surrounding the hushed table. All but Nicole avoided his glance.

"Do you counsel revolt, Count?" Catherine's quiet query emerged in a more dangerous tone than anger.

"No! No, of course not." The count paused and ran a finger around his cravat. "But unscrupulous persons might seize upon the issue as a cause for rebellion." A cunning flicker darkened his eyes, vanished before it could be recorded. "There is much to be accomplished on this issue. Taxes are in arrears because villages must choose between remittance and starvation. Millions are regarded as beasts of burden whose only purpose for existence is to produce an endless stream of food and goods they cannot themselves afford to purchase."

"I grieve for them, but no intelligent person can advocate equality. The superiority of the noble above the non-noble is a primary and indisputable truth, is it not? Would you advise the noble to starve because a serf claims hunger? Would you knout a fellow aristocrat because an occasional serf is the victim of abuse?" Catherine enjoyed intellectual stimulation, but her gaze hinted the controversy approached the limit of her tolerance.

"Your Majesty, I beg you not to draw inferences where none are intended!" A troubled expression etched deeply into the count's sharp features. He had stepped into a quagmire. Drawing a long breath, he followed the only possible course; he continued. "If the noble is so vastly superior, then it would follow that no abuses could occur. But they do." The atrocities of the well-known gentleman whose name had sparked this uneasy discussion leaped into several minds. A few of the ladies affected charming shudders.

"And that is precisely why I continue to preach gentleness and humanity. We must all accept our obligation to provide humane and paternal care for our serfs. Only then will they worship us with obedience and increased production."

Nicole focused upon the sweep of lawns, as bright at ten in the evening as they had been at midday. The long thin shadows crept into her mind. She wondered if Catherine refused to recognize the distended bellies along the roadsides. Was it possible that the empress did not see the women bowed beneath heavy shoulder yokes? The hollow-eyed men

worn out before their years? The journey to Oranienbaum
had wound through a countryside sliced by stony plots of
land, past slow-moving peasants sowing buckwheat and barley beneath the rays of the hanging sun. Had no one
observed the weary slump of saddled shoulders? Or the sullen
blankness in eyes turned toward the procession of richly dec-
orated carriages? With some difficulty Nicole returned her
attention to the tail end of the conversation.

"So you see, Count, the serfs are not as miserable as you
contend. They have their *izby*, their huts, and their turkey in
the pot each Sunday." An airy hand dismissed further dispute, though the count stared incredulously. Catherine's smile
returned, curling across her lips like a bright ribbon. "Men
have died of overeating in Russia, but never of hunger."

Deeply disturbed, Nicole lowered her head and examined
her napkin ring as memories of Vadim's stories surfaced in
her thoughts: famines, terrible lengthy droughts, entire villages becoming ghost towns. But murmurs of agreement
whispered about the table like a sigh. Count Zeprin unhappily
accepted his defeat. He stared into his wine, wondering if he
was still well-placed at court, suspecting he would not again
be seated at the empress's table.

Alexander Vasilchikov, who had endured the conversation
with scarcely concealed boredom, tactfully elected this moment to lighten the mood. Catherine beamed at him as if in
praise of a clever child. "Well, what now? Shall we dance?"
He inclined his head toward the occupants of other tables,
who had deserted their raisin cakes and sherry for an orchestra tuning their instruments beneath a silky crimson awning.
"Or a picnic by the shore?" A chorus of groans echoed from
full stomachs. "A ride in the forest?" His eyes sparkled eagerly. "Or perhaps a bath to erase the dust of the journey?"

"*Da!* Just the thing!"

"Are the stones hot yet?"

"There's a charming *bania* just outside my . . ."

With cries of pleasure, the company rose to their feet. Nicole joined them slowly. She noticed Catherine settle a
restraining hand on Vasilchikov's uniform sleeve. It appeared
the empress entertained plans of her own; Vasilchikov would
not be joining the frolic.

Nicole lingered behind as swaying hoops scampered across
the lawns. The pastel gowns cast long gray shadows across
the dimly lit grass carpet. The men made a pretense, which

was not entirely a pretense of chasing the silvery laughter and the teasing eyes peering over bared shoulders.

"Will you join us, Natasha?" Lilia Ulanova's sultry dark eyes gleamed with anticipation.

"I . . ." Early on Nicole had developed a distaste for the *bania*.

"Run along, dear, and enjoy yourself. Summer is a time for pleasure." Catherine's clear calm gaze measured Nicole's hesitation. "You must be gay. Only thus can life be endured." She voiced her own oft-stated philosophy. "Surely your worries will keep until autumn." If she referred, however obliquely, to Nicole's parentage, no hint disturbed the shadowed pools of dark blue.

"Thank you, your Highness." Nicole bowed deeply; then, feeling forced, she gathered her mink-trimmed skirts and ran lightly toward Lilia, yielding to the shouts of the men who had waited to chase them. She gave herself up to the game with a silent grimace, resenting the fleeting touches at waist and breast. However, she allowed no trace of her indifference to appear in the saucy smiles she flung over her shoulder as she raced toward a rainbow cluster of gowns jamming the women's entrance to the baths.

In keeping with the rustic illusion of summer, the *bania* was constructed of weathered logs such as one might observe in any peasant village. The only concession to nobility was the size of the structure, and, of course, the lavish fittings, which included a platoon of servants to perform the ablutions.

Amid the squeals and giggles, the women wriggled free of stays and laces and voluminous underskirts, calling suggestive replies to the bantering innuendos vaulting the partition between the men's and women's compartments.

"Oh, Lilia," cried a small dumpling of a woman. Her merry laugh lifted with malice. "What small breasts you have! Not nearly as large and rounded as mine!" Her dimpled face plainly hoped her voice would be recognized beyond the partition.

"Ah, but who would desire breasts that drag against the knees?" Lilia purred. "Poor Sophia, I didn't realize you had reached such an advanced age! How many years have you sagged so revoltingly?"

Purple splotches mottled Sophia's blown-out cheeks. She fought to suppress sputters of rage as the game which was never a game soured in a burst of raucous hooting from the men's side. Cheeks flaming, Sophia tossed her head and flounced into the inner chamber, vanishing into a solid wall of steam.

Lilia leaned to Nicole's ear. "Sophia's father lost his fortune at the gaming tables . . . she has no dowry and no prospects. She forgets she can no longer afford arrogance."

An overloud voice called across the boards in a musing tone, "Natasha Stepanova . . . I wonder if she has breasts that bump the knees?"

The women handed frothy piles of silk and lace to the servants as they studied Nicole from the corners of their eyes. And a few lashes narrowed as the owners privately swore they recognized the interested male voice.

Flames of scarlet darted along Nicole's cheekbones as her slim, perfect body emerged from the tangle of undergarments. She urgently wished to cover herself, responding to the depths of her New England roots. Instead her chin firmed and she determined not to bow to the long silent stares of envy. Drawing a breath, she attempted to diffuse the submerged tension. Injecting a forced gaiety, she called, "Princess Natasha has the figure of a boy—which is no figure at all." She examined the staring faces. "And warts! Everywhere, warts and lumps."

An explosion of male laughter shouted disbelief. On the women's side, silence prevailed.

"You're very beautiful," Lilia observed quietly, studying Nicole with a practiced eye. "It is no surprise that all the men send you expensive gifts. Have you selected your summer lover yet?"

Nicole blinked and cursed the intimacy of communal bathing. Russian morality continued to astonish. She faced away from the envious stares. "Love does not interest me." She accepted a pair of wooden sandals and slipped them onto her feet. Then she unplaited the long golden braids looping her small head and allowed a silken curtain to swing past her eyes.

Lilia shrugged elegantly rounded shoulders. "A pity. What else is there?" Her dark eyes questioned the circle of silence. "Don't you agree?"

The inquiry tapped a wellspring of opinion, diverting sullen glances from Nicole's firm full breasts and long shapely legs. She shot Lilia a grateful glance, then followed an undulating pair of white buttocks into the steamy interior. And tried desperately not to think of giant pale hams slapping together.

Inside, clouds of pearly steam obscured her vision. It required a moment before she recognized the dark shape of a servant pouring ice water over the crackling hot stove glowing in the corner. As the ice water dribbled through slits in the stove top, bursts of damp white heat erupted to catch in moist thickness within the tunnels of the throat. The fog curled about naked figures reclining along wide toweled benches or sitting cross-legged upon a wooden floor.

Nicole gritted her teeth. It was incomprehensible why any sensible person would prefer this torture to a fragrant tub filled with sudsy warm water and privacy. She was certain she could reside in Russia for the remainder of her life, heaven forbid, and still fail to understand the predilection of nobility and peasantry alike for hot, choking steam.

But the worst was yet to come.

When the women's bodies gleamed like buttered bread, they lazily surrendered their tender flesh to the ministrations of servants wielding birch twigs. Ostensibly the twigs were to beat any loose dirt from the body, but to Nicole the emphasis seemed to stress the beating.

She yielded with clenched jaw as a grimly smiling servant swung the twigs against her shrinking flesh in sharp stinging arcs. The servant evinced every evidence of thoroughly enjoying the task. When her body glowed a fiery pink, Nicole snatched up a towel, and gasping for a breath of cool night air, hurried after Lilia. They ran across a stretch of lawn toward two mountainous piles of freshly chipped ice.

With a cry of pleasure, Lilia stripped the towel from her body and flung herself into the ice chips, rolling and laughing in throes of delight. Nicole's cry did not register delight. As the shock of cold met her overheated flesh, her skin contracted and her mind shouted rebellion. She gingerly smoothed ice chips over her breasts and along her bare legs only because it was expected and not from the tiniest personal inclination. She watched the other women wallowing joyfully in the ice, and felt utterly convinced they pretended, as she did.

"Ah, God . . ." moaned a long sighing voice. And the cavorting women swiveled to peer toward a tunnel appearing through the ice from the men's side. Handfuls of ice flew over the ridge separating male and female, and a laughing blizzard ensued. Eventually someone stuffed chips into the tunnel, but without any noticeable urge toward haste.

When Nicole related her indignation to Pavla, she ground

her teeth and vowed never again to participate in such group adventures. It rasped against the grain of her staid New England morality. And she hoped with all her heart that none of her friends ever learned of this night. For an instant she attempted to visualize the very proper Major William Caldwell rolling naked in the ice chips. She didn't know why she had suddenly thought of him, but the image was so incongruous that she laughed aloud.

"But why not?" Pavla inquired. Genuine bafflement clouded her eyes as she flared a filmy nightgown of ivory gauze across the bed. "I don't see anything out of the ordinary about what you described. It's just an innocent pleasure." She considered Nicole's preference for privacy as indescribably dull.

"It isn't right for men and women to . . . to see each other . . . like that. You know what I mean." A warm flush stained Nicole's throat. In their own fashion, the Russians were exceptionally clean people. Perhaps because the baths provided as much entertainment as cleanliness. With a sigh, Nicole recognized that Pavla could not comprehend her objections.

"Well . . . it's the season of white nights," Pavla offered finally, as if that explained everything.

And perhaps it did. Nicole pressed her forehead against the windowpanes, almost wishing she had accepted the pleading invitations of young Count Praxin. Almost. The soft magic of the night which was not a night sounded a siren song to lovers. Silvery glades beckoned from the forest edge, and pools of shadow spilled shimmering blankets upon the lawns. Although the clock bells had long since struck midnight, strolling figures wandered two by two along the stone terraces and lingered to embrace beneath leafy overhangs. The dull sun illuminated seductive trysting alcoves, but masked the participants in cloaks of privacy.

Watching as a pair of shadows blended into one beside a tinkling fountain, Nicole reflected that she alone spent the dreamy white night by herself. She alone climbed between cool pale sheets without the comfort of strong reaching arms. "Oh, Dimitri!" she whispered, the words a ragged ribbon of despair. "My heart, my love!" Then Pavla gently led her from the windows, returning to release the thickness of velvet against the night.

A long week of restless white nights elapsed before Nicole encountered Dimitri. And when she saw him, her heart

153

stopped, and all the pent-up longing of the mystical crystal nights leaped into her eyes. Dimitri had not attended tonight's banquet—she had searched for him as always—but now he appeared in the theater box across from her as if at the wave of a sorcerer's wand. And from the instant his smoky eyes caressed her, Nicole abandoned the play even though Catherine had authored it and would expect appropriate comments at the card party to follow.

Dimitri. She silently savored the name. Without turning her golden curls to confirm it, Nicole sensed the women's eyes lingering on him, observed as princes and ambassadors stopped by his box to court his favor. Denisov was like the hub of a wheel, radiating spokes of masculine confidence. And she loved him. She loved him with a sweet and constant ache which infused each breath with yearning.

And hopelessness. Always the specter of Darya rose between them like a wedge.

Nicole cast a quick glance to either side of Dimitri's emerald satin shoulders. On his left, old Countess Kamarova flashed her black-toothed smile in a parody of coquettishness; on his right sat someone's young daughter, peeking at Dimitri above the lacy edge of a painted fan. Nicole would have traded instantly with the young girl. She released a breath of relief at Darya's absence. The confrontation she dreaded had again been postponed, but she knew her curiosity would be satisfied eventually. As surely as God had opened the abyss, Nicole would one day smile and curtsy before Dimitri's wife.

"Princess Natasha?"

A light hand brushed across the blue ruffles below her powdered shoulder. Nicole shrugged absently, hoping the fingers and the voice would withdraw. She watched as Dimitri's eyes narrowed into a frown. He crossed his arms over his chest.

The low whisper insisted. "Princess Natasha?" And now Nicole felt a wisp of hair stir on her cheek as the man leaned closer. His arm slipped along the back of her chair.

Resenting the familiarity, she tilted her head slightly to recognize Count Boris Zeprin's profile. His eyes focused upon the actors, but she understood his senses were attuned to her and not to the play.

"The other night," he murmured, the words for her alone. "You kept silence when the others agreed to imperial foolishness. Such an act required courage, a conviction of belief."

Nicole's mind cast backward; then she drew a startled

breath. She stared at the bristling black line of his mustache and wondered uneasily where this conversation led.

"There are . . . people . . . well-placed people with high connections, who are urgently interested in your views. People who predict the end of the economy as we now know it, unless relief is provided an oppressed peasantry. Lacking better conditions, these people believe the serf population will one day rise against the nobility. They believe it wiser to offer minor concessions now than to face oblivion later. If the nobility is to be preserved, action must be taken!"

Nicole's eyes widened in shock. She understood perfectly where the conversation led. Dryness clogged her throat, and she uttered an incoherent sound.

"These people are very interested in backing one of similar views. If such a person were discovered to possess royal blood . . . a throne could be promised in return for certain political considerations. It would not be necessary to offer greater proof than a remarkable resemblance to her late majesty, our little mother, Elizabeth."

Nicole gasped. "Do not speak of this!" Hastily, she lowered her outrage as jeweled heads turned upward to stare. "Tell your people you know of no one foolish enough to desire a crown!"

The stage light heightened the contraction in his sharp features. He looked at her then, a long thoughtful stare. "I assure you I am not the czarina's agent testing your loyalty."

Nicole's gloves fluttered above her lap. "Who you represent does not interest me. My response would be identical in any case!" She fixed stony eyes upon the scenery behind the actors, dismissing him.

Disbelief curved into a cynical smile. "Every woman yearns to wear a crown," he said softly. "Our plans are in the final stages. We shall discuss the matter again, Princess. Perhaps then my people will permit me to present their names as a gesture of our good faith. I think you will be both surprised and suitably impressed."

He inclined his head and slipped from the box before Nicole could frame her refusal in stronger terms. Those seated nearby examined her curiously, then returned their attention to the play below. Setting her jaw, Nicole pretended to follow suit, but she saw nothing; her pulse raced and her fan shook between her fingers.

Cautiously she glanced about the theater box, scrutinizing those who had observed Count Zeprin's whispered interest.

155

Would they recall the event? Would her name now be linked to his?

Touching a glove to her moist forehead, Nicole marveled at how easily one became ensnared in the mazes of intrigue. She resented this intrusion deeply. In one uninvited stroke Count Zeprin had involved her in a dangerous situation. If he revealed the names of his coconspirators, she would be thrust squarely into the center of the matter. Treason. She chewed her lip behind the lacy camouflage of her fan. Morally, the correct response would be to inform Catherine immediately. However . . . would Catherine believe Nicole innocent of involvement, or would she seize upon the incident as a fortunate excuse to eliminate the threat of a rival? Would she choose to believe Nicole a central figure deserving of the dungeons in the fortress?

Disturbed and angry, Nicole tapped her fan against her teeth. If Catherine found the slightest reason to suspect Nicole of engaging in plots, Nicole harbored no doubt that the empress would strike swiftly and conclusively. The box suddenly shrank around her, choking and hot.

Two items surfaced with abundant clarity: she could not allow another encounter with Zeprin—he must be avoided at all costs; and she must take care to involve no one else in this madness. Her troubled blue eyes strayed toward Dimitri's box. Until Zeprin admitted the futility of his insane scheme, it was imperative that she not be observed in private with anyone, lest the danger imperil that person as well. If her longing to be near Dimitri inadvertently endangered him, she would never forgive herself.

Between acts, Nicole rose unsteadily and sipped glasses of iced champagne with friends and drifted from box to box, exchanging greetings and bits of gossip she instantly forgot. Although she was aware Count Zeprin tagged her steps, she steadfastly ignored him. Her senses vibrated toward a tall dark man whose eyes questioned hers above the sea of twinkling diamond tiaras. She smiled reassuringly, hoping her slight shrug was convincing, suspecting it was not. But Zeprin watched, and Grand Duke Paul. And heaven knew how many others. Frustrated and angry, she moved beneath the chandeliers, maintaining a constant distance between herself and the one person with whom she longed to be. And she raged impotently at the injustice of that greatest trickster of all—fate. As if Dimitri's command marriage were not obstacle enough, now destiny conspired to make Nicole's presence an additional danger. The very world seemed to rise up against them.

When the lights mercifully glimmered and went down, she returned to her box and stared blindly toward the stage. Instead of seeing the actors, she saw Grand Duke Paul, Zeprin, Darya, and Catherine. All the obstacles barring her happiness.

The solution to the ache in her heart was obvious. But emotion spurned intellect; she couldn't forget him. She could not.

Nor could she endure an evening of whist in the empress's apartments. After murmuring compliments for the play and excuses for herself, Nicole fled into solitude, walking beneath the shadows of the midnight sun until her feet were as exhausted as her mind.

If Nicole cherished any halfhearted resolve to avoid Dimitri, the resolve crumbled in the following weeks. Nicole remained within the circle of Catherine's intimates, as did Dimitri Denisov. It was Catherine's pleasure to surround herself with the brightest and the most attractive people.

Nicole endured the inevitable encounters with her head held high and an artificial smile to disguise the pain inside. And when Dimitri's dark brows drew together questioningly, she laughed and concealed her expression behind her fan and swiftly joined another group. The encounters were achingly painful, but she constantly reminded herself they might have been worse; Darya might have been clinging to his arm. Darya's continued absence puzzled her; there were moments when Nicole's frazzled nerves would have welcomed a confrontation to settle the wild speculation of a jealous imagination. She comforted herself by assurances that the Darya she visualized was probably more provocatively lovely than the actual woman could ever be. And she did not believe this for an instant.

When Pavla suggested inactivity was the breeding ground for troubled thoughts, Nicole heartily agreed. Henceforth she immersed herself in a fatiguing swirl of social events, accepting invitations as they appeared, dancing and flirting mindlessly with a succession of men. And occasionally she glanced over a shoulder and read bafflement in the silvery eyes of one who watched from the sidelines. At such moments her heart churned wildly and she held herself rigidly, commanding her body to remain in place and not to run into his arms. Always there were those who watched, those who would paint the blackest motives across the canvas of impulse; she dared not weaken.

As the weeks passed, it gradually occurred to Nicole that she labored to avoid an ever-increasing number of people: men whose attentions she rejected, women whose men she had unwittingly stolen, Paul, Dimitri . . . and always Count Zeprin. Count Zeprin worried her constantly. He dogged her steps as persistently as the young nobles who flooded her rooms with flowers and gifts and passionate letters. Thus far she had eluded any private conversation with the count, but she wondered anxiously for how long. And how long before Dimitri confronted her? And what would she say to either of them?

She rested her head against the cushions of Catherine's carriage and closed her lashes over eyes hinting the strain of the last weeks. Faint violet shadows bruised the hollows below her lashes.

"Natasha, dear, you're as pale as a Siberian hare. Are you resting well?" The carriage lurched, and Catherine laughed as she bounced against Vasilchikov's regimental tunic. She righted herself and straightened her hat, smiling deeply into Vasilchikov's eyes.

Discreetly Nicole shifted to examine the countryside, releasing a quiet inner sigh. The carriage outings were designed for relaxation, but she considered them a chore. Particularly when a mischievous fate decreed she share Catherine's carriage instead of occupying one of those following behind.

Others considered sharing Catherine's carriage a mark of favor, but Nicole did not. Especially as she was also forced to share the carriage with the lively Alexis Bobrinsky, Catherine's illegitimate and publicly nonexistent son by Gregory Orlov, and Sir Tom, of course, and Vasilchikov. All too frequently Sir Tom tracked mud or dust across Nicole's hems, Bobrinsky climbed in and out of her lap with the childish disregard of a ten-year-old, and Catherine and Vasilchikov indulged displays of affection which wrenched a lonely heart.

"I find it difficult to sleep," she answered above Bobrinsky's bobbing head. And then leaned deeply into the cushions as the child lunged to hang his head from the carriage window. Nicole would have traded the contents of her jewelry box to be in her own chambers at this moment. The white nights had surrendered to brief periods of darkness, but even so, the sun did not slip below the horizon until ten at night, only to reemerge before two in the morning. The shimmering of semi-permanent dusk disturbed lifelong patterns of sleep.

Catherine smiled archly. "As do I," she concurred. But the remark was a double entendre intended for Vasilchikov's amusement. She had forgotten Nicole.

Observing them without appearing to, Nicole isolated Catherine's baffling infatuation in a sudden flash of intuition. Vasilchikov restored Catherine's faded youth. The brightness in her eyes, the light grace of hand and head—they now had a focus, a fresh exhilarating purpose. With a touch of sadness, Nicole suspected Vasilchikov would be only the first of a series of young lovers.

And Vasilchikov? He adored his empress as only a youth can adore an older woman. Catherine was mother, sister, mentor, lover. His boyish face reflected a glow of disbelief at his remarkable good fortune. If his secret heart yearned for dewy younger faces, for smooth firm flesh, no scandalmonger had yet uncovered evidence of such an indulgence. That would surface later, when the flush of pride and gratitude had dimmed, when his eyes opened to wrinkles and graying hair and a thickening waist. Later still, Catherine would pace the palace corridors, silently despairing of a male intellect as vigorous as the flesh.

Sighing, Nicole patiently guided Alexis from her lap and struggled to explain the substance of shadows in answer to the boy's hundredth question. Before she concluded, he'd lost interest and was teasing Sir Tom with the tip of his boot. Delighted, Catherine and Vasilchikov laughed and exclaimed at the charm of a boy and a dog.

Nicole thought it anything but charming. In the excitement of play, Sir Tom had wet copiously upon Nicole's gold satin slipper. Her smile froze and she gritted her teeth in silent irritation. The day darkened from bad to worse. Opening her eyes in a glare, she wriggled her wet toes from beneath the dog, and a murderous glint hardened her gaze to sapphire.

Perhaps if she hadn't been angrily daydreaming of means to dispose of dogs, she might have anticipated the sudden wild swing of the carriage. As it was, she found herself totally unprepared when the horses swung into a turn at too great a speed. For one terrifying instant the coach tilted out of control, and Nicole stared in horror as the roadway rushed toward the windows. Then, miraculously, the carriage body lurched back onto its springs without toppling.

The carriage careened to a shuddering halt, enveloped by

loops of choking gray dust. The adults stared at each other, too shaken to speak; then Nicole touched a trembling hand to her forehead. A crimson stain seeped into her glove. She stared at the blood in astonishment, retaining no memory of the injury.

Catherine bolted forward. "Bobrinsky!"

A tangle of limbs and paws indicated the child and dog had been thrown between the seats. When the boy emerged, his face was as white as his collar and he clasped his arm protectively against his chest. Catherine gasped, and both gloves flew to press her lips.

Bobrinsky's brimming eyes focused upon Vasilchikov's uniform, and his wobbling chin lifted. "It doesn't hurt, Mama . . . not too much." A slow stain blackened his blue satin sleeve.

Catherine inhaled deeply, and her eyes softened with pride and love. Displaying the wisdom for which she was famed, she refrained from gathering the child to her bosom. Instead, she granted him his fledgling manhood and pretended to accept his lie. "Very good," she responded weakly. "Then you'll be brave and patient while we seek help."

The boy nodded valiantly, his gaze fixed upon Vasilchikov's gold buttons.

Before the swirls of dust settled, the imperial guards surrounded the carriage and plucked the hapless driver from his perch. Nicole swallowed hard as they dragged the man into the bordering field and knouted him until he fell unconscious across the shoots of young barley. The unfortunate footman, whose crime had been proximity, swiftly met an identical fate.

In the road behind, the drivers of the following carriages reined tight; horses reared and coaches spun across the lane in a jumbled tangle. Once halted, the carriages disgorged a dusty multitude of silk gowns and flaring coats. The ladies and gentlemen of the court rushed forward to encircle the royal coach.

With no memory of descending, Nicole discovered herself standing in the roadway. Only Bobrinsky remained within the carriage. A shouting mass surged forward, reaching toward Catherine to personally assure themselves of her safety, and thus endangering the safety of all. A woman screamed and a man swung his cane. Appalled, Nicole pressed her handkerchief to the laceration above her eye, then squirmed forward until she attained Vasilchikov's side.

"Alexander!" Her shout disappeared in the excited babble of confusion. She jabbed him sharply with her fan. The soldiers might have aided Catherine, but the tidal thrust of people had cut them off. "Alexander!" Nicole screamed into his stunned expression.

"She might have died!"

Nicole read the words but could not hear them. She clawed his tunic sleeve until he bent; then she cupped her hand and shouted into his ear. "Lift her!" A boot trampled her toes; an elbow would have knocked her sprawling, had space allowed. "Lift the empress to the carriage so they can see her!"

Comprehension dawned on his chalky face; then Vasilchikov spun and shouldered into the crowd. His strong young hands circled the empress's waist, and he swung her to the carriage door. Catherine understood at once. She raised her palms, an innate authority in the gesture, and a semblance of order hushed the shoving, pushing throng. Nicole exhaled a long breath of relief and sagged against Vasilchikov.

"My friends . . . as you can observe yourselves, I am unharmed."

A lusty cheer stirred fresh eddies of dust, drawing the attention of curious peasants, who paused in the fields and leaned on their hoes, welcoming the diversion.

"Princess Natasha has suffered a minor scrape, as has my small protégé . . ." As ruffled as she was, Catherine displayed the presence of mind not to acknowledge Bobrinsky. In spite of the fact that each face smiling up at her knew the truth. "We shall call at the first estate and beg the aid of a physician. No"—she smiled—"please don't follow. We cannot descend en masse upon our unknown host. I urge everyone to continue your outing."

Nicole rested against the carriage wheel, pressing her handkerchief above her eye and listening as Catherine skillfully quelled the murmurs of protest. Catherine was an opportunist. She had transformed the unfortunate event into an occasion to display a charming concern and consideration for others. Every eye admired her, every voice praised her unselfish valor.

With one noticeable exception. Grand Duke Paul had disdained the mad dash toward the imperial coach. He remained aloof, hunched above his cane in an open carriage. He stared at his mother through eyes sick with disappointment. For the briefest of moments he had fancied himself an emperor. Mother and son communicated silently above the heads of the court; then Paul barked a harsh command and his carriage wheeled in the road.

Catherine watched him depart; then she concluded her remarks and ducked inside the coach. She clamped her lips and waited impatiently for a fresh driver to be commandeered. The carriage swung into the lane, traveled a short distance, then turned slowly into a tree-lined driveway opening to the right. The graveled sweep led to a large pillared summer estate positioned like a jewel upon manicured lawns.

When the imperial coach halted before a curve of marble staircase, a dozen startled servants ran forward to assist the empress and her party. Others darted across a wide veranda and then into the house to alert the occupants of their unexpected guests.

Nicole peered from the coach windows, and her heart fluttered and sank. Her fingers plucked at the lace framing her face. Fate continued to stir chaos into her day. She stared at the wide double doors and expelled a low hopeless breath as she gathered her skirts to descend.

She recognized the Denisov crest.

13

BEFORE THE SERVANTS located Dimitri, the house physician had performed his tasks and departed. He bandaged Bobrinsky's arm and sheltered it within a silk sling, and he secured a small square of gauze above Nicole's eye.

Dimitri appeared in the salon doorway wearing tight-fitting gray riding breeches. His white shirt gapped at the collar as he tossed a riding crop on a table, then strode toward Catherine's chair. Nicole dropped her gaze from his quick glance, not lifting her eyes until he halted before the empress. A gentle breeze drifted from a bank of open windows, feathering his black hair across a deeply tanned forehead.

"Your Majesty. Please accept my apologies for not welcoming you personally. I trust Molka attended to the injuries satisfactorily?"

"Your man performed admirably." Catherine's plumed hat dipped in a pleased nod. She extended her fingers for his kiss. "There's no need for apologies." Catherine bloomed in the company of handsome men; her eyes sparkled flirtatiously. "Our visit was scarcely by invitation."

Dimitri responded in kind, his brow arching in a tease. "Are you hinting I've been remiss in attending to my social obligations?" As one of the favored inner circle, he was permitted such intimate remarks.

Catherine laughed and denied it, her blue eyes gliding across the sharp definition of thigh muscles straining his breeches.

"Perhaps a taste of vodka would chase any unpleasant memories of your mishap." He crossed easily to a sideboard, as if unaware that Catherine measured the fluid elegance of his stride.

Catherine hesitated; her aversion to spirits was well-known. But today was an unusual occasion. "Yes, thank you. Something to steady the nerves would be welcome."

Vasilchikov studied Dimitri uneasily and moved to touch the empress's shoulder. "She was magnificent! I don't believe she has any nerves!"

Catherine beamed, patting his hand absently. "It was you who saved the hour. If you hadn't thought to rescue me from the crowd, the consequences might have proven serious indeed."

Preening, Vasilchikov accepted the compliment, embellishing upon his inspiration. He accorded no credit to Nicole; but then, she had not expected that he would.

Dimitri served the empress and Vasilchikov, then crossed to lower the tray before Nicole. His gray intensity blotted the others from view. "You've been avoiding me," he accused in a soft voice. His smoky gaze examined her steadily.

Nicole's stomach tightened. Flustered, she looked away from his sun-darkened skin, his white teeth, and his questioning stare. But her eyes appeared to possess a will of their own, and returned to his face. She drew a shallow breath and silently pleaded for his discretion.

"A toast!" Catherine proposed gaily. "God grant us our desires, and grant them quickly!" It was her favorite toast, and they all smiled indulgently, then raised their glasses.

The shadow masking Nicole's eyes negated the smile curving her pale lips; God would not grant her desires, quickly or otherwise. Conscious that Dimitri watched, she swallowed her vodka rapidly, trying not to grimace as a stinging explosion ignited below her heart. She choked, and a hand fanned the air before her cheeks. "Excellent," she gasped, her voice catching and her eyes watering.

Dimitri laughed and refilled her glass.

Annoyed, Nicole wiped her eyes. And in a flash, her annoyance vanished. She didn't wish to spoil this rare moment in his company by indulging emotions which did not endure. A flush of pink brightened her smile, and she hastily lowered her head, lest Catherine read the message in her eyes. Then Catherine spoke and the warm radiance bled from Nicole's face and she watched the tremble return to her fingers.

"Where is your lovely wife today?"

Nicole's breath froze. The confrontation she dreaded flew forward on soft wings. She pressed her lips tightly, and calmly commanded her blank mind to formulate a plan. She would rise and bow. Of course. She would force her tongue around polite greetings. She would smile and frame sentences.

She would die by slow inches.

Dimitri's smile altered subtly. "The servants are seeking Darya now. Occasionally she desires moments of solitude . . ." Briefly his eyes lingered upon Bobrinsky dozing in the window seat.

Catherine studied his expression thoughtfully. "Darya's health and happiness are of great concern to me," she said slowly. "And to the state." No trace of her previous bantering tone remained to lighten the sober shifting of undercurrents. "I would be most displeased if Darya should discover Russia inhospitable." She paused. "Or if the princess should be unhappy in her marriage." Catherine cocked her head and swirled the vodka in her glass. "Very displeased," she repeated quietly, her eyes speculative.

Pinpoints of steel appeared in Dimitri's gaze, his shoulders tensed, and the white shirt defined a strain of muscle. Then he smiled and leaned into a bow which avoided mockery only by its elegance. "Have I ever disappointed you, your Majesty?" he asked lightly.

"No." Catherine stared. Her brows met in a faint line. "You intrigue me, Prince Dimitri." She ran a finger around the rim of her glass. Her body remained relaxed, but she positioned her head in the unconscious habit of royalty. "Thus far you have not objected to the demands of state and sovereign. But I sometimes wonder what will occur when you are requested to perform a service you find disagreeable."

"Are you so certain such an eventuality has not already occurred?" he answered softly.

He smiled into Catherine's startled eyes, and Nicole drew a sharp breath at the sheer masculinity he projected. Catherine met his steady gaze and it was the woman, not the empress, who wet her lips and leaned forward.

Catherine might have pursued the topic, but she did not. Instead she smiled quickly at Vasilchikov's frown and lifted her vodka. "Does Darya receive word from her aunt?" The empress led smoothly into a discussion of Maria Theresa, and then into Austria's stake in the Polish gamble.

Nicole relaxed slowly, glad the sparring had concluded. She attempted to follow the political discussion, but her mind persisted in wandering. The salon reflected the quiet elegance undoubtedly created by Darya Denisovna. White fur rugs were scattered across a gleaming mahogany floor; silk damask covered the sofas and chairs in cool shades of blue and ivory and yellow, the colors repeating in rich embroidered draperies beside a bank of windows overlooking the garden. Fresh flowers nodded from Oriental vases, and delicate china figurines reposed on the mantelpiece. The walls were hung in pale blue silk.

It was too much to hope that they might depart before the servants located Darya. Nicole shifted in her chair to better observe the hallway leading toward the salon doors. She fixed her gaze upon the corridor until she realized with an embarrassed start that she was staring at the same young girl she had first observed at the theater. The child was perhaps twelve years of age, dressed in green silk to compliment her luminous eyes and wearing a rope of pearls in her dark hair. Nicole smiled, reminded of a child who has been playing grown-up with the contents of her mother's wardrobe.

As yet unconscious of the important guests, she slowly approached, her attention centered upon an exquisite porcelain doll she cradled lovingly in her arms. She arranged the doll's miniature court dress and hummed a lullaby in a sweet youthful voice.

The scene was charmingly nostalgic, and Nicole's lips softened in the slightly melancholy expression of a woman recalling the hope and innocence of adolescence. How brief and how precious the period was; how quickly it passed.

Noticing Nicole's interest, Dimitri turned to follow her gaze, and his eyes faded to the color of rain. Then his mouth set, and he strode to the door, guiding the girl inside.

Her emerald eyes widened as she looked about the room, and a burst of embarrassed pink fired her cheeks. Hastily she thrust the doll behind her back, futilely attempting to conceal it within the folds of her skirt. Eyes wide with dismay, she looked up at Dimitri, her lower lip trembling.

Without expression, he removed the doll and tossed it on a chair.

Immediately the young girl hid her crimson face in a deep curtsy. "Aunt Catherine," she murmured. Her heavily accented French emerged in a high, unformed voice.

"You remembered!" Catherine's delight wreathed her features in smiles. She extended her jeweled hand for the girl's kiss, tactfully avoiding a glance toward the doll. "You must always regard me as part of your family, my dear. My door is open to you exactly as if I were your true aunt. I well recall how difficult it is to be alone in a strange country!"

No, It couldn't be. Nicole stared as the girl straightened, peeking shyly at Vasilchikov and then at Nicole. Her face lifted upward, as a flower following the sun, and her emerald eyes appealed to Dimitri. An inner glow warmed her cheeks as she smiled into his silvery gaze.

No. The joke would be too cruel.

Now the full intensity of Dimitri's gaze swung toward Nicole's white face. For a timeless moment their eyes held; then he bowed and spoke in a voice devoid of expression. "Princess Natasha, I have the honor to present Princess Darya Denisovna. My wife."

Shock froze Nicole's senses. Her smile wobbled into a ragged line of rejection. As if sleepwalking, she pushed to her feet and smoothed her skirts, and listened dully as her voice murmured the proper greetings. This was simply not possible, children did not marry, mature men did not . . . She smiled until her cheeks felt stiff and sore, and she focused on the child because she could not bear to meet Dimitri's level gaze.

Timidly Darya accepted her role as mistress of the estate. She inquired politely about the accident, she murmured solicitously over the sleeping Bobrinsky, she dispatched a servant to fetch blini and vareniky, sweet dumplings stuffed with fruit and sour cream. And as she performed gracefully if somewhat self-consciously, her eyes continually strayed toward her husband. She was a child actress portraying the woman. And when the lovely green eyes brushed her husband's strong angular face, no one could doubt the audience she played to.

Stunned, Nicole sought Dimitri's eyes above the girl's dark

head. A paradox of laughter and tears strangled her voice. She didn't know whether to laugh at the incongruity of the situation or weep for the tragedy of it. She was conscious of deep sorrow as she stood abruptly and edged toward the garden doors. "Forgive me, perhaps I sustained a harder bump than I'd supposed." She touched the square of gauze above her brow. "I think perhaps a breath of air . . . ?"

"The very thing, dear." Catherine extended her glass to Vasilchikov for another splash of vodka and smothered a yawn. "I believe I may impose upon our hostess for the use of a bed. Suddenly I'm drowsy—a brief nap exerts an appeal." She cast Vasilchikov a coy glance before looking toward Bobrinsky, who sighed and turned in his sleep. "We won't depart until Alexis awakens."

Nicole bowed deeply, then escaped.

She wandered to the foot of the garden, then rested her spine wearily against a broad tree trunk. There she paused to sort out her thoughts, spinning a rosebud between her gloves and staring at the thorns. A child. Princess Darya had carried a doll; she had been playing at tea parties. Good Lord! Nicole tilted her head and stroked her cheek with the dewy blossom. Schooners of clouds sailed across a vast blue-white sky.

She had feared and resented . . . a child. A child whose small hard breasts were as unformed as her voice; a child who grasped the world within her palm and didn't suspect her treasure. Nicole pressed her lashes against her cheeks, and the rose crushed within her fisted glove. A sadness deeper than pity stole across her thoughts. Although nothing was changed, somehow everything had altered.

"Natushka!" Thunder boomed from the head of the pathway. A giant silhouette flung a long shadow over the gardens, blocking the twilight shafts of afternoon sun. "They told me I'd find you here!"

"Vadim!" The rosebud tumbled from her fingers, and Nicole gathered her skirts in a headlong rush up the path. She flung herself into his arms, laughing as thick cords tightened around her. Then he swung her in a wide circle until her fur-trimmed skirts floated upward in a halo of gold velvet, and she laughed in delight, clinging to her hat. When Vadim replaced her on her feet, they smiled at each other, the affection a warm strong current between them.

"You've grown another foot!"

He grinned and reminded her of his age, but she could

swear he was taller than she remembered. But she admitted his age; perhaps it was a trick of the sunshine, but she noticed a few white strands pebbling his black beard.

"And you smell like dog piss." His huge grin fenced the dark beard below teeth as white and strong as pickets.

"Good heavens! I was afraid of that!" She related the story glumly, pausing when he threw back his head in bellows of laughter. When she concluded, they had arrived at the base of the pathway. Smiling fondly at each other, they leaned on a wooden fence overlooking an expanse of fields.

Vadim's black twinkle appraised her as he packed his pipe. "Don't worry, Natushka, true beauty always smells like perfume to a man."

Nicole idly picked at the splintering fence post and watched a wizened peasant scratching the soil with a *sokha*. The plow appeared to be a marvel of inefficiency. "Vadim . . . am I beautiful? Really beautiful?"

He studied the translucent perfection of a roses-and-cream complexion, then glanced at the lush curve of velvet tapering to a tiny waist emphasized by the flare of her skirts. "Natushka, you are enough to steal a man's breath away," he said softly. "What causes you to doubt the obvious? Have all the men in the palace died?"

She lowered her head and remained silent, examining the fence post.

"Ah . . . I see." The fence groaned as he leaned his massive elbows on the top rail. A drift of smoke curled toward the fields. "Would you compare a caterpillar to a butterfly?" he inquired gently.

"One day a caterpillar becomes a butterfly."

He nodded. "Eventually. But until it does, one cannot compare the two."

Not looking up from the fence post, Nicole whispered, "Princess Darya will be a very beautiful butterfly." Inwardly she raged at herself. It was idiotic, ridiculous, pointless to feel jealousy toward a child. She would change the topic immediately.

"*Da*," he agreed, "perhaps as beautiful as you." He blew a smoke ring and watched it float on a slight breeze.

Now was the moment; she would redirect the conversation. She drew a breath. "Dimitri . . . does he . . . I mean, do they . . . ?" A scarlet humiliation burned her face and throat, and she wished the earth would open and swallow her.

Vadim smiled. "Natushka, she is a child. She has not yet

begun the bleeding." He cast a sidelong glance toward Nicole's flaming embarrassment and began softly, "In my village there lived a man named Ivan Ivanovich . . ."

Covering her eyes, Nicole settled heavily against the post. She was behaving like a fool, like a stupid mindless fool! "Tell me about Ivan Ivanovich." She said in a small shamed voice. "I think I need to hear an Ivan story."

". . . a boy, actually, whose father presented him with a wife for his tenth birthday."

Nicole blinked and her hand dropped. "A wife for a boy of ten?"

"Of course. The earlier a son marries, the sooner a daughter-in-law joins the *izba*, bringing her strong back and another pair of hands." He shrugged away so elementary a truth. "The father chose a sturdy buxom young girl of twenty-two for his son, and she frolicked with the boy when she was not laboring in the fields or weaving linens for the master. In due course she formed an attachment to a handsome young widower, and in due course Ivan grew up and learned of the liaison. He did everything men have done since time began to woo his wife back to him." Vadim examined his pipe, waiting for her question.

"And did the wife return to Ivan?"

"No." Frank black eyes probed hers. "For, you see, although Ivan matured into an admirable young *kulak*, the wife continued to see the child she had married. Always she would remember bouncing Ivan upon her knee and pinching his smooth cheek. She saw him with the eyes of a mother or a sister."

Nicole contemplated the tale, understanding what Vadim sought to impart. A crack splintered the cold encircling her heart. "I think your story does not have a happy ending," she guessed reluctantly.

Vadim shifted his pipe to the corner of his lips. "There are but two forms of divorce in Russia," he explained. "Banishment or death. Had Ivan or his wife suffered the misfortune of exile, both would have been free to remarry. This did not happen. The unfortunate Ivan challenged the widower to knives. Ivan was killed, and the widower was blinded."

Nicole sighed heavily. There were no happy endings in Russia.

Vadim shrugged. "Ivan found peace; his wife and the widower were married." He lifted Nicole's chin and turned her face to meet his eyes. "Natushka, only sunshine and rain are free. Like so much else in this life, happiness carries a price."

Frowning, she scrubbed her stained slipper across the gravel, watching as the pebbles scattered. "The price of my happiness is guilt and danger and pain for many people. The price is too high."

"That is for you to decide."

Suddenly she felt a deep and debilitating weariness. She was tired of paying prices. She paid for the accident of her unknown parents in units of fear and anxiety. She paid for a hopeless love with restless sleepless nights. She paid for the gifts overflowing her chambers in dances and dinners with partners as boring as flat wine. She paid and she paid. "Vadim . . . what would you advise me?"

Vadim smiled. "Do I look like an oracle?" His ebony eyes sparkled like orbs of shiny coal. "Whatever the heart desires can be rationalized." For an instant his eyes turned inward; then the shadow passed and Vadim was again the Vadim she knew. "You consider the price and determine what you are willing to pay . . ." He shrugged eloquently.

Was her love worth the wrath of an empress? The pain and bewilderment of a child? Was her happiness more important than embroiling Dimitri in a dangerous plot? No. She sighed, admitting she was unwilling to generate so much suffering. Yet she was equally unwilling to pay the greatest price of all—losing him.

Vadim coaxed a smile to her lips, then swung her to a sitting position atop the fence. "No more upsetting topics," he promised. They chatted easily of nothing and of everything until Nicole glimpsed a flash of gray and white moving past the hedges. She drew a soft breath and held it until Dimitri reached them. He halted with hands on hips, his wide sleeves fluttering in the breeze.

He grinned at Vadim. "I see that you've plucked the loveliest blossom for yourself, as usual."

Nicole blushed prettily and smoothed her palms over her gold skirt. If she had guessed the day's destination, she would have chosen a larger-brimmed hat, one which framed her face in shadow.

Turning her head, she directed her gaze toward the fields. The sunlight and plowed earth shimmered with a brilliance of color and clarity they had lacked a moment before. An utter impossibility. Nicole smothered a tiny sound. Dimitri's physical impact quivered along nerves which tautened and

170

stretched. She was acutely aware of the small space separating them. And she felt his warm breath upon her lips even as she knew it to be impossible.

Smiling, Vadim knocked his pipe against the fence, scattering the ashes into neat rows of barley. "I just remembered that I didn't order the groom to brush down your horse, *barchuk*." He grinned at Nicole. "I'll see to it immediately."

Nicole opened her arms, refusing to allow him to depart without an embrace. "Thank you," she whispered into his white hair. "Thank you."

His large hands dropped from her shoulders, and she watched until he disappeared around the curve in the hedges. Then she surrendered to the raw tension leaping between herself and the man next to her.

They looked at each other, and a miniature world lay within their eyes.

Never had he appeared more desirable. White stockings hugged the muscles below the gray riding breeches. Breeches which fit over sinew and bone like a second skin. He stood before her, not touching, yet she saw his reaction to her open lips, to her plunging bodice, in the swell of gray cloth growing between his tensing legs.

Nicole wet her mouth and her head fell backward, warm breath rushing past her lips. A tremor of weakness tingled through her flesh, followed by the feverish heat of yearning. And still their eyes held. She felt herself being swept into hot silvery depths whirling with passion and urgency. Her milky breasts rose in shallow breaths above the band of velvet; a moist glow shivered up her thighs. And she longed to touch him, to experience again his demanding body crushing against her, yearned for him as she had seldom yearned for anything in her life. The ache of desire was as painful as a wound.

His fists clenched at his sides until they whitened; then one hand lifted as if to caress the gauze near her hairline. The heat of it bathed her face, and Nicole swayed dizzily. One step. One tiny step, and she would lie within those powerful arms.

His hand dropped without touching her. And his brooding smoky eyes devoured her, ravaged her. "We can be seen from the house," he said hoarsely. "Or I would take you here. Now."

Nicole's mouth dried, and she flung out a hand, balancing her weakness upon the fence. "And I . . ." Her own voice

171

deepened with the impact of him. The scent of sweat and leather and horses made her feel faint.

She touched her collar with a shaking hand and closed her eyes to blot out the sight of sun-darkened skin and tousled hair and smoldering eyes. "Dimitri . . . I've been a fool. I thought . . ."

"I know what you thought."

Vadim's words echoed through the hollow spaces in her mind: banishment or death. "But nothing has changed, has it?"

"Nicole, look at me."

Her knuckles whitened where she gripped the fence, and she raised her gaze to a blaze of intensity which stopped her breath.

"I will not live my life without you."

A small choked sob escaped her throat.

"If having you means exile, I am prepared to accept that condition. I'm arranging my affairs now. When all is in order . . . will you come with me?" No hint of impulsiveness was reflected within his level bruising stare. "I can offer you every luxury that money can purchase. What I cannot offer you, Nicole, is marriage."

A radiant weakness stole across her limbs. Joy trembled along the soft contours of her mouth, and she felt faint with happiness. She whispered, "Catherine will never permit you to leave Russia."

His eyes locked to hers. "My life is my own. I've finished placing my destiny in the hands of another. No matter what forces of duty and obligation to state were brought to bear, I should never have agreed to marry Darya. I did so because the consequences of refusal were . . . unpleasant." His hands opened and closed, and the burning intensity of his stare leaped between them like lightning. "Tell me you will come with me, Nicole, or by God, I will take you away by force!"

Her eyes glowed with love. "You must know I'll go with you," she answered simply. "But, Dimitri . . . are you very certain? Can you abandon Temnikov? Your homeland? Forever?"

The white linen defining his chest and shoulders strained as if he yearned to crush her in his arms. He glanced toward the windows with moody eyes, then leaned on the fence and transferred his gaze to the fields. After a moment he said quietly, "This is a wonderful land, Nicole, with a brilliant future. The people, the soil . . ." Passion roughened his voice. "But no one should be subject to the whims and desires of one ruler. What mortal being has the wisdom or the right to legislate the private affairs of individuals?"

Nicole gazed at him with a startled expression. Identical convictions had echoed from the rafters of the Duchard kitchen, issuing from the lips of men who repudiated an English king and mapped an unheard-of experiment in freedom.

"Marriages should not be commanded for political convenience," he continued, his anger a quiet heat. "Residences should not be assigned by imperial fiat. Government positions should be awarded based on merit and not purchased through bribery or flattery." Gray fire leaped in his eyes. "Catherine dispatches hundreds of thousands of serfs to a war they do not understand or desire. Catherine decides Poland shall be carved up like a pie to serve the vainglorious appetite of history. One person should not wield that kind of power over individuals and nations." His anger turned upon Nicole's pale face and faded to weariness.

She longed to ease his tired face against her breast. Instead she laced her fingers tightly into her lap. "My love," she murmured, "you are speaking treason."

"Yes, treason." Dimitri's long fingers thrust into the blue-black curls tumbling across his forehead. "Logic becomes treason, a miscarriage endemic to all the world. There is no country on the face of this earth where man's need for something larger than himself has not stripped him of individual freedom!" His jaw knotted and the sun-deepened lines about his eyes tightened. "If such a paradise existed, where a king's signature could not consign men to slavery at a whim, I swear to Christ I would sail there and place my sword and my loyalty in the service of the giants who created it!" His fist slammed against the fence.

Nicole inhaled deeply and fought the tremor in her hands. She spoke slowly and carefully. "Dimitri . . . the seeds of such a place have been sown. Ideas identical to yours and mine are taking root there."

"It should have been here!" Nicole recognized his fierce love for Russia in the passion raising his voice—and she heard the betrayal of that love. He had anchored his faith in dreams without substance. His teeth ground and he stared into the fields. "Nothing will change in Russia until men understand they cannot achieve reform by installing new faces upon old thrones."

Nicole drew a sharp breath. Count Zeprin's sly features

loomed before her. She'd been a fool not to inform Dimitri of Zeprin's plot. "Dimitri . . ."

He passed a hand across his brow. "Tell me where individuals may walk as free men, tell me of this fantasy land."

She met his swirling eyes, and for a moment her mind was swept clean of thought. She swallowed hard and forced herself to the issue. Zeprin would wait. "Do you recall meeting Paul Revere before we sailed from Boston?" With building excitement she confided the secrets of the kitchen meetings; she fed his spiritual hunger with the nourishment of hope.

At the conclusion of her explanation, he regarded her thoughtfully. "I didn't suspect events had progressed to this point." The crunch of gravel caught their attention, and they glanced quickly toward a servant appearing at the head of the garden pathway. "As a spy, I failed dismally." His wide sensual lips parted in a wry smile. "I'll contact Revere immediately. There are methods to guarantee the privacy of correspondence—"

"I beg you to use caution! If Catherine . . ." Nicole bit off the warning as the servant bowed and announced the empress was preparing to depart.

Dimitri's strong warm hands circled her waist and he swung her from the fence, holding her briefly against him. His warm mouth lingered inches from her own. "When all is in order, Tasha, my love, I'll come for you."

"Yes . . . yes!"

Nicole bid him a reluctant farewell and climbed into the dim interior of Catherine's coach. Every ounce of will was brought to bear not to turn backward as the horses pranced from the driveway. But her elated thoughts lay beyond the reach of willpower. She counted the trees flashing past the coach windows as if she counted the days until he came for her. And it seemed her chest lacked the space to accommodate her swelling heart. Once at the Summer Palace, she floated across the lawns, lost within a private capsule of warmth and happiness.

Her distraction proved a dangerous lapse. She should have noticed the dark figure pressed into the alcove outside her door. But she suspected nothing until a hand shot from the shadows and banded her wrist like a cuff.

"Count Zeprin!" Pulse thudding, Nicole raised her fan and fluttered it before her pale cheeks. "You gave me a start!"

She expected him to release his grip, but he did not. Instead he lurched toward her, his face a purplish color made ghastly by the jumping light of the corridor torch. "I don't know what game you're playing, Princess, but my people grow weary of your childish delays."

"I don't know what you mean." Snatching her arm free, Nicole tossed her head and attempted to brush past him. With all her heart she wished she had discussed Zeprin with Dimitri and asked his advice. There hadn't been time.

The count stepped before her, solidly blocking passage. "You know very well what I mean! You've been avoiding me. But the time has passed for foolish games. Plans are made, events are scheduled. All that's lacking is a commitment from you."

Aghast, Nicole covered her ears, shaking her upswept curls violently enough to dislodge her hat. "I've told you! I don't want to hear this! You're committing a grievous error. I want nothing to do with you or your plots!"

Tiny bubbles of spittle foamed at the corners of his lips. "You little fool! Do you think anyone cares what you want?" He hissed like a serpent. "You're nothing but a puppet! A figurehead! All we require is your name. All we ask is that you appear to lead the insurrection! When the coup is completed, you may amuse yourself however your empty little head dictates, so long as you stay out of government affairs!"

"You are mad!" Where in God's name was the guard? What bribe had Zeprin paid? A rapid glance confirmed the corridor was empty. Drawing an unsteady breath, Nicole collected her wits and leveled an icy stare upon the man confronting her. There were weapons on both sides. "If you persist in annoying me with this insanity, Catherine shall learn of it." She drew herself to her full height. "If you believe this threat an idle one, I assure you it is not. What better way to prove my loyalty than to expose your plot?"

A sly smile twitched the uneasiness along his lips. "Ah, but you have no names, do you?"

This was true. Nicole forced a smile across her own lips. "But you do," she suggested evenly. "And I've heard there are rather unpleasant methods which might induce you to reveal them."

They stared at each other, eyes hard with loathing. Count Zeprin's fists clenched and released, the jewels on his fingers flashing in the dim light. "I see," he answered softly. "Now, allow me to assure you of something . . . an opportunity such as this arises but once in a lifetime. We can promote you as Peter the Great's granddaughter, you fool! Elizabeth's daughter! As such, the military and the commoners will rally to your cause in an instant. We will not allow this moment to slip through our fingers! All your stupid threat gains you is the promise that we will act quicker than originally planned." Ambition and fury tainted the breath striking Nicole's white face. His lips were as cold and hard as the diamonds sparkling at his throat and cuffs. "If you will not cooperate willingly, then we shall force you to declare yourself as empress!"

"There is nothing to declare. You can't force me to act against my wishes!"

"We shall see."

His harsh, mirthless laughter raised cold prickly bumps on her skin as she watched him bow and melt into the corridor shadows.

14

AUGUST RAINS DAMPENED the spirits of a pleasure-wearied court. Fireworks displays could not be scheduled with any degree of reliability, nor could hunts, picnics, or carriage outings. Roadways dissolved into mud wallows, horses sank to their ankles along dripping bridle paths. The court released an irritated sigh and imprisoned themselves indoors, seeking amusement in billiards, cards, and a repetitive cycle of concerts, masquerades, and balls. The lavish events languished beneath a lackluster indifference as summer romances waned and gowns limped and tempers shortened.

In the fields surrounding Oranienbaum, peasant families threshed the grain and sowed winter wheat and rye. In mid-August the court drove beribboned carriages into the fields to observe the peasants celebrate the day of Floris and Lauris. The peasants ignored the yawns and snickers; they herded their tired horses to a small outdoor chapel where a pock-faced priest blessed the animals and sprinkled them with holy water.

Slowly the summer drew to a close. Oranienbaum had yielded its pleasures; freshness was at a premium.

Irritable and bored, the Russian court erupted in sporadic outbreaks of vague maladies. Black-currant jelly, the recommended medium for gargling, could not be purchased for a thousand rubles. A raw scar appeared upon the English ambassador's jaw, rumored to have been won in a duel involving the last two pails of black-current jelly. Gossips predicted the victor would amass a fortune.

The court physician discovered himself much in demand. Those ladies who suffered cramping prior to their monthly indisposition followed Catherine's example and demanded to be bled. Others took to their beds complaining of headaches and backaches and stomachaches. Most occupied themselves with measures to obliterate the ravages of summer. They scrubbed lemon rinds across offending freckles and applied egg white and French brandy to the remaining traces of sunburn.

Pavla expressed a common opinion when she stared listlessly from the windows, her broad face shiny with heat and humidity as she prayed plaintively for snow.

Nicole smiled and glanced up from her open trunk. She folded her riding habit and packed it, deciding she would need a new habit shortly—one fashioned from a fabric sturdier than silk camlet. The camlet fitted to perfection, but it shrank in the rain and faded in the sun. She rested her fists upon her hips and surveyed the room for additional items she could pack. They would not depart for another week, but she too found herself anxious to place the summer behind her. For an instant the furious countenance of Count Zeprin flickered behind her lids, and a light shiver traveled across her ribs. Annoyed, she gave herself a shake; the incident was long past, an unpleasantness she hoped he had forgotten as absolutely as she had. As she had? Irritated with herself, Nicole closed the trunk lid with a satisfying slam. Straightening, she smiled at Pavla, who half-sat, half-reclined upon Nicole's bed. "Why would you wish away the summer?" The question was more to generate conversation than as a form of disagreement.

"We need something to spark the blood, something to wake us all up. There's magic in the first snow."

"Not for me!" The shudder Nicole exaggerated was not entirely pretense. "I hate the cold!"

Pavla smiled and wiped her forehead. "You, my princess, are in the wrong country."

"So I understand." Nicole sank to the lid of her trunk and fanned her face with her skirt hem. If someone had informed her a year ago that she would one day consider sixty-five degrees as a heat wave, she would have laughed and thought him crazy. "Would you like some lemonade?"

"Not enough to get up and prepare it."

"Fortunately for you, this princess possesses a few culinary talents." Nicole pulled to her feet and assembled the ingredients from a small chest they stocked for this purpose and she sliced the lemons, added sugar, and stirred water into a glass pitcher. She wished for ice, but not badly enough to dash to the *bania* and fill a bowl from the melting mound of chips. She arranged a silver tray with wedges of melon recently arrived from Astrakhan and dewy white grapes from the Crimea. "Will this tempt you?"

"The handsomest *kulak* in all the provinces couldn't tempt me today." Pavla sighed. But she popped a grape into her mouth. "How do you muster the energy to dance quadrilles every night, when it's all I can manage just to brush out my hair?"

Early-evening shadows masked the softness suddenly shining from Nicole's blue eyes. How could she explain that a promise in a garden lightened her step and fueled her spirits? As strongly as she cared for Pavla, she couldn't bring herself to confide her plans. Giving voice to dreams was a jinx.

Smiling at the foolishness of superstition, Nicole blotted melon juice from her lips and then laughed at Pavla's soulful expression. "Speaking of quadrilles, I'm to attend a masked ball in less than an hour. Is my costume ready?"

Pavla rolled her chin in her palm. "If you're still going as Queen Isabella, it's ready." She yawned hugely. "Do you really suppose Queen Isabella wore Russian damask and a powdered wig?"

Nicole shrugged. "Who knows? That's why this is an excellent choice." Stretching, she rose and contemplated herself in the mirror, frowning at a light sprinkling of freckles dusting her nose. Dimitri would attend the ball tonight. She smiled at the rush of pink raised by the thought of his name. Surely they could manage a dance. Happiness glowed in her eyes. Soon . . . soon.

She stripped her afternoon gown over her head, then roused Pavla to aid in hooking the Queen Isabella costume. "What jewelry would you suggest?" she asked. The lavender bodice pulled tight and molded her breasts.

178

"Oh, something official-looking. Queens have to look official." Placing a finger alongside her nose, Pavla considered the gown, her thoughts casting about for an official touch. "I have just the thing!" She bent to her pallet and withdrew a kerchief heavy with pilfered items.

"Oh, Pavla!" Nicole sighed heavily and rolled her eyes. "Bring the collection here. Let's see what mischief you've perpetrated this week!"

Pavla unfolded the kerchief on the dressing table and pushed through the items with her forefinger. "Here! I thought I remembered this." In her palm she extended a sunburst medallion lavishly inlaid with sparkling gems.

Nicole smothered a gasp. The medallion was far and away the most expensive item she had ever discovered in Pavla's cache. "Pavla! This is . . . this is reprehensible! Are you mad? Every guard in the palace will be searching for this!" She stared at Pavla in the mirror as tingles of apprehension raced along her spine. One day Pavla would go too far, one day she would surely be caught, and then . . .

Pavla snorted. "It's paste. Not worth looking for."

"Paste?" Nicole held the medallion to the light, feeling somewhat comforted. No one in her right mind would admit to wearing paste jewels. And poorly made ones at that. Pavla was right; no one would be searching for this piece—the admission would be far too humiliating. "All right, to whom did this belong?" She demanded weakly.

Pavla's dark eyes darted to one side in the expression she reserved for these awkward moments. "I don't recall exactly. . . ."

"The truth!" Nicole said sharply, her eyes flashing.

Pavla sighed, avoiding Nicole's steady stare. "Count Zeprin," she admitted. "I ran into him in the hallway, he inquired about your costume, and . . ."

Count Zeprin! Nicole dropped the medallion as if it had suddenly turned red-hot in her palm. She dropped her chin in her hands, and stricken eyes stared at Pavla's reflection. "Dear God, you don't know what you've done!" She began an explanation, then abandoned the effort as too lengthy and too time-consuming. She commanded her mind toward the problem at hand.

Tapping a finger against her teeth, she regarded the paste medallion thoughtfully, her mind racing. Perhaps the incident could be turned to her advantage. Gradually a plan formed behind her eyes as she recalled evidence of Count Zeprin's vanity. Suppose she wore the medallion and openly claimed to have found it; she could make certain the court gossips were aware she sought the owner, and she could laughingly underscore the fact of the medallion's artificial manufacture. Then, when the gossips were wondering who among the court wore paste, Nicole would openly accost Zeprin and return the piece. A slow smile curved her lips as she imagined the scene. Zeprin would flee the court in disgrace, and she would be rid of him.

She turned the piece in her hand, wondering if it were wiser to wear the piece or to conceal it. With a decisive nod she pinned it below her breast. If someone recognized the piece as Zeprin's, so much the better; it would only make the confrontation easier. Leaning toward the mirror, she admitted the sunburst design added exactly the right official touch to her costume, even though a cursory glance revealed it to be artificial. She fluffed the ruffles floating about her breast and smiled, anticipating Zeprin's disgrace.

"Will Count Zeprin attend the ball?" Pavla asked nervously. Paste or no paste, it was her experience that no one welcomed being the victim of a theft. Very possibly she had erred in suggesting that Nicole wear the medallion. She had allowed her eagerness to be of service to run away with her common sense.

"Very likely," Nicole responded sternly. "I'll see that the piece is returned." She fought to establish a serious expression and launched into a familiar lecture on the evils of thievery, then halted as she recognized the futility of plowing barren ground. She broke off in mid-sentence with a sigh and changed the subject. "Do I look like a queen?" The mirror reflected an enchanting vision of lavender beauty, and Nicole smiled, wondering if Dimitri was fond of lavender.

Pavla dropped into a mock curtsy, grateful that the subject of the medallion was to be closed. "If I didn't know, I'd swear you were Queen Isabella herself!"

Nicole laughed and stroked the scent of roses behind her ears and between her satiny breasts. It would be a wonderful night, she was sure of it, and the more she anticipated Zeprin's humiliation, the more eagerness she felt for the evening to commence. "You didn't learn of Queen Isabella until two days ago."

Pavla rocked on her heels and examined the ceiling. "Maybe so, maybe not. Did I ever tell you about the time I attended a convent school in Spain? The priest was so handsome you could just—"

"Pavla! You are absolutely incorrigible!" Smiling, Nicole edged her hoop through the door, then spun lightly and leaned into the bedroom. She lowered her eyebrows and attempted a scowl. "I expect you to replace every single item in that kerchief before I return!"

"I will. I swear it."

"Including the fan with the broken handle."

"But Princess Lilia gave it to me, I swear!"

Nicole sighed. "Even the fan."

Pavla affected a wounded expression, then shrugged broadly. "Don't forget your mask."

"Oh, yes, thank you." Nicole raised a black domino sewn to an ivory wand and fitted it over her eyes, covering the offending freckles. A blue sparkle twinkled behind the mask, readily identifying her despite her disguise.

Humming softly, she gathered the cumbersome lengths of lavender damask and entered the corridor, following the twists and turns until she emerged onto a lattice-covered walkway leading to the main palace. A stream of jesters, queens, Tatars, pirates, and clowns converged upon a torchlit entrance strewn with orchids. Nicole waved and nodded, at too great a distance to identify those who returned her greetings.

Behind the mask she searched for a tall, powerfully built man garbed in cossack attire. It suited Dimitri, and she smiled at the idea of the queen and the cossack. Her step quickened and her pulse thudded softly in the hollow of her throat. Anything could occur at a masked ball. And often did.

As Nicole approached the arched doors, costumed heads turned to stare. A pall of silence rippled backward like a wave. She tossed her head gaily, attributing the open mouths to her costume. The plunging neckline was deeper than any she'd previously dared, and the heavy pearls sewn to her skirt caused it to sway provocatively from the hoop strapped to her waist. Waving merrily, Nicole swept through her audience as queenly as the true Isabella. She stepped into the crowded foyer, a pleased smile curving below her domino.

Immediately, all conversation dwindled as every eye fixed upon Nicole; masks dropped and jawlines fell slack.

Her step faltered. The lavender costume was fetching, but not stunning enough to warrant an abrupt silence. A terrible sense of unease began at her slippers and washed upward. She wet her lips and peered through the mask, tensing in growing confusion and alarm.

A dark figure clad in flowing trousers and a black sheepskin cap emerged from the stillness, moving swiftly toward her, the sound of boots loud upon the marble floor. Bruising fingers gripped her arms above the elbows. "Nicole! In the name of Christ! What are you thinking of?"

She stared upward, searching Dimitri's hard angry eyes. "I don't understand. What . . . ?" A velvet bear stumbled against a milkmaid as people hastened to open a space between themselves and Nicole. She blinked in astonishment. Had she been exposed to a plague?

"The medallion! My God, the medallion!" Dimitri's face frightened her. "You don't know?" Releasing her arm, he passed a hand quickly over his eyes. "You must be the only aristocrat in Russia who doesn't recognize that medallion! It's part of the cluster of medals dedicated to St. Anne."

She didn't grasp what he was saying. "Dimitri?" Beneath his arm she glimpsed Count Zeprin leaning against a pillar, his arms crossed on his chest. His sly smile of satisfaction chilled her blood. As she watched, he mouthed the word "Tonight." A hard knot of fear tightened about her heart.

"Only the Empress of Russia is authorized to wear the order of St. Anne."

"Oh, my God!" Blood and air seemed to rush from her body, and Nicole flung out a hand to steady herself. Muscle and tendon dissolved in the white heat of fear, and her head spun. She blinked rapidly at nothing, fighting the waves of black threatening behind her eyes.

"Nicole! Nicole, can you hear me?" Dimitri shook her. Dimly she noticed that his fingers pressed flaring red marks into her arms. "Listen to me! This changes everything. We must leave tonight!"

Her domino clattered to the floor, and she pressed her forehead, feeling beads of perspiration form beneath the tips of her gloves. Her triumph, her wonderful evening, congealed into a nightmare. "He tricked Pavla," she whispered through bloodless lips. "They used Pavla's weakness against me." Of course the medallion was paste. The real medallion was no doubt safely resting in Catherine's jewelry casket. Zeprin had anticipated every action, every thought. She looked at his satisfied smile through sick eyes.

"Nicole! Return to your rooms as rapidly as possible without attracting undue attention. Dress in comfortable dark clothing. I'll come for you the instant I've arranged horses and ship passage. We'll sail from the gulf within an hour!" Gray eyes blazed into hers. "Nicole! Have you understood a word I've spoken?"

"Yes." No sound passed her lips. Nerveless fingers plucked at the poisonous medallion, but it resisted her weak efforts. Spinning, she fled through a thick wall of silence, pressing her glove over the damning sunburst even as she knew it was too late. The damage was done: she had declared herself an empress, paste or no paste.

Exactly as Count Zeprin had promised. In her sickened heart, Nicole comprehended that even now his people were moving stealthily into position, marshaling their forces. Within minutes Count Zeprin would appear at her door, demanding that she either lead the insurrection or surrender herself to the Peter and Paul fortress as her fate. A government would topple tonight. Or the plotters would die.

Shimmering dizziness wobbled across her vision as she ran along the latticed walkway. If harm came to Catherine, she would never forgive herself for this stupidity! "Dimitri!" She chanted the name beneath her breath in a half-sob, like a talisman with the power to protect and rescue. And an image of the brass angel atop the fortress danced wildly in the winds tumbling through her mind. Biting back a frightened cry, she quickened her pace, racing pell-mell toward a group of people emerging from the palace wing.

It wouldn't do to have them question her. Fighting desperately for control, Nicole forced her gait to slow. She clamped her glove firmly over the medallion. And felt her heart crash to her knees as she recognized Grand Duke Paul occupying the center of the group.

"Ah, Princess Natasha." He leaned into a desultory bow. Ugly little eyes touched her breathless white face before dropping to the hand she pressed below her breast. "Are you unwell, Princess? Or have you lost your sense of direction?" Titters of laughter traveled through the small grouping. All but Paul affected elaborate jeweled costumes. Paul had chosen the uniform of a Prussian general, a choice certain to enrage his mother.

"Excuse me, your Highness, I'm certain you're anxious to join the court, and I . . . I'm feeling unwell." She coughed into her free glove, sounding as desperately wretched as she felt.

The grand duke evinced no haste to attend his mother's ball. He clasped his gloves behind his tunic, his narrow eyes repudiating her choice of costume. Then his expression altered, becoming suddenly thoughtful. Wisps of gold escaped the edges of her powdered wig; a lavender ruffle trailed behind the hoop; and unless he was mistaken, it appeared the princess had lost a slipper. "What are you hiding beneath your glove?" he demanded, his senses sharpening.

"Hiding? Why, nothing, your Highness, I . . . I have a stitch in my side . . ." It was a gamble, a terrible risk, but if the gods were with her . . .

They were not. "Liar," he hissed softly. The faces about him sobered and exchanged curious glances. "Take your glove away."

The gamble was lost. "Your Highness! I implore you . . . you must believe that I was deceived! I didn't know!"

A greedy glint leaped into his eyes, the heat of a hunter closing on the scent. "I command you to remove your glove!" Eagerness shrilled his tone.

"Oh, sweet heaven!" Nicole breathed. Terrified tears glittered in her lashes; her eyes shone like drowning sapphires. Her skirts rustled from the tremor shaking her body.

Impatience quivered along the grand duke's wizened form. His arm shot forward and he violently slapped her hand from her breast.

The party went rigid with shock; even Paul had not expected what his bulging eyes beheld.

"You brazen bitch!" he choked. "Are you so sure of yourself that you dare . . . that you dare . . . to flaunt your evil ambitions?" His voice ripped on a scream, and he tore the medallion from her gown, shredding the bits of lavender and lace beneath. "I'll kill you!"

He jumped forward, but a dozen people leaped to restrain his fury, holding him as taloned fingers clawed toward Nicole's throat.

"Think of the empress! Perhaps she's altered the line of succession!"

"Never!" Paul shrieked. "The crown is promised to me! To me!"

"If Princess Natasha is harmed, it will appear that her claim is genuine! A civil war will ensue!"

The chorus of voices urged caution. "Advise your mother of the bitch's outrage and let the empress decide!"

Rage blackened Paul's features. "I am capable of acting without that whore's advice!"

"Think! If you harm Princess Natasha, she could become a martyr—like your father!"

Paul's head snapped and his lips curled back from his teeth as he searched furiously for the author of the last phrase. He screamed, "Who dares mention this harlot in the same breath as my father?"

Nicole seized the respite to gather her skirts and dash into the palace corridor. She trusted saner voices would stall Paul for the precious minutes she needed, and she prayed to God that the grand duke would listen. Paul might fear Nicole's supposed aspirations, but she knew he feared his mother more. Given a choice, Nicole preferred to throw herself on Catherine's mercy; in her heart she believed Catherine would grant her a fair hearing. She held to that thought like life itself.

Gasping for each torturous breath, she tumbled into her room and spun to bolt the door behind her. Shaking fingers stumbled over the lock. "Pavla!" Her shout choked on a sob. "Pavla, I need you!"

But her rooms were empty. Both Pavla and the kerchief of little baubles were missing.

"Damn! Damn, damn!" Pressing both hands hard against her temples, she forced herself to draw a long shuddering breath. "Think! For God's sake, calm yourself and think!"

She ripped at the lavender gown, halted abruptly, then tore the wig from her head and hurled it across the room. The diamond tiara tinkled into a corner; one of her braids tumbled across her shoulders and swung down her back. She clawed at the tiny hooks running down her spine. They gave way with maddening slowness. Her fingers scrabbled at the straps of the hoop; then she kicked free. Flinging open the armoire, she pulled out a black grisette skirt and a wine-colored blouse, shrugging into them and then finding her boots. She thrust her arms into a dark jacket with a fox collar.

She had but a moment to catch her breath and pin the loose braid into place before a knock hammered at the door. A thudding heartbeat thundered in her ears, and her hands shook uncontrollably. "Who is it?" She tried again, striving to vanquish the tremulous croak. "Who's there?" Dimitri? Count Zeprin? Grand Duke Paul?

Silence rang heavily in her inner ear. Then a sharp command sounded and a heavy shoulder struck the door. Once, twice, and then again. A long jagged crack splintered inward.

The chunk of shattering wood broke Nicole's paralysis and she bolted toward the windows. The door gave way and crashed against the wall. Soldiers in Prussian uniforms poured into the room, and two of them captured her wrists, twisting her arms cruelly behind her back. They shoved her forward toward the doorway.

Grand Duke Paul stepped through the pieces of broken wood. He halted just inside the doorway as though he didn't trust himself to approach nearer.

"This is all a mistake," Nicole whispered. "Count Zeprin . . . he tricked my servant. I swear to you I didn't know!"

"Shut up!" he snapped, grinding his teeth.

A menagerie of animals paraded through Nicole's wildly swinging thoughts. His small pig eyes were the eyes of a boar chasing down a rabbit. His stunted upturned nose reminded her of a Pekingese. The hunched body was that of a monkey; his face was as sly and cunning as a ferret's.

He smiled, and her blood chilled to ice. "I am not going to kill you," he said softly.

Nicole sagged in relief. Fear of his mother's reaction stayed his hand.

"But you will not trouble us any longer. Mother will learn that I can act as decisively as she. She will be proud of me." He nodded to the soldier behind Nicole. "You will simply disappear." He spread his palms. "Poof. Gone. And everything will be as it used to be."

An evil-smelling cloth swept down, smothering Nicole's nose and mouth.

Paul laughed at her futile struggles. "Not even Mother will learn what happened to you. I'll tell her I took care of the problem, that is all." His eyes glittered. "No one will ever find you. No one!"

Nicole's eyes rolled upward, and she stumbled against the soldiers. Each sucking breath earned a wave of blackness, as a darkness of despair closed over her.

15

"NADIA STEPAN!"

The name possessed a vague familiarity, like something glimpsed from a distant dream. Nicole glanced at the two women waiting behind her, then pressed her fingertips to a reeling head. The drugs had not entirely dissipated; her perception remained maddeningly fuzzy and disoriented. Flashes of a long journey flickered through her consciousness: wagon beds heaped with straw, disembodied hands raising food to her lips, nights in stony fields.

She blinked at a stocky man pacing a wooden platform and then toward the dozen men gathered below. Sheaves of drying grain were stacked in neat tiers along high walls. A barn? Where the structure might be located, in what city, she couldn't guess. She examined her surroundings like an accident victim who awakens far from the last-remembered scene.

"Nadia Stepan, step forward!"

Nicole turned slightly, wondering why neither of the two women obeyed. A sudden weight pulling at the base of her slender neck surprised her. Her hair had been plaited into a single heavy braid which swung nearly to her waist. Peering downward, she struggled to recall donning a coarse brown skirt and wooden shoes. None of this made sense; not her appearance, not this place.

Confused, she appealed to the woman on her left, switching from French to whispered Russian when the woman's broad peasant face did not respond. "Where are we? Why are those men staring at us?"

Indifferent eyes displayed no curiosity. "It's a marriage auction, of course." The first woman exchanged a shrug with the second. "If you don't answer, the bailiff will come for you with the knout."

Nicole's jaw dropped, and she spun to face the man on the

platform. A long narrow cord dangled from his waist sash. His impatient stare narrowed.

"Am I Nadia Stepan?" Another identity? She pressed her temples, feeling the headache behind her eyes. How many people had fate decreed she must be? How many times could she adjust to new names and new circumstances? The anchor of self she longed for had never appeared so frighteningly elusive.

The first woman rolled her eyes toward the overhead rafters lost in a musty gloom. "Addle-witted," she commented, shaking her kerchief.

A slim patience exhausted, the bailiff paced a step in the women's direction and his hand threatened at the whip handle. Swallowing hard, Nicole bolted forward. She climbed the platform hastily and halted, staring into the critical faces below. Beneath sweat-stained felt hats, beards jutted and hard eyes judged. The men wore homespun linen tunics above coarse blouses and fitted trousers. Knives and short axes swung from their wide sashes.

"This is a mistake," Nicole whispered.

"Shut up!" The bailiff glared, his fingers closing upon the hilt of the knout. Nicole swayed, and her damp palms rolled the brown skirt into clumps. "Now, then," the bailiff called. His voice disturbed motes of dust drifting in the close atmosphere. Shafts of sunlight leaked through wide cracks in the barn siding. "What am I bid for this one?"

Nicole closed thick trembling lashes, mentally seeking an avenue of escape.

A fierce-eyed man spit on the dirt floor and ground the globule beneath a tree-bark shoe laced to the knee. "She's nothing but skin and bones! I wouldn't give you two kopecks for that one!"

"*Da*! She wouldn't last a day in the fields!"

"We want wives with the strength of an ox and the endurance of a horse! Give us wives with muscle!"

Indignation stiffened the bailiff's bearded chin. He scowled at his audience. "Are you too stupid to recognize beauty when you see it? This woman is fit for a prince; she's a prize! When have you ever in your whole miserable lives seen hair this color?" He lowered his voice and winked. "Picture this one on a cold winter night!"

If beauty lay in the eyes of the beholder, then no one beneath the platform edge recognized beauty standing before him. Beauty consisted of heavy muscle and chapped red hands; beauty was a broad back coupled to the mental dullness of stamina.

Disgust accompanied a vigorous spasm of spitting. "Picture her stacking a ton of sheaves or loading a wagon. Ha!"

The bailiff waved a paper. "It says here that she's a skilled domestic! She'll tend your animals and produce more *arshines* of woven goods than you can sell in an entire summer!"

The men hooted their disbelief; they could see the paper was as blank as a summer sky. "Show your hands," they demanded of Nicole.

Over the bailiff's scream of protest, Nicole raised shaking palms. For once in her life, she prayed no one wanted her.

"Smooth as a baby's butt! Christ!"

"A lazy woman isn't worth the effort to beat her!"

"One chicken."

Curious heads turned toward a thin man leaning against the barn door. Through the murk and dust, Nicole squinted to define a clean-shaven face younger than the others. A fringe of straight dark bangs hung below his hat brim, ending in a ragged edge above quiet brown eyes.

"One chicken?" The bailiff pounded his heart and staggered about the platform. "One stinking chicken?" His amazement was absolute, delivered in a groaning shriek. "*One* chicken? For this treasure?"

Callused brown hands rose to hide an outbreak of grins. No one questioned the master's right to require marriageable men and women to wed, but everyone resented the bailiff enriching himself in the process.

"One chicken," the young man repeated evenly.

The bailiff judged the shuttered faces below, then shrewdly ended his performance with a defeated snort. "Sold to Yuri Janov, the right to wed Nadia Stepan. But it's robbery! By all the saints, this is robbery!"

"It's God's will," a voice corrected. A dozen dark tunics smirked and shrugged agreement.

The bailiff shoved Nicole down the platform steps and shouted another name, his voice confident with fresh hope. A few of the men cast Yuri Janov pitying glances, then focused their attention on the squat woman occupying the platform, the strong one with shoulders like a bull's. Now, this was a beauty! Vigorous bidding ensued.

Dazed, Nicole stumbled toward the barn door. The wooden clogs felt heavy and awkward on her stocking feet. And she blinked rapidly, unable to accept what had just occurred. She desperately wished her head would clear. And with all her heart and soul she yearned to be a thousand miles from this place.

Yuri Janov pushed the barn door with the heel of a rough palm, and they stepped outside without speaking. A panorama of stark beauty opened before Nicole's confused gaze.

September sunlight sparkled across a winding river threading through the golden countryside and connecting small villages like beads on a string. She shaded her eyes and counted four villages within sight of the hill upon which they stood. The villages were small, comprising perhaps a dozen or two *izby*; only one boasted an onion-domed church and the awnings of a small marketplace.

"Where are we?" she asked without looking at him. She bit her lip and sought the courage to examine the man who had purchased her.

Janov had waited patiently as she studied the terrain, his thumbs hooked in his sash. When she spoke, his thick dark brows rose toward the fringe of bangs. Curiosity gentled his stare. "These are Prince Repinsky's holdings."

"But where? Are we near St. Petersburg?" She forced herself to look at him now, freshly surprised by his youth. Despite the lines etching his face, she guessed him but a year or two older than herself. The wrinkles fanning his dark eyes and full-lipped mouth were more the result of sun and weather than age. His tunic bloused at the sash, but Nicole's glance confirmed he was thin and lanky. His body had not yet fleshed out a raw-bone structure.

"St. Petersburg?" Incredulity lifted a pleasant voice of medium pitch. "I don't think so—someone would have mentioned it. Is St. Petersburg near Moscow?"

"Moscow? Is this Moscow?"

He smiled, his sober face suddenly boyish. "*Nyet.* Moscow is far to the north. Much grander than this." Waving, he encompassed the collection of wooden villages scattered near the river. "Moscow is larger than anything you can imagine. When my father was alive, he visited there once. He told us they have a giant snow slide and many beautiful churches. Too many churches."

Nicole drew a deep breath. They were traveling in circles of confusion. Perhaps if she phrased it differently. "Is this a city?" She too indicated the distant villages. She couldn't imagine any of them classed as a city, but then, she couldn't imagine any of this.

Janov appeared as perplexed as she. "*Nyet*." His dark eyes touched her gold braid, then slid away. And Nicole recognized that he too was beginning to suspect she was addle-witted. "These villages belong to the master. The nearest true city is Penza."

Penza. Now they were getting somewhere. Except the name meant absolutely nothing. Her mind racing, Nicole fought to place Penza. If Penza lay to the south of Moscow . . . then she now stood on a hill more than six or seven hundred miles below St. Petersburg. Buried in a collection of forgotten serf villages. Her heart plummeted, crashing in the vicinity of her toes. No one would ever find her.

Dear God! Pressing trembling fingers to her white lips, she fought for the next breath before she met his puzzled dark eyes. "I'm trying to understand. But all this . . . You see, I don't belong here. I . . ." She halted. It was useless. No matter how sincerely or how explicitly she explained, Yuri Janov would never believe the truth. The truth existed in a universe beyond his experience to comprehend. She would sound like Pavla constructing fairy tales from thin air.

Nicole swallowed the hot stone in her throat. "I . . . Must we marry?" She asked it in a small shaking voice, knowing the answer. And knowing she was helpless. Sliding a hand into her apron pocket, she discovered it as empty as she had guessed it would be. With no money and no accurate idea of where she was, escape lay outside the realm of possibility. The heavy gold braid swung over her shoulder as her head dropped.

"I paid a chicken for you." Pride squared his thin shoulders and tightened his jaw. "But if you prefer one of the others . . ."

"*Nyet*," she whispered. Recalling the fierce bearded faces in the barn, she admitted fate could have dealt a far worse hand. She glanced at him through damp lashes. Though he was slight and wiry of build, she suspected Yuri Janov possessed a strength of endurance. Quiet pride shone in his dark eyes. And although his clothing was faded and patched, the patches were neatly sewn, his tunic and fitted trousers scrupulously clean.

Janov turned his profile to the river and spoke in a level tone. "As a husband I can offer a respectable name and a tight *izba*. My mother is hard but fair." The sober brown eyes altered subtly beneath the line of straight black hair. "There are no sisters, but you won't be expected to shoulder

191

an unreasonable load. My brother's wife will share the women's burdens."

"We . . ." The word appalled. Nicole rubbed a chill from her arms and stared across the picturesque beauty of the river and the villages. She had viewed a painting similar to this scene in Catherine's Hermitage. "We . . . will live with your family?"

Surprise deepened the hollows below his cheekbones. "Of course. Where else?"

Behind them the barn door banged open and a jubilant man shoved his prospective bride into the afternoon sunlight. His hands ran over her like she was a prize animal, testing for muscle tone, feeling for flaws. His black beard jutted toward heaven and he shouted, "Thank you, God! She's an ox!" The woman beamed proudly.

Yuri Janov shyly touched Nicole's arm and nodded toward a worn dirt pathway leading down from the rise toward the smallest of the villages perhaps two miles distant. Nicole expelled a short breath of utter hopelessness, then directed her wooden clogs toward the ruts.

They had walked for several minutes before she heard him cough and clear his throat. "I don't recognize your accent. Are you from Moscow? Is that why you asked about it?"

Nicole bit the inside of her cheek. Sensibility warned against the truth, but her thundering heart felt near to bursting with the need to explain. She blurted her story without allowing herself to dwell on its credibility. Or the omissions. She could not bear to speak Dimitri's name. A disconsolate blackness sliced too deeply.

Yuri walked behind her, listening politely. A smile twitched the corners of lips unaccustomed to frequent levity. When her cracking voice trailed, he removed his hat and ran short hard fingers through his hair. "You're a fine storyteller, Nadia Stepan, I enjoyed it."

Nicole started at the name, then silently tested it upon her lips. There was nothing to gain by resisting. Releasing a distraught sigh, she concluded that her only hope for sanity lay in acceptance.

"I'm sorry to tell you the village already has a storyteller." He considered her tale, his expression plainly rejecting the possibility of a land beyond the sea. But he'd heard rumors of an ocean, and he applauded her for including mention of it. Known facts added a touch of believability to a story. "The part about St. Petersburg would appeal more without so much frivolity and plots. That portion is confusing." His suggestions were thoughtful and unhurried. "And you should mention the czarina's efforts to free the serfs . . . tell how the landowners prevent her from doing so."

Nicole halted in the path, her brown skirt swinging over the tops of tiny wildflowers. Her wide eyes pleaded. "This isn't a story! Every word is true, I swear it!" She sounded like Pavla.

"Of course." He smiled. "Still . . . it's too bad we have a storyteller." Slanting rays of sunshine gleamed reddish-black in his hair before he resettled his hat.

Nicole's shoulders slumped, and she turned back to the pathway, dejection slowing each step carrying her nearer the watering pond at the lower edge of the village. She'd known he couldn't possibly believe her. But somewhere deep inside, she had hoped. A quivering sigh escaped her lips. At least he hadn't ridiculed her, and for that she was grateful. He had listened and then attempted to help in his own way. She suspected she would learn to respect his tact and gentle consideration, qualities she didn't credit to the other men attending the auction. But, Lord . . . oh, Lord, she resented the need to accept any husband!

They paused for breath a few yards from the well above the watering pond, and a cluster of women grouped about the bucket studied Nicole curiously. Half a dozen barefoot children ran to greet them. "Yuri bought a wife," they chorused. Small dirty hands smothered giggles, and they stared at Nicole's long gold braid.

She offered the children a ragged smile; then her lips froze as her gaze flew to examine the collection of wooden *izby* facing across a dirt lane. One of the leaning huts would be her new home. The thought nearly buckled her knees.

Each *izba* appeared depressingly identical; only the painted carvings beneath the leaves distinguished one from the other—that and the elaborate individual shutter designs. Each *izba* featured a gate leading into a small inner yard cluttered with animals and farming equipment and weathered sheds of varying size. Scraggly kitchen gardens scored the land immediately behind the structures; otherwise no vegetation relieved the stark profiles. No trees, no shrubs, no grass. The village sprang from miles of stubbled fields which rolled outward unbroken by any silhouette until one's eyes touched the distant northern horizon and a faint jagged ridge of treetops announcing the edge of the *taiga.*

Unable to bear the boundless desolate sweep, Nicole turned hastily toward the winding Moksha River below the village. Whatever lay in the hidden pockets between the rolling hills beyond the river was obscured from view. Golden-brown fields stretched as far as the eye could perceive.

The vast enormity of the empty sky above and the endless carpet of fields below was overwhelming. Nicole sat abruptly upon a charred tree stump and blinked hard at the trembling hands clasped in her lap.

She was unaware that one of the women had separated from the gathering beside the well and shyly approached Yuri, listening with widening eyes as he spoke. Not until Yuri repeatedly cleared his throat did Nicole become cognizant that she stared at his linden-bark shoes and a woman's embroidered hem.

"What? I . . ." She lifted a blank face, then choked on a breath of shock. She stared into the sweet open face of the girl with sunshine in her soul. The woman Yuri gently pushed forward was exactly the person Nicole had conceived Vadim's adored wife to be. The girl returned Nicole's stare through lustrous dark eyes of such kindness and gentle sympathy that Nicole intuitively knew nothing had ever disturbed the simple purity of this woman's heart. Her lovely rounded face and wide generous mouth were fashioned for quiet smiles and golden laughter, her hands sculptured for soft touches and reassuring pats.

"This is Larisca Janov," Yuri murmured, "my brother Simeon's wife." Nicole looked up curiously, wondering if she imagined the hint of pain and sorrow. His eyes brushed Larisca's blue headdress; then he turned abruptly toward the river.

Larisca wiped her palms on her apron, then pressed both Nicole's smooth hands between her own roughened fingers. "We'll be sisters," she offered timidly.

The diffidence was surprising. Nicole felt as if she had known Larisca always. "Da, I . . ." The auction, the huts, these people . . . Her head whirled, and she swallowed a sudden unbidden rush of tears.

Concern softened Larisca's eyes to black velvet. Nicole felt as if she looked into the deep quiet heart of a violet. "Yuri repeated your story." Larisca's face shone with the wonder of it. "I hope you'll tell it again to Katya and me. I'm certain Yuri didn't tell all the details."

"Katya?"

"*Matushka.*"

Nicole remembered; Yuri's mother. The woman who was hard but fair. She tilted her head and listened to the children laughing from the mud thickening the rim of the watering pond; she inhaled a pungent tang of manure and kitchen scraps and freshly mowed fields. No, she was not imagining any of this.

Larisca watched her. "You must be frightened," she observed gently.

Nicole's braid swung heavily as her head snapped upward. "Do you believe me?" Eyes blazing with renewed hope, she probed Larisca's velvet gaze and recognized that the girl yearned to believe. But the effort required accepting that copper could be gold. Nicole pushed from the stump and spoke in a rush. "Please, I need help! Everything is so strange to me. If you can't accept my story, could you . . . could you pretend that it's true?" She pressed her lips and ignored Yuri's frown of disapproval. "Would you pretend I know nothing of your ways and . . . and help me?"

Uncertainly Larisca turned the suggestion in her mind. Pretending would strengthen the fantasy of court balls and fairy gowns and all the impossible enchantments of an unreachable world. "Like a game," she said finally. The novelty of the idea appealed, and her generous lips curved in a smile. "We'll pretend." She raised her face toward Yuri; then a sudden shadow dimmed the sunshine in her smile. "Katya is waiting," she murmured, lowering her face.

Nicole concealed her surprise at the abrupt alteration of tone and expression. But as Yuri guided them toward the end of the lane, she listened carefully as they spoke, and observed from the corner of her eye as Yuri and Larisca Janov avoided direct glances. They meticulously prevented an accidental brush of hands or clothing.

Sudden understanding positioned a dart of sorrow beneath Nicole's heart. Fate had acted capriciously with more lives than her own.

Acting on impulse, Nicole clasped Larisca's callused hand. The girl smiled a shy pleasure; then her smile faltered as she read the knowledge in Nicole's sad eyes. A blush heated her rounded cheeks and she dropped her head with a small shake of denial. She returned the pressure of Nicole's fingers, then pushed through the gate with a quickened step.

Yuri Janov swept his hat from his dark hair and his jaw knotted. "This is our home."

Nicole recognized the stubborn pride in his voice and posture. Yuri did not fully accept her story, but enough doubt prevailed that he offered the Janov hut with a hint of defensiveness.

"It . . . it's very nice," she murmured. And prayed the lie was not as obvious as it sounded to her own ear. She lowered her eyes from a planked roof and peeling log siding to examine a noisy family of scrawny chickens scratching near the steps. Yuri's *sohka* leaned against a wooden porch; she glimpsed additional farm tools between the legs of sheep wandering the enclosure at will. Recently shorn, the sheep appeared as naked and vulnerable as Nicole felt. Her jaw tightened and she firmed a tremulous chin. Someone, perhaps Louis Duchard, had once told her that one must accept what cannot be changed. "Very nice," she repeated faintly.

Inside, the hut smelled of generations of living. Nicole inwardly winced at the heavy blend of cabbage and groats, smoking animal fat and cooking wastes, old straw across the floor and the thick scent of too many people crowded into too little space. There was only one room.

Larisca leaned near her ear, assuming her role in the game "Cross yourself toward the *krasny ugolok*—use two fingers, in the old way."

Nicole drew an unsteady breath. "The *krasny ugolok*?" she hadn't learned this expression.

"The beautiful corner," Larisca whispered, phrasing it another way.

There was no beautiful corner. A quick glance determined one corner to be undistinguished; another housed a water barrel and a collection of household utensils. The *pech*, an enormous earthen oven, occupied the third corner. Choosing by elimination, Nicole blindly swung toward the remaining corner and awkwardly crossed her breast.

Wryly, she congratulated herself on choosing correctly. On the wall above a whitewashed table hung a battered long-handled ax and a fading icon of St. Nicholas. A sheaf of dried rye rested on a small shelf below the icon. Here the family ate, prayed, and entertained.

A harsh voice erupted near the *pech*. "Ulcers on my soul! Is this the best you could do?" Katya Janov fisted both chapped hands on wide shapeless hips. "She's skinny, pale as the first snow, and she isn't even Orthodox, even I can see that!" The eyes of an eagle narrowed in the weathered face of a hawk.

"*Matushka*, this is Nadia Stepan, my intended bride." Yuri met his mother's flashing eyes. "It's God's will."

Nicole involuntarily drew back as Katya marched forward to thrust a chunk of black rye and a chip of salt into her hands. Uneasily her wide eyes sought Larisca over Katya's massive shoulder. Larisca pointed to her lips. Nicole nodded imperceptibly and placed the salt chip on her tongue and bit into the bread. And stood as still as a stone while Katya circled her, lifting the gold braid, then pinching Nicole's upper arm, testing for muscle.

At the conclusion of the examination, Katya heaved a sigh which began inside her heavy wooden shoes and traveled upward toward her second-best headdress, a framed structure of embroidered red linen. "It's God's will," she muttered in a resigned voice. She stared darkly at Nicole. "Well, sit down, sit down." She waved toward the table and returned to the *pech*. "Tonight I feed you as a guest, Nadia Stepan; the day after tomorrow you take your place in the household." Reaching across the hearth, she attacked a large crock of simmering buckwheat groats, stirring the spoon with short resentful strokes.

Uncertainly Nicole approached the table. Larisca hastened to lay out wooden bowls and four wooden spoons. Yuri carried in an armload of firewood, then washed at the water barrel. Watching them, Nicole felt acutely conscious of her idle hands. Katya slammed a steaming earthenware tureen in the center of the table. Then Yuri solemnly seated himself at one end of the table and the women occupied the other, opening a space between themselves and the head of the house.

Yuri Janov bowed his head and offered a brief prayer; then he reached for a long hot loaf of dark sourdough bread. He positioned it upright and regarded the loaf with reverence before he broke it into chunks and extended the pieces toward the women. Katya ladled groats into the wooden bowls and Larisca passed a platter of salted cucumbers and sliced beets. As it was Friday, there was no meat in the pot. The church proscribed meat on Fridays and Wednesdays, a prohibition working little hardship in the village, as there was seldom meat on any day.

Katya chewed slowly and studied Nicole. "You aren't true Orthodox—what are you?"

"I was raised in the Protestant faith," Nicole answered. The groats balled in her mouth like lumps of glue.

They stared from blank faces. "Is Protestant another word for *Skoptsy*? That crazy bunch which castrates the men and carves out the women?"

Nicole choked. "*Nyet!* A Protestant believes . . ." She looked into their waiting eyes and knew they would think her mad. ". . . very much like the Orthodox." She didn't dare glance at the icon of St. Nicholas. Hastily she bent to spoon more groats into her mouth.

Katya considered this information. "Well, so long as you live in my house, you're Orthodox." That was that, in her mind.

Nicole nodded, accepting her conversion with a tiny sigh. She listened with half an ear as the Janovs scorned various sects. Her attention wandered about the single room as darkness settled beyond two small windows. A lighted wick inserted into an earthen saucer filled with smoking animal fat offered scant illumination beyond the table, but Nicole could identify shadowy sleeping shelves ringing the room.

And suddenly it required enormous strength not to bury her face in her hands and surrender to a storm of hopeless weeping. With all her aching heart she rejected her new destiny. Dimitri hovered behind her lids, and she saw his sensual mouth and strong chiseled face as clearly as she saw the totality of her loss. They had come so close to happiness! Something wrenched inside, dying in a spasm of despair and hopelessness. "Good-bye," she whispered silently, her grief a bleeding canker in her heart, "Good-bye, my love."

At the conclusion of the meal, Larisca cleared the scraps and tossed them outside for the chickens. She returned from the *pech* carrying wooden mugs of *kvas*, a near-beer made from bran, malt, flour, water, and the dried crusts of heavy rye bread. After the first startling sip, Nicole set her jaw and concluded she had tasted worse things. She lifted her head and forcefully sealed a mental door on all that had elapsed before this moment. Tormenting herself with memory would only make a hard life more unbearable.

Drawing a breath, she pasted a smile on her lips and posed a question to Larisca without looking toward Yuri. "Will your husband . . . Simeon, I think you said . . . will he join us later?"

A silence opened. Yuri turned his mug in damp circles on the table. "Simeon was recruited five years ago, part of the village quota." As Larisca appeared near her own age, Nicole calculated she had been married very young. "He's fighting the Turks. We don't know where."

Katya sighed heavily and shrugged. Her dark shift rustled across broad shoulders. "It's God's will."

The dim smoky light heightened a shy blaze of hope flaring Larisca's velvety eyes. "Nadia! I just thought! Can you read?"

Nicole ground her teeth at the strange, unfamiliar name. "*Da.*" She almost added "of course," but caught herself. Items and events she had regarded as givens could not be assumed here.

Larisca flew up from the bench and withdrew a folded page from her blouse. Fingers trembling, she leaned above Nicole and flattened a yellowing letter on the table top. "I received this four years ago." Her gentle eyes searched Nicole's face. "But no one in the village can read it."

When she gazed at the letter, Nicole's heart sank. She looked at them apologetically. "It's written in Russian. I can read only English and French." They stared from uncomprehending eyes. They knew nothing of England or France.

But Larisca understood the letter couldn't be read, it would remain a mystery. She passed a hand over her face, and a tiny bitter groan escaped her lips. She had difficulty relinquishing the brief flame of expectancy. Her shaking forefinger touched a sentence. "Here. This is Yuri's name, and this is mine. And here is Katya's." Her whisper was fierce, imploring, praying this small clue would aid Nicole in deciphering the page.

Nicole shook her braid helplessly. She too stared at the letter hoping it would miraculously reveal its message. Of course it did not. However, one enigma resolved itself when she examined the childlike scrawl at the bottom and realized it was not the same hand that had penned the body of the letter. Simeon Janov had dictated the page; he had not written it himself.

"I'm sorry," she stammered. "I wish I could read it . . . but I can't. Surely someone in all these years . . . your priest, maybe?"

A twist of bitterness chased the sunshine from Larisca's soft features. "Even if the priest were sober long enough to be trusted with my letter, he says he can read only Latin." She touched Nicole's shoulder heavily. "I'm sorry." Dark lashes feathered across her pale cheeks. "All these languages I've never heard of . . . and no one to read the words we speak every day. I just don't understand!" Shaking her glossy dark head, she sat hard and folded the letter back into her blouse, nestling it protectively against the firm fullness of her breast. Yuri studied his hands.

"I . . . It's God's will," Nicole responded weakly. Now she was doing it. How quickly one adopted the fatalism of the peasant.

They agreed soberly. Then Katya pushed from the table and pointed Yuri toward a stool beside the *pech.* "If you're to be married in the morning, you need a haircut." She dropped a wooden bowl over his short dark hair and tested a knife against her thumb.

Tomorrow. Nicole squeezed her eyes shut and her heart fluttered painfully. Would this miscarriage actually occur? She dropped pleading eyes from Yuri's carefully blank expression.

Beyond the window facing the lane, a flicker of torchlight caught her eye. A blend of women's voices lifted in a song titled "The Horn," a mournful melody regretting the lost freedoms of maidenhood. The tradition of centuries sang in the high lilting voices.

Katya glanced up from the bowl and nodded briskly to Larisca. "It's time to brush out her hair, the women are coming."

Nicole lifted imploring eyes to Larisca, clinging desperately to the fragile bond between them. Without the answering support promised in Larisca's eyes, she thought she would have leaped to her feet and fled into the night.

"There's nothing to fear," Larisca reassured her. Her strong capable fingers loosened Nicole's long braid, and she brushed the shower of gold around the quiver in Nicole's shoulders. And her eyes pained as she touched the silken tresses Yuri would soon stroke. No one spoke until Larisca clasped Nicole's hand. "It's time to go." She guided Nicole past Yuri and Katya and into the outer yard.

Nicole held tightly to Larisca, not knowing what to expect as the village women surrounded her. Flickering torchlight glowed through her hair, transmuting the flowing strands to spun gold and raising smiles of pleasure to the lips of those who lined the lane to watch. From every side the women's voices sang the ancient marriage laments. "How will you live among strange people?" The words echoed the grief pulsing through her heart. "How will you endure being ruined by a man?" They waved warning fingers toward her white face. "Don't expect your mother-in-law to issue orders nicely. She will howl at you like a wild beast, she will hiss at you like the snake in the field."

The steady pressure of Larisca's fingers reminded Nicole the chants were but a tradition stretching back into the caverns of time. But her heart hammered in her mouth and her pulse rang in her ears. She followed blindly where the women led.

They guided her to the village *bania*, a crude wooden shack unlike the splendor at Orienanbaum or St. Petersburg. Inside, the women stripped her clothing and ritually beat her clean with swinging birch twigs; then they rebraided her hair in a long shining length interwoven with colored ribbons. They sang her back to the Janov *izba*; then the voices and torches disappeared into the darkness.

Katya had unrolled straw pallets upon the sleeping shelves, and Nicole hastened into hers and turned her hot face to the wall, grateful for the blackness and the heavy silence. Scalding tears leaked from her lashes and ran unchecked down her cheeks. She grieved for the death of Nicole and Tasha, for the unbearable loss of a man with smoky eyes and a hard warm mouth. She did not know who she was or where she was, and the utter loneliness of dislocation shredded her inner spirit.

As the hours slipped silently past, measured by a bar of moonlight slowly retreating across the straw floor, she abandoned the effort to sleep. Restless rustlings from the pallet at her feet and the pallet near the *pech* confirmed that two others also found sleep impossible this night. Her heart flew toward them in kinship, and she ached with recognition of the pain they must be suffering. Sticks of straw crumbled in her fists. And Nicole imagined a cadre of brass angels scorning the folly of human hearts.

In the morning a dozen men escorted Nicole to the church in the South Village. They accepted her exhausted silence and red-rimmed eyes with good humor. "Weeping bride, laughing wife; laughing bride, weeping wife." Her downcast eyes and reluctant steps augured well for the marriage. One of the men circled the party, waving a mounted icon to ward off evil spirits. Nicole watched him through dulled eyes. She lived out the minutes of a surrealistic dream which contained elements of reality for everyone but herself.

Inside the church, the priest's droning words flowed over her like air blowing through a sieve. None registered within her numbed mind. She sensed the stranger beside her and understood the ceremony was very real and binding to Yuri Janov. She heard confirmation in his solemn resigned tone as he voiced the responses. And she wondered wildly at his acquiescence when she herself felt so far removed from the proceedings, protected by the insulation of alienation.

At the conclusion of the service, the priest placed a hand upon both their shoulders and turned them simultaneously. Had one turned before the other, the first to turn would be the first to die. Church and superstition had formed an amiable alliance.

Katya cleared her throat importantly. She marched down the aisle attired in her holiday finery. Beneath the critical eyes of the villagers, she loosened the bride's hair, then replaited it into two long twists, which she pinned into a triumphant coronet and then covered the married woman's coiffure with a matronly headdress.

The ceremony had ended. Everyone agreed the couple was properly wed.

The remainder of the afternoon passed in singing and dancing and feasting in the Janov yard. The village women brought gifts of food for a table groaning with steaming fish tarts, bowls of wild berries and mushrooms, hot cabbage stuffed with sausage, wheels of golden cheese, and tiers of rich dark bread. Platters of cucumbers appeared, and beets swimming in sour cream and blini and green onions and pickled vegetables and thick white rice cakes.

Music plucked from a variety of homemade instruments smothered the laughter and ribald jokes. Yuri opened the dancing by pulling Nicole into the center of the yard, where she stumbled through a whirling tzigane, tripping on the hem of her borrowed skirt as she struggled to follow the wild music and clapping hands. Then she and Yuri licked a salt cube together to ensure fertility, and someone pushed a small boy into her lap to guarantee strong healthy sons.

Nicole endured, watching through a miragelike haze. She responded only to the slow dying thud of her heart, recognized only the flaring embers of pain as Larisca and Yuri's eyes met, then fell away.

When the moon had risen high in an empty sweep of sky, Katya grasped Nicole by the hand and led her before Yuri. The bride knelt before the company and removed her husband's shoes, demonstrating her submissiveness, amid cheers of approval. As she slid the shoes from Yuri's feet, avoiding his embarrassed grin, she decided dully that she would have balanced upon her head had ritual demanded it. She did as they instructed, appeared where they pointed. She was a sleepwalker praying for release from the dream.

Then Larisca and the best man led the couple to the cow shed, where they would spend their first wedded night. The first joining would exert a fertile influence upon the watching cows.

Nicole stepped inside the shed and stared at the closing door. Whatever emotions wrung her soul, they were no more terrible than the agony swimming in Larisca's moist wounded eyes. For a moment they gazed at each other, understanding but helpless; then Larisca strangled a sob and softly closed and bolted the door.

Nicole swayed. She rubbed her hands over the chill in her arms, then inhaled a long shivering breath and stepped deeper into the shed. She raised a pale face to her husband.

16

THEY BALANCED ON milking stools, facing each other across a dim patch of moonlight falling past a gap in the thatched roof. Beyond the shed, the noise and laughter of drunken revelry continued unabated into the night. Two indifferent cows chewed lazily and occasionally opened soulful eyes and shifted weight.

When the silence became heavy and unbearably awkward, Yuri combed a hand through his short dark hair and cast Nicole a brief forced smile. "I always wondered what a man said to a woman on their wedding night."

Lowering her gaze, Nicole removed the new headdress and placed it in the straw near her feet. She rested her head against the planks at her back and directed her eyes toward the distant glitter of starlight showing past the gap in the roof. The night was sharp and chill. She wished she had accepted Larisca's offer of a shawl.

"Why?" she asked in a small voice. "Why are we here? Why did you agree to this?"

Yuri selected a stick of straw from the floor and spun it between his palms. He did not answer immediately. "Every nine years the village elders reapportion the land according to need. With Simeon in the army and Pa dead . . ." Embroidered linen rustled around a shrug. "We needed another adult in the household to keep as much of our land as possible. We'll still have to relinquish some."

Nicole studied his bent head. Starlight gleamed in the straight dark hair hugging his hidden face like a bowl. "Death or banishment." She dropped her lashes, strangling on the whisper. A devastating sense of finality slowly poisoned her hope. The gaiety beyond the walls sounded a jarring, discordant note. Voices laughed as one small soul shriveled and died. Her fingernails cut half-moons into her palms as she restrained an urge to jump from her stool and scream at the revelers to halt their foolish dancing and merrymaking—they celebrated a travesty, a mockery of fate. She released an aching breath. "There was another reason, wasn't there?"

When he didn't respond, Nicole sighed deeply and raised swimming eyes to the patch of starlight. The moment had arrived for true good-byes, for the last bittersweet release of dreams and memory. "I understand hopeless love. I think I know what you're feeling." The words tore upward from the bowels of despair.

And suddenly, without having planned it, she discovered herself speaking of Dimitri Denisov, the choking memories more for herself than an explanation for Yuri. And her lips framed Dimitri's name in a kiss of farewell. She remembered their first meeting and lovingly reconstructed the weeks aboard the *Kreml*. No small event was too insignificant to escape the funnels of memory. She spoke until the pale square of starlight had crossed their bare toes; she relived her happiness and her heartbreak and presented it from the perspective of loss.

When her voice faded into strangled silence, she lowered her gaze toward twisting fingers, and liquid diamonds hung in her lashes.

Yuri shifted his eyes to the dozing cows, and his thin chest expelled a quiet breath. Her confession elicited his own. "When Simeon first brought Larisca home, she was just a shy gangling girl." He rested his head against the wall, and faint light painted his features in hollow shadows, creating an illusion of great age and weariness. "Then Simeon left with the recruits, and the years passed. She matured into a beautiful woman." His jaw knotted. "She never complains. The fear and loneliness of those early years never passed her lips, but she must have missed Simeon in the beginning. She always awakens with a smile and a word of cheer. Never has she asked to return to her own village or family. She makes my life better just by being here."

Nicole squeezed her lashes and nodded dumbly. Dimitri had made her life better just by being there.

"For years I refused to acknowledge what was happening. I swore I loved her like a sister." Now ragged shards of pain deepened his tone. "Then one night . . . I couldn't sleep because . . . and I looked across the *izba* to where she lay, and she was awake too . . . and I saw in her wonderful eyes the same pain of longing that I felt in my own. It was wonderful, and it was terrible."

"Did you . . . ?"

He was shocked. "She's my brother's wife!"

"Katya knows," Nicole said quietly.

"She probably saw it before we did. When I understood that I . . . what I felt, everything changed. I can't be near her without wanting to . . . Christ! It hurts—in here." He tapped his chest. "I'm afraid to look at her or to talk to her, lest I dishonor my brother and her." He dropped his head into his hands, and his knotted knuckles pressed against his eyes. "*Matushka* told me privately that we couldn't go on like this, and she was right. She insisted I attend the auction. She thinks if I have a wife of my own, there will be less chance of . . . an accident . . . which we would all regret."

Nicole stared at the apron hem she pleated between her fingers. So much heartache. She grieved for Yuri and Larisca, for Dimitri and herself. For all the disconsolate souls who bound their hearts to the unattainable. The words "death or banishment" tolled a death knell in her ears. "Why me?" she asked in a scarcely audible voice. "Why did you choose me?"

His fingers dug at his temples. "God forgive me! You're slight and fragile . . . I thought maybe . . ."

Nicole recoiled in horror. But she understood. Her kindred heart understood and forgave. Hot silent tears rolled down her white cheeks and she dropped her head, surprised when she felt his arm slide around her shaking tunic. She had not heard him move his stool. "I've never been so alone in my life," she whispered.

"I know." A heavy sigh lifted his thin chest. "I know." Gently he guided her head to his neck and patted her heaving shoulders in long comforting strokes. "I'm sorry, Nadia. By all the saints, I'm sorry for what I hoped, and for . . . for everything."

She clung to his collar, sobbing until a wet patch spread beneath her cheek, until no more tears existed and her breath hitched in long burning shudders. Above her golden braids, he stared at the chill starlight and silently uttered his own good-byes. Then his arms tightened beneath her body and he carried her to a mound of fresh sweet hay. When he placed her on a white rectangle of linen, Nicole stared at his kneeling figure through wide damp eyes.

"We can't change our destiny. I can't be Dimitri and you can't be Larisca," he explained softly. "Who we are is God's will. But perhaps we can comfort each other." Almost timidly he opened her blouse and drew a quiet breath as her breasts spilled free. He gazed at the rounded perfection of moonlit ivory tipped with rose. Nicole turned her face to one side and closed her eyes, but his hand touched her wet cheek and guided her pale face toward his. "I'll never beat you or hurt you, Nadia."

"*Da*," she answered, her throat dry and closed. It had not entered her thoughts that he might. Yuri Janov was a gentle man; she sensed the basic goodness in his heart. He was a quiet, sensitive man of the soil. But she looked into his calm eyes and knew what would follow: a betrayal, an adultery. They each belonged to another. And yet . . . And yet the terrible emptiness of solitude drove them toward a closeness, toward a warm touch and a sympathetic presence.

Slowly he slid his blouse over his head, revealing a thin hairless chest. And she tried desperately not to think of crisp dark curls; but she did. And as her face brushed against the taut cords of wiry muscle banding his arms, she commanded herself not to remember hard bulging shoulders tight with sinew and power. But she did. Nicole moaned and covered her eyes with her arm.

She gasped as his callused palm cupped her breast and she experienced the rasping scratch of roughness against her soft tender flesh. He waited, then gently he lowered her arm and guided her hands to his neck. Her brimming eyes fastened to his pleading face and she read a need for warmth and acceptance as deep as her own. A small anguished cry burst past her lips as her arms circled his neck. They clung together in a fierce embrace, holding tightly to understanding and compassion.

When he quietly moved above her and entered her, the act lacked the urgency of passion. Their lovemaking was an expression of one sorrow reaching into another, a gentle caring instead of a yearning drive. They performed self-consciously, strange with one another, enacting a joyless ritual of obligation.

But when Yuri rolled away from her, he opened his arms and drew her head to his shoulder. The sharp outline of his collarbone pressed into her cheeks, and Nicole moved lower, seeking the firm hollow which pillowed her memory, but finding only the hard definition of ribs. She closed her lashes in a tight fringe. She and Yuri would never experience the raw animal urgency of physical magic, but somehow they had become friends in the last quiet moments. She felt the threads of sympathy between them as surely as she felt the crackle of straw bending beneath their combined weight.

Later, when the music and outside voices had lapsed into starry silence, he came to her again. And this time they were not embarrassed strangers. He unplaited her hair, scattering the ribbons across her breasts and bare legs. And he smiled as the shimmering waves of gold tumbled about her waist. He lifted a long curl and watched it twine around his finger, and Nicole realized he had never touched a woman's hair. Drawing a quiet breath, she folded her hands beneath her head and offered her slim body to his marveling eyes, smiling shyly as he traced the swell of her breasts with a trembling hand, then the gentle curve of her stomach, and finally the golden triangle between her thighs.

They explored each other slowly, without the haste of passion, whispering quiet words, guiding tentative fingers. They offered and timidly received the warm comfort and gentle pleasure each sought. And if they cried the wrong names in the final joyful moment of release, neither begrudged the other nor considered the error a betrayal. Eased at heart, they nested into the straw and slept.

If Nicole had feared the morning might erase their calm bond of companionship, the first full bar of sunshine dispelled her anxiety. Yuri stroked her cheek in shy gratitude; then he rose and quickly dressed. Without looking at her, he removed a dead chicken from inside a hinged bin, where tradition had placed it—to be used or not, at the husband's discretion. As Nicole hastily donned her borrowed blouse and tunic, Yuri slit a tiny incision between the chicken's breast feathers, and he dribbled a few drops of blood upon the white linen which had lain beneath them. No one would know for a certainty where the blood had originated. A flush of color blazed across Nicole's cheeks.

"Thank you," she whispered. "You're a good man, Yuri Janov." She settled the headdress upon newly plaited braids and murmured a prayer of thanks to the icon hanging above the cows. It could have been so much worse, so very much worse. She could have awakened to a hard slap from one of the fierce angry men she'd observed from the auction platform. A shudder rippled the dark tunic across her small shoulders; then she firmed her chin. "Are the ceremonies complete now?"

"They'll parade the linen through the village and you and I will be escorted to the *bania*." His dark eyes sobered with concern. "Then life returns to normal. Work and more work. Nadia . . . your story . . . it's true, isn't it?"

Nicole's features constricted. Eventually St. Petersburg and all it represented would recede from her thoughts, but not yet. Not yet.

Yuri's callused brown hands closed upon her shoulders. "Poor Nadia. From a princess to a peasant." The tale was so incredible that trailings of doubt continued to linger behind his eyes. "You'll find this life hard. Very hard."

Her chin lifted and she met his eyes squarely. "I'll survive," she promised softly. "I'm stronger than I appear."

He misunderstood. "I'm sorry for what I was thinking . . ."

"Please." She raised a finger to his lips. "It isn't that. I just don't want pity. I don't think either of us does." Pity was an emotion she couldn't tolerate. She rejected an excuse to cling to the past. If she was to survive, she had to forget the existence of any life but this one. She ground her teeth and vowed to accept what she could not alter. She would do whatever was necessary to endure.

Outside, the wedding guests yawned to life and picked themselves from benches and piles of straw. Soon a cacophony surrounded the shed as shouts lifted above a persistent banging on the bottoms of earthenware pots.

"Ready?" Yuri asked, lightly touching her shoulder. At Nicole's determined nod, he rapped sharply on the door, then stood aside as the bolt slid back. He thrust the bloodied linen through the crack and an elated cheer rose toward the heavens.

The guests ran the linen up a pole and marched it triumphantly before the bride and groom as the couple was led

208

to the village *bania*, where they bathed together before being paraded back to the Janov *izba*.

And Nicole's heart shrank from the anguished sight of Larisca's empty smile.

As the days blended monotonously into weeks, Nicole conceived a sorrowing admiration for Larisca and Yuri Janov. They were forced to share the limited confines of one small room; they slept an arm's reach from one another. They ate at the same table, washed from the same barrel. And did so without a single accidental brush, without a solitary impulsive word. Unless one carefully examined the tortured drop of glances, no one would have suspected the tormented longing and ache of loss lying below the surface.

However, there were moments when the hurt flamed into evidence. On those infrequent occasions when Yuri's body demanded release and he led his wife by the hand to the shed, then Nicole bit her lip hard and avoided Larisca's staring eyes. Larisca's chalky frozen smile was too agonizing to bear observation.

For days following the visits to the shed, Larisca sat over her letter as if her need would decipher the words, and she buried herself in the acid catharsis of labor. Long after Nicole and Katya and Yuri had dropped in exhaustion on their pallets, Larisca worked beside a single flaring wick. She labored until her spine snapped and her hands chapped raw and red. And the *izba* reverberated with the white ache of unfulfilled yearnings and unspoken words.

Nicole seized upon Larisca's example and submerged her own painful memories in work. She learned the unique rhythms of village patterns and a woman's place in them. And a crushing fatigue seeped into her bones which she believed would remain there forever.

In October the village men hitched their horses to sagging wooden carts and devoted most of the month to chopping firewood in the distant *taiga*, then returned the logs to the village to be split and stacked. When the winter's supply overflowed the yards, they climbed over their *izby* with axes and wooden nails, repairing, tightening, sealing the cracks against a sharp chill the sun could no longer vanquish.

The women mixed mud and manure for chinking, and stirred great steaming vats of *kvas*, filling, then storing the barrels beside the *izba* doors, where they could easily be dug out when the snows came. Nicole and Larisca put up crocks of sauerkraut, stuffed the entrails of pigs and sheep with spicy winter sausage, stored wheels of cheese and baskets of beets beneath the hut in the cellar. They cleaned the ash from the *pech* and dipped fat tallow candles in preparation for the winter holidays. The chores were endurable only because of Larisca's encouragement and constant good humor. In Larisca's view, there was no task without an enjoyable aspect, and it was this she keyed upon.

"*Da*, the manure lodges beneath the fingernails." Larisca laughed, leaning over the tub with Nicole. "But think how good it will feel when we're finished!" Her velvet eyes caught the autumn sunshine. "And how snug the *izba* will be all winter."

Nicole envied the ability. There were days she felt too tired to swallow, when only Katya's sharp tongue drove her to lift the spoon to her lips and to chew the heavy dark bread.

"You must eat," Katya warned from the *pech*. She ladled extra helpings of *kasha* and cabbage into Nicole's wooden bowl, then shook the drippings into the hearth to nourish the house spirits. "We'll put some meat on your bones before summer!"

Nicole wearily eyed Katya's fluidly efficient movements and despaired that she would ever learn to make each motion serve in place of two. Sighing, she tore her bread into chunks and bit into it. She ate a pound of bread a day, like the others, but no additional weight fleshed out her slender curves. The grinding daily labor burned the food as quickly as she consumed it.

Near October's end a gray curtain drew steadily across the sweep of cobalt sky, and the temperature plunged alarmingly. When Nicole or Larisca stepped onto the porch to gauge the clouds' progress, their breath plumed outward in a silvery mist.

And then, two days later, great cold puffs of white lace drifted toward the earth, falling in lazy spirals against upturned faces. Smiling ruefully, Nicole joined the joyful rush into the lane, shivering beneath the folds of Larisca's dark woolen shawl as she observed the villagers dancing in the street. Children caught the snowflakes upon their tongues with squeals of delight, and adults nudged one another with gleeful winks as if they had never witnessed such a wonder.

Nicole tightened the shawl about her shoulders and gazed toward the fields slowly disappearing behind a thickening veil of white. And she recalled Pavla, dear Pavla, once claiming magic existed in the first snow. Watching as the snow frosted the *izby* and transformed the village squalor into sparkling freshness, Nicole sighed and admitted there was indeed a magic in the sight.

But her heart wrenched beneath the folds of the shawl. The damp crystals drifting soft and chill against her cheeks and hair signaled the final dissolution of what she now recognized had been a tiny kernel of hope. Winter settled over Russia like a cold tight shroud, locking the inhabitants within flimsy manmade barriers—hidden from sight and contact. No one would ever find her. If anyone was seeking her. No, she could not bear to whisper his name. Finally her heart admitted what her head had long known.

Nicole returned to the *izba* with slow, disheartened steps. She hunched above a mug of heated *kvas*, her golden braids bowed, and she remained silent as neighbors crossed themselves before the *krasny ugolok*, then toasted the winter with cries of pleasure and delight. The time of idleness had arrived; they welcomed the snow like a cherished lover too long absent.

Larisca's arm slid about Nicole's shoulders. "Come join us," she urged, her soft eyes worrying over Nicole's pale dejection. When Nicole shook her head, Larisca kissed her cheek and slipped away. She understood which sorrows were not to be intruded upon.

Within a week Nicole learned that the scant illusion of idleness did not apply to the women. The bailiff trudged through knee-deep drifts to visit the villages, distributing material to be woven for the master before the spring thaws returned the villagers to the fields.

"Twelve *arshines* from each of you," the bailiff instructed briskly, and admonished them to produce quality goods, before he vanished into the wet cold of a fresh storm, his sheepskin cap sunk near the collar of a warm *tulup*.

Nicole eyed a mountain of raw material with a sinking heart. "How much is an *arshin*?" she queried in dismay.

"I forget you don't know these things." Larisca smiled. She extended her palms to approximately thirty inches. "This is one *arshin*." Velvety eyes laughed at Nicole's gasp. "We have all winter. And it isn't so bad—the women gather and tell stories while we work. They all want to hear your story." A rough hand patted encouragement. "We'll finish in time and have a week or so to make ourselves new tunics and maybe some linens to sell in Penza."

Nicole sighed and applied her energies to a birch-twig

broom. The work never ceased. She could not envision how they could complete the goods demanded by the master with any time remaining to fill their own needs. Yuri's work blouse was a collection of patches on patches; Larisca's skirt was deplorable. Her own gathering of village hand-me-downs wasn't fit for the rag pile. The arduous hours ahead weighed heavily, and she expelled a discouraged breath. But then, perhaps the relentless work roster was not as appalling as it appeared. She knew what Larisca claimed: work swept the mind free; thoughts were too weary to ponder disturbing issues.

Late in November Yuri finished the evening meal and waved aside his mug of *kvas*. He didn't select one of the blocks of wood becoming soup bowls or ax handles beneath the skill of his knife. Instead he looked a steady question toward Nicole, and she lowered her head as a stain of crimson rushed upward from her throat. Without a word, she turned from the tub of dirty dishes and shrugged into a *tulup*, removing the heavy sheepskin coat from a peg near the door. She followed Yuri down the path he had shoveled to the cow shed. Her fingers tingled within the mittens Larisca had given her at the door, and the pain in Larisca's pale smile remained behind her eyes.

Inside the shed, Yuri lit a wick in a saucer of animal fat and stamped the snow from his winter *lapti*. He sat on a milking stool and tugged at the laces ending just below his knees. When the shoes were kicked off, he sighed, expelling a mist of cold cloudy vapor, and he wriggled his toes, hoping the simple pleasure would coax a smile to Nicole's shivering lips.

He watched as she spread a thick blanket over the straw, and his voice was gentle when he spoke. "If you're too tired . . . ?" He studied the weary slope of her shoulders, the dark smudges beneath her blue eyes.

"*Nyet*," Nicole answered softly. Quickly she removed her own bark *lapti*; then she slid beneath the blanket, her teeth chattering in the cold. Outside, snow fell in a steady thick curtain. Large drifts nearly touched the low eaves of the shed. Soon they would need the snowshoes Yuri had carved, in order to fetch water from the well and to tend the animals. The paths shoveled by the men drifted over faster than they could keep pace.

Yuri stepped from his trousers and dived beneath the blanket. He gathered Nicole into his arms and they huddled closely, drawing upon each other's warmth. Each tacitly acknowledged this would be their last visit to the cow shed until spring; in another week the deep cold would be prohibitive. And it was unthinkable to indulge more than a smile within the *izba*. Neither could have borne Larisca's small brave expression.

"We haven't talked recently," Yuri murmured against her hair. "Are you feeling well?" He would not take her greedily, as his instincts urged. He would wait until they were easy with one another, until the cold needles of straw warmed beneath their bodies. Closing his eyes, he inhaled the wintry fragrance of her hair.

"*Da.*" Nicole pressed her face into his warm neck. He was too thin; she traced his ribs beneath her cold fingertips. Yuri Janov lacked the barrel-chested stockiness of most peasant men; nature had played the trickster, giving him the slender ascetic build of a scholar. She suspected his wiry physique prompted him to avoid the nightly brawls in the village *kabak*, where the men gathered for a glass of vodka and a companionable pipe. And often released their frustrations and disappointments in an eruption of fists and ax handles.

Yuri's character preferred the more tranquil atmosphere of the Janov *izba*. He spent the winter evenings carving utensils. And occasionally he could be persuaded to spin yarns about the great bears tracked in the *taiga*, or he might relate legends whose history stretched into a far ancestral past. Not for the first time, Nicole silently grieved for Yuri's ignorance. The waste was appalling. Yuri's strong intelligent mind would have gathered spiritual nourishment from the printed thoughts of the world's great thinkers. He would have quietly exulted in recognizing many of his own ideas expressed and shared by others.

He lifted her hand from his chest and rubbed a thumb across her palm, smiling to himself. "Calluses. I remember when this little hand was as soft as new butter." They lay together in comfortable silence. "Do you miss the other life, Nadia? St. Petersburg?" He carefully avoided naming Dimitri; they had not mentioned Dimitri or Larisca since their wedding night. Quietly he answered his own question. "Of course you do. Who would willingly choose this life? You were created for something better."

Smiling at the compliment, Nicole burrowed deeper into the warmth of his arms, but her mind traveled backward. In St. Petersburg the winter season would be well launched with

opulent balls every night and theater parties and grand ban-
quets. Elegant little sleds would flash along the frozen Neva,
transporting nobles in beaver hats and ladies swathed in rich
furs. She responded slowly to Yuri's question, thinking it
through.

"No . . . I don't miss St. Petersburg." She fought the persistent image of teasing silver eyes. "But I miss home," she
continued, surprised at the statement but recognizing the
truth. "Sometimes I miss Boston so badly I hurt inside,"

More and more frequently her thoughts seemed to dwell
on New England and the warm security of Louis Duchard's
modest brick house. The concept of home tugged a sore
heart. She would have traded ten years of her life for a single
glimpse of Marie and Louis Duchard. Varina, Elizabeth—
they were shadowy ghost figures; the Duchards were her
parents, her roots. In their care she had never questioned her
identity or her purpose. Her arms tightened about Yuri's
neck, and she hid her face against his warm skin. New England was as lost as St. Petersburg.

"Are the winters severe in New England?"

The Janovs never tired of listening to her remembrances of
New England. Again and again they queried Nicole as to the
validity of her astonishing claims. They could not envision a
land without peasants to till the soil, a land where every man
could own the ground he worked. New England was the
promised land, heaven across the sea.

Nicole traced the firm line of his jaw. "Must we discuss
that now?" she whispered. Knowing this would be their last
visit to the shed elicited a surprising regret. She would never
love Yuri as she loved Dimitri Denisov, with fire and breath-
snatching passion, but her affection and respect for him ran
deep. And the pleasures in this life of hardship were few; the
brief hours of warmth and sharing and quiet tenderness were
moments to treasure.

His voice roughened and his lips found the sweet pale hollow of her throat. "Later," he murmured. The intense cold
had prevented them from disrobing, but she felt the heat of
his palm penetrate the coarse cloth covering her breasts, and
then his fingers raised her skirts and he covered her with the
length of his body. He smiled gently and brushed a honey-
colored tendril from her cheek. "You've made a good wife,
Nadia Janov."

"Worth one chicken?" she teased, tugging the hair falling
over his eyes.

"At least two chickens," he replied. But a sadness sobered his jest.

Then he kissed her eyes and the corner of her mouth, his touch as soft as the falling snow. And he entered her quietly, moving to a slow stroking rhythm, his eyes caressing her face as he watched to ensure he provided the same pleasures he received.

Nicole raised her hips as his thrusts quickened, and she cupped his narrow face between her palms. And when he had spent himself, she cradled his dark head upon her shoulder and stroked his back until his breathing returned to a normal cadence. The smell of warm straw and sleeping cows and the snow-fresh scent of his straight hair filled her nostrils. She rested her cheek against his head in drowsy contentment. Outside the shed, a curtain of white drifted across the darkness; tiny puffs of vapor misted their lips. This was not the man her heart longed for, but as the long winter months wore on, she knew she would miss the private hours in the shed. The sharing moments with this man, her quiet gentle husband.

They kissed at the door and closed it behind them until spring.

Larisca, too, sensed the occurrence of the last visit to the shed. The sunshine returned to her lovely pale face, pleasing them all, and her velvety dark eyes resumed their radiant glow. Nicole and Katya depended upon Larisca's good humor to lessen the burdens of the grueling workload. And influenced by Larisca's gentle teasing, the trek to the well became not a clumsy floundering hardship, but an excuse to enjoy the sharp crisp frost in the air, to install roses in house-bound cheeks. Embroidering the master's linens was transformed from a disagreeable drudgery into an opportunity for pride in the skills of the needle. With unflagging good cheer, Larisca unerringly pinpointed the silver edge to every cloud.

"Find the silver in this cloud if you can!" Katya challenged, grumbling from the *pech*. She threw a narrowed glance over her wide shoulder toward the table where Nicole and Larisca bent above the hems of petticoats fit for royalty. Their needles flashed above the material, and occasionally they amused each other by describing the imagined ladies who would wear their creations. "Two days until Christmas, and every man in the village is down at the river instead of helping with the preparations! Ulcers on my soul!"

Prince Repinsky planned a holiday extravaganza for the

neighboring aristocrats, and every able-bodied man above the age of twelve had been commandeered from the villages. Two hundred and thirty-eight men assembled each morning on the frozen banks of the Moksha. They began in the frigid predawn hours and labored until the last chill rays of winter sun vanished.

As the week progressed, a snow carnival had sprung from the riverbanks. Ice sculptures of giant bears and wolves and prancing horses as high as the tallest *izba* lined a quarter-mile stretch of the river, which had been meticulously swept free of loose snow to create a skating rink. At one end, a glittering pavilion had been painstakingly constructed from heavy blocks of carved ice. It would house a forty-piece serf orchestra to provide music for the skaters. At the opposite end, an enormous snow slide complete with a train of handcrafted sleds had been built for the entertainment of the nobles' children. Jugglers were expected, and clowns and a trained bear. It was rumored that diamonds and emeralds would be awarded as prizes for the best skaters and the winners of the troika races.

Larisca glanced up from her needle and smiled. "The preparations are well in hand, *Matushka*. Yuri caught the fish for Christmas Eve dinner a week ago; we have plenty of firewood." The fish waited in a box on the porch, frozen as solid as granite by nature. "I miss him too, but . . ." Her head dropped concealing her expression. "But Yuri says they are creating a wonderful spectacle by the river." Her head tilted and she winked at Nicole. "Wouldn't you like to see it?"

Nicole dropped her sewing into her lap. "Oh, yes! *Matushka!* Could we? Could we go see it?"

Katya poked at her steaming pots. Most of the holiday cooking was complete, the *izba* boasted fresh straw on the floor and a new coat of whitewash on the table. And she was curious too. Her eagle eyes mellowed and she allowed herself to be persuaded. "One of you hitch the horse to the sledge."

With cries of pleasure, both girls pushed their arms into the heavy sheepskin *tulups*. Nicole hurriedly laced her *lapti*, and Larisca produced their kerchiefs and the fox-fur caps Yuri had tanned for them.

They reined the horse well below the frozen watering pond, and trudged through drifts of snow toward a line of women and children who had also appeared to examine the project taking their men from the *izby*.

Larisca clapped mittened hands. "Oh, look! It's wonderful!"

Indeed it was. A fairyland spread before their wide eyes. Nicole gaped in astonishment at the towering snow sculptures and the magnificent lacy ice pavilion. The structures glittered a crystal blue in the dwindling sunlight. The day after tomorrow, children would shriek laughter down the slide, fur-clad skaters would spin and glide across the ice, and dashing troikas would race past the crimson flags dotting the river course. A fairyland for nobles.

"Wonderful? Three men die and more suffer frostbite, and you think its wonderful?"

They swiveled to inspect the speaker, Anashula Verenski. The woman stood with arms crossed upon her breast, her stony eyes as hard as the ice below them.

"Who died?" Katya demanded. She filed a mental note to castigate Yuri for being too exhausted to relate all the news.

"Marya Hamka's husband died beneath a block of ice, and two men from the South Village. My Molka will lose two toes and a finger. Is that wonderful?" Anashula Verenski turned bitter eyes upon Katya. The line of women listened in silence. "Marya Hamka has two babies and carries the third in her belly. Who will plow her fields? Who will feed the little ones?"

"I didn't know this," Katya responded grimly.

"Better the ice blocks crush that bastard the prince than fall on our men!" Anashula's mended mitten waved. "All this for a single afternoon! Three men dead, and a dozen too crippled to pull a plow!"

Katya's eagle eyes sharpened. "Such talk will earn you stripes on your back. Hush!"

Anashula Verenski's eyes blazed. "How long, Katya Janov? How long will we remain slaves? I say *volia!* Let the revolution come! *Volia!*"

The woman stared; some sucked shock into their lungs, others nodded agreement behind tight stares. *Volia* translated loosely as "having one's way." It was a destructive concept of freedom—the freedom to burn, to pillage, to plunder the countryside.

Katya rejected such inflammatory ideas. She issued a warning through pinched lips before she stamped through the snow to the Janov sledge. "A revolution eats its own children, Anashula. Remember that. And afterward, conditions are harsher than before. Nothing is gained."

"But it will come," Anashula predicted bitterly. A frosty

edge of desperation cracked her tone as she transferred her stare to the glistening marvel gracing the riverbanks. "It must come!"

Christmas dinner was marred by Yuri's dull-eyed fatigue and by the sober unrest in Katya's astute eyes. She shaped the cross of grain beneath the tablecloth with her own hands, slapping away Larisca's offer to help. And Katya herself served the Christmas *kresty*, golden crosses of baked bread. Nicole and Larisca observed their mother-in-law's uncharacteristic silence with concern, attributing the distracted scowls to her grief for Marya Hamka and the fatherless children.

When they seated themselves before the roast fish, Katya usurped Yuri's prayer and voiced fervent pleas for peace, lifting imploring eyes to the icon of St. Nicholas. Then Yuri cast a handful of precious grain upon the table and pronounced the Christmas litany: "Health to all men, to the cows and to the sheep and to all the animals in the sea and sky!"

Later, the village young people caroled from *izba* to *izba*, singing songs invoking a plentiful harvest and wealth and luck. They crowded the Janov hut with laughter and fresh snow and songs honoring Yuri as head of the household. Nicole and Larisca passed refreshments and Yuri scattered grain over the carolers' snowy caps before they departed for the neighboring *izba*.

Then it was time for the traditional casting of fortunes for the new year, and they looked to Katya expectantly. But Katya occupied her chair stiffly, staring into the flames crackling within the *pech*. She refused to toss the grain on the painted squares. Katya Janov did not wish to gaze into the future.

17

JAGGED LINES SPLINTERED the surface of the Moksha. Tongues of forked lightning shot across the ice, accompanied by heavy groaning and sudden loud cracks. The loosened floes ground together and sprouted upward in glistening needles of blue-white crystal before the currents swirled them away.

The spring thaw arrived with startling abruptness. Nicole would have believed it impossible had she not witnessed the event with her own eyes. One day, heavy white blanketed the fields; a week later, all traces of snow had vanished and vigorous new life burst from the earth. The countryside blossomed with tiny wildflowers; tender green shoots sprang up in the fields.

A copious runoff transformed the lane into a muddy bog, and the village men sank logs in the street to facilitate walking and riding. The bailiff collected the master's woven goods, and later, Yuri drove the cart to Penza to sell the women's additional handiwork, produced as Larisca had predicted. The money went for taxes, as did many of the Janov's spring animals. Those animals not owed the master as his right were seized by the bailiff in payment against an unpaid balance of taxes. The remaining deficit was added to the Janov debt, a staggering total which reached backward into generations.

Nicole stood wide-legged in the lane, her ankles sunk in mud and her fists clenched on her hips. She glared resentment as the bailiff collected animals from each *izba*, then drove them past the watering pond and toward the bridge over the Moksha, leading toward the master's manor. She couldn't see the manor house from the village, but she could imagine it, a splendid pillared mansion sheltered between two gently rolling hills.

"It isn't fair!" she exploded bitterly when Yuri and Larisca appeared at her side. "I helped birth that calf, I saved his life! That calf is mine! And the new sheep are yours, Yuri, and the chickens belong to Larisca!"

Gently Yuri cupped his roughened hands around her shoulders and studied the flushed face blazing up at him. "Nadia," he said quietly, "nothing belongs to us. Not the *izba*, or the fields, or the animals. We have the use of them, that's all."

She concealed angry tears behind a shaking hand. "Well, it isn't fair! That calf wouldn't be alive today if it wasn't for me. No one should have the right to take him!" The calf's birth had seemed a miracle to her; she'd made the mistake of making a pet of him.

A warm arm slid about her waist, and Larisca brushed a flying tendril of gold beneath Nicole's dark kerchief. "This is how it has always been." She pressed her cheek to Nicole's, and the steady pressure of her arm directed Nicole into the yard. "It's God's will."

Nicole flung out an arm. "Do you believe that? Do you believe God wills the plunder of our animals, our weaving, our grain?"

Resignation registered upon the two faces watching her distress. Yuri fumbled for an answer, exchanging a glance with Larisca. Finally he shrugged and tugged at his cap. "That's how it's always been."

"But that doesn't make it right! Don't you ever want to refuse?" Her shoulders slumped in discouragement. No one refused in Russia; individuality earned the knout.

Larisca pressed Nicole's hands and drew her toward the porch. "Don't think about this. It's Shrovetide! The last celebration before Lent. And then nothing but sober faces and prayers and work." She attempted to frame a sad face, and the expression was comical on sunny features designed for smiles and song.

Despite herself, Nicole joined Yuri's burst of laughter, and Larisca frowned at them, then added her gaiety to theirs, pleased to have lifted Nicole's sour mood. She directed Nicole inside and dispatched Yuri to the shed; their preparations for the holiday were not yet complete.

While Yuri hitched the horse to the cart, the women worked at the *pech*, fashioning dishes to symbolize the returning spring sun. They heaped platters with blini, small round pancakes, and fried two dozen eggs, discarding those with broken yolks.

During the ride to the cemetery they scattered the blini along the roadside, and twice they halted so Katya could fling lark-shaped cakes into the fields. Katya thrust her arms wide and cried, "Fly to the fields and bring health! First to the cows, second to the sheep, and third to man!" Katya insisted no ritual be overlooked; such a blunder courted disaster. She ordered Nicole and Larisca into the Janov land strips to spread a white cloth and present the remaining lark cakes. Larisca delivered the standard invocation with a smile. "This gift is for you, Mother Spring, smile upon us." Then she and Nicole skipped back to the waiting cart, singing bird calls to each other amid outbursts of laughter, and consequently earning Katya's hawk-faced disapproval.

At the cemetery they joined friends and neighbors, calling soft greetings as they placed their fried eggs upon the graves of loved ones. Many new mounds pocked the earth; the winter had been harsh. The Janovs arranged their eggs, then hurried back to the village for the bonfires and dancing, the last spurt of merrymaking until the traditional three-day drinking spree at Easter.

In late April the field work resumed in earnest. The women bid Yuri good-bye before dawn, watching as he pushed his *sohka* into the cart; then they prepared the day's food before they trudged two miles to the threshing barn. There they threshed the grain to be used for sowing. Before supper they hoed manure into their kitchen garden, and by May the vegetables were planted both in the square behind the *izba* and in the Janov cabbage patch in a low damp plot near the river.

Nicole had never felt as bone-weary in her life. Once the seasonal duties were completed, the daily chores remained. The animals had to be watered and fed, eggs gathered, cows milked. Fresh water for cooking and washing had to be fetched in heavy buckets from the well, and the food prepared and cleaned up, and the *izba* aired and straightened, and fresh straw added to the floor and to the sleeping pallets.

Though the weather warmed considerably, Yuri exhibited no haste in summoning her to the shed, a thoughtfulness for which Nicole was deeply grateful. She was asleep each night before her tired head settled into the straw.

In June the village granted itself a holiday to celebrate the day of St. John Kupalo. The hemp and flax were in the ground, the barley and buckwheat sown. A collective sigh of relief expanded weary chests. The men passed the holiday crowding into the *kabak*, dancing, drinking vodka, and playing *gorodki*, a game much like skittles. The women packed lunch baskets and drove the carts to the *taiga* to rummage for herbs on the forest floor. The older women announced the herbs were now at their height of medicinal potency.

Nicole rested her spine against the trunk of a wide larch and released a sigh of pleasure as she opened a cloth in her lap containing a loaf of thick dark bread, cheese, pickles, and salted cucumbers. The day was a sinful luxury. Content, she closed her eyes and delighted in the fresh sparkling air and the spicy scent of pine needles matted beneath her body.

"Are you falling asleep?" Larisca smiled. She poured two containers of *kvas* and curled Nicole's limp fingers around a mug.

Nicole returned the smile. "When *Matushka* promised we could sleep until six, I felt like kissing her!" Her smile turned

221

rueful. "But I woke at four-thirty as always and couldn't get back to sleep." She made a face.

Larisca laughed. "Tomorrow morning you'll kick yourself, wishing you'd slept today." She swept off her headdress and shook out skeins of glossy black hair. "It's so peaceful here! I wish we could come more often . . . but then, who would do the work?"

They sipped their *kvas* in companionable silence, lazily listening as the older women loudly debated the qualities of various herbs. After a time Larisca rolled onto her stomach and withdrew her letter from her blouse, smoothing it on the bed of pine needles. She cupped rounded cheeks within her palms and stared at the letter.

"Isn't there anyone . . . ?" Nicole bit her tongue. They had discussed the subject innumerable times before. There was no one. She folded their lunch scraps into a basket and drew her knees up under her chin. "Do you think he's still alive—your husband?"

Larisca stared at the letter. "If he isn't . . . it would be such a cruel travesty . . ." A flush of color spread over her cheeks and her jaw tightened as if the words had slipped out unintended.

Nicole hastened to breach the sudden awkward pause between them. "What is he like?"

Larisca replaced the letter with a resigned sigh and then stretched on her back, gazing upward toward white puffs of cloud drifting above the treetops. "Five years is a very long time," she replied at length. "I try to remember Simeon at night sometimes, or when I'm in the fields, but . . . I can't bring his face into focus anymore." She frowned in concentration, ashamed of the admission. "He was an inch or two shorter than Yuri, I remember that. And I think Simeon's eyes were darker than Yuri's. But I'm not certain anymore. He wasn't as thin." She continued speaking, searching the drawers of memory and discovering the contents faded beyond repair.

Nicole bowed her head, experiencing a familiar sorrow as Larisca unconsciously described Simeon in terms of Yuri. She withdrew a sprig of mint from her sack and pressed it flat against her knee. Then she closed her lids and tried to recall the pattern of the veins in the leaf.

Failing, she tilted her head backward and gazed at the sky. She understood Larisca's dismay. No matter how tenaciously Nicole clung to her own memories, she could no longer recall

Dimitri's chiseled profile with true clarity. She knew his wonderful eyes were a silvery gray, but the exact shade eluded her; she could no longer visualize the hard sensual line of his mouth or the confident elegance of his stride. And the loss sickened her.

But she loved him, and that would never fade. Her love remained a sweet constant pain which was with her always. Disturbed, she packed the lunch basket in the cart and followed the women deeper into the forest, but the pleasure of the day had vanished.

Following a relaxed supper, the first in weeks, Yuri shyly clasped Nicole's hand and led her to the *izba* door. Neither dared a glance toward Larisca's tiny sad smile or watched as she transferred her gaze to a distant point in space.

Inside the shed, Yuri gathered Nicole into his arms and held her tightly before his lips brushed her forehead. "You're upset tonight," he observed, examining her pale face. "Would you like to talk first?"

Nicole felt the months of abstinence straining against her body and knew she could not refuse him. She bit her lip. Besides, it wouldn't be fair to burden him with the memories of another man, indistinct memories which blackened her mind with confusion and loss. She drew a soft breath and forced her mouth into a curve. "We'll talk later."

Yuri's dark eyes glowed. He carried her to the mound of hay and drew her into his arms, holding her fiercely. "God in heaven, but I've missed you! The winter never seemed so long!" Closing his eyes, he pressed her soft form along the length of his body as if memorizing the imprint of firm breasts and slender hips. His hands moved with trembling eagerness, stroking her golden hair, her cheeks, the tiny hollow pulsing in her throat.

After helping her to sit up, he tugged her tunic over her hair, gasping as full creamy breasts spilled into his palms. "My God," he whispered hoarsely, and his dark head bent to kiss the ripe flaring nipples. "You are so beautiful!"

Nicole closed her eyes and bit off a moan, hearing another man's deep murmur in her inner ear, trembling to another man's skilled fingers teasing along the silkiness of her thighs. Yes, the winter had been long. And suddenly she needed a man with a desperation which frightened her. She craved the straining urgency of two bodies wild with exertion and desire, yearned for the fiery rapture of a soaring violent release. She kicked free of her skirts and urged Yuri to hasten as he

223

fumbled at the string of his summer trousers. Then her arms circled his neck, and she pulled him into the straw as his lips covered hers and she arched her pale slim body.

But fire and mind-sweeping passion were not qualities prized by a gentle man. Although Nicole felt Yuri's swelling need, he acted without hurry, stroking her golden skin and softly kissing her breasts and stomach until she thought she would scream. Her nails dug against her palms as her hands clenched into fists. A silent plea of frustration turned acid on her tongue, begging for the blissful pain of a man's punishing demands.

When Yuri entered her gently, with characteristic consideration, she believed the stab of disappointment would kill her. Beneath his tender stroking, her body quivered with a deep urgency to leap and plunge and fight and thrust. Tears stung her eyes. Her fists beat against her hips and she battled the urge to strike out, to inflict pain if she could not incite the fire and fury of unbridled passion.

When he lay beside her, his narrow chest gradually slowing, Nicole flung an arm over her eyes, hiding the bitter disappointment she did not want him to observe. A cool evening breeze flowed through the cracks in the shed, drying the moisture on her skin. But she continued to burn with an inside fire. And recognized with a groan of despair that only one man could quench the flames. And that one man was lost forever.

Yuri lifted on an elbow and stared down into her hidden face. His short straight hair ended above his brows in damp strands. "Did I hurt you?" he inquired anxiously.

And Nicole lowered her hands to smother the small desperate sound pressing hysterically behind her lips. "*Nyet*," she choked. Tonight she would have welcomed a man's bruising kisses, his crushing embraces. She stared into Yuri's concerned frown, then dropped her eyes.

"Nadia . . . what's troubling you?"

"I . . . Larisca can't remember Simeon's face!" The blurted confession erupted from deep within, unplanned and instantly regretted.

He stared into her stricken eyes, and his face sobered in painful understanding. He lay back on the straw and folded his hands beneath his head. "I see," he responded quietly.

Nicole buried her face in her hands. One of her braids pulled loose and swung to her waist. Hot tears flowed between her fingers. "Oh, Yuri, forgive me. I've hurt you, and

I'm sorry!" She pressed the end of the braid against her eyes. "I don't know what's wrong tonight. Most of the time I'm too tired to think about anything, but sometimes I . . . sometimes I look around me and I realize this is all my life will ever be! Everything else is lost. And I don't know if I can bear this . . . this . . . mix-up of people and things and . . . and . . ." Regret and embarrassment turned her face aside as he pulled on his trousers, then silently extended her skirt and tunic.

Once begun, the river of words tumbled unbidden from her pale lips. "There must be more to life than endless work! And it's not even for our own profit! Yuri, there's a whole world out there! Filled with wonderful sights and people!" Her lashes met her cheeks so tightly they ached. "I think sometimes I would sell my soul to hear one more orchestra play one more polonaise, to eat until I was full, to feel the softness of silk against my skin once again!" Ashamed of her selfishness, her palms lifted in a helpless gesture of apology. "And yet there is so much good here! A richness of life I hadn't imagined. And the people! You and Larisca and Katya and Boris Mikov and Anashula Verenski and Molka Shuman and Marya Hamka and . . . and all the others. I love you all; I would miss you like my heart if ever . . ." She scrubbed furiously at the humiliating tears, rubbing her braid over her eyes and wet cheeks. Then she leaned miserably over her knees. "The wasted luxury at court is an abomination, and so is this endless drudgery. Somewhere, someplace, there must be a middle ground!"

Yuri's eyes slid from the long smooth curve of her bare spine. He dropped her tunic over her hair and presented his back as she adjusted it over her breasts. Then he poured two tin cups of *kvas* and silently twisted one into the straw near her skirt. He seated himself a small distance from touching, his eyes focused on the cows, who watched with lazy indifference. And he followed her lead, not speaking of the two ghosts who had shared their lovemaking. "It's easier on those of us who have never known another life," he offered finally. "We know who we are and where we belong."

"That's it!" Swimming blue eyes lifted in a white face, and Yuri stared, then dropped his gaze from her blazing loveliness. "I don't know who I am! I don't belong anywhere!" She swallowed deeply from the tin cup, choking as the *kvas* burned down her throat. She wrapped her arms tightly about her knees. After a short silence she spoke to her toes. "Some-

225

times I feel like . . . like a rainbow. But no one views the rainbow in its entirety. Catherine saw only the pink stripe; Paul imagined only black. You see one color, and Pavla and Vadim saw another." Her fist pounded the straw, and her voice sank to a whisper. "I don't know. Perhaps there isn't an entire rainbow. Only one person ever . . ." But she refused to speak his name aloud. Dimitri was her private talisman—not to be shared, or her dreams would shatter into a million fragments.

They lapsed into a clumsy silence, listening to the medley of summer sounds humming in the darkness, each absorbed in private thoughts.

"Nadia . . . I think sometimes you would be happier being one solid color." He considered the allegory, swirling the liquid in his cup. "Fate has pressed the rainbow around you, and you rebel. It would have been better to be born a princess or born a peasant. It is the shock of both which troubles your mind. You cannot fit the pink onto the green."

She lifted her forehead from her knees, startled but not really surprised by his insight. For she agreed with his observation. She resented being Nicole, Natasha, and Nadia. She wanted to be one person alone; she craved the security of one band of color. She rejected the idea of red suddenly bleeding to pink and the process lying outside her control.

Wide liquid eyes fastened to Yuri's sober study, pleading for a glimmer of hope. "Will I ever find the right color for me?"

Closing the distance, he gathered her gently into his arms and pressed her hot face to his shoulder. "Does anyone?" he asked, not expecting an answer.

When her tears dried, they rose to return to the *izba*, but Yuri stopped her in the doorway of the shed. His hand lifted to stroke her cheek. "Do you understand that I care about you?" He cleared his throat awkwardly. "Will caring be enough for you?"

"Oh, Yuri!" Again Nicole's eyes swam, and she flung herself upon his thin frame and embraced him fiercely. "I care for you, too! And if it isn't . . ." His collarbone pressed into her cheek. "At least we're friends!"

Gently he held her away from his body, and his sad smile wrung her heart. "I'm sorry that Larisca . . . no longer remembers a certain face."

A flush of misery stung her cheeks, and she lowered her

eyes. "I hurt for you both," she whispered. "I wish things might have been different. You deserve so much more."

He expelled a resigned breath. "We all do, my little friend, we all do." Then he kissed her forehead and they entered the darkened *izba*, silently approaching their separate pallets upon the sleeping shelves. And listened to the muffled weeping from the pallet near the *pech*.

The summer unfolded in a sizzling blur. Blisters bloomed on Nicole's palms and broke painfully over the handle of her hoe. A scorching sun painted her cheeks fiery red and spread shimmering waves atop the fields. When next Yuri led her to the shed, they fell onto the pile of straw too exhausted to attempt more than a quiet clasping of hands.

In early July everyone in the villages, from the eldest to the smallest, streamed into the field to cut the hay. Women and children followed behind the men's swinging scythes. They raked the hay into mounds, then tied the mounds into shocks. Nicole carried the heavy shocks to the platform near the road, determined to keep pace with the others. Her arms shook with fatigue, and her spine cracked and protested on those rare moments when she tried to straighten.

"It's the time of toil," Katya announced. Weariness stripped her hawk face of its fierceness. Her eagle eyes were glassy. The family no longer divided one loaf of bread. Each member consumed five pounds daily, requiring several loaves for each. The women rotated at the *pech*, rising in darkness to begin the day's baking.

When the haymaking concluded, the men departed to harrow the fallow ground, and the women moved into bordering fields to reap the winter rye and then the remaining cereal grains. The labor was excruciating. The women worked into August, their movements dull and slowed.

Nicole moved like a sleepwalker through the rows of golden wheat, her hands puffed and swollen around a small woman's scythe. Dimly she registered the sight of Katya crossing the rows to fetch their lunch basket, and her throat worked, anticipating the jug of cool well water. Heavy sun hammered against her kerchief, and her skirts swung like lead weights around her dusty *lapti*. She swayed, perceiving the sun as a deadly enemy, the endless rows of rippling wheat as lines of massed foes. Nicole wiped a grime of sweat and dust from her brow and drew a breath, the air hot in her lungs. She shaded her eyes and looked toward the road, wondering if Larisca was as anxious for rest and water as she. Larisca bent to gather an armload of severed wheat; her full breasts swung against her blouse, and dark stains ringed her arms.

And despite a mind-numbing exhaustion, Nicole admitted the beauty of the scene, full-bodied women moving through a sea of golden wheat. Undulating tides of wheat and oats and barley flowed as far outward as the eye could see. All waiting to be reaped and stacked and threshed. Nicole sighed heavily, the beauty dispelled by her last thought. She briefly closed her eyes and released a weary breath, seeking the strength to continue. And marveled how this would be the poor harvest everyone predicted. She couldn't envision how any of them could have survived a bountiful harvest.

The next instant a flying dark body knocked her sprawling into the hot dust between the rows. And a hard callused hand smothered her cry. Nicole's eyes widened in astonishment above clenching taloned fingers, and she stared up at Katya in alarm, believing the older woman had surely taken leave of her senses.

"Not a word!" Katya hissed. She released Nicole and dashed forward, halting before she'd taken three steps. A long despairing groan broke from her chest, and her wide shoulders slumped. Blinking rapidly, she lifted Nicole's scythe, performing the motions of reaping without doing so, her eyes riveted upon the road. "Stay hidden," she warned sharply, one brown hand waving Nicole down.

"*Matushka*, for heaven's sake! What's wrong? Are you ill? Too much sun?" Cautiously Nicole raised her head and peered about the field. To her surprise, nearly all the younger women had vanished, presumably into the scorching dirt like herself, hidden between the rows of wheat.

"God, God! He's seen her!" Now Katya abandoned any pretense of reaping. She stood frozen, her eyes dying, watching Larisca, who continued to gather the wheat without looking up.

"Who?" Nicole parted the stalks of wheat and stared toward the road. An open carriage had parked beside the field. Inside, a grotesquely obese man reclined on the velvet cushions, a wig perched on his head, a gold-tipped cane between massive outspread legs. He watched Larisca, his small greedy eyes glittering as Larisca bent, her breasts straining the fabric of her blouse. The man licked his lips.

"No!" Nicole was unaware she had groaned aloud. "Dear God! No!" She didn't need to be informed this was the master. She'd heard him described often enough.

A footman descended from the carriage, nodded at a flow of instructions, then entered the field, wrinkling his nose in distaste as a layer of dust spread over his polished leather boots. He tapped Larisca on the shoulder, and she straightened painfully, her hands pressing against the small of her back. As the footman spoke, Larisca glanced toward the carriage, seeing it for the first time. Her knees buckled and she sat abruptly, falling on a mound of wheat stalks. Her kerchief sank between her shoulders. The footman returned to the carriage, and it turned in the road, proceeding toward the village and the bridge leading to the manor.

Nicole's mouth dried, and stalks of wheat snapped in her fists. A terrible dark suspicion flooded her tongue with a brackish taste, and her mind shrieked. "Prince Repinsky," she whispered, the name a poisonous worm twisting through her heart. And suddenly she placed it. Images swirled before her eyes, spiraling backward, and she watched bits of a shattered pipe tumbling toward splashing waves, listened as a man's angry whisper spoke of a girl with sunshine in her soul and the landowner who had extinguished that sunshine forever. Gregory Repinsky.

Screaming, she clutched her skirts and ran, stumbling over stubbled rows, crashing through the sea of wheat until she reached Larisca. Wordlessly, Larisca caught Nicole's hand and stared up at her through eyes gone opaque with shock. Weeping and shaking, Nicole and Katya lifted Larisca to her feet and led her home, abandoning their tools in the field. They dispatched one of the village children to the north fields to fetch Yuri, and they waited, hunched around the table, unable to look at each other, listening to thunderings of fear and impotence pounding against their ribs.

When Yuri arrived, wild-eyed and distraught, Katya waved him to the table and produced a bottle of vodka they hadn't known she had. They drank it neat, staring into faces that had bleached white beneath the fire of the sun's scorch.

And Nicole wept quiet bitter tears as history repeated. She anticipated the futile plans before Yuri finished framing them, and she knew the objections before Larisca's frightened whisper faded. There was no escape.

They waited in private pools of despair, watching as the sun sank below the window frame. At twilight Larisca rose unsteadily from the table. "I . . . The *bania* . . . He said . . ." Her cloudy velvet eyes turned a plea toward Nicole. "I can't think. Nadia . . . ?"

Nicole wrapped her arm about Larisca's waist, supporting her as they stumbled down the lane toward the *bania*. A line of village women parted before the door. Silently the women lowered their eyes and returned to the village, offering Larisca their most precious gift. Privacy.

Gently Nicole peeled the dusty field clothes from Larisca's small rounded body, and she washed that limp form with tender soothing strokes. She could not bear to swing the birch twigs, and instead threw them aside. After the steam, she ran a cloth soaked in cool water over Larisca's shrinking skin; then she sponged the tears from both their faces and dressed Larisca in her finest holiday skirt and tunic. The bright embroidery at hem and breast offended their eyes, mocked the still quiet night.

When the manor cart arrived, a dozen men materialized at the Janov gate, summoned by Katya. They held Yuri, dragging him toward the cow shed and fighting him to the ground as Larisca climbed into the cart.

Larisca sank to a stool in the cart bed behind the driver. She stared at Yuri; then her kerchief dropped between trembling shoulders and silent tears fell to the hands clasped tightly in her lap.

The village men restrained Yuri until the cart had crossed the bridge and disappeared between two hills brushed pink by the early evening. The men shuffled about the yard, kicking at stacks of firewood and spitting angrily at the chickens. Boris Mikov cleared his throat as if to speak, then thought better of it and scrubbed a hard brown hand through his beard. Someone thrust a bottle of vodka into Katya's shaking fingers. A resigned voice muttered, "It's God's will." Then the men melted into the lengthening shadows.

There was nothing to do but wait.

Tentative fingers of pale gray stretched along the eastern sky before they heard the cart clattering up the darkened lane. They stared at each other, then rushed outside. The driver hunched above the reins, staring at nothing, as they lifted Larisca from the back of the cart.

Each step jarred tiny whimpers past her bloodied lips. And the small choking sounds ripped at the raging hearts beside her. They had progressed but a few steps before Larisca begged them to halt. She lurched forward, and Nicole supported her forehead as she vomited a dark liquid against the shed wall. Pink stripes seeped through the fabric covering her back. Drops of dried blood stained the tops of her *lapti*.

Tears streaking his thin cheeks, Yuri swept her into his arms and carried her inside the *izba*, waiting while Nicole added an extra thickness of straw to the sleeping shelf. Then he tenderly lowered Larisca to the straw and dropped to his knees beside her. His fingers trembled past the rope burns scabbing her wrists, and he rubbed her icy fingers as Katya hurried to heat water at the *pech*.

"I'll kill him! I swear I'll kill the son of a bitch!" Yuri's voice broke on a raw crack of pain.

Larisca's hand lifted to linger upon his cheek, and a long look passed between them. Her answer was scarcely audible through her broken lips. "No. If you care for me at all, don't endanger yourself." For a brief moment her defenses crumbled and the sweetness of love blazed in her eyes. But when Yuri raised her hand to his lips, her gaze flickered and died and she turned her face to the wall.

Yuri's agonized cry savaged Nicole's heart, and she and Katya leaned on each other and their tears mingled and their hearts fragmented.

The cart came the next night and the next. And what shreds of hope they had secretly sheltered withered and fell away.

A small and beautiful piece of sunshine died before their eyes.

18

THERE WAS NO magic in the first snow. Not this year. No one from the Janov *izba* joined the merrymakers in the lane. Nicole leaned beside the window, watching dully as ice crystals feathered across the panes. Behind her, Katya fussed at the *pech*, spicing the hut with the scent of small sweet cakes. Katya attempted to inject an artificial normalcy by baking the traditional offering to the first snow. But there was no normalcy in the silence. They tiptoed through their chores anxious not to awaken Larisca, who moaned and whimpered in a restless painful sleep.

Gently Nicole adjusted the blanket over Larisca's battered flesh; then she returned to the window and pressed her hot forehead against the icy panes. The cart would not return until the bleeding between Larisca's thighs ended and the latest injuries had healed. But Nicole knew she would strain to hear the rattle of harness and iron just the same, quivering with a loathing that had lodged in muscle and bone. For the remainder of her life she would start up in fear at the clatter of a cart in the night.

She rolled her forehead against the frosty glass, closing her lashes on a weary sigh. The preparations for winter had been tedious and fatiguing. And this year the satisfactions had been few. She and Katya had harvested the kitchen garden and planted the garlic; they'd salted and pickled and packed and barreled. The *izba* roof was tight, the walls chinked; the sheep were shorn, and cords of firewood waited near the porch. The sheds were stocked with hay and mash. And while the harvest hadn't provided as many barrels of *kvas* this year as last, the brew was barreled and stacked outside the door.

Through the autumn labors, Nicole and Katya had exchanged miserable glances above Larisca's pale silence. And each had recalled last year's silvery laughter and gentle teasing.

Sighing heavily, Nicole dropped to the table and clasped her hands before her, her eyes straying to the ax on the wall beside the fading icon of St. Nicholas. And behind her the choking sounds of labored breathing rose, caught, then fell. Why did God permit such abominations? How did these things occur? She dropped her head. Larisca never spoke of the atrocities at the manor, but even a fool could guess the form of Repinsky's passion.

Pain excited the man. Pain as evidenced by the marks on Larisca's shoulders and back and buttocks. In addition she had suffered several fractured ribs. She hid in the Janov *izba*, shamed, shielding her bruises and lacerations from the villagers' pitying eyes. And she willed herself to die.

Nicole knew this as certainly as she knew the weight of full buckets swinging from a shoulder yoke. Larisca would not die soon; the immediate death she prayed for eluded her. But death waited patiently in the shadows. And Gregory Repinsky's obsession with pain and peasant women would not end until Larisca slept in her grave.

Nicole's fist slammed against the tabletop, and Katya hastily raised a finger to her lips, nodding sharply toward the sleeping shelf. But Katya understood Nicole's rage and impotence. After removing a sheet of cakes from the *pech*, she selected one and offered it to Nicole with a mug of warmed *kvas*.

"Eat," she ordered, sitting heavily. "It won't help anyone if you starve yourself."

Nicole picked at the cake and examined Katya in the dim snowy light. The older woman had shed weight, as they all had, and she had aged. Her hawk face was but a gray suggestion of what it once had been. The glimmer of fierceness had faded from her tired eyes. Nicole reached to cover her mother-in-law's hard wrinkled hand, and they sat in the silence of misery, watching as the first snow hissed against the windowpanes.

After a time, Katya heaved a sigh, then smoothed her black skirt and straightened her headdress. Absently she poked a strand of iron-colored hair beneath an embroidered edge. "Yuri is at the *kabak*?" It wasn't really a question.

Nicole nodded, and her eyes darkened to the color of a frozen pond. The blocks of wood for winter carving lay untouched in the corner. Carving occupied the hands but not the mind. And this Yuri Janov could not tolerate. He scooped the egg money from the bowl atop the *pech*, and he spent it at the *kabak*, swallowing vodka until the fiery liquid burned his mind free of unbearable thoughts. The village men carried him home each night, and Nicole and Katya put him to bed. As the egg money disappeared, so did their hope for embroidery thread and shoelaces and lye and a myriad of small items they would learn to live without.

Winter deepened. The Moksha froze and provided a roadway for transport sleighs carrying goods to distant Moscow. Snow rose to the top of the porch, and icicles grew nearly to the ground. The men chopped fishing holes in the river ice, and the women added pigweed to their flour, and everyone prayed that next year's harvest would be better. In the evenings the men crowded the *kabak*, and the women gathered to gossip and weave the master's *arshines* of cloth. Babies chilled and died, and old men chilled and died. Wolves howled from the edge of the snowcapped *taiga*.

And a fur-lined sleigh came and took Larisca away. Nights alone were no longer satisfactory; the master decreed Larisca would live at the manor.

Silence settled over the Janov *izba* like a heavy gray shroud. The remaining occupants wrapped themselves in anx-

233

iety and pain and moved about the hut like pale shadows. They ate and did not remember, slept and found no peace. And every nerve screamed to the surface when sleigh bells sounded beyond the gate, signaling that Larisca had been returned, too broken to be of use.

They nursed her and wept over her and tried to smile hope and encouragement into those terrible hollowed eyes. And they silently grieved at leaden skies and frosty gray air and knew their sunshine had forever died.

Always the sleigh returned. And, heartsick, they helped Larisca through the drifts and into her fur-lined prison, and they felt the tears freeze on their cheeks as they watched until the sleigh disappeared between snow-heavy hills.

"Yuri was right," Nicole exploded between clenched teeth. She bent to unlace her *lapti*, the tinkle of disappearing sleigh bells curdling her mind. She stared at the ax on the wall. "Repinsky should be killed. By inches." A sweet, sick pleasure soured her throat as she imagined it. No barbarism was too cruel for Gregory Repinsky. He plucked the sun from the heaven and crushed it slowly between his massive thighs. An impotent craving for vengeance carved slices into Nicole's soul.

"It's God's will," Katya muttered from the *pech*. Her shoulders rose and dropped. She stirred meager portions of *kasha* and *shchi*, groats and thin cabbage soup, mindful to dribble a drop or two for the house spirits.

Nicole's mouth opened, angry denials quick on her tongue. Then she snapped her lips together. A fatalistic belief in God's will anchored Katya's life. To strike at that foundation did the older woman a disservice. Disheartened, Nicole laid out the eating utensils, hesitating beside Yuri's seat, then slowly placing his bowl and spoon. Some nights he returned home, some nights he did not. They never knew.

The scant meal disappeared quickly. Within minutes Nicole and Katya were wiping the bottoms of their bowls with bits of pigweed bread. Both looked up as the door flew open and Yuri entered, bringing a swirl of snowflakes and cold crystal air. They watched silently as he stamped the snow from his *lapti*, then flung his sheepskin cap and *tulup* toward the peg. And they exchanged a quick hopeful glance, each seeking confirmation that the other saw what she did. Yuri wasn't intoxicated.

But he was drunk with excitement. A fire glowed in his dark eyes that neither his wife nor his mother had previously observed. The flush on his cheeks originated inside, not solely an effect of vodka or frost. They stared in astonishment as Yuri brimmed three mugs with *kvas* and joined them at the table. "No, no," he waved them into their seats. "No food—a toast!" Nicole and Katya stared uneasily, then touched their mugs to his. "To the revolution!"

Nicole's jaw dropped nearly as far as Katya's. "Yuri, what are you saying?"

Katya's shoulders stiffened, and she glared at her son. "I'll tolerate no foolish talk in this *izba*!"

"It's coming, *Matushka!* It has already begun!" Yuri's excitement glittered across his gaunt face. "Czar Peter III is marching to free us! Thousands of peasants have abandoned their villages to follow the great cause!" He leaned above clenched fists, staring jubilantly into their blank expressions. "The revolt began in September! In Yaitsk. The cossacks are marching toward Moscow!"

"And we're only now hearing of it?" December winds rattled the panes and whipped blizzard snows across the empty fields.

"The czar and his troops smashed General Kar's army and hung the officers! Did you hear me? They are marching toward Moscow!" He drained his mug in a gulp and refilled it. "Don't you understand? The revolution is here, it's a fact! We'll be free; we'll own our lands!" His dark eyes burned like flames of ice. "And Larisca will be saved," he added in a low hard voice. "They're roasting the landowners alive!"

Katya's stare flicked to the icon above the table. "Where did you hear this?"

"The news is sweeping the countryside. Everyone knows."

"Yuri . . ." Nicole shrank from dimming the emotion leaping across his pale thin features. "This can't be true, it must be some kind of hoax. Peter III is dead. He was assassinated years ago."

"*Nyet*," Yuri insisted, "the czar escaped his assassins and now marches to reclaim his throne. And he offers us freedom for our assistance."

The braids crossing her small crown captured the chill candleglow as Nicole slowly shook her head and stared into her mug. "I've seen the grave, Yuri. Whoever this man is, he cannot be Peter III. Catherine's husband is dead."

Yuri's eyes blazed. "I don't care who he is! He's a saint! This man is freeing the villages and routing the government troops. Aren't you listening? It's freedom! It's *volia!*"

Katya winced at the destructive word. "Stay out of this, Yuri," she whispered. "No good will come of it. Entire villages are following this man? How will your czar feed them all? Who will plant the crops come spring?" The wise eagle eyes implored. "Maybe they win a town or a village, but, my son, it is a long, long march from here to St. Petersburg. The government troops have guns and supplies, and they are experienced fighters."

"First Moscow and then St. Petersburg. And the cossacks are a match for—"

"But do you know how to fight, Yuri? Do men of the soil know how to plot battles? Will your scythe be equal to the government guns?" Katya's eyes closed and her wrinkled hands drew patterns in the air. "The cossacks win a skirmish here and there, but that does not win a revolution. *Nyet.* Before this futility ends, dead farmers will fill the bellies of the wolves. Wives and mothers will sing the funeral laments. And the landowners will exact their revenge." Her black eyes held him to his chair. "Ignorant men do not place a man, whoever he claims to be, upon a throne, Yuri. And ignorant men do not make or change the laws. We are who we are. It is useless to dispute God's will."

An edge of desperation choked Yuri's voice. "*Matushka,* we must try! So long as we bow our backs and accept slavery, we will always be slaves. We must rise up and show them we are men! We must fight for our rights and freedoms!"

"A serf has no rights and freedoms."

"*Nyet!*" His fist slammed upon the table. The candle and dishes jumped beneath the impact. And his face was terrible to observe. "All men have basic human rights and the freedom to live as men! We must have the right of refusal! There comes a time when a man must shout: 'Enough! I will bend my knee no more! I will call no man master!' "

The *izba* rang with impassioned silence. And Nicole bowed her head, remembering other declarations shouted around another kitchen table. Yuri spoke the truth. But so did Katya.

Katya was first to break the lengthy silence. Her heavy shoulders heaved upward, then slumped. "Do others in the villages agree? Has the *starosta* taken the sense of the people?"

Flickering candlelight marched aggressively through Yuri's short dark hair. His eyes narrowed to pinpoints of cold flame. "If Czar Peter comes, we will follow!"

Katya's head dropped. She appeared ancient. "Perhaps the revolution will end before it touches us." Apologetically she spread her palms. "No mother welcomes a war." Long after Yuri and Nicole had retired, they heard Katya praying into the cold night.

Swiftly it became abundantly clear that Katya's views occupied a minority position. The village hummed with speculation and anticipation; such a momentous event had not occurred in a century. Despite waist-high drifts obstructing the lane, men shoveled paths to reach the *kabak*. In times of trouble, the *kabak* enjoyed a brisk business. Noisy discussions bounced from the walls, and each scrap of news was endlessly dissected. Dejection misted the village when no news was forthcoming; elation cheered through the snowy lane when a fresh victory was announced for Czar Peter and his cossack troops.

Larisca confirmed that the manor house itself buzzed uneasily with rumors. She returned to the Janov *izba* for Christmas week and a desperately needed recuperation. "All the landlords about Penza gathered last week. The sole topic was the uprising." She adjusted a cloth soaked in healing herbs against a blackened eye. "Many of the landowners are moving to Moscow for the winter."

"The bastards are on the run!" Yuri leaned across the table. Eyes hard as the ice capping the Moksha stared at Larisca's purple bruises. His voice trembled with rage. "Repinsky . . . ?"

Larisca shook her head, her eyes tearing at the painful movement. She never referred to Repinsky by name, but the word "he" became a monstrous label as it passed her lips. "He claims history dooms the rebellion to failure. He says the serfs are not to be reasoned with, but brought to heel as efficiently and brutally as possible." For the first time in months, a fiery spark of life glimmered in the depths of pain-filled eyes. "But they worry . . . the landowners are uneasy."

Larisca's news swept the village like wildfire, adding the vote of authenticity the villagers hungered to hear.

A second exciting confirmation presented itself on Christmas Day. All villagers were summoned to appear at the well, where a priest read a public proclamation authored by Catherine herself. His voice puffed with importance, the priest read an astonishing document admitting that a Don cossack, one Emelyan Pugachev, had launched a serf rebellion in the Orenburg *gubernia* and proclaimed himself Peter

III. Catherine's address ridiculed Pugachev's assertion and admonished her subjects to scorn tales of the rebels.

The priest folded the proclamation into his *tulup*. "Be assured that General Bibikov is on the march to snuff out the last remaining traces of this infamous treason."

The villagers shifted in knee-deep snow and maintained carefully impassive expressions. But elbows nudged, and sparkling eyes winked, and glad hearts soared. If the government had been forced to acknowledge Peter III, or Pugachev, or whoever the rebel leader was, then the revolution constituted a serious threat indeed. The *izby* rang with rejoicing. Christmas carolers paraded in the lane, singing joyously of wealth and luck with spirited fervor. And no one turned them from the door without offering plentiful libations. The scattering of grain was more generous than anyone remembered from years past.

In mid-January army recruiters lodged in Penza and called up the men in the surrounding villages. Rumor ran rife. Some predicted the men would be dispatched to the Turkish front; others insisted the recruits would march against Pugachev. Everyone prayed to be passed over.

When Yuri returned from Penza, Katya smacked a fist against her heart and sank to the table. "Thank God! I was so afraid they'd take you." After sending a child to the manor house with a reassuring message for Larisca, Katya prostrated herself before the family icon, weeping in relief. Nicole bowed her head and added her soft prayers to Katya's. The day had been long and anxious.

Frosty color pinked Yuri's hollow cheeks. "*Nyet*," he confirmed, and crossed his breast. "As the sole male in the household, I was spared."

Others had not been. Dismay flickering in their downcast eyes, two dozen village men bid their families farewell and marched to Kazan to engage the insurgents. They departed with slow shuffling steps, reading betrayal in the glances of friends and family and feeling the sting in their own hearts.

But . . . Kazan! The villagers seized on the information and clasped it to wondering bosoms. The cossacks and peasant force had advanced a considerable distance. Their conquered territory was significant—Moscow lay within reach.

"St. Petersburg watches, and the German skirt trembles," the villagers assured themselves gleefully. Everyone knew the harvests would continue poor so long as a woman occupied the throne.

Throughout spring and into summer, no traveler could pass through the village without being unceremoniously plucked from the lane and whisked into the *kabak*, where he was grilled until the men satisfied themselves that every last scrap of news had been extracted. Southwest Russia eagerly followed the long siege of Kazan, exulting in tales of skirmishes won and despairing at skirmishes lost. The government troops holding Kazan had stubbornly held out through the winter, and then into the ripening summer.

"Yuri, what will happen?"

They lay on the hay mound in the cow shed, stealing a moment alone while their strength permitted. The time of toil was nearly upon them. Soon the hayfields would steal their energy and they would be too exhausted to indulge one of their infrequent trips to the shed.

Yuri gazed up at her, admiring the gleam of starlight playing through her loosened hair. Summer had painted both their faces a reddish brown. "If the rebels take Kazan . . ." His eyes hardened, and weathered lines fanned from the corners. "And if they can hold it . . ."

Watching him, it occurred to Nicole that she had not observed his characteristic gentleness in a long while. That too had died with the sunshine. "Kazan is the turning point, then?" Like everyone, Nicole anxiously followed the news with a mixture of hope and dread.

A short bitter laugh coughed from Yuri's thin chest, and he adjusted his naked limbs in the straw, folding his hands behind his head and staring toward the gap in the thatching. "Each stand is a turning point—either for the rebellion or against it. But we'll take Kazan. Peter's army is twenty five thousand strong, and more of our people join him every day."

Nicole smothered a sigh. The villagers rejected Catherine's claims. They couldn't bear to place their faith in a runaway serf named Pugachev; they wanted to believe in Czar Peter.

"Nadia . . ." Yuri caught her hand and cradled it against his cheek. She felt his stare piercing the soft darkness. "When the harvest is in . . . I'm leaving to join the cossacks."

Nicole's hand tightened against his face, pressing into the hollow below his cheekbone, dropping to touch his wide full lips. In her heart she had known this moment would come. She drew an unsteady breath and held it. "Have you discussed your decision with Katya and Larisca?" Katya and Larisca had given one man to an army; would they willingly surrender another?

He fell backward in the straw, and her hand dropped away. "I spoke to Larisca last week," he answered levelly.

Nicole nodded. She did not press for Larisca's response. "And *Matushka?*"

Yuri frowned and plucked at the straw. "I need your help."

Nicole released a long breath and tilted her head toward the distant shine of starlight. How many similar dramas had unfolded beneath the indifferent gaze of heaven? And when all was said and done, did the eventual outcome alter anything? Was the fight for freedom worth the bloodshed and the pain? Yes. But only if they won; only if Pugachev placed new policies as well as a new face upon the throne. In her heart, she did not believe they could win, and she did not believe Pugachev would wield power any more wisely than any other king or emperor. Her chest collapsed in a rush. "I'll do what I can."

Now the excitement returned to Yuri's eyes, and Nicole drew back from his blaze of intensity. And she understood that only a deeply rooted sense of duty kept him in the fields and off the road to Kazan.

"Nadia, look after *Matushka* while I'm gone. And if you learn the fighting has turned this direction . . . take the brown horse, the fast one, and ride to the manor. Get Larisca out . . . whatever it takes, get her out of there! The fighting will converge at the mansion. Fetch Larisca and bring her to the village. You'll both be safe here."

She nodded dumbly, wondering if the fighting could actually dip toward Penza and this village. A quiet hum of buzzing insects thrummed in the darkness around the shed. The cows shuffled peacefully in their stalls, and distant voices laughed from the *bania.* She could not visualize this ageless world invaded by a killing, plundering mob.

"If Pugachev comes south, won't that mean the rebellion is lost? Isn't Moscow to the north of us?"

Yuri gripped her hands so painfully she winced. "The rebellion is not lost until the last free man is dead!"

His stare frightened her, and Nicole slipped downward in the straw, pillowing her hair upon his bony shoulder. Tonight he took her with force, with fire and punishment, and she

240

stared into his passionate eyes and wished for the gentle man she had married.

Recruiting had left the village shorthanded, and each night more men slipped away to join the rebel forces. There were not enough hands to reap the hay and harrow the fields and sow the fall and winter crops. Although the women worked longer and harder than Nicole would have believed humanly possible, they could not accomplish it all. They abandoned hay to rot in the ground, and they reluctantly moved on, driven by the calendar to reap the grain crops. And they knew the rains would come before they could complete the harvest.

Katya paused beside Nicole and lowered her scythe to wipe her forehead. "It's hopeless," she despaired. Eyes glazed by sun and fatigue, she stared unseeing across the rippling sea of stalks. "We sleep only five hours a night, and still we can't get it all cut and off the ground."

The merciless sun pounded against Nicole's kerchief. Dark wet rings sagged from her arms to her waist, and sweat dripped into her eyes as she bent, stinging and blurring her vision. She straightened slowly, her face constricting as her spine cracked and popped. She pressed her hands hard against the small of her back, but no relief was possible. And, God in heaven, she was exhausted! Her limbs were fashioned from stone; each step involved forcing a granite block to move. Cocking her head to one side, she closed her eyes against the sky. The empty heavens curved above them like an inverted bowl painted a vivid, deep cobalt blue, without a cloud to mar the vast vacant sweep. Without a cloud to blot the torturous, relentless sun—a blazing, blinding eye from which there was no escape. "It's God's will," she muttered.

Katya didn't respond. Her weary eyes fixed to a puff of dust traveling swiftly along the road. They watched as the dust eddy grew, unaware they stood motionless, their scythes dangling limply from swollen hands. Exhaustion played tricks with time and perception.

The horse skidded to a halt beside the fields and a dusty rider waved his hat in the hot swirls of sun and floating chaff. "Kazan has fallen! The city is burning!"

For an instant his astonishing words had no impact upon the silence. Then a hoarse cheer screamed from thirsty throats, and bodies too depleted to lift another armload of grain, too exhausted to eat or sleep, found the strength to run across the stubbled furrows and onto the road. Eager hands dragged the rider from his horse, and the men paraded him toward the village upon their shoulders. The scorching eye of the sun blazed across emptied fields.

The men carried the rider into the *kabak* and fought each other to buy him vodka, and they shouted a thousand questions. The women danced in the lane and clustered about the well, splashing each other and singing of the bountiful times to come.

Katya sagged against the Janov gate. "Fools!" she spat. "They dance and sing while the crops burn in the fields. Will they dance when the snow bites deep and their babies cry for food?"

Nicole would have traded the rest of her life for the icy touch of a snowflake against her cheeks. She vanquished the image with a series of thirsty hot swallows.

"Well," Katya sighed, "if you want to dance and wade in the watering pond—go join the celebration." She raised a puffed brown hand and watched it fall. "I'll tend the animals and do the wash. Perhaps I'll catch up the baking so the day won't be a total loss."

To work beside the *pech* in this heat was to stand at the furnace of perdition and roast before the flames. Nicole watched Anashula Verenski raise her skirts and dance Marya Hamka past the gate. She was amazed at the reserve of energy fueling the dance. After wiping her streaked face with the edge of her kerchief, she shoved at the gate and followed Katya inside. "*Nyet, Matushka.* I'll help with the baking." The words cost dearly. "I want to be here when Yuri brings us the news."

The news allowed for a variety of interpretations. The wick in the center of the table illuminated conflicting expressions as Yuri excitedly imparted the rider's information.

When the siege of Kazan had been gloriously detailed, he added reluctantly, "A peace has been negotiated with the Turks."

Katya's eyes leaped and she straightened abruptly. "Simeon will be coming home!"

Nicole picked at a bowl of sliced beets and cucumbers. Her golden head dropped. And she remembered a tall powerful man who aided in delicate negotiations. A silver-eyed man whose military talents would have been appreciated at the Turkish bargaining table. Or had Dimitri sailed to America without her? Dark lashes pressed against cheeks reddened and dusted with freckles. The pain of memory never lessened.

"You don't understand," Yuri almost shouted. His troubled eyes darkened with anxiety. "The Turkish peace means the government now has the returning troops to send against the cause!" He hunched over his fists, staring intently into their faces. "The czar needs more men; he must not fail! He's our only hope!" When their expressions didn't alter, he rushed on, attempting to persuade, to convince. "The czar issued a manifesto promising free land to all the peasants! He gives us the forests and the fishing rights and the salt pans! He exhorts us to rise up and hang the landowners!"

Larisca's scarred form jumped into their minds. "Will they know this at the manor?" Nicole asked.

"*Da*." Yuri's gaze narrowed. The dim light carved shadows and hollows and transformed his features into a fierceness Nicole did not recognize. "Repinsky dismisses our advances as meaningless. The fool, in his arrogance, assumes the returning troops will quell the danger before it imperils him. Instead of escaping, he makes speeches!"

Each was familiar with Prince Repinsky's statement, read out in all the villages. He minimized the rebellion by refusing to view it seriously. Prince Repinsky deigned to turn tail and run before a common serf and his motley rabble. He pronounced the uprising an exaggerated scuffle; it would be put down immediately and without mercy. And he promised death or Siberian banishment to any Repinsky souls daring to join the insurgents.

Katya rose and cleared the supper bowls. "If you join them, I am looking at a dead man." Her voice emerged flat, expressionless.

"*Matushka* . . ." Yuri's eyes implored his mother, then turned to Nicole. She dropped her gaze, uncertain of her own feelings. "What is one less person in the fields? Will it make all that much difference?"

Katya lashed out, her eagle eyes flaming to life. "And what is one more grave in the cemetery? Will it make all that much difference? Would you desert us, with no man to sow our crops? With winter but three months distant? Who will chop firewood in the *taiga*? Who will mend the roof and chink the cracks?" Her face snapped shut in hard hawkish lines. "If a man fights, he fights to win. And this fight cannot be won!"

Yuri stared at her, then dropped his head between his hands. Nicole heard his elbows grinding against the tabletop. "I'll stay," he whispered. "Until the fall crops are in and the *izba* is tight for the winter." Nicole bit her lips and looked away from the despair in his murmur. "I'll be nothing but a news carrier."

News arrived daily. The sun did not rise without blazing across a rider whipping his foaming mount through the villages and pleading for men and supplies.

Pugachev lost Kazan. Expanded government troops pushed the rebels away from Moscow, turning the thrust of battle south. Without more men, the rout would continue.

Each night, men embraced their families and slipped along the darkened roads to join a disorganized retreat moving toward them. Those remaining in the villages abandoned their *sohkas* and scythes and devoted their energies to edging their axes and honing wooden stakes and fashioning clubs from firewood. The hot air crackled with excitement as each day strengthened the probability that Czar Peter's fleeing band would sweep through Penza.

Nicole wearily scattered a reduced portion of grain for the chickens and watched Yuri sharpen his ax against a pumice wheel. Her shoulders ached from swinging the scythe, and her mind reeled with the hopeless exhaustion of each day's field labor. But Katya insisted they could not quit. Gradually the women had returned to the dusty endless rows, waiting out the days in the manner they best understood—through labor. But more grain would fall from nature's blows than from the hand of man. The threshing barn was less than a quarter filled, and the winter crops had not been sown. No green shoots would bless the land when spring chased the winter snows.

"Please don't let them come here," Nicole prayed, not realizing she'd spoken aloud until Yuri responded.

"The czar will come."

She stared at him. "But that means we're losing! If they come here, they're in retreat—we're *losing!*" He refused to comment, and Nicole swallowed and lowered her voice. "Will you fight?" She knew the foolishness of the question before it departed her lips.

Yuri Janov would lead the assault upon the manor house, if God granted his prayers. He couldn't think Repinsky's name without a sickness of hatred blacking his eyes. The lust for revenge gnawed his mind and soul.

"First, I'll rescue Larisca . . ." His lips stroked the name, agonized over it.

Nicole paused with her hand in the grain bowl. Yuri didn't

plan as he spoke. Each action had long been mapped in his mind. She contemplated the raw emotion ravaging his features as he detailed his plotted sequence. And she shuddered as he discussed in loving detail the death he prepared for Repinsky.

The rebellion had been doomed from the beginning. She saw that now. The underlying principle was wrong. The slanting sun spread a halo of gold about Nicole's face as she swung away, unable to bear Yuri's expression. And she silently repeated her prayer with fresh vigor.

The cossack army invaded Saransk, a scant ninety miles north of Penza. Breathless riders reported the furious czar had hung two hundred gentry and fired the town. The villagers cheered until their throats turned raw. And they waited for the czar to descend upon Penza.

The cossack fury came.

19

COSSACKS, KIRGHIZ TRIBESMEN, Kalmyks, Bashkirs, and an army of marauding peasants poured into Penza. Aided by the local peasantry, they swiftly overcame an outnumbered resistance. When the brief battle ended, the rebels raped the gentry's women, then hanged them beside their men. They burned the governor's palace along with the governor and twenty frightened guests who had sought official protection.

Beneath the ghostly flicker of crackling flames, the hungry army plundered the town. The granary emptied within minutes; the state liquor warehouse was drained of its contents.

The celebration began.

First the rebels opened the jails. Then they dispensed three hundred and seventy tons of state salt to the populace. Tents and bonfires and dancing sprang up in the smoke-filled streets. A local delegation officially welcomed Czar Peter by parading crosses and icons; they buried the base of an impromptu throne beneath baskets of bread and salt.

As expected, the czar granted freedom and a parcel of land to his loyal children. He strutted beneath flaring torches, tugging a black beard and displaying his fine red coat and a fur cap heavy with medallions. He waved a silver scepter and thrust out his chest to boast the red sash of St. Anne. In a lengthy speech the czar gave vent to a host of frustrations, explaining the disorderly retreat in disjointed terms. He deplored the treachery of his wife, Catherine, and waxed sentimental over his misunderstood son, Paul. He exhorted Penza's populace to join the great cause; then he dismissed everyone to an evening of unrestrained *volia*.

Cheers drowned the excitement of screams and explosions and leaping fires. The populace flung themselves into an orgy of self-indulgence as Penza burned. They danced and raped and drank themselves into a stupor.

Gloriously drunk, banner-waving cossacks raced through the flickering streets, displaying their superb horsemanship and imperiling equally drunk Kalmyks, Bashkirs and peasantry. By morning, as many men had died in the ensuing fracas as had died in the brief inglorious siege of Penza.

An electrified countryside waited anxiously as news of the triumph trickled to the outlying villages. Before noon of the following day, every *kabak* in every village had learned the rebel army was again on the move, fanning across the countryside, pillaging in search of supplies and the cowering nobility.

"They're coming here!" Yuri burst into the Janov *izba*, his eyes hard and hot. Swiftly he crossed the room and ripped his ax from the wall above the table. "Nadia! You'll ride with me to the manor and bring Larisca home!"

Nicole dropped her broom and stared. Abruptly her mind released the tasks she'd been scheduling; urgent chores shrank to specks of insignificance. Nothing mattered but the terrible words on Yuri's pale lips and the sharp expectancy stinging the air. The dreaded moment had arrived. She nodded dumbly, swaying as the blood rushed from her head. Icy fingers squeezed her heart. She couldn't breathe normally.

"God in heaven!" Katya sagged against the *pech* as her appalled eyes widened.

"*Matushka!*" Yuri gripped her hands. "I ask your blessing."

"My blessing." Katya's echo was a hoarse croak.

"*Matushka*, look well upon your son. For the first time in my life I act on my own free will, as a man!" Fierce pride blazed from his stare. His spine was as stiff and as straight as the pines in the *taiga*. "Today I stand before you a free man—a man of choice!"

Katya's frightened eyes hungered over his face. Her fingers fluttered to his shoulders, his thin chest. "Don't do this," she whispered. "Don't go. Many landowners have gathered at the mansion, you know that. And there are peasants who will fight to preserve the old ways. Have you considered how many will die?"

Yuri's hands curled; he itched to be gone. "We have right on our side, *Matushka*. We will win!"

"You have *volia*—and that is not right." The color bled from her gray cheeks. Her eyes closed; then she sighed heavily and pulled Nicole forward and placed hard callused palms against the cheeks of her son and her daughter-in-law. "Go with my blessing," she whispered, the words a blasphemy in her heart. "Go if you must. It is God's will." Her eyes filled and swam.

They held to each other; then Yuri and Nicole broke from Katya's clutching embrace and ran. Yuri raced toward the brown horse, sliding on the bridle in one fluid motion. "A weapon," he shouted to Nicole. "Bring a weapon!"

Nicole's pulse beat against her temples in thunderous waves. Sun and dread washed the world of color; she perceived her surroundings in tones of black and gray and dull white. She snatched a pitchfork from a pile of hay and lifted her free hand to Yuri. He swung her up behind him, and his heels dug into the mare's flank. They jumped the gate, and Nicole clasped an arm around Yuri's waist and pressed her forehead against his shoulder as the horse stretched into a pounding gallop down the lane and over the bridge. Dimly she was cognizant of other horses, other clubs and axes and pitchforks. And a screaming wind shrieked around them, issuing from the throats of the riders. She clung to Yuri and prayed, and could not make her mind believe this was happening.

The brown mare skidded into the turn and bore down on a scene of hellish confusion. The rebel troops were meeting greater resistance than anyone had predicted. Gunfire exploded from the manor's broken windows; the west wing was burning, and flames shot from the roof. The gathered gentry fought to protect their women and their birthright, battling both on foot and on horseback. Before the flames, horses reared and plunged in whirling spirals of dust. Axes clanged against sabers. The combatants hacked and slashed indiscriminately, appearing, then vanishing within the choking clouds raised by the screaming horses. Swords flashed and descended, firearms exploded, the Bashkirs released showers of flaming arrows upon the mansion. A confused peasantry slashed at the gentry and at each other, uncertain who remained loyal and who had joined the insurrection. Lifeless bodies sprawled in the dirt, a trampled carnage of flowing wounds and missing limbs. Puddles of thickening red gleamed dully on saturated ground.

"Oh, my God!" Nicole's fingers turned white around the handle of the pitchfork. A gush of brackish black acid scorched her throat. And her eyes sickened in horror as a woman ran screaming from the mansion, her hair and gown a torch of fire. A man caught the woman and flung her violently upon a patch of yellow grass before the veranda. He ripped up her smoking skirt and fell on her. A horseman swept toward them, leaning, his saber descending. The man blinked once; then his bloody head toppled onto the woman's charred breast. Wild-eyed, she clawed to her knees, stood, then stiffened and pitched forward. A forest of arrows sprouted from her shoulders.

"No! Oh, no!" Nicole chanted between grinding teeth without being aware her lips moved. She heard nothing but the clashing, shouting din, the shrieks of men and horses. She squeezed her burning eyes shut and sagged against Yuri. This was not a grand and glorious cause, this was mayhem; this was senseless slaughter.

The horse stumbled and slid, halting near an open corner of the veranda as yet free of flame. Yuri dragged Nicole to the ground before the horse plunged to a full stop. "Wait here!" he shouted, leaping onto the smoking porch.

"Yuri, no!" Nicole screamed. He crouched, running beneath windows erupting gunfire. A flaming arrow caught the tip of his cap, tearing it from his head and pinning it to the wall.

Nicole could not bear to watch and could not look away. A babble of sound tumbled from her lips, lost in the din. Then a flash of movement caught her eye, and her terrified gaze swung from Yuri to the manor doors. Three flaming figures dashed onto the porch. One dragged a ruined foot.

"Larisca!" She saw Yuri's lips frame the name at the same moment as her own. He leaped forward and caught Larisca in rough, firm hands. Lifting her, he threw her over the balustrade and rolled her back and forth on the patch of sparse grass, smothering the flames.

"Yuri! Oh, God! Yuri!" Nicole knew he couldn't hear her warning shriek, but he responded to the vibration of pounding hooves. Yuri jumped to his feet, and his ax deflected a swooping saber. A bearded horseman swept past and bore down upon the fleeing women. The women fell as Yuri jerked Larisca to her feet and dragged her toward Nicole and the foaming brown horse. A window shattered above Nicole's head, and she cried out and bent away from a shower of glass and shooting plumes of black smoke.

Then she was stumbling forward to grasp Larisca's hands, and she sucked in a dust-choked breath at the sight of Larisca's swollen face. One eye was battered shut; her lips were puffed and bleeding. "This way," Nicole screamed frantically. Larisca's good eye was cloudy and confused. "Come this way, away from the fighting!"

Nicole slapped at Larisca's smoking hair while Yuri dragged her toward the horse.

"Hurry! Hurry!" The battle surged toward them. Nicole pressed her hands against her rolling stomach and wondered desperately if she could ride around the combatants or if she would be forced to risk taking herself and Larisca through the worst of it. "Hurry!" Wringing her hands, she watched Yuri bend to cup his palms for Larisca's boot. And suddenly everything leaped forward with unnatural clarity. She saw the individual stitches on the patch below Yuri's collar. His thin shoulder blades protruded like wings. One of his shoelaces was broken and dangling.

His simple familiar action of helping Larisca mount denied the chaos around them. Wildly Nicole promised herself they occupied an isolated pocket of protection while hell raged beyond a narrowing perimeter. She quivered at the clang of slashing metal and the screams of the dying. But she was not a part of that reality.

And then she was. Irreversibly, horrifyingly, reality crashed through the barriers.

A gun barrel glinted from the broken window above them. And Nicole's hands flew to her eyes. Something flashed as bright as the terrible eye of the sun blazing through the swirls of dust.

Shock ripped through her mind as a red flower blossomed on the back of Yuri's dark hair. As if in slow motion, she watched bits of red fly outward in a halo, saw Yuri jerk toward his cupped hands. And she heard a terrible scream, a nerve-scraping, shrill keening that shredded the soul. And she knew it issued from her own heart. Her knees collapsed, and she fell, covering her face as Larisca jumped forward to catch Yuri's body. Larisca screamed, the sound a shriek of ice and fire. She clasped him to her breast in one fierce motion and screamed his name again and again. Stunned tears of denial savaged her eyes.

"No, God. Please. No." Nicole shook her head violently as Yuri's thin chest convulsed once, then collapsed. A sticky wet stain widened across Larisca's shoulder. "Oh, please! Please, no!"

Larisca's shaking fingers brushed the hair from Yuri's brow, and she stared into his face. And she screamed and screamed. And she hunched over him, protecting him from the dust and the sun, cradling him to her bloodied breast and rocking back and forth. Tiny babbling sounds whimpered past her lips. "I love you. I love you. I love you."

Above them the crack of breaking glass sounded. The butt of a gun knocked shards from the frame, and an obese body squeezed through the opening, dropping heavily to the ground.

Larisca's stare clotted. "Bastard!" she shrieked. She dashed the tears from her streaming eyes. "Filthy perverted bastard! Murdering son of a whore!" She pushed Yuri's body into Nicole's arms and leaped to her feet. Her limp vanished as she raced toward the grotesque retreating figure. Like a spitting, screaming demon, she climbed his back and kicked and gouged and clawed for Repinsky's eyes until he snarled and hurled her to the ground. His heavy boot slammed against her ribs, and the snap of breaking bones exploded Nicole's mind into fragments of horror.

Larisca blazed up at him. "Finish it!" she screamed. She rolled onto her knees and crawled toward Yuri, her eyes fixed on his sprawled body. "There's nothing left. In the name of God! Finish it!"

Repinsky watched her dragging herself over the ground. His fleshy lip curled.

Nicole clutched Yuri to her chest, and a terrible cry erupted from the swell of shock and horror. She threw out a hand and screamed. "No!"

Repinsky waited until Larisca's shaking hand reached toward Yuri's cheek. Then he aimed and fired. The explosion ripped through Nicole's soul. That one execrable crack reverberated through her head in tidal waves of red, a black surge of crimson and heat.

The impact of the ball flung Larisca face forward into the dirt; her stretching hand dropped inches from Yuri's fingers. Repinsky smiled and reloaded. Then he spun, and his massive body waddled swiftly toward the rear of the mansion, fleeing the battle.

Sobbing hysterically, Nicole opened her fingers, unaware of the blood welling from the crescent cuts on her palms where her nails had pressed. She laid Yuri beside her skirt and crawled to Larisca, easing the girl's glossy dark head into her lap. Rusty smears of blood stained her fingers. "Oh, God, how can this be happening!" Acid tears sliced through the dust and smoke on her cheeks. "No! No, no, no!" She wiped her eyes furiously with the back of her hand and stared at Yuri's sprawled body and then down into Larisca's glazed expression. Her shaking palm covered a ridge of fresh scar tissue on Larisca's cheek. "Please, please don't let this happen!"

Larisca swallowed and attempted to speak, the shadow of death graying her features. "Yuri," she whispered. Her dark head rolled heavily against Nicole's knee.

Nicole scrubbed frantically at the tears obstructing her vision. Trembling hands pressed Larisca's cheeks with a violent force, as if she could infuse her own life into Larisca's broken body. She could do it if her willpower was strong enough; she knew she could. "Wake up," she begged, "wake up, now." She didn't realize she was holding her breath until something struck her arm and hot dark air rushed from her lips. The salty taste of tears and blood lay beneath her teeth.

She released the pressure on Larisca's cheeks and stared upward through a haze of blind rage. The battle surged about her in tides of blood and metal and heat. And always the coppery smell of death. She covered her ears and screamed until her throat rubbed raw. And a cold hard knot formed in her stomach and she laid Larisca near Yuri, away from the danger of slicing hooves. She arranged them with clasped hands as if she had all the time in the world; then she dashed heedlessly into the fray, mindless of the danger, seeing before her a broad fatty spine disappearing around the corner.

"Repinsky's escaping!" She cupped bloodied hands around her lips and screamed up at a horseman. His black eyes were wild and hot. Nicole pointed and screamed, but he did not hear.

And her mind flamed as fierce and hot as the fire at her back; she focused upon one searing thought. Repinsky must die. Whirling, she recognized the battle would spill around the back of the manor, but not in time. Teeth grinding, tears choking her breast, Nicole yanked up her pitchfork and ran.

She rounded the corner and halted, sliding in the dust, her skirts billowing out before her. And a smile of malicious pleasure curved her lips. Gregory Repinsky had managed to lead a horse from the stable, but the horse pranced in an uneasy circle, eluding the master's bulk. Gregory Repinsky could not mount without assistance. And now there was no serf to bend his back and provide a step. The prince cursed and kicked at the horse, his face purpling with rage. He struck the horse between the eyes with the butt of a gun, then aimed and fired. The horse stumbled and went down as Repinsky reloaded.

Nicole bared her teeth. An animal growl formed at the base of her throat. And the clash and the screams of battle faded, replaced by the terrors of a cart rattling up a darkened lane. Whimpers of pain roared through her memory, and a parade of atrocities flashed past her staring eyes. She saw Larisca's torn thighs; she saw Yuri's tortured eyes. And she closed the distance in a rush, reduced to the status of a mindless she-animal attacking the malignancy which had viciously destroyed the sunshine.

The snarling growl built until it vibrated her mind in quakes of raw urgency. She aimed the quivering tines of the pitchfork, leveling them toward Repinsky's broad back.

The sound of pounding feet and her hissing snarl penetrated Repinsky's fury. He swiveled to face her. He had a second to fire one of the guns before the pitchfork plunged into his stomach.

A brand of fire scraped along Nicole's rib cage, an intense knifing slash then forgotten. She gripped the handle of the pitchfork and lunged her weight against it, then blinked at the widening rings of red circling the buried tines.

The guns dropped from Repinsky's hands, and he sagged. He clasped the wooden handle above the tines. But he did not die. A foaming roar erupted from his fleshy lips, and tiny yellow eyes focused hatred upon Nicole. He jerked forward, and the handle dug into her rib cage, thrusting her backward. They stared at each other along the length of the handle. Then Nicole forced her white hands to open, and she ran behind him. Fingers scrabbled in the dirt and she found one of the guns and lifted it in both shaking hands and she fired at his back. Her trembling sent the ball wide, striking his shoulder. Repinsky spun with the impact, and the swinging pitchfork handle knocked her sprawling to the ground.

Pain transformed Repinsky. He possessed the strength of ten. A twisted smile curled wet lips. Nothing existed outside of himself and this wild-eyed creature with the bloodied hands and the swinging gold braids. And the pain—the delicious exotic pain. Gasping, his smile a hellish grin, Repinsky wrested the pitchfork from his massive stomach.

Nicole stared up at him, panting, seeing a bloodied wall of flesh. She located the second gun and fell backward. The ball ripped into his chest, and still he came. He lifted the pitchfork above her and drove it down with all his force.

Nicole screamed and wrenched violently to one side. The tines missed her flesh but pinned her tunic to the ground. She clawed at the material, frantically twisting to tear free. She could not.

Repinsky grasped the pitchfork handle, supporting his sagging weight. His boot lifted and smashed down upon Nicole's arm. But his dwindling strength failed to snap the bones. A bubbling shriek of rage foamed pink around his lips. Then, holding on to the pitchfork handle, he slowly slid toward the ground. He sat heavily, blinking stupidly at the rolls of stomach as his shirt soaked through and his life drained into a thirsty earth.

Nicole stared in stunned disbelief. He could not be alive; he was a disciple of Satan. With nearly superhuman effort she ripped free of the tines and rolled to her feet. Someone caught her and dragged her toward a shed. Anashula Verenski propped her against the shed wall, and when Nicole lowered her shaking hands from her eyes, a mounted cossack was galloping between the sheds and the flames shooting from the mansion. Repinsky's head stared from the tip of the cossack's pike.

Then it was over, finally over. A great cold numbness blanked Nicole's mind.

She pushed blindly from the shed and wandered across the battlefield, seeking the brown mare. Bodies littered the ground. When she found the brown horse, it was dead. Flies buzzed about a deep seeping gash, and she stared at them blankly. The scorch of August sun and the heat of the flaming mansion burned against her cheeks. She stared unseeing at bodies she recognized and many she did not as she proceeded aimlessly until the sea of bodies piled too thick to pass. And she blinked at them and attempted to think how she would cross the tide of hacked flesh and find her way home.

A commotion near the road pierced her weary thoughts, and she turned with the others to peer through the dust. A man wearing a red coat and a fur cap glittering with medallions pranced his horse into the carnage, followed by a personal guard of fierce-eyed, bearded cossacks. He surveyed the results of victory and raised his silver scepter. "My children, I congratulate you! The white-bellies are dead! When we have destroyed all the guilty nobles, each man will be free to enjoy a life of peace and ease!"

Hoarse cheers stirred fresh spirals of dust, and a wave of peasants converged upon the self-proclaimed czar.

Nicole stared at him, the man who had instigated so much killing in the name of freedom. He was short and stocky, disfigured by white scrofula scars and missing teeth. A coarse man living half in reality, half in a dream world. Surrounded by the shouting, adoring crowd, his dignity incongruously dissolved into a spasm of winking and gap-toothed grins. Sickened, Nicole covered her eyes and turned aside. She desperately wanted to escape the sight and smell of death.

But it was not to be. A throng pressed forward, running to surround her. She cried out as reaching hands swung her atop bloodied sweating shoulders. The cossacks paraded her around the burning mansion as onlookers cheered and applauded, dodging bits of flaming ash floating through the hot air. Dazed, Nicole clung to the black caps and begged to be released. She couldn't understand why they displayed her.

Finally the cossacks deposited her on her feet before the man they addressed as czar. Someone pushed Nicole into a deep bow, and a hysterical bubble of wild laughter scraped her throat, the sound lost in the noise. People had died to gain the freedom to bow before a peasant like themselves. They traded an arrogant nobility for a coarse pretender. It made no sense, no sense at all.

She looked at the man and whispered, "My husband is dead." He smiled and nodded, unable to hear. And then she screamed it, and when his smile broadened, she pressed her knuckles against her lips and swayed, blinded by rage and grief and the urge to kill him with her bare hands.

Regardless of the man's identity, he understood mob management. Within minutes he calmed the cheers and shouts and centered all eyes upon himself. A wild dark gaze glittered above his black beard, and his voice soared into the silence he'd commanded.

"I commend this woman for destroying the guilty oppressor Repinsky!" As the audience erupted into fresh cheers, he leaned to one side and a cossack whispered into his ear. "Nadia?" he repeated. The cossack nodded, beaming at Nicole's white face. "Let the name of Nadia Jankov be revered in these villages for as long as the *taiga* stands!"

Cheers exploded in Nicole's ears. But she watched from a protective shell of detachment as he removed a medallion from his fur cap and ceremoniously pinned it above her breast. For the first time she noticed the gash above her elbow. A dark wet stain plastered her blouse to her rib cage. And the relentless searing sun beat like a sledgehammer on her bare head.

The czar graciously assigned men to aid the villagers; then he and his personal guard departed in search of food and fresh ammunition.

Moving in a slow daze, Nicole and the surviving villagers loaded their dead and wounded into carts. The appalling number shocked sensibilities and mercifully numbed hearts and minds. Dimly Nicole concluded that axes and clubs were no match for sabers and firearms.

She pulled herself into a cart and sat heavily beside the dark cossack at the reins. They drove toward the bridge in silence. But because it was easier to speak than to think of the two people in the straw behind her, Nicole drew a breath and said dully, "That man is not Czar Peter. His name is Pugachev." She glanced at the cossack's full blue trousers, his sheepskin cap, and the broad leather strap filled with cartridges crossing his chest.

The man shrugged. "It doesn't matter. With enough men and guns, we can make a czar out of a goat turd."

"Are there enough men and guns?"

He shrugged again. "If not this time, then the next. Or the next. But they will remember us."

Nicole clenched her jaw as the cart approached the bridge. Up ahead, those villagers who had remained behind strained toward the rattle of cart wheels.

"What will you do now?" The cossack slid a curious glance toward Nicole as she ripped the medallion from her breast and flung it over the wooden bridge rails. "You're one of us.

Removing the medallion doesn't change anything. Your name is known. Come with us, I need a woman."

"*Nyet.*"

Another shrug lifted his tunic; then he added, "The government troops are a day or so behind us. They're hanging rebels. If they let you live, they'll knout that pretty back or cut off your ears or slit your nostrils. If they let you live." Black eyes fastened hungrily on her breasts. "Come with me or you'll die here."

"You'll all die."

The cossack's spine stiffened, and his black eyes grew hard as obsidian. Pride fired his voice, "But we die free! As men!"

Nicole lowered her head and remained silent until the cart jolted into the lane. "Stop there," she whispered, her voice a wound. "Where the old woman waits beside the gate."

Katya stared into Nicole's dead eyes as the cart creaked to a halt. "Both of them?" she croaked. Her eyes implored Nicole to tell her it was not true. At Nicole's nod, a mantle of ancient weariness settled permanently across Katya's fallen cheeks. "Bring them inside," she commanded harshly.

When the cossack vaulted back into the cart, Nicole and Katya stood beside the gate, leaning on one another and watching as the cart reined before another *izba.* A keening anguish wailed into the hot motionless air.

"There's work," Katya whispered. Her sick eyes flicked to Nicole's arm and ribs as she directed slow steps to the *izba.* "First we tend the living, then our dead."

She cleaned Nicole's wounds and treated them with herbal compresses before binding the gashes with strips of boiled cloth. "I should send you to the *bania,*" she muttered, "but I need you here."

When Nicole had dressed, they heated water at the *pech* and silently approached the two sprawled forms laid across the sleeping shelves. Katya smothered a high scream as she gazed into Yuri's shattered face. Shaking fingers crushed her white lips against her teeth as she swung from Yuri to Larisca.

"*Matushka . . .*" Nicole slid an arm around the quivering woman's thick waist. She felt a hundred years old; old and sick and dead inside. "Let me do this . . . I . . ."

"*Nyet!*" Katya filled an earthenware basin and grimly dropped to her knees. She bathed the blood and bone from her son's face.

Together they washed the bodies and dressed them; then

they lit candles before the icon and prepared the offering of cooked rice and raisins. A few villagers arrived to weep and sing the laments, but not many. Most families had candles and rice in their own *izby*.

Nicole watched a length of moonlight creep across the floor. The night was the longest in her memory. She hunched on a stool between Yuri and Larisca and listened to the wailing emanating from the surrounding *izby*. She listened to the dull pounding of Katya's forehead against the floor planks, and she listened to the smack of carpenters' hammers as the village men labored through the night to produce a dozen coffins. And she listened to the soft anguish of her own tears.

At dawn she and Katya lifted the bodies into the coffins. Before they nailed the lids with wooden pegs, they placed a loaf of bread and a lump of salt beside quiet white cheeks. And they arranged Yuri's fingers around the handle of his ax.

It was important to keep busy, not to think, so they argued where the opening would be sawed in the *izba* wall to remove the coffins. This was done to confuse the departed spirits; when the opening was resealed, the spirits would be unable to track their path home. They would depart in peace.

At sunset the caskets were removed through the raw openings yawning from the *izby* along the lane. A long line shuffled toward the cemetery, a tearful cacophony of laments singing the lives of each departed soul. Nicole sang of Yuri and Larisca, holding to the ancient rituals as the fabric of centuries rent apart. She stared at the fresh twin mounds in the Janov plot and clenched her jaw until it throbbed, and wondered why she could not cry.

Yuri and Larisca lay together in death as they had not in life. Nicole tilted her head toward a fiery sunset and prayed they had found each other beyond the clouds. The small sad dramas of humanity froze her mind and she withdrew into a mercifully numb corner of herself. She bowed her head and trudged home behind Katya, following the old woman's dragging hem.

When they returned to the village, Katya and Nicole purified the *izba*, each finding a modicum of relief in the physical labor. They pulled Yuri and Larisca's bedding and clothing into the yard and burned it, shading their eyes as the smoke spiraled upward to join the haze of other funeral purifications. They swept the *izba* floor clean of straw and scattered grain across the planks. They discarded all the water in the hut.

Only then did they and their neighbors sit down to the funeral repast, leaving vacant the spaces Yuri and Larisca would have occupied.

"He died as a man," was the frequent proud condolence.

"It is God's will," Katya responded dully.

"It is God's will," echoed a solemn agreement.

Nicole bit her tongue and remained silent.

Before the few guests departed, a crier passed through the village, and everyone leaned on the gate in response to the summons. They listened to the crier's announcement, then peered at each other past the shadows and read stirrings of fresh fear.

"Her Majesty's troops occupy Penza! Each soul is commanded to present himself before Count Mellin's representative and there to account for his actions and whereabouts throughout the previous three days!"

The instant the crier moved toward the next *izba*, the funeral guests slipped into the rustling darkness. Katya and Nicole stared at each other above the glow of the embers crackling in the yard. Before morning the remaining village men would vanish along the dusty roads, seeking refuge with the retreating cossack army.

"*Matushka!*" Nicole wet her lips and gripped the old woman's hands until Katya winced. "Will anyone whisper my name to the investigators?" Her shoulders tingled, imagining the terrifying whistle of a swinging knout. Wildly she wondered if death by hanging was as painless as claimed. She doubted it.

Pride squared Katya's shoulders, and a hint of the eagle fierceness narrowed her eyes. "*Nyet*, child. You will not be betrayed by any of ours." Her weathered palm stroked Nicole's soft cheek. "Come inside. It is time you spoke to me of vengeance. I need to know how the pig died."

Katya pinched the candles, and they sat in moon-shadowed darkness. One did not speak of killing and revenge with warm light softening the horror.

Nicole sank to a stool, her hands covering her eyes. She began slowly; then her voice quivered with rising passion as she emptied the residue of black emotion knotting her soul. At the conclusion of the blood and dust and flames, she wept with her golden braids buried in Katya's lap, her shoulders convulsing uncontrollably.

Katya stroked long loose strands from Nicole's wet face. "There, there," she soothed. "There, there. I'm proud of you. You bring honor to our name."

"But, *Matushka* . . ." Moonlight silvered the tears streaking her cheeks. Her arms tightened about Katya's waist. "I *killed* a man! I murdered him in the heat of rage and revenge!" Her lashes pressed against her cheekbones until they pained. And she remembered Vadim stating that revenge was never enough, and she knew it to be true. Repinsky's death did not equalize what had been done to Larisca. "And . . . God forgive me . . . I would do it again!"

"Listen to me!" Katya's hard palms cupped Nicole's face, the ridges of callus leaving an imprint. "You killed a beast, not a man! Never a man!" Katya's intensity swept the dark *izba*. Then she rose to her feet and fumbled in the deep shadows above the *pech*. When she returned to the stool, she pressed a folded page into Nicole's trembling hands. "Take this and remember! When you think the animal you killed was a man, touch this page! I know Larisca would want you to have it."

Nicole scrubbed the tears from her lashes and turned the yellowing letter between her fingers. It smelled faintly of soap and sweat and broken dreams. And was worth more than all the shiny worthless medallions any czar could give.

Katya's voice softened as she watched Nicole slip the letter inside her blouse and adjust it over her breast. "A letter is not much to give . . . but when it is all a person owned . . ." Her shoulders lifted and dropped in a quiet sigh. She touched a golden streak of moonlight glinting through Nicole's hair. "Nadia, no one will betray the name of one who took vengeance for all."

Nicole clasped that assurance to the front of her mind as she guided the Janov cart into the stream jamming the Penza road. There were few men in the procession. And the women and children were unnaturally silent. Nicole flicked the reins and tilted her head toward a blazing sky. The day would be hot. They rattled past empty wilting fields heavy with grain. Soon the rains would come, and the grain would rot. After a time, Nicole kept her eyes firmly upon the road, like Katya and the others; she did not look into the fields.

In Penza they joined a long line forming before a large tent flying Catherine's colors from the highest post. "No one will betray me," Nicole whispered beneath her breath as the line edged forward. But a sour taste of doubt looped through her stomach. The villagers would remain silent, but strangers had seen her and heard her name when the cossacks paraded her before Repinsky's smoking manor. If it came to a choice between the knout or speaking a certain name, would they maintain silence?

"I'll go first." Katya squeezed Nicole's arm, then stepped inside the tent. And Nicole stared at the burned-out shells of Penza's shops and homes and did not see the rubble. Nor did her blind eyes recognize nods of covert encouragement from the people waiting behind her. A red veil clouded her vision; her heart thudded unsteadily in her ears. She had killed a member of the nobility; the crime carried the highest punishment.

When Katya returned, she mutely pressed Nicole's icy fingers, then trudged toward the Janov cart to wait.

Nicole drew a halting breath and firmed her shoulders; then she bent inside the tent flap. When the glare of sun faded, she saw a young officer wearing a crisp green-and-gold tunic seated behind a desk constructed of planking stretched over two sawhorses. A canvas partition divided the tent behind him, but the canvas door was closed and Nicole could not see if more soldiers waited behind the partition.

"Step forward." The man waved her toward the desk without glancing up from a stack of papers. "Name?" His quill hovered above a blank page.

Nicole wet her dry lips. "Nadia Janov." She held her breath as he penned the name. He lifted another page and ran his finger down a list. Only when he reached the bottom without pausing did Nicole shift her weight and release a soft rush of air. No one had named her. Yet.

"Did you participate in the sacking of Penza?"

"*Nyet.*" Her answer was barely audible.

"Did you participate in the sacking of Prince Krackov's estate?"

"*Nyet.*" Frantically Nicole's thoughts leaped forward. How much truth? Someone might place her at Repinsky's manor. Should she admit to that much? Her hands wadded her apron into moist clumps, and a trickle of perspiration zigzagged down the cleft between her breasts.

"Did you participate in the sacking of Prince Repinsky's estate?"

Nicole tasted salt beneath her teeth. "I was present." The words whispered like the rustle of dead leaves. Circles of white appeared upon her cheeks.

Now the man's head lifted. He leaned backward in his chair with a startled smile of pleasure. "Well, well, well," he breathed softly. "What have we here?" Appreciative dark eyes admired her high cheekbones, slid to the open collar of her work blouse, then lingered at the lush curve of full ripe breasts. His appraisal swung upward toward the shining gold wisps escaping her kerchief. "You don't look like any peasant woman I've seen. Where are you from, my dear——?"

"In the name of Christ, Ostermann! Are you conducting an investigation or a seduction? Get on with it!" Irritation exploded from behind the partition. The authoritative command deepened in annoyance.

And Nicole pitched forward, grasping the edge of the desk to support a suddenly leaden weight. Color flared upon her cheeks, then paled, and she fastened wide anxious eyes upon the tent flap, watching as a lace-edged hand flung back the canvas. It couldn't be! Her ears played a cruel trick. But she'd heard that deep rich voice a thousand times in memory, knew it like the beat of her own heart.

A man bent to enter the main tent, and Nicole stared at blue-black hair tied at the neck with satin ribbon. Her nerves vibrated on the surface of her skin. Then her disbelieving eyes locked to a smoky stare set above the hard lines of a powerfully angular face.

"My God!" Pinpoints of light leaped into his gray eyes, and a mouth whose rapture Nicole had tasted in her dreams dropped in astonishment. "Nicole? Tasha!"

The heat in the tent crushed the air from her lungs. Darkness raced forward from all sides until she saw only two burning silver suns.

She slipped to the dirt in a faint.

20

"DIMITRI?" NICOLE RAISED her head from his shoulder and tossed back her hair, staring into his starlit smile. And the words on the tip of her tongue vanished as she gazed into the strong lines and shadowed power of his handsome face. She drew a soft breath and pinched her arm. "I forgot Katya. She'll be worried sick!"

"Who's Katya?" he murmured against her palm. He kissed each fingertip and playfully bit the area between thumb and forefinger. "I can't get enough of you! Come back down here." Powerful hands pulled her beneath him, and she cried out and laughed. His lips slid along her cheek and found the pulsing hollow of her throat.

Nicole smiled softly. "Dimitri, my dearest love, we must talk. . . ." She stroked his thick black hair, unable to believe she wasn't dreaming. But the tensing thighs pinning her against the silk sheets were not a product of her imagination, nor were the smooth, muscled shoulders beneath her fingers.

Moaning softly, she slipped her hands to the crisp hair curling over his chest and lifted her hips toward the velvety strength growing against her lower stomach. A tiny groan built in the back of her throat as a heated weakness sapped her dwindling willpower, beginning between her outflung legs and flowing upward. "Dimitri . . ."

His tongue teased her nipples into budding ripeness, then traveled in slow coaxing circles toward the gentle curve of her stomach. Skilled fingers played teasing games along the tender flesh inside her thighs, approaching, then withdrawing, until she quivered like a drawn bow.

"Later . . ." she gasped, reaching for him. "We'll talk later."

This time he pulled her atop his body, guiding her until she locked over his hips. His palms brushed the tips of her breasts, then stroked downward until his warm hands circled her slender waist. And he rocked her in deliciously torturous motions, thrusting upward slowly and deliberately until a scream built in her flung-back throat and a sheen of moisture gleamed on her skin like satin.

He held her teetering on the edge of a rapturous release, refusing to progress or retreat, until her nerves shrieked and deep shivers heated her flesh and tiny whimpers groaned past her open lips. Then he rolled her onto her back and her fingernails dug into his straining shoulders, leading him again into the damp hot emptiness and crying his name as the urgency swelled and he plunged above her in deep powerful strokes until his body tensed and a tidal force of ecstasy swept them both toward a sea of blissful oblivion.

Later, when her breath had slowed and they lay in a sated

tangle of arms and legs and rumpled damp silk, Nicole drew her forefinger slowly down the sinewy curve of his shoulder. "Dimitri . . . were there other women?" She could have kicked herself. Biting her lip, she congratulated herself on displaying the foresight to pinch the candle; she didn't want him observing her grimace of self-disgust. Of course there had been other women. She recalled at least a dozen court ladies eager to satisfy his appetites. What imp lived in the female breast which demanded the pain of jealousy?

"Thousands." His wide sensual lips curved in a grin. Then his tone sobered, and the smoky eyes softened. "And none of them were you. None possessed eyes as lustrous as a pond at twilight, or hair like a spun cloud—"

"Oh, Dimitri!" Nicole buried her face in his warm neck and clung tightly. "Why do you always smell like the sea?" She inhaled deeply, loving the fresh scent of him, the touch of his firm skin, the very idea of him. "You smell like sea spray and good leather and . . . and . . ."

He laughed and his arms tightened, holding her close enough that two heartbeats sounded as one. "I think you'd rather smell food." He stroked the honeyed tendrils floating around her smiling face. "We missed dinner. Are you hungry?"

"No." Her voice muffled against his chest. She didn't want to leave his room, didn't want to share him with anyone. For the first time in over a year she felt as if her spirit and her body occupied the same space.

"Liar." He laughed. Reaching above their heads, he tugged a velvet cord. "We'll see what the kitchens can provide at this hour."

Nicole glanced toward the silent burned-out town beyond the window, seeing the shadowed boards in faint starlight. All that Penza represented lay firmly behind her now. She nestled in his arms and told herself she would not experience guilt at waking some poor serf to raid the kitchens. But she did.

When chilled vodka arrived, accompanied by a variety of cheeses and a loaf of crusty bread and spicy sausages, Dimitri placed the platter on the bed and leaned into the pillows. "Here is to discovering life." He touched his glass to hers.

Nicole smiled, then sipped the vodka and made a face. To her dismay, she decided she would have preferred a mug of *kvas*. She'd developed a taste for the sour beverage. Even the bread disappointed her; the airy texture lacked the substance of heavy rye. She shook her head, recalling how often she'd yearned for more delicate fare than coarse brown bread and goat cheese.

"So." Dimitri grinned as she tasted the cheese and sausage with a tentative nibble followed by a sigh of genuine pleasure. "Who is this Katya you're so concerned about?"

The cheese dropped from Nicole's fingers, and her head fell backward with a groan. "As soon as it's light, I must send her a message!" She glanced at his quizzical brow and her lashes dropped. The story had to be told, but she resisted breaking the warmth and intimacy binding them. "I . . . Katya is my mother-in-law."

Dimitri stared. After a brief silence he sat up and lit a candle, then stepped into his trousers and extended a white linen shirt to Nicole. "I think it's time we had that talk."

Nicole nodded. She fastened the shirt over her breasts and rolled up the cuffs, lost within the folds of linen and ruffles. Mutely she stared into the clear depths of her glass, then drained the vodka in a gulp. "I don't know where to begin."

Dimitri sat before a small lacquered table, the vodka bottle within easy reach, one leg crossed over the other at the ankle. The single candle flickered, casting somber shadows over the lines and hollows of his face, "That last night in Oranienbaum," he prompted. "Count Zeprin broke into your rooms—"

"Count Zeprin?" Nicole's mouth dropped in surprise.

"When I arrived, you were gone—obviously there had been a struggle. Pavla and I pieced together the plot, then requested an audience with Catherine." He leaned to refill her glass and then his own.

"Dear Pavla . . ." Nicole attempted to imagine Pavla in Catherine's presence. She smiled. Pavla's plain wholesome face rose behind Nicole's lids as clearly as if Pavla stood before her.

Dimitri's eyes darkened to slate. "Pavla admitted stealing the medallion. It was obvious her weakness was used to entrap you." He swirled the vodka in his glass. "Pavla's admission of theft cost dearly."

Nicole drew a sharp breath and leaned forward. "What happened?"

"They cut off her right hand," Dimitri answered quietly. "She understood the penalty when she agreed to the audience with Catherine."

Sick, Nicole covered her eyes and bent over her knees. Russia was the epitome of barbaric cruelty. Logic and sanity achieved strange new dimensions here. Her fist struck the mattress, a frustrated gesture of protest, futile and pointless.

"Pavla was granted freedom for stepping forward to expose the plot."

A wild shrill of laughter burst from Nicole's dry lips. She shook her head and pressed her knuckles against her eyes. "They chop off her hand and then reward her—for the same incident. It's insanity."

Dimitri agreed, then continued. "Catherine ordered Zeprin's arrest. In prison he revealed the conspiracy, and he exonerated you from any taint of complicity. But no amount of torture elicited any information regarding your whereabouts."

Torture. Prison. Nicole swallowed and wet her lips. "Zeprin couldn't provide any such information, because he didn't possess it." She couldn't allow herself to contemplate Zeprin's fate, or she would scream.

Dimitri's thick dark brows drew together. "If Zeprin didn't kidnap you, then who?"

"Paul."

"The grand duke?" He stared, the pieces flying together in his mind. "Of course." He slammed the vodka bottle hard upon the tabletop. "That explains why Catherine quietly allowed the matter to drop—why she didn't pursue the efforts to locate you."

Now the words spilled forth in a rush. Nicole spoke until streaks of pink thinned the stars, until the vodka bottle emptied. Dimitri woke the man outside their door and ordered a jug of coffee and thick rich cream and a platter of pastries.

They sat at the table and stared at each other above steaming cups, listening as the guards changed beneath the window. A rooster crowed from the edge of the town.

Finally Dimitri spoke. "How many people know you killed Repinsky?"

Nicole released a weary sigh and pushed the hair from her face. "I don't know. Maybe fifty. Maybe more."

Looking into his cup, Dimitri nodded thoughtfully. "The story will spread."

"Repinsky deserved to die!" Nicole's hands gripped her cup, and she leaned forward, her face hard. She tensed as a cart rumbled past the house, proceeding toward a predawn errand.

"Tasha . . . little love . . . I don't condemn you," he said softly. "I want to protect you."

Sudden tears sparkled across Nicole's lashes. "I couldn't bear it if you thought less of me or if you . . ."

"Nicole. The system corrupts. Until the system changes and each man is granted the right to pilot his own fate, then uprisings will continue to erupt and abusive landowners will die," His warm hand covered hers.

"I don't understand. How can you direct the interrogations if you believe as I do? How can you hang men whose crime was searching for freedom?" She scanned his smoky eyes, confused and seeking reassurance.

Dimitri poured the last drops of vodka into his coffee. "I go where Catherine dispatches me," he responded tersely. "I have no more choice than a serf." He stood abruptly and paced toward the window, where he stood looking out over the town, his arms crossed on his bare chest. "Many of the rebels deserve to hang. Their atrocities are as appalling as anything ever done by a landowner. Rape. Plunder. Mutilation. Murder. This isn't a battle for freedom, Nicole; this is a marauding band with *volia* as their guiding principle. Pugachev doesn't seek freedom, he seeks power and revenge!" The silvery eyes glittered, hard and unyielding. "Perhaps he began as one man against a corrupt system, but what has his rebellion become? He advises the peasants to abandon their livelihood, and thus dooms them to famine and starvation. Does he promise education or grain or a better way of life? No. He grants his followers land he does not own. He bestows forest and fishing rights which he does not possess. He issues blessings upon scenes of rape and pillage and plunder. And, finally, he gives the people only another czar to obey."

"Katya was right," Nicole observed wearily. "A revolution eats its children."

Dimitri nodded shortly. "To succeed, a rebellion must promise educated men a voice in their destiny. A man needs the right to refuse—he does not need yet another czar!"

Nicole tasted her coffee, rolling the richness on her tongue and savoring the nearly forgotten flavor. After a short silence she asked, "What will happen to me?"

Dimitri wheeled from the window and knelt beside her chair. A finger lifted and traced the deep sunburned V at her throat, then stroked the thick sweep of freckles curving across the bridge of her nose. "No more field work for you," he said softly, kissing the calluses dotting her palms. "You ard I are returning to St. Petersburg." Alarmed protests tumbled from

266

her lips, and he smothered them with a light brush of kisses. "The incident here will be buried, and the earlier trouble with the St. Anne medallion is forgotten."

"But . . ."

"Catherine won't welcome the reemergence of the peril you represent to her—there are still those who would displace her if it could be proven you're Elizabeth's daughter. Zeprin was not unique in his ambitions. But you possess information Catherine is eager to learn. The serf rebellion obsesses her. She'll welcome your inside account as invaluable."

Nicole's eyes clouded, and resignation depressed her tone. "Dimitri, Catherine won't hear the truth. The truth surrounds her, it always has, but she refuses to acknowledge it."

He gathered her into his arms and pressed her head to his shoulder. "There's another reason for traveling to St. Petersburg."

She felt his smile against her flowing hair. "To place a distance between Nadia Janov and Natasha Stepanova?" A quiet sigh escaped her lips. Both identities faced danger. And in her own mind both lives had been lived out and concluded. They existed on a distant stage, roles outdated and no longer viable. Discarded bits of a rainbow.

"You and I once planned a sea voyage . . . remember?" Gently his large hands covered her shoulders, and he held her away from his body, reading the leaping response in her shining blue eyes. Then he laughed. "Haven't you noticed my surprise?"

"What . . . ?" Nicole frowned; then her mouth rounded and she drew a sharp breath. Her brows shot upward. "Dimitri!" She stared up at him in astonishment as she suddenly realized he was speaking perfect English! Her eyes glowed, and her fingers fluttered over his laughter. "When . . . how did you . . . ?"

"The English ambassador has been tutoring me. And your Mr. Revere passed along my correspondence to a Dr. Joseph Warren, who has been most helpful."

"Dr. Warren!" Everything was happening too rapidly to assimilate. "We're sailing home?" Wide excited eyes probed his smile; then she threw herself on his neck and sobbed happily. "Oh, Dimitri, my dearest love! When? When can we leave?"

Gently he brushed the tears from her cheek with his thumb, and he kissed her forehead. "Soon. Throughout the last year I've been settling the Temnikov peasants on their own land. I've enlarged my holdings in Salem and commissioned a house to be built through Dr. Warren's kind offices. There remain but a few loose threads to tie." A sparkle illuminated his eyes, and his voice sank to a teasing register. "Would six weeks, eight at the latest, suit your fancy, my princess?"

"Yes! Oh, yes!" She clapped her hands and danced around the room, listening happily to his laughter and glorying in a world suddenly turned right.

Dimitri caught her shirttail and tumbled her across the bed, holding her tightly in his arms. "If I wasn't already late . . ." he murmured huskily, his strong hands cupping her breasts.

The bed felt wonderfully soft and inviting. Nicole smothered a yawn and stretched languorously into the pillows, arching her slender curves into his hands. "Do you have to leave immediately, commander?" she murmured. Her eyes lingered hungrily on the hard sensual line of his lips.

"Yes"—he laughed—"and so do you."

"Me?" She cast a longing glance toward the deep feather pillows, attempting to recall when last she'd slept with a pillow not stuffed with straw.

"I'll assign someone to drive you to the village, and then . . ." Nicole sat up, her face sobering at the thought of Katya. "And then I'd suggest you find a lady willing to part with a gown or two." He crossed the room and lifted her peasant skirt and blouse. A grin flashed over his even white teeth. "You'll need something more substantial for traveling, something more in keeping with your rank." Larisca's letter fluttered to the floor, and he bent to retrieve it. "What's this?"

"It's Larisca's letter . . . but no one can read it." Her heart skipped, and she stared at him "Dimitri! You can read Russian!"

Flying across the room, Nicole pressed the page on the table, her hands shaking. "Please . . . read it to me!" But unexpectedly, a reluctance sprang into her thoughts. A vision of Larisca, lovely sweet Larisca, appeared on a screen of memory. Nicole pictured Larisca lying on the pine floor of the *taiga*, a shaft of sunlight shining through her hair as she stared down at her letter. And suddenly Nicole wondered at the breach of privacy in deciphering the mystery. Perhaps it would have been better to bury the letter along with its owner.

Before she could voice her reservations, Dimitri leaned

268

over her shoulder and began to read, and then she had to know it all.

" 'To my wife. The scribe is writing this in his own words, so if it does not sound like me, that is why. I am dying.' " Dimitri paused and examined Nicole's stricken face. "The letter isn't dated. When did she receive it?"

"Five years ago," Nicole whispered. She sat down hard, sickened to learn of Simeon's death—five long years past. He had been dead years before Nicole arrived in the village. A sting pricked her eyelids. Fate had dealt cruelly with hearts and emotions. "Go on."

" 'The army surgeon predicts I won't live past tomorrow. Tell my father he is to have my ax. Tell my mother I will die with her blessed name upon my lips.' "

Nicole made a small sound and squeezed her eyes shut. Her fingers laced tightly in her lap.

After touching her hair, Dimitri continued. " 'My dear wife, I love you, as everyone loves you, for your goodness and your beauty of spirit. But I have long been aware that your heart belongs to another. Yuri loves you too. I've seen it in his eyes. He is too fine a man to admit loving his brother's wife. Promise him that it is my wish for the two people I love most in this world to find happiness together. I give you both my blessing and wish you many healthy sons together. . . .' " In the heavy silence, Dimitri scanned the remainder of the page. "He concludes with an account of the battle in which he was wounded," he said quietly.

Tears wet her cheeks. "If only they had known! If only someone could have read this before I . . . They could have married, and all the pain would not have . . ." Nicole's face crumpled and she fell across the table, burying her tears in the hollow of her arm. She wept for life's tragedies, for Yuri and Larisca and the bond of love and honor between them. "Not once . . . not even . . ." Helplessly she pounded the surface, sweeping the platter of pastries to the floor. And knew she would find no comfort.

Throughout the carriage ride to the village, she repeated the letter's contents in her aching mind. And dreaded revealing its substance to Katya.

The carriage halted before the Janov gate and was immediately surrounded by a dozen ragged staring children. Curious villagers appeared on their porches to gape. When Nicole stepped from the interior, mouths dropped and eyes widened. Confusion drew Anashula Verenski's features; then her expression curdled and she shouted across the lane, "Are you gentry now? Did you strike a bargain with the government? A velvet carriage in exchange for a few whispered names?" She spit in the dirt. "We don't forgive betrayals, Nadia Janov. As ye do, so shall ye receive!"

Nicole stared in disbelief, then firmed her chin and rapped on the *izba* door.

"You knock at your own door? Ulcers on my soul! Has everything changed?" Katya jerked her inside and smothered her in a massive embrace. "Let me look at you! I haven't slept a wink! All night I prayed . . . I thought they'd hung you!" Her shaking hands ladled buckwheat groats into a wooden bowl and she pushed Nicole toward the table, then filled two brimming mugs with *kvas*, spilling more than entered the cups. "Eat. And tell me what they did to you! Why did they keep you? What names did they want?"

"*Matushka*, no names were betrayed, and I'm in no danger." A light shiver fingered up her spine. Danger was everywhere; life was never free of it. "But I won't be staying," she added gently. "I'm leaving." Nicole pushed aside the food and slid along the bench until her arm circled Katya's broad waist. She flinched at the fear and alarm flickering behind the old woman's fading eyes. Drawing a breath, Nicole quietly recounted her reunion with Dimitri. "We're departing for St. Petersburg tomorrow morning." She covered Katya's cold fingers with both hands and pressed. "We want you to come with us. Please, *Matushka*! There's nothing left here. Come with us."

Katya's shoulders slumped and she fixed her gaze upon the icon above the table as she digested Nicole's information. St. Nicholas appeared weakened and unbalanced without Yuri's ax alongside. "*Nyet*," she replied softly. "I began my life here; I will end here. This is my village."

Nicole chewed her lips and unconsciously increased the pressure on Katya's work-roughened hands. "*Matushka*, I beg you! Did you see the clouds in the west? Today the rains come. The snows won't be far behind. There's no hope for the crops, none!" She couldn't penetrate Katya's closed expression. "There's nothing here but starvation!"

Katya nodded dully. "The wolves will fatten before we see another spring."

Desperation pinched the color from Nicole's drawn features. "*Matushka*! What purpose will it serve to remain here and die?" She waved a frantic hand. "Who will chop the firewood for you? Who will chink the cracks and shovel a path to the well? There aren't five men in the village! *Matushka,* please! There isn't enough grain in the sheds to survive three months. The people and the animals will die!"

A grim smile pleated the seams in the old woman's face. She addressed the icon. "Sun fries the cheeks, and she worries about winter."

Nicole pressed her temples and drew a choking breath. If she could only find the right persuasive words . . . Her heart implored St. Nicholas for aid. "*Matushka,* you must come with us! If you stay here, you will die." She fought to establish a reasonable tone of voice. The image of Katya dying alone ravaged her senses.

"The war with the Turks is finished now. Simeon will come home soon; I won't be alone." The statement emerged without expression or conviction. Katya sipped her *kvas* and looked steadily at St. Nicholas.

The moment had arrived which Nicole dreaded with all her heart. She leaned her elbows on the table and supported her brow in her hand. And she read the letter by rote, each word a stabbing wound.

"So," Katya breathed when the silence became unbearable. "So. Both my sons are dead." Her gaze examined an invisible point in space. "It is a terrible thing for a mother to outlive her sons. It goes against nature." The quiet resignation in her shoulders and the lack of emotion in her empty voice suggested the news was not unexpected. She had long known Simeon would not be coming home.

Nicole leaned above her balled fists. "Please, *Matushka,* there is nothing to hold you here. I can promise you a dignified old age; I'll care for you! And you'll want for nothing!"

Katya shook her head slowly. "You've been a good daughter-in-law. Better than I expected. You're a hard worker." It was the supreme compliment she could pay. "I wish you well in your world. But . . ." The dark eyes she raised begged understanding. "My place is here. I am the last of the Janovs. There will be no more." Her hands fluttered above her dark lap like brown birds. "I'm not good with words, but . . . my place is here." She touched Nicole's wet cheek and added softly, "And if death rides on the snows . . . he won't be unwelcome. It is God's will."

An anguished cry tore Nicole's throat. She searched Katya's open gaze pleadingly, then dropped her face into her hands. She understood. Catching the wrinkled hand, she pressed it to her face, her hot tears bathing their clasped fingers. "Good-bye, *Matushka*," she whispered. She clung to Katya helplessly, pain blinding her vision. "Go with God!"

"And you, child. Go with God!" Katya stroked Nicole's shining hair, then bent away.

Nicole stood and gripped the table edge as she slowly turned her swimming eyes around a room that had housed generations of living. Faint echoes of Christmas laughter lay in the shadows above the soot-stained *pech;* so many conflicting emotions whispered softly from the sleeping shelves. The scent of cabbage and fresh bread, straw and grain, and life—vibrant life—filled her nostrils and she felt suddenly faint. Swiftly Nicole bent to kiss the top of Katya's bowed head; then she stumbled from the door, hurrying down the steps and across the yard. She flung herself into the waiting carriage, hearing the gate clang shut behind her, and she pressed her face into the velvet cushions and surrendered to a storm of violent weeping.

When the carriage had traveled beyond the village, Nicole signaled the driver to halt. She walked out into the fields, watching laden stalks bend before her skirts. Turning her back to the approaching wall of clouds, she gazed upward toward a vast empty sweep of sky; then her eyes dropped to the desolate miles stretching unbroken toward the horizon. A knot of despair wound about her heart. And she turned a final gaze upon the collection of wooden *izby* silhouetted against gray clouds and sunburned fields.

The terrible destructive loneliness of it plucked a barren chord. Gathering her skirts, Nicole fled blindly toward the road and the carriage, desperate for the presence of another human being.

21

NICOLE WAS ASTOUNDED to discover Dimitri's Temnikov lay but a scant two hundred miles northwest of Penza. If she had known . . . But she firmly thrust such regrets from her mind. Looking backward only gained her pain. Her existence as Nadia Janov had ended.

She surrendered joyfully to three delightfully restful days exploring Dimitri's childhood home and seeking the small boy in a rotting raft, in the crook of an inviting tree, in a hidden cave deep in the forest glades. At the conclusion of their all-too-brief visit, she and Dimitri hosted a banquet for the Denisov villages. Pits were dug and a dozen pigs roasted. Dimitri ordered food enough to feed the villagers for a week. The feast was his gesture of farewell, and the peasants sensed it as such. Shyly they approached to shake his hand, murmuring gratitude for the plots of land they had never dared dream of owning.

"Has Catherine learned you've parceled out your lands?" Nicole yawned and climbed into a large oaken bed which had once belonged to Dimitri's mother.

"No."

"She'll be outraged." The gifts of land might be interpreted as support for the peasant uprising. Refusing any troubling thoughts, Nicole stretched on fine linen sheets, then snuggled into the firm hollow of his shoulder. Quiet night sounds drifted in the cool air beyond their open windows. And she wished they could remain amid this peaceful beauty forever. But destiny always proved contrary, continually opposing the heart's desires. It was not to be. Quietly Nicole stored her impressions of Temnikov, a serene-forested chip of memory.

"We'll be beyond the English Channel before Catherine learns of it."

A gentle patter of rain sounded on the roof tiles, and they watched the curtains billowing from the windows.

"Warm enough?" Dimitri asked. He drew her into his sheltering arms, and Nicole smiled and surrendered her open lips to his as she arched her naked body. Tonight he displayed a gentleness that raised a tender ache to Nicole's heart. He stroked her quietly, wonderingly, as if each sweet hill and valley were a rare discovery not to be encountered again. And she understood that their shared passion was both a tribute and a farewell to Temnikov.

In the morning, a woman resembling Katya packed two boxes which Dimitri addressed to Dr. Joseph Warren in Boston. He closed the estate for the last time and ordered up their carriage. At the summit of a small wooded hill, Dimitri directed the driver to halt, and he gazed backward at the graceful pillared house set before the forest pines. Early-morning mist suspended above the river, imparting an ethereal shimmer to the stillness.

"Will you sell the house?" During their short visit, Nicole had conceived an abiding love for the grace and harmony of Temnikov.

"No." When Dimitri answered, his rich voice slid into a deeper register. "The forest will take it." For an instant his smoky eyes darkened; then he nodded curtly to the driver.

Nicole savored each day of the journey. When autumn rains dissolved the roads to impassable bogs, they sought shelter in country inns, exploring the countryside and each other. And when bright fall sun dried the roadways and they could proceed, they did so at a leisurely pace, experiencing no urgency to hasten their arrival in St. Petersburg. They dreamed aloud, shared their experiences, made extravagant plans for the future.

In Moscow, the city of bells, they toured teeming markets, and the Kremlin grounds, and a dozen onion-domed churches, laughing and enjoying each other's company as they waited for a platoon of seamstresses to complete Nicole's new wardrobe. Dimitri commissioned enough gowns to overflow three trunks, and he purchased satin cloaks lined in fur, sable muffs, brocade slippers, and smart little hats of sable and wool and velvet.

"This is far too extravagant for New England," Nicole protested, laughing.

"Then we'll buy you something drab when we arrive in Boston."

She unfurled an ivory fan etched in gold. Whatever trinket she chanced to admire appeared in their suite the following day. Her sparkling eyes flirted above the gold lacing the fan. "You're spoiling me dreadfully." And she loved it.

"Nonsense. It gives me pleasure to surprise you." Smiling, he clasped a rosy chain of pearls about her bare throat, burying his lips in her silky upswept hair. "Do you have any idea how remarkably beautiful you are?" he murmured hoarsely. His hands stole around her waist and rose to cover the crimson silk defining her breasts. She leaned against his chest and closed her eyes, then laughed as he teased, ". . . even with freckles."

"They're nearly gone," she insisted, smiling as she turned to nibble his chin. Nicole drew a soft breath. His teeth were as white as the lace at his throat and cuffs, and the rugged lines near his eyes and mouth served to heighten the strength of his features. Her knees weakened and she clung to his neck. Happiness glowed from her sapphire eyes, and when she allowed herself to think of being with him always, her heart swelled to bursting.

"I think we'll dine in tonight," he whispered.

Nicole laughed and reached to unclasp the pearls.

In the morning Dimitri dispatched a message to Catherine along with a second carriage containing the bulk of their luggage. They followed at an unhurried pace. The road from Moscow to St. Petersburg stretched through a gloomy uniformity of perpetual forest, but the inns and country *banias* along the side roads proved charming. A journey that elicited bitter grumbling from most travelers was, for Nicole, a time of enchantment.

"I wish we could go on like this forever. I wish we'd never reach St. Petersburg." She sighed and leaned her head against the velvet cushions of the carriage. A fragrant scent of pine and autumn sunshine delighted the nostrils. A cool tang crisped the air and pinked her cheeks. The promise of early snow freshened every breath. She adjusted the fur-lined hood of her cloak and snuggled into Dimitri's shoulder, careful not to spill a glass of chilled vodka as the carriage jolted over logs sunk into a bed of mud. The improved road signaled they approached the capital. As did the granite *verst* markers placed along the rim of the road.

"We'll be apart for only a week, my darling, two weeks at most."

A shadow dimmed Nicole's happiness. In St. Petersburg she would dwell in the drafty Winter Palace while Dimitri returned to his town house—and Darya. At fourteen, Darya had matured into a willful young woman, a young woman whose early sweetness had soured as she understood her husband would always perceive her as a child.

Nicole worried her lower lip. "Will Darya return to Austria?" She studied his sudden frown.

"I doubt it. Both Maria Theresa and Catherine want Darya in Russia to cement relations between the two countries." He answered slowly, contemplating the contents of his glass. "I imagine Maria Theresa will insist that Catherine grant an annulment. Darya will wed a new husband within six months." His odd expression sank a dart of jealousy beneath Nicole's heart. "I worry about her like a . . . like a father!" Dimitri's dark brows arched in surprise, as if he only now identified his emotions. "She's become reckless at the gaming tables, she's developed a sharp tongue, and if Vadim didn't guard her, I'm convinced she'd have ruined her reputation with a dozen lovers." He sighed and lifted his cap, running his fingers through his hair. He smiled ruefully into Nicole's upturned face. "Promise me we'll never have daughters—only sons."

Nicole laughed, then drew a breath, feeling a rush of color heat her cheeks. "Dimitri . . . would you be upset to learn we'd already begun?" She'd been hugging the joyful news to herself for a week, seeking the right moment to confess her suspicions.

"What?" Dimitri's chiseled face went blank. Then expression flooded back and he hurled both their vodka glasses out of the carriage and caught her shoulders in warm hands, holding her away from him to stare into her shining eyes. "Tasha! My dearest! Are you certain?"

A silvery laugh curved her lips. Dimitri appeared so absolutely thunderstruck. Blushing furiously, she nodded. "All the signs . . . that first night in Penza, when we . . ." Her fingers covered her mouth and she convulsed in joyous laughter. "Dimitri! You look so . . . so . . ."

He swallowed, speechless, then threw back his head and flung his fur hat high in the air, shouting his delight to the treetops. "You're wonderful!" He kissed her soundly on both blushing cheeks, then bolted forward and sharply smacked the driver with his cane. "For the love of God, man! Slower! You're rattling the lady like dice in a cup!" The driver cast a look of astonishment over his shoulder as Dimitri cupped Nicole's cheeks and stared deeply into her glowing smile. "Are you well? You didn't eat enough last night. We'll need more rooms on the house, and a nurse and a tutor, and—"

"Dimitri!" Laughing, Nicole smothered his plans with a kiss. "The last I heard, the process still requires nine months—we needn't concern ourselves with nurses and extra rooms just yet." She touched his lopsided grin with her glove and accepted the fresh glass of vodka he pressed into her hands. And she loved him so hard that it hurt inside. Tears of happiness suspended like jewels from her lashes and she flung her arms around his neck and attempted to voice her feelings. But mere words proved unequal to the task. "Love" was inadequate to define the emotion pulsing through each breath and every loving heartbeat.

When they halted for their last night prior to entering St. Petersburg, Dimitri insisted on carrying her into the inn lest she slip on muddy cobbles and stumble. And his roars echoed through the common rooms as he castigated the innkeeper for daring to assign them drafty quarters. He did not profess himself satisfied until they were settled in the innkeeper's own suite, with a generous fire crackling in the grate and an evening repast so sumptuous it would be discussed long after their departure.

Laughing, Nicole removed a feather pillow from her chair and seated herself quickly before he could protest. "I'm pregnant, not crippled. I won't break." She surveyed the array of food with amusement. All of her favorites were present, every possible item to tempt her appetite.

Dimitri leaned past the glow of candles to fill her goblet with champagne. "To Vadim Dimitrivich Denisov!" he toasted. His silvery eyes adored her.

"Or perhaps to little Natasha Denisova?" she teased. Her lovely eyes sparkled as brightly as the candlelight flashing through the wine.

"Tasha, my darling, I beg you to make the first one a son!"

She laughed, choking on champagne bubbles. "Oh, Dimitri, I love you so!" She ran to him, forgetting the splendid dinner as he swept her into his strong arms and kissed her deeply before he carried her to the large old-fashioned feather bed.

And there he fashioned an endless night of such exquisite tenderness that it would live in her heart forever, an unforgettable jewel of memory capturing the best that a man and a woman could share when a deep and genuine love coupled with physical magic.

Outside the gates of St. Petersburg, Dimitri instructed the driver to halt the carriage, and he swung Nicole to the ground. They strolled a short distance into mist-shrouded woods; then he leaned her against a tree trunk and kissed her soft lips until her knees weakened and her eyes deepened to the shade of a turbulent pond.

"I'll miss you like life itself," he murmured against her hair.

She touched his sober face with trembling hands. "Each day will seem like a year!" The two weeks broke into increments of longing. Now that she had been granted her heart's dearest wish, she could not bear to contemplate the impending separation.

Again within the carriage, they carefully maintained a decorum of distance as the carriage wheels rattled through the gates and bounced over the city's log paving. But beneath the lap robe, their hands tightly clasped. And they ignored the sights and sounds of bustling St. Petersburg, absorbed in each other as they marshaled small memories for the upcoming two weeks.

When the carriage rocked to a halt before the Winter Palace, Dimitri vaulted to the ground and gently swung her beside him, his powerful warm hands remaining on her slender waist. "I'll send Vadim the instant the sailing arrangements are in order." His bold silvery eyes made love to her lips, her soft eyes, her throat.

And then further conversation was prohibited. Guards moved forward, serfs scurried to remove their luggage, and a contingent of court ladies ran down the steps to circle Nicole.

"You've created a sensation!"

"Where have you been all this time . . . we were so worried, and no one knew what happened to . . ."

"Attend the ball at Prince Pretzkov's tonight and solve the mysteries for us!"

Princess Lilia Ulanova pushed between the chattering excitement and clasped Nicole's arm. A light fall of cold rain dripped from her hood. "Now, now, give the princess room to breathe." To Nicole she said, "It seems you always appear in St. Petersburg in the company of a certain devilishly handsome prince. A married prince." Sultry dark eyes flicked speculatively to where Dimitri conversed with the guard captain. Smiling at Nicole's crimson cheeks, Lilia embraced her and waved aside the disappointed ladies, leading Nicole toward the palace entrance. "Her Majesty desires an immediate audience. She suggests you dine in your quarters, then attend her at nine o'clock in her office."

Nicole nodded uncertainly. The glittering opulence of the

Winter Palace depressed her. She observed the gold and marble and malachite with a new bitter perspective. Soon the snows would come. And the peasants whose labor and taxes maintained this splendor would starve. No one who had lain sleepless on a snowy winter night and shivered as hungry wolves howled from the edge of the *taiga* could ever forget that plaintive sound. It embodied the hopelessness of cold and want and despair. But no one within the Winter Palace recognized cold and want and despair.

"I . . . What did you say? I'm afraid my mind was wandering." Nicole forced an apologetic smile and wrapped her satin cloak more tightly against the damp chill in the palace corridors.

"A great deal has occurred since you vanished." Lilia arched an inquisitive brow but tactfully refrained from voicing the questions in her eyes. Instead she imparted a torrent of news, some fact and some gossip, detailing events transpiring throughout Nicole's lengthy absence.

Nicole's mind leaped ahead, anticipating her reunion with Pavla as Lilia spoke. Only two items engaged her interest. Vasilchikov had been replaced by a new favorite, and to Nicole's astonishment, Grand Duke Paul had married nearly a year ago.

"But who . . . ?"

Lilia smiled at Nicole's expression. ". . . would have him? Wilhelmina of Hesse-Dramstadt. Chosen and persuaded by Her Majesty, of course." Lilia covered an unpleasant smile behind her glove. "Wilhelmina deceives the grand duke beneath his very nose, and the dolt is so stupefied by love that he refuses to see." Lilia laughed. "He follows her like a shadow—it's very amusing."

An inner sigh of relief lightened Nicole's step. At all costs, she wished to avoid Paul.

Pushing back her fur hood, she glanced down the corridor, recognizing it immediately. And another tiny sigh rustled about her shoulders. Discovering herself again in the west wing elicited a rush of familiar anxiety. She recognized cords of tension winding about her nerves. There were few happy memories here; the hallway was awash with vague undercurrents and perils which she had allowed herself to forget.

She paused before the door with her glove on the latch and directed a pale face toward Lilia. "Forgive me, but I think a rest is advisable. The journey was long and taxing."

Lilia nodded with understanding. "But pleasant, no?" She laughed. Her dark eyes rolled wickedly, and she winked.

Nicole stared after Lilia's retreating cloak, resenting the Russian habit of twisting every event into an intrigue. Then she gave herself a shake and forgot everything but greeting Pavla. She pressed the latch and rushed inside.

A wave of heat from the corner stove struck Nicole's cheeks with the impact of a blow. The windows had been sealed for winter; the cracks and drafts required maintaining the stove at full force. "Pavla? Are you here?"

A sound of breaking crockery crashed from the bedroom; then Pavla appeared in the doorway. "Is it really you?" Joyful tears sprang into her dark eyes, and Pavla released a shout, then stumbled across the room and dropped to her knees, wrapping her arms around Nicole's waist. "Thank God! I thought I'd never see you again! Thank God!"

Then they were embracing and both were weeping and laughing and touching hair and cheeks and arms.

"I'm so glad you're . . ."

"I didn't think I'd ever . . ."

"It was so long! And all the while I . . ."

Laughing happily, they wiped the tears from their eyes.

"*Chai*! Would you like some *chai*? Or coffee? Or something to eat?" Filled with happy energy, Pavla fairly danced about the room.

"Such luxuries! *Da*, I haven't been able to satisfy a thirst for tea since . . ." Nicole dropped her cloak; then suddenly she remembered, and she spun to catch Pavla's arm, staring in horror at the stump below Pavla's right wrist. "Dear God!" she whispered. A shaking hand covered her eyes; then she looked again. "Oh, Pavla!"

Pavla's broad shoulders shrugged. Her brows arched indifferently. "It's God's will." Smiling, she approached the bubbling samovar and filled two cups with tea. One she carefully balanced in the crook of her right arm, the other she served Nicole with a small flourish. "I'm managing." Her dark eyes refused pity.

"So you are," Nicole choked. Watching Pavla cope broke her heart, even though the girl obviously was accustomed to her loss and compensating beautifully.

"I hardly notice anymore. After all, it's been a long time now, over a year." She smiled gently. "I've had time to learn new ways of doing things. To practice."

Swallowing hard, Nicole patted the cushion next to her

skirts. "Sit down and tell me how this happened." Her blue eyes swam each time she glanced at the bony stump protruding from Pavla's tunic sleeve. "How could anyone do that to another human being!"

"It's the law." Pavla stared into her teacup and soberly related a tale of brutal interrogation and the horrors of the dungeons. "I was lucky they didn't take both my hands, the man said. . . ." Days had elasped without food or sleep. "Finally my oldest sister petitioned for mercy, and . . ."

Nicole peeked through her fingers. She had been tensed upon the edge of the cushions, her wounded eyes aching. Now her gaze narrowed suspiciously. "Pavla . . . you don't have any sisters."

Pavla blinked innocently. "Did I mention a sister?"

A smile twitched Nicole's lips, and suddenly she was laughing so strenuously that she found it necessary to place her cup and saucer hurriedly on the table. When she caught her breath, she mopped her streaming eyes and patted Pavla's knee with exasperated affection. "Now . . . what really happened?"

At the conclusion of a far less dramatic tale, Nicole kissed Pavla's cheek, and her sorrowing eyes dropped to the stump. "I'm sorry. I feel responsible for this."

Distressed, Pavla hastened to offer reassurance. "You aren't responsible in the least! I was the cause of all your troubles, it was I who stole the medallion—it's only right that I . . ."

Nicole covered her face and shook her head violently. *"Nyet!* It was all for nothing! It wasn't because of the medallion that I was kidnapped—that was only a small part of the reason. They shouldn't have taken off your hand!" It was appalling, an abomination. She squeezed her eyes shut and reminded herself she would soon put this barbaric land far behind her.

"Really, it's all right. Wait, I'll show you!" Pavla dashed into the bedroom and returned with her kerchief. She opened it before Nicole's damp eyes, and a collection of small items spilled over the tabletop. A broken earring rolled to the floor. "See?" Pavla offered proudly, pointing to the stolen items. "I can do everything left-handed that I used to do with my right!"

Nicole's mouth opened and closed soundlessly. "Pavla! Are you mad? Do you want to lose the other hand?" Sputtering, she searched for words emphatic enough to create an impression. Then her eyes touched the pink stump and her shoulders slumped. Nothing she said would create one iota of difference. She gazed at Pavla helplessly. "For heaven's sake, don't get caught!" she murmured weakly. And shook her golden curls wonderingly, listening to words she had never thought to hear pass her lips.

Pavla smiled happily. "Now, tell me all about you," she insisted. "Tell everything that's happened since I saw you last."

Periodically she crossed to the samovar, keeping their teacups full as Nicole spoke of the village and the people in it. Occasionally Pavla nodded and murmured. When Nicole concluded her story, Pavla clapped her hands and turned shining eyes on Nicole's waist. "A baby! We're going to have a baby!" Revolt paled beside this momentous news.

"Pavla . . ." Nicole clasped Pavla's hand between her palms as she explained Dimitri's plan. "Will you consider sailing with us?"

"Of course." Pavla's dark brows shot toward her braid in surprise. "Why wouldn't I go?"

"You're free now. Free to make your own choices and decide your own fate."

A sheepish smile stole over Pavla's wide peasant cheeks. "I'm not free. I never filed the papers with the registrar's office."

"But . . . but why not?" Nicole stared. Her spirit remained too near the uprising to understand why anyone would refuse the freedom othes had died to gain.

Pavla's blue tunic adjusted about an elaborate shrug. "Where could I go? What would I do?" Her expressive eyes explained everything. "I can't read or write or do much of anything. My only skill is as a lady's maid. But why would a lady pay for tasks her own serfs will do? Besides, I want to stay with you. "We . . ."—a shyness crept into her voice— "we're friends."

"Has my estate paid your living all this time?" For once Nicole blessed bureaucratic delay, a chronic condition in Russia.

Pavla nodded. "Your guards were reassigned, but no one seemed to remember me. I've sewed and cared for your belongings." She smacked her forehead. "Which reminds me, you have a packet of letters."

Nicole's eyes strayed toward the clock. Enough time remained for a quick trip to the *bania* and a change of clothing, or . . .

282

"Bless you, Pavla, and thank you. If you don't mind, I believe I'll glance through the letters."

She experienced a sudden fierce hunger for news of home, and she pored eagerly over Louis and Marie's letters, some dated as far as a year in the past. The letters plucked her heartstrings. The spacing increased as time had elapsed without a reply, but Louis and Marie had not relinquished hope: ". . . Her Majesty is kind enough to inform us of all efforts to locate you. We won't give up. Our prayers are with you, daughter, and we are confident that . . ."

Nicole dropped the letter into her lap and pressed a bit of lace to her lashes. She no longer cared who her mother had been. Louis and Marie were her parents. Parenting wasn't merely a function of breeding. A parent was that selfless person who lovingly answered a child's cry in the night, who freely gave of time and love and heart. A parent loved whether or not the recipient was worthy. A parent never abandoned hope. Dashing the tears from her cheeks, Nicole read on. She drank in the news of neighbors and friends, of small events and large: ". . . and the mob converged on Griffin's Wharf. A group boarded the ships and hurled 226 chests into the harbor. We destroyed ninety thousand pounds of dutied tea. The British will learn our protests are serious, not to be regarded with the disdain of the past . . ."

The letter was dated nearly a year ago. Thoughtfully Nicole reread the passage, her sharp eyes noting the "we." And a fond image of Louis rose behind her lids. Then her spirits dampened. The situation in Boston had worsened beyond all expectations. Was there no place on earth free of strife? The remaining letters detailed alarming conditions in all the colonies. When she finished reading, Nicole rested her curls against the cushions, relaxing the tension which had built as she read. In Louis's oft-stated opinion, war threatened but a short span into the future. Nicole covered her eyes and placed a hand on her stomach. She could not imagine Englishmen fighting Englishmen, ripping apart the fabric of civilized life. They were not ignorant slaves with nothing to lose and everything to gain. With enormous effort she vanquished an image of a quivering pitchfork. . . . Surely the safe streets of Boston would not bear witness to a revolt such as Nicole had experienced. It wasn't possible. Sanity would prevail.

"It's nearly time for your audience," Pavla reminded, touching Nicole's shoulder.

"There's only one more." Nicole turned the last envelope between her fingers, frowning at the unfamiliar cramped handwriting. Curiously she slid her fingernail beneath the seal. And her mouth pressed in annoyance as she read:

Nicole:

I order you to return immediately. You promised your journey would not exceed one year's time; it now approaches two. My patience wears thin. I dislike admonishing you by pen, but your lengthy absence is humiliating and inexcusable. Another man would long ago have dissolved our engagement and sought comfort elsewhere. That I have not is evidence of a character of which I have lately considered you undeserving.

For both our sakes, I pray I can find it within my heart to forgive you once we are married. But you must be prepared to perform your wifely duties in an exemplary manner.

At this time, demands upon my career are severe. It is your duty to return at once to provide a haven and a home. Frankly, I am bitterly vexed that it is necessary to remind you of your obligations.

An explanation is expected.

Your injured fiancé,
Major William Caldwell

Nicole crumpled the page in her fist and released an irritated sigh. She didn't know whether to laugh or to give way to the anger behind her eyes. How like William to "order" her home! And how fortunate that fate had spared her a disastrous marriage to such a martinet. She could no longer recall William's features, nor did she wish to, but his somber character returned to memory with full force. Shaking her curls, she tore the letter and tossed the pieces into the stove. As the fragments curled and blackened, she decided her annoyance was misplaced. William was to be pitied. He clung to a fragile bond which had been tenuous at best, and did so in the face of rejection and silence. In a small manner she viewed William's actions as parallel to the overall situation in Boston. The British refused to recognize independence.

The tower clock struck the quarter-hour and Nicole started. If she didn't hurry, she would be tardy for the audience with Catherine, and that wouldn't do at all. She kissed Pavla hastily and rushed through the dim palace corridors, arriving in the east wing breathless and more than a little nervous. She smoothed her hair and patted down her skirt, admonishing herself for not reserving a moment to change from her traveling attire.

"You're late," the secretary announced curtly. Behind thick spectacles, his eyes slid disapprovingly over her rumpled wool skirts. He rose from his desk and pushed open heavy carved doors. "Princess Natasha Stepanova."

Princess Natasha. Nicole played the chameleon, assuming new identities at will. Inhaling deeply, she squared her shoulders, then stepped firmly into Catherine's office.

A blaze of candlelight illuminated Catherine's massive desk in pools of glowing yellow, but the remainder of the large opulent room remained in night shadow. Heavy fog beaded a bank of windowpanes; suffocating heat wafted from the large stove in a far corner.

Catherine evinced no notice of Nicole's presence. She did not glance upward from a stack of papers. Nicole hesitated, wetting her lips; she hadn't the slightest notion what to expect. Would Catherine welcome her? Or would the empress view Nicole as the resurfacing of an old and uncomfortable problem? Nicole paused uncertainly beside the large utilitarian desk.

Tonight Catherine had chosen to appear as the empress. She wore an elaborate diamond tiara in her graying chestnut hair. And she had not changed from her formal dinner gown; the deep navy blue was as cool and stiff as the expression she finally lifted. For a long moment Catherine studied Nicole without speaking, her features unreadable. Then she placed her quill beside the inkwell and waved with practiced grace. "You may be seated."

Nicole arranged her skirts in the chair before the desk. Her nerves tightened uneasily and she bit the inside of her cheek. Catherine had not offered her hand, and this omission signaled a cool beginning. As did the somber face with which Catherine regarded her. No trace of the famous smile softened the empress's thin lips.

"I understand you resided in a peasant village for a year or more." The words were uncharacteristically blunt.

Nicole nodded. It was unlike Catherine to forgo polite openings to a conversation. She shifted in the chair. "Yes, your Majesty." Her mind raced, wondering if Catherine would inquire about the kidnapping—and what her answer should be.

As if anticipating the direction of Nicole's thoughts, Catherine stated flatly, "I am not interested in the details of your disappearance. That matter was disposed of to my satisfaction long ago. I am, however, vitally interested in what you know of the serf revolt."

Nicole stared into Catherine's steady gaze and read the truth. Catherine knew the circumstances of Nicole's kidnapping. She had known of Paul's interference from the beginning.

Nicole dropped her eyes and clasped her hands tightly against the pleats of her skirt. She hadn't anticipated this sober expression and icy tone. She should have, but she had not. In the past the empress had treated their difficulties with grace and kindness; Nicole wasn't prepared for this distance, this scarcely repressed anger. A growing alarm sharpened her senses.

"When did you first learn of Pugachev, and what was the reaction of the rural villages?"

Nicole concentrated on Catherine's rapid-fire questions, answering as truthfully as possible. And she experienced a rising resentment toward Catherine's obvious bias. A temptation to justify and to defend the peasants' actions hovered about the tip of Nicole's tongue. An urge to plead their cause and press her own opinions constricted her chest. So many suffered beneath Russia's oppressive system. She swallowed hard, instinctively recognizing that her opinions would enrage the empress.

"Then they truly believed Pugachev was my late husband, Peter?"

"Yes, your Majesty."

"But why?" Catherine exploded. Furious, she shoved from the desk and paced angrily before the misted windows, her heels striking the floor with sharp annoyed clicks. "Why would they believe such an obvious and blatant lie? Do they hate me that much? To believe in ghosts rather than reality? Don't they understand that I have their best interests at heart?" Hard blue eyes leveled upon Nicole.

Nicole watched the performance through carefully impassive eyes. Sadly she concluded that Catherine believed what she was saying. "Yes," she answered slowly, "the peasants do believe that you care about them. And they return your love. They believe you would relieve their misery if not for the influence of the landowners." She attempted to skirt the more uncomfortable questions.

A short mirthless laugh passed lips thinned by frustration and annoyance. "If they believe I love them—which is true—then why did they follow Pugachev? Why choose to believe a common cutthroat is a czar? Pugachev does not resemble Peter in the least; he does not speak like Peter or . . . Nothing about him resembles my late husband! Yet the peasants believe him and would depose me to put him on the throne!"

"He promised them freedom, your Majesty. The freedom to be men instead of slaves! The freedom to own their small plots of land, the freedom to keep the fruits of their labor and to have a voice in the amount of taxes they must pay! You can't imagine the abuses and the poverty and the hardships the peasants are forced to endure! Hunger and deprivation and—"

"Do you propose to lecture the empress about her realm?"

Nicole drew back from the abrupt frosty tone. Catherine's intense interest was not for the plight of the peasants, but was founded in the specter of her murdered husband returned to haunt her. Long after the conflict with Peter had been resolved, he had again risen as her adversary in the figure of Pugachev. Once again she struggled for a throne. Nicole expelled a soft breath. "The peasants believe the grain won't flourish with a woman occupying the throne," she finished lamely.

Catherine threw up her hands and returned to the desk. "How can one reason with such superstitious stupidity? How can one hope to understand it? They love me but they fight to overthrow me. They use me to excuse their laziness in the fields!" She sat heavily, and her fingers curled into fists. "They betray my love with ingratitude and treachery! Well . . . when they observe their comrades' severed limbs and empty heads nailed on posts at the crossroads, they shall think twice about defying me in the future!"

"Your Majesty . . ." Nicole was shocked that anyone could claim Russia's peasantry was lazy. The calluses had not faded from her own roughened palms. Catherine's expression froze the protests on Nicole's tongue, and she licked her lips and transferred her troubled gaze to the foggy windows. The temperature was dropping rapidly. Thick frost would coat the ground before morning.

Catherine flung backward in her chair and dropped her hands into her lap, drawing a long calming breath. After examining Nicole with quiet speculation, she asked softly, "And did you participate in the uprising? Considering your remarks, I think it necessary to explore your sympathies."

Dimitri had warned her this question would arise. Nicole steadied her chin and met Catherine's gaze evenly. "I was present at the Repinsky mansion when it was burned. I was attempting to rescue a woman being held there against her will."

The diamond tiara dominated the candlelight as Catherine nodded shortly. "Did you participate in the uprising?"

"I witnessed it."

"That is not my question." The words were encased in ice. "Did you participate?"

"I . . . No, your Majesty, I did not." The lie departed her lips uneasily, but she had earlier concluded this was the path she must follow. No one must learn of her role in Repinsky's death, if she were to survive.

A tiny smile relaxed the corners of Catherine's lips. A smile which against all logic imparted a chill of triumph to her stare. "I see," she commented idly. Her forefinger absently traveled the length of a closely printed page. "You and Prince Dimitri journeyed to St. Petersburg to inform me of the rebellion's progress, is that correct?"

Nicole's sense of unease leaped and lodged painfully in the base of her throat. Her pulse fluttered at wrists and temples. "Yes, your Majesty."

Catherine tapped a finger on her chin. She tilted backward and idly scanned the ceiling. "Do you find it as odd as I that your journey required four weeks? Do you think it strange that several couriers passed your carriage with information far fresher than your own?"

"I was unaware of . . ."

Catherine's gaze leveled pleasantly upon Nicole's white face, and her smile was frightening, the smile of a woman who enjoys the hunt, the final kill. "Prince Dimitri considered your information pertinent and valuable enough to reassign his post and personally escort you, but he did not consider it urgent enough to warrant haste. I find that a curious contradiction."

A sour taste pinched Nicole's lips. She concealed the tremor in her hands within the heavy folds of her skirt. And she gritted her teeth, vowing to stumble through this interview somehow, even though she suspected Catherine was toying with her. "Your Majesty, I—"

Catherine lifted a paper, then dropped it on the desk, cutting Nicole's words with a sharp wave. "It may interest you to learn that Pugachev was captured while you and the prince were dallying about the countryside." Nicole sat up straight, her nails biting into her palms. Then Catherine's eyes hardened. "Pugachev is being transported to Moscow in an iron cage. There he will be drawn and quartered." Catherine's gaze held and pierced. "Pugachev has been most cooperative—as cowardly in defeat as in battle. He was . . . persuaded . . . to reveal the names of his cossack leaders. Who in turn revealed further names of particular interest."

Nicole's mouth dried to dust and her heart crashed like a lead weight to her knees. Now she understood. This hadn't been an interview, it had been a trial . . . with the verdict previously decided. She closed her eyes. Please, God, grant us two weeks . . . two weeks of freedom and we'll escape this land forever.

"One of the names Pugachev's men connected with Prince Repinsky's untimely death was one . . . let me see, here . . . Ah, yes, one Nadia Janov. A blond woman whisked from the interrogation tent by Prince Dimitri. It appears that Nadia Janov was transformed overnight into one Princess Natasha Stepanova." Catherine's cold smile froze the blood. "You lied, my dear," she said softly.

A shallow groan issued from chalky lips. The lie had been a terrible blunder. Perhaps if she had admitted the truth and thrown herself on Catherine's mercy . . . But no, she had known from the beginning that Catherine sought an event outside the question of lineage. "Your Majesty, please allow me to explain myself." A velvet curtain of unreality swathed her mind. "Gregory Repinsky was a monster. He did things no human being should be allowed to . . ." Her lips clamped. No, she would not beg. Not once had she experienced remorse for her act, and she did not now.

"I don't concern myself with your assessment of Prince Repinsky's character. Your views are unimportant. The penalty for murdering a member of nobility is banishment . . . or death. The reason prompting the action is immaterial."

Nicole gripped the arms of her chair and ground her teeth. She would not faint. She would see this through to the end with dignity. Please, God. "You've considered the circumstances?" The room appeared to swirl closer until she stared at Catherine through an odd tunnel effect. "And decided to . . . ?"

"I've examined every possible resolution. If I order your execution, familiar rumors will be provided fresh credence. It will be whispered that I employ this incident as an opportunity to eliminate a legitimate rival."

Nicole's gaze swept the room; there was no portrait of Elizabeth among the many wall hangings. Her chin firmed stubbornly. "That is the truth."

"Of course," Catherine responded flatly. Pitiless eyes flickered. "We have understood one another on that point from the first, have we not?" She paused. "Therefore, I have elected banishment."

Banishment. The word echoed down a dark cavern, a breath-snatching concept of relief and dread.

"I am exiling you to Yakutsk in northern Siberia. Most unpleasant, I'm told, but as far from this room as I can imagine." Catherine watched as Nicole's face paled to the color of snow. She continued. "Earlier this evening I granted an appointment to Prince Dimitri. It may be of interest to learn that I have chosen to banish him to the mines near Irkutz." She answered the leaping question in Nicole's bruised eyes. "No, it is not near Yakutsk."

A sickened cry burst from Nicole's bloodless lips. "This isn't fair! Dimitri had nothing to do with Repinsky's death! I beg you not to punish Dimitri for my crime!"

Catherine's eyes contracted sharply. "I am never unfair! I can hardly overlook the fact that Denisov knew of Repinsky's murder and chose to share the duplicity rather than report it. This makes him part of the conspiracy!" Undisguised rage mottled Catherine's cheeks. "Prince Dimitri has been a great disappointment. He forgets his duty to me and to the state. I can no longer tolerate his negligence of Maria Theresa's niece! This was not our agreement. As an exile he is divorced—a more tractable husband will be found who will remember his duty and obligations as a husband and as a loyal subject!"

Nicole's world shattered into fragments. When she opened her lashes, Catherine was staring at her. "Your Majesty . . . all of this is so unnecessary. I was never a threat to you. I never desired a crown, never."

For an instant Catherine's face softened, and then she sighed. "That is the pity of it—I believe you. You were never personally a danger—it was the idea of you which imperiled." Her gaze reflected a sudden sad affection. "You wish to be the woman . . . I wish to be the empress." A deep sorrow pained her eyes, a flash, then vanished. "Perhaps you are the more fortunate." She tugged the cord hanging beside her desk.

The interview had concluded.

Catherine folded her slim hands on her papers as Nicole rose on unsteady legs. "I think we shall not encounter one another again. Go with God," she added softly.

"And you, your Majesty." Summoning a reserve of pride and dignity, Nicole bowed deeply, then gathered her skirts and raised her head high. Iron flowed into her spine and she backed from the room as gracefully as if the audience had addressed only pleasant themes.

But once the heavy doors clanged shut, her step faltered. Six uniformed guards fell into step both before and behind, raising a wobbling smile to Nicole's pale lips. The number appeared excessive for one small frightened woman. The secretary cleared his throat and formally informed her that she was under house arrest. The next exile train departed St. Petersburg on foot in two weeks. She was instructed to dispose of all personal holdings within this period.

Two weeks. Her wavering smile turned to irony. An hour—a lifetime ago—her heart had soared at the mention of "two weeks." Now ... Now the phrase signaled an ending.

Her shaking fingers dropped protectively to her stomach, and her eyes were hot and shiny with unshed tears.

Her baby would be born into a vast frozen wasteland. Siberia.

22

PAVLA WAS FIRST to spot the *etape* through a thick primordial growth of snow-covered larch and pine and birch trees. Following Pavla's mittened finger, Nicole released a small tired sigh; this rest house was as dilapidated as the others had been. With all her heart she craved a hot bath and a clean soft bed and a wholesome meal. But she knew the stockaded enclosure would be filthy, cold, and vermin-ridden, the food an abomination.

"We'll stretch our legs here, I think." Dimitri reined the horses to one side, allowing space to pass for those unable to afford the luxury of transportation. He swiveled on the driver's seat and looked into the boat-shaped bed of a *tarantas* which had been divested of its wheels and mounted on sled runners. As the *tarantas* was devoid of passenger seats, Nicole and Pavla balanced precariously on their luggage, shivering and vainly attempting to discover a position of relative comfort. There was none.

"*Da*," Vadim answered for all. After knocking his gloves free of ice, he lifted giant arms and swung Nicole to the snowpack, then stretched a hand to Pavla. "But don't walk too far," he cautioned, touching Nicole's cheek. "We don't want you tiring yourself."

"You're worse than a mother hen," Nicole teased. She raised her mitten and pressed it to his dark beard. "And so are you," she added, smiling at Pavla.

Pavla stamped her feet and slapped at her shoulders. Gradually a sluggish circulation returned to cramped muscles. She winked at Vadim. "We've never had a baby before."

"Correct." Vadim beamed. His cheeks were fiery with the cold. "This old *diad'ka* isn't ready for pasture. There'll be another Denisov to tutor." Rummaging in his coat, he produced his pipe and leaned against the side board of the *tarantas* with a sigh.

Nicole could well imagine his weariness. There wasn't space in the *tarantas* to accommodate them all. Throughout the last thousand miles, Vadim and Dimitri had spelled one another at the reins, one driving as the other trudged beside the sled. Vadim insisted upon walking more frequently than he rode; he'd exhausted three pairs of boots between Moscow and the Ural Mountains.

He shrugged when Dimitri admonished him to accept his turn in the sled. "It'd easier for me—I'm not wearing leg irons." Because Pavla and Vadim were voluntary exiles, neither was forced to endure the five-pound fetters constraining Nicole and Dimitri. The leg chains transformed walking into a painfully slow and fatiguing process.

Taking Nicole's arm, Dimitri kicked through the snow to a fallen log, then knelt and massaged the tender flesh above the iron bands cuffing her ankles. "If I could, I would kill the man who locked these on you!"

"They don't hurt," Nicole lied. She reached to tuck a lock of black hair beneath his fur cap. "Don't worry so much. I'm healthier now than I've ever been." A contradiction lay in the dark bruises beneath her eyes and was repeated in a persistent shiver trembling along her shoulders. Her stomach growled, and she wrapped her cloak tighter about her body, secretly hoping the added pressure would appease a constant hunger.

Dimitri dropped to the log beside her and stared at the line of exiles struggling through the snowdrifts near the *tarantas*. "Liar," he accused softly. "Even if you were healthy, how long would you remain so on a diet of sour bread, no meat, and a few ounces of gruel?" Hard, brooding eyes studied her cold face and the faint bluish tinge shading her lips. The color of his eyes matched the smoky gray of the heavy damp mist drifting in the treetops. "If we stay with the exiles, Nicole, you'll weaken and die. Already your cheeks are hollow. Not enough nourishment is provided to sustain a woman with child."

Her senses sharpened and she studied the angry lines drawing his face. "*If* we stay with the train. . . . Then you're still plotting an escape?"

"Of course." They watched a green-coated guard rein his horse beside the *tarantas* and address Vadim. Puffs of silvery vapor concealed his lips. The forest absorbed noise like a moist sponge; they couldn't overhear the guards' conversation nor did they hear the desolate clank of the prisoners' leg chains. "I won't have my son born in exile."

Nicole inhaled slowly, feeling the deep cold burn her lungs. "Dimitri . . ." Laying her glove on his arm, she searched his eyes. Each night they were locked in the miserable *etapes*, and a dozen guards patrolled the lines throughout the daylight marches. Death was the only form of escape Nicole had observed. Death by freezing, death by starvation, death by disease. She shivered and clasped her arms about her stomach, unconsciously protecting the gentle mound lifting her heavy wool skirt.

"Escape." She tested the word. If they failed to escape, she would end in Yakutsk, while her husband—she savored the word "husband"—would labor in the mines near Irkutz. She would never see him again. Never. She could not conceive of "never." "Is escape possible?" Twin lines furrowed her brow as she struggled to prevent her doubt from showing.

"Anything is possible." Dimitri adjusted her hood over her hair, cupping the fur next to her pink cheeks. "Vadim and I have nearly completed the details." He kissed her forehead and held her tightly. "God in heaven, but I miss you!" he whispered huskily.

"It's been so long . . ." By day they were allowed to share the sled, but at night men and women were segregated. The sight of husbands and wives touching hands before being prodded toward separate cells was painful to observe and worse to endure. Nicole rested her head against his fur collar and drew on the strength of his steady heartbeat.

"We'll reach Ekaterinburg in two days." Dimitri spoke in a normal tone, though the guard watched them. The thick growth of *taiga* swallowed their voices. "We'll make our escape from there."

Nicole's heart lurched and her grip tightened. "So soon!"

"The next major stopover beyond Ekaterinburg is the forwarding prison at Tiumen. Once beyond Tiumen, we're too deeply into Siberia to hope for success. It must be Ekaterinburg."

Shifting on the log, Nicole stared at their fetters. Ice clogged the links lying on the snow crust. Although the exile system appeared a chaos of disorder, with accident and caprice playing equal roles, Nicole had learned of few successful escapes. Distance and climate favored the guards over the prisoners. But escapes surely must occur. And she trusted Dimitri's judgment. Firming her chin, she met his questioning eyes. "How will it happen and what can I do?"

"The key is preparation. And money," Dimitri answered flatly. He patted his coat, indicating the gold coins sewn into the lining. The coins had purchased the *tarantas* and horses, luxuries most of the exiles could not afford. "Bribes." Assisting Nicole to her feet, he nodded toward the guard conversing with Pavla. "He's been bought. There are others. We'll purchase supplies in Ekaterinburg, and two fast sleds. I'm arranging now for horse relays." He stared intently into her wide sober eyes. "We'll use the rivers as much as possible. Frozen, they're better roads than any in the world. We'll travel fast and hard, my little Tasha, we'll accomplish in two weeks the same distance covered by the exile train in several months. I have a French ship waiting in Riga. Can you endure it, my darling?"

"Yes," she answered firmly. "Whatever you ask, I can do. Pavla and I will be ready." She lifted her face for his warm, hungry kiss; then they directed reluctant steps toward the *tarantas*.

"Conserve your strength; the journey will be brutal." He

held her tightly, his lips buried in her hair; then he swung her atop the luggage and turned to argue with Vadim.

Vadim grinned, his black eyes twinkling above the frost sparkling in his beard. "You drive, *barchuk*, and I'll walk. After that rest, I can walk to China!" Clasping the edge of the *tarantas*, he snorted like an ox and raised the sled upon one runner—luggage, occupants, and all.

Pavla clung to the side board with her good hand. "Put us down, you imbecile! The point is made!" She grinned at him and made a face.

Nicole smiled and silently thanked God for their loyalty and kindness. Pavla and Vadim had insisted upon accompanying the Denisovs into exile. No amount of argument had dissuaded either. And Nicole guiltily admitted she was glad it had not. As Dimitri shouted the tired horses back onto the path, she reached beneath the lap robe and found Pavla's hand, giving it a grateful squeeze. Pavla returned the pressure with a smile, then waved her stocking-covered stump at Vadim, urging him to keep pace. Vadim pelted her with snowballs, attempting vainly to appear remorseful when one of the hard balls knocked Dimitri's cap askew and Dimitri roared in mock outrage.

Tears of affection froze in Nicole's lashes as she bowed her head. Their efforts to divert her sinking spirits touched her deeply.

All traces of levity vanished upon attaining the stockade. Inside the pointed wooden fence, horses and sleds and dragging feet had churned the yard into an ankle-deep soup of mud and manure and human offal and kitchen scraps. Even in winter, a noxious stench announced the *etapes* long before they emerged from the thick surround of *taiga*.

While Dimitri and Vadim quartered the horses, Nicole and Pavla lifted their sodden hems and picked through the muck toward the entrance to the common room. A blast of fetid overheated air choked them as the iron door squealed open. Only the promise of warmth and food forced their steps into the dark foul interior. As always, the common room was crowded with gray-coated prisoners. A scent of despair and hopelessness as powerful as the stink of urine and vomit stung their nostrils. Peering through the smoke, Pavla located a barrel of *kvas* and returned with a bowl for Nicole and one for herself cradled in the crook of her arm.

Without expression, Nicole dipped a fingertip into the bowl and removed a black beetle; then she lifted the *kvas* to her lips and drank, directing her gaze toward the log wall. The figures hunched over the tables depressed her. Faces flickering in the dim illumination of smoking animal fat reflected impotence and resentment and bitter desperation. If Nicole met those eyes, it was as if a transfer occurred, and she too surrendered to the desolation of despair.

A camaraderie of common catastrophe bound them all; over the last months their faces had become as familiar as the yellow diamonds stitched to the spines of their gray coats. At the *verst* post marking the division of European Russia and Siberia, they had all joined hands and wept on each other's shoulders, each understanding the other's pain at leaving home and family behind. All were united in the day-to-day struggle for survival. And in their hatred for the indifferent guards and for appallingly primitive conditions.

Nicole stared into the gaunt faces, and a shudder swept her small frame. Many of the people in this room would not survive the long trek. They would succumb to fatigue, cold, starvation, and the myriad diseases lurking in the filth and the food. A silent prayer wrenched her heart: Please, God, protect those I love.

When Dimitri and Vadim entered, she shoved through the sea of gray coats and flung herself into Dimitri's arms as Vadim's bulk and hostile stare cleared a space at one of the tables.

"Are you feeling all right?" Weary shadows of concern flickered across Dimitri's face; the hollows in his cheeks sank deeper as an effect of the uncertain smoky illumination.

"Yes, I just . . ." She probed his tired eyes and welcomed the perils of escape. No risk outweighed the devastation of a separation. "All this . . ." Her wave encompassed the dirt and the hunched figures and the choking atmosphere. "None of it matters as long as you're here with me!"

His hand, still cold from the frigid temperatures beyond the door, stroked her pale cheek tenderly. "My wife."

Nicole kissed his palm and pressed it to her cheek. Then she ate the wretched bread and *kasha*. And bitterly resented the approaching nightly segregation.

The women's *kamera*, cell, was an unheated long barrack, indistinguishable from other *kameras* in other *etapes* along the exile trail. Dried mud and hard-trodden filth blackened the floor. The air was so poisoned and foul it hurt to breathe. Pale chill moonlight provided the only illumination, emanating from three cracked panes set in a heavy grate near the ceiling. An enormous sleeping platform occupied the center of the room, perhaps twelve feet wide and thirty feet long. An uncomfortable slant elevated the head above the feet. It was the only furniture provided other than a large wooden tub used for excrement.

Nicole climbed onto the platform beside Pavla, and they curled together for warmth. Long ago they had abandoned wishing for blankets or pillows; had any been provided, the items would have vanished before dawn.

As the *kamera* quieted for the night, Nicole lay sleepless, listening dully to the rustlings of exhausted bodies seeking an elusive comfort upon the hard bare planks. Leg chains rattled. A child whimpered. Someone wept softly. And Nicole bit her knuckles and remembered silk sheets and a man's hard warmth.

She started when Pavla pressed her shoulder and whispered. A frosty vapor issued before her cold lips. "Here." Pavla reached around Nicole's body, pushing a piece of greasy cloth into her hand.

Careful not to disturb the woman whose spine lay three inches from her nose, Nicole lifted her hand and unfolded the cloth around a chunk of roasted meat. "Oh, Pavla." A choking wave of emotion smothered her voice as she turned to position her mouth near Pavla's kerchief. "You take this. I know you're as hungry as I am." How Pavla produced the occasional bits of meat remained a mysterious thievery of near-miraculous proportion.

"*Nyet.* The baby needs nourishment." When Nicole mounted a whispered barrage of protest, Pavla yawned elaborately. "Shhh. You'll wake the others." She closed her eyes and pretended sleep, the matter concluded.

Nicole sighed and then gobbled the meat, savoring each small bite, chewing it slowly until it nearly disappeared, and longing for more. All the while experiencing stabbings of guilt—everyone was hungry. "Are you still awake?" she whispered. She too had a gift.

"*Nyet.*"

"There's news." Nicole cupped an icy hand about Pavla's ear and whispered Dimitri's plans. Even in the faint chill light she could observe the excitement leaping into Pavla's dark eyes. "And when we're free, I promise you will never go hungry again! I'll never forget your devotion!"

A troubled spasm erased the pleasure from Pavla's features. "If it wasn't for me, you wouldn't be here! One thing led to another, but the whole chain began with me!"

"Who is to say? It's God's will." Once one was indoctrinated with the peasant fatalism, the concept was difficult to relinquish. Nicole adjusted her cheek into her mitten and sought vainly to relax cramped muscles. She prayed it was God's will to favor their escape.

The plans lifted sagging spirits. Snowdrifts didn't appear as insurmountable, the stinging cold didn't bite as severely at cheeks and toes. Hardships could be endured. Because a ship waited in Riga. The knowledge conquered cold and hunger, made bearable that which previously had seemed intolerable. When they glanced into each other's eyes, hope flourished there, the anticipation increasing as the *verst* posts announced they approached Ekaterinburg.

As the *tarantas* broke from the snowy edge of a dense larch forest, Dimitri reined the horses and studied the town below, memorizing the street grid and the surrounding terrain. He and Vadim conversed soberly, their fur caps bent together, as Pavla and Nicole climbed down to stamp cold feet and slap at thighs and arms. A light fall of fresh snow dusted their cheeks and hoods.

"Back in line!"

At the guard's shout, both women hastily returned to their cramped perch atop the luggage, but the guard ignored Dimitri and Vadim with a broad wink and concentrated his shouts on the painful struggle of those who walked. Suddenly freed of the sound-swallowing *taiga*, the prisoners' chains became audible. The mournful clanking drummed a shuffling dirge. Nicole cringed and bowed her head.

"Everything is arranged," Dimitri promised quietly. He walked beside the *tarantas* as Vadim returned the horses to the path. Vadim held the horses to a slow gait, allowing Dimitri to keep pace with the sled. His chains dragged and sank in the snow, snagging on underlying branches and stones. "All that remains is to bribe the guards in Ekaterinburg."

Nicole stretched to brush new snow from his cap. He'd lost weight. Caverns sank below his high cheekbones; new lines fanned from his silvery eyes. The aura of lean command had intensified. The new gauntness fashioned a face men would fear as well as respect. Power and force jutted across his countenance like a challenge; one would think twice before opposing this man. And Nicole loved him so intensely the violence of emotion pained.

"Dimitri . . . can anything go wrong?" Despite determined efforts, anxiety crept along the edges of her mind.

His glove lifted and a thumb caressed her lips. "Nothing is without risk, my little Tasha." A shrug adjusted the heavy *tulup* about his shoulders. "If a man is corrupt enough to accept a bribe, he is corrupt enough to renege upon whatever the bribe purchased." His reassuring smile quashed the alarm flaring her wide eyes. "We will get out." Suddenly the smile vanished and hard promise tightened his jawline. "Our son won't be born in a prison!"

"Our son?" Valiantly she attempted to tease away his frightening intensity, but her small effort failed. His acknowledging smile was taut, distracted. And she understood his thoughts shot ahead, occupied by a thousand details.

Dimitri held her glove and trudged beside the *tarantas*, struggling against the chains limiting his stride. An expression of cold fury knotted his brow when he stooped to untangle the obstructive links. Snow frosted his cap and shoulders. He seemed unaware of the frigid air and dripping trees.

Before they gained the city gates, he detailed his plan in terse, clipped statements. Nicole would complain of stomach pains when she and the other women were settled into the *kamera* for the night. A guard would then escort Nicole and Pavla into the prison yard and look aside when they ran toward the stables instead of proceeding to the common room. Vadim and Dimitri would be waiting with two sleds and supplies. They would abandon the luggage.

"If anything goes wrong . . ." Dimitri's hard, unyielding eyes locked to hers. "Vadim will take you to Riga and on to Boston. The ship passage is paid. When you reach Boston, call on Dr. Warren immediately. He's holding a chest of gold in both our names."

Nicole's fingers tightened convulsively about his glove. If anything terrible happened to Dimitri, her world would blacken and decay. "Dimitri, without you, I . . ." She couldn't voice the unthinkable words. It was selfish, she knew, but if one of them was fated to die, she prayed it would be herself. Death would be more acceptable than facing life without her heart.

As if reading her mind, Dimitri stroked her cheek. "You're strong, Nicole. Stronger than you realize." He brought her glove to his lips. "Nothing will go wrong." But the core of intensity hardening his stare quivered along her nerves. She was not reassured. "Remember always that I love you. I have loved you from the first moment I saw you. And I will love you even after God stills this heart!"

He was saying good-bye! Her heart lurched painfully. "Dimitri!" But he had dropped behind the *tarantas* as the exile line thinned to enter the city gates. They could not speak, but their eyes held, communicating their love as if the light curtain of snow did not lay between them.

Nicole's anxious stare remained riveted to his face as Dimitri swung aside to study the wide unpaved streets of Ekaterinburg. Dimly she perceived square log houses separated by high wooden fences, white-walled churches with colored domes, a noisy bazaar undaunted by the worsening climate. People of every description paused to jeer the line of exiles, high-cheeked Yakutes, Orientals, peasants, soldiers, and women whose haughty chins and heavy warm furs identified them as nobility. Some hurled balls of ice at the shuffling exile train, taunting them with the hardships to come. Those who would remain in Ekaterinburg to labor in the gold and copper and pig-iron mines bowed their heads beneath the assault. Nicole dodged an ice ball and protected her cheeks with her hood, as did Pavla.

The road fronting the high walls surrounding the prison was a lake of semifrozen mud. The sled dragged and pitched, the runners sinking, then bucking forward. Razorback hogs foraged in the squalid garbage heaps outside the walls. Both Nicole and Pavla gasped and pressed their mittens to their nostrils as a foul stench assailed their nostrils long before the gates swung out to admit the exiles. Nothing helped. As they entered, a detail of guards passed the *tarantas*, whipping a horse-drawn sled heavy with lifeless forms. The naked bodies would be dumped in the snowdrifts outside the city gates, to be disposed of by marauding wolves.

Nicole shuddered and a cold stone of fear lodged in the pit of her stomach. To end as fodder for the wolves shocked the soul. Wildly her gaze swung about the yard, seeking Dimitri. She needed his strength now, when the risk of escape loomed with terrifying reality, no longer a verbal exercise. He stood at the far end of the enclosure, deep in conversation with a guard whose small greedy eyes glittered as he listened. "Dimitri!" But the noise of clashing chains and shouted commands swallowed her cry. A dozen exile trains funneled into Ekaterinburg; nearly two hundred gray-coated prisoners milled about the muck layering the yard, staring at the new arrivals through blunted eyes.

Unlike the *etapes*, the Ekaterinburg prison segregated men and women immediately upon arrival. Nicole and Pavla were herded into a stumbling line of women and children and marched to the prison *bania*. When the women realized their destination, lagging steps quickened, anticipating the damp heat against cold-stiffened bones.

Once beyond a cursory examination for lice and disease, Nicole rested her golden head against the inner *bania* wall and sighed deeply, filling her lungs with the wonderfully warm steam. Forcibly she ejected all troubling thoughts, allowing nothing to divert her weary flesh from soaking in the moist heat. It was her first bath in three weeks.

"Already you're rounded." Pavla smiled, examining the satiny curve extending below Nicole's full breasts. A wise nod swung her loose dark hair across dripping shoulders. "He'll be a big one." She tossed back her hair and secured it with her stump, while her left hand deftly separated the strands for plaiting.

Nicole's lips formed a private smile, and she gently traced the mound swelling her waist. Or what had once been a waist. Her skirts fit snugly about her thickening body; they needed adjusting. The task would provide an occupation, once aboard ship.

Instantly a chill of fear raised bumps along her naked skin. The cold lay inside, resisting the clouds of steamy heat. The journey to Riga was long and arduous, fraught with opportunities for peril. Would they actually reach the ship? Her wide eyes locked to Pavla's stare, and she read an identical kernel of apprehension.

"We will make it, won't we?" Pavla whispered, her eyes beseeching assurance.

Nicole swallowed and concealed her expression as she toweled her hair. "Of course." She willed an image of hard slate eyes, and her voice firmed. "Of course we'll make it."

"I'm not really worried . . ." Pavla offered weakly. "I've escaped before. Did I tell you about the time I was held prisoner by . . . ?"

Nicole shook her damp tresses with exasperated fondness. "Pavla, you're hopeless!" She kissed Pavla's wide grin and they dressed quickly, responding to a burly matron's hostile prodding.

The heavy cold outside the *bania* shot needles of ice deep into their lungs. Snowflakes struck sharp and stinging against overheated cheeks.

Protecting their faces, the women marched to a long narrow room, dark and foul, where they would eat, sleep, and quarrel for the next three weeks until another, larger train formed for the next leg of the trek. Nicole and Pavla gingerly seated themselves on the edge of the sleeping platform, balancing bowls of suspicious gray soup upon their laps while trying desperately not to breathe. The poisoned air seared chests and burned nostrils.

Babies cried and children vomited and the women argued fiercely for space. Dim snowy light filtered past iron-grated windows illuminating a scummed water barrel placed next to an overflowing excrement bucket. Nicole shivered violently as her stomach rolled. It would require little pretense to convince anyone that she was ill.

Minutes stretched into hours as Nicole and Pavla silently awaited nightfall. Gradually the women settled into the *kamera*, establishing their territory, tending hopelessly to their small needs. The excrement bucket overturned and flooded across the frozen mud floor. No one had the stomach to right it. Two women and three children collapsed and were dragged away. A wild-eyed creature cowered in a corner, squatting in the black cold muck chewing on her chains until her teeth splintered and blood froze on her chin and someone alerted a guard. The guard struck her repeatedly, then kicked her through the iron door.

When Nicole believed she could bear no more misery, when the scream sticking in her throat threatened to explode, the last vestige of light faded and the women stretched wearily along the bare platform. Their breath formed a chill silvery mist at head level.

"Now?" Pavla whispered. She blew on her fingers, eyes wide and almost feverish above her mitten.

"*Da.* Now."

As Pavla slipped from the platform, Nicole sat forward in the blackness and leaned over her knees, drawing a long toxic breath. A moan issued from between her bluish lips, and she wasn't certain if the sound was entirely manufactured. The woman nearest her shivered and whimpered in her sleep as if she sensed the approaching guard. He stared down at Nicole.

"Are you Natasha Denisovna?" he asked in a low tone.

"*Da.*" His feet had sunk to the boot tops in the mud and inky foulness freezing across the floor. Nicole averted her eyes, certain he must hear the increased drumbeat of her heart. A flush of nerves stained her cheeks. She told herself the escape would be successful. Everything was arranged; it was God's will.

"Follow me." The guard's voice lifted for the benefit of any sleepless listeners. "I'll take you to the hospital." He cleared his throat. "Across the compound and up three flights."

Nicole slid into the muck and felt Pavla's strong arm circle her waist. Once outside the *kamera*, both paused for a quick breath of clean air, sickened to discover it nearly as poisonous as that inside. Nicole blinked through a veil of thickening snow, seeking the dark outline of the stables.

"That way," the guard hissed. A rough hand shoved Pavla.

Pavla spit at his boots, then pulled Nicole through windtousled drifts as quickly as Nicole's leg chains allowed.

A shaft of yellow light spilled into the dark night as they approached a door set into a log wall. Vadim swept them inside, his powerful arms a familiar comfort. He bolted the door.

"Over there," he directed. Quickly he lowered Nicole onto a low stool and produced a key, brandishing it triumphantly before he uncuffed her leg irons and threw them toward a second discarded pair. "Better?" he inquired, rubbing his large hands gently over her ankles.

"Dimitri?" Alarm flared her eyes. A masked lantern cast enough light across the piles of hay for her to observe Dimitri's absence.

Vadim captured her fluttering hands. "Outside, hitching the horses to the sleds. He's fine." As Nicole closed her lashes in relief, Vadim touched Pavla's fiery cheeks, then pulled them both to their feet, hurrying them toward another door and then outside into the frigid black night. Two sleds appeared from the swirl of snow and rising wind.

"Dimitri!" Nicole ran forward, and suddenly she was in his warm strong arms. His hard mouth found her lips, crushing hungrily as eddies of snow swirled about their caps. She clung furiously to the taste and touch and smell of him. She knew they hadn't the time to spare, but she pressed against him with fierce need, wishing she could melt into him, wishing she could become a part of each breath, each steady heartbeat.

Lifting her chin, he smiled into her eyes. "Draw on the courage which is so much a part of you, little Tasha. Think of this"—the smoky challenge in his eyes indicated the compound—"as only an ugly memory." He kissed her again, tenderly now, as soft as the snowflakes melting on her flushed cheeks. "Soon, my love . . . soon!" Sweeping her into his arms, he cradled her against his chest for a timeless moment, staring deeply into her shining eyes; then he lowered her into the straw bed of a small fast sled and adjusted a thick robe about her body. In the adjacent sled, Vadim settled Pavla. Dimitri touched Nicole's lips briefly; then he called quietly into the snow-shrouded blackness, "Ready?"

"*Da, barchuk!*"

Within the muffled silence enclosing the stockade, the horses' hooves and the jangle of harness sounded unnervingly loud as Dimitri and Vadim walked toward a dark gate, guiding the horses by their bridles. Nicole bit her lip and prayed silently. She wouldn't believe they were truly safe until Ekaterinburg lay far behind them, not until they had traveled deep into the protective camouflage of the larch forests climbing the Urals, not until they stepped onto the deck of the ship waiting in Riga.

The sled glided to a halt, and she held her breath as Dimitri commanded in a low harsh tone, "Open the gate!"

"One moment."

Nicole's senses quivered, balancing on the nervous voice emerging from the dark curtain of snow obscuring the gate.

Something was wrong. The gate did not open.

She wet her lips in a ringing silence.

"Open it. Now!" Dimitri growled.

A rustle of movement responded from the deep shadows, and Dimitri's hand dropped to a sword Nicole had not noticed until this moment. Her heart lurched at the sudden tension cording his jaw and sharpening his voice.

"*Barchuk!* We've been betrayed!"

At Vadim's roar, Nicole struggled upward, kicking free of the fur robe. A half-dozen soldiers rushed from a niche in the wall, their swords drawn. Before Nicole could drop from the sled, the sharp ring of scraping metal exploded in her ears. Eyes wide and terrified, she collapsed to her knees in the straw and clung to the edge of the sled as Dimitri positioned his back to her. Skillfully he parried the thrusts of three rushing soldiers. But he was outmanned.

With a mixture of pride and freezing fear, Nicole pressed her knuckles to white lips and stared at the glint of far torchlight flashing from the blades. Vadim's bellow sounded battle behind her, but Nicole didn't dare turn. Her pounding heart fastened to the furious fight unfolding before her frightened eyes. And a stream of words poured from her lips, but she did not hear them.

One of the soldiers cursed and sank to the snow clutching his side; another blinked at a gash ripping across his shoulder. "Yes!" Nicole's fists clenched, beating at the sled's side boards. "Yes, yes, yes!"

Then she screamed and her heart stopped.

The two soldiers lunged as one, and Dimitri stiffened. As if in slow motion, his sword slowly toppled, limp in his fingers. One hand grasped the sled board, so near that Nicole could have touched him. The other hand lifted to his face.

And came away red.

Red. The color of shock; the color of fear and horror. That smeared red hand would haunt the remainder of Nicole's days. She stared without breathing, a whimper of denial beginning low in her throat. No. From the corner of her eyes she saw Vadim loom up from the snowy darkness. He rushed behind the two soldiers and smashed their heads together, crushing them like ripe melons. They fell silently, and Vadim leaped over their bodies and raced to Dimitri's side. "Easy, now." His giant hands guided Dimitri to the snow beside the sled. Dimitri slid down, and a layer of new snow turned pink on his coat.

"No!" The paralysis ended suddenly. Nicole clawed over the boards and dropped to her knees in the snow, angrily dashing a blinding moisture from disbelieving eyes. "Oh, God! No!" Her cries lifted on the wind, muffled by the falling snow. The blade had slashed his cheek and opened his jawline. A second wound seeped across the front of his coat. If he lived, there would be a scar, a terrible scar. And his right eye was in danger, the blade had come so close! "Dimitri!" If he lived. "Oh, God, please! I beg you—I'll do anything you ask! Dimitri!"

One hand covered the horrifying wound; the other lifted and Nicole snatched it, pressing it to her cheek, kissing the palm desperately, cradling his hand to the burning tears streaking her face. His eyes caressed her; then his stare slipped upward. A calm intensity signaled Vadim.

Vadim's mitten closed upon Nicole's shoulder. "Come! We haven't a second to spare!"

"No!" Nicole shook her head violently. Her hood flew back, and snow glittered through her hair. "I won't leave him!" It was unthinkable. Her hands shook so badly she didn't dare touch him for fear of increasing his pain. They had to have help immediately. Somewhere in the depths of this hellhole there must be a doctor! Glancing upward, her eyes wild, she screamed into Pavla's frozen horror, "Run to the guardhouse! Get help!"

"No." Dimitri's whisper cracked upward. Willpower and need soared above the pain. "Go with Vadim. I'll follow when I can."

Nicole stared at an opaque veil descending across his eyes; then she buried her face in her mittens, weeping hysterically. He was dying. And hungry wolves patrolled the countryside. "No! I won't leave without you. You need care . . . and medicine . . . and . . ." It couldn't end like this, blood and snow, lost in the wasteland of Siberia! No, no! Not when they had found each other, not when the future beckoned so brightly.

Above her babbling, Vadim and Pavla conferred rapidly. "Listen to me. It's best if I stay," Pavla insisted. "You can't get medicine or bandages, but I can. No door is locked against me!" Even now a pride of conviction underscored the truth in her voice.

Vadim agreed hastily. His massive bulk sank into the snow and his voice emerged urgent but steady. "*Barchuk*? Can you hear?" Dimitri's eyes settled on Vadim's face. The blood had begun to freeze on his cheek. "Rest well, *barchuk*. I'll take her home."

Dimitri's expression eased, and for a brief moment the terrible glassiness retreated before a sharp clear expression of gratitude. His gaze swung toward Nicole and softened. Cold lips moved, forming "I love you." But no sound emerged. A small rush of air puffed silvery above his mouth; then his eyes closed and his dark head dropped.

Nicole screamed. She flung herself across his body, her hands flying over his face, his hair, his chest. Incoherent words bubbled like acid upon her lips. Wildly she begged him, then commanded him to respond. "Dimitri! Wake up!" Tears strangled her screams. A numbness as bitter cold as the ice beneath her knees closed about her heart and squeezed the breath from her chest. "Dimitri, please!" She utterly rejected what her eyes and hands confirmed.

"Pavla! Open the gate!"

She heard Vadim's tense command as if from a vast distance, watched Pavla run into the dark curtain of snow concealing the gate. Across the compound a door opened and a guard leaned into the spill of light. Instantly a shrill whistle split the air.

Giant hands gripped Nicole's shoulders, ripping her upward and onto her feet. Teeth bared, she fought like an animal, smashing and clawing at Vadim's face and arms, stretching her mittens toward Dimitri's still form. A thin coating of snow lay over his face, and it offended everything decent and good; it was vital, the most important act in the world, to brush the cold snow from his lips and lashes. "Let me go! Dammit! I order you to let me go!"

Vadim stared into her hot wild eyes; then he whispered, "Natushka, forgive me." His massive fist drew back.

White-hot pain exploded along her jaw and erupted upward, searing her mind in agonizing waves of black and gray. Her knees went slack, and Nicole pitched forward, blinking in shock.

A merciful oblivion washed over her mind.

23

SHE OPENED HER eyes to frigid air and blackness. If she held herself perfectly still, the cold was bearable, but if she shifted outside the envelope of her body warmth, even slightly, needles of ice stabbed past her clothing. She blinked rapidly, fighting the wisps of fog floating through her brain. Gradually she became aware of a dull throbbing ache along her jaw. And gingerly she touched her cheek, grimacing at the resulting leap of pain.

Her movement disturbed the artificial darkness, and Nicole realized her head and body were covered by a heavy black fur. Thrashing upward, she fought clear of the robes and lifted her head. Icy wind clawed at her face; a bitter cold lashed her cheeks.

But neither terrified her as did the hunched bear towering above her on the seat of the sled. The world spun, and she felt the creaking sway of the pirate ship, stared in horror at a

307

mountain of furred flesh. A shattering cry burst from her stiffening lips. She thought of

The bear swiveled on the seat, and Vadim's black eyes peered down at her, narrowed against the biting wind. Frost rimed his brow and beard, icing them as white as the tufts of hair escaping from his black fur cap. An icicle hung from one nostril. "Stay covered!" he shouted, waving her into the thick robes. He pushed a wool scarf over his nose and mouth and turned back on the seat, cracking a long whip above the heads of racing horses.

Nicole's fear dissolved in short gasping breaths, but her confusion remained. She protected her face with the lower edges of her fur-lined hood and stared at the frozen landscape flashing past the sled. She couldn't estimate the time, but night had surrendered to day. A frozen white day. Snow piled in high drifts along the banks of the icecapped river; snow lay a foot deep beneath the hooves of the flying horses. Dry white pellets blew out of a leaden sky. The blankness of white engulfed her. And the resulting disorientation played chaos with her confusion. Unless she fixed her gaze steadfastly upon Vadim's broad fur-clad spine, she felt as if she were swimming in a cold white sea, lost and directionless.

Then memory returned like an exploding sun, shooting rays of scarlet pain deep into the flesh and mind.

A razor agony, sharper than the screaming wind, more bitterly penetrating than the slashing cold, slammed across her senses. Reeling, Nicole doubled into the straw and wrenched into a tight ball. Raw whimpers froze before her lips, cracked, and vanished on the wind. Wet red smears flickered before her eyelids, a gleam of bone.

And she pleaded to die, to follow wherever her heart had gone. She wept and cursed and bargained with God, and felt a biting emptiness carve out the space which once had housed her soul. Dimitri was dead, and time elapsed in units of anguish.

When the sled shivered to a halt, she was unaware of the change in motion until a woman's heavy mitten stirred beneath the furs, then lifted Nicole's wild face. Tears froze to crystal beads on her cheeks, the process almost instant. A cup appeared, and vodka choked down her throat and burned across the pit of her stomach, imparting a false energy.

"Vadim!" Nicole struggled against the bulky robes, kicking and slapping at them in frustration. She had to speak to him, had to explain that they must turn back immediately. It was imperative! If they returned in time, they could rescue Dimitri's body from the death carts. She thought of the wolves prowling the *taiga*, and a deep horror constricted her breast.

Not until it was too late did she notice the ropes lashed across her furs. She couldn't extricate herself without assistance. "Vadim!" Her gloved hands formed into fists, and she leaned as far forward as the ropes allowed.

Vadim appeared in an intermittent blur, a snowy figure hitching fresh horses to the sled, examining them critically, dropping a small purse into the woman's mitten. The woman approached Nicole, her sheepskin cap bent against the savage wind; the indefinite outline of a rest house appeared, then vanished in the blizzard behind her bundled form. She tossed a food package over the side of the sled and hurried away, ignoring Nicole's sobbing pleas.

Vadim's whip cracked and the sled leaped into the storm, gliding up an incline, then hurtling down a long steep slope. A wide frozen roadway of river ice uncurled before them, and the sled gained speed until the brutal wind ripped the breath from Nicole's lungs and burned her exposed flesh. She screamed at the dark bent figure hunched above, but the wind whipped away her cries, burying them in the relentless white swirl. With a helpless wail she plunged beneath the robes and surrendered to the feral ravages of grief.

It came in waves, a surging black tide, a hurricane of wind and fury that smashed at the soul. She rocked in the straw and sobbed and screamed into the wind until her mind was blank and depleted and her limbs weak from thrashing.

When again she struggled upward through the tangle of robes, night had overshadowed the white. The stinging snow whirled out of blackness.

She blinked at the icy darkness; then her eyes settled on a glimmer of light flickering through the snow curtain, and then another, silhouetting Vadim's swaying figure on the seat above her. She could see he was dizzy with fatigue, and for a frantic moment Nicole feared he hadn't seen the lights. She released a long vapory breath as he reined the horses, and the sled glided to a silent halt before a log hut.

Vadim did not move, not until a man wearing a heavy *tulup* and a fur cap tugged his sleeve; then Vadim stumbled to the snowpack and lurched toward Nicole. His stiff gloves fumbled uselessly with the ropes securing her robes. Slowly he lifted his hands before dulled eyes, blinking stupidly, wondering why his fingers did not function. The man in the *tulup* gently shouldered Vadim aside and released Nicole, lifting her from the sled bed and half-carrying her through mountainous drifts and then into an *izba*, where he indicated a stool before the *pech*.

Nicole didn't question where they were; it didn't matter. Nothing mattered. She extended her hands toward the stove and closed her lashes until Vadim staggered inside and crossed himself before the "beautiful corner." He fell onto the bench before the table and buried his head in his hands. His face was a fiery red above the line of his scarf.

Nicole looked at him and remembered his promise to Dimitri. And knew with a twinge of despair that he would never agree to turn back.

"Here. Take this." A sturdy young peasant woman thrust a steaming cup of *kvas* into Nicole's shaking fingers, then timidly placed a larger container on the table before Vadim.

"Give them vodka, woman! Can't you see they're half-frozen?" The man slammed the door, pushing the howl of snow and wind outside. He stamped the snow from his *lapti* and tossed his cap and *tulup* toward a wooden peg. Gesturing impatiently, he directed the woman to assist Nicole while he pulled off Vadim's dripping coat.

With no memory of crossing the room, Nicole discovered herself seated at the table across from Vadim. She stared at a loaf of fresh crusty bread and an earthenware tureen of *kasha*. Not the foul gray *kasha* of the *etapes*, but a thick hot gruel studded with plump raisins and bits of cabbage.

Nicole's dull gaze appraised the food without appetite. It astonished her that Vadim retained the energy to eat. He broke the loaf and spooned *kasha* between his black beard and mustache, the movements wooden and mechanical. And repellent. Even the idea of eating cramped Nicole's stomach; watching sickened her.

All she could think of was a silent man lying on snow that slowly stained pink below his ribs, a man who, if he was alive, needed hot wholesome food like that sitting untouched before her. If he was alive. Nicole lowered her head and stared at her folded hands. She didn't care if she starved or froze. It didn't matter. Her grief craved punishment; it was morally wrong to eat and enjoy the warmth, to smile or taste or feel. Dimitri was dead or dying, and it was wrong—wrong!—that the world went on.

A baby's cry relieved the close quiet, and Nicole lifted a blank face toward the *pech*. A length of sturdy cloth had been suspended from the rafters, and the woman removed an infant from the folds of the sling. Murmuring soothing nonsense words, she sank to a stool before the warmth, opening her blouse with one hand as she cradled the infant in her other. In a moment the baby's tiny mouth closed over the source of nourishment and he gurgled in drowsy contentment.

Unconsciously Nicole's fingers dropped to cup the growing swell below her waist. She had forgotten. As impossible as it seemed, she had forgotten.

Shyly the young mother looked toward Nicole's stare. "His name is Petka—he's our first." Her dark eyes smiled toward her husband, who fed wood into the *pech*. Lightly he touched her kerchief before returning to the table.

Nicole's eyes brimmed. Letting her head fall backward, she blinked at the smoke darkened rafters and forced herself to consider the baby inside her womb. The baby meant she must endure; she must accept a life she no longer desired. And for one intense guilt-ridden moment she bitterly resented the child beneath her heart.

"Eat," Vadim commanded wearily. "The world looks better on a full stomach." A more normal color had reappeared above his beard, but not even the vodka could erase the glaze of fatigue masking his eyes.

Nicole shook her head. The world could never be better, never again; it would be gray forever. Her body stiffened in pain, recalling gray eyes which had acted as a barometer of emotion, sliding from gray to silver to slate to smoke.

"Punishing yourself proves nothing," Vadim observed quietly. He glanced pointedly at her stomach. "Would you punish the little one too?"

Blinking at resentful tears, Nicole lifted her spoon. She paid scant attention to the conversation until she comprehended that Vadim and the man discussed the possibilities for a successful escape.

". . . be out of the Urals tomorrow." Vadim's dull eyes flickered toward the sleeping shelves rimming the room. He rubbed his lids continually.

"The worst is behind you. As far as the Siberian government is concerned, the instant you pass the boundary *verst*, you have effectively escaped. They haven't the jurisdiction to pursue beyond the border. The chase will be taken up by the Russian soldiers." The man smiled. "The Russian soldiers care little for Siberian politics, even less for Siberian prisoners. If the blizzard continues, I'll wager your chances are excellent—the soldiers won't risk this weather for two prisoners."

"We'll find out," Vadim responded grimly. He didn't bother to explain their circumstances, but his eyes steadied upon Nicole and she knew he was thinking of Catherine's special interest in this particular prisoner. Regardless of the savage climate, it was more likely the Russian soldiers would pursue than that they would not. It would be dangerously foolish to assume otherwise.

"If we stay far enough ahead," Vadim muttered, "we'll never see them."

Nicole stroked aching temples. They would leave the Urals behind? Tomorrow? She couldn't believe it. The exile train had required several weeks to complete the snow-clogged trek across the low mountains. A slow stumbling drag of chains echoed through the hollowness of her mind. And she stared at Vadim with undisguised respect.

He pushed from the table and painfully stretched popping shoulders. Then he clapped the man on the shoulder and favored him with an exhausted smile. "Thank you, my friend, for assisting us."

The man, dwarfed alongside Vadim's bulk, shrugged. "You're paying enough." He waved Vadim toward the sleeping shelves. A hard point narrowed his eyes. "Years ago I vowed that if I survived my term in the mines, I would spend my life helping others escape."

Vadim sank to a straw pallet with a long low sigh. "You survived."

"*Nyet*, my friend. I would have died if I hadn't paid someone more wretched than myself to assume my name and my place in the shaft. I escaped."

"I am glad for you. Wake me at dawn." He was asleep instantly.

"That's less than two hours." Seeing that Vadim did not move, the man covered him with a heavy wool blanket, then plumped the straw for Nicole.

An unexpected sense of comfort stole over her as she lay sleepless in the darkened *izba*, listening to the wind howl around the corners. The *izba* represented life. Generations had flowed through this small room, had lived and loved and quarreled and labored and faded to create space for new generations. Such was nature's design. One generation surrendered to the next. But, oh, Lord, it was hard, so bitterly hard. She pressed her knuckles against her breast as a parade of faces marched across the *izba* ceiling. Irina, Larisca, Yuri, Katya, Dimitri. So bitterly hard, Lord. Weeping softly, Nicole curled around her stomach and closed red-rimmed eyes.

It was still dark and the cold was intense when they resumed their places in the sled, equipped with fresh horses and a basket of food which the woman advised Nicole to shelter with her body or the bread and cheese would freeze. Clouds of vapor rose from the warm bodies of the horses, and Nicole had occupied the sled but a few minutes before her silvery breath enshrouded the vehicle in mist.

"Good luck to you both. Go with God." The man waved a lantern against the predawn blackness, watching as Vadim swung the horses down the dark village lane and then on toward the frozen river.

Within minutes the tiny village had vanished far behind the flying sled. Sometime during the chill sharp morning, the snow thinned to a sparse fall; Vadim predicted it would cease entirely before late afternoon.

He leaned wearily against the sled as a man and a boy from a solitary post-house changed the heaving horses. The post-house resembled the others at which they had paused, a snowbanked isolation of log huts and stables. "If anyone is chasing us, we're giving them a good run for it." Vadim's deep voice was harsh. Then he smiled and urged Nicole to drain her cup of vodka. "Keep warm, Natushka, it's a long way yet."

Reluctantly Nicole did as he instructed. The flesh possessed a fierce will to survive, a will which surpassed the mind's despair. She drank the vodka and despised herself for living.

As the days and nights flickered past in a numb, quickly forgotten succession, she huddled, shivering, in a ball within the bed of the sled, and she endured the savage stages of grief. Disbelief yielded to utter rejection and then to torment. For days she struggled with a rage so virulent she teetered on the edge of violence. She longed to strike out at the good people who sheltered them, at Vadim, at the world.

Then finally her sore heart quieted into a dull, resigned acceptance. Nothing could alter the course of events; nothing would turn back the hands of time. And nothing truly mattered anymore. She wondered at the courage Dimitri had praised. Where was the woman who had wielded the pitchfork? She didn't know anymore.

A giant hand probed beneath the furs, rousing her from restless dreams of prowling wolves and flaming mansions. Nicole pushed upward through the robes and shielded her eyes against the hiss of a torch, bright against the black snowy night. Someone assisted her from the sled and kicked a path through the snowdrifts.

Another *izba*. Curious faces. Hot food. They blurred through her mind in a weary hash. And she thanked God for Vadim, her constant amid a confusion of shifting impressions. She reached across a wooden table to press his hand, and she peered affectionately into his glassy black stare. The grueling exertion of the last two weeks had sunk his eyes in dark rings; his massive shoulders slumped and his face was gray beneath the burn of wind and cold. He was too exhausted to finish his meal.

"Lie down," Nicole murmured. "You're asleep on your feet."

He nodded slowly, white hair swinging toward his black beard, covering the dead white tip of a frostbitten ear. "Rest, Natushka." He examined her pale face. She too wore blue bruises beneath her eyes; deep shadows lay in the hollows carved beneath her cheekbones. "Rest."

"I have the remainder of my life to sleep," she answered, guiding him toward the shelf. When his eyes closed, she placed a finger to her lips and whispered near the kerchief of the woman beside the *pech*. "Wake us in five hours."

"He said two hours."

"*Nyet*. Five." Nicole pressed the woman's fingers around a coin; then she covered Vadim with his coat before she stretched into the straw. But her hot eyes would not close. Eventually she swung her long legs over the shelf and looked toward the woman knitting quietly beside the warm glow of the *pech*. The woman's children slept on the high shelf above the *pech*, beneficiaries of the additional warmth. Occasionally the woman glanced upward, cocking her head and listening as mothers do.

"It isn't necessary to keep vigil on our account," Nicole said softly. "Why don't you sleep?"

The woman shrugged and glanced up from her knitting needles. "I don't mind. I don't sleep well anyway. Not since Sasha left—Sasha is my husband."

"Do you expect him soon?" As sleep proved impossible, Nicole crossed to a stool near the woman. She accepted a mug of *kvas* and cradled the warmth between her palms.

The woman's mended shawl rustled about a second shrug. "Sasha left the village to join the czar's troops. When the revolt is won, he'll come home." Her expression pinched upon itself, and Nicole guessed the woman had opposed her husband's decision.

Without thinking, Nicole blurted, "But the revolt ended months ago! The government crushed the rebels!"

Now it was woman's turn to stare.

"I . . . I'm sorry." Nicole bit her tongue furiously, cursing herself for the impulsive words.

The woman covered her face and coiled within herself, appearing to grow smaller before Nicole's distress. One of the children murmured and turned in his sleep.

"I see," the woman said finally. After a silence, she continued, her voice steadying. "Then Sasha will be coming home soon."

"But . . ." Nicole swallowed. If Sasha wasn't home now . . . She thought of the rebels she'd seen dangling from high posts at the crossroads. She didn't know how best to proceed. "Should you allow yourself to believe . . . I mean, aren't you worried that . . . that . . . ?"

". . . that Sasha is dead?" The woman lowered her knitting into her lap, and her level eyes examined Nicole's dismay. "Sasha is not dead. Wounded maybe, but he is not dead."

"But . . ."

The woman tapped her thin chest. "I would know it. Here." She studied Nicole curiously in the dim flicker of the *pech*. And she read the message behind Nicole's anguished stare. "Is your husband dead?" she inquired gently.

"*Da*," Nicole whispered. "Maybe. I . . . I don't know!" Without her intending it, the story rushed from her lips in low impulsive bursts, halting and choked by the hot stone blocking her throat. She didn't understand the raw compulsion to share her misery, she simply yielded to it. ". . . the gash below his ribs, and his eye . . . oh, Dear God, his eye!" She buried her face in shaking hands, rocking on the stool and battling the small gasping sound tearing her voice.

The woman waited until Nicole had quieted and drained the mug of *kvas*. "The heart is a strange thing. Have you looked inside it?" she asked softly, placing a chapped red hand above her breast. Gently she dismissed the doubt in Nicole's empty gaze. "Do it . . . and then you will know. Search for that hard kernel of truth . . . and if you do not find what you fear . . ." She took up her knitting and lowered her head.

What could the heart do but confirm what the intellect had recognized? Nicole released a long breath, feeling maneuvered into a game she rejected. But knowing the woman watched, she closed her eyes self-consciously and attempted to do as the woman advised. At first her stiff muscles resisted; then gradually, reluctantly, she surrendered to the deep stillness of the snowy night, broken only by the rhythmic click of knitting needles and an occasional sigh from those who slept. Her golden head relaxed backward upon the column of her throat. Cautious fingers of emotion probed her heart. And a frown of building concentration furrowed her brow as she opened her mind to an uncomfortable raw vulnerability.

A steady strong beat pulsed in her ears. And she curled deeper into herself, searching for that dread agony of truth.

Fearfully she examined the hidden spaces of her spirit, seeking to confront the cold blackness of loss.

It was not there.

"Is this true?" she whispered. Nicole stared at the woman, afraid to believe.

"The heart does not lie." Placing her knitting to one side, the woman leaned to press Nicole's trembling fingers. "But does it truly matter?" she asked wisely. "Hope is all that matters. If you can discover hope, you can go on."

Disappointment shattered her, and Nicole's breath released in a bitter rush. "Is that all it is? Just hope?" Suddenly she felt foolish and childlike. Hiding her expression, she scrubbed angrily at her eyes.

The woman tugged Nicole's hands from her face. "Is hope such a bad thing? I think it is more than you had before."

Nicole stared.

When Vadim yawned awake and stretched beside the sleeping shelf, the *izba* had come to life. He glanced about him; then his jaw dropped.

Wearing a flour-streaked apron over her wool skirt, Nicole leaned above the *pech*, ladling hot groats into the children's wooden bowls. She dribbled a smidgen for the house spirits, then dropped the spoon into the pot and swung a tiny moppet high above her curls, laughing into the small delighted face. "Marya, I believe this one takes after you. Look at that smile!"

Marya's own smile was pleased as she herded the children toward the table and a platter of freshly baked bread. She complimented Nicole extravagantly on the perfect loaves.

"It's all in the wrists." Nicole laughed. "The kneading is all."

Marya waggled a finger. "Now, Natushka. The hoping is all." They smiled at each other.

"By all the saints!" Vadim roared. The children paused with their spoons near their mouths and gazed at him in awe. "What happened while I was sleeping? A miracle?" He rubbed his beard and stared hard at Nicole.

"*Da,* a miracle," Nicole responded softly. She squeezed Marya's hand affectionately, then briskly ordered Vadim to the table. "Eat. Someone promised me the world looks better on a full stomach." The children's eyes widened as Vadim's bulk shadowed the table.

"The world has long ago passed dawn! Why didn't you wake me?" Vadim glared out a window frosted in icy fern-leaf patterns. "What in the hell time is it?" A string of mighty curses erupted from deep inside his barrel chest, and the children covered their mouths and giggled, nudging each other.

"Vadim!" Nicole fisted her hands on her hips. Vadim blinked at the giggles. "You said we'd arrive in Riga tomorrow. A few hours' delay will do no harm. You look one hundred percent better."

Life had returned to his vivid black eyes, the color in his cheeks was pink and natural, and the slump had eased from his broad shoulders. He nodded slowly. "So do you." A large hand cupped her cheeks, and he examined her calm smile thoughtfully. "It appears we both received what was needed." As the women smiled, he lowered his thick black brows and glowered at the children. "Why aren't you eating like your mother told you to?"

"Why is your hair white and your beard black?"

"Are you a giant?"

"Were you as big as me when you were ten?"

The tiniest girl climbed on his knee without invitation and yanked his beard. Vadim leveled a glare which would have sent an adult scurrying for cover. Dark velvet eyes smiled up at him. "Do you know any stories?"

Helplessly Vadim flung out his palms and directed a pleading gaze toward Nicole's laughter.

"Tell them about Ivan Ivanovich," she gasped.

"Why are they doing this?" He growled menacingly, and the children giggled.

"Because they know how to read hearts," Nicole replied softly.

Tears stung her eyes when she embraced Marya and the children, then climbed into the sled. The shouts of farewell repeated in her mind long after the small village had disappeared and the sled was the only blur of color against a sparkling expanse of wind-crusted snow.

A day, a night, and another day. Fields blended into thick stands of forest crowding the banks of the Dvina River. Then the frozen roadway veered and they could glimpse the wooden church domes of ancient Riga above the treetops. And through the gaps glittered the icy sparkle of the Baltic.

They didn't pause. Vadim skirted the town, whipping the horses directly toward the wharves. Few ships risked the Baltic this time of year; the *Caravel* was easily identified among a sparse collection of masts.

As were they. A man dozing atop a rotted post jumped to his feet as the sled halted and Vadim hurried Nicole toward the pier. Measuring eyes gauged Vadim's size; then the man approached them quickly. "Identify yourselves."

"I am Princess Natasha Denisovna," Nicole answered. Her eyes traveled across the harbor to a trim ship smaller than the *Kiev* had been. The *Caravel* was built for speed.

"Where are the others?"

"There are no more," Vadim answered. Nicole bowed her head and pulled at her mittens. "You'll have two passengers instead of four."

The man nodded and hastened to the end of the wharf. He waved a red scarf, and immediately a rowboat descended along the side of the French ship.

Vadim and Nicole stared at each other. Against tremendous odds, they had made it. Nicole turned her face toward the brightly painted church domes, their onion shape suddenly foreign to her eye. An image of graceful Boston steeples rose before her vision. Home. Home, where the language appeared upon the tongue without thought; home, where the simple wholesome food rode easily on the stomach. Home to a land where men owned their farms and homes and the women and children could read and write. She was sailing home!

And leaving her heart behind.

"Vadim . . ."

He ignored her beseeching tone. "I intend to sleep for a week." His weary black eyes focused on the ship's banners flapping briskly in a cold brutal wind. "And I intend to enjoy every second of it." Nothing in his taut expression indicated

318

he would enjoy anything. Another heart would remain in Russia. He stood with his arms crossed firmly on his chest.

They watched as a half-dozen men bent over the oars and the rowboat shot toward the wharf.

"Vadim . . ." The rowboat struck against the dock, and the man with the scarf waved impatiently. Nicole placed her small mitten on Vadim's arm, halting his forward step. "Vadim . . ." Pleading blue eyes locked to his.

Vadim stared down into her white face. "Natushka," he reminded gently, shaking his shaggy head. "You were there—I promised him I'd take you home. I didn't promise that I'd see you to the boat."

"He needs you. He'll be dangerously weak; he won't be capable of escaping or making the journey. Not without help."

"You're assuming he's alive." Vadim's eyes searched. "And if he is, Natushka . . . he'll never forgive me if I leave you and go back for him."

"And I won't forgive you if you don't." She pressed her shaking hand to his frosty beard. "More important . . . you will never forgive yourself."

They stared at each other.

"The tide will be against us if you don't come now!" the man with the scarf shouted angrily, his face darkening.

Vadim looked at the ship and then toward the city. Then he stared down at Nicole. And she knew. "Thank you! God bless you and keep you safe!" She flung herself against his massive chest and wept into his collar.

"I'll bring them out," he promised thickly. "I'll bring them home to you in late spring." His bear arms tightened convulsively and he buried his face in her hair; then he released her and rushed her toward the rowboat, lifting her up and lowering her over the side.

"Vadim!" The rowboat pulled away, the distance widening. She was suddenly distraught at leaving him. She cupped her hands about her lips. "You never told me. Gregory Repinsky—was he . . . ?"

Vadim stood wide-legged upon the dock, a sturdy indestructible oak. Though his figure steadily diminished, the roar which sounded across the water appeared just beside her ear. "The same. I wish it had been my hand on the pitch fork!"

Nicole bowed her head and touched her forehead, closing her lashes against the sting of icy salt spray. She dashed her eyes and stared upward as his distant bellow floated upon the wind: "Life does not always grant our dearest wishes."

A shudder rippled her frame and she shaded her eyes with her mitten. And a silent prayer unfolded within, begging that Vadim's farewell was not a portent.

Once on board the *Caravel,* Nicole rushed past the laboring sailors and dashed to the bow as the sound of winding chain squealed above a snap of unfurling sail. Gripping the rail until her palms ached, she strained toward a black furry dot on the wharf. She'd forgotten to make him promise to engage a room and rest before he began the long brutal return to Ekaterinburg.

As the *Caravel* swung slowly toward open sea, she realized Vadim would never have agreed to a delay. The furry dot waved, then ran toward the sled. Nicole imagined she heard the sharp crack of his whip, and she watched through a blur of tears as the sled turned back the way it had come, disappearing through the trees fringing the riverbanks.

"Watch over him," she whispered hoarsely. "Watch over them all and bring them home safely to me."

Captain Henri Blanc appeared at her side. He bowed and extended a crystal goblet of French wine. "A barbaric country, no? There is always a storm brewing in Russia."

Nicole followed his gaze, but she was uncertain if he referred to the thickening clouds overhead or to a street brawl which had spilled onto the wharves, attracting the attention of a knot of soldiers who had just arrived at the dock. Her heart lurched, and her eyes darted swiftly toward the river. Then she sighed and forced a wavering smile to her lips. "Storms frighten me," she admitted softly.

"Then it is fortunate you've chosen to leave Russia." He gazed into her face, openly admiring her clear eyes and wind-burned pink complexion.

"Yes." As she reluctantly turned from the rail, responding to the polite pressure of the captain's hand, she yearned for a calm, untroubled future.

But a storm was gathering.

24

CAPTAIN HENRI BLANC had followed Dimitri's instructions exactly. He'd provided every amenity, including a wardrobe containing men's and women's clothing. Dimitri had foreseen every contingency.

As Nicole examined the trunk in her cabin, she further discovered that Dimitri had requested English fashions more suitable for staid Boston than the lavish gowns and elegant cloaks they had purchased in Moscow. After a deliciously hot tub, her first in weeks, she donned a simple gray wool and fastened a white apron above it, hoping a sewing kit had been provided. The waist of the skirt gapped over her stomach. She adjusted the apron to conceal the gap, then examined herself in the mirror as she placed a snowy dust cap over hair still damp from washing. There was an undeniable charm to the ruffles framing her lovely pale face.

But for whom? With a catch in her throat she tugged the cap from her hair and tossed it toward the trunk; then she wandered to the windows and placed her palms flat to the panes. The choppy cold waves were as turbulent as her thoughts. A solitary tear slipped down the curve of her cheek; the voyage would be long and lonely.

Throughout the first weeks Nicole seldom ventured from her snug cabin. She altered the skirts and gowns to fit her burgeoning stomach, she stared tearfully at the men's clothing hanging in the wardrobe beside her own, and she tormented herself by constant anxiety, worrying over the events in Siberia. Had Vadim arrived safely? Had Pavla managed the necessary medication and care? Would the escape proceed without danger, or would history repeat? Most important, was Dimitri alive? The worry was endless. The not knowing was worse.

She clenched her fists and ground her teeth and bolstered the lonely days with hope. But occasionally a crack split her defenses and severe depression swathed her mind. Was it wise to cling so desperately to unsubstantiated hope? Did she open herself to the devastation of losing him again?

On such dismal days, Nicole politely refused Captain Blanc's dinner invitations, choosing to dine alone, judging herself unfit for company. She prowled the small cabin as intellect waged battle with emotion. And when she pinched the candle and fell across her bed, she felt exhausted and bruised by the forces battering her spirit.

During the moments of doubt, she yearned to climb the forecastle and face into the biting winds, remaining there until her feverish mind was as cool as the icy waves. But the bitter climate precluded walking above deck. Ice-caked ropes and sleet-glazed planks invited a mishap she dared not risk. When the urge to stretch her legs became compelling, she circled the perimeter of her cabin and attempted to convince herself she was exercising, not pacing. The difference between the two was too minuscule to measure.

The close confinement of the cabin would have seemed easier to endure had she been blessed with Pavla's company. Dear Pavla. How often her prayers flew toward Pavla's ministrations. And she cursed herself and wept with guilt that it had been Pavla who remained behind, and not herself.

As her stomach blossomed and her thoughts focused more intensely upon the child she carried, she desperately missed the comfort of a woman's understanding. She wanted to talk of babies and dreams and babies and upbringing and babies and babies and babies.

Dimitri's baby. It was her link to him, a cherished proof of the love they had shared. And when she curled into her lonely bed each night, she stroked her nightgown and murmured to the child within, relating memories and dreams, recalling a man's courage and integrity and indomitable spirit.

"Your father was . . ." Her whisper caught and choked. And she covered a horrified expression with her fists as she realized she referred to him in the past tense. Groaning, she smothered her despair in the pillow, haunted by ghostly accusations.

Had it not been for Henri Blanc's company, Nicole concluded that the isolation would have driven her mad. But Henri's charm, and more specifically his memories of a lifelong friendship with Dimitri, became the focal point of her long empty days. She anticipated the dinner hour and an excuse to depart the cabin, which occasionally appeared to shrink until the breath squeezed in her chest.

"You look lovely tonight, as usual. Blue suits you." Henri escorted her beyond an oaken desk piled high with charts and seated her at a table glittering with silver and delicate china.

"Thank you." Nicole smoothed the ruffles at her throat and wrists. She couldn't observe his bolted table and chairs without that first sea storm flashing through her memory, not without remembering herself trapped and struggling in Dimitri's lap. She smiled at the foolishness of beginnings. It all seemed so long ago, a remnant of a stranger's past.

As always, Henri extended himself to ensure that the dinner hour was agreeable, entertaining her with tales of his long years at sea or relating mildly titillating escapades of the French court. Nicole understood he attempted to amuse her, and she was grateful, but tonight she decided that one more account of French ladies trysting with French gentlemen and she would scream. Her intellect craved stimulation, a topic to steer her thoughts from troubled wanderings.

"Henri . . . I wonder, could we discuss something more meaty than scandals? Your accounts are fascinating, of course, but . . ."

Henri Blanc possessed a storyteller's talent for wresting the maximum from any incident, no matter how trivial. His talent, charm, and aging good looks had made him a great favorite in drawing rooms throughout the seaports of the world. Nicole examined his seamed face apologetically, experiencing a dart of guilt for her implied criticism. He didn't deserve censure. She opened her lips to withdraw her comment, then halted as an unmistakably relieved smile pleated the lines across his face.

"My dear, you have made me a happy man. What would you prefer to discuss?" He waved aside her murmurs of apology. "Literature? Theater? Politics? Business? Religion?"

Immediately Nicole understood his enduring friendship with Dimitri. Both men possessed the gift of curiosity. Their interests ranged across the spectrum.

"Politics or business, I think." If Dimitri was dead—she frowned and hastened past the thought—she faced the task of supporting herself and her child. The more she learned, the better equipped she would be.

Henri's graying brow arched over warm eyes. He lowered his fork and raised his wineglass. "A toast to all women who develop interests beyond flirtations and fashion! Would that God had seen fit to create more of you!"

Nicole smiled and touched her glass to his. She liked this open capable man; he reminded her of Vadim. They were similar in age and in their hard sensibility of outlook.

"I'll wager you haven't encountered many American women," she responded. "Flirtations and fashion exert an appeal, but in the colonies, business and politics play a vital role in a woman's concerns, equally as important as the cut of her gown or the sparkle in her eye."

The cabin boy stepped forward to refill her glass, balancing against a gentle roll. Nicole smiled and thanked him in a distracted tone. Upon consideration, she wondered if her statement was entirely accurate. Her own life had revolved about political considerations more than most. Most women had not been exposed to secret gatherings in a darkened kitchen, nor been involved with the inner machinations of a great court like Catherine's.

Henri smiled. "An English officer, may all the English rot in hell, once boasted that ten British regulars could conquer the colonies in a week—unless they raised the ire of the women. In that unhappy event, ten American women could drive the entire army into the sea."

Nicole laughed. She abhorred the English disdain for colonial military prowess, but she was pleased by their clear respect for the colonial women. She wondered if she might class herself among them. In truth she had not succeeded in coming to grips with her elusive identity. Her biological parents had been Russian, her adopted parents were French, she had been raised as an Englishwoman. She had been a princess and a peasant and an exile. She was a rainbow with emphasis first upon one color and then upon another, but never a constant, never a whole to which she could anchor herself.

"I'm not convinced American women are as ferocious as you imply." She smiled. What color of the rainbow were the American women? The Russian women? Were they always one shade and never another? She watched Henri finish his meal and blot his lips. "But our women are supportive of their husbands' concerns, and often take part, whether political, social, or economical."

Henri observed the shadow of pain as she uttered the word "husband." "You miss him very much, don't you?"

"Very much."

Henri studied her bowed head; then he asked softly, "How did you meet?"

Tonight she was not fated to increase her knowledge of business or politics. Skillfully Henri Blanc led her to speak of that which lay closest to her sore heart. And he listened patiently until the clock struck midnight.

Nicole started in surprise and her cheeks colored as she hastily pushed from the table. She placed a grateful hand on Captain Blanc's sleeve and apologized for keeping him so late. "Your Suzette is a fortunate woman. I can't tell you how greatly I appreciate . . ." A lump choked the words. His consideration and kindness touched her deeply.

Henri escorted her to the door, where he entrusted her to the charge of a work-weary sailor. "I'm confident Denisov would see to Suzette's comfort if our situations were reversed." He kissed her lightly on the forehead. "Don't torment yourself, Nicole. Dimitri is too damn stubborn to die." A grin widened his lips. "One day he'll appear on your doorstep as arrogant and overbearing as he ever was."

Nicole pressed his hand and smiled. His assurance lacked the true ring of conviction, but she liked him for his genuine concern. And lacking his company, she would have surrendered to the depressions on a more frequent basis.

It wasn't until late February, a week from the New England shores, that they returned to politics.

Nicole waited until the cabin boy cleared the dishes and filled Henri's wineglass. "My father's letters spoke of tension and deteriorating relations between the populace and the British." When she found it difficult to sleep, which was often, she passed the dark hours attempting to recall everything Louis had mentioned in his letters. She suspected the Boston she sailed toward was not the Boston she had departed three years ago. What it might offer herself and her child occupied growing space in her thoughts as they approached the end of the voyage. A tiny fist prodded, and Nicole lifted her teacup to conceal a private smile.

Henri nodded toward the tea caddy, his gray hair bobbing across his shoulders. "Enjoy every sip, my dear. Once we dock, there will be no more bohea. I understand the colonists prefer coffee or local herb teas."

Nicole arched an eyebrow. "The boycott is still in effect, then?" She recalled inflammatory broadsides posted about Boston, admonishing the citizens to spurn British imports. She had attended spinning bees where friends and neighbors vowed to wear nothing but homespun. In actual practice, however, she also recalled that English tea had continued to fill private tea chests and English fabric had swished about the ladies' boots. But if she understood Henri, the boycott was now being seriously observed.

"Have you learned of what everyone is now calling the Boston Tea Party?"

"I believe my father mentioned it, yes."

"Although the destruction of the tea was a rather small event in itself, it has become the symbol and perhaps the catalyst for colonial unrest, seized upon by colonists and British alike as a trial confrontation. Since then, relations have steadily worsened."

"I would have imagined the tea party, as you call it, would be over and forgotten by now." Nicole frowned, casting backward to recall the date of Louis's letter.

"I'm afraid not. England insists upon restitution for the lost tea. Last May General Thomas Gage was appointed governor of Massachusetts. He arrived in Boston armed with a list of restrictions to be enforced until the city repays the East India Company for their losses. Gage closed the Boston harbor—it remains closed now, nearly a year later—and he shifted the capital to Salem, for a short while at least." Nicole gasped and her eyes flared. "The upper house of the colony's legislature is now appointed by Gage, troops are being quartered in private dwellings, and all town meetings are unconditionally prohibited. In spite of everything, Boston refuses to repay a single shilling."

Nicole stared. "How dare the British invade private homes and ban public meetings? That is intolerable," she stated flatly. A stubborn pride firmed her tone. "The people of Boston will not submit to coercion. Mark my word, the East India company will never be reimbursed. Never." Her jaw set. In this moment she saw little difference between King George and Catherine: both expected absolute obedience; both believed they knew what was best for their subjects, despite evidence to the contrary. "And England will rue the day she meddled in American commerce and individual freedom."

Henri Blanc laughed. "I see now how ten women with broomsticks could sweep the British army into the sea. The flash in your eye is alarming."

"Don't tease." Nicole responded more sharply than she'd intended. He raised his palms and apologized, still smiling.

Nicole frowned at the night sea tossing beyond the cabin windows; then she probed for additional information.

"I wish I could answer all your questions, but my primary interest centers on events affecting trade. I haven't paid as much attention to political reports as I might have."

Nicole tapped a fingernail against her teeth. "Henri . . . do you think the situation could escalate to open rebellion?" It was unimaginable, and yet . . . She recalled predictions stated around her father's table, forecasts many had disbelieved, and they had now come to pass.

"Relations are tense. There's bitterness on both sides." He shrugged. "You know your countrymen better than I. The question, as the English perceive it, is one of obedience. The colonists must obey their king. But will they? Or will they insist upon dictating their own laws, their own taxes, their own destiny? And where will such demands lead?"

It all had such a familiar ring.

The questions troubled her throughout the brief remainder of the voyage. Nicole discovered that the concept of "obedience" rankled, as had the Russian concept of twenty-five years' service to the state, of absolute unquestioning obedience. With a pleased smile Nicole concluded she was indeed American; blind obedience offended her spirit.

But how would issues be solved? And how would her life be affected by the conflicts? One query raised another. She worried the possibilities until her head ached, finally concluding that personal observation was necessary to adequately assess the impact upon her future. Anxiously she anticipated a long thoughtful discussion with Louis.

When a cabin boy informed her the *Caravel* had entered the Salem harbor, Nicole swiftly donned a voluminous warm cloak and glanced about the small cabin she had occupied throughout the preceding two months. The cabin represented a slow healing, a conquering of doubt and tears and bittersweet indulgences of memory. Now it was time to step forward, to reenter life.

Satisfied she'd forgotten nothing, she joined Henri on the forecastle, enjoying the shouts from the high rigging, the leadsman's curt sounding of depths, and the growing eagerness of a weary ship putting into port.

"Happy to be home?" Henri asked. The quartermaster had the ship firmly in hand, but Henri continued to lean against the railing, watching critically as the *Caravel* trimmed sail and slowly maneuvered through the crowded harbor. Ships which normally would have anchored in Boston fanned across the water, their rocking masts a forest of rope and wood.

"There's still the coach ride to Boston," Nicole reminded him. But, yes, this was home. Her heart sang at the sight of New England shores. The bustling seaport of Salem gladdened her eye and overwhelmed her initial disappointment at not docking in Boston. There was nothing foreign in the low sprawling town, no onion domes, no strange costumes, no harsh-sounding languages. Salem was solidly and gracefully English. English carriages rolled through snowy lanes, English spires soared against a vivid blue sky, and English curses shouted across the waves as the dockmen labored to shift barrels of unwieldy cargo. Nicole smiled contentedly, and her thoughts flew forward to that wonderful moment when she stood on her parents' porch and reached a hand to the brass knocker.

"I've been saving a surprise for you." Henri grinned. His expression was so like Dimitri's that Nicole caught her breath and stared. "When Denisov wrote to engage the *Caravel*, he also instructed me to dispatch a letter to the colonies." Henri's grin widened at her sharp intake of breath. He watched the color drain from her cheeks, then return in a rush of excited pink. "To a Mr. and Mrs. Duchard."

Nicole's hands laced tightly across her breast. Dimitri had thought of everything. She blinked misted eyes. "Henri, I thank you a thousand times!" She whirled toward the rail and shaded her brow, straining to isolate two beloved faces from the figures crowding the wharf area. Her pulse raced joyfully.

Henri laughed. "You can't see a thing from this distance. Here. Use this."

She accepted a telescoping eyeglass with a rapid word of thanks and adjusted it with shaking fingers. Eagerly she trained the glass upon the shoreline and swung it slowly along the wharves. Any instant, Louis and Marie would leap into the lens.

The glass wavered, traveled backward, and froze. Nicole lowered the glass and caught her lip between her teeth. She blinked at Henri, then stared hard across the water, a puzzled annoyance constricting her features.

Neither of her parents waited on the docks. But Major William Caldwell did. His stern expression and scarlet uniform were unmistakable.

25

Some moments speed through time like a comet, spent before they are grasped; others are endless, they strain the limits of endurance. Time halted as William extended his arm and assisted Nicole onto the wharf. The moment froze, and for a panicked instant Nicole believed she was condemned to eternity, her glove in his, her gaze locked to his scrutiny.

A surge of relief briefly lifted her breast as he finally spoke, and time resumed its normal cadence.

"I told myself no mortal woman could be as beautiful as I remembered you. But you are." Pain and joy, accusation and adoration; a variety of emotions fleetingly appeared, then vanished beneath the shadow of his hat brim.

William's full-dress uniform was a startling splash of scarlet amid the wharf's drab colors. Nicole judged it a defiant gesture certain to inflame sullen dockworkers. It wasn't as much the uniform as it was William's flair for wearing it. He made of the hated red coat a deliberate symbol of superiority, of unquestioned supremacy. Studying him from the corner of her eyes, Nicole concluded that what she had once regarded as confidence was nothing more than abrasive arrogance.

She cleared her throat uncomfortably. The rigid set of his hat, a dull gleam of braid and polish, his sash and immaculate white satin breeches—all proclaimed rank and authority. And when his pale gaze brushed the throng crowding the docks, contempt was disturbingly evident.

Nicole wondered how she had ever admired him. Perhaps Marie had been correct: Nicole's youthful infatuation had centered more upon the romance of a uniform than upon the man wearing it.

Averting her gaze, she endured the cold March wind billowing her cloak and fluttering the stiff powdered curls formally arranged on either side of William's narrow face. And she recalled a dozen people she would have preferred to encounter.

As he flicked aside his jacket and bowed over her fingers, she murmured a polite greeting. "It's a pleasure . . ." The falsehood stuck to the roof of her mouth, as her glove appeared stuck in his hand. Frowning, she withdrew her fingers and anxiously scanned the crush of people milling about the docks. "I'm expecting my parents . . ." She wet her lips and spoke with false heartiness, in the manner of one slight acquaintance addressing another. To her embarrassment, she could think of nothing whatever to say to him.

"A pleasure?" An eyebrow rose and thin lips disappeared into a twist. Nicole started as she recognized his evident irritation. "Why didn't you write?"

His bluntness dismayed her. Concealing the spread of pink across her cheeks, she waved at strands of wind-tossed gold blowing from the ruffles framing her face. Polite society avoided direct confrontations; she was uncertain how best to respond to his breach of etiquette. And resented being placed in this awkward position. Striving to suppress her annoyance, she plucked at her gloves and stammered, "William . . . that was all so long ago . . ."

"Yes, indeed! You've behaved outrageously. I believe you owe me an immediate apology!"

Astonishment and anger flared in Nicole's eyes. She drew back as his mouth clamped into a hard slash, and it flashed through her mind that he loathed her; yet the hunger in his eyes contradicted that conclusion. She attempted to comprehend what she was observing, but quickly abandoned the task as impossible. Hastily she scanned the docks, seeking her parents and silently thanking God that William Caldwell was no longer a part of her life. An apology, of course, was unthinkable. Stiffening her spine, she turned away and stared toward the wharf.

"I see," he said coldly. He raised a hand toward two soldiers leaning on a stack of rum barrels. "Take Miss Duchard's luggage to my coach." The soldiers saluted briskly and grasped the handles of Nicole's trunk.

"This is uncalled-for!" She inhaled slowly and smoothed the anger from her voice. "I'm grateful for your concern, William, but it isn't appropriate. My parents—"

His pale eyes regarded her coolly. "The Duchards are in Boston."

"I beg your pardon?" Too much occurred at once. The excitement of arriving home, William's clumsy confrontation; the information required a moment to penetrate. When she understood her parents were not coming, a sense of alarm constricted her breathing, and her voice rose. "Has something happened to them? An accident?"

"Lower your voice. You're attracting attention." His frown intensified.

"William!" His greater concern for a scene than for her parents flooded her cheeks with angry color. "Why aren't they here? Henri said he wrote to them . . . William! I demand an answer!"

His spine straightened and he drew to his full height, transforming her worried questions into a contest of wills. "All in good time. Now I command you to proceed."

Nicole's hands clenched into fists as she stared at his knotted jawline and then into eyes that had become icy and intractable. But New England was not Russia; his coach was not a cart she was forced to climb into. And she refused to be intimidated by his uniform or his anger. She raised her chin in defiance. "I do not respond to commands, Major Caldwell! I'm not one of your underlings. And I'm not proceeding a single step until I learn what's happened to my parents!"

William flushed with anger and embarrassment and hastily glanced toward the soldiers. He hissed, "Don't play the fool! I ordered them to remain in Boston. Isn't it obvious? You and I require privacy to reconcile our future!"

"You *ordered* them . . .?" She couldn't imagine Louis agreeing, unless he had no alternative. The defiance in her stance evaporated, and she fastened a bewildered stare upon William's taut profile. A frown creased her brow. Events in Boston had undergone a drastic turn indeed.

"It is my honor to direct the Boston Pass Authority. No one enters or leaves Boston without my signature." Obvious pride underscored his explanation; his chest expanded visibly.

"Passes are required?" Nicole experienced difficulty grasping what she was hearing. Passes were necessary to travel between Russian cities, but not in New England, not in an English country. What on earth had transpired in her absence? She wished Louis were present to explain these bewildering changes. And she wished Louis were here to solve her immediate problem.

Facing away from the sharp breeze, she rapidly assessed her situation. She could hire transportation to Boston, as she had originally intended, or she could engage a room at an inn and dispatch a message to her parents. She cast a resentful glance toward William—Louis and Marie might or might not be granted a pass to fetch her. Or she could accept William's forceful invitation and arrive home within hours.

Her lower back throbbed; her stomach weighed a thousand pounds. She wanted to go home.

William glared at the soldiers. "What are you staring at?" he snapped. "Do you seek a charge of insubordination? Take the lady's trunk to my coach as commanded!"

The soldiers hurried past, the trunk swaying between their scarlet jackets. Nicole watched them moodily; her decision was made. Given a choice, she would have countermanded William's order; on the other hand, sharing his carriage would see her home immediately and in relative comfort. But she deeply resented the high-handed manner in which the decision had been denied her.

Rejecting William's proffered arm, she marched beside him in tight-lipped silence. And when they reached his coach at the edge of the wharves, she disdained assistance and climbed inside without aid. She settled herself against worn leather cushions and arranged the lap robe over her body and the surrounding expanse of cushions. She wished it clear that he was to sit facing her and not at her side.

This did not approach the homecoming she had envisioned. And she suspected the journey would be dreadful.

The coach bounced on its axle as the soldiers wrestled her trunk into the boot, and Nicole pursed her lips and released a long low breath. Had she considered the matter, she might have guessed a confrontation with William was inevitable. But she hadn't thought of him once since she had burned his letter. As William had long ago ceased to exist for her, Nicole had naively supposed herself to be of no further interest to him. She stared from the window and nibbled the tip of her glove. She had blundered.

Neither spoke until the coach jolted beyond Salem's boundary hedges. Nicole pretended an interest in the rolling countryside and indulged a vain hope the trip might be endured in silence. Glaring from his window, William brooded and chewed a fingernail.

She erased his annoyance by closing her lashes and pushing her feet near the small charcoal foot-warmer. She wished for a pillow to ease her back. She hoped her energy would revive when she was reunited with Louis and Marie; for the moment, she felt tired and drained experiencing the exhausting effects of seven months' pregnancy, little of which time had elapsed in a restful manner.

Twenty minutes passed, and then thirty. William turned from the snow-dusted landscape and removed his hat, placing it on the cushion beside him. The heavy hat had imprinted a ridge; pomade had darkened his sandy hair to a muddy shade of brown. He cleared his throat and stared at her, drinking in the radiance of her complexion, the thick fringe of lashes pressing her high cheekbones, the sweet pink curve of her lips. A sound wrenched from his chest. "Nicole . . ."

Wary eyes blinked open. Soon this awkward companionship would be nothing but an unpleasant memory. She thought it unlikely they would meet again—she would make certain they did not.

"Nicole . . . God! I didn't want it to be like this!"

She raised an eyebrow toward a naked vulnerability which surprised her. Her most vivid memory of William Caldwell was his cool control, his tight harness on emotion. Wetting her lips uneasily, Nicole dropped her gaze to the woolly lap robe. Perhaps if she remained silent, he would abandon this line of conversation.

His stubby fingers combed over the ridges left by his hat. He stared in disgust at the resulting smears of pomade and hastily wiped his hands on a white handkerchief. Laced fingers dropped between his knees, and his head fell backward until he stared toward the coach ceiling.

"I imagined your homecoming a hundred times, maybe a thousand. We would gaze at each other . . . we would smile . . . you would beg my forgiveness . . . and following a suitable delay, I would grant it. We would marry and be happy." An embarrassed silence opened between them, and Nicole turned her face to the window, speechless. "You can't imagine what I'm forced to endure each bloody day of my life! General Gage is a fool. An idiot! He grants the Whigs whatever stupidity they demand and punishes his own soldiers for infractions a reasonable man would scorn. He's making us a laughingstock!" He looked at her. "I need you, Nicole. I need a home and a wife to provide a slice of normalcy in the midst of this chaos."

In the embarrassed quiet following his outburst, he studied his knees, watching them sway with the tilt and bounce of the coach, watching them swing toward her lap robe and then away. "Dammit! Why don't you speak?"

How could she respond? Consternation pinched her lips. A Russian folk saying surfaced from a swirl of dismayed thoughts. The sharpest knife cuts cleanest. She inhaled deeply, feeling the color blazing on her cheeks, and swallowed hard. His declaration stunned her. "William, please . . . I would prefer we didn't continue this conversation. I . . . We ended this relationship before I sailed."

His astonishment appeared genuine. "We discussed delaying our plans—I recall that conversation very well—but dissolving our relationship was never a consideration." His voice heated with conviction, his memories rearranged to support his desires.

Nicole's gloves fluttered above her lap. "But I returned your pledge ring!" She tamped the desperation tingeing her tone. Reason would prevail. She fervently wished she had engaged an inn in Salem.

"An oversight. I understand and I forgive you. The explanation is simple—you were facing a long and perilous journey, you were distraught at discovering your parentage in question, you were experiencing a great deal of mental turmoil . . . you gave Madame Duchard the ring before you and I discussed the matter fully."

The blaze of conviction warming sallow cheeks to pink alarmed her. "No, William. I intended to break our engagement."

The sharpest knife did not slice cleanly. His voice rose. "Why do you insist on raising these unpleasantries now? All that matters is that you came home to me!"

Good Lord, the situation went from bad to worse. Nicole pressed into the cushions, shrinking from his eyes. A nervous stare widened her own gaze, and she pondered William's mental state. Something had tampered with his logic. Pressure, ambition, frustration? Her eyes darted toward a leather cord dangling near her window. The far end threaded through a notch in the coach roof and was knotted to the driver's ankle. If she required assistance . . .

"Don't you understand? I love you, Nicole. I love you!" An obsessive heat congested his face; his eyes pleaded. "I can't get you out of my mind! Not a day passes that I don't remember the sweetness of your lips, that I don't long to—"

"Stop!" Shaking hands muffled her ears. She regarded him with pity and shock. The sharpest knife—yes, but how terrible to wield, how brutal the act. She plunged ahead quickly, conclusively, before he could worsen the situation, if such was possible. "William, I'm married."

His stare was blank, uncomprehending.

"Married, William. Do you remember Prince Dimitri Denisov? He and I . . ."

Shock transformed the blankness. "I don't believe you." His thoughts traveled along a visible path. He saw himself dragged from the Duchard pantry, recalled Denisov's laughter. Denisov had witnessed a British officer's humiliation. "No. This isn't true. Don't make jokes, Nicole!" He blinked. A dawning of betrayal and rage glimmered behind his heavy lids, belying his words.

"I love him."

"No." The denial was flat, without expression.

"Oh, William . . ." The scene was worse than she could have imagined in a month of trying. Hot color burned across her cheeks as she struggled with the lap robe. Without looking at him, she pushed the robe to the floor and molded her cloak about her pregnancy. "It's true," she whispered. The heat of embarrassed modesty deepened to crimson, but she could think of no other method to convince as swiftly and conclusively.

William's shock was absolute. His stare froze, his lips opened and closed. He yanked his hair and blinked at her swollen stomach as tears of fury sprang into his eyes and furthered his mortification.

"Someone else . . . you gave yourself to . . . Goddammit!" He struck the cushions with terrible force and then his fist slammed against the coach window. A web of cracks splintered into a wheel. He pulled a sliver from the heel of his palm, then dropped his head into clawing fingers.

Nicole's shock was nearly as great as his. Lowering her gloves from her lips, she edged along the seat, drawing nearer to the driver's cord and away from any accidental brush against his knees. Hastily she raised the lap robe and covered herself.

The sharpest knife had stabbed and gouged; his pain pummeled her senses, radiated outward in black violent tides. She'd had no idea, none at all, of the depth of his emotion.

"Slut!" he hissed. "Whore! Lying teasing harlot!"

"William, please . . ."

"No more! I command you to silence! Just . . . be silent!" His hands knotted into white hammers shaking with the need for violence. Red lumps welled along his jaw, and his breath exploded in shallow bursts. He blinked deeply before the famed control slid across his countenance like a granite mask. British officers did not grieve over a mere woman. He straightened in his seat, adjusted the gold officer's gorget about his neck. He replaced his hat on the pomaded ridges. "If you speak one word, one single word, before I grant permission . . . I cannot be held responsible for my actions." He spoke through grinding teeth, his pale eyes a frozen pond.

Nicole felt the white blanching her cheeks as tangibly as powder. She lowered her head, unable to withstand the dark wave of hatred. Following an endless stiffness of silence, she closed her eyes and rested her head on the cushions. But her body quivered beneath his cold fixed stare. It was a living force, ravaging, punishing, loving, and despising.

Never had she breathed a deeper sigh of relief than when the coach rumbled down the Charlestown peninsula and was maneuvered onto the Boston ferry. She felt as if she had passed a lifetime within the dark interior of this carriage. Soon, thank God, it would end.

When the coach rolled from the ferry and onto the cobbled lanes of North Boston, Nicole leaned eagerly toward the window. Some changes were evident from the ferry—British ships patrolled the harbor, the wharves were deserted—but she was unprepared for the changes within the city itself. Immediately she sensed an air of tension and expectancy as dark and pervasive as the pall of smoke overhanging the steeples and rooftops. The noisy bustle and commerce she remembered so fondly had diminished to a sluggish trickle. The atmosphere was pungent with mistrust and suppressed hostility.

Her expression sobering, Nicole studied the street scenes with a thoughtful eye. An inordinate number of scarlet-clad soldiers strolled the cobbled streets, their polished muskets prominently displayed. Boston's citizens skirted a direct encounter, but eyes narrowed and bold stares leveled over shoulders. The tension was tangible.

Nicole's concern gradually intensified to alarm, increasing with the passage of each block. Here and there she observed shuttered houses, vacant and dark, shop fronts boarded over and deserted. She caught her lip between her teeth. Where were the chestnut vendors? The butcher wagons? The strolling couples and the housewives hurrying home from market? There were fewer people along the narrow streets than she remembered. And less traffic. The horses' hooves and the iron wheels rumbling over the cobblestones were distinctly audible, whereas normally they would have been swallowed by the bustling street noise.

Pressing her nose to the window, she held her breath and counted the blocks. Another turn, then on beyond the winter skeleton of the Wilsons' big oak, then into the final turn . . .

A smothered cry of joyful relief strangled her as the coach reined finally before the modest brick two-story. The driver assisted her to the street, and Nicole stood without moving, blinking at a threat of sentimental tears. The picket fence needed a coat of whitewash, the weather vane leaned from the roof at an odd angle. The lilac bush beside the porch would require pruning before spring. And the house appeared to have shrunk somehow.

It didn't matter. She loved the snug trim lines, the weathered brick. She loved the sheltering elm which she and Louis had planted so long ago, and inside, the crowded high-ceilinged rooms painted in light cheerful tones.

Silently she urged the driver to haste, watching anxiously as he wrestled her trunk from the coach boot to the cobbles. She fidgeted beside the gate and wished for nothing more than to run up the steps and into the door. But William must be dismissed, and for the life of her she couldn't think how best to accomplish the act. It seemed ludicrous to extend her hand and murmur a polite thank-you. And she could hardly express gratitude for the pleasure of his company.

Together William and the driver swung her trunk from the street up onto the walk; then William straightened and knocked the slush and mud from his boots. "You go on inside. I'll join you when we've finished here."

His assumption that he merited an invitation absolutely stunned her. Had he already forgotten the dreadful journey? What more could they discuss? "Papa will see to my trunk, William. In view of . . . of everything . . . I think it best for us to part here."

A thin unpleasant smile twisted narrow lips. He pushed open the gate, and to her vast annoyance he followed her through. "We won't be saying good-bye." Before her irritation could sink toward anger, he continued. "I live here too." The unpleasant smile broadened. "The quartering act—have you learned of it? I had planned to surprise you."

That he had; she was thunderstruck. Nicole's mouth rounded and her dismayed eyes widened until they ached. Dazed, she watched him swagger up the walk and mount the porch. And she promised herself this must be a dream. It had to be.

William paused and turned, his movements a precise military execution. One boot rested possessively on the porch, the other on the step below. "Aren't you coming, my dear?" His pale eyes glittered, enjoying her consternation. "Or is it acceptable to address a married woman by that form?"

She couldn't have responded if life depended upon it. Thankfully, she was spared the necessity. The front door banged open and Louis and Marie tumbled down the steps and Nicole was suddenly engulfed in tight moist embraces followed by a flurry of excited voices and warm hugs.

Louis beamed over his wife's shoulder as Marie wiped her eyes with her apron hem, then tucked wisps of gold beneath Nicole's hood. Nicole smiled. If a manual existed for mothers, the first rule required every mother to fuss over her daughter's hair. Nicole tossed back her hood and held Marie. Her mother. She inhaled a wonderful warm scent of yeast and soap and lemon wax. Yeast and soap and lemon wax were the comforting smells of home; they always had been, they always would be.

Marie returned the embrace with embarrassed pressure, and her face went slack. Soft wrinkles sagged, then bounced upward in a joyous smile. "Nicole!" She pushed Nicole the length of her arms and stared at the voluminous folds of cloak. A hopeful question leaped into her eyes.

Nicole laughed and nodded happily.

"Oh, my dear!" Marie pulled her into a rough embrace, her reticence forgotten. Then she cupped her hand and whispered into Louis's ear.

The seams in Louis's face pleated into a broad smile. "Well, well. So our little girl is going to make grandparents of us." He grinned at Marie.

A sharp crack interrupted, and they swiveled toward the slamming door and empty porch. Louis's expression sobered and he thrust his hands deep into his pockets.

Marie rubbed her hands across her apron and exchanged a quick glance with her husband. "Well, now. Just look at us, standing here in the street! Come inside, come inside. We want to hear about everything! Are you hungry?"

Nicole smiled. The second rule in the mother's handbook demanded food be offered at the slightest provocation, especially during moments of discomfort or crisis. As Marie listed the delectables waiting in her kitchen, Nicole shifted her gaze toward Louis, and a thousand questions brimmed along the arch of her brow.

"There are changes," Louis responded quietly. His eyes

flicked along the deserted street, then returned to Nicole. And his steady gaze conveyed more than words. "We'll talk later."

Nodding, Nicole walked slowly toward the porch, wondering how in heaven's name she and William would share the same small house. Why hadn't General Gage commandeered the abandoned houses for his troops? But of course that solution would not have punished the citizens of Boston. She sighed and lifted her skirts.

The house was exactly as she remembered, mellow tones of polished wood and copper, gleaming oak floors, warm splashes of red and yellow and green. Lived in and loved.

But there were changes. The parlor was off limits.

Marie had converted the parlor into temporary quarters for William and his current aide, a silent pallid man referred to as Shadow.

"If he has another name, no one knows it," Marie shrugged. Her dark eyes flashed resentment as she stared at the closed parlor doors. "Well." Ten years dropped from her smile as she turned toward Nicole. "I kept your room exactly as you left it. Perhaps you'd like to freshen up before dinner?"

"Mama . . ." Fate could produce ten new mothers, and Marie would still be the only one who mattered. Not even the Empress Elizabeth could hold a candle to the small wrinkled face smiling with love and joy. An affectionate twinkle misted Nicole's gaze as she observed Marie's embarrassment at the emotional tone in Nicole's voice. "I'm glad to be home." She noticed the shine of unshed tears as Marie pressed her arm and nodded wordlessly. Marie touched a timid hand to her daughter's cheek; then she hurried toward the kitchen, dabbing her apron to her eyes.

Nicole might have stepped from the door of her room just minutes ago. Her dust ruffle and pillow shams were freshly laundered and starched, the pale yellow flounces beneath her white curtains were crisp and fluffy. A book lay open on her bedside table, pressed to the page she had last read.

Three years ago.

Three long turbulent years. Nicole closed the book, then glanced into the cracked mirror above her bureau and ran a finger across the chip on the washbasin. She opened an empty drawer and inhaled the dusty scent of a forgotten sachet. Slowly she removed her cloak and hung it on the peg behind the door; then she squared her shoulders and smoothed her palms over her skirt, facing into the room.

It was her room, and yet it was not. A different person had slumbered in the polished four-poster, had warmed chill toes upon the small hooked rug. A girl had occupied this room; a woman had returned to it. A bittersweet ache banded her chest as she confronted her vanished innocence. So much had happened since last she stood beneath these rafters.

Chiding herself for foolish meanderings, she dashed cold water over her cheeks, arranged her hair, then descended to the dining room, following the smell of boiled beef, turnips, and parslied carrots.

Louis and Marie occupied one end of a gate-leg table; William and Shadow were seated before the other. Avoiding William's flat stare, Nicole slipped into the chair beside Louis and bowed her head for grace.

Other than murmuring "amen" to Louis's brief prayer, Shadow did not speak throughout dinner; he ate with single-minded purpose, his thoughts remaining private. After two bites, Nicole forgot his presence entirely. William also spoke little, but it was impossible to ignore his brooding.

"No politics tonight, gentlemen. Please."

Marie's request placed the burden of conversation squarely upon Nicole's slender shoulders. An obvious tension crackled between Louis and William, the Whig and the Tory, an uneasiness precluding discussion of troubled Boston. Marie's expression suggested a discussion might easily escalate into an argument. Ceding to Marie's wishes, Nicole swallowed the inquiries hovering about the tip of her tongue.

Instead she responded to a deluge of questions. Some she answered fully, some she sidestepped; all memories of Russia elicited varying degrees of pain.

At the conclusion of a spotty tale which had omitted Yuri and Larisca and any detailed mention of the serf uprising, William leaned forward and lazily replenished his wineglass from a decanter near the candlesticks. "I'm uncertain as to the reason for your exile," he commented, "but I found it extremely interesting that your . . . husband . . . is dead." He mocked her, a gleam of triumph shining in his pale eyes. "Dead."

He made the word sound so final. Nicole's chin firmed. "I prefer to believe Dimitri is alive. I know it in my heart." Put into words, her reasoning emerged as wishful petulance. Biting the inside of her cheek, she lowered her head and frowned at her clasped hands.

William's lip curled, and he smiled.

"Of course Dimitri's alive," Louis agreed gruffly. He touched her shoulder and glared at William; then he placed his napkin beside Marie's Sunday china and stood. "I haven't tasted a meal like that in I don't remember when, Mother." He patted his stomach and smiled at Marie.

"I guess not," Marie sniffed. "Not when meat is a guinea a pound."

"A guinea a . . . ?" Nicole gaped at her empty plate in astonishment. She had consumed a small fortune. "Mama, you shouldn't have—"

"She didn't. I provided the meat." William tilted backward on his chair legs. The mud drying on his boots nearly brushed Marie's lace tablecloth. Almost, but not quite. "To celebrate our . . . or rather, this . . . happy occasion." Sarcasm soured the sentiment.

"Thank you." It galled her to imagine the homecoming he had envisioned. His arrogance exceeded belief. She had returned his ring, had broken their pledge, had not corresponded. A reasonable man would have relinquished such a phantom engagement. Gazing into William's belligerent face, she regretted nothing.

"I believe a stroll is in order—to walk off this fine meal," Louis announced. "If Mother doesn't need you in the kitchen . . . ?" He lifted a brow.

"You accompany Father," Marie promptly agreed. "And when you return, I have apple pie and cheese."

William held Nicole's chair as she rose. "I believe I'll join you," he said casually. "Unless, of course, you object?" Etiquette guaranteed no objection would be forthcoming. He reached confidently for his jacket.

"I do object." Crimson flushed Nicole's cheeks; she was unaccustomed to acting with deliberate rudeness. "I'd like a few moments of privacy with my father, if you don't mind. Surely we don't require your permission to leave the house?"

Sandy brows shot toward William's hairline, then clamped together. After a slight hesitation, he responded as a British officer. His bow was elaborate, though he answered through clenched teeth. "As you wish."

"Thank you."

The night air was crisp and frosty, an invigorating contrast to the closeness within the house. The cold raised circles of bright pink above Nicole's collar. It felt light and pleasant, unlike the heavy oppressiveness of Siberian cold. She threaded her arm comfortably about her father's sleeve and listened to the crunch of new snow beneath their boots.

"I was wrong to offend William," she said when they left the Duchard gate behind. Cold air warmed in her lungs and emerged in silvery puffs of vapor. "But I just . . ." Her voice trailed. "William insists on believing I betrayed him."

Louis glanced at her stomach from the corner of his eyes. He pressed her gloves. "Pride can be destructive. Especially when coupled with ambition, frustration, and a sense of impotence. William's pride is suffering. None of the British are having an easy time of it." His mitten lifted and waved. "The regulars are bored and idle, suffering constant harassment from the townspeople. The officers are frustrated and angered by the lack of action. They view General Gage's efforts at appeasement as betrayal. Tempers hover on a cutting edge."

He fell silent as they approached a sentry patrolling the corner. The soldier shifted his musket, and frosty moonlight flashed along the bayonet. He watched warily as they turned into a quiet side street. Nicole arched a question toward Louis, and he shrugged.

She looked back at the sentry and then at the houses they passed. "Where did the Marshalls go? And the Batterseas?" Many homes were vacant and dark, the windows boarded over with planking.

"Maybe to relatives in the country, maybe to friends." He assisted her across a patch of ice. "Many believe war is simply a matter of time. Perhaps it is. Boston will never repay the East India Company; the dispute has jelled into a matter of principle. And now Gage has fortified the Boston neck and Copp's Hill. Not the actions of a peaceful man. Cautious, yes, and probably what I would do in his position, but his actions cannot be interpreted as peaceful. We have information that he's requested additional troops from England." Louis squared his chin thoughtfully. "If war comes, it will begin here, in Boston."

War. The acrid coppery smells of war leaped into her mind. The deep-seated crush of dread born from experience. Speaking quietly, Nicole drew a frosty breath and confided her sojourn in the peasant village and her own experience with war. Louis listened in silence, and the pressure of his mitten on her hand increased. She felt his understanding and sympathy, though he said nothing.

"Papa, do we stand any better chance against the world's

finest army than the serfs did? Our people are farmers too." Voices echoed down the corridors of memory.

"We're enough of a threat to worry Gage. Six months ago he seized the gunpowder from the Charlestown magazine, and he's removed several cannon from Cambridge. We weren't prepared for that. But it does indicate he's worried." He rubbed her fingers. "There are unmistakable parallels here to the situation you've described: excessive taxation, lack of representation in government, a large population at the mercy of a few. But there are differences as well. Most of us have the benefit of an education. We have munitions. We don't seek to replace one king with another. And not all of us are strangers to battle. Many of our people fought in the Indian wars and distinguished themselves on the field."

The cold air dried her throat. "But war . . ."

Louis held her arm tightly against his side. "I'm no longer young," he observed slowly. "And war is a young man's game. When I offered my home for meetings, when I supported the views I heard aired there, I didn't expect the situation to escalate toward war; I hoped for a peaceful solution. No one desires war. But if our liberty as a state and as an individual stands at issue—then I agree with your Yuri: let the war begin!" His impassioned voice rang in the sharp crisp air.

"The others . . ." Nicole listed them: Paul Revere, Dr. Joseph Warren, as many as she could recall. "Do they agree?"

"And more. When Gage closed the harbor, all the colonies pledged their support. They honor our shipping contracts, they send us fresh supplies. All New England watches the Bay Colony and waits. Men are organizing, a militia which can be activated within minutes of an alarm. All the colonies are quietly making preparations."

They turned slowly at the end of the block and retraced their steps. The cold and the night seeped inside Nicole's cloak as the impact of Louis's words sank home. Louis's information was not entirely unexpected. Hadn't Henri hinted as much? Hadn't she confided similiar principles to Dimitri? But the reality of impending action wound a chill about her heart. Sentries at the corners. Cannon atop Copp's Hill, British soldiers occupying her home. Brave words were one thing, reality another. She stared at the darkened houses and quickened her step.

"If we must fight, Papa, then I predict we will win," she offered softly. "If not this fight, then the next. Or the next.

343

We will win because we won't quit until we do. Because all men have an innate right to determine their own destiny, because no man should be bound by taxes or laws he has no voice in enacting. Because no king and no empress has the wisdom or the right to decide what is best for you and me."

Louis soberly appraised the determination firming her small rosy face. When he spoke, the words emerged with a strange reluctance, as if he discharged a promise he regretted. "I won't deny that your words please me, but . . ." He frowned. "If you really believe this, Nicole, perhaps you can aid the cause. . . ."

"I would be proud to do so, Papa. I promise whatever aid is asked of me." She would spin yards of homespun and replace all her English gowns. She would eschew English tea and learn to brew the harsh local blends or insist upon coffee. She would spurn meat at a guinea a pound. She would cheerfully welcome whatever sacrifices were required.

Louis studied the warm spill of light falling from the Duchard windows. "We'll discuss the matter again. When I'm a grandfather."

Before she entered the house, Nicole filled her lungs with sharp cold air and stared upward toward a sweep of stars, icy white against the black night. "Forgive me, Yuri," she breathed silently. "I've learned so much since you went away." She chose a particularly brilliant star and addressed her thoughts toward its sparkle. "I was too foolish to understand there are ideas which reach beyond individuals, ideas worth dying for. I rejected the magnitude of your dreams. Now I know that your fight will continue until men are granted the freedom to choose and until no man calls another his master." She seldom allowed herself to think of Yuri, but tonight she felt his gentle spirit beside her.

"He was a good man, Papa. He died free." She pressed Louis's arm, and then her moist eyes lifted in promise. "You may count on me to do whatever is needed."

As they stamped the snow from their boots and hurried toward Marie's apple pie, neither suspected how bitterly hard fulfilling her promise would be.

26

APRIL ARRIVED SOFTLY, spreading delicate tints of green across the tumbled hills and valleys glimpsed from Boston's deserted harbor. Rocks and woods, straggling villages, gradually secluded themselves behind unfurling leaves and fleshed-out branches.

From her upstairs window Nicole marked the progress of the earth's spring ritual. New England's spring was not the startlingly abrupt spring of Russia, but rather a gradual transition toward renewal. She felt at one with the process, an integral part of life's productivity. Her advanced pregnancy mirrored the swelling buds on tree and shrub.

As public appearances were now beyond the realm of propriety, Nicole did not accompany Marie to market, nor was she expected to return the calls of friends. She occupied her days by engaging in simple tasks, since Marie stoutly refused to allow her any chores more strenuous than dusting, mending, light cooking, and the knitting of small caps and gowns.

"You must guard your health," Marie insisted. Had her mother been granted her desires, Nicole would have passed the next month in bed awaiting the great event in an environment of total bed rest. Marie suspected Nicole's stubborn energy as dangerously modern. The old ways were best. "You looked like death when you came home," she grumbled. "Hollow cheeks, lackluster hair, skinny arms . . . Now that we've filled you out some, it's foolish to risk what you've gained!"

Nicole smiled, glancing upward from the small blue booties materializing beneath her knitting needles. "I feel fine, Mama," she reassured Marie at least a dozen times each day. "Perhaps a little warm . . ." she added, touching her apron hem to her brow. Regardless of the warming weather, Marie maintained a blazing kitchen fire, and she pushed Nicole's chair as near the warmth as safely possible.

"A chill could kill you." Muttering, Marie ground a stone

pestle into a bowl of dried corn, preparing a meatless corn pudding for dinner.

"You be looking good to me, ma'am," the new servant girl volunteered, pausing above a hot flatiron and a basket of laundered shirts. Molly had run off last year with a British deserter. The new girl was named Cassie. She too hoped to snare a dissatisfied soldier and elope to Pennsylvania or perhaps to one of the Carolinas. She'd been batting her lashes at Shadow, but thus far the self-immersed Mr. Shadow had not comprehended he was under siege.

"Thank you, Cassie." The cracked mirror above Nicole's bureau had confirmed Cassie's observation. Her cheeks had rounded, her hair had regained its rich golden shine, and her clear eyes contained the maturity of promise. Each time the baby moved, her complexion lit from within.

Bowing her head above her knitting, Nicole surprised herself by admitting a quiet happiness. Her growing preoccupation with the baby had diminished her frantic worry for Dimitri. She could think of him now without a rush of panicked tears, without the sour dread weighing like a stone against her heart. The anxiety remained always, but the level had receded.

There were, however, flawed areas marring her precariously balanced ease of mind.

She paused to watch Cassie bend and select another starched white shirt from the basket. And an unconscious frown disturbed her brow as she recognized one of William's uniform shirts.

Each evening Nicole was aware the instant William returned to the house. A gathering tension snapped through the rooms. His brooding tainted the atmosphere.

No one knew what to expect of William from one day to the next. Occasionally he was pleasant, wooing her with interesting anecdotes of his day, seemingly anxious to please; more frequently he cast her as a target for bitter sarcasm.

She marveled that she had ever thought him controlled or emotionless. Perhaps once, but these qualities had been eroded by frustration, anger, thwarted ambition. Restraint, control, lack of emotion—these were not qualities she would now have chosen to describe him.

In an effort not to provoke William, the Duchards adjusted their habits to his moods. Breakfast and dinner hours were modified to match his schedule; they pinched the candles and retired before ten o'clock. Marie served William's favorite dishes; Louis attempted to avoid explosive topics.

Because the sight of Nicole's extended stomach caused William to become physically ill, she seated herself before he entered the dining room, and she fled immediately upon finishing her coffee, returning to the kitchen or retiring to her room. Her flight enraged him. But as he appeared annoyed whether she remained or fled, Nicole chose to pass the balance of her evening beyond the reach of his moody stares.

As the time approached for her confinement—mid-May, by her best estimate—she withdrew to her room more frequently. There, amid the comforts of familiarity, she shrugged out of her cap, apron, and gown and wrapped herself into a loose quilted robe, brushed out her long hair, and settled into a small rocker near the window, gently rocking the ache from her lower back. Louis had carried the chair up from the parlor; the arms were worn smooth of finish from years of comfortable use.

Accompanied by the gentle creak of the rockers, Nicole sat in the darkness and allowed her thoughts to drift over the small events weaving her days, and the larger event to come. From there it was but a small step to conjecturing about the world into which she would birth a new life.

Her conclusions were both conflicting and alarming.

The British troops, bored with inactivity and pushed near their limits by harassment, failed to understand General Gage's reluctance to crush Boston's continuing insolence. Appeasement had failed; the troops clamored for force. Along with many fellow officers, William expressed a growing contempt, referring to General Thomas Gage as "Tommy," a term rife with indignity and dissatisfaction.

"Old Tommy had best protect his flanks," William had recently declared in tones of disgust, "or he'll discover himself brought up on charges of treason. His pandering to the so-called patriots smacks of collaboration!"

Gage's concessions to the populace were bitterly resented by officers and regulars alike. As discipline grew lax, the soldiers turned to gambling and drinking. Cheap New England rum ignited tempers; boredom fueled grounds for drunken duels; street brawls erupted with tiresome regularity, involving officers, regulars, and equally frustrated townspeople. Desertion become commonplace. And British morale suffered a disastrous decline when the deserters were captured, then flogged or executed. The British troops unanimously believed

Gage should smash the recalcitrant Bostonians rather than punish his own men, regardless of their infractions.

William employed the Duchard dining table as a forum to air disgruntlement and chagrin. "Gage should be replaced immediately!" he fumed.

"Gage is doing the best he can," Louis had responded quietly.

Louis steadfastly maintained that Gage was a good man, performing as well as could be expected in a complex and difficult situation. Perhaps better than most. Gage evinced an honest effort to understand the colonists' needs and demands. An attitude William abhorred.

"Some democracy is certainly beneficial," William had recently admitted. "But too much democracy opens the state to mob rule. Surely the events in Boston have adequately proven this. Don't you agree?" No one at the table had agreed, and William's tone had darkened. "This entire bloody colony is pledged to sedition! If this be democracy, then let it be damned!"

The challenge was too tempting, Louis had been unable to suppress a rebuttal, and an argument had ensued. "We'll never agree," he said finally. "You support the royal prerogative, William, and refuse to allow any disagreement. But many of us believe the people would be better served by self-government rather than by a king several thousand miles distant who may be misinformed as to our situation."

"Ridiculous! Utter rubbish!" A thin smile had curled William's lips. "And to what lengths are you prepared to extend yourself to achieve this colonial government you continually harp on? War?"

Louis had stroked his chin, answering thoughtfully. "No reasonable man seeks violence, and we prefer a peaceful solution to the issues at stake. But if war is the ultimate price of liberty . . . we won't shrink from that terrible price."

William choked on spasms of harsh laughter. "Our drummers display more military prowess than the Americans!" He'd lifted his napkin to his lips, smiling into an angry silence. "Recall if you will how deplorably inept the Americans have been in previous skirmishes. They weary of battle and desert; they lack any hint of discipline; Americans are farmers, for Christ's sake, not soldiers!"

Nicole and Marie had toyed with their silverware; Louis's lips had tightened. "Do you mock the courage of Americans, sir?"

William grinned. "Certainly not. One can't ridicule a quality not proven to exist."

Louis had risen slowly from the table. He'd leaned his weight upon fists flattened beside his plate. "You are a guest in my home. Not by choice, but a guest nonetheless. It is for that reason alone that I do not challenge you."

William had tilted backward on the chair legs, undaunted. He nudged Shadow, who continued to eat placidly, exhibiting no interest in the heated exchange. "Bring on your war . . . we itch for a little practice." William had examined his fingernails. "We'll repel you as easily as flicking a gnat from our shoulders." A pretended yawn stretched his lips. "Frankly, we'd welcome the opportunity to put you in your places, to settle this nonsense once and for all."

Louis had leaned forward, speaking softly beneath snapping eyes. "You may very possibly have your opportunity, sir. We wait."

"Aha. You wait. And for what, sir?"

"For the first shot. No war shall be instigated by an American! We will not be first to fire on our fellowman."

William's chair legs had struck the floor with a sharp crack. "Then for your sake I pray you wait in vain. Farmers aligned against professionals . . . your people would be massacred!"

"I think not. I think you dangerously underestimate American courage and determination, sir."

The men's eyes locked. An expression of icy fury congested William's face. "Let the confrontation come, then. We shall take great pleasure in demonstrating our superiority. Gage will not dally forever! And when he makes his move . . ."

Recalling the disturbing exchange, Nicole shivered and tilted backward in the rocker, easing the weight from her spine. William's brash confidence was founded in fact; she did not for a moment doubt his boasts. The awesome British army was recognized as the finest in history.

To their credit, few of the colonists shrank from the British army's fearsome reputation. Friends and neighbors lauded American valor and commitment. And none more so than Dr. Joseph Warren.

Once a week Dr. Warren called to examine Nicole and to pass along encouraging news of meetings in Cambridge, the colonial headquarters. The colonists were not sitting idle. They amassed munitions, published broadsides, organized town militia.

"Joseph, do you believe the issues can be settled peacefully? Or do you believe war is as inevitable as Papa claims?" Nicole had raised the subject during his latest visit. War occupied everyone's thoughts.

Young, handsome, something of a dandy in his choice of attire, Dr. Warren had shrugged. "Many of us believe the likelihood of war increases with every passing day." His expression clearly stated that if war came, he would be found in the thick of it. He had peered into Nicole's eyes, gauged the healthy color of her lips, hair, and fingernails, then nodded and professed himself satisfied. "To fully answer your questions and mine, we'd require a crystal ball . . . or a well-placed spy in Gage's camp." He'd bent above his bag. "Have you spoken to your father?"

"Every day." Nicole had laughed and filled his coffee cup. "Papa lives here too, remember?"

Immediately Marie had thrust her short plump body between them. "A raisin bun, Dr. Warren?"

He'd glanced into her frown, then accepted a bun, biting into the warm center with a small murmur of pleasure. "On a more personal note, Nicole, I transferred your gold to Salem, as you requested, and peeked in on the house. It's coming along nicely. . . ."

Our gold; Dimitri's and mine. She'd considered correcting him but had not. As president of the recently formed Provincial Congress, Joseph was granted the passes to shuttle back and forth at will. She'd sighed, wishing that she herself could supervise the building of the house Dimitri had commissioned. She'd yet to see it. "Thank you. I think the gold will be safer in Salem in the event . . ." She'd bitten her lips. "I hope you retained a small purse for your trouble."

He'd waved the bun. "Nonsense. When I agreed to act in Denisov's behalf, I did so as a friend." He'd regarded her through sympathetic eyes. "I conceived a great admiration for your husband through our correspondence. I deeply regret his loss. A man of his intelligence and experience would have been a great asset to our cause."

It wounded her that everyone assumed Dimitri was dead. Nicole had drawn a long breath and held it. "He speaks highly of you as well."

They'd discussed the devastation of loss, the various manifestations of grief; then Joseph had risen and adjusted a maroon cloak with an emerald velvet collar. Not for Dr. Warren the coarseness of homespun; he'd abandoned English fashion in favor of French. "In the event I'm unavailable . . ." No one could confidently schedule tomorrow. He scribbled a name on a scrap of paper and placed it on the table. "This doctor is familiar with your case and will assist your delivery."

"I can birth my own grandchild!" Marie had snapped. She'd fisted floury hands upon her hips and glared.

After a wink for Nicole, Joseph had slid an arm about Marie's indignant shoulders. "I'm certain you can, Madame Duchard. In fact, I'm depending upon your assistance."

Nicole leaned into the rocker and replayed the conversation, experiencing a vague unease. The rockers creaked gently as she stared at the budding elm beyond her windowpanes, tracing a wash of moonlight across the branches. A slice of white filtered past the darkened windowsill, falling pale and spring-chill upon her robe. A light breeze chased darting shadows along the empty streets. Closing her lashes, she pondered the doctor's visit, seeking an elusive something—something—which had scratched up a prickle of ill-boding. Something in the conversation mystified her, but she could not isolate exactly what.

A soft rap at the door startled her focus of concentration. Immediate alarm flared behind her eyes, and she struggled from the rocker to hasten across the room. No one knocked in the middle of the night to deliver good news.

"William!" Her surprise was total. She clasped the throat of her wrapper and leaned into the corridor, glancing anxiously down the darkened hallway. "Has something happened? What's wrong?"

"No, no, nothing like that. I just need to talk to someone. May I come in for a moment?"

She stared upward, wrapping her arms about her shoulders. He was still dressed in his uniform; she could see the faint ridge where his hat had pressed a circle around his hair. A barely contained excitement vibrated along his thin frame, leaped from sparkling eyes.

Nicole frowned and edged backward. "This is most unseemly, William." It was downright scandalous. And out of character. "If we must talk . . ." She let the words trail, hoping he would withdraw when he observed her reluctance. He did not. ". . . don't you think the kitchen would be more suitable?"

"Of course. Yes. Forgive me . . . my mind is traveling in a dozen different directions."

One of the directions was embarrassingly evident. His gaze stroked the loose curls flowing to her waist, hungered toward the glimmer of moonlight captured within golden strands. When he spoke, his voice had coarsened. "I'll go on ahead and poke up the fire."

Puzzled by his excitement, and offended by the intimacy of the late-night encounter, Nicole leaned against her door, closing it.

She felt half a mind to climb into the four-poster and snuggle into her pillows. But she couldn't be confident of William's reaction; he might return and pound on her door, might create an awkward scene. How she had once judged him as predictable was an enigma, unless obsession was predictable in a manner she did not immediately recognize. Sighing, she braided her hair and coiled it beneath a nightcap. No method existed to disguise her stomach. She fluffed her robe as best she could and descended the staircase.

"Sit here." William seated her at the far side of the kitchen table, near enough the hearth to enjoy its feeble warmth, but not so near that her bulk would be in silhouette if he passed behind her.

She frowned into the mug of cider he pushed into her hands. "I'm very tired, William . . ."

Either he did not hear or chose not to. He lifted his cup, and the sweetish smell of rum wafted toward her nostrils. His eyes shone in the glow of revived embers. "To King George!" he cried. "To the British army and its proud history of victory, both past and present!"

Similar toasts had ignited brawls throughout all the colonies. Had William been less distracted, he would have objected to Nicole's lack of haste and enthusiasm as she slowly raised the cider to her lips. But he paced before the fire, striding toward the shadowy spinning wheel, then swiveling and marching toward a shelf of crockery and utensils, running short stubby fingers through his hair. Nicole suspected the rum he waved was not his first.

"It's a grand evening! A glorious evening!"

"William . . . it is the middle of the night."

"A lovely night." His arm soared, and droplets of rum sloshed over the sides of his mug. "Here's to the night. Not too cold, a moon to see by, fog before morning!" Flinging open the base of the dry sink, he refilled his mug from the jug Louis kept hidden there.

Nicole stared. William was as gay and feverish as if he attended the season's most coveted ball; except she didn't recall William being gay at parties or, for that matter, anywhere. "William, is there something specific you wish to discuss?"

"Wouldn't you like to know," he cried merrily. "Wouldn't you just like to know!" His tone extended an invitation to coax. He was fairly bursting to reveal the source of his ebullience, even as a natural caution urged silence.

Nicole sighed and pushed aside the mug of cider. "I'm too weary for guessing games. If you will excuse me . . ." Placing her palms on the table, she prepared to rise.

"Wait!" William chewed his lips, shifting from one boot to the other. He watched the firelight flickering rosy across her scrubbed loveliness. "I suppose it won't harm if I tell you. . . . They've already departed." Speculative eyes darted over her cap, her robe, the tips of her slippers showing beneath the table. He smiled. "You're hardly dressed to go calling."

"William . . ."

He raised his palms. "And I know you wouldn't betray a confidence." He stared at her, then offered a hasty apology for his sarcasm.

Summoning an effort toward patience, Nicole stroked her forehead. It had been a mistake to join him. Only a ridiculous sense of guilt had prompted her to agree. And only her advanced pregnancy saved her reputation from ruin.

She watched him replenish his drink, and resented the manner in which he'd made the Duchard home his own, striding about and poking into cupboards as if he belonged here. She didn't relish the confiscation of the parlor or his obvious disdain for her parents' opinions. And she considered his scarlet jacket particularly offensive.

The omnipresence of swaggering crimson throughout Boston represented everything she had grown to despise; the soldiers' fitted coats symbolized absolute rule by authority and force. She regarded them as embodying Catherine's elitism, Repinsky's abuse; when she observed the red coat, she saw closed harbors, excessive taxation, the tyrannical inflicting of one will upon another.

"Who has departed?" Resigned, she gazed into the fireplace, acknowledging that he would not release her until he'd shared his news. She was glad when he removed the red jacket and flung it toward a low stool before the spinning wheel. She was also glad he had not bothered to light additional candles.

He sat across from her, his hands clenching the mug of rum, his pale eyes shining. "Troops! Old Tommy has finally made his move!"

Nicole's lips dropped, and her throat dried to sand.

"By God, I would give ten years of my life to be on the march with them! That's where the glory is, on the field! Not stagnating in a cramped office issuing passes!" His momentous news would not tolerate stillness. William sprang from the table and resumed an excited pacing, arms waving, firelight painting his white satin breeches the hated color of red.

Nicole's mind raced. She recalled Shadow slipping from the dinner table before Marie had served pie and coffee. William, too casual, departing for an evening staff conference at Province House. Odd rustlings of movement in the streets. Tall shadows gliding between the houses. Not imagined; real. She stared at him.

"We shall discover just who underestimates whom! Arrogant bastards! When the munitions at Concord are sitting on Boston Common, we'll see how quickly egos deflate! The potential for a colonial army will be totally disabled. We'll suffer no more foolishness concerning resistance or war."

Concord! How had the British learned of the stockpile housed there? How did they dare to seize private property? Beyond the kitchen window a cloud drifted across the moon, blanking the yard and the stubble of last year's kitchen garden.

"When the roosters crow, Concord will awaken to soldiers!" His voice soared with glee. The level in the rum jug sank steadily.

Nicole held her breath and calmed the pounding against her ribs. Someone must have noticed the strange night rustlings. Surely. Soldiers had slipped from other dinner tables. Many beds would be empty tonight. Someone would notice.

Immediately she thought of Louis, whose senses were acutely attuned to worsening developments. He slept soundly above their heads. Innocent of troops set in motion.

What if no one had remarked the night's absences? A light patina of perspiration beaded upon Nicole's brow. She pressed moist palms against her robe.

"The soldiers will march all night," she whispered. The people living along the roads would notice them.

William nodded, explaining the distance and routes of travel. Proudly he emphasized the suggestions he had offered

Gage. It had been William's idea to adopt a longer route, one that skirted the major population centers.

Tendrils of gold escaped Nicole's cap and adhered damply to her temples. By morning the soldiers would be weary, perhaps too exhausted from the all-night march to attempt the fatiguing task of hauling cannon and shot back to Boston. She considered the famed British discipline and realized the foolishness of her hope.

William underscored his points with a stabbing finger. "The so-called patriots desire a confrontation? A test of abilities? Of determination? By God, they shall have it!" He drained his mug and slammed it triumphantly on the tabletop.

Nicole jumped. She promised herself that even now the patriots were converging upon Concord, preparing. They were removing the carefully hoarded supplies and concealing them elsewhere. She prayed this was true.

As William paced and reviewed Gage's planning session, Nicole splashed a sturdy dollop of rum into her mug. Her hands steadied as the raw liquid warmed her stomach. What if . . . ? What if! A thousand possibilities thudded through her brain. Then shock. She, Nicole Duchard Denisovna, possessed vital information. Information which could affect the course of future events if . . . if the alarm could be sounded swiftly enough.

Fresh shock drained the color from her expression as she realized her news could not be passed along. She could scarcely run into the midnight streets wearing her night-clothes. It was too late, in any case; the soldiers had too advanced a start. What was needed was a determined rider with a fast horse.

She stared at William, unaware of the stream of smug predictions pouring from his lips. He would not sleep tonight. He would prowl the darkness waiting for morning, waiting for confirmation of British supremacy. No message would leave this house.

Tension crawled along her shoulders, drawing the muscles into tightly bunched knots.

"Remember what I say—we'll march into Concord; we will strip the munitions depot; we will load the supplies; and we shall return unopposed. Without a shot being fired. Without encountering greater resistance than a few angry stares and a few disgruntled mutters."

She had never felt so frustratingly impotent in her life! An urge to strike out, to hurl her cup through the window, trembled along her taut frame. She longed to scream and shout and raise enough noise to be heard in Concord!

William's lip twisted. "American courage? Nothing but boastful sputterings, fiery speeches. Wind through the ears. Let them gaze upon the scarlet columns, and they will fade toward their farms, seeking the safety of trees and fences!" He raked his sandy hair with digging fingers. "God! I wish I could be there to see it! Tomorrow, first thing, I'm requesting a transfer to field duty. Absolutely!" His eyes strayed toward her face, hoping she would object; then he could assure her by speaking of glorious deeds, of reputations to be made in battle, of advancements in rank and respect. Ambitions fulfilled; merit finally rewarded. "I'm wasted in my current position. My intellect should be directed toward larger issues than who enters or leaves the city!" He sought confirmation. "Don't you agree?"

Nicole stared past the window and into the blackness beyond. An entire army could have tramped through the Duchard backyard and she would not have seen them. And William had predicted morning fog. Fog to swallow movement; fog to muffle sound.

"Don't you agree?"

"I . . . What? Excuse me, I wasn't . . ."

He exploded. "You weren't listening! You never do! When I speak, you retreat within yourself!" Pinpoints of resentment centered upon her pinched expression. "I'm trying to share with you! Can't you grasp that? I wanted you here to explore the opportunities arising from tonight's incident! But I wanted a discussion, not a monologue!"

Nicole pulled her wrapper closer about her body, withdrawing from the blend of frustration and reproach.

He covered his brow and sank to the table, his excitement diminished. "Dammit, Nicole!" The stare he leveled accused her. "Everyone else, my friends, my subordinates, they all have someone! Someone to talk to, someone who listens and responds and cares!"

She turned her face to the shadows, shifting from the revealing glow of dying firelight. "Please, William. We've discussed this previously. There's nothing between us. If there ever was, it is ended and forgotten." She cursed herself for being here. She should have guessed that any moments of privacy would lead to this.

"If it wasn't for that baby . . ." Bitterness harshened his tone as he nodded toward the bulge of her robe showing above the table edge. "You wouldn't insist what we feel for each other is over if it wasn't for that baby! If you didn't carry the Russian bastard's seed, you would admit that he's dead. Dead! Then you would beg my forgiveness and return to me!"

There was no reasoning with him. No point in replying. Logic could debate illogic until the oceans dried to desert, and neither side would convince the other. Nicole cupped her stomach and struggled up from the table. She made no pretense of concealing her pregnancy from his rejecting stare; she would never do so again.

"Good night, William."

"Just hear me out!"

She replaced the rum jug in its hiding place—it was nearly empty—and she dropped the two mugs into a tin pan of cold soapy water atop the dry sink.

"Nicole, listen!" The shredding of pride came hard. "I . . . I'm lonely!"

She recognized the desperation in his whisper and she felt a responsive twinge of sorrow, as for anyone who stared into a deep quiet night and whispered of loneliness. But she did not answer. Nor did she acknowledge that she had heard. Instead, she leaned above the hearth and banked the fire.

"I love you! What must I do to prove it? God in heaven! Don't you hear me? I love you! Do you fear I can't forgive your betrayal? Is that it?"

A log tumbled forward, sending forth a shower of sparks, and she halted its progress with the poker and wrestled it back into place.

"Don't you realize yet that I would forgive you anything? Anything at all?" The final bastion of pride crumbled and his tone pleaded.

She couldn't decide which was worse—his prior arrogance or this terrible capitulation to emotion. Standing before the fire exaggerated the curve of her stomach; she could feel his repugnance crawling over the swell of her robe. And she hurried, performing a shoddy job with the coals.

"If it wasn't for that goddamned baby, things would be different! We could forget we'd ever been parted. We could begin afresh, as if that Russian nonsense had never happened."

Nicole's jaw tensed; she pressed her lips into a thin line and resisted the urge to lash out. Pity and loathing vied across her features. She replaced the poker on a nail protruding from the hearth stones, and without glancing toward him, without speaking, she crossed the kitchen and entered the dark hallway leading to the stairs.

White satin breeches, a white linen shirt, rushed beyond her and loomed to block her progress. "I want a wife and a family of my own. I want you. Is that so reprehensible?"

"Step aside."

The blur of white moved, stepping backward, remaining before her. "Every man needs a loving home. A haven to vent the petty frustrations of his day. He needs a wife to listen and to care about the smallest daily events in his life, because, dammit, no one else does. He needs the care and the advice and the solace of a woman!"

She could see a feeble fall of light illuminating the staircase and thanked God she had exibited the presence of mind to leave a candle burning at the top of the stairs. The candle sconce was positioned three feet from Louis and Marie's door. At the first hint of raised voices, at the first sounds of a scuffle, Louis would appear.

William mounted the staircase backward, facing her. "I know you love me, Nicole. You try to hide it, but I've seen the love in your eyes when you didn't know I was watching."

Deep shadow obscured his expression, but her own features were bathed in dim candlelight as she tilted her head backward and focused her amazement. "You are deranged," she whispered, halting with one hand upon the railing. "Understand me. I do not love you. I have no desire to be your wife. I am married, William, for this moment and for the rest of my life!"

She could not see into his face, but she sensed that her words flowed beyond him without impression.

"I understand you have to say that because of the baby. That's the reason, isn't it? You think somehow you betray the baby if you admit to loving someone other than the baby's father, don't you? You fear the baby will suffer in some indefinable way if you admit your true feelings!"

She blinked at him in disbelief, edging upward another step. "That is utter nonsense. It isn't plausible. Please let me pass." Two more risers, and she would stand firmly upon the landing. A short dash would carry her to her door and to freedom from this whispered babble, from these mad insinuations. She would curl into her quilts and pretend this midnight craziness had never occurred.

He leaned forward. Droplets of rum-scented mist assailed her nose. "If it weren't for the baby . . ."

"Sir. I demand that you step aside!" Escape in sight, she pushed against his shoulder, her eyes on the landing behind him. In two minutes this ugliness would end.

But he grasped her wrist suddenly, and she cried out, her gaze swinging to meet the anger in his eyes. "You haven't heard a word I've said!" His mouth twisted. "Because of this!" Abruptly his hand descended to press against her bulging robe.

The swift release of her wrist followed by the sudden unexpected pressure against her stomach threw her off balance. She would never be certain if she jumped from his touch or if he pushed.

She teetered on the edge of the stair, her arms wheeling, her face chalky and bloodless around staring eyes.

For an instant they gazed into each other's souls, and the instant stretched toward timelessness.

Then she was falling. Dizzying weightlessness. Light spinning away at the end of a black tunnel. Hard wooden edges slamming into her flesh. Darkness rushed upward, wind whistled past her ears. She heard a sharp high scream, then a hard thud, and finally a thick deep silence.

She lay very still, afraid to move, denying the cold fire spreading through her stomach. A gush of warm salty liquid, outside her control, rivered from between her legs and soaked past her nightgown and then into her robe.

The wet discharge terrified her, impelled her to movement. Slowly, cautiously, she lifted on one elbow, testing her battered flesh. Nothing appeared to be broken, but the fire in her belly obliterated sensation. She was too numb to be certain. The smallest movement shot fingers of pain past the numbness. Small aches were dwarfed by the involuntary ripples bearing down across her stomach in hard agonizing waves.

Blinking rapidly, she stared upward, gasping Marie's name. But there was only William.

He stood motionless at the top of the staircase, rigid with shock. A groan wrenched upward from his chest, and it might have been remorse or it might have been jubilation.

"I'll see you dead!" She didn't know if she uttered the words aloud or if they screamed through her mind.

William stared down at her crumpled form, his expression lost in shadow. Then he sank to the top step and pressed his forehead against the wall.

27

VADIM DIMITRIVICH DENISOV entered the world at approximately the same moment as seven Americans bid it farewell; British and American forces clashed upon the Lexington green five miles from Concord. April 19, 1775, would long be remembered both privately and historically.

"He's beautiful, isn't he?" Nicole murmured proudly. She relaxed against a mound of pillows as tiny fists kneaded her breast. Black curls lay silken soft against her skin. Once again she thanked God that her son was healthy and perfect and exhibited no ill effects from his premature arrival. "I'm so glad he has hair. Bald babies remind me of tiny old men."

Chuckling, Louis leaned backward in the rocker and winked at Marie, the candlelight imparting an additional sparkle to his crinkled eyes. "As I recall, you were as bald as a bucket, but we still thought you were the prettiest thing we'd ever seen. Didn't we, Mother?"

Marie agreed happily, hovering about Nicole's bed, plumping the pillows, brushing a loose tendril toward the blue ribbon restraining Nicole's curls.

"I wish Dimitri could be here." A man should know his son. Nicole touched the infant's small aristocratic nose with the tip of her finger, then drew a long breath and held it until her voice steadied. "He has Dimitri's strong features. Don't you agree, Mama?"

"Not at all. I think he looks exactly like my Grandpa René. See that brow? Already it shows intelligence. Grandpa René was the magistrate in our village when I was growing up. He was the shrewdest man for miles around."

"Well, now," Louis commented, rocking forward. "I'd say he favors the Duchards. He'll be tall, anyone can see that.

And my Uncle Jacques had a dimple on the chin same as Vaddie does."

"Vaddie?"

"Father and I think Vadim is too stilted a name for a baby." Marie shrugged apologetically. "For a man, yes, it's a good strong name. But for this tiny mite?" Vaddie it was; her tone brooked no argument. She extended her arms, and Nicole eased the sleeping bundle against Marie's pillowy breast. Humming softly, Marie slid into the rocker Louis hastily vacated. She opened the corners of a small bright quilt. "That's Grandpa René's brow for certain, and, yes, Father, I think he has your nose."

Louis beamed over her shoulder in modest agreement. "I believe he does, Mother. And your ears."

Nicole laughed helplessly. There wasn't a drop of Duchard or René blood in her son's veins. But Louis and Marie would never admit it. And if one stretched the imagination to the limit, Vaddie did resemble the painting of Grandpa René. Faintly.

In Nicole's mind, however, Vadim Dimitrivich was a three-week-old miniature of his father. She saw Dimitri in Vaddie's blue-gray eyes, in his tiny strong jaw and broad baby chest. He wore Dimitri's black curls and waved Dimitri's long tapered fingers.

A trembling hand lifted to her eyes, and she pressed her face into the pillows. Every beat of her heart sounded a cry of longing. "Oh, my love, where are you? We need you."

Vadim had promised to bring Dimitri home to her in the spring. . . .

But the tulips had bloomed and died. The scent of lilac blossoms drifted on the evening breeze. The air teasing her curtains was soft and warm and hinted of early summer. Nicole plucked the lace edging her wrist, and she listened to the thrumming night sounds of late spring. Vadim had promised—if Dimitri was alive.

Catching her lip between her teeth, she transferred her gaze to Marie and Vaddie rocking quietly in a pool of mellow gold candlelight. Vaddie—she tested the name silently, deciding she liked it. She released a restless sigh and frowned at the ceiling.

This should have been the happiest period of her life. But she lay in the four-poster and watched the days lengthen and the elm thicken—and her heart wept.

"Mama . . . I'm going to dress tomorrow, I've been in bed long enough."

Marie was scandalized. "It hasn't been a month yet! I've never heard of a lying-in period of less than a month!"

"Dr. Warren says I'm fine. He said I could get up if I didn't overdo." Nicole privately believed the lying-in period could be halved without harm. Weeks of bed rest lulled the mind and weakened the muscles.

Marie sighed, recognizing the determination setting Nicole's jaw. "You always were a willful child." She smiled.

"I know you're shorthanded." Cassie had eloped with Shadow, to no one's surprise but the intended groom's. "I can clean and help with the cooking . . ."

Marie agreed reluctantly. "Only the light tasks." She rocked her grandson in her arms and visibly brightened. "We can carry Vaddie's basket along with us while we work."

Louis listened in sober silence as they arranged a schedule. An odd resigned expression descended across the back of his gaze. When he spoke, he sounded older than just minutes ago. "You're quite certain you're out of danger? Dr. Warren agrees?"

Curiosity arched Nicole's brow. "Yes, Papa." He still wore the leather breeches and leather vest he worked in. She liked the smell of tanned leather and the solid honest stains of bootblack upon his hands. The smells and sights of home.

Louis drew a breath and injected a tone of heartiness into his suggestion. "Mother, why don't you give young Vaddie a tour of the kitchen? If he'll be helping out, he should know something about pots and lug poles."

Marie hesitated. Her brows clamped together, and Nicole's curiosity heightened. Marie met her husband's eyes; then she bowed her head and extended the infant for Nicole's kiss before she softly closed the bedroom door behind her.

Hitching the rocker nearer Nicole's bed, Louis settled himself and mustered a thin smile. "Feel up to some politics?"

Anything was preferable to tormenting herself with the significance of spring. Nicole tugged the ribbon from her hair and shook a shower of gold around her shoulders. She had enjoyed her brief respite from the world, but it was time now to return. "Yes, Papa. Tell me the news."

Louis spoke quietly, detailing the events of the night Nicole would never forget. Nor, it seemed, would history.

Someone had indeed noticed the empty soldiers' beds, the shadows slipping toward the wharves. Paul Revere and others had alerted the countryside that the British were on the move. Patriots sprang from their beds and converged upon various gathering points to argue the best course of action and how firm a resistance to mount. In the morning, to the surprised horror of both sides, musket fire had erupted upon the Lexington green. Men had died. Shaken, the Americans had withdrawn and the British had marched on to Concord, where they seized the patriot's supplies.

"Dear God!" Nicole whispered. Fisted hands rose to her lips.

As the exhausted British soldiers began the long return to Boston, nearly a thousand enraged patriots had gathered along the Concord road. They followed the crimson columns, darting behind trees and beneath stone fences, firing continually.

Unfamiliar with the countryside, the stunned British were forced to hold to the road. This tactic ensured their return to Boston, but made of them easy targets. Many were wounded, some died. Had General Gage not hastened to dispatch reinforcements, few soldiers would have survived the march intact. Dragging their wounded, firing blindly, they fled toward Boston in full retreat.

The patriots touted the day as a rousing victory; the British fumed with humiliation and swore revenge. They considered the rout a fluke, one which deserved deadly answer.

Nicole's eyes sobered gravely. "It's war, then."

The waiting had ended; shots had been exchanged. Men were dead.

Louis nodded. "Both sides claim the other fired first at Lexington." He shrugged, the leather whispering about his shoulders like a sigh. "Historians will argue the incident for decades. What matters most is that our men came when they were called. And they rousted the finest army man has gazed upon. We desperately needed that boost of confidence."

"Thank God for Revere! That night . . . when William told me . . . all I could think of was sounding an alarm. And it was impossible!"

Something in her words turned Louis's face toward the window, and Nicole wondered suddenly if he was ill. He looked his age tonight, old and weary and disillusioned. "The value of inside information cannot be underestimated," he said.

Nicole heartily agreed.

He continued in a flat voice, explaining the consequences

of the Lexington-Concord confrontation. New England ports now refused to clear any British ships; as a result, Boston was cut off from food and fuel. Hay for horses and domestic animals was running scarce; people depended on salted provisions, as fresh had become nearly impossible to obtain at any price.

"Earlier this week General Gage agreed to abolish the pass restrictions, thereby allowing any Whigs to depart Boston who wished to do so. Every citizen was commanded to surrender all personal weapons to the selectmen in Faneuil Hall."

"Did you . . . ?"

"No choice was given."

It would seem strange not to see Louis's musket hanging above the kitchen hearth alongside the strings of drying herbs. The space would appear as unbalanced as the icon of St. Nicholas without Yuri's ax beside it. The repetitive quality of history overwhelmed Nicole. Identical dramas played out again and again; only the actors changed. She drew a breath and focused her attention.

As Louis continued speaking, many small puzzles were solved. For the past week the streets had sounded as Nicole remembered. Coaches and carriages and wagons had rumbled across the cobblestones below her window; she had attempted to nap despite the noise of children and greetings and shouts. Preoccupied with Vaddie, she hadn't thought to question the increased activity.

"People are leaving?" Her mind leaped forward. The Duchards had no country relation to take them in, but Dr. Warren had reminded her of the house being built on Dimitri's Salem estates. If the roof was on, they could live there.

"They were," Louis answered before Nicole could fully explore the idea forming in her thoughts. "Over four thousand Bostonians boarded their homes and crossed the Boston neck before Gage rescinded permission."

Nicole blinked. "Then we can't leave now?"

"No. The people in Boston are effectively hostages."

Nicole stiffened against the mounded pillows. She wished she had been informed of this news earlier, although she didn't know what difference it might have made.

Louis sighed. "When General Gage tallied the large numbers departing the city, he became alarmed, and justly so, that only Tories and soldiers would remain. In such an event, Boston would invite attack. The city can easily be bombarded from the Dorchester peninsula or the hills above Charlestown. By holding the remaining Whigs in Boston, Gage believes the patriots won't burn the city."

The situation had escalated alarmingly. "We should have gone with the others."

He leaned to cover her hand. "Mother and I didn't wish to risk your health or Vaddie's."

"Is it possible to receive any passes now?"

"Do you really imagine William would authorize passes for us?" Louis asked gently.

William. Her mouth soured. "He's still here, then."

"Of course." Louis stroked his cheek. "We haven't seen much of him recently . . . staff meetings, training exercises . . . the British are busy."

Nicole fixed her gaze to the jumping wick of a near candle. She wouldn't think of facing William until it was absolutely necessary. "Is there any more news?"

"Only that Charlestown is being evacuated. The populace is moving inland. It's far too dangerous to remain. The cannon atop Copp's Hill are sighted along the ferry path directly toward Charlestown." He paused, then added in a troubled voice, "Additional British troops are expected any day."

"It really is war." She stared at him. "Englishmen fighting Englishmen. Papa . . . is this really true?" She wished to God that he would throw back his head and laugh and admit the story was but a fairy tale he had concocted for her amusement, the way he'd done when she was small.

"Both sides are committed, Nicole. Men have died. We will go on to win liberty or we will suffer an oppression never before seen on these shores."

The night of her return to New England, Nicole had predicted the patriots would triumph in the unlikely event of war. But everything had appeared simpler then. Gunpowder had not floated on the wind.

Louis inhaled deeply. "Every person must do what he can, according to his or her ability and position."

Nicole agreed absently. Ladies' groups would form; bandages would be needed. Tents, musket balls, canteens, pouches to carry powder . . .

". . . many will be asked to endure grave sacrifices . . ."

"Yes." Nicole was no stranger to war's bitter sacrifices. She thought of Katya, wondering if she was alive, and a small serf village. They had sacrificed their grain and their future.

Offered their sons and their fathers. War did not make requests; war demanded.

When Nicole's mind returned to the present, she realized Louis watched her with a grieving expression. Suddenly the silence was unbearable. "Papa . . . ?"

"Nicole, I wish to heaven I didn't have to speak of this . . ." He leaned his forehead into his palm. "Dr. Warren and most of the others . . . they believe you could render the cause an invaluable service . . . it would require a sacrifice."

"Me?" Amazement vied with curiosity and amusement. She could not imagine what she might do that others could not do better.

"We have people . . . spies, if you will . . . in many areas of the British operation. But we have no one at the upper levels."

"You mean with access to Gage?"

"Yes."

"I don't understand. How might I help?" The fragrance of lilacs mixed with the scent of leather. A faint odor of pine wafted from the candles, a result of the crushed needles Marie stirred into the tallow. The smells of childhood and comfort and safety. "I certainly don't have access to Gage." She smiled.

"But William does."

Her smile froze, and the blood slowly drained from her cheeks.

"And . . . as you admitted, William yearns for someone with whom to discuss his daily travails, the meetings he attends, the ups and downs of a staff officer's routine . . ."

She could not speak. Her arms dropped heavily across the quilt. Her blue eyes were enormous and horrified in a chalky face.

"If the British elect to mount an offensive—and we believe they will, once fresh troops arrive—William may be included in the planning sessions. He will certainly be informed of the time and the place of the attack." Louis lowered his gaze from her shock. "If the patriots were to receive prior warning, General Ward would know where to concentrate our men."

"Dear God!" Nicole whispered. She recalled agreeing to the inestimable value of advance information. She heard her own voice promising she could be counted upon, no matter what was asked. She had drawn a noose about her own neck.

Louis lifted her cold hand and rubbed it between his own.

"It's no secret that William . . . ah, cares for you." His murmur was low and pained.

"Oh, Papa, you can't know what you're asking!" She blinked at nothing. She saw William's hand abruptly descend to her stomach, then light spinning down a dark tunnel. The scene replayed in her mind every day of her life. But no matter how carefully she examined those split seconds on the stairs, she could not determine whether or not her fall had been an accident. Basic instinct argued it was not, but . . . In truth, she would never know for a certainty.

"I would have to be an idiot not to know," he muttered. "It was I who found you at the foot of the stairs."

Nicole did not understand why her eyes remained dry. Tears choked her breast, welled in a hot lump in her throat, but they did not spill from her lashes. It was a small thing, but it troubled her.

"What do they want me to do?" It was necessary to repeat the question twice before her voice gained the strength to be heard.

Louis lowered his head. He stared at the small cold hand lying white against his stained palm. "Whatever you can." He paused for a painful tick of time, released a breath. "You could encourage confidences through conversation or . . . or maybe more," he finished lamely. Louis had been asked to sacrifice his daughter; the knowledge wounded his eyes and his heart.

"More?" Fresh shock drained her stare of color. The blue shaded to ash.

"You have the right to refuse. I want you to know that."

But did she? Could anyone claim the right of refusal when the fate of a nation lay at stake? Knowing she could help—was it moral to walk away? Was it possible? Dropping backward into the pillows, Nicole withdrew her hand from his rough palm and jerked the quilt to her throat. The warm May night had suddenly turned chill.

And her thoughts whirled toward William. His pale cool eyes insisted Dimitri was dead—those eyes that had stared into her own seconds before he . . . pushed? Major William Caldwell of the scarlet coat and the swaggering step.

"Papa . . ." Her mind bounded in a dozen confused directions. "If I agree, everyone will think I'm a turncoat, a Tory. My friends . . . No one will . . ."

The discussion was as painfully difficult for Louis as it was

367

for her. He leaned backward in the rocker, and neither looked at the other.

"Most of your friends have fled the city, Nicole. But, yes, to those who remain, it will appear you've switched sides." Now he looked at her. "But those who matter will know the truth, and when this is over, you will be vindicated."

War shot poison tentacles into homes and hearts. War was not only an exchange of glorious speeches and ringing cannon but also the sundering of families and friends and lifelong principles; it was compromise and small acts of betrayal.

Louis placed her robe near her clenched hands. "Come with me, I want you to see something. Across the hall."

Nicole longed to curl into a tight ball and reject what he had suggested, but she slid obediently from the bed and followed Louis into the darkened bedroom he shared with Marie. He drew back the curtains.

Below the window the ground dropped toward the shore of the Charles River. Stairstepped rooftops offered a clear view of the Charlestown peninsula on the far side of the river. Moonlight ribboned across the millpond to Nicole's right. To her left rose the menacing bulk of Copp's Hill, its battery of cannon aimed toward Charlestown. Dots of lantern light marked the position of British ships drifting in the river currents.

But this was not what Louis had invited her to observe. He held back the curtain and nodded toward thousands of campfires flickering like fireflies over and around the hills mounding the Charlestown peninsula. The darts of orange flame were thickest along the South Road near the waterside, then thinned, to cluster again atop Breed's Hill and Bunker's Hill.

"If we lived in South Boston, near the neck, you could gaze toward Roxbury and see the same sight," Louis said quietly. "Men from all the colonies have converged here. Waiting."

Nicole gripped the windowsill, and the distant firelight reflected in her wide eyes. It was as if all the stars had fallen from heaven and now twinkled over the New England countryside. "Boston is surrounded!"

"With more men arriving every day. You can see why the British are nervous," he added dryly. "However, it's common knowledge the British will receive reinforcements. Once they arrive, we'll be outnumbered." He ran a hand through his hair, not looking at her. "What you see is deceptive. Our people light extra fires to deceive the British. When the attack comes, we'll need every able-bodied man on the line. Even a few hours' warning would be enough to deploy our men where they're most needed. Enough to save lives."

Nicole stared across the dark river. In the silence she could hear the ticking of the grandfather clock at the base of the staircase and Marie's voice murmuring faintly from the distant kitchen. Her fingers whitened across the windowsill as she blinked at the campfires on the hills—tiny flaring circles of defiance representing men and ideals and a steady determined resolve.

A few hours' warning—it could save lives.

"Oh, Papa." A sigh of resignation rose from her toes. She walked into Louis's arms and rested her head wearily on his shoulder, inhaling the safe, comforting scent of leather. "Tell Dr. Warren and the others . . . tell them I will do what I can."

He held her tightly, unable to speak, but emotion quivered along the tremor in his arms.

Later, when the house was dark and silent, Nicole slid from her quilts and knelt beside Vaddie's basket. She looked into the sleeping face of her infant son until her knees cramped. Then, rubbing her temples, she wandered past the small hooked rug and paused beside her window before turning and pacing toward her bureau. And then again.

Because she couldn't bear to think of William—not just yet—she contemplated the men camped on the hills beyond the Charles River. Who were those men from New Hampshire and Connecticut and Pennsylvania? What were they thinking tonight? What type of man sacrificed his crops and his family's future to crouch on a hillside and wait? Who were the men who expressed themselves willing to lay down their lives for an ideal?

She knew the answer. They were ordinary men, farmers and shopkeepers and blacksmiths and printers. Men who desired a better world for their children and their grandchildren. Men of courage and conviction. Men of vision. Men like Yuri and Dimitri.

In the light of what others would forfeit, Nicole's sacrifice paled to insignificance. No one had suggested she risk her life. Only her integrity . . . possibly her morality.

"Dear Lord, please . . ." She leaned her elbows on the bureau top and rested her forehead against her arms. After a moment she slowly raised her head and studied the pale face reflected in the mirror. "You are a spy." It was ludicrous; ordinary people were not spies. A thin smile curved her lips, then wavered. Ordinary people did not take up their muskets and go to war.

The cracked mirror split her bewilderment into halves, one deeply shadowed, the other tinted ivory by the moonlight. She examined her split countenance a very long time, as if one of the halves might reveal the answers she sought. And it occurred to her that she was never what she appeared to be. She was not a Duchard, not a princess, not a serf. She was not a Tory, and it was possible she was not even married. Her mind shrank from the last.

"Who are you?" she whispered, watching twin lips move in shadow and moonlight. "Which color of the rainbow is truly yours?"

She didn't expect an answer, yet it grieved her heart when none was forthcoming.

Lying sleepless, staring at the dark ceiling, she eventually forced herself to explore the implications of her promise. William.

What exactly would her promise entail? What price would be paid for William's information? A shudder rippled her nightgown, and revulsion churned in her stomach.

Then came the crushing weight of betrayal, as she had known it would. If Dimitri was alive . . .

She flung an arm over hot dry eyes, blotting the sight of a soft seductive moon and the flood of memories it released.

A breeze whispered through the rustling elm: "Tasha . . . Tasha . . ."

28

Nicole needn't have worried that William would think her attitude strange. He accepted her thawing with unquestioning relief, as one welcomes the mending of a stubborn wound. Mystified by the vagaries of pregnancy, William credited her previous temper and intractability to that enigmatic condition. Delight, not suspicion, expressed his reaction to discovering Nicole waiting on the porch when he returned each evening. He accepted as his due the private hour in the kitchen following dinner and Louis and Marie's discreet retirement.

"Did I mention how lovely you are tonight?"

They sat facing one another before the glow of the hearth. Nicole tilted an embroidery hoop toward the light of the table candle as she fashioned tiny bluebirds along the hem of a summer gown for Vaddie. Occasionally she glanced toward Vaddie's basket in the shadows near the spinning wheel, and then her lips curved into a quiet smile.

"Yes, William, you mentioned it several times. Thank you." Last week she had folded away her Yankee homespun. Tonight she wore a pale green English linen adorned by rose-colored ruffles edging puff sleeves and hem. She had removed her apron and cap after washing the supper crockery, and bright candlelight played about the loose piles of hair pinned atop her small head. As the night was warm and mild, William had discarded his jacket and opened his collar, relaxing before a tankard of rum in suspenders and shirt sleeves.

Nicole correctly guessed that William reveled in fantasies of a comfortably married couple passing a quiet evening. The image was repellent. She drew a breath and affected a light and casual tone. "Will many people attend the reception tomorrow night?"

Yesterday the long-awaited *Cerberus* had anchored in the harbor, bringing Major Generals Howe, Clinton, and Burgoyne and the first of the reinforcement troops. A bolt of excitement had cracked through Boston and held. Shoulders straightened; steps quickened. The dispirited regulars displayed new hope, polishing their equipment and promising each other they had not forgotten the humiliation of Concord. Now that the generals had arrived, ". . . the story will be different, by God!"

"Everyone who matters," William answered. "I'd prefer you to wear your blue satin . . . the gown which matches your eyes." A flush of embarrassment heated sallow cheeks. "That is, if you care to. I don't know about women's attire, I..."

Nicole studied him from the corner of her lashes. The blue satin was decidedly low-cut. "Am I expected to seduce the generals?"

He stared at her. "Good God, no! That would be far too risky at this point. A seduction can advance a man's career or wreck it!"

Teasing did not occupy a space in William's character; Nicole should have known better. She released a quiet sigh. William viewed events in black and white; there were no gray areas of frivolity. He was dull in the manner of all self-centered people who view the world in terms of themselves. Each decision in William's life was balanced against the possibility of personal gain.

"I'd prefer the generals to notice you, certainly. But seduction? No, I don't think so. Your usual charm and grace will suffice." A hint of jealousy glimmered about the set of his mouth.

"I was jesting, William."

Vaddie yawned, and tiny fists flailed above the rim of his basket. From the uncomfortable fullness swelling her breasts, Nicole judged it nearly time to withdraw.

"I see." He frowned into his tankard, then cleared his throat before proceeding to brief Nicole as to the idiosyncrasies of the newly arrived generals, outling their characters, with emphasis upon General William Howe. "Howe is the one we wish to impress favorably. I've requested a transfer to his staff."

"Oh?"

William expected little more than an occasional "Oh?" or "Really?" or "How interesting." When Nicole allowed herself to realize how little was required to please him, her head bowed beneath a burden of sorrow and guilt. Guilt appeared to be her prevailing emotion of late. She experienced guilt at deceiving William, guilt at compromising her own integrity, guilt at appearing in public with a man other than her husband. Guilt caught her breath when she accused herself of abandoning Dimitri and Vadim and Pavla in Siberia. And intensified each time she enjoyed the freedom of walking the lanes unopposed, or consumed a nourishing meal.

A wry discouraged smile twisted her full lips. If she considered the matter thoroughly, she suspected she could convince herself the British conflict was somehow her fault; in her present frame of mind, she was willing to shoulder the guilt for all the world's troubles.

"Are you listening?" William demanded.

Ugly memories deepened Nicole's gaze. "Of course."

"Howe will direct the offensive. I should be on his staff, that's where the glory will be. It's vitally important that Howe accept my transfer application!"

Nicole studied her embroidery hoop; then her fingers pushed the needle through and drew it out the other side. Louis had stressed that every scrap of information was valuable. Carefully she phrased her next comment, misdirecting the emphasis. "That might be dangerous for you, William. Or are you referring to a small-scale skirmish?"

He snorted in disgust and raked a hand through his hair. "The plans won't be firm for another week or two, but the engagement sure as hell will not be small-scale! This isn't Concord!"

Nicole lowered her head and expelled a soft breath. Her hands steadied the embroidery hoop against her knee. A thousand campfires could be observed merely by shifting her glance to the kitchen window.

When and where? Would the British march across the Boston neck and seize Roxbury? Or would they first secure the Dorchester peninsula? Or the Charlestown peninsula? Everything depended upon knowing when and where the assault would be mounted.

"First the generals must jockey their importance, each striving to impress the others." William blew out his cheeks and shook his head. "Etiquette demands that Clinton, Burgoyne, and Gage submit their personal plans, and each will insist upon his own idea, even though Howe is senior officer and entitled to the final decisions. Courtesy requires that Howe at least pretend to seriously consider the suggestions of the others." He stared moodily toward the orange flickers beyond the window. "Sometimes I wonder how many battles we've botched because our generals were off somewhere drinking each other's health and tiptoeing about attempting to devise a battle plan without wounding each other's greatly inflated egos." He drank deeply from the tankard of rum. "There's been nothing but quibbling since they stepped off the ship! Each is convinced he alone is the most brilliant, the most skilled, the best qualified to ensure victory. It's a farce. Our water boys could crush the Americans, but to hear Gage tell it . . ."

William's face fell as Vaddie's fussing increased. He scowled toward the shadows as Nicole laid aside her embroidery and hurried to bundle Vaddie from the basket onto her shoulder.

"Ssh, love, don't cry. Mama's here, ssh. Mama knows you're hungry." Nicole pressed her cheek to her son's warm little head and inhaled the sweet baby scent of fresh skin and silken curls. Thinking of tomorrow night and the generals' reception, she missed Vaddie already. Marie had located a wet nurse for Nicole's necessary absences, but Nicole resented the need. She cherished her private moments, jealously wishing to care for her son without assistance from strangers.

"Can't you stay a little longer?"

It startled her to discover William standing directly before her. "No, William . . . we've discussed this. Vaddie will fuss until he's fed. I'm sorry, but . . ." She eased backward, distressed as always by the naked yearning intensifying William's gaze. But her son came first, before spying, before anything else.

William stared into her eyes, questioning; then he placed moist palms upon her cheeks. She felt the tremor cupping his fingers.

And she swallowed hard as the color rose in her cheeks. "Please, William, don't. I'm not ready for this yet."

Pale hard eyes hungered across her lips, and his jaw tightened. The tension jumping along his thighs shot waves of heat toward her own. And a rise of panic choked her breath. If he kissed her . . . Quickly she shifted Vaddie to her breast, positioning the baby between them.

His hands burned on her face and his breath quickened. "Is one kiss too much to ask?" he inquired hoarsely. "You're so beautiful! All I think about is . . ."

"I . . . Excuse me, I must feed my baby." Deftly she ducked beneath his hands, weak with the promise of escape. "Good night, William. Sleep well."

His brooding stare followed her hasty steps.

Later, when Vaddie slept contentedly in the basket beside her bed, Nicole mounded her pillows and folded her arms behind her hair, staring into the darkness. She could not avoid William forever; one day soon he would demand more than companionship. She closed her eyes and attempted to imagine his hands running along her skin, wondering if she could endure the shame.

A slow heat spread through secret hollows; it had been so long—too long—since she had known a man's hard touch. She tossed across the empty landscape of her bed, hating the tingle which raced along her limbs. Her heart rejected shameful thoughts, but her rebellious flesh knew nothing of Tories or personalities or vows or loyalties or guilts. The flesh knew only pent forces too long denied. Memory had become her worst enemy, she saw that now; memory stroked her golden skin and heated it to a silky moisture, memory explored deep recesses and whispered of vacancies rapturously filled.

Nicole buried her face in shaking hands. She thrashed across her pillows, feeling the tug of her gown across breasts and thighs, and she thought of the split image in her mirror, the two halves, one dark and one light. "Oh, Dimitri!" Unbidden, powered by the forces of yearning memory, her hands slid over her breasts, and she stroked the aching nipples thrusting against the thin material of her nightgown. Groaning, she snatched her hands away as if she caressed raw flame, and felt the guilt descend in waves. Weeping, calling his name, she thrust her traitorous hands beneath the pillows and battled the temptations of lonely women everywhere.

Consequently, she moved through the following day tired and cross and unequal to the task of washing and dressing her hair, pressing the blue satin, locating the correct gloves and fan. She surrendered Vaddie unwillingly to Mrs. Potter, the wet nurse, and ground her teeth and thought hard of sacrifices.

Louis leaned on the porch rail as William escorted her toward his waiting carriage. "Have an enjoyable evening," he called softly.

Nicole gazed over her shoulder and read the expectancy in her father's expression. And the concern. Forces were gathering; a tang of anxiety salted every breath. The British generals and troops had arrived. The first clash could not be far behind.

But when? And upon which front?

"You're distracted tonight. Are you unwell?" William settled into the cushion beside her, taking care not to wrinkle his satin breeches. Curls stiff with pomade framed his face; a long powdered tail was tied at his neck. A dozen brass buttons gleamed down his red jacket; he had clayed his gaiters and fitted them over his boots when wet to be certain they dried tight and without a crease. He's spent an hour polishing the ceremonial sword resting on the cushions across from them.

"I'm fine, William." She commanded her voice to remain light. "You needn't concern yourself. General Howe will be charmed."

A frown drew his sandy brows as he attempted to decide if she mocked him. "It is important, you know," he responded stiffly. "I've submitted my request for transfer. I want Howe to remember us favorably—my career depends upon it."

Us. William viewed them as an us. Nicole winced and gazed from the open window. Few of the Duchards' friends remained in occupied Boston, but she recognized one or two faces leaning from porches and squinting as William's carriage bounced toward Province House. The curled lips and accusing eyes hurt.

And she considered the envious leers of the street soldiers little better. Scarlet clusters grouped at the corners and before the pubs and shops. The soldiers shouted greetings to passing carriages and exchanged ribald comments about the women within. A blind man would have noticed the shift in morale. High spirits were evident in smartly squared shoulders, in brisk crisp steps, in the gleam of spit and polish. Discipline had sharpened. Everyone whispered that the generals were here; soon the upstart Americans would receive their just comeuppance.

Their carriage stalled in traffic, and both Nicole and William peered from the windows, watching as the Fourth Regiment, the King's Own, paraded its banners in the streets vying with the Royal Welch Fusiliers, each engaging in good-humored rivalry, to the delight of crimson-coated onlookers. The soldiers joined in the play enthusiastically. Only the tall elegant grenadiers disdained the friendly competition; their awesome reputation exempted them from boyish displays.

Nicole shivered delicately. Nearly six thousand soldiers, ten regiments, jammed Boston's cobbled lanes. Waiting.

And when she raised her lashes, she saw the ring of camp-fires across the Charles. Waiting.

Grinning, William leaned back inside the carriage. His eyes sparkled, and Nicole guessed he would rather have joined the jubilation in the streets than attend a stuffy reception.

"Are you warm enough?" he asked as the carriage reined before Province House.

Nicole gazed at the blaze of light spilling from the windows of Governor Gage's residence. Carriages lined the street. Without warning, her heart dropped to her knees. "I . . . Yes," she murmured, her voice frozen despite the warm night. The magnitude of what she was attempting overwhelmed her. God in heaven, she was here as a spy. A traitor would march through those wide doors.

A terrible scenario flashed before stricken eyes. She would enter on William's arm. The all-powerful generals would level shrewd eyes, and a ringing voice would denounce her. Nicole wet her lips and fixed a wide stare on William. A tumble of questions scorched her tongue. Did the British hang women? Stone them? Who would raise Vaddie? Did it hurt to die?

"You're trembling." William frowned as he handed her from the coach. He spoke from the corner of his lips as they mounted the stairs and waited in the foyer to be announced. "There's nothing to fear—not even Margaret Gage is as beautiful as you. Howe will be enchanted."

"Major William A. Caldwell and his lady, Mistress Nicole Duchard!" William had given them her maiden name. If she survived the evening, she would rebuke him for the lapse.

Nicole drew an unsteady breath and pasted a brilliant smile on her stiff lips; then she stepped forward into the grand hall, passing beneath glittering crystal chandeliers and into a lane of people, moving toward a scarlet line of gleaming brass and braid and medals.

Any instant, rough hands would grip her elbows and drag her away.

She exchanged bows with General and Mrs. Gage, with staff members whose faces and names she instantly forgot, and then with Major Generals Howe, Clinton, and Burgoyne, each of whom retained her hand longer than necessary. She could not comprehend why none remarked the thunderous pounding ringing in her ears.

To her utter disbelief, none of the generals peered into her eyes and denounced her for what she was. Gossip had elevated them to omnipotence, but they were mortal beings after all. A flood of relief weakened her limbs and she sank abruptly to the nearest settee, touching the corner of a lace handkerchief briefly to her brow. She felt as if she'd swum a moat thrashing with sharks and emerged unscathed within the castle. Dazed, she wondered how history's spies had survived the ordeal with nerves intact. Perhaps they hadn't.

"Mistress Duchard?"

She jumped, then looked upward into the smiling eyes of "Gentleman Johnny" Burgoyne, the oldest of the major generals and by far the most personable. Handsome, worldly, a man of fashion, Burgoyne moved easily in the company of lovely women and elegant society. The other generals appeared ill-at-ease by comparison, more accustomed to the male world of sweat and toil and musketry.

"May I offer you a glass of port?" He extended a crystal goblet. "My own stock, I might add, I can vouch for the quality." Vivacious snapping eyes explored her plunging bodice without apology. And when a blush of heat colored her cheeks a charming pink, he grinned with delight. "I would have sworn the Tory women had abandoned the art of blushing. What a treasure you are, my dear, a rare find!"

She stammered a reply and rose hastily to her feet, slowly regaining her sense of equilibrium. There was nothing in Gentleman Johnny's sophisticated smile to suggest he feared a spy in their midst. He wore the expression of all men when confronted with a beautiful woman: challenge, pride, and in the back of his gaze, speculation.

As if by magic, William appeared, flaunting his possessiveness like a trophy. He touched Nicole's elbow and cleared his throat. "General Burgoyne, may I present—"

"Mistress Duchard," Gentleman Johnny finished. He ignored William, fixing his gaze firmly on Nicole. "One doesn't forget eyes as blue as cornflowers, hair as gold and thick as a ripe wheat field . . ."

William frowned uncertainly and stepped backward as Burgoyne inserted himself between Nicole and William.

A bubble of laughter formed in Nicole's throat. Burgoyne was easily twice William's age and infinitely more experienced. He effectively excluded William from their conversation. Nicole recognized his game and joined smoothly. She played the game well, having honed her skills in the Russian court.

She covered smiling lips with her fan, exposing only teasing eyes. "Come now, sir. And what would you have said if my hair was black and my eyes were brown?" She swayed forward in a rustle of satin, trailing the faint intoxicating scent of roses. She peeked back at him over one bared shoulder, confident he would follow. Without appearing to do so, she led him toward the other generals.

Burgoyne laughed, understanding his hand had been called. Intrigued, he fell into step beside her, abandoning William to stare after them, his mouth rounded. "I didn't expect a sophisticate in the provinces, my dear. I'm delighted." He cocked his shaggy head. "Let's see . . . I would have compared you to a sultry velvet midnight." He smiled. "But between you and me, the dazzle of sunshine far outshines the shadows of midnight. There is no comparison. Of course, in the interest of science, I would require a moonlight examination to confirm my theory . . . ?" An obvious invitation lingered in his pause.

And was parried. Nicole smiled and tilted her curls, knowing the feather touch of candlelight enhanced the expanse of creamy white extending from breast to throat. "Why, General, I do believe you're a flirt!" The game proscribed easy conquest. Seemingly by accident, she paused a step from General Howe and lifted a sweep of dark lashes above her fan, drawing Howe into the conversation.

"Burgoyne a flirt?" Howe's black eyes smiled down at her. He was tall, a tendency toward stoutness concealed by his rigid military bearing. He seemed unaware he spoke in a shout. "That's like saying the Charles River is wet." The heartiness of his laughter drew discreet stares.

Nicole sensed Howe edited the comment in deference to the presence of women. Had he been in the company of men, the statement would have been couched in vulgar terms. Coarse features hinted Howe would have felt more comfortable among ladies of a type not found at formal receptions. His was a basic nature, an earthiness requiring open fields and grandiose schemes. Instinctively Nicole understood his troops would love him; he was a man's man in the fullest sense of the term.

General Clinton, however, stood apart from the others, his dark brooding eyes ready to take umbrage at the slightest offense. As Nicole chatted lightly with Howe and Burgoyne, her eyes strayed toward Clinton, attempting to form a sketch of his character to report to Louis. Comparatively, he was colorless and uninteresting. Younger than Howe or Burgoyne, he managed to impart an impression of weary age. Suspicion smoldered in his gaze; disillusionment lived there. Nicole suspected Clinton was his own worst enemy; he would protect his pride at the expense of all else.

But it was Howe who would make the final decisions. She touched his arm with her fan and smiled into his eyes, laughing at his comments when the others did.

Forming her lips into a pretty pout, she seized on a pause in the conversation and addressed both generals. "I do hope Mrs. Gage was able to locate meat for our dinner. Fresh supplies are nearly impossible to obtain." She wondered if she sounded as simple to them as she did to herself—a woman engaged with petty concerns while history swirled about her ignorance. Then she relaxed as she realized Howe and Burgoyne would have recoiled in horror from an intelligent woman. Women were for decoration, for idle amusement.

Burgoyne puffed his chest and smiled. "Now, don't you trouble your pretty little head about these hardships, Mistress Duchard. I can assure you the shortages are only temporary. It appears Boston is hemmed in, but now that we've arrived, we mean to make a little elbow room. Fresh supplies will soon be sailing into Boston harbor."

"How wonderful," Nicole murmured demurely, lowering her lashes. The question was: how soon?

"Gage has managed to seal himself up like a bug in a bottle, no room to move."

Howe laughed and nodded above the bright gowns and scarlet coats clustering about them. "Hear that, Tommy?" he roared above swiveling heads. "Johnny here claims he's going to give you a little elbow room. What do you say to that?" Excusing himself, Howe strode toward a glowering Gage, trailing amused listeners like a magnet pulling filings.

Nicole fluttered her fan. "May I assume we'll have fresh meat by next week?"

Responding from habit rather than suspicion, Burgoyne skirted the trap. "Would you rather decorate your platter or your lovely throat? Perhaps a diamond pendant . . ." He smiled as he extended his arm and escorted her in to dinner. "I could arrange either. I could also arrange a great deal more, once this little battle is behind us."

Nicole laughed, concealing her disappointment. She hadn't expected they would present her the attack plans on a silver tray, but she supposed she had hoped it would be easier than it was proving. She wished a hasty conclusion to her spying career—the sooner the better. She released an inner sigh; patience was the key. Accepting that little more could be gained tonight, she abandoned her role and gave herself up to a surprisingly enjoyable evening. The Tory ladies were charming and gay, Burgoyne was extravagantly attentive, the food plentiful, and the dancing a delight.

Not until a servant presented her shawl and she had thanked Mrs. Gage did she realize she had neglected William.

William handed her into the carriage and seated himself across from her in stony silence. The driver cracked his whip and the carriage lurched forward into a darkened lane.

Expelling an exasperated sigh, Nicole spoke first. "What is it, William?"

He stared at her. "I told you! I told you it was vital to impress Howe!" The words emerged amid a shower of spittle. "And what did you do? You spent the entire evening flirting with Burgoyne! Burgoyne will direct the battery on Copp's Hill, he's of no value to me. But Howe, dammit! Howe will lead the field troops—that's where careers will be made! If a man excels in the field, his future is assured!" His gloves dented the rim of the hat he held on his knees. "You greatly disappoint me!"

Nicole's eyes flashed. "What was I to do? Follow the general about like a tail-wagging puppy? I did what I could."

"Oh?" His stare intensified as he struggled to control his anger. "All night you were the center of attention, and many times Howe joined the group around you. But did you call out to me? Did you direct Howe's attention to me? You did not!"

"William . . ." She drew a breath and bit off the retort stinging her tongue. Suddenly Nicole felt tired. Her feet were sore from dancing, her breasts ached from missing Vaddie's nightly feeding. "William, you could have approached General Howe yourself."

He stiffened. "That would be poor form, a bit obvious, don't you think?"

"And wouldn't it have been obvious if I'd dragged you forward each time the general favored me with a remark?"

Pale eyes chilled and his lips thinned. "May I remind you of Proverbs Thirty-one, verse twelve: 'She will do him good and not evil all the days of her life.' Or verse Eleven: 'The heart of her husband doth safely trust in her . . .' "

Nicole passed a weary hand across her eyes. Only a saintly drudge could hope to fulfill the duties and obligations of a wife as outlined in Proverbs—a book much quoted by reproving husbands.

"I am not your wife, I did you no evil, and I am too fatigued to discuss this further." William's audacity and expectations sapped her energy.

William chewed his thumbnail in silence. His stare was illuminated in intermittent flashes by torches carried by the sentries patrolling the street corners.

"I wish to marry you."

Nicole's breath stopped. From the moment her attitude had warmed, his proposal had become but a matter of time, as inevitable as winter. His transparency of motives shadowed a ghost of bitterness about her lips. As his wife, she would be controllable, unlikely to flout his demands, as he insisted she had done tonight.

Instinct urged a prompt refusal. But unfortunately the issue was not simple. The generals were in Boston. The offensive would occur soon; very soon. Her troubled eyes strayed toward the distant campfires glimpsed between the dark houses. If she refused William outright, would he leave the Duchard home and seek quarters elsewhere? In that event, the patriots would forfeit their only link to the high command. The burden of responsibility slumped her shoulders. She stared hard at the orange dots reflecting across the ribbon of dark water.

She stalled the question. "Could you accept Vaddie?" Fresh guilt soured her mouth. Using her son in this delicate deceit dismayed her.

"Accept that bastard's son? Never!" The hat brim crushed in his fingers.

"Then a marriage is not possible." Was her relief as obvious as she feared? The game proceeded in advances and checks.

"I love you. And I believe you love me . . ." William paused for her confirmation, then exploded when none was forthcoming. "That damn baby spoils everything! Your loyalty to him exceeds your loyalty to me!"

Nicole thrust shaking fists within the concealing folds of blue satin and struggled to control a flash of temper. "And would you wish any mother to feel otherwise?"

"No! No, of course not!" William composed himself and drew a breath. "Nicole . . . for some time I've been considering a plan I'd like to discuss. I believe we should send your parents and the baby to the country."

"No." She stared, unprepared for this advance.

"It's awkward having your parents in the house . . ."

"The house belongs to them; you and I are guests. How dare you suggest they be evicted from their own home!"

"Everyone is aware that Louis is an avowed Whig. Surely you'll admit the awkward position this places me in. Not only does his presence impede my career, but it's necessary to censor every word, even to you. I find this inconvenient at the very least."

His reasoning brought her up short. Immediately she recognized the truth in what he claimed. Nicole swallowed hard. She hadn't anticipated the complexities of the situation when she had agreed to aid the patriot cause. "I refuse to send Vaddie away," she said quietly.

"Before making a hasty decision, please listen to what I have to say." He leaned forward and stroked her limp hand. "With the Duchards out of Boston, we'd have the house to ourselves."

Her heart lurched. "A scandal."

"We'll hire a girl for the sake of appearances until we resolve the questions concerning marriage."

Nicole's pulse thudded in her throat; a ball of lye formed in her stomach. "What do you hope to accomplish by this?"

"The trust of my coworkers. Freedom to speak openly. And I'd like you to realize how simple life could be without . . . distractions. How comfortable we can be together."

Nicole's jaw tightened and she turned her face to the window. "I could never marry anyone who refused my son." The entire discussion drifted toward nonsense; she was already married. Wasn't she? "And, William . . . I will never relinquish Vaddie."

"I'm not asking you to."

But of course he was. William resented any reminder that another man had touched her. He attempted to spin back the clock to a time which never was.

He cleared his throat. "Actually, I'm primarily thinking of the baby's safety. This would be only a temporary measure."

The lie was so blatant that Nicole's stare narrowed and her lips pinched. She wrenched her hand from his gloves and withdrew into the folds of her shawl, mentally urging the driver to hurry.

William raised a palm. "Consider . . . Boston is surrounded. With Howe's arrival, a full-scale battle is imminent, far more serious than the recent sniping." He paused, then played his trump card with a smile. "Would you willingly endanger your baby's life by insisting he remain here, in the pathway of shells, when you have an opportunity to remove him to safety?"

Dear God. Tears jumped into her eyes. He'd made the one advance she could not check. "You believe the patriots will shell Boston?" she whispered in a faltering voice.

"Possibly. Both Bunker's Hill and Breed's Hill have the range."

She knew he didn't believe for an instant the patriots possessed either the courage or the capability of shelling Boston. But Nicole did. Her mind whirled. The Duchard house sat nearly at the base of Copp's Hill, a natural target. A slight miscalculation and . . . She covered her eyes. And she hated him. Because he twisted his selfish motives into something which sounded fine and noble.

"I suppose you wouldn't consider my leaving with my son." The statement was wasted; even if he agreed, she could not leave. Not while the campfires winked like eyes, watching her, depending upon her.

"That is not possible," he answered gently. "I need you here."

She nodded, reaching a trembling hand to her temple. "I can't marry you, William, I can't give up Vaddie."

"And I can't accept him."

"Then why continue?" she cried. But she knew the answer. They would pretend. An atmosphere of unreality seeped into pores and infected everyone with a pretense of normalcy. Boston's citizens had mastered the art of pretense. The populace attended their daily business as if tomorrow was guaranteed. Tonight at Province House the melodies had been gay and unconcerned; the ladies and gentlemen had laughed and danced as if the surrounding campfires could not be glimpsed from every window. As if a city of tents had not sprung up on the green, as if soldiers did not jam the streets rattling their sabers and breasting their muskets. Because to accept the reality of looming war was a horror too grim to endure; pretending became a way of life, a defense. And resulting absurdities passed unnoticed.

Such as this. Such as sending away her parents and her baby and then pretending they did not exist.

William assisted her over the cobbles and opened the

Duchard gate. At the door he paused and studied her sorrowing face in the moonlight. "Do you agree, then? Your parents and the baby will leave Boston?"

Insects strummed beneath the porch boards, and a light breeze whispered through the dark shrubbery bounding the steps. Nicole swayed, listening to the distant sound of male revelry and the nearby barking of a neighbor's dog. And the cracking of one small heart.

"I agree," she whispered. They would pretend; they would suspend reality like so many others. And never think of the day when reality might return.

William's thin features lit up. "I'll secure passes immediately. My dearest Nicole, you have made me the happiest of men!"

Too defeated to resist, she offered no protest when his hard dry mouth descended and crushed her teeth against her lips. She stared dully at his closed lashes and she felt nothing. His arms tightened, flattening her swollen breasts against his jacket, and she felt absolutely nothing. A dark cinder occupied the space where her heart had been.

Shaken, he released her and blotted his brow self-consciously. "Soon, my darling, we . . ."

But Nicole rushed past him and bolted up the staircase, rejecting the promise in his husky murmur. Trembling hands tore away her ball gown and she yanked her nightdress over her hair, not bothering to brush out her curls or scrub her face.

Tenderly she lifted Vaddie from his basket and took him into her bed, comforting his drowsy cry by opening her collar and cradling him to her breast. "Ssh," she crooned softly. "Ssh, Mama is here."

Then the tears came.

29

THE HOUSE WAS bitterly silent.

As Nicole cleaned upstairs, she could hear the steady ticking of the grandfather clock below. When the stew pot hanging from the kitchen lug pole bubbled over, she heard the resultant hiss as she swept the front porch. Throughout the long quiet afternoons she fancied she could hear the blood pumping through her veins.

She had watched them go, standing on the ferry dock with tears misting her vision, and she had frantically promised herself that time would ease the pain of loss. But two weeks after their departure, she thought of Vaddie and her parents and felt the agony of amputation.

Perhaps it had been unwise to dismiss the servant girl she had hired so hastily. The girl had been a slattern, but she had provided company. And she had served as a buffer between opposing fields of building tension; she had been a third person in the house. And she was proving more difficult to replace than Nicole would have guessed.

Two weeks. She paused above the washboard in the yard and wiped a soapy hand across her apron. It seemed more like a lifetime. Was Marie also tackling the laundry today? Of course, it was Monday. If a laundry pole hadn't been built behind the Salem house, Louis would have erected one by now. As clearly as if she stood in the Salem yard, Nicole visualized Marie snapping laundry onto the line, then bending to stroke Vaddie's dark curls before flapping out another piece of wash.

A choking sigh broke from Nicole's throat, and she dropped onto a stool beneath the old apple tree and leaned her head into the shade, frowning at her hands. The day smelled of summer and sunshine, but she didn't notice. A deep gloom darkened her eyes.

Nothing engaged her interest. The kitchen garden badly needed weeding, ashes accumulated in the hearth, she hadn't touched the spinning wheel in a week. Boston's women performed the fair-weather rituals, beating winter soil from rugs, whitewashing parlors, setting out plants. None of it seemed important, nothing mattered.

She touched her breast, leaving a foam of suds on her apron front. Her breasts no longer ached or leaked their fullness onto her clothing. Her usefulness had dried; another woman nursed her baby. The knowledge lodged poison arrows below her heart.

And to what purpose? She was no nearer learning the site of the British attack than on the night of the generals' reception. Nicole ground her teeth in frustration. The entire town fidgeted and waited.

Including William. Oh, yes, William waited. She closed her eyes against the sun and thought of the mild sultry nights. William wouldn't wait forever—wasn't that why he was so pleased by the hired girl's departure? Nicole rubbed her temples.

Sleep was impossible. The blue shadows beneath her lashes attested to a persistent insomnia. She suffered through the long nights, listening to William's endless pacing below, tensing toward the expected pressure of footsteps on the stairs. Footsteps which hadn't yet occurred. But they would.

And when they did . . . ?

Slowly she pushed to her feet and emptied the tub of wash water into a rivulet which ran toward the kitchen garden. She packed the emptied tub with laundered shirts and dragged it toward the line. Then she stopped and straightened, staring at a row of bed sheets drying in the sun. A flock of sparrows had passed overhead and fouled her laundry.

"Damn!" Tears sprang into her eyes. The bird droppings meant she would have to fetch fresh water, heat it, carry it into the yard, and launder the bulky bed sheets again. Shaking hands lifted to her hot cheeks.

She stared at the thick white commas deposited upon the bed sheets, and something exploded in her mind.

Screaming, she threw herself at the linens. Fists flying, feet kicking, she attacked the soiled folds with fury. They flapped and snapped, and the wet corners wrapped about her body. Thrashing, fighting, her teeth bared and hissing, she battled them in blind frenzy.

When the spasm ended, she stood in trembling silence and surveyed the wreckage she had wrought. One line had fallen;

muddy linen crumpled at her feet. Two of the sheets were torn.

She sank abruptly to the ground and sobbed into her hands.

The footsteps would come . . .

When finally her heaving shoulders stilled, she peered through her fingers, and with the linen fallen, she could see across sparkling waves to the Charlestown peninsula. Beyond the abandoned town, small dark shapes moved over the hills and marched along the waterside. A ring of men stretched from Charlestown on the north to Roxbury on the south. The force steadily grew.

She sat in the dirt and watched the moving dots for a long time. Then she struggled upward, blew her nose, and kicked the laundry into a pile before she began again.

After a dinner of salt pork and beans, Nicole cleared the table and pushed a flatiron toward the embers to heat. June's long daylight hours extended a woman's working day.

"It's hot tonight." William sprawled beside the table in his shirtsleeves, a tankard of rum beside his hand.

"It's summer." Spring was but a memory. Spring, the symbol of hope and promise, had quietly departed. Shoving irritably at an errant lock of gold, Nicole shook out a uniform shirt and draped it across the board. She removed the iron from the hearth and set another in its place.

William watched her smooth a sleeve, then lean her weight on the iron. He smiled softly. "Do you know how lovely you are?" Heat flushed her cheeks and spread a sheen of delicate moisture across her brow and above her lips and upon the satiny skin flowing into her bodice.

She felt sticky and hot and on edge. "I doubt I am." After folding the pressed shirt, she bent and then smoothed an apron across the board. Beyond the kitchen window the sun slid below the horizon in brilliant ripples of golden pink and orange.

"Burgoyne certainly thinks so. I never encounter him but what he inquires about you." He tasted the rum, rolled it on his tongue, watched her exchange the flatirons. "I think you'll hear from him when things calm down a bit."

She deflected his jealous tone with a wave. "Do you see Burgoyne often?" The spy questions emerged without thought or expectation, a matter of habit. As the feathery shadows of twilight suggested an uncomfortable intimacy, Nicole paused to light a candle and placed it prominently upon the table.

William nodded. "Of course. Since I've been assigned to Howe, I see all the generals daily."

She bent above the iron. "And . . . ?" As always she maintained a light conversational tone. And promised herself one day the answer would be meaningful. Then perhaps the ache occupying Vaddie's space would be worth the sacrifice. Perhaps.

"And . . . more meetings. Eternal bloody circling meetings!" An impatient hand tugged at the sandy hank falling forward on his forehead. He crossed his legs and stared at white stockings running into his shoes. "The same discussion again and again. Gage should take the offensive. Gage should occupy and fortify Dorchester and Charlestown. Gage should do this, Gage should do that. All very polite, all very correct." A snort of disgust erupted against the rim of the tankard. "Nominally Gage remains in charge, but everyone knows Howe supersedes him. But we are Englishmen, by God, and correct form will be observed. And never mind that more bloody campfires spring up each night. If Gage possessed a grain of common sense, he would abandon this charade and cede immediately to Howe!"

Nicole had heard it before. Prior to Louis's departure, he had led her into the attic and shown her a string suspending from a slit in the roof. The string was tied to the weather vane. When the British assault plans were firm, she was instructed to tilt the weather vane, and someone would contact her immediately. She despaired of ever doing so.

"Patience is the key," she muttered. And wondered which of them she advised.

"Patience . . ." he echoed, his pale eyes lingering on the swing of her breasts above the board. His gaze turned inward and his breath quickened.

"The generals can't delay forever." She hoped. As the light was now too poor to continue ironing, Nicole placed the flat-irons outside the buttery door to cool and pushed the laundry basket into the shadows near the spinning wheel. After pouring herself a cup of Marie's cider, she sank to the table across from him and eased the muscles along her spine. She didn't recall household tasks proving so physically debilitating; she suspected they wouldn't be if approached on a full night's sleep.

"The generals . . . yes. Howe has promised to firm the plans no later than the middle of next week."

The cider mug hitched along its pathway to her lips, and Nicole stared, feeling a tremble begin deep inside. A leap of joy sprang into her gaze before she hastily lowered her lashes. By the middle of next week this unbearable tension would end. Thank God! She felt nearly euphoric, realizing the conclusion of her ordeal lay within sight. If she was lucky, the footsteps on the stairs would never come. If she was lucky.

William reached and stroked her hand lightly, as if the action was the most natural in the world. The simple motion froze Nicole; she stared at their hands without blinking.

"I'll be with Howe when we take the field—does that worry you?"

She wet her lips and withdrew her hand, dropping it into her aproned lap. Once, a spider had spun an enormous web across the corner of Louis's tanning shed, ensnaring a fly in the silken trap. Nicole recalled watching the fly struggle fruitlessly to escape the spider's drowsy vigilance. If the moment had been granted again, she would have smashed the web and freed the fly. "I . . . Yes, of course."

"It shouldn't. Howe and his staff will be well-protected. We'll guide the battle, but we won't be involved directly. I don't want you to be anxious."

Did he genuinely suppose he would remain uninvolved? Candlelight brushed the wrinkles from his face, transforming his countenance into a smooth, unruffled surface. This illusion, coupled with his excitement, led Nicole to the sudden realization that William had yet to experience war. The superiority of his stride was the swagger of ignorance; to William, war was glory and noble deeds. But Nicole had observed firsthand the horror of severed limbs and piled corpses—no one left a battlefield the same person as he who had entered. There was no glory, no nobility in war. Her lashes squeezed against her cheekbones.

"I hope you're right, William. I wish none of this was necessary." She would worry and grieve for them all, the British and the Americans. For the young soldiers who would not return to their regiments, for the young farmers who would not harvest the fruit of their labors.

"I love you, Nicole."

The simplicity of truth rang like a clear true bell. His obsession rejected her soiled apron and the unkempt tendrils straggling from her cap. Chapped hands and bruised eyes were amended in the flame of idealism. He saw what he wished to see. Depression erased Nicole's brief elation, and the guilt returned, heavy and oppressive.

"Please, William . . ."

"You must admit that I haven't rushed you. I've been patient, haven't I? But, Christ Almighty! How long must we endure this? I think of you all sweet and drowsy in your bed, and I long to run up those bloody stairs and—"

"William! I beg you . . ." Her hands twisted her apron; acid tension scoured the back of her throat. "I commend your patience and I beg you to continue . . ."

"I've allowed a reasonable adjustment period—now it's time we discussed marriage again." He drained the rum and placed the tankard near the candle. The pewter rim gleamed like a silver ring.

"I'm already married." She regretted her reply the instant it left her lips. She could not afford carelessness; could not risk driving him away when they were so close to the time and place of attack. It was imperative to maintain their fragile balance until the middle of next week. As the sunset faded to blues and lavenders, flickers of orange appeared on the hills across the river. Watching them through the window. Nicole felt utterly alone and trapped and tired. So tired. Responsibility rode her shoulders like a granite yoke.

"Are you really?"

Her head snapped upward, seeking his usual sneer of sarcasm. But William's gaze examined her quietly and soberly.

"If Denisov was alive, don't you think he would have sent word before now? It's been months, Nicole."

She slumped in her chair. It shocked her to hear him voice her innermost thoughts, as if a stranger had crept into her head and rummaged through her secrets. The earlier nibble of depression now bit hard, and for the first time in recent weeks a flood of overwhelming doubt assailed her spirit. Dimitri was dead. She had known the truth longer than she cared to admit. Finality seeped toxic droplets into her soul.

"You don't know Russia . . ." She faltered. "Letters are lost or . . . or seized. Maybe Dimitri posted a letter and it . . . Or maybe he's planning to surprise me. Maybe even . . ." Her dulled eyes stared toward the dying sun. She was so tired. Tired of listening for footsteps, tired of the emotional tug-of-war, tired of struggling to slam the door on truth.

William reached across the table and cradled her hand.

"He's dead, Nicole," he stated quietly. "It's time to bury the past and look to the future. Our future."

It was confusing. For an instant Nicole imagined genuine sympathy in William's tone. She could believe he attempted to comfort her despair. Until his next words.

"You belong to me, you always have. Denisov was nothing but a stupid lapse, a mistake. One which I am willing to forgive."

She withdrew her hand. There was no blame to forgive. Her marriage hadn't been a "lapse," a foolish indiscretion—it had been forever.

"Not many men would decide to be as generous . . . but you needn't thank me. With the baby out of our lives and Denisov finally buried, we can forget the unpleasant past. We can begin afresh. And no one need know . . .."

He continued speaking, but Nicole tuned out the words. He'd lied about Vaddie, exactly as she had suspected. If the war ended this minute, he would not allow Vaddie to return. William would justify whatever satisfied his selfish ambitions.

Swimming eyes flicked toward the glowing campfires, and her nails pressed crescents into her palms. Ten days—only ten more days. She could endure anything for ten days. "I'm exhausted, William. Please excuse me." If she remained another instant, she would explode, and her value to the patriot cause would be forfeit.

Annoyance darkened his expression. "But I wasn't finished . . ."

"You did say Howe would finalize the plans next week, didn't you?" If she had misunderstood, she didn't think she could bear it.

He nodded, one brow arching toward his hairline. "What does that have to do with . . . ?"

"Good night, William."

Upstairs she jerked off her apron and tossed it toward the corner basket along with her cap and her laundry-soiled gown. She didn't bother to light a candle, but slid into a summer nightgown and then into bed. As usual, sleep eluded her. She blinked into the darkness and listened for Vaddie's soft breathing, forgetting for an exhausted instant that he no longer slept beside her bed.

Gradually a shroud of depression returned to enfold her, chill despite the warm night. She had lost everything. Vaddie was denied to her; Dimitri was dead. She whispered the words aloud. "He's dead." Nothing in her heart stirred to protest. She waited for the strong leap of inner hope. And when nothing emerged, she hid her eyes in the crook of her arm and prepared for tears. But the tears refused to flow; her grief was a dry choking thing, indefinable.

The grandfather clock bonged midnight, and Nicole struck the pillows and tossed in twisted sheets. The deep resonant voice of the clock sounded a death knell, striking down hope and ringing in defeat. In the ensuing silence, Nicole ground her teeth and listened to the familiar pattern of William's pacing. Footsteps approached the staircase, hesitated, then returned to the parlor; approached the staircase, hesitated, then returned to the parlor; approached the staircase, hesitated . . ."

Nicole's heart stopped. She shoved up on her elbows, staring intently into the darkness, straining to hear. Silence. She held her breath, drawing comfort from the safety of childhood talismans. The hooked rug beside her bed, the cracked mirror splintering the moonlight, the light summer blanket clenched in her fists. Somehow these familiar everyday items would save her.

A new sound disturbed the deep seductive silence. The pressure of a boot on the stair.

Her heartbeat accelerated, ringing in her inner ear. She clamped down on her lip in frantic annoyance, striving to overhear the next step above the arid thundering inside her head.

The elm protected her window . . . the sampler had always hung above her battered trunk.

A creak groaned from the staircase.

Her favorite books crammed the glass case; she remembered the birthday Marie had presented her with the chipped basin and pitcher standing below the mirror.

Another creak.

Dear Lord. Nicole jerked to a sitting position and rubbed her hands across the gooseflesh rising along her arms. She stared hard at the door, seeing it in sepia tones of moonlight, wishing to heaven that Louis had installed a lock. And wishing her nightgown did not plunge low on her breasts. Wishing a third person was in the house, wishing her hair was pinned under a cap instead of shimmering below her waist.

Wishing. Wishing she didn't crave comfort in her sorrow, wishing her body had no memory of a man's embrace, wishing the strange weakness spreading from her center would vanish, vanish, vanish.

Steps traveled the length of the corridor, steps dragging

with hesitation, speeding with eagerness. Uncertain steps. Confident steps. They halted outside her door.

She stared at the latch until her eyes watered and burned, watching it slowly depress, then click open. And she clutched the bed sheet to her pulsing throat, hiding the rapid rise and fall of her breast as the door inched open and William filled the frame.

Neither spoke.

But she heard the rasp of his harsh breathing as he leaned against the door jamb, one hand covering his eyes as if they were the last hope of resistance. Then his hand dropped and he stared helplessly, a blur of white shirt and breeches.

Their eyes locked across the patches of pale moonlight, and their miniature war mirrored the larger one. Dominance against determination. Force against resistance.

Then his eyes flicked toward her smooth bare shoulders and a groan wrenched from his chest, intruding upon the soft winds of quickening breath. His fingers rose to pull the studs from his shirt front.

"No," Nicole choked. She shrank into the pillows, feeling lead weights where her limbs had been. Her flesh chilled and paralyzed. They were alone in the house; no one would hear if she screamed. Wide-eyed, she watched as he flung aside his shirt and bent to his boots. "Oh, no," She whispered, her voice catching between a sob and a plea.

Bare feet padded across the bars of shadow until he halted beside her bed. His pale eyes hungered over her hair spilling across the twin hills mounded beneath her bed sheet. His naked chest expanded and fell, his eyes burned upon her lips.

"Please, William, don't do this, I beg you!" It was hopeless. She had no place to run; fighting a man of his size and strength was futile. A spectral voice roared through Nicole's brain: "Dimitri is dead . . . he is dead . . ." Again and then again. Wildly she told herself that if she believed Dimitri was dead, then she could endure what she could not hope to prevent.

She clutched the sheets to her breasts, covering the swells of ivory satin, her teeth chattering in a tattoo of fear and loathing.

William moaned and swayed, his fingers fumbling thickly at the drawstring of his breeches. They whispered to the floor and his manhood leaped free, rock-hard and quivering with urgency.

Nicole strangled and jerked her head from the sight. Desperately she commanded her leaden body to wrench from his trembling fingers as he unhooked the soft material covering her nakedness. But the futility of it sapped her strength. Silently she cursed the physical power of men, the helplessness of women alone, and she felt the burden of centuries crush down across her spirit.

He opened her gown and stared, brushing away her protesting fingers, slapping down hands that sought to cover. And the thoughtless action drove home Nicole's powerlessness to resist, underscored the dominance of man. Despair flooded her mind.

"My God!" His voice was a hoarse croak. "My God!" His weight stumbled onto the bed, and he stretched a tremorous hand to her full breasts, stroking the hot dry silkiness beneath his palm, not seeing her mouth twist in revulsion. He caught her nipple between his thumb and forefinger and rolled it gently into hardness. And his breath exploded in rapid shallow bursts, a mixture between a groan and a gasp.

Shaking with humiliation and impotence, Nicole flung her head to one side and covered her eyes with the backs of her hands, pressing against the rage of tears searing her cheeks. She would have killed him if possible; she hated him with a violence of white-hot fire. And she loathed the campfires across the river as his hand slid over her soft belly and slipped toward the golden thatch between her thighs. This, then, was to be her sacrifice, an act of violation, taken and not given. Never given. Never, never!

Slowly, resisting the urge to haste, William explored a dry wall of denial. His fingers moved, seeking to coax an elusive sweet readiness. Small inarticulate sounds moaned from the depths of his throat.

Nicole battled in teeth-grinding silence, her fight one of the mind and will. He could force himself upon her, his fingers could stroke and probe, but he would find no satisfaction; hell would turn to ice before she responded to him. She willed forth a stoniness as hard and unyielding as the throbbing force pulsing along her inner thigh.

Bruising fingers gripped her cheeks and snapped her face to meet his as he understood. His gaze scrutinized her unmercifully, and a thick moist cry raked from his throat. "Whore!" Then his lips savaged her, no longer waiting for a response, and she cried out at the force of his brutal kisses. No longer was his touch reverent. His hands mauled, pushed, and slapped at her, arranged her flesh with appalling disregard, adjusted her body to receive vengeance.

For a quivering instant he stared intently into her hatred; then a rod of steely fire cleaved her body and she screamed. Her screams incited him to frenzy, and he clapped a rough hand over her lips and his body pumped relentlessly, thrusting, punishing, exacting a brutal revenge. The animal plunging expressed a core of humiliation, a bitter frustration of unforgiving loneliness, a bottomless well of resentment. He punished Woman with a man's weapons and received a primitive exultation from her cries. Gripping her buttocks, he rocked into her, using her without mercy.

She was both the cause of his frustration and the solution; the vessel designed to accept man's explosion of fury.

Nicole endured. Recognizing his physical superiority, she abandoned struggle; she endured. And in a numb corner of her shock she comprehended purgatory. Understood wounds leaving no mark upon the flesh, wounds which could never heal but which would fester throughout a lifetime.

When he finished with her, he buried his face in the pillows and she wrenched her body away from his struggle for breath, a bitter smile of triumph upon her lips. He had violated her flesh, but not her spirit. She had emerged the victor because he had touched nothing of her inner self. She had won.

But he was not finished with her.

He took her again, his frustration mounting at the limp form beneath his savage thrusts. And she fought back the curtain of exhaustion and stared at him through expressionless eyes, giving nothing.

At last fatigue wearied his body and dulled his stare, and he rolled from her with a curse. "I'll make you love me," he whispered hoarsely. "If it takes a lifetime . . . one day you'll open your arms and beg for my embrace!" His eyes blazed down into hers; then he fell away from her and dropped instantly into a heavy, sated sleep.

Nicole stared at his face on her pillow, her eyes like damp wounds. In sleep as in waking, his face was ordinary, the expression one of self-absorption. She shrank disgustedly from the heat radiating from his drying skin. Slowly, careful not to awaken him, she slipped from the bed and eased into her robe, testing the aches and bruises along her body.

Silently she descended the staircase and passed the open doors of the parlor without glancing into the dark interior. In the kitchen she grimly filled a tub with water, then stood in it and scoured her flesh to a raw flaming pink. And all the while she sensed the hopelessness of her actions; William had left an imprint no soap and no brush would dig deeply enough to expunge.

Seating herself at the table, she deliberately thought of nothing as she heated water for a cup of harsh herb tea. When the kettle steamed, she stirred her tea and stepped through the buttery door, sinking to the stoop and cradling the hot cup between her palms as she watched the darkness pale to a pearly gray and finally to pink and then to a warm clear blue. Small figures moved about the deserted town of Charlestown; the hills appeared empty and untouched in the sunlight. She wondered how many of the nightly campfires were shills.

And a shudder of self-loathing shook through her body. The world had segregated into layers of deception; nothing was as it seemed or should be. If all was right in the world, she would not be here, last night would not have happened. A heavy mantle of depression settled about her shoulders and she dropped her head, a tangled curtain of gold swinging forward to hide her despair. She couldn't bear looking at the Yankee hillside and knowing she could not run away. She would stay here with William until her job was complete, and she would ache with the wound of betrayal every day of her life.

She felt the betrayal even though Dimitri was dead. He had returned to the earth exactly as spring's promise had returned to the earth. Gone. A brief blossom had vanished as if it never existed.

Yet she cringed beneath the weight of betrayal all the same, experiencing it as a savage wolf ripping at her heart. She couldn't bundle her love into a tidy package and tuck it into the grave—love endured, reaching beyond the mind's acceptance of death. Dimitri was dead, but her love was not. Her love for him was a living vital force. And campfires and generals and the foolish games of men had driven her to betray that love.

"Good morning."

Nicole drew a sharp shallow breath and searched for the strength to face him. She combed her fingers through her hair and twisted it into a coil falling over one shoulder. Then she edged to one side as William settled on the stoop beside her.

He was dressed in a fresh uniform shirt and breeches, his hair neatly tied at the neck. He smelled of soap and pomatum.

Glancing at him from the corner of her eyes, Nicole tightened her jaw. The lines had vanished from his brow, and the deep etchings had smoothed from nose to mouth.

Smiling, he waved his tea toward the open sky. "A glorious morning!" Boyish enthusiasm glowed in his tone. "A day for anything! A day for conquering!"

Nicole frowned and bit her lower lip, searching frantically for something, anything, to say. "Are you hungry?" Mentally she ran an inventory of the items on the buttery shelves. Flour for biscuits, salt pork, one or two eggs for which she had paid a fortune.

"Famished!" He touched her hair as she rose from the stoop, and he followed her inside, where he maintained a running flow of conversation as she silently prepared his food.

He became aware of her silence as he tied his sash and closed the row of brass buttons running up his jacket. "You're tired." His pride was unmistakable. "Rest today. There's nothing pressing, is there?"

She hadn't completed the ironing, a basket of mending waited beside the spinning wheel, the garden rows cried out for thinning, if she didn't attend to the churn soon they would run out of butter, which reminded her that she needed to go to the market before the flour crock was empty . . .

"No," she answered dully, "there's nothing pressing."

"Good." His hands closed upon her shoulders. "I want you well-rested this evening." He kissed her forehead, strapped on his sword, and adjusted his hat before the hallway mirror. Then he was gone, trailing a whistle as he descended the steps and entered his carriage.

A thick stifling blanket of silence settled over the house. Nicole sat at the table, staring at the remains of his breakfast. This house had become William's home and had ceased to be hers. Home was not a dwelling where one dreaded to enter a room, and she dreaded to enter her own bedroom. Or was it now their room?

She leaned her forehead into her palm and closed her eyes. The barriers had fallen; how could she henceforth refuse him? On what basis? She had gazed into his eyes and read his assumptions. In William's mind, they were wed.

Weeping might have eased the desperation constricting her chest, but her eyes stubbornly remained hot and dry. After a time she pulled to her feet and cleaned the kitchen; then she blanked her thoughts and mounted the stairs. Without daring to glance into the cracked mirror, she made up the bed and then dressed hastily, choosing an unadorned gown the color of tears.

She had nearly completed the ironing when a knock startled the silence. Hesitating, Nicole wearily debated whether or not to respond. Resting her head against the hearth stones, she listened to the persistent raps. Then, sighing, she placed the iron against the grate and slowly approached the front door, the click of her heels loud against the oak flooring. She wiped her hands on her apron, drew a reluctant breath, and opened the door.

For an instant her mind did not register what her eyes beheld. A blue kerchief, a single long braid, dancing dark eyes, a canvas bundle slung over one shoulder of a sturdy shapeless body thinner than Nicole remembered. And a stump at the end of an empty cuff.

"Pavla!"

She dashed forward, and her gasp smothered against Pavla's broad shoulder. Now the tears gushed to her eyes. Laughing and weeping, she dashed at her lashes and patted Pavla's face, touched her braid, pressed Pavla's hand fiercely to her cheek.

Pavla kissed her soundly and wiped tears from her own eyes. Then she lifted her hand and screwed her face into an expression of intense concentration. "I be smile to eyeballing you," she announced proudly, then switched to Russian. "Vadim and I are learning English."

The impact of Pavla's reality stunned the breath from Nicole's chest. Clutching her stomach, she sagged against the doorway and clung for support. Her limbs dissolved to water, her face paled to the color of paste.

"For God's sake, Pavla!" Her whisper strangled. "Tell me! Dimitri—is he . . . is he . . . ?"

"He's here. He's with Dr. Warren in Cambridge. At the patriot headquarters." Pavla reached out her hand. "Just across the river."

Nicole swayed, and the blood rushed from her head. "Oh, my God!"

Pavla caught her as she fell.

30

ACROSS THE RIVER in Cambridge. The phrase rocketed through Nicole's mind as Pavla related the harrowing months in Siberia, the numerous times she and Vadim had given Dimitri up for dead. She spoke of the horrors in the forced-labor copper mines, of substandard rations and men dying and then of the perilous race across Siberia with Russian soldiers at their heels.

"But we made it, thanks to God's will, and here we are." Pavla smiled. "All we did on the ship was eat and sleep, sleep and eat."

Nicole replenished their teacups and pulled her longing gaze from the shimmer of water beyond the kitchen window. A flush heated her cheeks, and her hands trembled. "Dimitri's eye . . . ?"

Pavla's expression sobered. "He almost lost it, Natushka, but thank God that didn't happen." She reached across the table and pressed Nicole's shaking hands. "He wore a patch for a while, but now he sees perfectly. There's a scar, but I think you'll agree it only makes him more handsome and dashing than before."

Nicole breathed a heartfelt prayer of gratitude, then lowered her hands from her mouth and fixed large moist eyes on Pavla. "When will I see him?" Every pulsebeat urged her to fly to him. Across the river in Cambridge—so close and yet so impossibly far.

Pavla sidestepped the question. "We docked in Salem and drove out to the house. We met your parents and Vaddie." A soft wistful smile curved her lips. "He's wonderful!"

An ache of tears shimmered on Nicole's lashes. "Dimitri . . . did he hold his son? Was he pleased?" She had pictured the event a thousand times—and hadn't been present to see it.

Pavla nodded. "We all agreed Vaddie looks exactly like someone called Grandpa René." She winked above a grin.

"Personally, I think Vaddie resembles the prince, but I wouldn't dare admit that to Madame Duchard. Vadim is so proud he insisted on holding his namesake for hours. I never heard so many Ivan Ivanovich stories in my life!" She laughed above an odd flush of pink.

"I . . ." Nicole stared at her hands as the full implications of Pavla's tale penetrated her emotional churn. "Did my father explain why I couldn't accompany them to Salem?"

"*Da.*" Sympathy deepened Pavla's fine dark eyes.

Nicole struck the table, then concealed her face in her apron. Shame more painful than tears could soothe knifed through her heart. The magnitude of her betrayal gnawed the inner edges of her very soul.

"The prince is very proud of your courage."

"You don't understand! I . . . Last night . . ."

"Natushka . . . listen to me. The prince is proud of your courage and your commitment to liberty. In your place he would do the same." A wry smile twisted the corners of her lips. "Don't manufacture blame where none exists," she advised softly.

Nicole didn't respond. Small groans escaped her pale lips, and she rocked in the chair, her face hidden in the folds of her apron. He'd been alive all the time! Dear God! She should have fought William with all her strength; she should have at least tried. She'd been a fool to think she won by denying him satisfaction. She had not won, she'd lost everything. Could Dimitri possibly forgive her? Equally as important, could she forgive herself?

"Here . . ." Pavla rummaged quickly through the canvas bundle, producing a square of cloth and a folded packet.

Slowly, Nicole lowered her apron and examined the items through stinging eyes. Her unsteady hands opened the small square of cloth, and she stared at a tiny black curl. A sheen of tears brimmed along her lashes as she touched the silken strand with her forefinger. "Thank you," she whispered. No, she had not lost everything. Somehow they would survive; Vaddie was the link.

Embarrassed, Pavla shrugged from her chair and poured boiling water into the empty teapot. "I thought a lock of Vaddie's hair might ease your heart a little." She placed the flatiron on the hearth to heat and eyed the basket of laundered shirts, wondering if she could manage them one-handed.

Nicole wasn't listening. She stared at the packet of closely written pages, recognizing the hand which had penned them. Dimitri was in Cambridge, but a piece of him lay before her on the table. She felt unworthy.

Pavla flapped an apron across the board and bent for the iron. "Read it," she urged gently. Lapsing into silence, she smoothed the apron with her stump and clumsily ran the iron over the material. The chore was difficult, but she managed. "Read it."

Nicole swallowed and nodded, blinking furiously to clear her vision. First she pressed the pages to her breast. Dimitri had touched these pages, his breath had caressed the paper. Feeling foolish but unable to stop herself, she raised the packet to her nose and inhaled, imagining she recognized sea and salt and leather and horseflesh and all the various wonderful smells which were uniquely his.

As her fingers trembled too violently to steady the pages, she smoothed them against the table. Nicole drew a deep breath, held it, then lowered her gaze.

My darling, my dearest Tasha:
  I love you.
  How does one span the months of silence? By telling you the image of your loveliness and valor sustained me through the days of fever and cold? By relating how your love powered each futile swing of the pickax? But you know that.
  As you must know my instinct is to storm Boston and find you. The frustration of delay torments me even as I pen these words, even as I admit the strategic importance of your position.
  Louis and Joseph Warren have explained your sacrifice. And my heart swells with pride. And with the fury of imagining what your sacrifice entails. If Caldwell has violated your trust, he will die—this I promise you.
  It is important, my love, that we understand each other on this issue, for I deem it wise not to dwell on this subject in the future. War demands sacrifice from us all; we cannot assign blame in these difficult times, and we cannot castigate ourselves with guilt. I know your heart, my love. And I know your courage. Together we are strong enough to bear whatever ugliness must be borne—and then forgotten. The sacrifices offered by the good men and women upon these shores shall be repaid a thousandfold in the legacy we leave to those who come after us.
  We will not speak of blame or forgiveness for acts extending beyond the realm of individual morality. It is

402

God's will. Instead, you and I, little Tasha, shall concentrate on our strengths and on our convictions, on those qualities which will reverberate through the ages. I think of the lives which will be altered because you are who you are and where you are. . . .

Nicole closed wet lashes. She knew where she was but not who she was. After a long moment she lifted a cup of cold tea to her lips. She did not feel strong, and her conviction pulsed at a low ebb. God in heaven, how she yearned to be with him! Just for five minutes, Lord, just to see him and touch his face for five minutes!

But it wouldn't be enough. Her love was wild and selfish; she demanded a lifetime.

As she bent above his letter, her eyes blurred and overflowed with the tenderness of memory. He recalled their drive to St. Petersburg, the crystal days and rapturous nights; he spun dreams into a chain of tomorrows. She smoothed the last page, reluctant to fold away this link to her heart, wishing the letter could go on and on.

From the depths of my soul I thank you for our son. He is as strong and healthy as his namesake, as lusty and remarkable as his mother. His only fault lies in lacking a sister. I have promised the young gentleman to remedy this oversight at the earliest opportunity.

I cannot promise the future we both desired, my darling. Warren and General Ward have kindly expressed a conviction that my services will be of value throughout the term of conflict. I have pledged my sword and my loyalty for the duration. What is occurring in New England is the single most important event we shall witness in our lifetimes, my love. It is our duty and our honor to play a small role.

Burn this letter, sweet Tasha, and know that I shall come for you as soon as General Ward agrees your service has ended. Know also that I count the minutes until I hold you again in my arms.

Your Dimitri

Nicole read his letter repeatedly, hungering above each phrase, raging impotently at the winds of destiny. She had fought in the serf uprising; Dimitri had battled the Turks and suffered Siberia. It was enough. Why did fate insist they risk their lives here as well?

Because they believed in freedom. They believed in individual liberty; they believed in a better world than Russia or

England could offer. But if he died . . . if she lost him again, it would be the finish of her.

Nicole's forehead sank into her palm, and again she read his letter, tracing the ink with her forefinger. Then she crossed reluctantly to the hearth, kissed the pages, and touched them to the flames beneath the pots. She retained the pages until heat scorched her fingers.

Opening the cupboard beneath the dry skin, she filled a cup with rum and swallowed it neat. Then she seated herself at the table and watched as Pavla ironed. She marveled at the girl's one-handed dexterity, dismissing as nonsense Pavla's mutters of vexation.

"Do you know what was in the letter?" she asked.

"I can guess."

"Was he . . . was he . . . ? When he learned that I . . ."

Pavla smiled. "He jumped on your father's horse and was halfway to Boston before Dr. Warren caught up with him."

A sound more like a sob than a laugh closed Nicole's throat. It was so like him. And so like him to think it through before he wrote to her. "I don't know what to do," she said when she could speak. "My heart demands that I go to him, but my head cautions me to remain here." She felt exhilarated and numb and confused and on fire, and when she remembered last night and William, she felt the urge to commit some wild and violent act of denial and outrage. Anguish and shame choked her low voice as she confessed to the night and blurted her fears for the nights to follow. "What am I going to do?"

Pavla listened in silence, struggling to fold William's uniform shirts in a pile, applying the clumsy iron to others.

"Is there a choice?" she asked when Nicole had blotted her eyes and lapsed into a miserable silence. Pavla exchanged the irons and steadied the board against her hip. "Duty comes first, doesn't it? In my village the husbands have a saying: Man's curse lies in not being able to perform when he most wishes; a woman's blessing is her ability to perform even when she does not wish to." Her eyes touched Nicole, then dropped. "If you must share his bed, you must," she added without expression.

Nicole's head dropped backward until loose tendrils of gold dripped over her shoulders; she stared at the ceiling. "You and I . . . we've endured so much together." The pirate ship and the fears of St. Petersburg; the traumas of Oranienbaum and the grinding hardship of Siberia. "Have you ever questioned the purpose? The loss of your hand, the . . . ?"

"It is God's will. He does not burden us with more than we can bear. And he gives us selective memories; he doesn't allow us to remember pain. One day you will forget how you listened for a boot on the stair."

Nicole shuddered and shook her cap furiously.

Pavla glanced upward from a steaming sleeve. "Do you remember the heartache—exactly—of waiting for the cart to fetch Larisca? Do you remember the horror of plunging the pitchfork into Repinsky? The pain and sorrow of bidding Katya good-bye? Do you remember what you felt—exactly—when you woke in the sled and believed Dimitri dead? Can you even now recall with accuracy the pains of childbirth?" Pavla's wise dark stare knew the answers.

Nicole winced in defeat. Her breast rose and fell. "One moment at a time. Life must be faced one small moment at a time. . . ." Her eyes strayed toward the window and the late-afternoon sunlight sparkling across the river. A tingle raced along her spine, and her body tensed with longing. Dimitri was there, meeting, conferring, planning, doing whatever soldiers did. While she waited here, resisting, resenting, listening, doing whatever spies did.

Sighing heavily, she watched Pavla set the irons outside on the stoop to cool and then store the board in the buttery. A deep weariness settled across her shoulders.

In contrast, Pavla harbored no end of energy. Returning to the kitchen, she tended the hearth, bending above the soup bubbling within a heavy iron pot. She stirred the ladle vigorously and cleared her throat. "How old do you think I am?"

Nicole arched a brow. The question was plucked from thin air, pertaining to nothing she could identify. "Twenty-two? Twenty-three?"

"*Nyet.*" Pavla sounded annoyed. "I was thirty last month."

Nicole smiled at the lie. "Thirty," she repeated.

The ladle raced about the pot rim. "Do you think there is too great an age difference between a woman of thirty and a man of forty-five?"

Startled, Nicole intensified her stare. "Some would consider it ideal, Pavla . . . ?"

"Someone . . . thinks maybe the age difference is too great."

Someone? A frown puzzled Nicole's brow; then her eyes widened and a pleased smile lit her features.

Vadim.

It made sense. He and Pavla shared similar backgrounds, they had passed nearly a year in one another's company, and they were possibly the only Russian couple in New England. Thinking back, Nicole realized she had always sensed a mutual affection. Pavla and Vadim—it seemed as natural and as happily inevitable as a sunrise.

But forty-five. Vadim was fifty if he was a day, a youthful vigorous fifty, but fifty nonetheless. Smiling to herself, Nicole expended an effort to sound offhand. "I think your someone is wrong. In fact, I think age matters very little if two people truly care for each other."

Pavla flung the ladle into the depths of the pot. "That's what I say!" Wrists on her hips, she stared darkly into the soup pot.

"Uh . . . I don't believe you've mentioned Vadim's whereabouts. Where is he now?"

"He's in Cambridge with the prince." The anger in Pavla's voice matched the fear Nicole experienced when she imagined Dimitri facing the British muskets. "You might suppose he'd leave the fighting to the younger men, but *nyet*! He's as happy as a Christmas goose at the idea of bashing heads and mangling soldiers! He won't admit he could be wounded or even killed!" She stared at Nicole, and then her hand flew to her lips. "You guessed!"

Nicole laughed. "Of course I guessed. And I wish you both years of love and happiness!"

Pavla smiled. "I have to convince him first. We've spoken of marriage"—a flame of crimson flushed her cheeks, and she was almost pretty—"but he thinks he's too old for me."

"We'll work on him," Nicole promised.

"I'm doing everything I can. I don't lie anymore."

"Thirty?" Nicole smiled.

"Oh, that." Pavla's stump waved an airy dismissal. "That doesn't count."

"And stealing?"

Pavla lifted her left palm and solemnly swore she hadn't appropriated a single item not belonging to her. She thought a moment, then patted her pocket. "Except these. But I need passes to get in and out of Boston."

"Oh, Pavla!" Nicole laughed helplessly as Pavla fanned a pad of passes, all bearing William's signature.

Pavla grinned sheepishly. "And the Americans need ammunition. I promised Dr. Warren I'd do what I could . . . but after the war, I swear I'll never steal anything ever again!"

Nicole pinned up her curls, smiling. "I think Vadim would be well advised to tuck you far from the reach of temptation."

Pavla arched her brow. "He's bidding on the farm three miles from you and the prince. The land in Salem is good farmland, dark and rich and—"

"What language is that?"

Both women spun toward the intrusion. William filled the doorway with red and white and gold braid. Flinging his hat toward a peg, he unbuttoned his jacket and frowned at Pavla.

"For Christ's sake, Nicole, what are you thinking of, hiring a one-handed servant? What possible good is she? Ged rid of her." Displeasure creased his brow and he bent to the sink for the jug of rum. Each short gesture proclaimed his annoyance at not discovering his rum poured and waiting.

Nicole's jaw tightened. "William, I have the honor of presenting my longtime friend Pavla."

Pavla's mouth smiled, but her eyes sharpened. "I be smile to eyeballing you." She curtsied.

William stared. "What in the bloody hell did she say?"

"She said she is happy to see you." Nicole drew a breath. "Pavla will be staying with us." Her chin jutted defiantly, and stubborn eyes flashed. She read William's refusal and vowed not to budge from her position. This was, after all, still the Duchard house.

He examined her expression and swirled the rum in his tankard. "Does she speak any English?"

"She's learning."

"Not very well from the sound of it." His pale eyes locked on Nicole's defiant stare. "What language *does* she speak?" His dangerously soft tone suggested he had guessed.

"Russian."

"I see." Biting off further comment, he tucked the rum jug beneath his arm, bowed stiffly to them both, and withdrew. They heard the parlor doors slam.

Nicole released a breath, and her eyes flicked to the ashes in the hearth. "William can be . . . . difficult."

Pavla shrugged. "It's God's will." She fished the ladle from the soup pot and dropped the dripping spoon on one of William's freshly laundered shirts. Ignoring Nicole's bemused gasp, she used the shirt to wipe the ladle, then tossed the shirt toward the rag basket. "That is what I think of him."

Nicole pressed her lips but couldn't prevent the explosion of laughter, even though she knew William would hear and assume the worst. She laughed until helpless tears streaked her cheeks, and each time she glanced at the soup-stained shirt or toward Pavla's indignation, a fresh wave bubbled forth. When she caught her breath, Nicole mopped her eyes and gasped. "Oh, Pavla! I be smile to eyeballing you too!" The laughter brought a welcome release from shifting tensions. The relief, however, was short-lived.

Dinner was awkward and then openly hostile. If Nicole addressed William, Pavla was excluded; when she responded to Pavla's comments, William sulked in heavy silence. An invisible line had been drawn, and Nicole was the prize, tugged first this way and then that.

"Pavla, stop provoking him. Can't you see he's getting angry? You know I have to be civil!"

Pavla smiled and nodded pleasantly to William. "You are a skinny hairless pig with no eyelashes and a face like a mud wallow. Beneath your snout is an ugly little mouth which tells me you are a stupid insignificant man. Pig!"

"What did she say?" William demanded.

Nicole stirred her soup and gazed steadfastly toward her wineglass. "She said she dislikes pork."

"I can't imagine why—she has all the shape and beauty of a sow!"

"What did he say?" Pavla hissed, eyes narrowed.

"He was being polite. He mentioned that you possess a certain unique beauty."

Pavla snorted. "If he said that, I'll eat the molding off the walls!"

"Tell the sow that anyone with a shred of sensitivity would recognize we wish to be alone! If she wants to be useful, she can withdraw and . . . and wash the dishes or something." William flung his napkin across his empty plate and shoved from the table. He crossed his legs and brooded into his wine.

An evening of switching from English to Russian had given Nicole a raging headache. The tug-of-war for her attention did not amuse her. "I haven't seen Pavla in months, William. We have much to discuss. Surely you can understand that."

After a stiff hesitation he answered, "Very well." His eyes bored into hers. "But she sleeps in your parents' room."

A crimson flush began at Nicole's throat and climbed upward. "I thought—"

Ignoring Pavla's intake of breath, William grasped Nicole's wrist. "All day I've thought of nothing but last night." His voice dropped, and Nicole's distress deepened. "I've been anticipating . . ."

The desire in his eyes required no translation. "Pig!" Pavla spat.

Annoyed, William threw up his hands and scowled at her. "What is that bloody word she keeps saying?"

"William, please. About tonight, I beg you. Pavla . . ." Dimitri's chiseled aristocratic features sprang before her vision with a clarity which snatched at her breath and weakened her limbs. Then she looked at William and quickly lowered her gaze, hoping the swing of golden curls concealed her grimace of repugnance.

"Put her in your parents' room."

Nicole resented the harshness of command. A ragged sigh lifted her breast. William was capable of appearing in her bedroom and ordering Pavla out. The humiliation of the imagined scene was unthinkable. Standing abruptly, she gathered an armload of dishes and fled to the kitchen.

Then the waiting began. The terrible waiting. Magnified by knowing her adored Dimitri slept across the river. She pushed her hot face into the pillows and wept. And listened for the creak of a boot on the stairs.

And she wondered that the human heart could endure such dread and anguish and continue to beat normally. "Help me," she whispered as her door inched open. "Grant me tolerance and forgiveness."

William slipped into her bed, and a warm groan sighed against her ear as his eager hands cupped her breasts. Pulling her roughly into the curve of his nakedness, he ground his manhood against her body, boasting his readiness.

Nicole bit the back of her hand to smother the scream building in the pits of nausea. Her teeth cut tiny marks on her skin and she stared blankly at the ceiling as he wedged his knee between her legs. One quick movement and her nightdress vanished; his mouth and hands explored the creamy fullness of her breasts. Nicole squeezed her eyes shut and forced her thoughts to distant vistas as he labored above her. Vaddie. Her parents. Sunshine on the river. The road to St. Petersburg. Hemmed by quiet tall trees; the forest floor scattered with autumn wildflowers. Serene and tranquil. Protected from turbulence and violation.

Chest heaving, William rolled from her body and rested on

his elbows, staring into her pale blind face. His lips curled away from his teeth. "You weren't there!" he accused. "You just . . . weren't there!"

She didn't speak, didn't move. She directed the force of her spirit toward vanishing. The stickiness on her thighs burned like acid. She detested the stink of him, the violation of his seed upon her body and in her bed. She wanted him gone, as if never born. William could force her a hundred times, a thousand, and she would die before her arms circled his neck, before her lips parted in surrender.

She stared up at him. Their intensity meshed and held. And William slowly understood that nothing he did or said would crack the barriers of resolve. "Nicole!" Bewilderment thinned his mouth, and he wet his lips. "I don't . . . You and I, we . . . But why? Why are you doing this?"

Comprehension arrived swiftly. "That Russian sow." His countenance grew livid, and knots rose along his jawline. "He's alive," he said flatly. "That's it, isn't it?" Bruising fingers gripped her cheeks, and he wrenched her face toward a moonlit fury. "He's alive and he's here, isn't he? Answer me! The bastard is alive!"

"Yes!" Nicole cried. "A thousand times yes!"

"With the patriots." It wasn't a question.

She shoved to her elbows, her eyes blazing and her heart hammering in her ears. She didn't care about patriots or campfires. The battle was here and now.

William knocked her to the bed. His fingers dug brutally into her bare shoulders. And a misty shower rained over her wince of disgust as he swayed before her. "If Denisov is in Charlestown when we attack, I swear I will find him and I will kill him! Do you hear me? Are you listening now? I'll kill the son of a bitch! He won't claim what's mine!"

Her cold eyes expressed contempt. She smiled.

He hissed into her smile; then his hand cracked across her cheek. The pain was instant, fiery. But Nicole didn't cry out. She lay limp where the force of his blow had thrown her. She smiled at him, making no effort to conceal the imprint rising upon her white cheek. And her smile was more terrible than any words could have been.

"Good God! Look what you made me do!" A shaking hand touched her cheek; then he grasped her by the shoulder, exasperated by her silence and her smile. "Speak to me!" He shook her. "Dammit, say something!" Golden hair flew over them both, and sweat beaded on his brow. "Dammit to bloody hell! Stop smiling! Stop it!"

But she triumphed by refusing to respond to his shrieks, by refusing to resist when he struck her again. She swallowed her cries and repudiated him by a smiling silence. And watched as he blinked at his hands as if he could not comprehend the violence these strange appendages performed.

"Nicole . . ." Dim moonlight filtered a face congested with frustration and fury. "Denisov can't enter Boston, and you can't leave! You'll never see him again! Are you listening? I'm talking reason to you! I'll never allow you to leave." Seeing her lip twist, he shook her savagely. "Don't make me do this!" His stare swept her naked breasts, and his jaw clenched. He pulled her against his chest and a groan wrenched from the depths of his spirit. She felt his excitement growing between his thighs and closed her eyes in a shudder of denial.

With a cry he fell on her, and he punished her silence, punished her lack of responsiveness. He punished her for all his disappointments both real and imagined, punished her as only a man can. And he wiped the smile from her frozen lips.

She suffered his passion in white-faced silence. When he yanked her onto her knees and rammed her from behind, she bit off a scream as hot silent tears streamed. She uttered no plea; she closed herself to him despite the agony. And when he jerked from her with a choked sound and stumbled from her room, she knew the victory was hers.

Limping, she staggered slowly across the darkness and wrung a cloth in the washbasin, pressing it to the bruises swelling on her cheek. Gingerly she cleaned her thighs and her stomach and donned a fresh nightdress. Bare feet moving quietly, she crossed the hallway and tiptoed past Pavla's sleeping form, until she stood at the window.

A panorama of dark tranquil beauty opened below the sill. Distant silvery stars adorned the warm June night. Ships rocked gently on an ebony ribbon, drifting silently on the slow river currents. The rolling countryside winked drowsy orange eyes. All was still and quiet.

Nicole rested her arms on the windowsill, and her gaze softened with yearning as she focused on the reassuring warmth of a thousand fires. She thrust the last hour from her thoughts. Instead her mind and her heart flew across the river. Did Dimitri sleep beside one of the campfires? He and

Vadim? She stared until her eyes watered, imagining she could pierce the distance to Cambridge, wondering if he had remained there, or if he slept within her sight. Her heart winged outward, and she experienced a strong kinship with New England wives and mothers.

Other women stood at windows tonight, staring toward Boston and dispatching their prayers upon the night winds. Their men waited in Roxbury, in Cambridge, in Dorchester, in Charlestown. Waited for an unknown moment and an unknown site.

Nicole's breath caught sharply and froze. Her mouth dropped and she jerked upright as her mind raced backward. William. He had said, "If Denisov is in Charlestown when we attack . . ."

Charlestown! The British would attack at Charlestown!

She bolted from the window and craned her head, her narrowed gaze sweeping the ring of campfires. The men waiting in Roxbury, Dorchester, and Cambridge waited in vain!

But what if it was a trick? She eased inside the window and chewed a fingernail, thinking it through. No. William's remark was a slip of the tongue uttered in the heat of passion and most likely overlooked. So. He hadn't confided the truth; he had attempted to mislead her by promising next week. Her mouth tightened. Very well, she now possessed one piece of the puzzle, and William's vanity would provide the other. The officers would don their finery for the battle. Her shoulders straightened with confidence.

Touching her fingers to her lips, she blew a silent kiss past the Charlestown campfires and on toward Cambridge. "Good night, my love, my heart . . ." She returned to her bed with a small painful smile.

Pavla was dressed and enjoying a second mug of strong black coffee when Nicole descended to the bright sunlit kitchen. William, thank heaven, had already departed for Province House.

Pavla studied the bruises on Nicole's cheeks but tactfully refrained from comment. She had earlier watched William storm through the house. No explanation was necessary.

"No more coffee for me," she declined Nicole's offer. "It's time for work."

Nicole raised her eyebrow and sipped her coffee. "Work?"

"The ammunition. With luck I'll be able to complete two trips across the Boston neck today." Pavla shrugged. "It isn't much, but every small effort helps. The patriots are desperate for ammunition."

Nicole looked into her cup. She remembered a small ragged army who had gone to war with pitchforks and clubs and sharpened firewood. "*Da*," she whispered. "Every small effort helps. But how are you going to steal ammunition when you can't speak enough English to ask directions to Copp's Hill?"

Pavla grinned. "I'll manage."

Nicole watched her swing along the cobblestones until she was lost to view among the soldiers crowding the walks. "Yes," she agreed. "I believe you will."

She swept the porch, enjoying the fresh air and gentle breezes, training her mind on the household tasks and away from disturbing memories. She weeded the kitchen garden and chopped vegetables into a stew pot. After tidying the kitchen and the bedrooms, Nicole drew a breath, then pushed open the doors to the parlor, allowing a moment for her eyes to adjust to the dim interior. William's quarters were as she had expected.

The curtains were tightly drawn, shutting out the sights and sounds of the street. The light blankets of his cot were tucked down so snugly a dropped shilling would have bounced from them. Polished dress boots rested before the fireplace, a neatly pressed dress uniform hung from a hook on the mantel. A pile of folded stockings sat near a pile of gloves, each as perfectly aligned as if framed by a box. Toilet items were arranged just so upon a tabletop beneath a spotless shaving mirror. Everything was clean, tidy—sterile. There were no personal items; no pictures, no mementos, no papers. Nothing to indicate preference or personality.

Careful not to disturb the order, Nicole began with his uniform jacket. She loosened a brass button until it suspended from two strands of thread, ready to fall at a touch. One of his boots she scuffed against a stone in the yard. She meticulously opened the stitching of a finger on one pair of gloves; another she employed to dust the tabletops. His stockings received the same treatment before she folded them precisely as she had found them. She crumpled his sash into a ball and applied her weight until the wrinkles were deep and unsightly. Finally she depleted the supply of pipe clay used to whiten his shoulder belt and the facings on his jacket.

Satisfied, she smiled and dusted her hands, then quietly

closed the parlor doors. She occupied herself with dinner preparations until a knock interrupted her concentration.

"Pavla!" Nicole blinked, then leaned outside the door and scanned the street. "Come inside, for heaven's sake!"

At some point between breakfast and late afternoon, Pavla had sprouted a voluptuous figure. A great rounded bosom jutted from her bodice, and her hips had ballooned to a pillowy fullness. Watching from behind as Pavla swayed toward the kitchen, her skirts bouncing provocatively about an odd slow gait, was an experience not to be missed. Laughing, Nicole fell into a chair and shook her cap helplessly, at a loss for words.

"I didn't have time to make the last run." Pavla grinned apologetically. She postured, turning slowly. "You can't imagine the interesting offers I've received."

"I think I can." Nicole laughed.

Pavla glanced at the clock. "Better help me out of this before the major returns." She peeled off her gown, revealing the contraption underneath. A harness circled Pavla's neck and shoulders; it crisscrossed her broad back and swept toward two enormous canvas cups at the breast. Nestled within the cups lay two shiny black cannonballs.

In answer to Nicole's startled questions, Pavla shrugged. "They weigh four pounds apiece. It isn't *too* uncomfortable."

Nicole placed the cannonballs on the kitchen floor, grunting slightly. She regarded Pavla with open admiration, then unbuckled the hip pads from Pavla's waist. Pavla confirmed the pads were stuffed with powder. Nicole lifted clanking petticoats and tested the garments for weight.

"Shot," Pavla explained. "And heavy. I feel as light as a snowflake now." She stretched and grimaced, rubbing her shoulders.

Nicole contemplated the collection. "I can't imagine how you managed to walk at all, carrying that weight." A frown of concern drew her brows, and anxiety sharpened her tone. "Do you know the penalty for aiding the enemy? If you're caught . . ."

Gently Pavla patted the bruises on Nicole's cheeks. "Do you know the penalty for spying? If you're caught . . ."

They stared at each other. And then they embraced.

They hid the ammunition before William returned. The cannonballs disappeared into emptied crocks and were shoved high on the buttery shelves. The shot-filled petticoat vanished under Pavla's bed, and the hip pads they concealed behind a stack of old coats in the cubby under the stairs.

"Pieces of me are everywhere!"

Nicole smiled, but she did not underestimate the dangers involved. She wished them both behind patriot lines and the deceptions ended. Sighing, she admitted she had no idea how soon her wish might be granted, or how many nights fate had designated she must endure.

Tonight for certain.

She tossed in her bed and listened to the clock and thought of Russian nights. And waited. So much of life was spent waiting. She pondered waiting. Some waiting was the eagerness of anticipation, and some waiting was a dark pit of dread.

Heart sinking, she watched the latch depress and felt her muscles tense and grow rigid. William quietly crossed the shadows and stared down at her for a long moment before he slid into her bed. But he did not reach for her, nor did he speak. To Nicole's relief, he crossed his arms behind his head and ignored her, staring into the darkness. Before the downstairs clock bonged two o'clock, he rolled silently onto his side and slept.

The clock had sounded three before Nicole deciphered his behavior. William would not force himself on her again until he could boast Dimitri was dead. That had to be the explanation—it would be William's ultimate victory, his justification. She stared at the blur of sandy hair occupying her pillow, and a shudder leeched the warmth from her skin. It was a long time before she slept.

Both Nicole and Pavla heard the explosion when William returned at twilight on the following day. He rushed into the kitchen waving his jacket. "Look at this! And this and this! My uniform is an abomination!" Furious, he hurled a handful of gloves and stockings toward a chair and raked his hands through his hair. "And I'm nearly out of pipe clay! There isn't enough to do the shoulder strap!"

"That's your dress uniform isn't it?" Nicole asked. She ladled leftover stew into a tureen. "Are you ready for dinner?"

"I don't understand this. I am never careless with my possessions!" His pale eyes narrowed suspiciously. "Has anyone been in my room?"

Nicole straightened and leveled cold eyes on him. "Are you

accusing us of invading your privacy? For what purpose, may I ask?"

"Pig!" Pavla sniffed. She couldn't follow the conversation, but she recognized tight lips and sharp tones.

William watched as Nicole resumed working, her actions normal and unhurried. "Of course I'm not accusing you. It's just that you don't understand how important this is! My jacket needs a button tightened, all my small things need to be laundered, I'll have to go out tonight and purchase more pipe clay . . ."

Nicole pretended a sigh and placed a stack of plates on a tray. Her heartbeat skipped and her expression felt stiff and unnatural. "That's hardly anything to be this perturbed about, William. I'll sew on the button tomorrow, and if you'll place your stockings and gloves in the laundry basket, I'll wash them Monday."

"I can't wait until Monday—I need my uniform Sunday!"

Nicole paused a fraction of a second, and her breath burned as she held it in her lungs. She arranged spoons on the tray. "I hadn't planned to wash again until Monday."

"That won't do!" Realizing he had shouted, William glanced at Pavla and at Nicole's lifted brows, then cleared his throat. "Sunday would be better. I thought I'd attend church . . . that's all."

Commanding her hands to remain steady, Nicole lifted the tray and turned toward the dining room. "Leave your things in the hallway," she suggested softly. "And I'll see that everything is prepared for you."

He hadn't attended church since Nicole had known him.

The second piece of the puzzle slotted into place.

She hurried through dinner, finishing before the others, and when William finally departed to purchase the pipe clay, she dashed for the attic, leaping the stairs two at once.

She placed a shaking hand over a wildly pounding heart; then she pulled the string tilting the weather vane. And raced downstairs to sit on the porch step and wait.

Within minutes a lanky shadow paused near the gate. And a soft voice called to her. "Mistress Duchard? Where shall I deliver Dr. Warren's parcel, and when would you like it in his hands?"

Her knuckles whitened as she clasped her hands beneath her apron. "Deliver the package to Charlestown on Sunday morning."

31

NICOLE BOLTED UPRIGHT in bed, her heart hammering. Muscles tensed, she stared intently into the darkness, critically examining the deep silence. A pounding dread banded her chest like the stifling residue of a nightmare.

Nothing appeared out of the ordinary. The downstairs clock struck four, its familiar resonance fading into a predawn hush. Across the hall Pavla stirred in her sleep; William's chest rose in quiet even breaths at her side.

Slowly she returned to her pillow and cast about half-awakened thoughts, seeking the source of the disturbance which had roused her. A vaguely remembered sound refused to surface. Rolling as far from William's outflung arm as possible, Nicole strained to identify the night creaks settling about the darkness. Had something toppled in the kitchen? Did a loose shutter bang against the bricks?

A roll of thunder clapped across the harbor and Nicole's eyes fluttered open. Rain? Pushing to her elbows, she blinked toward the open windows, listening for the patter of raindrops through the elm. She heard nothing but a dry whispering rustle. Not rain, then. Frowning sleepily, she stared toward the exposed rafters overhead, tracing their rough contours in shadowed tones of moonlight as the thunder boomed once more. The noise sounded sharp, close, yet no clouds obscured the moonlight and she had observed no flash of lightning.

"William?" Puzzled, she tugged his shoulder, disliking the touch of his bare skin. Sleep and confusion blurred her thinking. Had she dreamed a thunder which didn't behave as thunder? It wasn't impossible; her dreams of late had unreeled in strange irrational patterns. "I heard something."

"Thunder," William mumbled. "Go back to sleep."

"But it doesn't sound like—"

William jerked upright as a fresh explosion erupted from

the harbor. This time the roar continued unabated for a full minute before lapsing into a ringing silence.

"Good God!" Flinging back the sheets, William fumbled in the darkness, hastily donning his robe. "That's cannon fire!" He dashed across the hallway and burst into Pavla's room, with Nicole at his heels, her eyes wide and anxious.

Pavla pushed up and tossed her braid over one shoulder. She scrubbed at her eyes and yawned. "It's dark . . . what's all the commotion?"

William tore the curtains aside and stared. "Christ!"

The *Lively* lay at anchor in the ferryway midway between Boston and the Charlestown peninsula. She was lighted from bow to stern, her lanterns silhouetting dark running figures. A persistent clanging of ship's bells shattered the stillness. As they watched, the *Lively* opened fire, and a haze of white smoke drifted across her lanterns and fuzzed her outline.

A bitter taste seeped into Nicole's mouth and she clung to the windowsill, feeling nauseous. "You said the attack would begin tomorrow, not today!"

William continued to stare at the *Lively*. "I said nothing about the attack plans." He didn't look at her. "As it happens, we did plan to attack tomorrow . . . but the attack sure as hell wasn't to begin by bombarding the hills above Charlestown!"

Nicole's heart froze. It was her turn to stare. "But you said . . ." he'd said nothing; she had assumed.

William had forgotten her. He joined neighboring residents hanging from their windows and peering through the darkness toward Charlestown. "Dorchester," he spit between clenched teeth. A hand dug at his hair. "Dorchester first, then swing up and cut off Roxbury. Charlestown was to be last." His thought processes raced across a pinched face. "Something is bloody well wrong!"

Nicole emphatically agreed. She felt sick; she had committed an appalling blunder. Wide cautious eyes swung to examine William's expression. Even in the throes of passion, William Caldwell had not abandoned control. He had fed her false information, given her the wrong site. The game had two players.

Holding her stomach, she edged to the window as the *Glasgow* navigated toward the *Lively*. Both ships flashed cannon fire, and Nicole covered her ears against the thunderous burst. Smoke floated above the river, ethereal and lovely in the moonlight.

Nothing made sense. She shook the tangle of hair falling around the shoulders of her wrapper, attempting desperately to puzzle it out. "But if Dorchester was the initial target, then why are they firing on Charlestown?"

"Exactly what I'd like to know!"

A violent pounding sounded at the front door, and William stared at her, then tightened his robe sash and raced toward the staircase, descending in a clatter.

"It's begun, hasn't it?" Pavla slipped to the window. Her white cap and nightgown lighted in a ghostly flash, reflecting the orange bursts in the harbor.

"*Da*," Nicole whispered. "I think so." Her teeth chattered as a sudden deep chill chased through her flesh. She caught Pavla's hand.

Together they hastened down the hallway and paused in a well of darkness at the top of the stairs. Nicole lifted a finger to her lips as William unbolted the door, but her caution was unnecessary. They could hear perfectly; the men's excitement crackled through the house.

"General Howe and General Gage request your attendance at Province House immediately, sir." The unseen voice was young and eager.

"The firing . . . report on the firing!"

"The lookout on board the *Lively* spotted activity on the peninsula's middle hill—"

"Breed's Hill . . ."

"It appears the colonials are raising a redoubt, sir."

"On Breed's Hill?" William's harsh laugh expressed a contemptuous scorn. "Their leaders are not only ignorant, they're mad!"

Nicole didn't need to observe the aide to recognize the grin in his reply. "Aye, sir."

Quickly she translated the exchange for Pavla; then both stumbled down the stairs in response to William's shout. The next half-hour was frantic. Reacting to William's terse instructions, they labored to clay his shoulder belt and gaiters, then polished brass buttons while William cleaned his cartridge box, waist belt, and boots.

When William stood before them resplendent in full parade dress, the transformation had been accomplished in record time. Nicole and Pavla studied him without expression.

Eagerness and excitement imparted a feverish glow to his eyes. "They think they have the advantage by selecting their ground." He hastily strapped on his officer's sword, a single-edged cut-and-thrust. "The folly of such stupidity will soon be evident. There is no advantage against the British army. We'll secure the peninsula before nightfall, mark my words. And tomorrow we'll proceed as planned and obliterate the southern forces."

Nicole brushed his hat brim with a damp cloth. Her heart crashed painfully against her ribs. "It will be that easy, then?" A tremor whispered through her voice. It was no longer a game; it was deadly real. For weeks the Whigs and the Tories had bowed and nodded to one another in Boston's lanes, refusing to allow political differences to puncture society's veneer. They played a game of careful courtesy. But now the period for pretense had concluded. Today the fabric of civilization would tear asunder.

"As effortless as sweeping ants from the front porch." Confidently William settled his hat upon stiffly pomaded hair. The ringlets on either side of his temples bobbed as his gloves settled upon Nicole's shoulders. He laughed. "You're trembling. I assure you I'm in no danger. If you and"—his disdainful glance included Pavla—"your friend desire an amusing interlude, climb out on the roof and watch if you like. You'll have an enviable view. The tides must be considered, but I'll wager we'll be across the river by midday. I'll be home for dinner as usual, expecting a victory celebration."

A deep anger kindled in Nicole's breast and sprang into flame. His arrogance born of inexperience appalled her. She wet her lips and stared, understanding he actually believed the nonsense he spouted. He admitted no recognition of the patriots' stubborn commitment and resolve; he didn't comprehend the seriousness of the waiting threat. He hadn't seen men with bloodied stumps and gaping holes, he had not suffered the shrieks of the dying. He didn't understand that committed men would fight with clubs and broomsticks and stones if necessary.

"Ants!" she breathed, shaking. "Men will die!" she blurted.

He winked. "And careers will be forged."

Nicole felt sick, too weak to resist when he stepped forward and swept her into a painful kiss of such passion that it left her breathless. William crushed her roughly against his satin breeches, and she felt the hard pulsing stab of excitement and knew he would have taken her on the floor had time permitted. A surge of bile soured her mouth and a deep abiding anger quivered within her breast.

When he released her, she wiped her lips and blazed toward the pinpoints of granite hardening his stare.

"I haven't forgotten my promise," he reminded her softly. "If opportunity grants, I'll resolve our personal triangle today as well."

It was the final breaking point; her fury erupted as the tensions of the last weeks spun outward and snapped. The continual shock of cannon fire signaled a beginning, but it also marked an end. Nicole's teeth bared. "You're an arrogant, conceited fool!" Once begun, the rush couldn't be halted. Her arms waved and golden strands flew about her flushed face. "You think today will be an amusing event to witness? *Amusing?*" Her voice shrilled. "Men will die! Don't you care about them? Is your precious career more important than those men's lives? Are you so certain you're invulnerable? Are you so certain you'll stand on the sidelines, outside the line of fire?" She leaned her fists on the kitchen table, facing him with blazing eyes and high color.

Suddenly her shoulders slumped, and she admitted the futility of her attack. There was nothing she could say he would understand. "Listen carefully, William. There will be no victory dinner. I don't care when you return or if you return. Because when today's clash is ended, I'm leaving. If I have to swim the Charles, I'll do it. I'm going home to my husband!"

His glove cushioned the sting of his slap. "Now, you listen! When I find the son of a bitch who dishonored you, and I will, I'll kill him. And then we'll both be free of the past!"

"I love him! I've always loved him. And no one else." She said it with pride and controlled quiet. Her hand lifted to her cheek, but she didn't give him the satisfaction of a wince. Nor did she notice as Pavla's arm slipped about the tremble across her shoulders. "I won't be here when you return." Her chin firmed and lifted and her stony defiance matched the hardness in his stare. It was over—finally and wonderfully over. She had done what she could, and now she was free. Loathing flashed from her eyes.

William's laugh was ugly. "Now who is the fool? Swim the Charles?" Contempt deepened his sneer. "And do you honestly believe any possibility exists that you'll slip past thousands of soldiers nerved for battle? A dog couldn't get out of Boston today!" His fingers dug into her shoulders, and she smothered a cry. "You'll be here. You will be waiting because I won't let you go and because when Denisov is dead you won't want to go!" The clock sounded the half-hour; an impatient voice shouted from the street. "But I won't forget that you wished me dead," he hissed. "You'll pay for that wish for the rest of your life!" He tugged at his glove, staring at her. "You'll beg my forgiveness. Tonight, when I hand you Denisov's ears."

Nicole gasped. And for a terrible instant she feared he would attempt to kiss her again. She backed swiftly away until her palms flattened against the hearth stones. Her fingers curled about the handle of a fish knife. His lip curled and he laughed. Then he bowed deeply first to her and then to Pavla, who had not understood the words, but who comprehended the slap and the tone. William's bow was a mockery offensive to them both, exactly as it was intended.

His gaze locked to Nicole's, piercing her soul. "Tonight I'll want a woman. I've heard that battle increases a man's vigor. You'll whimper my name and beg."

"Never!"

His teeth ground silently. "If it takes a lifetime, I will make you love me!" He smiled bitterly at her shudder; then he spun and raced toward the porch.

Nicole listened to the door slam. She heard the clatter of running feet in the streets, of iron wheels careening over the cobblestones.

Sickened, she sank to the table and buried her face in her hands. William was right. No one would leave Boston, not today. Not even Pavla's magic could arrange the impossible. She wiped her eyes with the sleeve of her robe as Pavla wordlessly poured coffee into pewter mugs. There was little point in spinning the clock forward; first today must be endured. Somehow.

They hunched above their mugs without speaking, watching the dawn sky pale, then deepen to a clear cloudless blue. The day would be hot. Nicole listened to the steady boom from the harbor, watched her coffee mug jump on the table. Today would be the longest in memory.

She and Pavla dressed in light summer clothing, covering their ears as Burgoyne brought Copp's Hill roaring to life above them and to the left. Floors shook and windows rattled in their frames. Dishes skittered from cupboard shelves and crashed to the floor as the monstrous pounding blasted through the morning.

The British fired continuously at the feverish activity on Breed's Hill, now obvious in the glare of bright sunlight. Despite the unnerving bombardment, the colonists toiled furiously and the redoubt slowly grew. Distance rendered the British cannon largely ineffective, but the continual firing exacted a lethal toll in nerves. As did the salvos roaring from the fleet guns positioned on the Charles. Great hunks of earth gouged from the Charlestown hills.

Nicole's ears rang continually as she swept broken crockery into a pan and tossed the pieces through the buttery door. Shading her eyes, she stared toward Breed's Hill. Tiny dots swarmed across the peninsula mounds. Ignoring the gun and cannon fire, the Yankees labored unceasingly in the building heat. A breastwork appeared, stretching to the north of the redoubt. Sun flashed on metal, and Nicole narrowed her gaze and squinted. She counted four small cannon being dragged over Bunker's Hill and down toward the Breed's Hill redoubt. Four. Only four.

A barrage of cannonballs whistled from the Copp's Hill battery as she watched. Deep gashes ripped into the green heights near the patriots. Loose balls careened along the slopes, knocking figures awry in a lethal bowling game. The redoubt was safe, but the men below it were not. The speeding balls tore legs from torsos in the blink of an eye. Nicole covered her forehead and listened to the thready pulse in her temples. The patriots' four small cannon were a pitiful jest; they were futile in the face of superior British artillery. And Dimitri and Vadim were on the hill; she knew it as certainly as she knew William was a fool.

She sagged against the door frame and surrendered to a drifting sense of unreality. All across Boston, housewives swept broken shards into pans. They tidied their beds and stirred their pots. While their men prepared for war. Hysterical laughter bubbled behind Nicole's fist—the image was so impossibly bizarre, so outrageously improbable. Surely someone would return to his senses in time and demand an end to this charade. The ear-splitting bombardment would cease and the leather-clad figures scurrying over the hills would tip their hats and withdraw to sanity. Everyone would smile sheepishly and shake his head and agree to find an amiable solution for the issues at stake.

It was too late. Such rose-colored dreams lay in the realm of yesterday.

Shortly before noon, exactly as William had suggested, people began to appear on the rooftops. Boston's citizens crawled out their windows, dragging parasols and lunch baskets and pails of rum punch, and they settled themselves for the promised spectacle.

"It's as if no one realizes men will die!" Nicole slapped at tears of frustration. "This isn't a farce staged for our entertainment! It's real!" She beat her fists on the windowsill as she watched a family on the rooftop below, arranging stools, awnings, and amusements for the children. And her heart wept for the dark figures streaming over Bunker's Hill and down toward the redoubt.

Was Dimitri among the men feverishly laboring to fortify the hill? She pressed her knuckles against her eyes. A sinking conviction warned her that Dimitri would be in the worst of it. Dimitri and Vadim and Dr. Warren and how many others whom she knew and called friend?

Pavla touched her shoulder. "We may as well join the others." Her dark eyes scanned the distant hills, seeking a giant form among the swarming dots. She chewed the end of her braid nervously.

Nicole's defenses crumbled; icy wasps stung the lining of her churning stomach. She admitted the impossibility of keeping pace with the breaking crockery and cracking windows. It was impossible to think of anything but the tense expectancy building upon an unseasonably hot breeze.

And the waiting eroded her spirit. The terrible taut lull of waiting. She jumped as a water pitcher crashed from Marie's bureau, and she stared at the broken pieces for a long moment. Then she caught up her sunbonnet and followed Pavla out onto the roof.

A cacophony of noise and shouts assaulted the senses. Cannon blasted overhead; wagons rumbled unceasingly through the streets, transporting the British cannon to the waterfront. Fifes and drums beat the troops into formation on Boston Common. People raced through the streets. And depending upon political persuasion, voices shouted derision or encouragement from the rooftops.

The level of noise and excitement was unlike anything Nicole had experienced or ever wished to again. Conversation was impossible. The din enfolded each into a shell of frightening isolation.

She tied her bonnet and swallowed an arid bitter taste as the sun climbed the sky, and she squinted anxiously toward the Charlestown neck, where British ships fired a storm of ringshot and chainshot. The lethal rain of shrapnel turned the narrow passageway into a death march for the stream of patriots hastening to join the exhausted men on Breed's Hill. The men in the redoubt had toiled throughout the night; reinforcements and provisions were desperately needed.

"Why don't we answer the cannon?" Nicole whispered, her hands balling into fists. Her eyes watered from an unblinking stare, her nerves felt like wire. "Why don't we return their fire?"

As if in response to her summons, the cannon in the redoubt roared. Two balls slowly curved over the harbor and smacked into the earth below the Copp's Hill battery. Despite the ineffectiveness of the patriot salvo, a thin cheer of Whig voices sounded from isolated rooftops. The patriots valiantly roared defiance into the maw of superior bombardment, into the body of the famed British war machine. David defied Goliath. It was a fine and glorious moment.

Two more rounds sailed harmlessly across the harbor, and then the Yankee cannon fell silent. Tory cheers rang from the rooftops.

"What happened?" Pavla shouted into a thunderous din of fleet guns, battery cannon, and cheering.

Nicole frowned and bit savagely at her thumbnail. "I don't know." Something had happened inside the redoubt, rendering the cannon useless.

Behind them in the streets, a swirl of fifes and the hollow rattle of drums swung the British troops through the lanes toward the embarkation points along the North Battery and the Long Wharf. On cue, the Copp's Hill battery held their fire and the fifers' whistling rendition of "Yankee Doodle" floated across the harbor waves, a deliberate mockery designed to taunt the men on Breed's Hill.

Nicole ground her teeth. "The main body is loading on the far side. Our men won't see them!"

"We'll all see them soon enough," Pavla predicted grimly.

They scrambled to their feet, holding to the chimney bricks and facing toward the ferryway. Waiting. As did the men in the redoubt. All activity dwindled to a halt, and dots of leather and homespun strained toward the music of fifes and drums. A thickness charged the hot humid air, and the waiting built until it quivered and strangled and hearts felt near to bursting.

The first rowboat rounded the tip of the ferryway. Then another and another. A heart-stopping armada of twenty-eight heavily loaded boats. Dizzily Nicole sucked in her breath at the sight of glittering steel bayonets and brilliant red uniforms. Gleaming brass cannon caught the sun from the prows of boats riding low in the water. Sun flashed on the bayonets and cannon and brass buttons. The sight was stunning. Awesome. Terrifying.

"Oh, my God!" Her whisper drowned in a shattering eruption as Copp's Hill and the ships of the line opened a murderous barrage to protect the rowboats. The balls smacked well short of the redoubt, and a fortunate wind prevented the larger ships from approaching to effective firing range—but few noticed. All eyes centered upon the armada disgorging boatload after boatload upon the shores to the right of Charlestown. The light infantry waded ashore, followed by the fearsome grenadiers, easily identified by their tall black caps. The unstoppable, awesome grenadiers.

The scarlet-clad killing machine, a well-disciplined engine of efficiency, assembled on the beach.

Nicole's knees buckled and she sagged, numb to the scorching shingles bruising into her flesh. What possible shred of hope had an undisciplined band of farmers against the finest war machine in history? She mopped her brow and pulled at the brim of her bonnet, watching intently as British artillerymen dragged their heavy cannon up the shallow slope of Morton's Hill and formed a line to secure the beachhead. And she knew William was among the scurrying red dots directing the soldiers into regiments.

As the rowboats turned back against the tide to fetch additional troops, Nicole inquired in a weak voice. "What time is it?" The time was of no compelling urgency. Her request was a craving to touch reality, to clasp something known and ongoing when confronted by terrifying uncertainty. Somewhere on those gouged and smoking hills Dimitri labored and prepared. Dimitri would face the killer machine. Nicole glanced at her shaking hands, then thrust them deeply into her apron pockets. How often could one man tempt fate and emerge whole? She felt alternately burning and then cold, cold to the bone.

"Nearly two. Time for lunch, apparently," Pavla answered, pointing.

They shaded their eyes and blinked disbelief as the British troops calmly settled along the shoreline and unfolded lunch packs. A line of two thousand hungry Yankees waited atop the grassy hills ascending from Charlestown toward the redoubt. They too watched in silence as the British consumed their midday meal. Stomachs rumbled; dry throats swallowed convulsively. And the heat intensified.

The lull tightened nerves into thready strings. Perspiration glued hair to necks and temples. Nicole slowly chewed the bread and warm cheese Pavla had produced, her ears ringing with the roar of cannon fire overhead. She welcomed the cool relief of sweet apple cider served from a chilled pail. Dark stains dipped below her arms and appeared on the spectators' backs.

She thought of the hot, thirsty men on the hills and her eyes searched hopelessly among the dots for a tall dark-haired man with a giant at his side. She looked at her bread and cheese guiltily. Many had labored through the night to erect the redoubt; she wondered when last they had eaten or slaked their thirst. Wincing beneath the blazing sun, she attempted to recall provision wagons crossing the narrow Charlestown neck. She could not. Few drivers would be suicidal enough to whip a wagon through the deadly hail of chainshot.

The bread and cheese stuck in her throat, and she quietly laid them aside.

Across the river the British folded away their lunch scraps as additional troops waded ashore. They contemptuously ignored a volley of sniper shot from the abandoned houses in Charlestown.

The drummers fanned out and swirled their sticks, and the rattle of drums beat the regiments into two brigades.

Nicole's heart froze; she mouthed a silent prayer. After the hours of waiting, it was about to begin. "Protect him," she whispered fiercely. "Please, please, please!" Pavla tensed beside her, a similar stream of prayer tumbling from her lips.

The fifes whistled and the drums rolled, leading the troops out of the beachhead. One brigade swung along the northern shore and was soon lost to view. The second brigade advanced toward Charlestown, the redoubt their objective. Lightning flashes of sniper fire coughed from upper stories and deserted shop windows. As spectators cheered, the British engaged in a time-consuming house-to-house struggle, expelling the Americans, only to have them stubbornly reappear, firing at the British flank.

The brigade veered from the musket fire, withdrawing to a safe distance. And a puzzling pause ensued. Two men with signal flags approached the shore. The sound of fierce gunfire erupted to the north. The first brigade had engaged.

Nicole licked dry lips; the floor of her mouth had turned to sand, "I wish to God we could see better!" She wished a thousand impossibilities. She wished Dimitri safe. She wished she knew if he crouched in the redoubt or along the northern fence. Every muscle ached with strain, and tension curled her body forward in the direction of her heart. The unseen gunfire peppered her mind, shot smoking holes through her thoughts.

"To the north! There's no cannon fire," she observed suddenly. Her fingers gripped Pavla's sweat-stained sleeve. "Listen!"

Pavla grinned. "I have an idea that right about now the British are discovering their twelve-pound cannonballs won't fit their six-pound cannon."

Nicole's head spun. Her mouth dropped and she stared. "How could you know that?"

Pavla shrugged modestly. "While I was . . . borrowing ammunition, I made a friend in the munitions unit. He didn't object if I wandered about on my own." She waved the end of her braid against the heat. Her dark eyes sparkled. "I think maybe I accidentally switched the labels on a few crates of balls. Many crates of balls."

Nicole was speechless; then she laughed aloud and swept Pavla into a tight embrace. She attempted to shout into Pavla's ear, but her words were drowned in a monstrous blast of fire and smoke. Copp's Hill exploded into a solid sheet of fire and thunder. Acrid smoke seared each breath on the rooftops below as carcasses, hollow balls filled with burning pitch, flew across the harbor and smashed into Charlestown. The ships of the line roared with one voice, bombarding the empty town with glowing hot shot.

Charlestown burst into flames. Nicole smothered a scream as the wooden homes and shops erupted. Fire leaped from house to house; pyramids of flame climbed the church steeples. Several dozen figures ran from the burning village and raced toward the redoubt. Plumes of smoke funneled toward Boston, carried on the hot breeze.

Nicole's knuckles whitened against her teeth. And she raged helplessly at the wanton destruction of decency and tradition. The British demolished private property: Charlestown would be leveled along with any snipers. She pressed a chalky face to her knees, sensing the shocked silence along the rooftops below the roar of the guns. Not even the Tories cheered the burning of Charlestown. She flattened her palms on the roughened roof shingles. If one private dwelling's destruction was sanctioned, no home was safe. More than anything else witnessed today, this unconscionable act drove home the irreversible course of the horror unfolding before them.

When Nicole raised her bonnet from her knees, rowboats heavily laden with munition crates were rounding the ferryway, pulling frantically toward the north shore.

Teeth biting into the back of her hand, Nicole peered intently through the drifting smoke to see the British brigade split into two scarlet columns. Slowly they advanced toward the redoubt. Their polished gun barrels and bayonets flashed in the relentless sunlight, the ships of the line boomed behind them, and Charlestown burned in the foreground. The faint commands of the fifes and drums traveled across the waves, regimental banners snapped smartly, and the scarlet columns marched into the dense hayfields stretching up Breed's Hill.

Her heart hitched and stopped. Gooseflesh prickled on her arms as if the breeze were polar cold instead of scorching.

Whatever happened to the unseen north, however, it was not the effortless victory smugly predicted by the British. Judging by a continuous storm of firing, the grenadiers were having a difficult time of it. A white haze overhung the northern shore. Again and again a nerve-shredding pause was followed by minutes of intense firing. And Nicole beat her knees helplessly in the terrified frustration of not knowing Dimitri's position. Pavla's fingers bruised into Nicole's arm. The two women clung together without being aware they did so. And each blinked continually, hoping to pierce the smoke and distance and find the men they sought.

The visible brigade stumbled over rocky terrain concealed beneath the waving hayfields. The stony ground and rock fences slowed their progress but did not halt them. The British advance was as steady and relentless as the passage of the blazing sun.

Breath burned in Nicole's lungs, pulsed against aching ribs. Trickles of perspiration slipped between her breasts, and she spared a fleeting thought for the heavy scarlet coats, for the tight leather vests and breeches. "Fire!" she urged silently, her eyes straining toward the redoubt. "For God's sake, fire!" But the redoubt remained as still as death. Waiting. And the British flowed up the hill like spreading fingers of blood. Bayonets flashed from the base of the earthworks, and still the Yankees held their fire.

Nicole jumped to her feet and sagged against the chimneytop, every nerve a jolt of pain, her eyes burning with the effort to see past the distance and the smoky haze. "Fire!" Pavla gripped the bricks until a line of red appeared beneath her broken fingernails. And the citizens of Boston waited in frozen silence or dropped to their knees and covered their faces.

A sheet of fire erupted from the redoubt.

An incessant stream of fire, an uninterrupted peal of fire and flame and roaring thunder. The stunned British dropped like ripe cherries. The front line fell and the next wave marched into a hell of whistling balls and spitting flame. They died in the hayfields beneath the sun and the redoubt, and their screams drifted on the wind-borne smoke.

The horror of it staggered the sense, stopped the heart. On and on the British came, line after line, column after column, marching into a hail of death and mutilation.

Upon the rooftops of Boston, not a sound was uttered. Shock molded flesh into stone, stirred a sickness into the soul.

David repelled Goliath. Neighbors fired death and smoky horror upon neighbors. Englishmen murdered Englishmen. The world was ever changed.

The scarlet lines broke and the British turned tail and fled down the hillside in wild disarray. They had sustained a staggering loss.

A salty taste appeared beneath Nicole's teeth as she watched the survivors reform at the base of the hill.

And her dazed mind could not comprehend the iron discipline required to march again into that holocaust of flame and smoke and screaming death. Unconscious tears rolled down her cheeks, and her fingers scrabbled at her breast.

British officers dashed along the lines, waving swords and screaming, and the drums rattled and the fifes swirled and the stunned soldiers waded again into the scorching hayfields, sidestepping the bodies of fallen comrades.

They advanced to the very lip of the redoubt before the Yankees opened fire.

A curtain of flash lightning exploded from the redoubt. A fire storm of death and destruction. And when the smoke drifted free, the British were in chaotic retreat, stumbling over mangled bodies concealed in the tall grass. They streamed down the hill in frantic disorder.

Their losses were appalling.

Eyes streaming tears and smoke, Nicole and Pavla scrubbed their lids and watched as a flotilla of boats spread across the harbor. General Clinton rowed over reinforcements.

"They can't continue," Nicole sobbed. She was unconscious of the tears wetting her cheeks or of the apron hem she shredded between her teeth. "They don't have the ammunition or the men!"

No reinforcements risked the deadly fire continually raking the Charleston neck. The desperate lack of patriot ammunition was well-known.

She blinked frantically through a watery curtain at the boats crossing the harbor. The British would throw fresh troops against the exhausted patriots. And when Clinton's men disembarked, the Yankees would be disastrously outnumbered.

The weary remnants of the second brigade reformed at the base of Breed's Hill for another assault on the redoubt. Nicole sank to her knees in disbelief. It was impossible, unthinkable, a death wish, a suicide contingent. Twice they had charged and twice been decisively repelled. At a terrible cost. Sprawled lumps of scarlet littered the hillside; a man couldn't walk three paces without stumbling over the dead or wounded. Nicole watched with a horrified expression, her nails digging into her arms. She expected the soldiers to bolt, to refuse the prospect of further murderous devastation. She prayed that they would. The carnage must stop; the horror must end!

The relentless drums hounded the men into the trampled hayfields, and a crimson tide washed slowly up the hillside. Cannon fire sounded to the north; Clinton's men swarmed onto the shore and divided into columns. One marched north, one plunged toward the hayfields.

The continuous thunder of gunfire and cannon riddled the soul. The first British line marched into the furnace of shot and fire, and they fell, and the next wave marched into hell. Again and again they charged the redoubt. One hundred fell, and one hundred more appeared in their places. And the men on Breed's Hill fired until their guns were emptied, and then they swung their muskets as clubs.

The tide of bayonets flooded over the lip of the battered redoubt, and a choking haze of dust and smoke rose above the battle raging within.

"God! Please, please, God!" Nicole wept frantically, scrubbing furiously at scalding tears as a hoarse cheer erupted from Tory rooftops. Her muscles cramped, her body ached.

Men retreated to Bunker's Hill, forming a musket line to protect the flight of the men in the redoubt. Smoke and dust and sun-flashed bayonets swirled and plunged in the chaos around and within the redoubt. A few men emerged, too few, and backed toward Bunker's Hill, fighting every bloody step of the way.

The crimson wave penetrated the breastworks, then swept inexorably toward Bunker's Hill. Screams of rage and victory roared across the harbor.

In full disordered retreat, the Yankees fled toward the Charlestown neck, with the British in close pursuit, slaughtering as they could for the butchery they had been given.

It had ended. David had faced Goliath and acquitted himself well; now David ran before the wounded Goliath's fury.

And history veered into a long and bitter pathway.

Nicole buried her face in her arms and sobbed.

32

THROUGHOUT THE LONG sweltering night, loyalists and patriots alike stared from their windows and stood in their doorways as coaches and wheelbarrows transported the dead and wounded from the waterfront to a makeshift hospital set up in the Manufacturing House, a large abandoned factory. The Manufacturing House overflowed before midnight, and General Gage commandeered warehouses and empty barracks to accommodate the continuing deluge of wounded and dying.

Returning the wounded became an exhausting and seemingly endless task, which would continue throughout the night and far into the next morning. The British had sustained more than a thousand casualties, and no transportation existed but the rowboats, clumsy and time-consuming to maneuver and severely limited in space. Once docked, the suffering wounded were stacked into wheelbarrows like crumpled lengths of cordwood and jolted over cobblestone lanes toward the nearest temporary hospital. If they survived the boats and the wheelbarrow ride, the injured were then forced to endure an often fatal delay as frantic doctors dashed along the lines judging which cases might wait and which could not. Men who had survived the battle on Breed's Hill died in the streets of Boston.

Stunned at the extent of the devastation, Nicole and Pavla sat on a porch step and watched the bloody procession file past the Duchard house. Someone had planted torches along the street, and war's appalling residue rolled beneath a ghastly leaping hiss. Nicole leaned her forehead against the banister, watching as a young British officer staggered toward the gate. His uniform was tattered and bloody; tears streamed down his face. He stretched a hand toward the women on the porch. "These brave men need water and bandages. I beg you ... have mercy on us."

Nicole's heart wrenched. Loyalists or patriots, they shed the same red blood. The suffering procession slowly creaking through the streets had no politics. But the sights and sounds limping past the flickering torches brought home, as nothing else could, the meaning and the terrible cost of this day.

She rose silently and tied up her skirts. While Pavla ripped bed linen into strips, Nicole hurried between the house and the street, carrying pitchers of cold well water to the tide of mutilated, broken, stretcher-borne men. After a time her apron reddened and her mind numbed to the horrors of suffering. She raised bloodied heads to cups of water, pressed squares of cloth to gaping holes, and she watched dying men move on and others appear in their places.

The line stalled after midnight; hospitals filled to capacity. Doctors ran along the torchlit streets commandeering private homes and stables.

A harried middle-aged man climbed to the Duchard porch with a heavy step. Before he pushed through the door, he waved the nearest row of wheelbarrows into the yard.

"I'm Dr. Shaw," he announced wearily. His coat and vest were soaked and clotted. "Forgive me, ladies, but we need your house." A shaking hand passed over his eyes; then he shouted to a man wearing a soiled bandage twisted above one knee. "Put them upstairs first."

Nicole and Pavla pressed well away from the path of activity as a platoon of men rapidly cleared the house. They hurled Marie's furniture into the backyard, then laid the injured end to end on the wooden floors. Upstairs, three men occupied each mattress. The house quickly soured with the smells and liquids and whimpers of dying men.

On and on they came, straining the perimeters of the walls, exhausting the capabilities of the medical aides. Those who were ambulatory stood or slumped against bare walls; those who could not stand covered the floors of every room.

Dr. Shaw shouted, "I need help here!"

"Me?" Nicole's hand flew to her breast, and her eyes widened in shocked rejection. But there was no one else—every aide was frantically occupied. She blinked dizzily at the pulsing artery clamped between Dr. Shaw's fingers.

"Hold this shut!" His arm flashed, and Nicole jerked to the floor. Her shaking hand pinched the wet ends as Shaw's fingers plunged deeply into a meaty hole. He dug out a jagged piece of glass and a twisted nail. "Christ! Holy bloody Christ!" Tears choked his fury. "Barbarians! Look at this!" He stared at the nail and the tooth of glass; then he hurled them violently against the wall. Lunging forward, he pressed his ear against the soldier's chest, then rocked back on his heels and stared unseeing into Nicole's chalky horror. "A ball . . . I might have saved him if it had been a ball. But glass and nails?" A string of strangled curses issued from white lips. Angrily he waved her aside and bent to the next man.

Gagging, Nicole staggered through narrow lanes of bodies in a headlong flight toward the kitchen. She discovered a tall crock near the buttery door and ladled a swallow of water, rinsing her mouth and hands. A continual film of moisture blurred her vision. What glass and nails did to a man's flesh was an atrocity she would carry into eternity.

But she rejected the image of the Yankees as barbarians. The broken glass and rusted nails evinced a desperation beyond rational comprehension. Helpless men lacking ammunition had fired whatever lay at hand rather than surrender. When their supplies were gone they had faced the awesome British artillery with glass and stones and nails. Her heart ached for their courage and bleak determination. But oh, Lord, the terrible unthinkable destruction and mutilation!

Moaning softly, Nicole pressed her forehead into her palm, unconsciously imprinting a red smear across her brow. Did Yankee homes along the Cambridge Road witness this same charnel scene? And did her love, her heart, lie quiet and bloodied upon a Yankee woman's floor? Her palm clenched into a helpless fist and her teeth ground audibly. Feeling faint, she splashed her face, then filled a fresh pitcher. And she averted her eyes as she walked past a growing mound of amputated limbs. Slowly she worked through the parlor, stepping cautiously around legs and slippery pools.

"Mary? Is it you, Mary?" the man at her feet whispered around a gaping throat wound. His voice bubbled.

"Yes," Nicole choked. "It's Mary." Kneeling beside him, she wet her fingers and gently patted driblets of moisture over his lips.

He took her hand. "Tell the boys . . ." A pink foam gurgled in his throat. "Tell the boys their dad fought well and died bravely."

She blinked fiercely at a watery curtain.

"Mary . . ." His head sagged and his hand fell away from hers. Blank eyes stared into nothing.

"Oh, dear God!" Candles placed at intervals on the floor threw nightmare shadows up the walls; a sweet-and-sour stench pinched her nostrils. She stared at Mary's dead husband and his features dissolved into another dead face and then into another. They flickered into an endless procession of dying men marching solemnly through the caverns of her mind. Nicole rubbed damp palms against her apron. More than anything in this world she craved the reassuring presence of a whole person, someone not groaning or dying or slick with blood. "Pavla! Pavla, where are you?"

"Don't shout!" Dr. Shaw admonished. He cleaned a crimson slash with a blood-soaked sponge before packing the wound with lint, then covering it with a poultice mixed of bread and milk and oil. "If you're searching for the girl with bad English . . . she left."

"She left?" Nicole repeated blankly. She watched as he lifted another man's bloodied head to a heavy jug of rum. The man swallowed greedily, his eyes wild and hot.

The doctor didn't glance upward, but his voice was sympathetic. "We're all tired." He tested a boring instrument, then clamped the soldier's head between his knees. "Easy does it, son." He remembered Nicole when he heard her sharp intake of breath. "The girl said she was leaving to find . . . I don't recall . . . someone. She begged you to accompany her." He studied the head wound and positioned the boring instrument. He would remove a piece of skull to relieve undue pressure on the brain. "You said you would follow later when the work was done. You said something about God's will and harvesting what is sown."

The soldier screamed, and Nicole stumbled away.

She remembered Pavla's departure as a gauzy dream from long ago. Vaguely she recalled Pavla embracing her and begging her to leave also. Then Pavla had vanished.

"Yes, thank you. I believe I do remember," she said politely. No one was listening.

Responding to a whispered plea, she knelt and raised a young man's head toward the water cup. And blinked about her with an expression of surprise, as if slowly awakening from a long and terrible nightmare. How many hours had she been winding bandages and lifting wounded heads? Wandering in a daze of shock and horror? She had no idea.

"Are you an angel?" the young man whispered. Both eyes were swathed in strips of bed linen. A trickle of clear fluid ran from beneath the bandages. One arm was missing below the elbow. Nicole was glad he couldn't see the hill of severed limbs. "Who are you?"

"I . . ." She stared into his blind face. Who was she? I'm . . ."

But she didn't know. She was a displaced person. A patriot in the loyalist camp. A wife without a husband, a mother without a child. She was a body without a heart, flesh without spirit. A rainbow gone mad, the colors twisting and knotting and bleeding together.

As she struggled to frame an answer, a shadow blotted the candlelight softening the young man's suffering. But when she lifted her head, the beginnings of irritation vanished and the sharp words died on her lips.

"William!"

It was not the William she knew. Hollow eyes stared from a face streaked by sweat and smoke. A bootlace tied back his hair. His jacket and shoulder strap were missing, as was the tip of his stained sword. Blood matted a strand of hair to his forehead; a black crust glued his shirt to his ribs. The satin breeches were grass-stained and blood-spattered.

"How badly . . . ?"

But he seemed unaware of his wounds. He blinked at her and his gaze coiled inward, staring into unspeakable scenes. "Fifty percent," he whispered. "We lost fifty percent of the men we fielded." Deadened eyes scanned the rows of wounded. "Half the officers . . . they fired at the officers first . . . and half the regulars . . . the grenadiers were decimated . . .

436

and the Royal Welch Fusiliers, they..." Red-rimmed eyes blinked rapidly and tears welled over his lashes. He choked. "Some of the men tried to desert, and Howe hung them on the field ... You couldn't advance more than three or four paces without stepping on a hand or a foot ... and the blood. Oh, God, the blood and the smoke and the screams! ... I saw a man's arm in the grass ... with the fingers still clutched around his musket! I ..."

Nicole's face paled. "Shhh." She grasped his arm and guided him outside into the hot night air and away from the smells and sounds. She pushed him onto the porch step and examined his wounds in the shadowy flare of the torches. Miraculously, neither were serious, not judged by what lay behind her in the house.

"We marched up that God-cursed hill again and again ... and ... and they slaughtered us ... ignorant farmers butchered the finest army in history. ... I tell you, they fought like devils, like demons loosed from the bowels of hell!" Bewildered eyes fastened on the line of creaking wheelbarrows passing in the street. The torches illuminated legs dangling from coach doors, staggering stretcher-bearers, weaving men half-carrying others worse off than themselves. "It was impossible ... it couldn't have happened ... but everything went wrong! The ships couldn't move in close enough to be of use ... the bloody cannonballs didn't fit the cannons ... and no one knew the terrain." Stunned eyes blinked his bafflement. "We didn't know the goddamned terrain! No one had bothered to map it or even to walk over it! The cannon sank in swamp bogs, there were stone fences hidden in the hayfields ... and we didn't know! It went on and on and on, endlessly ... and I saw ... I saw them fall and die! And I heard their screams! Sweet Jesus, I will always hear the screams!" He buried his face in his hands as Nicole sank silently to the step.

She waited until he quieted, until his dulled eyes stared at the parade of casualties with a semblance of calm. Then she drew a deep breath.

"I'm sorry, William. For both sides. No one wanted it to end this way." They listened to pleas for water and aid, to the dirge of iron wheels rattling over puddled cobblestones. "I have to leave—you understand that, don't you? I don't belong here—I never have."

A harsh sound bubbled in his throat. "I knew it was you all along. I knew you were a spy!"

Her breath hitched and caught. She stared at him.

His lip curled. "Did you believe me so stupid that I didn't guess? I always knew!" One hand pressed the dried crust above his ribs; the other violently indicated the suffering line limping past the torches. "You caused that. Yes, you! If you hadn't fed them information, today couldn't have happened! We would have gained the element of surprise. We would have marched through Dorchester and Roxbury with minimal resistance! The colonists would have crumpled . . ." His voice quivered. "Without all this! Look well at the blood and severed joints, but don't speak to me of leaving! Your duty is here, atoning for the hell you helped cause!"

Nicole stared at his balled fists and her face blanched to a snowy white. Her self control contradicted the emotion quickening her breast. "No, William, I'm not to blame. You don't understand even yet, do you? This was inevitable. You might have surprised the men in Roxbury, but they wouldn't have surrendered without opposition. Every inch of ground would have been yielded in blood! Roxbury . . . Charlestown . . . it's the same, don't you see? Can you think of today and still misunderstand the commitment involved? We're fighting for principles, for liberty and the right to live without coercion and . . ." She bit off the next words as his face congested with fury.

Wearily she pulled to her feet and stared down at him. "Good-bye, William." A tide of emotion flooded her breast, but she did not give it voice. She didn't speak of freedom or native soil or the love of democratic process. And she didn't admit that she finally had begun to glimpse Nicole Denisovna. And Nicole Denisovna did not belong in Boston tonight. She belonged with the scattered pieces of her heart and flesh and spirit.

"Go, then," he screamed. "Get out of my sight, whore! Run to your bastard husband if he's alive! Run, swim, crawl on your bloody knees, for all I care! I'm sick of your deceit! What do you think will happen to my career when Gage or Howe realizes there must have been a leak in security? And they will. And they'll track the leak to this house. I'm ruined because of you!" His head dropped toward his breeches, his hands dangled between his thighs. She heard his teeth grinding. "If you stay in Boston, you'll hang as a spy! So go . . . go before I kill you myself!"

Without a word she spun down the steps, her skirts flaring

behind her. She paused briefly at the gate and allowed herself one final glance for the house in which she had grown to womanhood. Then she lowered her head and dashed along the torchlit streets, moving against the line of coaches and wheelbarrows, following them to the source.

It was the most difficult journey of her life. Croaking whispers called out to her, bloody hands implored. "Water, miss! I beg you . . . a taste of water!" "Have you seen Martha Brady? Have you seen my Martha?"

She swallowed the thickness in her throat and ducked her head, dodging grasping fingers. Their cries would twist through her heart all of her days. And she murmured a grateful prayer for the women dashing from their homes with water pitchers and bandages. Others ran along the torchlit lines peering into torn faces and wailing. "Did you see Johnny Marble on the hill? Was he alive?" "My son, Robert Porter—he was with the Fourth Infantry. Have you seen him?" "Billy Able, my husband, he left with the first wave. Mister, have you . . . ?"

Sometimes the women found the men they sought. And then their screams ripped across the soul.

Shaking, Nicole paused in the shadows near the wharf and leaned her hands upon her knees, drawing deep gulping breaths in an effort to collect herself. A stream of rowboats brushed orange by the flames of burning Charlestown rowed back and forth between Boston and the peninsula. Exhausted men pulled the wounded from the boats and loaded them into wheelbarrows and stretchers; then the empty boats shoved from the dock and returned across the harbor for more. It was an endless nightmare, a ghastly scene of blood and carnage and leaping torchlight.

Nicole lowered her fists from her mouth and reached deep inside. She would not wait for Dimitri or Vadim or Louis to come for her. She accepted the responsibility for her own escape. And there would be no better opportunity than amid tonight's confusion. Slowly her head lifted and she brushed tangled strings toward the bun at her neck. She smoothed her bloodied apron and squared her shoulders; then she stepped firmly onto the wharf. She spoke to no one; she did not glance at the rows of moaning wounded. She was going home. Wherever Dimitri and Vaddie were, that was home. She walked straight to the first rowboat and waited silently as the last injured man was unloaded.

Then she lifted her skirts and jumped. She landed in the rowboat on her knees, and a line of oarsmen eyed her with weary curiosity. The rowing master stared down the length of the boat. "What do you think you're doing, lady? You can't go over there!"

"I have to find my husband," Nicole explained quietly. "I have to." She lifted herself onto a cracked board across the stern and folded her hands into her lap. A coil of rope hissed over her head and dropped into the slosh of blood and water at her feet. They drifted slowly from the dock.

The rowing master shrugged. "Pull!" he shouted.

A dark form flew over her shoulder and thudded into the first row of oarsmen. Nicole gasped and clutched the side boards as a sheet of water rushed upward before the violently rocking boat righted itself. The rowing master cursed and screamed.

And Nicole's composure cracked. "William!" Her wild eyes swung toward the dock, and she half-rose. But several yards of black river had opened between the boat and the wharf.

William balanced in the stern. "Turn this boat around!" The burning town flicked orange fingers across his rage, flashed from the blade he waved at the rowing master.

"Good Christ Almighty! Excuse me, ma'am." The rowing master shoved to his feet in the prow. He glared at William, then shouted to his men. "Pull, you whoresons! Excuse me, ma'am. This boat don't put about just because some idiot bastard says so! Excuse me, ma'am."

William shrieked. "I am Major William Caldwell, assigned to General Howe, and I command you to turn about this instant!" His sword threatened the first line of oarsmen as the strip of dark water widened. The men grunted. They bent as one and stroked, concentrating on the mechanical rhythms of labor.

"I don't give a rat's ass—excuse me, ma'am—if you're General Howe hisself!" The rowing master lifted a musket and leveled it at William's stomach. "There's wounded over there, and we, by God, are going after them—no stupid bloody delay is going to cost some brave man his life!"

William's teeth gnashed and he brandished the sword. "This harlot is a spy, you ignorant son of a dockside whore! You'll swing from the gallows for refusing a direct command!"

The rowing master spread his legs and raised the musket to

eye level, squinting down the barrel. "I don't see no major's jacket, and if that lady is a spy . . ." One eye flicked over Nicole's bloodied apron, slid across hair burnished coppery gold by the firelight. "Then I'm a cow's tit. Excuse me, ma'am." His finger tightened around the trigger. "You got two seconds to sit down and shut up."

William yanked at the gold officer's gorget hanging around his neck. "You stupid bastard, can't you recognize an officer when you see one?"

"Sit down!"

"You'll swing for this!" Seething with frustration, William sat hard. "What's your name, soldier?" He spat the words from rigid lips.

The rowing master grinned and nudged the man nearest him. "Name's John Smith, of the Royal Marines." Someone chuckled. "Got that, General? John Smith. Now, row, you sons of bitches, row! Excuse me, ma'am."

Nicole pressed her lips into a hard line and blinked down at her clasped hands. The word "spy" clotted in her throat. An image unfolded behind her eyes—a mob screamed down on her, waving coils of rope. She swallowed a dark taste. No, it was almost over. Safety lay with the dawn. She could walk the length of the Charlestown peninsula and find the Cambridge Road by sunrise.

The heat of the flaming town warmed her cheeks and filled her ears with a hellish crackling as they pulled nearer the peninsula. An acrid haze blotted the stars and stung her nostrils. A smoke ceiling diffused the glow of flames and cast an orange blanket over the waters and up the trampled hillsides. A wide jumping halo radiated outward, within which she could see tired men combing the hayfields for concealed bodies.

"It's over, William. Let it go." She spoke in a weary expressionless whisper as the shoreline approached. Exhaustion settled across her bowed shoulders, and she desperately wished she could open her eyes and discover it was suddenly tomorrow.

He fumbled for her hands. "Forget what I said about being a spy. I swear, Nicole, I'm half out of my mind. Listen to me . . ." He licked his lips and swallowed. "I have some money—we'll go west. Start over. Or we could go to Europe. Would you like that? Europe?" His grip mashed her fingers together as he groaned. "I can't give you up! I can't! If I can't have you, then no one can! I swear to you, Nicole, if you refuse me, I'll see you hang as a spy, I mean it. I'd rather see you dead than lose you to another man!"

She pulled her hands away with difficulty and stared at him, a long stare of repugnance and pity. "There's a sickness in you, a terrible obsessive sickness."

Flames reflected in the bottom of his eyes. "I love you—that's the sickness!"

She examined the fiery reflection with horrified fascination. "Even now . . ." She read the truth and shrank from it. "Even knowing what I did, even knowing that I love Dimitri, you would . . ."

Brutal fingers crushed into her shoulders, and his face frightened her. "Just give me a chance! You could learn to love me if you tried! You never tried." He shook her. "Are you listening? I'm willing to give up my *career* for you!" The rejection in her face shot a livid color across his cheeks.

Had the rowing master not growled and raised his musket, Nicole believed William would have struck her. She rubbed her shoulders and steadfastly refused to glance at him again.

The instant the boat bumped the shoreline, she gathered her skirts and dropped over the side. Dirty water filled her shoes and dragged at her hem. A few weary soldiers watched with disinterested smoke-rimmed eyes as she waded onto the beach and stepped carefully through the rows of wounded awaiting transportation.

No one questioned her presence or attempted to halt her progress toward the hayfields waving in a hot, smoky night breeze.

"Halt!" William shouted. "I command you to halt!" He stumbled after her, shaking water from his boots, holding his rib cage. "I charge you with aiding and abetting the enemy! I charge you as a spy!"

Nicole did not slow her step or indulge a backward glance. Traveling the waterside road would have provided a quicker route to the Charlestown neck, but she chose to walk directly over the hills of battle. A chill kernel wound into her heart. If Dimitri had died, he had died here, on Breed's Hill or on Bunker's Hill. And if he lived, he had taken his stand on this ground—and she would not skirt hallowed soil. One day she would tell her son that she too had stood upon the site of glory, and she too had spit defiance at the British.

"Stop! You are under arrest!"

She heard the whistle of William's sword slicing the air inches from her spine. But she did not turn. She lifted her wet hem and entered the hayfields, watching the stalks bow before her in the strange orange glow. The crackling fire and the moans of suffering receded behind her. But it was not a hell of her making. William was wrong. The British bore equal responsibility for the patriots' victory. Yes, victory. The patriots had ceded their ground, but they had done so with ferocious valor. They had shown the world what determined men could accomplish in the face of deplorable odds. Nicole had read the shock and disbelief in the eyes of the returning British. She had seen to whom the victory belonged. The British had won the peninsula, but they had lost the battle. And they knew it.

"I command you to halt this instant!" Hysteria thinned William's shout. He plunged through the hayfields, furiously swinging his sword at the grassy stalks, holding his rib cage and gasping.

A man sitting on a rock fence staring at nothing roused himself and shifted to one side as Nicole silently pulled herself over the stones and dropped into the shadows on the far side. He eyed William curiously as William followed, his sword ringing against the piled rocks.

"She's a spy," William cried. "Are you going to sit there like a goddamned statue and allow her to escape?"

The man didn't move. "I'm through fighting for today, gov'nor." He swiveled a matted head to watch Nicole advance steadily upon the redoubt. "You'll have to capture that dangerous spy all on your own." He chuckled and shook his head, anticipating the story he would tell his mates.

Nicole paused and caught her breath at the base of the ruined redoubt. Bits of dried grass clung to her skirts and apron hem; her wet shoes squeaked around torn stockings. She peered at the gouges in the face of the redoubt, and her heart wept. A broken bayonet gleamed in the grass at her feet, and dark stains streaked the lip of the earthworks. Bright flickering shadows danced across the outer walls; an ebony silence lay within.

She pressed both palms flat to the fire-warmed wall and closed her eyes, opening herself to the spirit of this site. Explosions of gunfire echoed in her mind. And with all her heart she wished every American could stand in her shoes tonight and pay homage to this battered wall.

It was the beginning; the symbol of liberty and freedom. It mattered not if history forgot the names of those who had battled here today—history would record in iron the principles these men had fought and died for.

"Nicole, I mean it!" William puffed up behind her. "I'd sooner see you dead than watch you take another step!" He spun her from the wall, and madness glittered from his eyes.

It was so petty; so dreadfully small and petty that she couldn't grasp his intent. An event transcending individuality had occurred here, an event which would live in men's hearts long after she and William were laid in their graves. Without a word she shoved past him and walked toward the yawning black entrance. She had to view it all; she had to see where they had crouched and waited.

Her step faltered at the entrance. Flickering orange illuminated the grass and walls, but a deep ebony void opened before her. She hallucinated the quiet sound of breathing, imagined her name whispered within. She was so tired.

William seized upon her hesitation. In two quick strides he stood before her, his face a mask of torment. "I loved you," he whispered. The crack of his fist sent her reeling backward. Her hem caught on a jagged stone, and she threw out her hands to break her fall.

A sob strangled his voice as he stood over her, straddling her sprawled body. The sword quivered in his grip, and he stared down at her. "Oh, God, I loved you so!"

Time halted. Shadows moved, odd rustlings sounded within her ears, but they did so within a strange panorama of slow motion. An odd calm stilled the tremble along her lips and limbs. She marveled at her lack of fear. There were regrets, yes—no one died without regrets. She would not watch her son grow to manhood; she would not run into her husband's arms.

Her eyes swept from William's tortured gaze toward the tranquil dark ribbon of water below. If she must die, then she had chosen her place. Here, among the ghosts of brave men, looking out upon the land she loved and whispering the name of the man she adored.

"I can't give you up to him! I'll see you dead first!" William's sword shook, and a twist jerked across his pale lips. "God forgive me," he choked. The blade whistled upward.

And struck a steely barrier as a second flash swung from the mouth of the redoubt.

"Drop it, Caldwell."

A swell of muscle tensed against the blade, holding it taut as a tall hard man stepped from the redoubt and into the flickering orange half-light. A faint ridge of scar began at his brow, dipped toward his eye, then faded in the direction of a knotted jaw.

"Stand away from my wife!"

33

DRAWN BY THE promise of fresh battle, patrolling soldiers and a half-dozen ambulatory wounded ascended the hill and gathered curiously in the brush near the mouth of the redoubt. They watched as Denisov and Caldwell circled cautiously. Swords and style were gauged, hard stares measured.

"Six shillings on the Yankee."

"Why not? They whipped our asses earlier!"

"A pound on the British officer! You got to believe, boys, even in an officer."

The soldiers thumbed back their hats and leaned on their muskets, and weary smoke-greased faces relaxed in anticipation of the unexpected entertainment.

Nicole flattened her palms against the wall of the redoubt. And her wide joyful eyes fastened upon Dimitri's granite challenge. Her heart pounded as she traced in actuality the sculptured profile she had caressed in a thousand dreams. He was alive! A wave of dizziness swept her senses. He was wounded, but he was alive!

The sleeve of a dusty white shirt had been cut away to apply a swath of bandages binding his left shoulder. His leather breeches were ripped and bloodied along the line of a bayonet slash crossing his upper thigh. His clothing was as torn and blood-spattered as William's. But he was alive!

While her pulse pounded like thunder in her ears, she stared at the ridge of scar tissue tracking from brow to jawline. And she longed to kiss away the old hurts and pains. As he circled in and out of weaving orange shadows, she gazed into the molten silver stare he riveted upon Caldwell, and a shiver chased through her flesh. He was the most powerfully handsome man she had ever seen. Her husband. Her heart.

The words whispered into an arid canyon as her body tensed and her muscles knotted into stone. She strained toward the two men, who judged light feints and parries as they circled a patch of hard-trodden earth. Testing. Preparing. A coil of anxiety exploded in the pit of Nicole's stomach and surged upward in black spirals.

She cried out as Caldwell lunged, his lips snarling back from his teeth.

And she released a quick agonized breath as Dimitri easily deflected the thrust. His lunge to one side opened a dark smear along his thigh wound. He grinned, and the tip of his sword swiveled in tight challenging arcs. He gestured with his left hand, urging Caldwell to try again. "Is that the best a British officer can manage, Caldwell? No wonder you lost today."

William pressed a hand to the fresh blood leaking over the crust sealing his rib wound. "We didn't lose! You ran like dogs with your tails between your legs!" Both men panted, their exertion severely testing exhausted bodies. "We won!" He sidestepped and clumsily parried Dimitri's sudden flashing thrust. The swords locked and scraped upward, holding.

Dimitri smiled. A ripple bulged across his shoulders. "You won? And how many men did it cost?" The swords quivered and strained beneath the pressure of combined weight. Flickering orange illuminated the hatred blazing from leveled stares. "The Yankees suffered a hundred forty dead and less than three hundred wounded," Dimitri offered softly. His silver glance flashed toward the steady stream of rowboats traversing the river. "One of your own generals is reputed to have claimed the British army could not survive many more victories such as this one."

"That's a lie!" William hissed. Beads of sweat glistened in the darting glimmer of distant flames. He leaped backward and swung; the ring of clashing steel sang out between them. "Our total casualties are less than three hundred."

The watching soldiers shifted and glanced at one another. One man spit into the brush and wiped his hand across his mouth. "Hell, we got more than that still waiting to be transported! And the oarsmen been at it since suppertime!"

"You know better than to believe an officer, boys. An officer lies when the truth is better! Make that ten shillings on the Yankee!"

Dimitri grinned and his blade hissed up the length of Caldwell's sword, toying with it; then his arm whistled upward and down, and Caldwell diverted his savage thrust by the narrowest of margins. They paused, filling their lungs with breath, and they stared hard as an invisible signal passed between them.

The period of conversation and testing had concluded. Now the contest began in earnest. Furrows of concentration creased smoky brows and tensed along jawlines and thigh muscles. Arms swung and plunged in blurred strokes, blades flashed firelight and clashed heavily before springing apart to hiss downward once more. Rivulets of sweat streaked their faces, wet circles widened beneath their arms and sprouted upon their backs.

Nicole could not bear to watch, nor could she bear to look away. Her fists pressed against ashen cheeks, and she slipped silently to the ground, leaning against the redoubt wall. A storm of labored breathing roared past her ears; her fear and anxiety flamed into a curtain of denial; she shook her head violently. The duel was insanity. Enough fighting and killing had occurred on this soil! She had never wished William dead; she had wished herself free. Free to leave Boston; free to choose her husband. Was the price of freedom written in blood? She stared at them through shaking fingers, two wounded men gasping and bleeding. Both appeared near collapse.

"Stop," she whispered. "Please stop!"

But they fought for deeply rooted opposing principles. And they fought for a woman's love. Neither would cede. Honor demanded total victory—death.

Holding his ribs and gasping, Caldwell lunged, off balance, and his blade slashed through emptiness, passing well to Denisov's side. Staggering, he turned to meet Denisov's stumbling rush. Denisov's arm shook with fatigue as the blades clashed and locked; his left arm dangled, blood dripped toward his wrist. Muscles quivered, lungs strained.

"All bets are off, boys. Them two are going to fight until they both die of exhaustion. Won't be no winner."

Nicole dashed tears of agreement from her eyes. But the speaker misjudged.

Caldwell jumped backward and then thrust forward, the broken tip of his blade leveled at Denisov's rib cage. Denisov's sword whistled in a flashing arc, met steel, and appeared to curl along the British blade. His eyes glittered and Denisov drew a breath, his chest expanding. In a powerful surge of hidden strength, Denisov's wrist flicked and Caldwell's sword ripped from his fingers. The blade spun in a pinwheel of light before crashing into the thick brush. Instantly the tip of Denisov's sword scratched beneath Caldwell's chin and held. A line of pink opened above Caldwell's collar as both men fought for breath, their chests heaving.

"Kill him!" William screamed, urging the spectators to action. He sucked air into his lungs and raged into Dimitri's panting grin. "I order you to kill them both!" The strangled command grated across the night. Bits of ash sifted from the orange-gray sky. "Kill them! They're both patriot spies!"

"That true, mister?"

Dimitri became aware of the spectators for the first time. A silvery stare swept the ring of onlookers. "I'm no spy, gentlemen, but I'm proud to be a patriot and proud to have fought on this soil!"

They regarded him soberly. It was a brave statement. Denisov stood on British ground, surrounded by British muskets. A grudging look of respect stole into their stares.

"I've come to take my wife home. I'm going to kill this scum, and then we'll leave. If any of you gentlemen object . . . line up by the redoubt and I'll fight you next!"

Nicole gasped and her hands flew to white lips. He stood wide-legged, swaying with fatigue. Blood streamed steadily from his wounded shoulder and dripped down his thigh. She stared at the defiance gleaming from his smoky eyes, at the determination knotting his jaw, and she knew he would fight them one by one until he dropped.

The soldiers examined him thoughtfully. Though exhaustion sagged in his stance and smoke-grimed face, his challenge had been delivered with the resonance and resolve of a man in prime condition. The soldiers shifted. One man spit. Another examined the bore of his musket.

"Hell, I don't want to fight no half-dead patriot. No honor in that."

William shrieked, "Didn't you hear my command? Are you going to stand by and allow this traitor to kill a British officer?" Madness darkened his flame-lit eyes; his hands opened and clenched. And hatred blazed above the blade pressing steadily against his throat. "You heard him admit he's a patriot—I order you to kill him! Kill them both!"

"Well, now, sir, I don't exactly see how we can do that. This here Yankee acquitted hisself with honor. He beat you fair. Don't seem right for a man to win fair and square and then have to fight off a gang of the loser's men in order to walk away clean." He hawked a glob of spittle into the brush. "No, sir. And it don't seem right for a British officer to dishonor hisself by suggesting it."

William's face purpled. "I'm not asking your bloody opinion! I'm giving you a direct order!"

"Seems like it won't be no loss to see the end of an officer what don't know the meaning of a fair and honorable fight. And one what orders decent men to kill a woman! Now, that don't seem right. It just isn't British!"

Another man lifted a thumb and settled his hat. He used his musket as a crutch to support an injured leg, leaning on it as he turned down the hillside. "It's been a long day, and this mother's son has had enough of fighting and killing."

"Me too. If you want him killed, sir, you kill him." Another man descended into the orange shadows wafting over the hayfields. And then another. Long black images stretched behind them.

"The boys are right. It's a sorry day for England when valor is rewarded with foul play." The last man snapped his musket to his chest in a stiff military salute. "I don't agree with one single patriot idea, mister, and if I see you in the next battle I am going to try my damnedest to kill you. But I salute your courage in coming here, and I personally guarantee safe passage off this peninsula for you and your lady." He nodded crisply to Nicole. "A fair fight is a fair fight. And I don't want no patriot saying the British don't honor a fair fight." He coughed into his hand. "I'll take a little stroll down the hillside a ways while you finish your business here, then I'll escort you to the neck."

Caldwell's mouth dropped. His eyes bulged. And then his shoulders slumped in the stunned acceptance of defeat. He watched the men melting into the hayfields.

When only three shadows remained in the clearing, Dimitri's silvery eyes blazed like liquid steel. "I am going to enjoy this, Caldwell. I've imagined it a hundred times!" The ridge of scar tightened and turned white.

"Dimitri!" Nicole's heart skipped and plunged.

As William had observed the soldiers turn their backs in contempt and then depart, a bewilderment of defeat and abandonment had swept his expression. For a brief instant his gaze had brushed Nicole's pale face, and she had read the agony of his humiliation. The arrogance and confidence had forever vanished from the slump of his shoulders. His will to live had curled into ash as dark and fragile as the smoky wisps drifting aimlessly in the night air. This day and this night had seen the destruction of all William Caldwell valued in life, including his self-respect.

An empty shell blinked before her; William's spirit had spun into the darkness along with his sword.

Dimitri's blade quivered as William's hollow gaze swung upward.

Major William Caldwell was dead. He had forfeited honor and career; he had been defeated by the man his woman preferred. If by a miracle he survived the sword thrust, it would be the greatest misery of his life, fate's cruelest jest.

William roused himself at Dimitri's hesitation. "You won your kill, now do it! Grant me the honor of a quick death." He stared at a point in space. "At least let me show her I can die well!"

Dear God. Nicole ground her forehead against the baked earth of the redoubt. It still mattered to him what she thought. A blackness of pity drained the blood from her face, and she felt weak and sick.

Dimitri's scrutiny stretched toward a silvery eternity. Then he said evenly, clearly, "In my eyes you possess no honor or dignity. I owe you no courtesy." A vitality of life and challenge blazed in his stare. In the strange orange half-light, the twisting scar imparted a satanic hardness to his fury. "Were it my decision alone, your death would be slow and unpleasant. But it is my wife you dishonored—the decision will be hers."

Nicole's heart crashed against her ribs.

"Speak, my love . . . does he die with honor? Or with none? *Da* or *nyet?*"

Thunder boomed through her head, and her fists rose to her breast as she pushed from the wall. She inhaled deeply, believing they were doomed to repeat the endless past. Swallowing hard, she stared into William's empty eyes.

If William survived, he would immediately demand a position in the first assault wave of the next battle. She knew this as absolutely as she knew the love swelling her breast as she swung her gaze to her husband's taut control. From this moment, William Caldwell would pursue death with the passion of a denied lover.

"There has been enough killing," she whispered. William would find his death, but it would not come at her command.

William sagged, and his face caved in upon itself. A shine of moisture filmed his eyes. He'd been rescued by a woman's pity—it was the ultimate debasement, mortifying ignominy no man of honor could accept. "Don't listen to her," he choked.

The muscles jumped along Dimitri's shoulders and thighs. Knots hardened along his jaw. He adjusted the sword in his fist, and he shook with the intensity of craving.

The blade trembled, dug a droplet of blood from William's flesh—then slowly fell away. Dimitri stepped back, his jaw working. He stared at William, and his lip curled. Then he flung his sword spinning toward the tall grass.

"You live because she asks it. If ever I see you again, you're a dead man."

The man with the musket popped his head above the rise and glanced at William. His mouth twisted, and he spit. "Are you ready, sir?"

Both Dimitri and William responded, and when the man's steady gaze indicated he addressed Dimitri, William choked and covered his face.

"In one moment. First . . ." Dimitri Denisov raised his head and looked at his wife. In three strides he crossed the clearing and stood before her, staring down into her shining wet eyes. His hand lifted and he stroked one soft cheek as if confirming a thousand memories. Gently, very gently, he drew her into his arms, and his warm lips brushed hers with the quiet tenderness of a deep and profound emotion. He held her slightly away to better observe her face, and he touched the joyful tears streaming past her lashes. Then he enfolded her roughly into his arms and pressed her head to his shoulder, holding her tightly, almost painfully, as if unable to believe the reality of her small frame. His eyes closed and he groaned her name, and the warm pressure of his fierce embrace told her he would never let her go.

And she fitted the curves and hollows of his body as if they had been fashioned solely one for the other. They clung together without the urgency of passion but with the deep tenderness of commitment and promise. And in that magic moment Nicole understood they would never outlive their need for each other. Youth would fade and the fire of passion might one day dim, but their union of spirit would endure. For theirs was a passion of kindred souls, a passion which delighted in physical blending but which was rooted firmly in the spiritual soil of love and caring.

Her fingers traced the ridge of scar before dropping to the firm outline of his wide warm mouth and then to the open collar of his shirt. She closed her lashes as her fingertips remembered the texture and warmth of his skin. "I love you," she whispered. He was dirty, smoke-stained, blood-spattered, exhausted. And he was the most splendid man she had ever known. "I love you."

They heard the sudden rush of a figure crashing through the fields, and they turned to watch William stumbling down the hillside toward the dying flames of Charlestown. A knot of men leaned on their muskets and eyed William's wild and reckless descent. Someone muttered from the side of a grin, and they all laughed. William veered toward the shoreline, his head down.

"It would have been kinder if he'd died, my love. You did him no favor by sparing his life." Dimitri watched as she tore her apron into strips and bound his shoulder. "Men will discuss the battle of Breed's Hill long after those young soldiers are grandfathers. What happened tonight will find its way into a hundred barracks." A smoky thoughtfulness studied William's flight. "He'll be labeled a coward and a laughingstock. A figure of ridicule. A man lacking honor and self-respect."

Nicole knotted the apron strips and examined her handiwork. She did not dispute Dimitri's judgment. Neither did she regret sparing William's life or the consequences which would follow. Her earlier pity had diminished as she recognized each person's responsibility for his own life situation. As Vadim had once stated, we all inhabit cages of our own making. She suspected William's cage was small, suffocating, and thickly barred. But he had chosen it; not she, not Dimitri, and not the men cupping their hands and hooting.

"Yes," she agreed softly. "But only for a short while."

Dimitri nodded. He too had read the eulogy in William's eyes. Strong rugged planes curved into a gentle smile. He extended his arm. "We have a long walk ahead of us. Are you ready, Princess?"

She returned his smile as her arm laced around his. With her hair flying about her cheeks, her torn and bloodied apron, her wet shoes catching on a dragging hem, she had never felt less the princess. "*Da*, my prince." Her gaze lingered on the promise of his lips. "I recall mention of a promise you made our son . . . something concerning a sister . . . perhaps when we arrive in Salem . . . ?"

He laughed and swept her off her feet, pressing her against his body to demonstrate his eagerness to perform as promised.

Then he carried her into the redoubt, and the man with the musket sighed and located his pipe and sat in the grass to watch the flames and the river. He waited patiently, and he envied the tall hard Yankee with the silver eyes.

34

THE SULLEN ROARS of the wounded British lion could be dimly heard as far distant as Salem throughout Sunday morning. At midday a gray rain stilled the cannon and the heavens wept throughout the afternoon. When the tears dried, a rainbow of hope spread across a purple sky.

Nicole and Dimitri strolled across the wet lawns and paused atop a grassy rise, their arms twined about each other as they looked back at the house. A burst of sun shot past the dark edges of a cloud bank.

"Do you like it?" Dimitri drew her against his chest. His arms wrapped about her slender waist, and he rested his chin upon her curls.

"I love it." The Temnikov house had been pared in size, but it retained the grace and harmony of line. It was a house designed to be lived in, to be filled with rowdy boistrous boys and spirited laughing young girls. Nicole smiled and covered the hands on her waist, leaning comfortably into the broad solidity of his warm chest.

As they quietly watched, Louis carried two chairs onto the

lawn and placed Vaddie's basket between Marie and himself. Louis scanned the latest broadside, Marie knitted, and tiny fists snatched at the sunshine. Pavla and Vadim wandered along the veranda, hand in hand, speaking earnestly in low voices. Occasionally a giant boom of delight bounced across the lawns.

"Do you think they'll marry?"

Dimitri nodded, the action nestling her head into the hollow of his neck. "Vadim won his bid for the farm." A grin shifted the line of white along his cheek. "Were you aware that Pavla is a farmer's daughter? At one time she and her sisters single-handedly operated the largest estate in southwestern Russia."

Nicole burst into laughter. "She's hopeless! I imagine she's trying to reassure Vadim that she'll be able to manage when he returns to the war."

Warm hands closed over her shoulders, and Dimitri swung her to face him. "Will you?" he asked softly, examining her eyes.

A whisper of breeze ruffled his wide sleeves and teased the black curls falling across his forehead. Soon he would go—when his injuries healed. Soon.

She watched the breeze chase across the yard and meander toward the rich farmland stretching behind the house. The fire storm of war had only begun; her man would follow the thunder and lightning. He would seldom be home to direct the sowing and tending and harvesting.

Could she? Could she operate her household, raise a family, and attend to the business of a large farm? Could she cope with aging parents and the pregnancies she anticipated? With drought years and flood years and the hopes and heartbreaks of harvest? Could she gracefully accept a life of hellos and good-byes, a life of wartime separations and agonizing worry? Could she be daughter, mother, wife, businesswoman, lover, nurse, servant, teacher . . . ?" The list was endless.

And which was the true Nicole Duchard Denisovna? Which role did she best fit? The princess or the peasant or the patriot? Who was she?

She rested her golden curls on her husband's shoulder, and a tiny frown traced the brilliant arch of the rainbow glowing bright against the sky. Was she red or green or yellow or . . . ?

A stillness of concentration creased her brow as she studied the bright palette of colors. Close examination revealed something she had previously failed to notice. The colors were not sharply defined. One blended into another so subtly that a clear line of definition could not be distinguished.

She drew a surprised breath and her mouth softly rounded. There was no isolated band of blue. Or green or yellow. The colors flowed together, blending and merging into one smooth entity.

Straightening in Dimitri's arms, she stared hard at the sweep of color. To select one arch from the meld was merely an illusion. It could not be done. The colors could not be separated without destroying the integrity of the whole—as qualities of character could not be isolated without distorting the whole.

The princess blended into the peasant and then into the patriot, and they were the same. They were merely different aspects of the whole! Daughter, princess, wife, businesswoman, mother—they were identical! The entire spectrum of potential existed in every heart; it was impossible to isolate one fragment and label it whole.

Filled with wonder, she raised her face to Dimitri, her eyes shining with the glow of discovery. "Yes," she answered firmly. "Yes, my love, I'll be all right when you go. I'll manage."

His thumb caressed her cheek. "You may be required to perform tasks you've never attempted, to accept responsibility for maintaining the constant thread in our lives." His face sobered and his silvery eyes made love to her. "These are the war years, Nicole, the stormy years. We must admit the possibility that one day you may have to face them alone. . . ."

Her heart lurched and then slowly steadied. There was no black band in the rainbow. If ever the time came when she must march through the years alone, she would remember. And she would rely upon the ghostly secondary shades within herself. Her eyes flicked toward the rainbow's dim afterimage, and she sensed its pale strength.

Her arms circled his neck as his smoky gaze traced her lips and his hands fitted her body against his hips.

And her glance traveled across the lawn, lingering on a wicker basket and tiny fists waving toward a butterfly. Then she gazed deeply into her husband's love. And before his hungry smolder deepened, before his warm eager lips crushed hers, she lay back in his arms and asked softly, "Do you remember when I didn't know who I was?"

His lips teased the corner of her mouth. "And who are you?"

A blaze of radiance illuminated her loveliness. She glowed with the richness of discovering all she had hoped, and more.

"I am Dimitri's wife. I am a rainbow."

ABOUT THE AUTHOR

MAGGIE OSBORNE was born in 1941 and grew up in Kansas and Colorado. After attending Ft. Lewis Junior College in Durango, Colorado, she worked on a newspaper and then as a stewardess. She currently lives with her husband, a manager with State Farm Insurance, and her son in Colorado. In addition to community activities, her leisure projects include painting and renovating old houses with her family. She is the author of *Salem's Daughter, Alexa,* and *Portrait in Passion,* historical romances also available in Signet.

More Bestsellers From SIGNET